The

Reader's Companion
to
The Year of the Red Door

by
William Timothy Murray

The Reader's Companion to The Year of the Red Door

For permissions, review copies, or other inquiries, write to:
Penflight Books
P.O. Box 857
125 Avery Street
Winterville, Georgia 30683-9998
USA

infodesk@penflightbooks.com

Be sure to visit:
www.TheYearOfTheRedDoor.com

rcl_Ed01/rev2.2408

Preface

The world of *The Year of the Red Door* is wider and deeper in scope than I could reasonably relate in its five volumes. As detailed and expansive as that tale may be, much was left out or highly abbreviated to keep the five volumes to a manageable, and readable, length. It is hoped that this Companion will give the interested reader an even deeper experience of that tale, and a greater appreciation of the people and events involved. Or perhaps it will at least entertain you with other tales and information.

There is much here that was only slightly referred to or never mentioned at all. The Flying Rug of Zan, for example, or the tale of Felthain (who became king of Altoria), and the intrigues and tragedies of the final days of Tulith Attis.

Those of you who have not yet read *The Year of the Red Door* are certainly encouraged to do so. Use of this Companion might be helpful, but be warned you will find here many "spoilers."

Please note that portions of this Companion have been previously published, most notably within *Eighteen Objects of Power* and *The Fall of the Faere and Other Stories* (both available as separate books). Over the years, I have also made available certain early drafts of notes in the form of "back stories," mainly as treats for my readers. Be aware that any previously released materials may have been edited or revised for this Companion.

Finally, I wish to offer my heartfelt thanks to all of my readers. You are patient, persistent, and kind. You have been tolerant of my limitations, sympathetic to the story and its characters, and continue to be supportive of this endeavor, as you have been from the very beginning. That is saying a great deal in this age of fleeting and shallow attention, and speaks to the unique and special qualities of the readers of *The Year of the Red Door*. Your messages of encouragement, your notes and letters, have meant a great deal to me on a deeply personal level. So I humbly thank you for giving *The Year of the Red Door* a special place, a real home in your hearts.

William Timothy Murray
2024

Table of Contents

The
Reader's Companion
To
The Year of the Red Door

Introduction & Acknowledgements
from the Compilers and Editors of this Companion

Year 316 of the Third Age

This work is based on the five-volume text of *The Year of the Red Door*, written by William Timothy Murray, along with many of his notes and other previously published work. Copies of these materials mysteriously appeared in what would become the Great Library of Darini only a year after the end of the Second Age. However, as will be mentioned in a moment, much of our work is also derived from other materials that were discovered and gathered together.

A great deal has taken place in the centuries since the end of the Year of the Red Door, the close of the Second Age and the beginning of our own Third Age. Our remaining population is still a tiny fraction of what it once was. All of the great cities are gone, as well as most small communities, and any roads and paths once constantly trodden are now swallowed by the advance of woods and fields. The world is very much still a new place for us, and as we strive to delve into its beauties and mysteries, we continue in our wonder at how our present state came into being. So much culminated during that last fateful year of the old world. So much was remade. We hope this Companion will assist you to better appreciate the tale, the times, the people, and the world of *The Year of the Red Door*.

The author of the five-volume work that we know as *The Year of the Red Door* is a person that we know very little about. We do not know how he came to possess the necessary intimate knowledge of the people he wrote about. We have reason to suspect that he was not a dreamwalker, but had some other skill or Sight that he employed. While some of his notes made their way to the Great Library at Darini, there is every indication that he was somehow supplied with much that remains lost or undiscovered. It is as if he was present before all that he described, even that which he related that was within the hearts of others. When *The Year of the Red Door* first appeared, it was something of a shock. Ullin Saheed Tallin, who made the discovery, found its contents quite unsettling, and many of those he shared it with considered it fanciful, the author prone to conjectures that he weaved into his tale. But we now know better. His work has been corroborated by many findings, and contradicted by very few. At the time of this writing, he was amiable to cooperating with us, but only up to a point. While he made available some of his notes to Darini's library, he has steadfastly refused to be interviewed himself, preferring to allow others to follow their noses and inclinations, coming to their own conclusions.

Meanwhile, the once-abandoned city of Darini has been reinhabited, and will perhaps become the first great city of this new age of the world, although its dwellers remain few compared to the mighty cities of the old world.   Yet the people of Darini have devoted themselves, under thoughtful leadership, to preserve and share whatever they can of the history and literature of the past.

And so it is to Ullin Saheed Tallin that we own much, if not most, of the information and many of the stories contained in this Companion. After the world-changing events that brought the Second Age to an end, Ullin established a Great Library in the restored city of Darini, located in the former lands of the Dragonkind.   With the enthusiastic assistance of former Nasakeerians, Dragonkind, Elifaen, and Men—many of whom were accomplished dreamwalkers—he led a series of expeditions throughout the world that spanned over fifty years. His mission was to locate and gather books, records, and archival materials of every description that were abandoned when the world was so radically depopulated. What he gathered was brought back to Darini to be carefully preserved, organized, catalogued, and made available to all.

In addition, under Ullin's direction, many people who were eye-witnesses or participants in various events were interviewed to garner additional information and perspectives not documented elsewhere.

Ullin himself made extensive use of these resources, aiming to compose a history of the world and the events leading to and during the years prior to 870 of the Second Age, the Year of the Red Door. This work he referred to as *"The Prequalia."* He was always reading and studying, and even while in saddle he was often making or editing his notes. His progress was steady, careful, and incessant, and the tale of his efforts and expeditions is a worthy epic of itself, full of adventures, discoveries, strange encounters, and mysterious incidents.

Ullin at last departed from the world in the Year 238 of the Third Age, at 273 years of age. "I wish to age gracefully, if at all possible," he wrote in his journal, "and in a manner that allows me the chance for study and contemplation. In this way, I hope to make some amends for the mistakes of my past, to better appreciate the long endurance of the Elifaen, and, through work and diligence, to obtain for myself and for others some bit of wisdom and some modicum of solace concerning the world and the events that encompass life."

Ullin was haunted by the perplexing events that had engulfed him, and the world, during that final year of the Second Age. He expressed regret that he could not, or did not, do more. According to his wife, Micerea, "He thought he should have been a better friend, a better soldier, a stronger swain to me. He regretted how ill-prepared and trained his militia in Passdale was, and how so many died and suffered as a result. He always regretted how he succumbed to the curse put on Esildre, and how that episode of weakness on his part, according to him, confused and lessened him in the eyes of others and in his own self-regard. He thought, or so he told me, that had he been a better man, Robby would have confided to him more, would have had someone to talk to about the burden that he obviously saw well in advance of arriving at Griferis, and in so doing Ullin may have done more for him. So, in later years, I suppose he thought the least he could do was to continue serving Robby, King Philawain, or at least serve the memory of those days."

Ullin never completed his *Prequalia*. But the work was taken up by others, most notably by his daughter, Mira. She has generously made available to us not only the vast collections gathered to Darini, including transcripts of many interviews, but also Ullin's own copious notes containing his commentaries, questions, and outlines.

As far as Ullin himself, his life touched upon and affected so many events, and was so rich in experience and scope, both before and after the coming of this Third Age, that we editors of this Companion have decided to render only a bare outline of his life (see Biographical Sketches). We must defer the fuller story of his life to some other work that might do justice to its scope, to his character, and to his achievements.

Meanwhile, there are several aspects of this Companion that users are asked to bear in mind. It will be quickly noticed that we rarely cite the sources of our information. We discovered early on in our work that doing so would be somewhat tedious to the reader, would be rarely pertinent, and would unnecessarily lengthen the already bulky size of this Companion.   Sources that are mentioned are sometimes pertinent, if only to give the context of when or how a topic is related. However, for the inquisitive, we have left all of our notes and references to the care of the Great Library of Darini, which is accessible in person or via dreamwalking to any and to all who care to visit it. By doing so, others can review all of our materials and sources, as well as our findings.   Since we had to contend with many contradictory or conflicting stories, particularly those about the early histories of the world, visitors to Darini would surely better appreciate the scope and travails of our endeavors, aspects of our work to which Ullin Saheed Tallin was certainly well acquainted!

How to Use This Companion

As mentioned above, it remains a mystery to us how the five-volumes of *The Year of the Red Door* ever came to be written, or exactly what means the author of that work had to discover what he related, particularly those internal matters of the minds and hearts of those involved. We certainly expected to find passages to correct or contradict, but we did not, which only increases the mystery of it, and our amazement.   Upon review, we saw that the people involved in that epic adventure made many mistakes, many false assumptions, and quite a few bad or misguided decisions. But the author relates them not as his but their errors, rather matter-of-factly, and with little judgment. It was up to us as readers to see those mistakes and errors, at least eventually, as the story unfolded before us. So now, our task is more or less only to clarify, perhaps expound upon, matters the author did not deem necessary to fully articulate.   And to give the contemporary reader a fuller understanding of the context of those long-ago days and years, or at least to render some useful tool for a closer look at those people and events.

Therefore, this Companion is intended primarily for those interested enough in *The Year of the Red Door* to read it again, or to read and contemplate a bit more about its world.   This is both a reference work of sorts and a supplement.   As such, there is no real reason to begin at this Companion's first pages.   One may browse to a section or passage that is of immediate interest, or one can turn to the glossary for a quick reminder of who is who and what is what.   Or one can delve into the stories and sketches rendered here for deeper insights, or perhaps a bit of entertainment.

Be mindful of these points:

• The order in which items appear in this Companion does not imply that one item is more important than any other.   Instead, they appear in the order that they do for the sake of managing the tedious aspects of layout and formatting for publication.   It is hoped that the Table of Contents and the Index will aid you in locating sections and passages of interest to you.   That is, as a reference work, there is no plot here—this is not "a story." So you need not read or peruse the Companion "in order" from front to back, but are free to decide for yourself how to use this Companion according to your own needs and desires.

• When *The Year of the Red Door* is in italics, we refer to the text manuscript of that name.   When in normal print, we refer to the time period of the Year of the Red Door.

• We have also made an effort to provide a few details about some of the lesser-known figures that played important roles in the history or the outcome of events. However, virtually every person, place, thing, and event is connected in some way to every other one. For this reason, we obviously had to confine our cross-references. But we hope that the layout of this Companion will help offset any such editorial shortcomings by allowing you to locate such connections.

• Some sections of this Companion contain passages that are somewhat redundant. Also, one section may contain a description or information about a particular that is different or lacking elsewhere. As explained above, the variety of source materials and points of view account for such variations.

• As more information becomes available, future editions of this Companion may contain revisions that provide new information or corrections. Nature takes its due course. Memories fade, books decay, and records are lost. But it is possible that more stories and information may yet come to light.

• This Companion does not "contain all." There was simply too much material to sift through, too many aspects and details to be sorted and sometimes deciphered, and too little time. Indeed, much has been left out of this work. For example, you will find no commentaries of the author of *The Year of the Red Door*, and not every tale pertaining to it has been included. Naturally, questions may arise that are not answered in this Companion. That is why we heartily invite you to contact us (and the author) directly at:

Email:
asktheauthor@penflightbooks.com

Or via Post:
Penflight Books
P.O. Box 857
125 Avery Street
Winterville, Georgia 30683-9998
U.S.A.

We realize that the above addresses are not within our world, but we have been assured that your mail will "get through" to us. We do make every effort to answer each note, letter, and inquiry that we receive!

On Behalf of William Timothy Murray,

Cornelius Beckmann, Supervising Editor,

With Assisting Editors:

Marina Anne Elfinson	Haran Toluz Orluss
Simon Barthus	Charlena Riceman
Yursagaki al Binsalud	Andrea Simons-Leigh
Arnold Chanyshenko	Mark Simons-Leigh
Salez Degamba	Reinholt Spatz
Lodewijk van Kyrtadt	Mira Tallin

Maps

Many of the following maps were prepared and published late in the year 869 of the Second Age. The map depicting County Barley was derived from work performed by Ullin Saheed Tallin.   It seems that the other maps were derived from various others gathered from a variety of sources. When published within an atlas, the following note was included.

A Note from the Cartographers

The geography and place names depicted on the following maps are generally accepted to be accurate as of the year of their preparation (869 Second Age). Distances are approximate, given the scales of the maps. However, these are only intended to give a general sense of the scale and relationship of the various regions and features. They are not intended for travel or navigation. Any mishaps as a result from the use of these maps for such purposes of travel are the responsibility of the user, not the mapmakers.

For maps more suitable for travel within particular regions of the world, all interested parties are invited to inquire at our establishment.

Brannon & Gray Cartographers
No. 16, Miller's Pond Lane
Duinnor City

County Barley

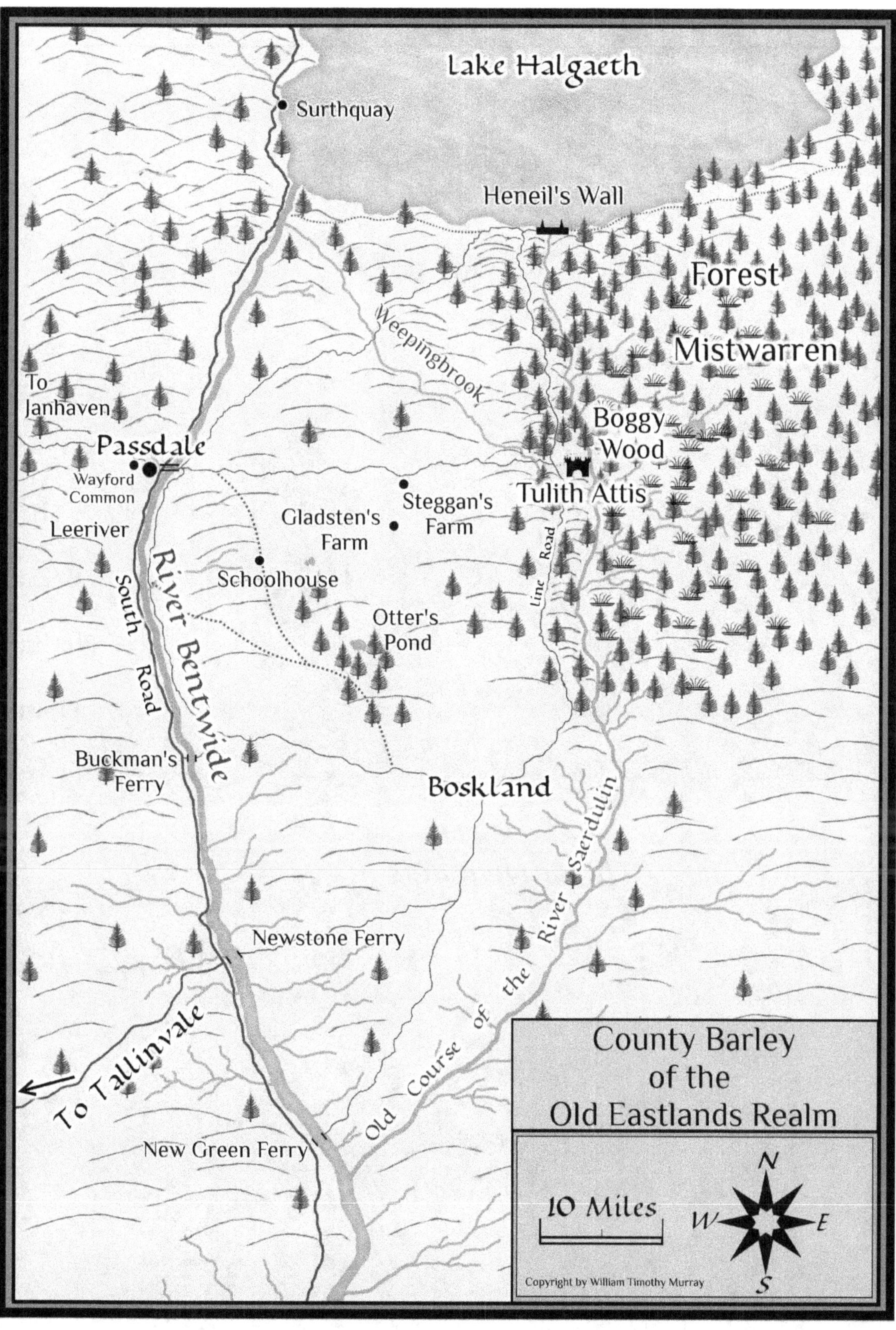

The Western World

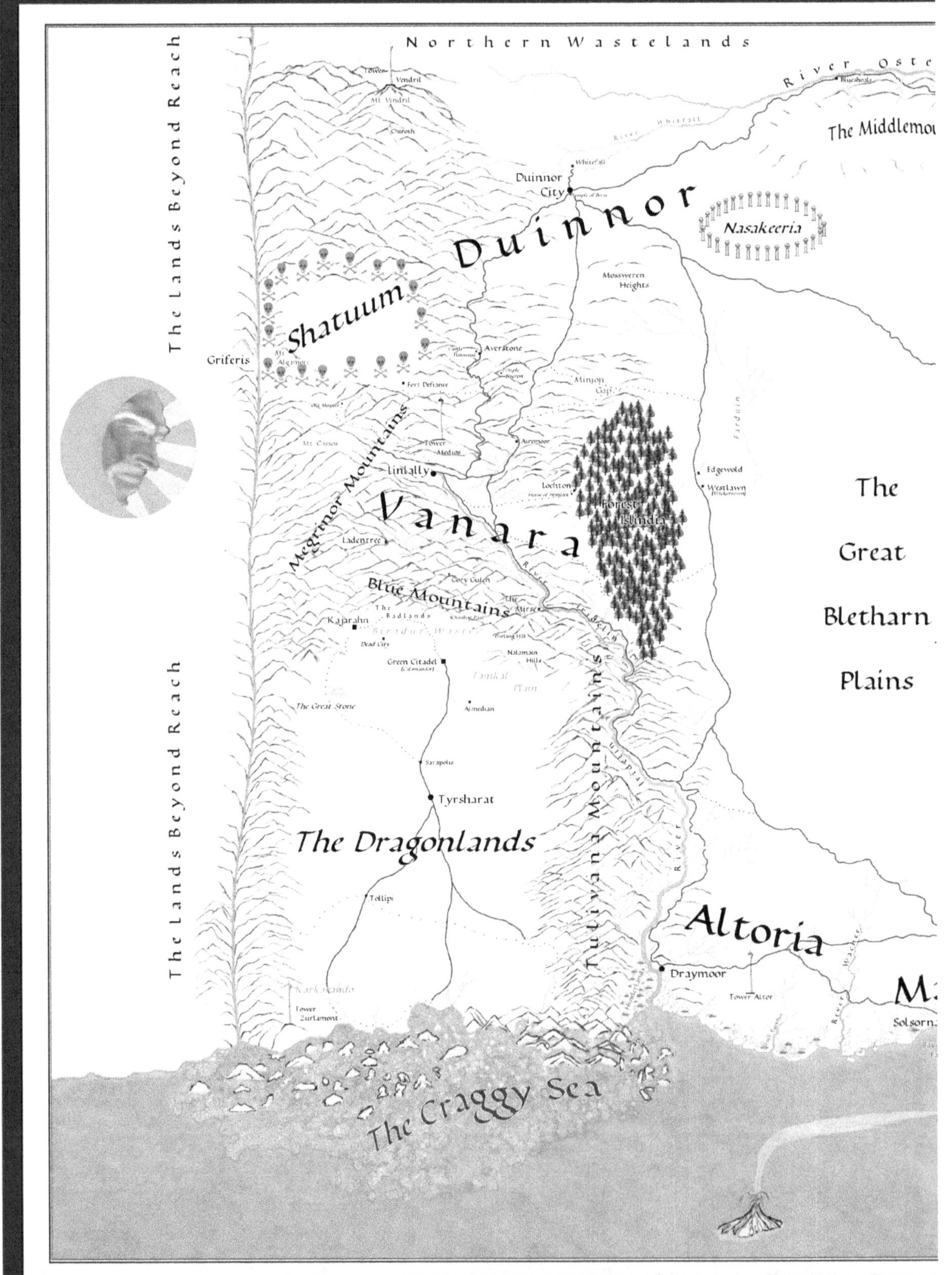

The Eastern World

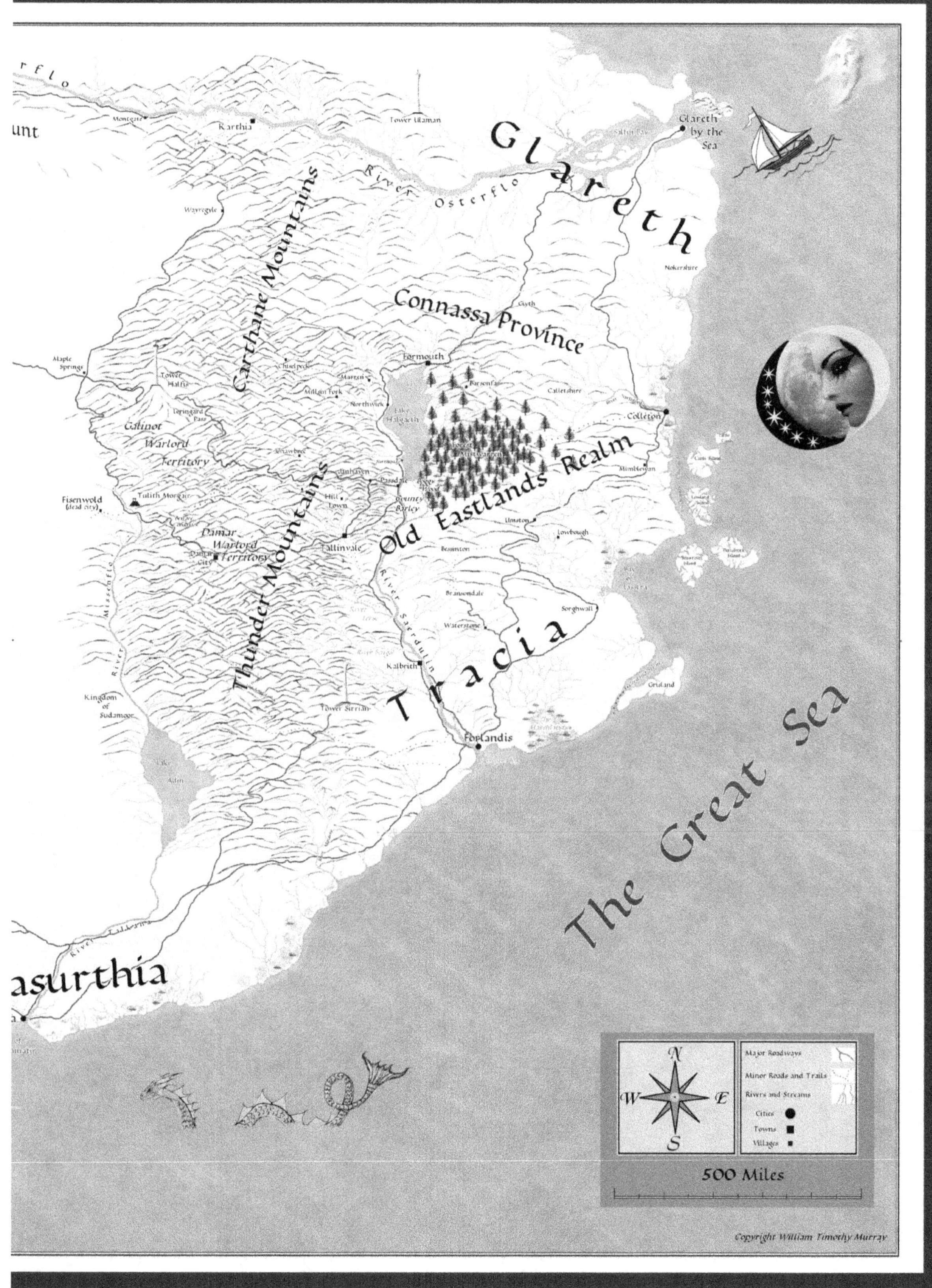

Duinnor and Shatuum

Northern Wastelands

River Whitefall

Whitefall

Temple of Beras

Duinnor
City

Duinnor

Mossweren Heights

Minion Gap

Averstone

Temple Belcron

Castle Elmwood

Fort Defiance

Shatuum

Griferis

Mt. Algamori

Old Mazner

...ains

Tower Vendril

Mt. Vendril

Chiroth

200 Miles

Middlemount and Nasakeeria

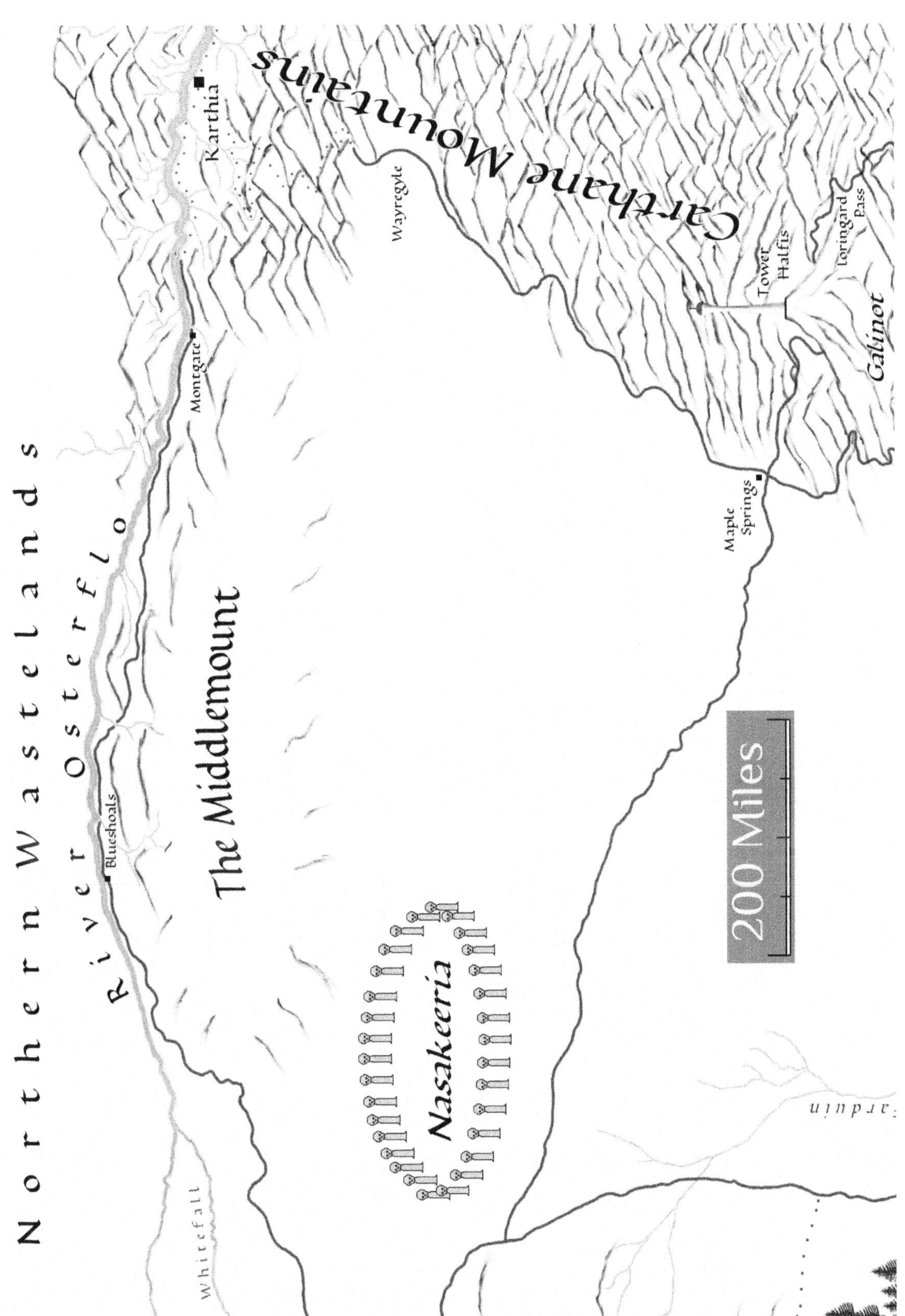

Glareth

Glareth by the Sea
Nokershire
Colleton
Northford River
Salfin Bay
Glareth
Calletshire
Connassa Province
Giyth
200 Miles
Barsonfar
Northern Wastelands
River Osterflo
Formouth
Lake Halgaeth
Tower Ulaman
Maerren
Northwick
Mitlsin Fork
Chiselpeck
Carthane Mountains
Karthia

Vanara

Farduin
Edgewold
Westlawn
(Wickertown)
Forest Islindia
Gup
Airemoor
Lochton
House of Hemlock
Tridetin
Mountains
River
Tridetin
Mirse
The
Nalamain Hills
Tamkal Plain
Gory Gulch
Dartang Hill
Almedian
Vanara
Blue Mountains
Khanhar Pass
Biradur Waste
The Badlands
Tower Medios
Tintally
Green Citadel
(Calamandor)
Sarapolis
Tyrsharat
Megirnor Mountains
Ladentree
Kajarahn
Dead City
Old Mayar
Mt. Cassos
The Great Stone
200 Miles

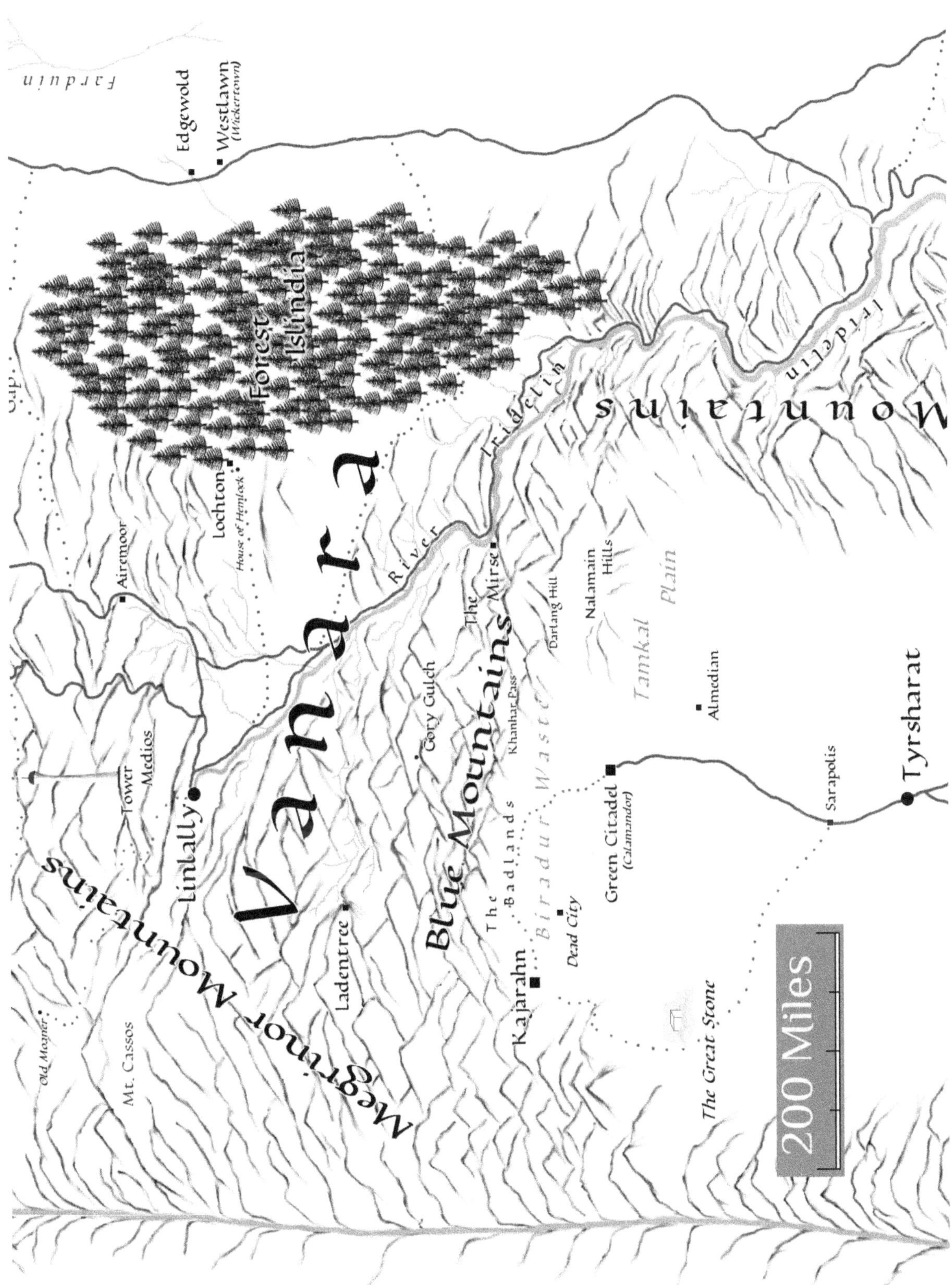

The Great Bletharn Plains
Fardu
Edgewold
Westlawn (Wickertown)
200 Miles
Loringard Pass
Galinot Warlord Territory
Chawbree
Fisenwold (dead city)
Tulith Morgair
Beware of Pixies
Damar Warlord Territory
Damar City
Missenflo River
Kingdom of Sudamoor
Thunder Mountains
Lake Adin

Tracia and the Old Eastlands Realm

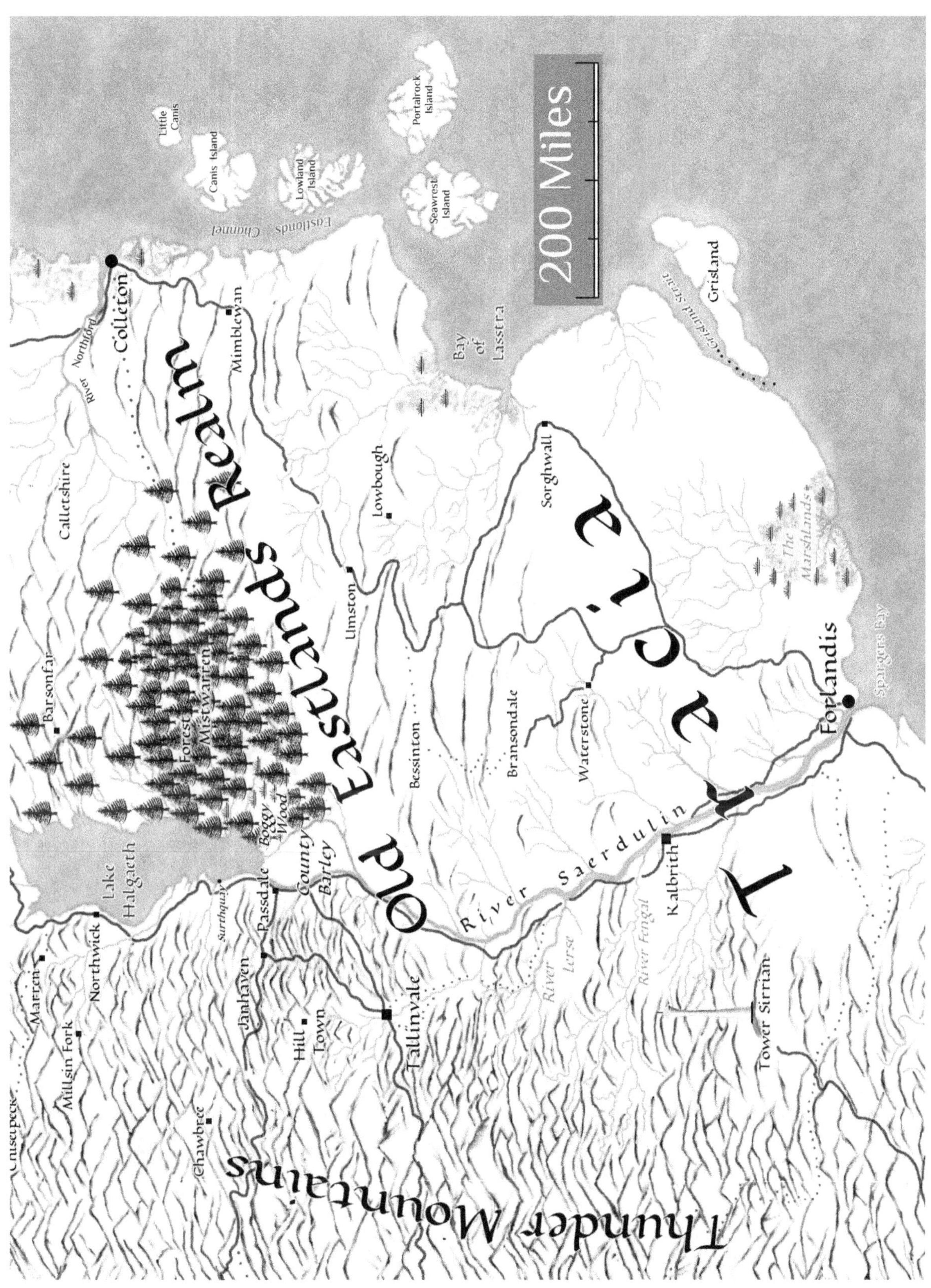

The Dragonlands

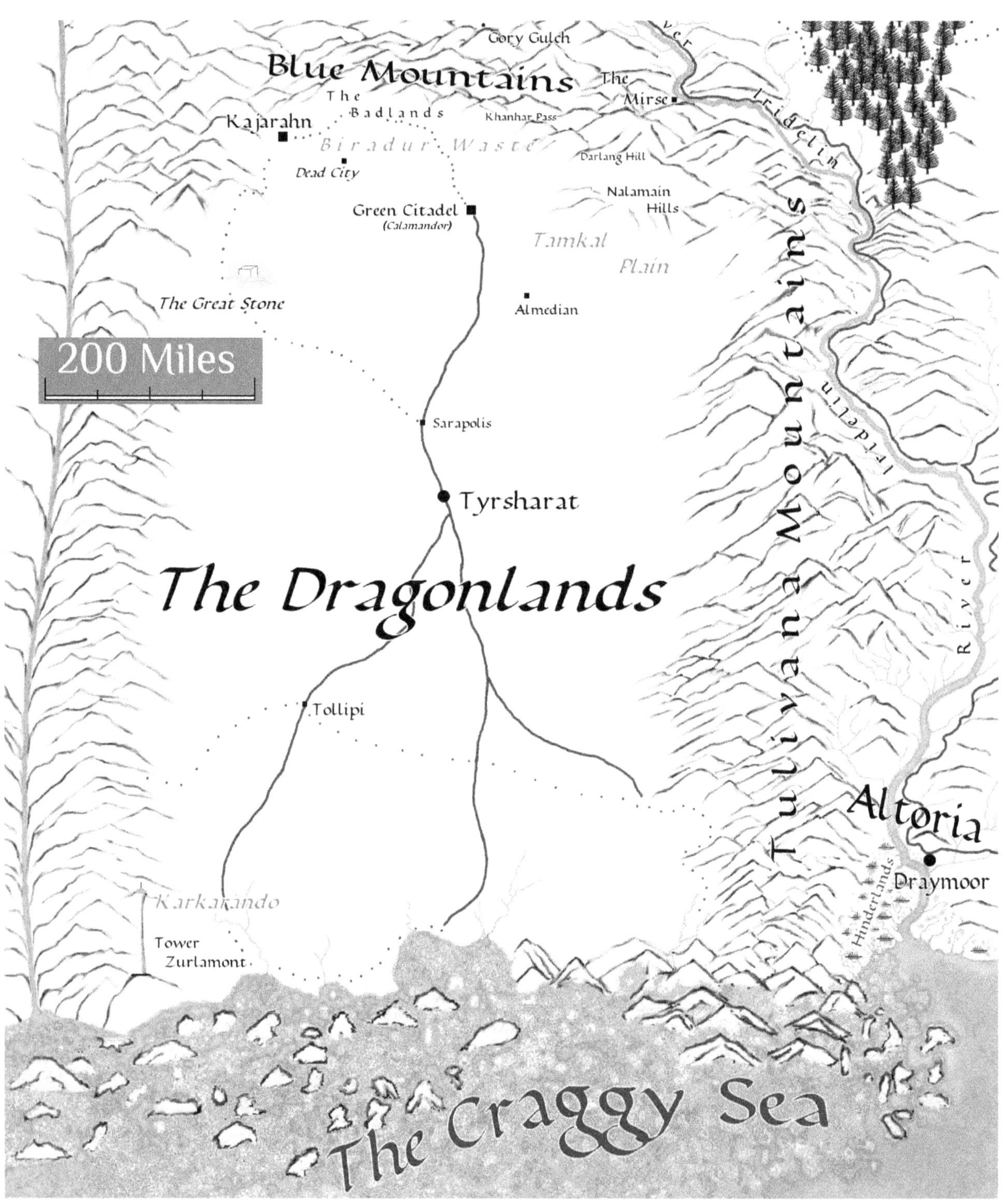

Altoria and Masurthia

The Frontier between Tracia and Masurthia

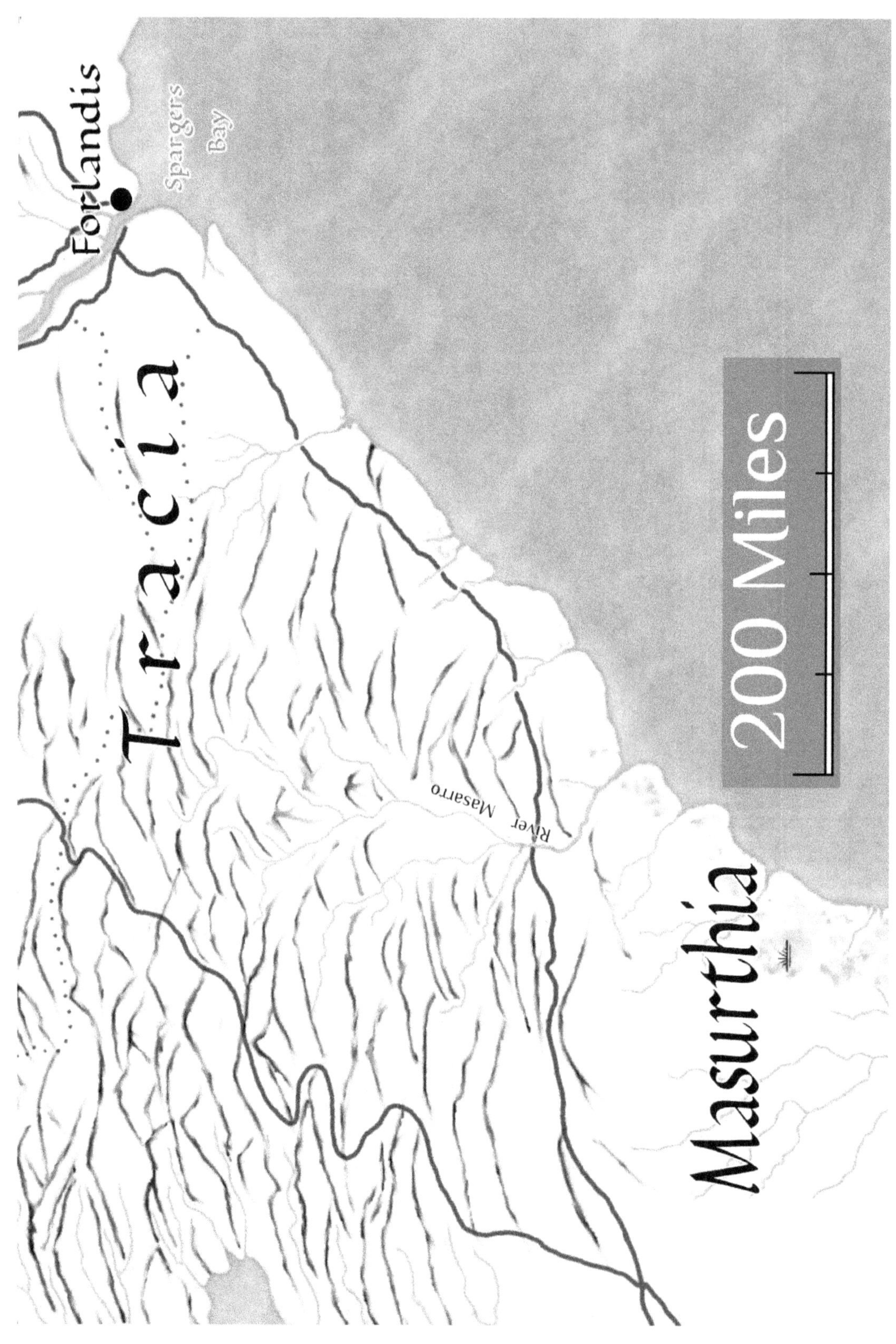

GLOSSARY

This glossary contains only brief definitions of the terms listed. In some cases, a more in-depth discussion is contained within The Year of the Red Door, while for other terms we refer you to various other sections of this Reader's Companion.

Adin A remote large lake on the eastern side of the Bletharn Plains, on the southwestern side of the Thunder Mountains. It receives waters from the Missenflo and from streams running down from the Thunder Mountains, and its level rises and falls sharply according to seasonal snow and rainfall. On its northern shores is the Kingdom of Sudamoor. The lake forms the headwaters of the Talkana River that flows southward through Masurthia.
See Also:
Eighteen Objects of Power (The Cornucopia of Sudamoor)

Airemoor A village on the road between Vanara and Duinnor.

Al Sairs The personal household army of Gurasa, the great Dragonkind general. Though small in numbers, comprising only three hundred at most, this elite force drew its members mainly from Gurasa's own tribe centered on the region of Almedian. Fierce and loyal to Gurasa, they followed him throughout his rise to power and fame, participated in many battles, often as shock troops during assaults or as guerilla fighters to harass the enemy. When Gurasa's career was ended, the Al Sairs continued to serve him during his unofficial exile in Almedian.
See Also:
Biographical Sketches (Gurasa)

Alaberbra (Kajarahn) An ancient city of the Dragonlands, located in the far northwest of the deserts. It was officially renamed Kajarahn, the Free City, following the devastating attacks of witches and demons that decimated the city during the early Second Age.
See Also:
Historical Sketches (Kajarahn)

Aldergiest Toll An account of the battle of Tulith Attis recorded by Aldergiest the Blue. Written in the years shortly after the battle, the ancient writer was apparently at Tulith Attis or knew some of those who survived to relate the details of the battle. It is known that he was a youngster at the time of the battle, and although it is not known when he wrote the Aldergiest Toll, a copy of it was first cataloged in the Royal Archives of Vanara in the year 420 S.A.

Aldred Great grandson of Eldwin of Nowhere.

Alglaeth nelar In the Ancient Tongue, means "proceed nobly" or "proudly go forth.".

Almedian A small walled town of the northeastern Dragonlands that was the home of Saltani Gurasa of the House of Golden Sand, a famous Dragonkind general. Its history is ancient though undistinguished, and its people lived chiefly by growing flax and meager wheat crops by using water drawn from its wells. By the Second Age, Almedian had grown somewhat, and was producing rugs and pottery in small quantities as trade commodities. The town was raided several times by renegades, which prompted the construction of its walls and the organization of a militia. During the late Second Age, when Gurasa became a famous and powerful general of the Dragonkind, he saw to the development of Almedian, providing funds to dig additional wells and to create a water distribution system that, along with plants smuggled from the north, served to bolster the available food in the community. He also rebuilt his family palace there, and employed many of the town. Although far from the centers of power, and therefore from the distribution of darakal herb, its people became remarkably robust and healthy compared to others in the Dragonlands, leading some to believe that Gurasa somehow provided more than the town's normal share of the healing herb. In spite of their modest status and wealth, most Almedians were considered Alziekfria. When Gurasa was forced into retirement, he returned to Almedian to live. Though he endured the tragic loss of his wife and sons, Gurasa and his daughter Micerea did much to increase the prosperity and security of Almedian's people. At the same time, through various subtle diplomatic maneuvers, Gurasa managed to protect his people from the oppression of the Emperor's court.

In the final year of the Second Age, Gurasa and the people of Almedian were warned of the encroaching flood and the entire area was evacuated, moving en masse to Darini. There they met with the Nasakeerians and along with them were the first new settlers of that city. Almedians did much to help restore Darini, and they brought with them not only their tools and many supplies, but also their knowledge, including nearly all of Gurasa's collections of books, records, writings, and artifacts.
See Also:
Biographical Sketches (Gurasa)
Glossary (Alziekfria, Darakal, Darini, Nasakeeria)

Alonair   One of the Firstborn of the Faerekind, a maker of fabulous statues and carvings of stone. It was Alonair who set before the Dragonkind the challenge of the Great Stone that preceded the first great conflict between Faerekind and Dragonkind and eventually led to The Fall of the Faere. Like Cupeldain and many others, Alonair lost his wings and became one of the Elifaen, remaining in the world when the faithful of the Faerekind departed with Aperion. Afterwards, Alonair was reviled by some of his race and driven to isolate himself.
See Also:
Biographical Sketches (Alonair)

Altoria   One of the Seven Realms, located southeast of Vanara, south Islindia, and along the shores of the southern Iridelin River. Its capital was the port city of Draymoor, just inland along the Iridelin, a major center of trade.
See Also:
Historical Sketches (Altoria)

Alzeeran   Dragonkind scribe to King Philawain of Griferis.   He delivered Chantay's (Lucinda's) amethyst Bloodcoins to Tower Altor.

Alziekfria   The ruling class and elite of the Dragonkind, mostly the wealthy or those favored by the Emperor. The name means "free from sickness." Because this wealthy and influential class received healing darakal extracts in greater quantity and frequency than other Dragonkind, they enjoyed much better health. As a result, most Alziekfria were very different in appearance than others of the Dragonkind who are less fortunate and receive the elixir less often. They commonly had long shiny black hair, clear and smooth, tan skin with no blemishes, and strong, muscular bodies. The women of the Alziekfria class were renowned for their legendary beauty. Because they were relatively free from the debilitating "desert sickness," the Alziekfria lived longer and were more physically active than most

others. And, because of their relative wealth and status, the Alziekfria also enjoyed higher literacy rates. Hence they held most of the positions of power, and most of the doctors, engineers, scholars, and high-ranking member of the armies and civil servants of the Dragonlands were Alziekfria.
See also:
Glossary (Darakal)
Historical Sketches (Karkarando)

Amandoel The name given to Heneil by people of his time, meaning The Builder.

Ancient Speech The language that was spoken by most during the First Age and somewhat into the Second Age. Sometimes it is referred to as the Second Tongue (after the First Tongue, also called Faerish, which was all but lost after The Fall).
See Also:
Essays & Explanations (Literacy and Education)

Anerath   A spirited horse that belonged to Ullin Saheed Tallin. The name was derived from the Ancient Speech and means "water prancer" because it was noticed how much the colt loved to splash and play in streams and ponds. He was one of the famous Majestics, a breed that was famous for their endurance, agility, and strength. Anerath was a gift to Ullin Saheed from the Thrubolds, Duinnor's renown horsemen and breeders of the Majestics, in gratitude for his having saved their son's life at the Battle of Garmitor.

Ullin received Anerath some years later, in 863 SA, just when he was transferred to the King's Post and assigned to Collandoth. For the next seven years, the two traveled all over the world, usually without other company, and traversing long stretches of difficult terrain. Anerath developed a special sensitivity to Ullin and his habits and needs, often sensing danger or the correct way forward before Ullin did. In some of his notes, Ullin relates how Anerath, more than any other animal he had encountered, seemed always to have a keen sense of whatever situation was at hand. Ullin was certain that, somehow, Anerath understood what was said to him.
See Also:
Glossary (Thrubold)

Aperion   A Firstborn Faerekind and the First and True King of the Faere, so appointed by Beras during the Time Before Time. Aperion sought to stop the bloodshed between the Dragonkind and the Faerekind, and he led the faithful and loyal Faerekind out of the world. It was Aperion who caused those who remained upon the earth to be Scathed of their wings, becoming the Elifaen, or Fallen Ones. It was also Aperion, so legend tells, who gave protection to the people of Nasakeeria by creating the Ring of Fire that surrounded that land. Aperion, too, gave to the Seven High Houses the Forty-Nine Keys of the Nimbus Illuminas as an offer of peace and as a way that the Elifaen might depart from the earth and take up their abode with him and with the other Faerekind in their heavenly home.
See Also:
Glossary (Aperion's Fire)
Tales of the High Houses (The Fall of the Faere)

Aperion's Fire A term used by occupants of Nasakeeria. It is what they called the mysterious wall of flame that ignited and surrounded Nasakeeria whenever a person attempted to enter (or leave) Nasakeeria. When a person attempted to pass through Nasakeeria's border, Aperion's Fire would shoot forth from the ground upward. It spread rapidly from the place it first appeared, and within seconds formed a searing wall of flame some hundred feet or more high and about fifty feet deep. The flames incinerated any intruder with such effectiveness that nothing but the bones were left, which were then thrown by the force of the flames beyond the edge of Nasakeeria's border. Over time, these bones formed a grisly ring around Nasakeeria, a reminder of the danger.

The exact nature of Nasakeeria's origin remained a mystery from its founding until the end of the Second Age. However, soon after it was established, it was quickly learned that any human who crossed its border on foot or on horseback would be consumed by hot flames that quickly sprang up from the ground trespassed upon, and the flames would spread almost instantaneously around the entire circumference of Nasakeeria. The force and the heat of the flames were such that the baked bones of trespassers were thrown outward to land some yards away from the flames. Over time, so many have inadvertently or intentionally crossed that these bones form mounds surrounding the lands. Mysteriously, while the bones were thrown outward, very few objects carried by such interlopers were blasted in that direction, and it was thought that such items were either wholly consumed by heat or else thrown into the interior of Nasakeeria.

This phenomenon was responsible for the destruction of at least two armies, one from Duinnor and the other made up of Dragonkind, that inadvertently encroached Nasakeeria's border. Countless others were also killed as a result of losing their way. Twice in history, entire armies were lost to Nasakeeria's fires. On the first occasion it was an army of Duinnor, dispatched eastward to join with those who sought to turn the tide of the Dragonkind Invasion of 322 S.A. The generals apparently knew but ignored the danger, and were consequently consumed, along with all three thousand of their men. This debacle led Duinnor to begin constructing warning pillars around Nasakeeria in an effort to prevent any future loss of life.

In 493 SA, Duinnor began a project of erecting warning markers around Nasakeeria. The markers were pillars of stone, standing eight feet high, each with a large carving of a skull at the top. Also, each marker was inscribed with a written warning for all to turn back. Beginning at the westernmost border of Nasakeeria, Duinnor placed a marker approximately every three to five hundred yards, proceeding north and eastward.

The construction and installation of the warning pillars was a momentous project beset with many difficulties, controversy, and delays. Each warning column was some eight feet high, capped with a likeness of a human skull, and they were installed some 500 yards apart along the perimeter of Nasakeeria. Owing to various problems, it took over sixty years to complete. In spite of this, there have been accounts of witnesses claiming to have seen the fires of Nasakeeria light up, probably the result of foolhardy adventurers or hapless travelers who ignored or failed to see or understand the warning pillars.

After the world was remade, Ullin Saheed Tallin discovered in Vanara copies of reports (apparently stolen from Duinnor) concerning some grisly secret experiments conducted by Kingsmen who wished to gain a better understanding of Aperion's Fire. In 436 SA, they used a powerful trebuchet to toss dead bodies across Nasakeeria's border. They learned that, dead or alive, whether touching the ground or not, any human crossing would trigger Aperion's fire. They also drove fully accoutered war horses, wagons filled with a variety of weapons and goods, cattle, deer, and a myriad of other animals across (none with riders or drivers), but all passed safely. The report was attached to another report dated 868 SA, which recommended a new set of tests. These would involve stealing a flying apparatus from Vanara. An extremely high tower would be built, and the flying device (along with the pilot) would be launched from atop this tower in an attempt to cross over to Nasakeeria at very high altitude. However, it was noted in the report that even Vanarans had difficulty understanding how to gain altitude with their best flying devices, and likely an altitude could not be reached that was significantly higher than what the trebuchet experiment had achieved. And, it was noted, even if a flyer succeeded in crossing over, his chances of returning were very low, essentially making the mission a suicidal one.

See Also:
Eighteen Objects of Power (Nasakeeria's Ring of Fire)
Glossary (Nasakeeria)

Applewait Family of Greenfar.

Aram see Tallin, Aram Saheed

Arata In the late Second Age, Lord Arata was one of the seven Supreme Judges of Duinnor. He was outspoken about issues of corruption and crime.   His rulings often flew in the face of the desires of Lord Banis, and on several occasions Banis sought to have him removed as a judge. There were even attempts on his life, the investigations of which seemed to implicate Banis or his agents.

Aremon A Nasakeerian hunter of the late Second Age.

Arkstan Proprietor of the Rivertree Tavern in Passdale.

Arldewain One of the Elders of Nowhere.

Ashlord Common name of Collandoth, a Melnari. This name is primarily used by Men.
See Also:
Historical Sketches (The Melnari and Their Familiars)

Atlana Daughter of Lord Banis and Lady Tiryna of the House of Elmwood and sister to Navis and Esildre. She was the mother of Coreth and Faslor. Along with her siblings and her father, she refused to go with Aperion and was Scathed of her wings. During the First Age, Atlana was a staunch supporter of Cupeldain and, later, his son Parthais. When her father was dismissed from Parthais's court, she left with him but returned shortly afterwards to remain in Vanara. She became a powerful and trusted advisor to Queen Serith Ellyn. When Serith Ellyn led an army east to confront the Dragonkind, she fought next to Serith Ellyn at the Battle of Saerdulin. Upon her return to Vanara, she continued to serve the Queen as a military advisor. She married Mathos and had two children by him. In the late Second Age, she and Mathos went to relieve a beleaguered garrison in the Blue Mountains and were both killed at the Battle of Gory Gulch.

Attis Thought to be the name of the original builder of Tulith Attis, an ancient fortress near Lake Halgaeth in the Eastlands. It was later the name for the town at the base of Tulith Attis, all of which was destroyed during the Dragonkind invasion of 322 S.A.

Avatar An uncanny apparition and mysterious servant of Unknown Kings that changed in form at the beginning of each regnal year. Eventually, the form taken by the Avatar would lend its name commonly given to a regnal year (The Avatar never had the same form as during any previous year.). The Avatar served the Unknown King in mysterious ways, not all of which are known. It is known, however, that the Unknown King sometimes sent the Avatar to summon someone to the King's High Chamber. The Avatar then floated through the streets of Duinnor City until it arrived before the person being summoned. As it passed through the city, so uncanny was its movement and appearance, that the Avatar filled people with fear whenever they saw it, even when its form was not itself very threatening. It was also somewhat mysterious that anyone thus summoned has not the will to resist, and would follow the Avatar back to the Unknown King.
　　Sometimes, especially during the reign of the First through Fifth Unknown Kings, the King and the Avatar would go about the city of Duinnor together, with the King following the Avatar in his sedan or sometimes in a carriage. With the King in his resplendent and eerie Golden Mantle and the Avatar, uncanny and fearsome, leading the way, such processions struck fear, awe, and compliance into the populace. However, with only one or two exceptions very early during the reign of the Sixth

Unknown King, such processions ended. Thenceforth, only the Avatar, often with a company of Palace Guard, would go forth into the city.

It is assumed that the Avatar could not be sent beyond the walls of Duinnor City unless in company with the King, because it was never seen to do so.
See Also:
Eighteen Objects of Power (The Avatar)

Averstone   A small village in the frontier between Vanara and Duinnor. It was situated along the old mountain road that runs from Vanara to Duinnor, and was only a few miles away from Elmwood Castle. For a number of years, Averstone was an important waypoint, particularly with those traveling to Elmwood Castle, with several inns, stables, coach houses, and blacksmiths vying for customers. For a few years, a horse race from Duinnor to Linlally passed through Averstone, something of a rival to the Mulberry Race. But participants were few and it never gained much popularity. During the latter part of the Second Age, Averstone began to decline when Lady Esildre suddenly stopped receiving guests. This coincided with road improvements that were made along other routes between Duinnor and Linlally. By the end of the Second Age, Averstone was a quaint and much-forgotten community of only a few dozen families. When, at the end of the Second Age, Secundur's legions were unleashed from Shatuum, Averstone was overrun and completely destroyed, and all its people consumed.
See Also:
Glossary (Mulberry Race, Elmwood)

Ayreltide   A winged horse in the service of Lady Islindia, Queen of the Wood. He existed as such only during the periods when Islindia brought forth her memories into actuality. Ayreltide rescued Ullin Saheed Tallin twice, first by taking him away from the Crack Between Worlds and, later, by bringing Micerea to him and helping them fend off the captain of Shatuum that pursued him.

Bailorg   **(Braig Bailorg Denuth Delcorman)** One of the Elifaen, perhaps a Firstborn, but not a member of any known House. He was a mysterious figure, an acquaintance of Pellen in Duinnor during the early Second Age. He was also seen from time to time in various courts, traveling extensively throughout the realms. It is suspected that he traveled into the Dragonlands on several occasions. He was involved in many nefarious activities, delicately balancing his service to several patrons at the same time, including Secundur, King Balsalza (of the Dragonlands), Lord Banis, and the Unknown Kings of Duinnor. He seems to have been chiefly interested in increasing his own wealth, power, and influence.

Certain facts about Bailorg emerged during the late Second Age. He was involved in the sack of Tulith Attis, serving at the time as a kind of adjunct advisor to the Dragonkind. It is almost certain that he was a double-agent, serving also Secundur and the Fifth Unknown King of Duinnor, playing each off of the other for his own gain. He delivered Pellen from certain death on the battlefield of Tulith Attis, turning Pellen into a formidable traitor (Pellen had been in the clutches of the Fifth Unknown King, ordered by the King to deliver Lyrium's Bloodcoins to Duinnor. Pellen's plot had resulted in the murder of his wife, Myrium, his brother Heneil, and many others.). Bailorg delivered to Pellen a special suit of armor, supposedly to help disguise him, but was instead enchanted in such a manner that eventually forced Pellen into the service of Secundur. Pellen then, at Bailorg's direction, imitated his brother Heneil's voice and had the gates of Tulith Attis opened to the Dragonkind horde, which immediately set about the massacre of all they found within. As his reward for helping the Dragonkind overthrow Tulith Attis, Bailorg and Pellen joined in the looting of the place, but the Bloodcoins were missing. However, during his journey away from the region, Pellen, who knew he was doomed in Duinnor by his failure, left Bailorg on his own. Shortly afterwards, Bailorg's slaves revolted against him, resulting in the loss of all his stolen treasure and, ultimately, the creation of the land and people of Nowhere.

Bailorg was known to have in his possession the Storm Bag of legend. Using this, he apparently conjured certain weather conditions to assist him, including a dense fog over Tulith Attis, and various other storms.

After the loss of his loot and slaves, Bailorg escaped capture and disappeared for many years. However, by the mid-Second Age, he was a known associate of Lord Banis of Duinnor, and even acted as a guide for Banis's son, Navis, showing Navis to the borderlands of Shatuum on an ill-fated mission to rescue his sister, Esildre. Evidence later emerged that Bailorg murdered Navis at the behest of Lord Banis, who feared that his son might succeed in the rescue and thus spoil his relationship with Secundur. This murder remained hidden for hundreds of years, however, and Bailorg returned to Duinnor to report that he had successfully guided Navis and the rescue party to Shatuum. Generously rewarded for the feat, Bailorg became a person of unsavory business, and he was reputed to have negotiated for the lease of deeds for various Vanaran properties and estates to Duinnor holders. Although implicated in many crimes over a long period of time, Bailorg was never arrested and tried. This is because he enjoyed the simultaneous protection and patronage of powerful figures, including Secundur, Lord Banis, and the Unknown Kings of Duinnor.

In a strange turn of events, Bailorg committed a botched kidnapping which resulted in his death in the year 870 S.A. Yet his life and actions had a profound influence on people and events far separated from one another, on countless families who fell victim to the evils he perpetrated, and thus on the events related within *The Year of the Red Door.*
See Also:
Biographical Sketches (Esildre, Pellen)
Eighteen Objects of Power (Storm Bag)
Glossary (Banis, Navis, Nowhere,)
Tales of the High Houses (House of Fairfir)

Balfast (see Ribbon, Balfast)

Ballista   An engine of war used to hurl stones or missiles at an enemy. It makes use of a torsion system of bands of rope that are tightened by various cranks to bend an arm or bow which slings or propels the missile when released. Others are more technically referred to as catapults, making use of a swinging arm to throw stones, pots of burning oil, or other blunt missiles. Ballistae came in various sizes and configurations, and were used in both defensive and offensive operations. At the Battle of Tallinvale, both types of ballistae were used (true ballistae as well as catapults), whereas at the Battle of Soltani Pass, the ballistae were actually catapults. In both battles, trebuchets were also used. Smaller versions of both were also used by various navies to good effect, especially those in the late Second Age that made use of spring steel rather than ropes for torsion or wooden arms.

Bandit   The horse of Bob Starhart, an Eastlands Post Rider.

Banis   A Firstborn Elifaen of the House of Elmwood. Father to Atlana, Esildre, and Navis. His wife, Tiryna, departed with Aperion. Banis did not join with any other houses during the Time Before Time and lived throughout the Vanara region. As his children became warriors for Cupeldain, Parthais, and Serith Ellyn, Banis served in their courts in various nonmilitary capacities. He was a staunch supporter of Parthais, serving as Vanara's Minister of Justice for many years. In the latter period of Parthais's reign, Banis was removed from his position for insubordination to the throne and became something of a recluse from the Vanaran courts until Serith Ellyn became Queen. He briefly served her as a judge, but moved to Duinnor early in the Second Age, and rarely returned to Vanara thereafter. In Duinnor, Banis rose to power through wealth accumulated by leasing Vanaran lands from Elifaen and collecting the unpopular Lease Taxes from those who did not depart those lands. Through various intrigues, he filled the parliament of Duinnor with his own supporters and served as Second Lord of the Royal Exchequer for many years, where he came to control much of Duinnor's financial policies, including the expansion and enforcement of the controversial Leases of Forfeiture. His power was further increased as he served as the chief advisor to the King's First Lord of the High Chamber, Lord Harstaff. Upon the death of Lord Harstaff, Banis was elevated to First Lord, and took the place of Harstaff, becoming second in power only to the King himself. It was Banis who was responsible for the loan of the black eagles of Shatuum to Duinnor, and he used them to spy on Duinnor's enemies and friends alike. The eagles of Shatuum were, in fact, given in trade by Secundur to Banis for his daughter Esildre. When his son Navis sought to free Esildre from Shatuum, Banis, in fear for the loss of those eagles and much of his power, engaged Bailorg to murder Navis. However, when Esildre eventually did come out of Shatuum, Secundur had found the arrangement with Banis so useful that he allowed the loaned eagles to remain in Duinnor.

Over time, Banis became the subject of much displeasure due in chief to his free abuse of power. It was well understood that he encouraged corruption among the Regular Army of Duinnor, and wielded great control over the military. Although the Kingsmen reported directly to the King himself, Banis continually sought to subvert them from their duties. He also sought to remove judges who would not favor his associates in their rulings, and was himself on several occasions implicated in murder, attempted murder, extortion, and corruption. He was never tried for any of these crimes, likely due to the protection given him by the King.

During the final years of the Second Age, Banis became increasingly desperate, audacious, and overt, often doing little to hide his acts of revenge, murder, fraud, and theft. He came to control the leadership of Duinnor Regular army, and, by the time of his death, he was making inroads to exert control over the Kingsmen. At last, desperate that his role in the Navis affair would become discovered and made known by Robby Ribbon, Banis ordered his agent in Vanara, Count Dialmor, to assassinate Robby using special operatives already in place who were preparing to assassinate Queen Serith Ellyn. As described in *The Year of the Red Door*, the operation failed, but at great loss of life and tremendous damage to the White Palace in Linlally. One of the attackers was captured and it almost immediately became known to the Sixth Unknown King that Banis had ordered the assault without the King's approval. This resulted in a rift between the King and Banis, and in his last months Banis became paranoid to the extreme and began to show signs of a growing madness.

At last, not long before the Sixth Unknown King was overthrown by King Philawain, Banis threw himself (or was thrown) from a high window of his apartment. Although Elifaen, he died instantly upon impact with the street below. During the investigation which followed, it was found that Banis had obsessively kept extensive and meticulous records of all of his activities and those of all his associates in crime. The discovery of these records led to the arrest of many of his accomplices, including high-ranking officials.

See Also:
Biographical Sketches (Esildre)
Glossary (Bailorg, Dialmor, Faradan, Navis)
Historical Sketches (Duinnor)

Banshee   Witches or messengers of the afterlife who are thought to beckon the living into death or whose appearance forebodes extreme danger. It is said that only certain bloodlines of Men are visited by banshees when near death or sometimes when threatened by mortal crisis. Banshees were unknown in the world until the coming of Men, though some say that they are witches of the First Age who struck some bargain with Beras for their redemption. This tale has it that, in order to redeem themselves of the evils their kind committed in the world, they must act as harbingers to the bloodline of certain dying Men whom they wronged. Other legends say that the banshee are not witches at all,

but another kind of spirit somehow bonded to the fate of Men. The most notable banshee was Caparrashee, attached to the Ribbon family of Men.
See Also:
Glossary (Caparrashee)

Barian   Known as Barian the Counter, he was a Melnari of the early Second Age, famous for his knowledge of the heavens.
See Also:
Historical Sketches (The Melnari and Their Familiars)

Barindon   Second King of Solsorna of the House of Cypress in the region that would become Masurthia Realm. Barindon was the son of Marfain and Terisi. It was his father, Marfain, who established the House of Cypress in the Time Before Time. Marfain and Terisi settled in the region of Solsorna when it was a fishing town governed by a clan of Elifaen. After a number of disputes, Marfain slowly took control of territories surrounding Solsorna until he laid siege to the town in 550 F.A. Shortly afterwards, he made it his kingdom, pronouncing himself King of Solsorna. In 925 F.A., Marfain died as a result of a hunting accident, and his son, Barindon, ascended the throne. Barindon continued his father's policy of expansion, pushing the boundaries of his domain north to the Plains of Bletharn, east into the lower Thunder Mountains, and westward into Altorian territories. In 931, after years of conflict with Altoria in the Wachee River territories (between Altoria and Masurthia), Barindon led a small army across the Wachee to sack and burn several Altorian garrisons. This act quickly led to war between the two realms. At the same time, both Altoria and Masurthia sought to wrest control of the trade routes passing through the territory that connected Tracia and Vanara. In 936 F.A., several Vanaran barges laden with trade goods bound for Solsorna were confiscated upon their arrival in Draymoor. This came at a time when King Barindon sought to also block Tracian overland caravans from carrying goods to Vanara. As a result of these actions, Parthais assembled a large army and drove them south into the Wachee river valley and effectively separated the warring parties. He then split his army and while he remained encamped along the Wachee, a third of his army marched toward Draymoor while the other third marched to Solsorna. He sent messengers ahead of each vanguard to warn King Barindon and Queen Therona that unless they immediately sued for peace and sent their envoys to Parthais, each city would be sacked. The plan worked, and both Therona and Barindon were humiliated. Before Parthais would remove his armies, the two feuding sovereigns were forced to agree upon the Wachee as the border between their realms. They were also forced to agree upon trade conditions and terms favorable to Vanara.

After the conflict ended, Barindon embarked on a road and bridge building campaign while at the same time began developing his trading fleets. In 947 F.A., he invited Lady Lucinda to bring her House to Masurthia, since he had heard of her troubles in Glareth. Many believe this was a ploy to obtain her Bloodcoins in an effort to legitimize the House of Cypress. However, Lucinda's ships never arrived as several were lost along the way and the final three were shipwrecked on the coast between Tracia and Masurthia. Although Barindon would spend years searching for Lucinda's two sons, who supposedly survived with the Bloodcoins, they would never be found.

Barindon himself died at sea in the year 996 F.A. Childless, the throne then went to his niece Gina.
See Also:
Biographical Sketches (Esildre, Felthain)
Tales of the High Houses (Lucinda, Therona)

Barley County   A rural county within the old Eastlands Realm south of Lake Halgaeth and just east of the Thunder Mountains, bordering the lands west of the ancient fortress of Tulith Attis. It was so named because of the main crop grown in the region. Barley was once merely the regional name for the area, but was adopted as the county name when the Eastlands Realm was organized (under the

regency of Glareth) itself into counting districts for the purpose of performing the First Census in 483 SA. Nearly all of the lands encompassing Barley were once part of the vast Bosk estate holdings, but over time much of the former Bosk lands were sold or deeded away. Its principal town is Passdale, formerly known as Dalefath.
See Also:
Glossary (Dalefath, Passdale)

Barsonfar   A village in Connassa Province of Glareth known for its dairy products, including a pungent, hard yellow cheese.

Bartow   One of the captains of the Fourth Army of Kingsmen under General Teracue during the late Second Age. He served in the Dragonlands, fought against the Wickermen at the Battle of Soltani Pass, and at Tallinvale against the Redvests.

Battalion   A military unit normally consisting of between 1200 and 1800 men, including military support staff (but often excluding civilian support personnel such as wranglers, blacksmiths, wagon drivers, etc.). However, the size and makeup of the battalion level military unit varied greatly from realm to realm, and from army to army. In Duinnor, a battalion is usually no less than 1500 soldiers, but in Glareth a battalion may have as few as 800 men. Several battalions may comprise an army unit or division. Battalions sometimes acted as semi-autonomous units under a battalion general or other command responsible to a higher general or commander. Battalions were usually subdivided into companies, variously consisting of between 150-500 men. Sometimes battalions were organized in support of specific types of operations or duties. For example, the 1st Battalion of the Kingsman Fourth Army was a Heavy Assault Battalion, while the Third Battalion of the Kingsman First Army was an engineering battalion, and specialized in fortifications, mapping, bridging, and the like, often in service to other units outside the First Army.

Military organization changed and varied greatly from place to place and over time. Thus, the term varied wildly in actual meaning. By the late Second Age, Duinnor was considering reorganizing its forces under a new structure that would combine certain battalions into divisions, and those divisions would then form a particular army group. Other organizational, tactical, and strategic units and structures were also being considered.

Baygast   Company commander of Sparrow Company, First Battalion, Fourth Army of Duinnor. He distinguished himself at Westlawn when he commanded a small ballista that helped destroy the monster of the Wickermen.

Beauchamp   Familiar to Raynor the Melnari; Beauchamp took the form of a rabbit. Beauchamp was captured sometime around 700 S.A. while on an errand for Raynor and was taken into the Dragonlands as a part of a menagerie of exotic northern animals. He survived the ordeal and managed to escape, working his way northward over the course of many years, eventually returning home to Raynor in Duinnor in 870 S.A. Beauchamp often served as something of a spy for Raynor. As described in *The Year of the Red Door*, Beauchamp carried out one of his most audacious "missions" when he infiltrated (with Raynor's help) the High Chamber of the Sixth Unknown King. There he discovered a great deal that would later be of use to others.
See Also:
Historical Sketches (The Melnari and Their Familiars)

Begrimlin   Often referred to as Begrimlin the Kingmaker, although it is not known why he was called Kingmaker. A Firstborn Elifaen, he was renowned for his ability to bring feuding parties to treaty, though he found little success when it came to bringing peace between his people and the

Dragonkind. In the latter part of the First Age and into the Second Age, he was active in many realms. He helped negotiate peace between Altoria and Masurthia and was also instrumental in the recognition of the kings of Glareth, Tracia and Masurthia. He was the tutor to Collandoth (Ashlord) for a short time. In the year 537 of the Second Age, while traveling in the Eastlands, he suddenly fell ill and died a few days later. Many speculate that he was poisoned with Sigh Mortabilis (foxdire), since no Elifaen dies of natural causes.

Behemoth A constellation of the northern sky, so-called after the legendary monster that roamed the earth during the Time of Strife and was said to have been thrown into the heavens by Cupeldain (though Cupeldain denied any such feat).

Bekund Captain of the House Guard of Tallin Hall.

Beleron An Elifaen prophet of the early Second Age who forewarned the Elifaen against joining with Men. A cult sprang up around him that persecuted Men and created divisions between Men and Elifaen during the early part of the Second Age. He eventually renounced violence and called for peace between the races, but was himself assassinated, along with several others of his cult who joined in his renunciation. For a few years, the implausible rumor persisted that the murder was carried out by agents of the Dragonkind. However, circumstances seem to point to those members of his own cult who were angered by Beleron's renunciation of his previous teachings. Members who were openly unrepentant soon became the subject of reprisals, and many met with mysterious deaths. Others, it is thought, formed a secret society dedicated to thwarting any peace between Men and Elifaen. Some, it is speculated, even allied themselves with Secundur. A few years after Beleron's death, a beautiful temple was built in his honor in the northern hills of Vanara (the Temple of Beleron, within the Valley of Dreams) and remains a place of worship and contemplation. It was a particularly popular destination for those seeking a change of heart (as Beleron had) and wished for a change in their life's direction. For some, particularly among military survivors, it was a place where they could have time and peace to grapple with the traumas and violence they had experienced or witnessed.

Belmira One of the daughters of Heneil and Lyrium, twin sister of Elmira, though they were not identical twins. Tradition has it that Belmira and Elmira were ordained by Beras to advocate for life and death, when called upon by the Elifaen to make such a determination for the sick, distressed, or condemned.

Belmira and Elmira were rarely separated from one another and seem to have had a shared thought process. When one spoke, the other often completed the sentence, and back and forth. Nearly all of their "duet" speaking is in rhyme.
See Also:
Biographical Sketches (Belmira and Elmira)
Tales of the High Houses (House of Fairfir)

Belsalza During the late Second Age, King of the Dragonkind. Son of Salzadur and supposedly a descendant of Kalzar the Great. Belsalza rejected the reforms of his father, rebuilt the armed might of the Dragonlands, reunited the sundered tribes, and carefully prepared for a renewed war against the north. In the final years of the Second Age, Belsalza sent special teams into the north to secretly prepare wells that would be needed by his armies and to make maps and scout good routes to Duinnor City, which Belsalza aimed to conquer. While some members of these teams did return to bring back maps, many others moved into hiding places, particularly along the escarpments of Middlemount, to await and take part in the coming invasion. At least one team, however, inadvertently crossed the border of Nasakeeria. Their bodies were entirely consumed, but their accoutrements were blasted into Nasakeeria where they would be found. The examination of these

items alerted Prince Nightar of Nasakeeria that they must prepare for their end of days in Nasakeeria and their return to their homeland in Nasakeeria. Thus, inadvertently, Belsalza set in motion the return of those who would take back the city that his own forebear, Kalzar, sought to destroy.
See also:
Glossary (Darini, Kalzar, Salzadur, Nasakeeria)

Bentbend   A village south of Passdale on the river Bentwide.

Bentwide   The stream that flows from the headwaters of Lake Halgaeth to the Saerdulin to the south. When Heneil's Wall was built, damming Lake Halgaeth where it fell into the Saerdulin, the lake level rose considerably, eventually spilling into the Bentwide. The Bentwide then flowed as a river, deep enough for boats to dock at the town of Dalefath (later the site of Passdale), where a bridge crossed the river permitting goods and traffic to go to Attis. When the dam burst late in the Second Age, the Saerdulin retook its course and power, and the Bentwide was reduced to a stream as the lake quickly fell to its ancient level.
See Also:
Glossary (Barley County, Dalefath, Passdale)

Beras   The personification of the Creator; sometimes called Intent. He was worshiped by Elifaen, Men, and the Dragonkind, all having separate views, lores, and ideas of Beras. Beras was also referred to as the personification of the Creator's Intent, seeing to the balance of the world. It was Beras who commanded the earth to be formed and for life to emerge upon it. Beras was regarded as the father of the Faerekind. The Dragonkind peoples also worshiped Beras who was, in their religions, the force behind their liberation from the ancient dragons who had enslaved them. Men worshiped Beras as their savior, who directed their departure from their Lost World and guided their epic passage across the boundless sea to the shores of the Found World.

Berralasa   One of the Elders of Nowhere, the outspoken wife of Herbert the Blue.

Bessinton   Farming region in the southern Eastlands, south of County Barley.

Bilaylin   1. a founder of the Bosk clan of Men, also called Bilaylin the Hammer. Along with several other Men, he joined with the Elifaen to fight the Dragonkind in the Second Age. He gained a reputation for valor on the battlefield and cantankerousness everywhere else. He died at Tulith Attis during the Dragonkind siege of that place, but was survived by a son and three daughters.

2. The right name of Billy Bosk, a descendant of Bilaylin the Hammer. Billy Bosk was one of those who accompanied Robby Ribbon and his party westward in 870 of the Second Age.
See Also:
Biographical Sketches (If Not For Galafronks)

Biradur   (Biradur Waste) The desert wasteland to the southeast of the Blue Mountains of Vanara in the northernmost reaches of the Dragonlands. It stretches from Kajarahn to the west to the Nalamain Hills and the Tamkal Plain to the east, and reaching from the Badlands southward to Calamandor (the Green Citadel). The Biradur is notorious for its vast flat stretches, sometimes covered by shifting dunes of sand, and for its violent sandstorms. Ever-changing in its particulars, where a sea of dunes may be one month may the next be scoured of all but the heaviest grit and dust. It is hot and inhospitable, and because there are few wells and no oasis between the Badlands and Calamandor (the Green Citadel), it was once thought a natural barrier against invasion from the Northlands. However, twice in the Second Age, armies managed to cross it and lay siege to Calamandor (the Green Citadel). Since then, it has sometimes been called the Crossing Plain.

Blackelm   One of the ancient Houses of Vanara traditionally in service to the House of Fairoak.

Blain   (Blain Farby) Father of Grantham Farby of Duinnor

Blaney   Surname of brothers Gargeoff and Markum Blaney who were residents of Hill Town and expert scouts. The two brothers migrated from Tracia during the rise of the Triumvirate and served under Martin Makeig in the fighting that took place when Redvests invaded the Eastlands.

Bletharn   (Bletharn Plain, or The Great Bletharn Plains) The great grassy plain that divides east from west, with Duinnor and Vanara on the north and west at the edge of the world and the other realms to its south and east. It is virtually uninhabited and has few trees and no significant surface water in the form of streams or lakes. In addition, a peculiar blight lays upon this region so that any game taken from the place and eaten will make a person violently ill from an intestinal malaise that might last for days but rarely results in lasting harm. Only those people who have been born in the region are immune to the malaise. For that reason, there are few occupants of the Bletharn Plains because none can sustain a community for a generation without having food constantly brought to them from elsewhere. However, there are a few groups who have managed to live on the Plains, mainly in the southern regions nearest to Altoria and Masurthia. These are various nomadic hunting tribes, generally called the Cuwali, who have little to do with the outside world and follow the herds of bison and antelope to hunt for their subsistence.

Legend has it that the Bletharn Plain was the place where Aperion called together all of the Faerekind of the world and where he offered them the choice of departing or remaining in the world. It is said that when those who decided to depart released their grip upon their bloody weapons, the weapons fell upon the plain and poisoned the land.

Bloodcoins   The common name for the Forty-Nine Keys to the Nimbus Illuminas, often called simply The Forty-Nine.
See Also:
Historical Sketches (Bloodcoins)
Tales of the High Houses

Bluepine   A village in the northern extremes of Tallinvale.

Bluepipe   Resident and councilman of County Barley, a maker of cabinets and boxes.

Bodwin, Sally   Girl of Hill Town, Goddaughter of Martin Makeig.
See Also:
Biographical Sketches (Sally Bodwin)

Boggy Wood   A densely wooded and boggy region of Forest Mistwarren on the eastern side of the River Saerdulin opposite County Barley at Tulith Attis.
See Also:
Glossary (Mistwarren)

Bonewalker's Valley   Also called Griferis Vale or Grigferith Vale. Since for a long time little was known about Griferis, many tales and legends surrounded it. It was not known that Griferis was not a floating island.   But tales of it were very often mixed with the most terrifying descriptions of hideous creatures. It is now thought, though, that Bonewalker's Valley was conflated with tales of Griferis, but originally derived from the tales pertaining to nearby Shatuum.

Bordy   A Passdale councilman.

Borwain   Ward of Lord Threshmere of the House of Hemlock. He had the talent of drawing and painting in such a way as to make the image seem to transform while gazing upon it.
See Also:
Glossary (Hemlock, Threshmere)

Bosk   One of the Ancient Honored Houses of Men, though not a Named House. It is descended from the earliest Men that arrived on the world's shore. The family estate is located in County Barley of the Old Eastlands Realm. Its most famous member was Bilaylin the Hammer who fought and died at Tulith Attis. His descendants were granted vast land holdings not far from Tulith Attis.

In the late Second Age, the Bosk family consisted of Garend and Frizella Bosk and their two children, Raenelle and Bilaylin (Billy). Their land holdings comprised much of County Barley, and consisted almost entirely of cultivated farmland, with barley being one of their most important crops. Called Boskland, the estate employed over 300 workers of all trades.

Boskland was destroyed during the Redvest invasion of 870, and its people scattered or were captured by the Redvests. Many became slaves, some became resistance fighters, and others became refugees. Garend Bosk survived the destruction and organized partisan resistance against the Redvests. Raenelle was captured and abused severely. Frizella, along with many others, fled to Janhaven where she became one of the leaders of the refugee community there. Billy Bosk accompanied Robby Ribbon westward on their quest.
See Also:
Glossary (Bilaylin, Bosk, Frizella, Bosk, Garend, Bosk, Harrald, Bosk, Raenelle)
Biographical Sketches (If Not for Galafronks)

Bosk, Bilaylin   (Billy)   Son of Garend and Frizella Bosk, close friend to Ibin Brinnin, Robby Ribbon, and Sheila Pradkin. He would accompany Robby Ribbon's party on Robby's quest for kingship. He was known to be somewhat of a talkative and playful rapscallion. But as related in *The Year of the Red Door*, he was intricately involved in Robby's quest, participating in many salient events.
See Also:
Glossary (Bilaylin, Bosk, Frizella, Bosk, Garend, Bosk, Harrald,, Bosk, Raenelle)
Biographical Sketches (If Not for Galafronks)

Bosk, Frizella   (nee Starfind) Wife of Garend Bosk of Boskland, in County Barley of the Eastlands during the late Second Age, mother of Bilaylin (Billy) Bosk and Raenelle Bosk. Close friend of Mirabella Ribbon (nee Tallin). Frizella was of a frank and practical disposition, intolerant of fools and carefree attitudes. She ran Bosk Manor, and much of Boskland, from her kitchen. She cooked all of the household meals, and she provided meals, medical attention, and assistance to the men and families of Boskland and Passdale whenever needed.

Before her marriage to Garend Bosk, Frizella became acquainted with Mirabella (then Tallin) after Robigor Ribbon asked for her hand in marriage. Knowing the conditions that her father (Lord Tallin) imposed during a year-long wait, Mirabella was able to learn through Frizella the events of County Barley and the ways in which Robigor was overcoming the obstacles that Lord Tallin threw against him. Frizella and Mirabella both married at about the same time, and Frizella taught Mirabella much as to the practicalities of keeping house, cooking, and other domestic skills. She attended and aided Mirabella when her husband and son were severely ill. She was also present when Belmira and Elmira came to the Ribbon household, and it was she who opened the door to them and led them to Robby Ribbon's sickbed.

She befriended Sheila Pradkin and tried to help her, but Sheila was reticent and self-conscious of her own poverty. When Sheila was with child, she was raped and beaten by her uncle, Steggan, and after escaping his clutches she managed to get to Bosk Manor where Frizella took her in and tried to save her life and that of the unborn baby. The baby died, but Frizella tended to Sheila's wounds and condition until Sheila parted company with her to go to Ashlord (Collandoth).

When the Redvest invasion took place, Frizella was instrumental in organizing the evacuation from Barley to Janhaven. She and Mirabella became the leaders of the refugees and together they organized an armed resistance against the Redvests.
See Also:
Glossary (Bosk, Bilaylin, Bosk, Garend, Bosk, Harrald, Bosk, Raenelle)
Biographical Sketches (If Not for Galafronks)

Bosk, Garend   Laird of Boskland in the late Second Age. Son of Harrald, husband of Frizella, father of Billy and Raenelle.

Garend Bosk received most of his education at home, but completed his schooling (briefly) under Gustan Broadweed. Garend's father, along with a few others of County Barley, were instrumental in bringing a school to the area, and Garend required that all children in Boskland of parents in his employ must attend school or show that they could by the time they were twelve, read and write adequately and had at least a basic competency with arithmetic. He did this in an effort to increase the industriousness of Bosklanders, especially since Boskland sought to increase both its agricultural and artisanal productions as well as secure trade with other regions. These goals required skilled workers who could keep records and accounts and understand written communications and instructions. When his father died and Garend became laird, he continued his father's policies, and even expanded them so that adults within Boskland could be offered reading and writing lessons.

Garend also served for a brief time as Sheriff of Barley County. With all but petty crime being almost unheard of in the county, there were incidents involving a group of young men and boys who were particularly troublesome, provoking fights and disputes, drunkenness, and theft. This resolved itself when they were mysteriously murdered near Tulith Attis. Garend investigated but only discovered that a stranger, name unknown, had been seen with the boys. Garend continued his duties as Sheriff until shortly after his father died, by which time he was also married and had two children, Raenelle and Billy.

As a young man, Garend was instrumental in the rebuilding of the bridge across the Bentwide located at Passdale. He and his father backed the scheme because he needed easier and cheaper access to the Janhaven road than using the local ferries provided. Boskland not only helped finance the work, but also provided materials and labor, with Garend supervising much of the project.

In 870 S.A., and as a result of raids that had taken place in Barley, Garend succeeded in convincing Passdale in establishing a militia based in the town to compliment his own Boskland Militia. These two forces, very small and terribly outnumbered, would be virtually annihilated when the Redvests invaded later that year. Garend succeeded in escaping capture and would go on to lead a partisan group which harried and harassed the occupying Redvests.
See Also:
Glossary (Bilaylin, Bosk, Frizella, Bosk, Bosk, Harrald, Bosk, Raenelle)
Biographical Sketches (If Not for Galafronks)

Bosk, Harrald   Laird of Boskland, father of Garend. Harrald Bosk, a forward-thinking man, was instrumental in establishing a county school and bringing in Gustan Broadweed as schoolmaster. It was Harrald's contention that a better-educated workforce would make for a more productive estate. But he was also sensitive that many children were otherwise doomed to menial work from an early age, work that was often dangerous and inappropriate for children. Once the school was established, and with much resistance and resentment on the part of many parents, he made employment in Boskland contingent on having some schooling. The Bosk estate paid for the lion's share of the school's expenses, and the children of those employed by Bosk had most of their school books and supplies provided to them at no cost by the Bosk estate. The plan paid dividends back to Boskland as the first generation of children who attended grew up, and, now able to read, write, and do mathematics, became valuable workers, supervisors, managers, and overseers on the estate. Other people of the region, elsewhere in Barley and Passdale, followed suit in an effort to help their bourgeoning shops, trades, and other businesses.

Harrald was also one of the strongest advocates for rebuilding the bridge over the Bentwide at Passdale, which would increase trade opportunities and general commerce.
See Also:
Biographical Sketches (Gustan Broadweed, Ned Arbuckle)

Bosk, Raenelle   Daughter of Garend and Frizella Bosk, older sister to Billy Bosk. Raenelle was captured by the Redvests during the invasion of 870 S.A. She was severely abused by one particular Redvest, Pargolis, and would eventually kill him.

Braig Bailorg Denuth Delcorman   Full name of the one commonly known as Bailorg.
See Also:
Glossary (Bailorg)

Branard   One of the militia of Boskland.

Bransondale   Town renowned for its pottery, located in the northern region of Tracia along the border with the Eastlands. The region surrounding Bransondale is claimed by Tracia but considers itself part of Eastlands Realm.

Bream   Resident of Hill Town, one of the Thunder Mountain Band.

Brennig   (Russard Brennig) Commander General of Tallinvale, Lord Tallin's chief aide and military advisor, died at the Second Battle of Tallinvale.

Brinathar   (Brinathar the Lion) Summer constellation to the east of Behemoth. Brinathar was a lion, and was the legendary protector of Ererdid the Princess, whose constellation is nearby. This constellation depicts Brinathar watchfully crouching nearby to the sleeping Ererdid.

Brinnin, Ibin   Man of County Barley, close friend of Billy Bosk. It is thought that a sickness while a young child scarred his mind so that even as an adulthood he seemed childlike and slow-witted. He had difficulty speaking, and he did not seem to grasp many common-sense concepts. However, he was gentle and kind, sensitive to his surroundings, and had a talent for verse and song. He was orphaned when his parents died. He was taken in by the Bosk family. He became, in effect, like a brother to Billy Bosk, and the two were almost inseparable, so much so that he accompanied Billy on Robby Ribbon's quest (as described in *The Year of the Red Door*). He survived the quest, and elected not to transform and depart the world as so many did. Instead, he remained in Barley, took a wife and had a family.
See also:
Biographical Sketches (If Not for Galafronks)

Broadweed, Gustan   Schoolmaster in the town of Passdale, County Barley in the late Second Age.
See Also:
Biographical Sketches (Gustan Broadweed)

Brolith   Elder of Nowhere.

Buckie   Powerful pony of Barley, favorite of Ibin Brinnin. Would allow no other person to ride him.

Buckman's Ferry   A ferry located near to where the Bentwide meets the Saerdulin.

Buckmarl   A type of large antlered deer or elk ridden by many Elifaen. They are swift and light on the hoof, strong and nimble in the wood and on rocky mountainsides. They are renowned for their ability to leap from crag to crag, much like a ram, with surefooted ease.

Byrn (Byrn Tallyck) Tradesman and resident of Greenfar.

Byrniece   Daughter of Pyros and Duiniece of the House of Fairmyrtle. When her mother and father died during the First Demon War (around 880 F.A.), Byrniece took the Bloodcoins of their House, and she led the remnants of Fairmyrtle into territories that would later become Tracia. There she would abide, marrying a Man in the Second Age. She died in 196 S.A. when a boar charged her horse and it reared and fell backwards upon Byrniece, crushing her to death. The Bloodcoins were stolen by King Kapol of Tracia, and then subsequently lost.
See Also:
Tales of the High Houses (House of Fairmyrtle)

Bywaters   Resident of Greenfar.

Calamandor   Known as the Green Citadel by Men, a great city in the northern deserts of the Dragonlands, that was sacked and destroyed twice in the Second Age.

Calamandor was one of the oldest and largest cities of the Dragonkind, with plentiful wells. It was a trading center and also produced fine pottery, copperwares, and finished textiles and clothing. Calamandor was also renowned for its elegant and rare overhanging gardens, fed by a system of water channels and pumping stations. Due to its milder climate relative to other areas within the Dragonlands, it was a favorite retreat for the Dragonkind royalty and for the wealthy. Under Queen Nebalasa, it flourished as her summer residence and when she died, she was entombed there within a lavish mausoleum, which became a popular and almost sacred site for the city and for visitors.

Calamandor was called the Green Citadel because of the tower that once held the Glowing Stone of Bazradur which emitted a bright green light both day and night. Legend had it that as long as the Glowing Stone shone over the city, it would be safe from attack from the north. It was also deemed safe by virtue of its distance from Vanara. In 790 S.A., the tower mysteriously crumbled and fell, shattering the stone so that, even when reassembled, it did not glow as brilliantly as before.

In 837 S.A., an army of Men and Elifaen managed to cross the Biradur Waste and lay siege to the city. It fell three months later, after horrendous and bitter fighting. After its fall and the subsequent sacking by the victorious Northmen, the long march back north saw even more fighting and soon became a route as fresh Dragonkind armies arrived. Few of the invading army survived. As a result of these events, Gurasa was held to blame for the fall of Calamandor, eventually to be acquitted of the charges which nonetheless ended his military career.

Not learning lessons from the past, the Dragonkind rebuild the city but continued using it as a base for intrusions into Vanara. Eventually, the Northmen marched again, and another siege took place with much the same results. The city was destroyed again, and just like before, the withdrawal from the conquered city became a shambles with heavy casualties suffered by Vanara and Duinnor. "Shannan ar Calamandor!" or "Remember Calamandor" became a rallying cry for the Dragonkind people. However, whenever the Green Citadel is mentioned in the north, it is often with in connotation of futility and shame; for although each of the two sieges were victorious, and the city sacked each time, such was the cost in blood and treasure that few believed that it was worthwhile or that any further attacks should be made.
See Also:
Biographical Sketches (Gurasa)
Glossary (Gory Gulch)

Calletshire   County in northeastern Eastlands Realm close to the border with Glareth Realm.

Calman   A captain of the King's Post stationed at Janhaven during the late Second Age.

Caparrashee   A banshee attached to the mortal family of Ribbon. She was one of several banshees that appeared to Men, mostly during a time of mortal danger, illness, or at death. Caparrashee appeared to Balfast Ribbon upon his deathbed, and was seen by Robigor Ribbon (Balfast's grandson). When Sheila Pradkin, pregnant and severely injured, tried and failed to make it to Boskland for help, Caparrashee appeared, to take the unborn child (of Robby Ribbon) across death's threshold, and she was witnessed by Robby Ribbon and exchanged words with him. She appeared twice more. Once, she was fooled by Robby in to thinking that he was near death, and so taken across the threshold of death in order that he might speak with his great-grandfather, Balfast. Finally, she appeared to assist Robby upon his own death. Perhaps this fulfilled her destiny and gave her redemption and freedom, for since then she has not been seen.
See Also:
Glossary (Banshee)

Captains of Shatuum   These were powerful warrior-lords who served Secundur as generals under Throgallus's (Pellen) authority. Secundur often used them independently and without the knowledge of Throgallus. There were originally thirteen of them, created from the spawn of Secundur's witches and their union with Valkose the Demon.   They were all very large, tall, and powerful, encased in black armor from head to toe emblazoned with Shatuum's emblem, a red hourglass. They rode equally large black horses. These captains were equipped with a sword of hot metal and a long whip of magic fire made, it was told, from the spirit of the vanquished Valkose. When struck by the whip, any creature would immediately explode into burning cinders. With these, they held in check the vast legions of witches, wraiths, and other creatures of Shatuum, preventing them from breaking out of that place before their numbers were sufficient to fulfill Secundur's plans. The captains remained obedient to Secundur until he was captured or destroyed by King Philawain, then they gave their allegiance to Throgallus.   One of the captains was destroyed when exposed to the reflected sunlight cast by a Bloodcoin in Ullin's hand. Another was destroyed when, while attacking Ullin, he fell through the ice of a mountain lake. The others were destroyed (or transformed) along with Throgallus and all of Shatuum's creatures when the Nimbus Illuminas was opened and the world was remade.
See Also:
Biographical Sketches (Pellen)
Glossary (Shatuum, Valkose the Demon)
Tales of the High Houses (House of Fairfir)

Carbane   Ruling Prince of Glareth, father of Prince Danoss. Carbane is of the Elifaen House of Beech. Carbane was the son of King Thalamir's daughter, Megan, who assumed the role of Ruling Princess after Thalamir's abdication. Megan carefully groomed Carbane to take charge of Glareth Realm and eventually abdicated to him, making him Ruling Prince of Glareth. Carbane oversaw many reforms, some that were initiated by his grandfather and others that came about during his own time. He worked to strengthen Glareth's maritime power and reach by supporting the construction of many new ship designs, including fast trade ships and innovative warships. Correspondingly, Carbane's policies bolstered shipbuilding, naval stores industries, training centers, and the development of new navigation methods and techniques. He created a separate province, called Connassa, to be ruled by his son, Danoss, and to serve as the administrative center to oversee the defunct Eastlands Realm. Carbane instituted many reforms in the legal system, extended rights to many, punished corruption and deceitful trade practices.

Under Carbane, by the late Second Age, Glareth became less dependent on trade with Duinnor along the Osterflo, and was routinely sending hundreds of trade vessels to every port in the Seven Realms.   Thus regular trade and the exchange of products took place between Vanara, Altoria, Masurthia, Tracia, and the Eastlands.   During the growing internal strife within Tracia, Carbane strengthened ties with Tracia's Ruling Prince Lewtrah, in spite his growing concern over Lewtrah's corruption and incompetence.   Many suspect that, well before the Tracian civil war that led to the Redvests taking power, Carbane was intentionally strengthening relationships with Prince Lantos, who was Lewtrah's brother and was opposite in character and capability.
See Also:
Glossary (Danoss, Glareth, Thalimir)

Carella   A bright star of the constellation Brinathar the Lion, often called the Eye of Brinathar.

Carriage of Ilex   A magical carriage conjured into existence by Ilex, King of Forest Halethiris, to be used by his family while traveling to and from Vanara to attend the conference of the Seven High Houses called by Cupeldain. Pulled by white oxen, the carriage moved twenty times farther on one turning of its wheels than an ordinary carriage would. It was much larger on the inside than its outwardly dimensions, containing a forest grove complete with a lively stream and gentle waterfalls within a woodland park.
See Also:
Eighteen Objects of Power (The Carriage of Ilex)

Carth   Farmer in County Barley known for his apples and cider.

Carthane Mountains   (The Carthanes) Lofty mountains to the west of Glareth and the Eastlands Realms. The range is bordered in the north by the Osterflo River and stretches south to the Thunder Mountains, west to the Plains of Bletharn, and eastward to Lake Halgaeth. Its highest peaks are ever capped with snow, as they rise precipitously in the middle region of the range and drop away as rapidly to the north. Its high passes, particularly Loringard Pass, were once a favorite summer route to and from the Eastlands and the west, but they were closed from late summer through late spring by ice and snow. Mount Halfis, its highest peak had upon its summit one of the Seven Towers.
The Carthanes were rugged and densely forested, encompassing a variety of forest habitats, laced with thousands of streams and rivers, and riven with deep gorges, and many isolated valleys. In the far north, along the Osterflo, it was mainly wooded with spruce and mountain pine. Hardwoods increase in numbers as one goes south, especially in the more sheltered elevations. In the middle Carthanes, and the Thunder Mountains, hardwoods dominate. Then toward the southernmost reaches, where the mountains were of rather modest height and not nearly as rugged, the forests were mostly of pine. All throughout the Carthanes were mines and quarries. Marble, granite, flint, iron ore, silver, gold, and later coal, were all mined to some degree. Rubies, opals, topaz, some amethyst, citrine, and a few emeralds were also found. Of course, the Carthanes were a prime source for lumber, too, with Glarethian companies operating extensive lumber operations and mills along the Osterflo. Among its natural denizens were deer, rabbit, bear, raccoons, squirrels, chipmunks, mountain lions, many kinds of birds, and an abundance of fish.
According to legend, the northwestern region of the Carthanes around the town of Wayregyle was once home to the High House of Fairmaple, under the leadership of Katrina. It was there that Katrina brought her people to settle in the year 816 F.A., seeking to distance her people from the encroachments of Lord Ormace (House of Fairbirch) and settlers from the Duinnor region. However, in the year 1260 of the same age, the region was found to be abandoned of all Fairmaple people, and rumors indicated that Katrina had once again led her people away, this time into the northern wastes beyond the Osterflo.

The region east of Mount Halfis was the home of Pyros and his House of Fairmyrtle. Legend has it that around the year 880 of the First Age the lands of Fairmyrtle were infested by witches. A few of Fairmyrtle's people escaped to Tracia. However, in an effort to eradicate the land of the witches and their lairs, Lady Duiniece made all the lands of that region freeze, even though it was summer. She made it so cold that the air itself froze, it is said, and even rocks cracked and crumbled. Such was the destruction this act caused that the mountain forests were almost entirely destroyed, and the land itself was changed due to avalanches and floods when the ice melted the following year.

In the early Second Age, a portion of the southern mountains of the range were inhabited by trolls, creations of Alonair that he more or less abandoned to their fate. Such was the noise they made that those mountains were thereafter called The Thunder Mountains. By the late Second Age, the trolls were gone, a few towns and settlements of Men were scattered throughout the Carthanes, and several warlords vied for power in the mountains.

It was in the Carthanes that Collandoth and company encountered Paltera, a mountain witch that he soon dispatched. Collandoth then discovered her lair and that she was concubine to Valkose the Demon, with which he did battle.

See also:
Biographical Sketches (Alonair)
Glossary (Karthia, Thunder Mountains, Tower Halfis)
Tales of the High Houses (Katrina, Pyros)

Cartu A warlord of Thunder Mountain hillsmen who, in the late Second Age, took power over the Damar people, instituted enforced conscription, and force a few other clans to serve under his banner. He built up his stronghold, called Damar City, and ruled despotically, forcing heavy tributes from farmers and tradesmen, taking slaves for his service, and directing attacks against Hill Town and other settlements. He also vied for territory and control of the roads with the Galinots, a warlord clan located north and west of Mount Halfis in the Carthanes. In 870 of the Second Age, Cartu allied with the Triumvirate of Tracia and joined with the Redvests in the siege of Tallinvale, where he was killed.

Cataract A legendary and invisible river that flows through the bottom of the Crack Between Worlds, the deep divide where the world ends and another world begins. It was called the Cataract due to the sound which was deep and powerful as a mighty waterfall. Explorers of the place tell that the sound of roaring water was interspersed with thunderous booms, as if mighty boulders were cracking and tumbling. Many others maintain that it is a vast and swift river of icy-cold water that pours into the Craggy Sea to the south of the Dragonlands nearby to Karkarando and that it is this torrent that creates the powerful and deadly currents of the often mist-shrouded Craggy Sea.

The earliest reliable account of the Crack Between Worlds was recorded in the First Age by Nimwill, royal scribe to King Parthais, who went to find Griferis. They arrived and spent weeks at the edge of the Crack Between Worlds, but Nimwill in his writing did not mention any sound coming from the depths of the chasm. While this caused some to doubt earlier reports of the Cataract, some wondered if perhaps Nimwill's party happened to visit during a period of relatively calm water flow. Some say he may have simply failed to mention any sound.

During the late Second Age, rumors began to circulate that a Dragonkind expedition had discovered a huge waterfall spanning the chasm at a point some two hundred miles southwest of Kajarahn. Its precise location is not known, but many think it was at or near the place where Thunderfoot's trolls would build a vast dam, the result of which caused the waters of the Cataract to overflow and spill through the mountains to pouring forth and washing across the Dragonlands. This was all done according to King Philawain's instruction, and his intention was to have the flooding waters wash away much of the desert sickness that was a result of the dust and sand of the Dragonlands. In this, he was correct, and in the centuries since the remaking of the world, the desert

is now covered with lakes, streams, and marshes, the sand is all but washed away or covered with vegetation, and the sickness that once plagued the inhabitants of the region is no more.
See Also:
Tales of the High Houses (Last Book of Nimwill)

Celefar   1. One of the Firstborn Faere who stayed behind with Cupeldain and the others of the Faere who were determined to fight the Dragonkind. It was Celefar who was loved by Aperion's daughter, Laeleth, and the love of Laeleth and Celefar and their travails to be reunited are recorded in many songs, poems, and tales.

2. A buckmarl ridden by Prince Thurdun, brother of Queen Serith Ellyn of Vanara. He is named for one of the legendary Firstborn, a great warrior and the lover of Laeleth, daughter of Aperion.

Certina   One of the Familiars. She accompanied Collandoth in the world during the Second Age. Certina's form was that of a small screech owl, not much bigger than one's hand.
See Also:
Historical Sketches (The Melnari and Their Familiars)

Chadler, Van -- Head of the Duinnor City Kingsman Constabulary in the late Second Age.

Van Chadler, born in Duinnor, enrolled in the Kingsman Academy in 823 SA at the age of 18. Upon graduation in 827, he was immediately assigned to serve in the Kingsman Second Army and took part in the siege of the Green Citadel. During the bloody final assault, Chadler was separated from his company and found himself with Dalvenpar Tallin, of the 4th army. With Tallin as his protector, they survived the siege, witnessed looting and atrocities. Dalvenpar saved Chadler's life by shielding him from arrows during their retreat. Dalvenpar died, but Chadler escapes, taking Dalvenpar's sword. Chadler was later wounded in the leg, but he survived and eventually returned to Duinnor. He immediately sends Dalvenpar's sword to Lord Tallin with a letter telling of Dalvenpar's fate. Chadler gradually recovered from his wounds, although he would permanently walk with a pronounced limp. As he convalesced, and while his health was being assessed to determine if he could resume his duty in the ranks, he was assigned to the King's Constabulary of Duinnor City. At the Constabulary, Chadler quickly proved adept at solving crimes and was given a "tenured" assignment. He rose in the ranks and eventually became chief investigator with the rank of City Commander. Later, he was promoted to general and assigned to serve as the head of the Constabulary, but within the year he was lotteried to serve as Palace General Commander of the Guard for the King. It was a term of service of five years, after which he resumes his normal duties as head of the Constabulary.

During the last years of the Second Age, Chadler worked diligently as the head of the Constabulary, and was active in many investigations. He also was very careful about training new Kingsmen assigned to the Constabulary, not only by providing additional training as might be needed to conduct criminal investigations, how to interview witnesses, and how to gather and safeguard evidence. He also insisted that all members of the Constabulary show good knowledge of the law, the courts and all procedures by insisting that each member submit every two years to a written and oral test on such matters.

Of course, Lord Banis and his followers constantly sought to undermine the Constabulary and to thwart any investigations or arrests that might harm his own endeavors. For example, besides the Constabulary, only Lord Banis had the power to issue warrants for arrest or summons, and he frequently used this power to suppress or to punish those who opposed him. Chadler thwarted much of Banis's arrest efforts by instigating a Kingsman rule that stated that any such warrants or summons issued by parties outside the Kingsman ranks had to be reviewed and authorized by a Kingsman of the rank of general before being carried out. This permitted the victims time to be warned. Thus, Banis began using Duinnor Regulars to carry out his arrests. As well, there were many investigations that Chadler conducted that clearly implicated Banis or his men of involvement in criminal acts, and in many cases Chadler was powerless to make arrests or to even interview those protected by Banis.

All of this, along with his normal duties, made his participation with certain conspirators quite difficult. Using his authority as the head of the Constabulary, it was easy for him to send his own agents into other lands, ostensibly to perform normal duties, such as seeking fugitives or requesting the transfer of captured wanted criminals to Duinnor. But they just as often delivered and received coded reports pertaining to all manner of military and domestic activities. He thus enhanced the information obtained and shared by other means.

He and his conspirators knew that peace with the Dragonlands was possible and a worthy goal, but quite unlikely given the political and social climate in Duinnor and Vanara. But they succeeded in establishing reliable Dragonkind contacts who were willing and able to help develop the possibilities for peace. Chadler and his co-conspirators also knew that Lord Banis himself was openly despised by growing numbers across the social, political, and economic spectrum. And, they understood that, outside of Duinnor, many of the King's policies and laws were unjust and unfair, especially those pertaining to Leases of Forfeiture, travel restrictions, and fees charged to other Realms that amounted to tribute. Through his discretion of enforcement, Chadler was only somewhat successful in softening the effect of such laws.

By the time Collandoth, Sheila, Ibin, and Billy arrived in Duinnor in the year 871, Chadler was quite ready to react to the news that they brought and to the crisis that they would precipitate, including the death of Lord Banis. He quickly realized that a new King was coming, and he threw himself wholly in support of it. Chadler and Captain Thrubold moved very quickly to assemble evidence pertaining to the activities and cohorts of Lord Banis which resulted in many arrests in the last days before the world was remade.

Chaldron A constellation of the northern sky, named by the Dragonkind after a legendary warrior. As legend has it, Chaldron was thrown into the sky by a dragon and is doomed to forever chase the beast around and around. It is one of a group of constellations that can be seen throughout the year as it circles so closely to the North Star. It was within this constellation that the Sword of Chaldron first appeared.
See Also
Glossary (Sword of Chaldron. Glossary (Wanderers)

Chancellor In most realms, the title is given to a ruling lord of the land. In all regions except Duinnor and Vanara, it is a position filled by group selection, the groups consisting of lords or other high ministers of government. This person is normally the second most powerful in the land, after the Ruling Prince.

In Vanara, the Lord Chancellor was the very highest lord, second only to the Queen in power, and was selected by the Queen herself to serve as her head of state. He was charged with overseeing military, diplomatic, judicial, and economic matters and carrying out the Queen's Rule of Law, acting as the Chief Judge of the Land with the power to overturn the verdicts and rulings of Vanaran Judges. The Lord Chancellor of Vanara was also Regent of Vanara whenever the Queen was absent from court, and spoke with the same authority as the Queen. This position, one of utmost trust, was created by Queen Serith Ellyn in 756 SA to alleviate many of her growing administrative duties, but was given more power and authority over time. In 849 S.A., Lord Rolland Seafar was named Chancellor, the first mortal to hold that title. The House of Seafar continuously held the title thereafter, with Brandis Seafar, at the age of thirty-four, becoming the youngest Chancellor in Vanara's history in 865 S.A.

In Duinnor, there are a variety of chancellors, all with limited power and purview, such as the Chancellor of the Exchequer, in charge of financial and banking matters. Other chancellors were appointed by the Hall of Houses (the civil governing body) for various roles, usually of a temporary and limited nature. In effect, however, the First Lord of the Realm was chancellor, holding virtually all powers in lieu of any specific edict or order from the King himself.

Chanter   One of the captains of the Household Gray Guard of Queen Serith Ellyn, brother of Gaiyelneth (who was a companion and maid to the Queen).   Chanter was an expert swordsman and taught his sister how to fence (and who quickly out matched Chanter). As a young soldier, Chanter fought at Gory Gulch.
See Also:
Biographical Sketches (Gaiyelneth)

Chawbree   A region west and north of Janhaven where oilwood was harvested from the stumps of old pine trees.

Chiroth   Region to the west of Duinnor that mined silver of exceptional purity.

Chiselpeck   A village in the Carthanes that mined silver and produced modest jewelry. It was known as Darforin until sometime in the middle of the Second Age, when it took the name of the chief mining concern located there.   This community was where Lyrium hid after her escape from Tulith Attis.

Chulwinkie   A resident of Bluepine.

Clingdon   Blacksmith of Passdale, County Barley, father of Gina. Blacksmithing was a family trade, and Clingdon was a master of his craft. He made the large signaling bell used by the Passdale Militia. Even though no metal was produced nearby to Passdale, the Clingdons always seem to have ample supplies of iron, steel, and copper. They mainly made tools and implements for farming, shops, and household use of a sturdy and utilitarian nature.   Occasionally the Clingdons would produce somewhat ornate items of wrought iron or brass.
See Also:
Biographical Sketches (How the Blacksmith Got His Iron)

Collandoth   Also known as Ashlord, mostly among Men. Collandoth had a varied and long career, and he was instrumental in shaping the lives of Sheila Pradkin, Robby Ribbon, and others. He was one of the key figures that influenced the way in which the Second Age concluded.
See Also:
Historical Sketches (The Melnari and Their Familiars)

Colleton   A port city on the Eastlands coast at the mouth of the River Northford. It was once the capital of the Eastlands Realm, from where various royal lineages ruled. During the middle Second Age, Colleton began to lose its status as an important trade port. This was partly due to the advent of larger and more efficient Garethian trade ships, and partly due to the rise of Attis as an important trade town. Colleton's importance was further eroded by the inept rule of several kings, particularly Inrick I and II. After the demise of King Inrick II, the Eastlands became a protectorate of Glareth, and Colleton continued to decline.

Common Speech   Also referred to as the Common Tongue. By the late Second Age, it was the dominant language of Men and Elifaen, and the native language for most Men of the eastern realms. It

became the standard language of trade and commerce during the Second Age and as its use spread, it almost fully displaced other languages. It was a heterogeneous language made up of many aspects of the Ancient Speech and various dialects, combining words and phrases brought by Men to the world with those spoken by the Elifaen. Virtually every region had its own dialects of Common Speech, some of which were difficult for outsiders to understand. In spite of this, and much due to its use in commerce and academia, it was rapidly being formalized by the end of the Second Age, with spelling and grammar fairly standardized across the world, at least in school settings. However, dialects persisted, especially in the old Eastlands and among relatively small and isolated communities.
See Also:
Essays and Explanations (Literacy and Education)

Common Tongue See Common Speech

Conjurer-king The magical kings of legend and myth who reigned over marvelous and mysterious lands unseen by ordinary mortals or Elifaen. Children's stories abound with such figures, sometimes evil, sometimes solitary individuals rarely seen. There is a basis for these tales in the kingship of Duinnor, for that king has an unknown name, is rarely seen, and rules through mysterious and, some say, magical powers. But such tales of conjurer-kings predate Duinnor by at least four centuries. Some scholars attributed its genesis to the Kings of Sudamoor, a mysterious place that is remote and has little interactions with the wider world. Collandoth the Melnari was sometimes called a conjurer-king because of his role in the history of Alaberbra (Kajarahn).
See Also:
Eighteen Objects of Power (The Cornucopia of Sudamoor)
Historical Sketches (The Melnari and Their Familiars)

Coreth Daughter of Atlana, sister of Faslor, and niece of Esildre. A member of Vanara's Fellfaere and the Gray Guard, Coreth became Robby Ribbon's unofficial guide and escort while visiting the White Palace at Linlally.

Cormund Valley A fertile valley in Vanara to the east of the Iridelin River.

Cornucopia of Sudamoor A possession of the Kings of Sudamoor. It was a large horn from which food and necessities flowed during times of need and want.
See Also:
Eighteen Objects of Power (The Cornucopia of Sudamoor)

Corunimus Delarus Means, in the Ancient Speech, "strike me dumb," usually used as an expression of grave surprise.

Craggy Sea The stretch of sea to the south of the Dragonlands and Altoria. It is a region filled with reefs, shallows, and jagged rocks that jut up from the surface. The combination of these obstacles with powerful currents, frequent fog, strong tides, and violent storms makes navigation through this sea nearly impossible, even by small vessels. Since wood is scarce throughout the Dragonlands, the people of that region rarely venture far from the few safe bays along their coast. It therefore serves as a natural barrier protecting Altoria from any large-scale sea-based invasions from the west.

The Craggy Sea has been the scene of many shipwrecks. Even though the region teems with all manner of fish, the hazards of fishing there prevent all but the most daring or foolhardy fishermen from the attempt. There were several attempts by Altoria to construct lighthouses and markers to warn away seafarers, but none were successful. For one, none of the bordering crags have any source of fresh water, besides rainwater. For another, the approaches to suitable rocks and reefs were, and by all accounts still are, extremely difficult, making construction and resupply very haphazard at best. For example, Altoria attempted to build a modest lighthouse on one of the nearest crags in 762 of the Second Age. It took a eight months to simply make a foundation for the planned stone structure, during which over thirty people died, with the loss of three vessels. Work halted for almost two years, but the second attempt fared even worse, with greater losses of men and ships, and no further attempts were made.

Crevasse of Fire Located along the eastern slopes of the Tulivana Mountains, the Crevasse of Fire was formed in the First Age when a volcano erupted there and spewed flowing lava. The lava cut a deep channel between two sharp cliffs and pooled somewhat before cutting under the mountain that blocked the lava, then it flowed farther eastward into the western edges of the watery Hinderlands. The volcano remained active for several years, and the Crevasse of Fire was the place where, in 918 F.A., Navis of Elmwood did battle with Jatarak the Ogre. Navis prevailed, and it is told that he cut off Jatarak's head to take back to Altoria, and tossed the giant's body into the Crevasse. Legend has it that Jatarak's body was not consumed by the molten pool, but was eaten by the dragon that put forth the fiery bile that made the volcano. The dragon, so the story goes, was satisfied with the meal, and went to sleep. By the time Navis had returned to Altoria through the Hinderlands, the volcano had become quiet.
In 870 S.A., a new eruption began spilling rivers of lava down the eastern slopes and into the Hinderlands. The flow was so steady and rapid that it created many natural causeways across the swamps and marshes, amid huge clouds of steam, and were well over halfway across the Hinterlands when the world was remade. This eruption ended not long afterwards, and the lava fields have formed a myriad of islands and small plateaus, many connected to one another by ridges.

Cronosis Also Semiluna, known as the Fortnight Flower or as Half Moon. A delicate flowering salvia of the Dragonlands. It has a large bloom that lasts for fourteen days, gradually changing color from brown (when it blooms) to red, to dark green, to blue, light blue, and finally, it turns white before it quickly decays.

Cuffdare A worker at the Hall of Ministers Library in Linlally. Although he was quirky and odd, he was extremely knowledgeable and skillful and was helpful to Robby Ribbon when he visited the Library seeking a copy of the Last Book of Nimwill.

Culfinor One of the ways in which the Unknown King of Duinnor was addressed, meaning "the one who is alone," or, "lonely one," presumably because of his isolation and rare public appearances.

Cupeldain One of the Firstborn of the Faerekind and founder of the House of Fairlinden. It was Cupeldain who led the Faerekind to make a war of retaliation against the Dragonkind, against Aperion's command. He and those who followed him were punished by being stripped of their wings. Cupeldain did much to bring about the end of the Age of Strife (the period just after the Fall) by establishing a center of learning in Vanara where his people could learn the skills of planting, construction, forging, and other crafts needed for a more comfortable life. It was during this time that the Elifaen received the Forty-Nine Bloodcoins and the Seven High Houses of the Faerekind were established. When Silmain established himself First King of all the Elifaen, Cupeldain opposed his efforts to unite the Houses and to use the Bloodcoins to open a way for his people to leave the earth. Cupeldain and his followers did not openly oppose Silmain's kingship, but they did little to support his efforts. However, when Silmain was killed in battle, Cupeldain was urged to take the king's place as ruler, and he eventually did so. A tenuous cooperation among the Elifaen enabled Cupeldain to continue warring against the Dragonkind and his victories did much to establish and secure Vanara's southern borders.

Cupeldain, like Silmain before him, called a Great Council to debate and decide the use of the Forty-Nine Bloodcoins. Sick of war and longing for a return to Aperion, Cupeldain urged that they use the Bloodcoins and depart from the earth. But a dispute arose and instead the Bloodcoins were divided among the houses so that each took possession of one of the seven different Bloodcoins in order to make it more difficult for any single House to depart on its own (which was actually impossible). This agreement, ironically, helped to unite the people since all Houses then depended on the others for the safety of their coins.

For a long while, Vanara prospered under Cupeldain's rule, and the city of Linlally grew in the security of its borders. During this era of peace, however, the strength of the Dragonkind grew and many of the foul creatures created during the time of Morgasir (those who survived Morgasir's destruction) began spreading into the world. Their assaults were unorganized and unpredictable, and usually not coordinated. Cupeldain established special fast-acting military groups organized to annihilate them and he mostly succeeded in clearing Vanara of their presence.

When a territorial feud broke out into violence between the Elifaen House of Laurel and that of Hemlock, Cupeldain sought to mediate a peaceful settlement between them. While traveling through their lands, he and his wife Loura were set upon and drowned, their bodies weighed with millstones and cast into a lake. The murder took place in the lands of Hemlock, but many pointed the finger of blame at Laurel. Regardless, a series of reprisals threatened to spark a wider civil war among the Elifaen Houses. However, Parthais, Cupeldain's son, raised an army and crushed the warring Houses, executing many chief members of the feuding clans and their wives, too, as punishment and as warning against future feuds that might threaten Vanara.

See Also:
Biographical Sketches (Loura, Parthais)
Glossary (Silmain)
Tales of the High Houses (House of Fairlinden)

Cuwali   A name for the strange nomad tribes and the name of their language. They are hunting tribes, living primitively along the southern reaches of the Bletharn Plains. The Cuwali tribes have an immunity to the sickness that befalls others who eat fruit or meat from the plains. They normally remain south, along the borders of Altoria and Masurthia, but sometimes move northward to hunt, and on rare occasions they have even been seen as far north as the Osterflo. During the Second Age, they were suspected of having frequent dealings with the Dragonkind, and knew secret paths through the Hinderlands and hidden passes in the Tulivana Mountains through which they could travel to and from the Dragonlands. Some evidence of this was found by Collandoth among the letters he acquired that had been written by Bailorg. One letter strongly indicated that Bailorg used the Cuwali as helpers or intermediaries with the Dragonkind.

Dalefath   The former name of the site where Passdale now stands, on the western banks of the Bentwide River in the County Barley of the old Eastlands Realm. When Heneil dammed the Saerdulin at Lake Halgaeth, the lake waters to rose and spilled into the Bentwide, forming a river that was before merely a stream. At that time, the old bridge at Dalefath was rebuilt and made higher and stronger. As a result, Dalefath became an important crossroads since it was the farthest north that heavy trade barges could come (smaller boats could still travel up the Saerdulin as far as Tulith Attis, but only if they were rowed by skilled oarsmen.) The name went out of common use sometime after the battle at nearby Tulith Attis, when Dalefath and the surrounding lands were destroyed. After its destruction, it would be almost a hundred years before the site was reoccupied and eventually called Passdale.
See Also:
Glossary (Barley, Bentwide, Passdale)

Dalvenpar see Tallin, Dalvenpar

Damar   A warlord region in the Thunder Mountains that sprang up in the latter Second Age; it allied itself with Tracia during that realm's revolt against Duinnor's rule. The Damar was a large group of lesser warlord clans ruled by the Cartu clan, and its most powerful ruler and overlord was Lang Cartu. Damar power was utterly destroyed in the late Second Age when Damar city and their strongholds were assaulted and overrun by Kingsmen who were on their way to the relief of Tallinvale during the siege of that place. Lang Cartu himself was killed at Tallinvale and most of the Damar fighters as well.

Damar City   The chief city of the Damar. The fortified city became the seat of power for the Damar warlords. It was burned and destroyed by Kingsmen in the late Second Age.

Danig   see Tallin, Danig Saheed

Danoss   Prince of the House of Beech, son of Glareth's Ruling Prince Carbane. Prince Danoss was the prince and governor of the Connassa Province of Glareth Realm during the late Second Age. He made his home at Formouth, on the northern shore of Lake Halgaeth. He organized the Connassan Lakemen into a paramilitary naval force tasked with patrolling the lake against pirates, and with carrying on trade with the south, and transporting passengers and trade-goods across the lake. In 871 SA, Danoss led an army of Glarethians and Loyalist Tracians (under Prince Lantos) against the Redvests in the Eastlands, coordinating the offensive with other Glarethian-led armies that invaded Tracia's coasts, quickly defeating the Redvests across Tracia.

Danthis   A military engineer, builder, and sculptor of the middle Second Age. He was responsible for the design and construction of many watch towers and minor keeps and fortifications in Vanara. He also built Tulith Morgair, a watchtower on the western Carthanes overlooking the Missenflo and the Bletharn Plains to guard the river crossing along the route to Fisenwold.

Darakal   A flowering herb that is native to the Karkarando region of the southwest Dragonlands. In the year 491 of the First Age, it was discovered that an elixir made from the herb alleviated or cured the sickness that normally plagued the Dragonkind. Immediately, attempts were made to grow darakal on a large scale. However, cultivation is difficult, requiring special techniques combined with the unique characteristics of soil and humidity found only within the Karkarando region.

Within two years after darakal's discovery, Emperor Tajahnaman mobilized to take over all cultivation of the herb and soon controlled the production of the elixir. His son, Churadu, established the Priesthood of the Dragon, a religious order, with himself as its head. Through his priests, Churadu established rites and ceremonies by which the darakal elixir was distributed.

Darakal is primarily given to the ruling class of the Dragonkind, who came to be called the Alziekfria. Taken as a kind of sacrament, the darakal elixir prevents those who partake of it from forming the characteristic scabs and scales, loss of hair and hair color, and other debilitating physical characteristics of ordinary Dragonkind. Those who are already stricken by the sickness can be alleviated of its symptoms by partaking of it. After Churadu, the cultivation of the herb and the production of its elixir was strictly controlled by subsequent Emperors as the priesthood gained power and authority. Soon after, unauthorized possession of the herb or the elixir was made a capital offense. But, due to the demand, a lucrative black market was more or less permanent. Shipments were stolen, illegal fields were cultivated, and smuggling was commonplace. However, black market darakal was as or more expensive than that obtained through the Emperor, and the danger of illegal possession was so great, only the desperate or wealthy could purchase it. Many attempts were made to cultivate darakal in regions outside of Karkarando, including in the Northlands, but with little or no success.

See Also:
Historical Sketches (Karkarando)

Dargul   Chief civilian advisor and counselor to Lord Danig Tallin of Tallinvale during the late Second Age.

Darini   A city of the Dragonlands that was established sometime during the Time Before Time, abandoned for thousands of years before it was resettled after the world was remade.

Darini is located in the northwestern Dragonlands, just south of the Biradur Waste and not far from Kajarahn. In the Time Before Time, it was a beautiful and prosperous city located at a location where natural springs gushed to the surface. This water was cleverly directed throughout the city, and irrigated the many fields and gardens surrounding Darini.   The climate was fairly moderate, compared to other regions, and among other crops, flax and grains were grown, as well as orchards of date and orange trees. These crops, along with linen and ceramic products, were important exports. Darini was renowned for tile-production, which was used in the design and building of its elegant homes, palaces, and walkways. The stonemasons and builders of Darini were renowned throughout the Dragonlands, and they were often hired in the great building projects of other cities.

During the time of Kalzar the Great, however, Darini came under greater pressure to provide food and supplies for use by him. He had already taken away many of the city's stonemasons and workers to quarry the Great Stone, and as his efforts to move it continued to fail, Kalzar demanded confiscated more and more of Darini's crops and products to supply his conscripts and slaves. The city revolted and refused to supply any more men or products to Kalzar. The small force that Kalzar sent to put down the rebellion was wiped out by Darini's fighters, so he assembled a large army to entirely conquer Darini.

But Darini was already starving and weakened by Kalzar to the point of near collapse. So the people of Darini decided to leave the city and to sabotage its source of water. This they did, guided, it is said, by an emissary from Aperion. Taking all that they could manage with them, they set off on a long and arduous trek northward, through the mountains, moving their mass carefully and secretively, in constant fear of discovery by Faerekind and Dragonkind alike. It took years, but they eventually arrived at the lands where they would settle, which would become known as Nasakeeria.

Meanwhile, having found an abandoned and arid city, worthless to his schemes, Kalzar was enraged. After a futile search for those who had defied him, he abandoned the Great Stone, turning his efforts instead toward attacking the Faerekind.

When the people of Darini eventually learned of the great war between the Faerekind and the Dragonkind, and when they learned of the Fall of the Faere, they were filled with fear. They knew that they could not defend themselves against an onslaught of vengeful Elifaen. And, as legend has it, Aperion heard their pleas and put around their land his fire to protect them, which they called Aperion's Fire.

The old city of Darini remained a dead city. Dust and sand encroached, covering over the canals and streets and much of its beauty. Very few people ventured there to look upon it. Search as the might, none found water. That is to say, not until Ullin Saheed Tallin and Micerea arrived in the year 862 SA and found a trickle of water. This trickle was the key to unlocking the ancient springs, and this feat was accomplished by Seleesa, a Nasakeerian who returned with all her people to reinhabit Darini.

Since the world was remade, Darini has become a home for many who wished to remain in the world rather than be transformed into the next world. Those who came and began restoring the city and surrounding lands included not only Nasakeerians, but also many Men, Elifaen, and Dragonkind. With a great and steady supply of water, the sands were washed away, and many fields were restored. Eventually, Darini would be the location of a Great Library, established by Ullin Saheed Tallin. Today, Darini continues to be a vibrant and beautiful place, and its people healthy, happy, and welcoming to all who may come to visit or to live.
See Also:
Glossary (Kalzar, Nasakeeria)

Darlang Hill A steep rise on the southeastern face of the Blue Mountains, south of The Mirse, jutting out roughly five miles into the desert. It overlooks the important Garthorn Pass that leads into the Mirse region. Darlang Hill was occupied by the Vanarans in the Second Age after the Great Invasion with the intent to use it as a base from which the nearby passes leading to The Mirse could be watched and patrolled. In 506 S.A. it was overrun by the Dragonkind who then sent another army through The Mirse. The Dragonkind marched northward up the Bletharn Plains toward Duinnor, but the army was swallowed and destroyed when they inadvertently marched into Nasakeeria.

After this incident, Darlang Hill was once again taken and refortified, occupied by a coalition of Fellfaere, Kingsmen, and local militia. However, by the late Second Age, many of the Duinnor troops stationed there were pulled away to other duties. Thereafter, only a token force of Fellfaere was permanently stationed there, and it fell to local militias raised from various estates in the Mirse region to man and defend the Hill and to repulse any incursions through Garthorn Pass.
See Also:
Historical Sketches (Great Dragonkind Invasion)

Deedle Tavern keeper of Bluepine in the late Second Age

Delcorman See Bailorg.

Desira Firstborn Elifaen, and sister to Tiryna (wife of Banis). It was rumored that Desira and Banis had an affair, which resulted in the birth of Desira's daughter, Shevalia, although Desira never identified Banis as the father. Desira was quite beautiful, a fact which belied her abilities as a warrior. Her prowess earned her high rank among Elifaen fighters, and as many tried to woo her as desired to fight alongside her. In spite of her skill, and under somewhat mysterious circumstances, she was killed at the Battle of Tamkal Plain.

Dialmor (Count Dialmor) Dialmor was a member of the Duinnor legation to Vanara during the final years of the Second Age. His duties were to manage several spy operations along with a covert military unit under the command of Captain Faradan. He operated under the authority of Lord Banis, who usually passed along Dialmor's reports (but sometimes did not) to other authorities in Duinnor, sometime including the King. Dialmor's history is not known, but he apparently had served the Sixth Unknown King as a spy in the Dragonlands, in Vanara, and for a time in Glareth. In 857 SA, Dialmor was elevated to the rank of count, a somewhat unusual title, and was given ownership and authority over some small properties in Duinnor.

In 866, Dialmor was assigned to Linlally, under the guise of Special Attaché to the Duinnor Ambassador. He took up offices at the Hall of Ministers in Linlally, within the confines of the Duinnor wing. As a contingency plan that Banis devised, Dialmor was given the task of overseeing the organizing of an elite armed unit charged with finding ways of attacking and assassinating Queen

Serith Ellyn. This Dialmor did over the next few years. One of Dialmor's successes was in learning that the Queen would be traveling to Glareth and likely carrying her Bloodcoins with her. This he reported immediately to Duinnor and, with the King's approval, Banis ordered Dialmor to direct Captain Faradan's group to track and to attack the Queen's travel party, once they were well away from any large protecting forces of Vanara. This Faradan attempted to do, but this happened to be on the very night that Robby Ribbon rang the Great Bell which, far away as they were, alarmed the Queen's company which formed into a very formidable defense perimeter around the Queen. Since Faradan's only hope was to take them by surprise while sleeping, he was foiled and retreated. Dialmor, exceedingly vexed at the failure, nonetheless reported it to Duinnor. Banis responded by ordering Dialmor and Faradan to prepare to assassinate the Queen upon her return by a direct assault on her White Palace.

For several months, Dialmor and Faradan's force prepared, using a secret location in Vanara to practice and train using maps and floorplans of the Palace acquired by Dialmor. Then Dialmor received word from Banis to target a different person, Robby Ribbon, to be urgently eliminated by any means. Dialmor was instructed that Ribbon was likely to arrive at Linlally to perhaps seek Vanara's assistance. So, when Robby's presence was discovered by Dialmor shortly after his arrival, and when it was learned that Robby would be guests at the White Palace, all was in place.

As described in *The Year of the Red Door*, this plot also failed. Faradan was captured, all his men killed during the attack, and Dialmor fled. Intending to go to the Free City, Dialmor was himself captured by renegades. They traded him into the hands of agents of Secundur who were gathering slaves. He and other captives were moved along the trail at the Crack Between Worlds toward Shatuum, but were rescued by Robby Ribbon. Upon discovering Dialmor's identity and prior activities, Robby Ribbon arranged for Dialmor's delivery to Lord Seafar in Linlally. Arrested and threatened with execution if he did not cooperate, Dialmor gave Seafar all of the information he had about all of Duinnor's secret activities in Vanara, with lists of all remaining agents. It is not known what became of him afterwards as the world was soon remade and everything changed.
See Also:
Glossary (Faradan)

Diamases   Son of Kalzar the Great. Diamases lived and died sometime during the Time Before Time. He inherited an empire that was severely damaged by the Faerekind and weakened by Kalzar's harsh rule. Diamases managed to retain power in spite of increasing political divisions and other problems. When he died, the empire that Kalzar built began to crumble as various tribes broke away.
See Also:
Historical Sketches (Thrones of the Dragonkind)

Dirkshire   A county in the Eastlands Realm located southeast of County Barley across the Saerdulin River. It was known for its soft white cheese.

Donniger   Family of County Barley in the late Second Age

Dorcilla   Resident of Greenfar in the late Second Age. She was the wife of Garnor Stavin, a cobbler and maker of leather-goods.

Drago   The ordinary class of Dragonkind. Mistakenly thought by some of the north as a separate race from the Alziekfria since the Drago and Alziekfria were often different from one another in appearance and health. That is because the Drago did not regularly receive the darakal elixir in sufficient quantity to be healthy and were thus more coarse in appearance, lived with pain, and generally had a harsh existence, often reflected in their fierce demeanor. They suffered scales of the skin, thinning hair, and, if they had the desert sickness long enough (and most did), their facial features changed. Most notable was a thinning of the lips, thickening of the tongue, and the loss of the bony structure of the proboscis, which resulted in a flat nose with narrow nostrils. As a result of the sickness, few Drago reached physical maturity and became over time increasingly weak and prone to other illnesses, thus their mortality rate was quite high. In the late Second Age, even with darakal in relatively high rates of distribution (historically), the Drago's average lifespan was about 30 years. For this reason, they tended to have many offspring, most of which would die very young. The poorest of the Dragonkind, who could not afford to purchase much supplemental darakal, were trapped by a cycle of poverty and illness. Of course, this was often taken advantage of, or even enforced, so that the Dragonkind kings and lords, by promising more darakal, could have steady replenishments into their armies and their ranks of servants.

See Also:
Glossary (Darakal)
Historical Sketches (Karkarando)

Dragon Terrible, fire-spitting creatures spawned by Morgasir during the Time before Time. Most of the dragons, along with Morgasir and a host of his followers, were destroyed by Beras in a great conflict, but some escaped into the bowels of the earth and into far places. Legend has it that the dragons sired a race of slaves to serve them, and, when the dragons were destroyed, the slaves were set free, becoming the Dragonkind. Dragons are thought by some to still abide deep within the earth, sometimes spitting such heat that molten rock and fire burst from the earth to form volcanoes.

Dragonkind Mortal inhabitants of the southern deserts, calling themselves Drakyr. Their legends tell that they were created as offspring of Morgasir's dragons, created to serve as slaves. When Morgasir was destroyed, along with most of his creatures and followers, these people survived by eking out a living in the vast forests and plains. Later, those lands were blighted by the Faerekind and became deserts and wastelands. But the Dragonkind survived and eventually multiplied, and built great cities, developed engineering and mathematics, writing, and other arts. Since the time of their first great king, Kalzar, the Dragonkind have warred with those of the northern lands.

Although the lifespans of the Dragonkind were very short, and child mortality was very high, they typically had many children, and proved resilient and very adaptable to the harsh conditions of the desert. Long before the Elifaen did so, they developed writing, mathematics, engineering, and various agricultural practices. They were artistic, imaginative, and inquisitive, as evidenced by their works of art, their literature, and their centers of learning. Their desert cities were among the most beautiful ever built, easily rivaling, or exceeding, those later of the Elifaen. Sarapolis, Calamandor, and Tyrsharat all possessed imposing and elegant palaces, courts, and gardens.

The Dragonkind were plagued by a sickness peculiar to the desert lands. This sickness, unknown in northern lands, robbed the people of vitality and strength, deformed the skin, hair and facial features of its victims, and limited population growth by a high mortality rate. Prior to the discovery of darakal, it was estimated that three out of five children died before reaching childbearing maturity. When darakal elixirs were discovered, it was found that even infrequent doses lengthened lives by an average of seven to ten years, increasing the average lifespan to twenty-five years of age. However, the Dragonkind leaders deliberately limited the distribution of the elixir in order to wield power over their people. Those in favor generally received darakal more frequently and eventually became known as Alziekfria, a class virtually free of all symptoms of the desert illness. Ordinary people, called Drago, only received small quantities of darakal, in wide intervals, enough to strengthen them for labor but not enough to eliminate their vulnerability to diseases that would otherwise not be life-threatening. Because of this, the Dragonkind were always extremely susceptible to epidemics and plague.

As a result of the ever-constant spectre of death, or even in spite of it, they developed several religious customs and beliefs. They were believers in Beras, a supreme god who was responsible for releasing them from bondage to their dragon creators. They also practiced elaborate burial rituals that emphasized the continuity of life. These were eventually formalized and organized by various kings, particularly Churadu, who imposed the religion on all his subjects in order to dole out, limit, and control the distribution of darakal in an effort to enforce and ensure loyalty.

Drakyr   The ancient and proper name for the Dragonkind and often used as the name for the lands of the southern deserts; also called Dragonlands. In some texts, the name sometimes refers to the people of Drakyr who claim to have originated as offspring of the dragons and call themselves the Dragon People.

Draymoor   Capital of Altoria located on the Iridelin River about forty miles upriver from the sea. It was established as the capital of Altoria by Therona and the House of Fairwillow.

Drayworth (Ramund Drayworth)   Former Duke of Drayfield of Tracia, a famous (or infamous) swordsman and adventurer of the late Second Age. Fiercely loyal to deposed Prince Lewtrah, he was hunted by the Triumvirate's assassins. Drayworth remained in Tracia for several years, fomenting insurgent attacks against the new rulers, but was eventually forced to flee Tracia and later took up residence in Hill Town along with other refugees.

Dreamwalker   Also called a lunesaari, a person who is said to have the power to control his own dreams and the ability to enter the dreams of others, thereby controlling or influencing those, too.

Dreamworld (Realm of Dreams)   The dream world is both a place and a state of being. There are three distinct types, or levels, of the dream world. The first is the normal dream state that everyone is familiar with. Everyone dreams. This area is enclosed by a bubble-like shield, encapsulating the dreamer within. The second area is lucid dreaming. This is when the dreamer is both aware of the dream and has some control over it. The dreamer sees and senses the dream as if projected before him. In fact, this projection is on the inside of the aforementioned bubble. The third level is when the dreamer moves outside of his own bubble and enters the dreamworld, proper. Knowingly or not, the dreamer can then move about the real world, albeit in an ethereal state, to see and hear that which is happening. Travel, to the practiced "dreamwalker," is easy and can be done by various means akin to flying, or walking, or by almost instantaneous self-transportation. The dream bubbles of others are visible to the dreamwalker, and the astute can enter the dreams of others, can even manipulate them, can communicate with the other dreamer, and can even transport the other dreamer to another place within the dreamworld to witness the actual world.

While it is thought that all humans have the ability to dreamwalk, it is apparent that the ability ranges widely from person to person. Some aspects can be learned, and one's abilities can be increased. Still, it is a fact that some people have almost no ability to dreamwalk, at least without assistance. On the other side of the spectrum, there are others who are masters of dreamwalking and are so well-developed in the skill that they find it second-nature. At the extreme end of this are a very few individuals who can dreamwalk while they are awake, existing in both the normal world and within the dreamworld at the same time. Examples include the Oracle of Beras as well as Traveshia (of Nasakeeria).

The extent of the dreamworld has never been firmly determined and many questions arise. What animals, if any, can dreamwalk?   Does the dreamworld extend beyond the borders of the known world? How high into the sky may a dreamwalker go?

One of the most mysterious aspects of the dreamworld surrounds the types of creatures that seem to inhabit that world, that have no corresponding corporeal existence within our "normal" world of wakefulness. Yet there is ample evidence that such creatures have some influence on dreamers. Of note are insect-like creatures that seem to either feed on or stimulate dreams of a positive or negative character. Blue ones, somewhat like fireflies, are associated with pleasant dreams. Red ones, giving off a red light and sometimes called cindergnats, are more often seen congregating on the bubbles of unpleasant dreams. Most frightening are dreamdogs, creatures variously described as part-bear, part-dog, that apparently feed on nightmares. How nourishment is gained, and whether it comes from the dreamer, is a mystery.

The dream world, and dreamwalking, were instrumental in bringing about the remaking of the world by King Philawain. It was through dreamwalking that he gained much of the vital learning that he needed to understand and carry out what was required of him. Most important to his efforts was his tutor, Micerea, the daughter of Gurasa (and later wife of Ullin Saheed Tallin). Indeed, Philawain assembled an army of dreamwalkers and it was within the dream world that they carried out and coordinated Philawain's plan of action.

Duinnor A landlocked realm in the northwest of the world. Its principal city was Duinnor City. By the middle of the Second Age, Duinnor was the most powerful realm due to its military and economic might.
See Also:
Historical Sketches (Duinnor)

Durlorn Resident of Janhaven, stockade foreman to Furaman the Trader, in the late Second Age.

Dyersly Saljem Dyersly, a scholar and learned man of Tracia in the late Second Age. Dyersly established a special school for arts and culture in Tracia and was close to the Royal Family. When they were ousted from power, Dyersly fled and took up residence in Hill Town.

Eddard A Barleyman, foreman of Boskland during the late Second Age.

Edgewold An agricultural and trading town of Men located in the west near to the Plains of Bletharn on the Long Road from Altoria to Duinnor. During the late Second Age, it feuded with nearby Westlawn when that town was overtaken by Wickermen rebels. Eventually, Edgewold was garrisoned by an army from Duinnor which saw to its defense and eventually overthrew the Wickermen rebels.
See Also:
Historical Sketches (Battle of Soltani Pass)

Eglan Soldier of Tallinvale in the late Second Age.

Elder A title given to the leaders of Nowhere in the Second Age. These were the original survivors of forced servitude under Bailorg, and the ones that received the set of curses that would follow. As a result of these curses, they and their offspring were diminutive in stature, long-lived, and could not travel away from the mountain forest lands that became their new home. Only the Elders of Nowhere gained the ability to move instantly from place to place within their lands (an ability not passed down to their offspring, though the other curses upon them were inherited by all).

Eldwin An Elder of Nowhere, one of the people originally cursed after the battle of Tulith Attis. Eldwin was a woodworker and carpenter who made tables and chairs and other such things. He became a friend of Esildre and was with her at the Second Battle of Tallinvale and afterwards he attended her death and saw to her burial. Eldwin then struck out on a quest for revenge and was joined by the spirit of Esildre, who had become a ghostly apparition. Together with King Philawain, they brought about Secundur's destruction. This act lifted the curse of smallness from Eldwin, and he resumed his full and original stature.

Eldwyna   Resident of Nowhere in the late Second Age, granddaughter of Eldwin the Elder.

Elf   Or Elfkind. Short for Elifaen. A slang term used to refer to the Elifaen, usually used by Men but sometimes by the Elifaen.

Elifaen   The Fallen Ones; those of the immortal Faerekind who refused to leave the world at the command of Aperion and who were "scathed," meaning they were stripped of their wings for their disobedience. This event is usually referred to as "the Fall," or sometimes "the First Scathing," which took place during the Time of Strife (before years were counted by the Faerekind). Afterwards, the Elifaen struggled to learn how to do those things necessary for survival, such as standing on their feet, hunting, making tools and clothing and shelter.

After the Fall, the Elifaen slowly lost the use of the First Tongue, that language and power that permitted the Faerekind to communicate with the objects and living things of the world. Eventually they developed another way of speaking which became known as the Ancient Tongue.

Since the coming of Men and the mixing of the two races, it was discovered that Elifaen are only produced by female Elifaen. Whereas those born of both Elifaen mother and father endure their Scathing within the womb (and many do not survive to be born), those born of Elifaen mother and Mortal father are not Scathed until later in life. Regardless of when they are Scathed, an Elifaen does not age beyond physical maturation or, if already mature, beyond their physical condition at the time of their Scathing.

Elifaen are considered immortal, although that is not strictly true. They do not age as other races do, and have prodigious healing abilities. However, they cannot survive loss of a great amount of blood or severe damage to vital organs. They may be poisoned by certain concoctions (particularly Sigh Mortabilis), and they are susceptible to bouts of severe depression, often leading to suicide.

Vanara was the chief land of the Elifaen, with the highest population of that race. At the time of Parthais, it was estimated that there were two Elifaen living in Vanara alone. However, the Vanaran population was greatly reduced over time by war and, as elsewhere, by a low birthrate. A distant second to Vanara, Glareth also had a high population of Elifaen. The ratio of Elifaen to Men has never been determined, as such, but it is thought that roughly three-quarters of Vanarans were Men by the late Second Age. At the same time, the Glareth population was made up of nearly eighty-percent Men. Altoria and Masurthia rank next with around ninety percent Men. Duinnor and the Eastlands had far fewer Elifaen, with less than four or five percent, and Tracia the least of all, with less than two percent claiming to be Elifaen on the last census available.
See Also:
Essays & Explanations (Being Elifaen)

Ellyn (Serith Ellyn)   Daughter of Parthais, Queen of Vanara throughout the Second Age. Usually referred to by her formal name, Serith Ellyn. Serith means "most high."
See Also:
Glossary (Serith Ellyn)

Elmira   One of the daughters of Heneil and Lyrium, twin sister of Belmira, though they were not identical twins. Tradition has it that Elmira and Belmira were ordained by Beras to advocate for life and death when called upon by the Elifaen to make such a determination for the sick or distressed or condemned.

Elmira and Belmira were rarely separated from one another and seem to have had a shared thought process. When one spoke, the other often completed the sentence, and back and forth.

Nearly all of their "duet" speaking is in rhyme.
See Also:
Biographical Sketches (Belmira and Elmira)
Tales of the High Houses (House of Fairfir)

Elrasil   A hunter of the First Age who discovered the Gate of Griferis and led King Parthais there. Later, he was made a warden of Vanara under Queen Serith Ellyn. He was born and lived in a mountain community within the region that later became part of Shatuum. When Parthais moved to persecute them, Elrasil was forewarned by Thurdun and so Elrasil led his people out of the region to a safer place nearer to Duinnor. Elrasil was last seen when he went back to find others of his people who had become separated from the main group.
See Also:
Tales of the High Houses (Last Book of Nimwill)

Endeweir   Lands of the far north where winters are long and summers short. It is said that in some regions ice never melts, and, during half of the year the sun does not fully set while during the other half it never fully rises. Several efforts to explore the region have been made.

Various legends tell that Katrina led her people of the House of Fairmaple into these regions to escape the turmoil and threats of Ormace and Vanara. They first settled in the northern Carthanes (perhaps in the region of Wayregyle), but that community later disappeared, with persistent rumors that Katrina had led her people across the Osterflo and into the far north. Stories persist that the Endeweir people are descendants of the House of Fairmaple, a people who live by hunting and fishing, and who have mastery of the icy lands.
See Also:
Glossary (Northern Expeditions)
Tales of the High Houses (Katrina, Ormace)

Ererdid   The sleeping princess, a constellation of the northern skies. She is watch over by the lion, Brinathar.

Esildre   A Firstborn Elifaen of the House of Elmwood who would play a pivotal role in the events that concluded the Second Age. Her life was long and varied, as was the case with many Firstborn. Near the end of her life, she befriended Eldwin of Nowhere. After her death, and with the help of Eldwin and King Philawain, Esildre's spirit brought about Secundur's destruction.
See Also:
Biographical Sketches (Esildre)

Esin dur te Lumenii   Translated, means Hope of the Stars, a famous collection of tales, legends, poems, and songs from the First Age, before the coming of Men.

Ethliad   (Ethliad, the Sword) A famous sword belonging to Silmain, first King of Vanara. Of magical qualities, it could cut through any material, even the thickest armor. The sword was lost when Silmain was killed in the Dragonlands, but was found years later by Lyrium.
See Also:
Eighteen Objects of Power (Ethliad, the Sword)
Tales of the High Houses (House of Fairfir)

Everis   The name of an ancient land that existed during the Time of Strife or perhaps the early First Age, well before the coming of Men. Some believe Everis was a village located in western Vanara, while others hold that it was the ancient name for a region within Masurthia Realm. It is now known only as the place from where the poet Starlerf came.
See Also:
Glossary (Starlerf)

Faddus, Connor (Connor Faddus) Chief steward to Lord Waterstone of Weatherlee.   Faddus and Waterstone were very close, and their two daughters, the same age, frequently played together. This was during a time when the Redvests, who Waterstone opposed, were rising to power. It was Faddus who discovered Faeanna's body, killed by a botched attempt by Redvests to assassinate Waterstone. Then, shortly after, Faddus's daughter became suddenly ill and died. He knew that Waterstone was thinking of enlisting his half-brother Steggan to look after his own daughter, Shevalia. So it was Faddus who suggested that he take Shevalia secretly to Steggan and make the arrangements while Waterstone buried his (Faddus's) daughter as if it was Shevalia who had died, a ruse to further protect Shevalia from being hunted by the Redvests.   And so it was Faddus who took Shevalia to Steggan and made the arrangements on Waterstone's behalf for Steggan to go with his wife and Shevalia into the Eastlands to County Barley, where Waterstone had secured a farm for them. After this, and after Waterstone's imprisonment (and subsequent death), Faddus and a few other faithful servants of Waterstone would attempt, unsuccessfully, to intervene on Sheila's behalf. However, Faddus himself was doggedly hunted by Redvest agents and he was finally captured and forced to become a slave laborer. He managed to escape, and he set out to find Sheila. This was after the Redvest invasion of Barley County, and well after Sheila had departed westward with Robby and company. Faddus made it to Janhaven, where he revealed to Mirabella his own identity and the true identity of Sheila Pradkin. He also revealed that seven Bloodcoins had been entrusted to Sheila and Steggan. These were the Bloodcoins given into Faeanna's safekeeping by Lyrium, to be taken away from Tulith Attis during the Dragonkind siege of that place. Faddus eventually made his way to Hill Town to join other Tracians in exile.

Fae A word most often used to refer to the Faerekind. It is part of the word "Elifaen," with "faen" being in the Ancient Tongue one of the plurals for "faere" Fae can refer to a person, a people, or sometimes a mysterious or magical quality. It is sometimes spelled "fay" in the Common Speech.

Faeanna Daughter of Shevalia, and serving maid to Lyrium. She was an accomplished fighter, having served with Cupeldain in the Dragonlands alongside her grandmother, Desira. However, she did not enjoy battle or strife, preferring the garden and the harp over sword and trumpet. She met Lyrium when her mother, Shevalia, was invited to visit Lyrium's home in Linlally. There, Faeanna played the harp for Lyrium and, it was said, immediately entranced the audience. Heneil (who knew of Faeanna's fighting skill and was concerned for his wife's safety after a confrontation with Ormace) encouraged Lyrium to take Faeanna into her service as her lady's maid, which Faeanna was only too happy to do.

When news of the murder of her parents, along with Cupeldain, came, Faeanna was with Lyrium in Vanara. Needless to say, she was distraught and when Parthais took an army to quell the uprisings and to bring the assassins to justice, Faeanna, Lyrium, and Heneil followed but none took part in the fighting. However, when Parthais executed those he held responsible for the murders, the threesome were present and they were shocked and revolted at the sight, and filled with doubts concerning the guilt of those who were accused and executed. This resulted in the House of Fairfir's effort to distance itself from Parthais. When Parthais became king, Faeanna remained in service to Lyrium, but as Parthais sank into madness and despotism, she was glad to go with Heneil and Lyrium to Duinnor. Eventually, she accompanied the armies led by Serith Ellyn and Thurdun to take the throne of Vanara from their father. Faeanna was among those with Serith Ellyn who witnessed the slaying of Parthais.

When Lyrium and Heneil went to Tulith Attis to live, Faeanna was made a member of Heneil's household guard, detailed with the protection of Lyrium and the children. She was at Tulith Attis until the day before the fortress fell to the Dragonkind, but was given the task by Lyrium to escape with the Bloodcoins of the House of Fairfir. She and the Bloodcoins disappeared. Of the several warriors that accompanied her, only one, Tyrillick, survived and would eventually be reunited with Lyrium. But he could not shed any light on the whereabouts of Faeanna or the Bloodcoins.

However, based on evidence that was revealed hundreds of years later, it was learned that Faeanna managed to avoid capture, retained the Bloodcoins given into her charge, and she remained in hiding, unable to locate Lyrium. Faeanna likely thought, as everyone did, that Lyrium had died at Tulith Attis. It seems plausible that it was this same Faeanna who married Lord Waterstone of Tracia Realm in the year 849 or 850 of the Second Age, even though Waterstone's wife was not declared to be Elifaen, as was the law of that land. She bore a daughter, named Shevalia. This Faeanna died in the year 852 S.A., poisoned by Sigh Mortabilis by Waterstone's enemies.

Faeanna's daughter, Shevalia, was later smuggled out of Tracia and put into the care of Lord Waterstone's half-brother, Steggan Pradkin in the Eastlands. Waterstone sent the seven Bloodcoins entrusted to Faeanna with Shevalia likewise for safekeeping as part of Shevalia's possessions. However, the Bloodcoins would be discovered and stolen by Steggan, one of many misdeeds and injuries he did against Shevalia. Lord Waterstone, ignorant of Steggan's behavior and propensity for drink and violence, was arrested and later died in prison. For herself, Shevalia remained ignorant of her heritage, of the Bloodcoins, and even the identity of her parents until the very end of the Year of the Red Door. Lyrium's Bloodcoins, protected so long by Faeanna, would be recovered and used as they were intended to remake the world.

See Also:
Tales of the High Houses (House of Fairfir)

Faere Properly speaking, the First Ones, meaning the children of the spirit of the Earth. Those beings who came to inhabit the world in the Time Before Time and who embodied the joy and harmony of creation. But there was a Falling away, and the Faere race was sundered from one another, some departing the world to a heavenly abode while others, cursed and removed of their ability to fly, remained behind. Those left behind were more properly called Elifaen ("the Fallen Ones"). However, the terms "Faere" or "Faerekind" are often used interchangeably, if technically incorrect, in referring to them.

The word "faere" is from the Ancient Speech and in that language is pronounced "fAY E' rEE" with three syllables, the middle "E" carrying the accent, and a "tapped r" sound. Originally, house names of the Faerekind used this form of the word ("House of Faerelinden"), but by the middle of the Second Age, with the prevalence of the Common Speech and influences of the dialects of Men, the pronunciation and spelling was changing among the Elifaen to match that of Men. In the Ancient Speech all vowels were long and pronounced, but this practice was already falling away before the coming of Men. Since few Elifaen knew how to read or write, spelling was inconsistent, even when the same pronunciation was used. Various dialects had emerged by the end of the First Age, with distinct regional differences between Vanara, Tracia, The Eastlands, and Glareth. Upon the coming of Men, with their own various dialects, Ancient Speech quickly began changing to eventually become the Common Speech, and the words "fair" and "faere" were most often pronounced alike.

The meaning of the word in Common Speech is somewhat confusing, especially when it is not written but used in speech. When spelled "faere," it refers to the Elifaen or their ancestors. But when spelled "fair" it might (or might not) refer to the Elifaen, depending on the context. However, when interpreted as meaning "pretty" or "just" or "more than average," it is most often spelled "fair." But there is no doubt among linguists that both words were derived from a common root used by early Elifaen to approximate a word or meaning in the lost First Tongue.

When used and spelled "faere," there is often a magical connotation because Men considered the Elifaen as magical beings. When the word "men" is used in writing, it is only a general noun for human males, regardless of race. When capitalized, however, it refers to the non-Elifaen and non-Dragonkind race of Newcomers to the world. When spoken, the meaning can sometimes be vague,

and might refer to all people or all males regardless of race, or it might refer to Men, the Newcomers. So the context for the use of "faere," "fair," or "men" is important, especially when spoken.
See Also:
Essays & Explanations (Literacy and Education)
Tales of the High Houses (The Fall of the Faere)

Faerum   Derived from "Faere," and now variously used, this was once synonymous with "world." Later, it more generally came to mean those ancient territories of the Faerekind centered upon the vast Forest Halethiris. That is, Faerum was once all of the lands from the northern Osterflo River (and somewhat beyond) to the mountains bordering the Dragonlands. It stretched from what is now Vanara to the farthest reaches of the eastern world to the bordering seas.

Fairbirch   One of the Seven High Houses of the Elifaen, founded by Ormace who received Seven Emerald Bloodcoins from Aperion.
See Also:
Tales of the High Houses (House of Fairbirch)

Faircedar   One of the Seven High Houses of the Elifaen, founded by Chantay who received Seven Amethyst Bloodcoins from Aperion.
See Also:
Tales of the High Houses (House of Faircedar)

Fairfir   One of the Seven High Houses of the Elifaen, founded by Lyrium who received Seven Amber Bloodcoins from Aperion.
See Also:
Tales of the High Houses (House of Fairfir)

Fairlinden   One of the Seven High Houses of the Elifaen, founded by Cupeldain who received Seven Sapphire Bloodcoins from Aperion.
See Also:
Tales of the High Houses (House of Fairlinden)

Fairmaple   One of the Seven High Houses of the Elifaen, founded by Katrina who received Seven Topaz Bloodcoins from Aperion.
See Also:
Tales of the High Houses (House of Fairmaple)

Fairmyrtle   One of the Seven High Houses of the Elifaen, founded by Pyros who received Seven Ruby Bloodcoins from Aperion.
See Also:
Tales of the High Houses (House of Fairmyrtle)

Fairoak   One of the Named Houses of the Elifaen. When their Vanaran lands were lost to war and economic distress, Kahryna Fairoak married Danig Saheed Tallin, making the Joined House of Tallin and Fairoak.
See Also:
Glossary (Kahryna)
Biographical Sketches (Danig Tallin)

Fairwillow   One of the Seven High Houses of the Elifaen, founded by Therona who received Seven Diamond Bloodcoins from Aperion.
See Also:
Tales of the High Houses (House of Fairwillow)

Falgo (Falgo Kalpis)   The son of a Tracian fisherman of the late Second Age during the time of the Redvest Triumvirate. In 865, at age 15, he won the Spargers Cup in the Dingy Class, piloting his 14 foot sloop-rigged Spray (which he and his father built). As a winner, Falgo should have received a commission as a midshipman aboard a Redvest warship. However, due to a dearth of ships, most of the young competitors were instead drafted into the Redvest Army. Falgo was sent at first to Kalbrith, then reassigned under General Vidican's command shortly before the Redvest invasion of the Eastlands. Unbeknownst to Falgo, shortly after General Vidican led his army northward, his father and most of the other fishermen of his village were also drafted into the army. It is not known what became of Falgo's family, as the women and children were all taken away to work in various places. Falgo was part of the Redvest contingent that invaded the Eastlands and conquered County Barley and Passdale. But he was captured by Robigor Ribbon, who forced Falgo to accompany him on a trek to Glareth to warn of the Redvest invasion. Along the way, Falgo betrayed his word to go peaceably, and he attempted to murder Ribbon but failed in the effort. Instead, Falgo was eaten by Slimeback, a serpent of Lake Halgaeth.
See Also:
Glossary (Slimeback)

Fallen Ones   The Elifaen, both those Firstborn who were originally stripped of their wings and all their offspring who bear the scars of Scathing. The word "Elifaen" in the Ancient Tongue means "fallen Faerekind," or "fallen ones."

Fallendine   A Familiar in the form of a vulture. It was thought that he originally was bonded to Tolimay the Angry, a Melnari, but was released from service when Tolimay's anger got the best of him and he exploded. Fallendine later willingly served Alonair, but also Micerea the Dragonkind daughter of Gurasa, and perhaps others as well.
See Also:
Historical Sketches (The Melnari and Their Familiars)

Famatir   The broad shallow bay at the mouth of the River Talkana in Masurthia Realm. It is where the Kingdom of Solsorna was established in the coastal city of the same name.

Familiar   Familiars were the mysterious creatures that were companions to members of the Melnari race. They had animal forms, human-like personalities, and the ability to communicate directly with others without the need of audible speech, although they preferred to communicate only with their particular Melnari companion. The known Familiars were:

Beauchamp, a woodland rabbit, Familiar to Raynor the Wise.
Certina, a small owl, Familiar to Collandoth the Wanderer.
Fallendine, a vulture, Familiar to Tolimay the Angry.
Hanion, a praying mantis, Familiar to Micharam the Poet.
Telliniece, a chipmunk, Familiar to Barian the Counter.
Wink, a firefly, Familiar to Ishtorgus the Mariner.

See Also:
Historical Sketches (The Melnari and Their Familiars)

Faradan (Titus Faradan)   Captain Faradan was a zealous and fanatical supporter of the Sixth Unknown King. Convicted of high crimes against Vanara, and for murder and attempted murder, he was executed at the Falls of Tiandari by being pushed from its summit.

Titus Faradan claimed that, as a little boy, he was a member of a delegation of students invited to the High Chambers of the High Palace of Duinnor. This was part of an annual ceremonial tradition where

Duinnor children present the King with a medallion in thanks for his protection of the people of Duinnor. It is said that, when departing the High Chamber, Faradan cast his eyes back and looked directly at the King. This brief glance so muddled the boy that he fainted and had to be carried home, not recovering his wits until some days later. Although his school grades improved somewhat afterwards, he became a somewhat sullen and resentful person, prone to fits of anger And he became a ferocious defender of the King, intolerant of any criticism of the King or his ministers. This led to various fights, and there were rumors that he was involved in a duel. He was expelled from school, and immediately applied, but did not gain admission, to the King's Academy. He then joined the Duinnor Regulars and was sent on patrol into the Blue Mountains. There he proved to be a skillful fighter, a good leader to his men, but somewhat insubordinate. His zealous devotion to the King of Duinnor won him few friends, but his skill and talent in the field, unusual within the Regulars, was recognized and he was promoted. Soon Faradan was acting more or less independently of command, he and his men spending months in the deserts and Badlands ambushing vulnerable Dragonkind patrols. They took prisoners only as sport before torturing them to death. They gained a reputation, therefore, of cruelty that exceeded the bounds. Faradan was twice recalled, at the outrage of Kingsmen, to answer for his conduct, but was exonerated of charges of unlawful conduct and exceeding orders. These confrontations made Faradan extremely resentful of the Kingsmen but also even bolder and insubordinate.

By chance, his company was one of only a few Duinnor Regular Army groups at the Battle of Garmitor. They fought ferociously, most of the company were killed, and Faradan was seriously wounded.

Faradan was promoted to captain, then put in charge of his own special unit, under the authority of Count Dialmor. Officially, Faradan was listed as a special military advisor for Duinnor stationed in Vanara. However, Dialmor, likely under the direction of Lord Banis, had Faradan train his men for covert actions. One involved the attempt to attack Queen Serith Ellyn's party as she journeyed eastward in 870 S.A., an attack that almost went off but was spoiled by the ringing of the Great Bell which alarmed and alerted the Queen's party. Another plan, much more elaborate, was for an attack on the White Palace which would involve a coordinated assault by infiltrators as well as a precise strike from without using trebuchets. This plan was originally intended as an all-out effort to catch the Queen unawares upon her return, to assassinate her and, if possible, to take the Bloodcoins. It was this latter plan, somewhat revised, that was put into play, but with the aim of killing Robby Ribbon, per orders from Banis.

The attack was carried out within days of Robby's arrival in Linlally and almost succeeded. It was only barely thwarted, but resulted in many deaths and injuries and severe damage by fire to the White Palace. All of Faradan's men were killed, but Faradan, who was wounded, was captured. Dialmor, meanwhile, had fled Linlally as soon as he gave Faradan his orders, and thus he was far away by the time the attack commenced.

Faradan was immediately charged with many criminal counts, tried, and convicted and sentenced to death. He steadfastly refused to name any of his co-conspirators, and only maintained that he served his King. He was executed in the ancient way by being dropped from the summit of the Tiandari Falls.
See Also:
Glossary (Dialmor)

Farbarley The northernmost area of County Barley closest to Lake Halgaeth.

Farbrick Court A street in Duinnor City, in the business district of West Noringtown. It was the street where the lending house of Norogus and Harmalway was located, who were co-conspirators of Bailorg.
See Also:
Glossary (Bailorg)

Farby A family of northwestern Duinnor. They were miners who in the middle to late Second Age made their fortune in mining iron ore, silver, and gold. Lucens Farby increased this fortune when he expanded the business by acquiring foundries and building new ones. His son, Blain Farby, increased their wealth by acquiring the chief interest in several coal mines. As a result, Blain Farby became a powerful and influential citizen of Duinnor, though he refused to hold office or to accept any title. He became a good friend to Lord Highleaf of Duinnor, and eventually fell in love with his daughter, Elyna. Lord Highleaf pressured Farby to accept an offer to be made Earl of the Realm, but Farby steadfastly refused on the grounds that he and his family were proud of their working-class roots, and he would not wish to seem pretentious. Nonetheless, Lord Highleaf gave his blessing to the marriage of Farby to his youngest daughter, Lady Elyna. Not long after their marriage, the Farbys would have a son who they named Grantham, after Lord Highleaf's given name.
See Also:
Biographical Sketches (Grantham Farby)

Farduin A seasonal river, subject to rains and meltwater, that flows from Duinnor Realm southward along the western reaches of the Bletharn Plain. By late summer it is usually a mere stream, if any water flows at all. It marks the border of the Great Bletharn Plains in the northwest, and no lands to its west are blighted by the illness that befalls people who consume game or cattle taken upon the plains.

Fascomb (Leander Fascomb) Post Rider of Duinnor. He was one of only a few Duinnor Regulars who was accepted into the ranks of Kingsmen and who did not fully train at the King's Academy. These applicants had to endure a rigorous testing and evaluation before full acceptance by the Kingsmen. Such Kingsmen are put on a kind of probation for a period of five years before being assigned to any fighting unit, most often serving as Post Riders or other challenging duties. When serving as Post Rider, such "provisional" Kingsmen were often given unpleasant routes and duties that would not be entrusted to a local or regional Post Rider, such as swiftly carrying military dispatches, serving official summons, or delivering decrees. Fascomb was typical of these recruits, and during his service, he delivered many summons to far-flung places.

During the final year of the Second Age, Fascomb was assigned to deliver Summons to the son of Lord Threshmere of the House of Hemlock. As it happened, he was accompanied by Robby Ribbon and his party.

Faslor Son of Atlana, brother of Coreth, and nephew of Esildre. Faslor was a member of the Nine Banes and was wounded by a witch called Mariglia. Centuries later, as a member of the Fellfaere, his scouting party came across Ullin Saheed Tallin who was attempting to make his way through the Blue Mountains from Kajarahn.   Finding Ullin unconscious, weak, and suffering from many minor wounds and exposure, Faslor's small party of scouts saved Ullin's life, then transported Ullin on a litter back to Vanara where he would slowly recover. Faslor had two sons, twins named Kranneg and Tulleg who Raynor arranged to be escorts for Esildre.

Fate-Seers A term given to certain fortune tellers of the First and early Second Ages. They were not an organized group in any way, and probably did not even know one another. They wrote verse or recorded arcane and cryptic writings concerning future events of the world, often in a state of mad rapture. It is said that they foretold the downfall of Parthais, the loss of the Bloodcoins, and the coming of Men. Many of the Fate-Seers wrote anonymously, attributing their words to Beras, or Aperion, or some other of the departed Faerekind.

Fellfaere Elifaen warriors of Vanara, renowned for their cold, efficient fighting skills. This term was adopted during the time of Cupeldain to refer to the official armed forces of Vanara, as opposed to

those fighters who had before been commanded or loyal to various houses or clans. Over time, particularly during the reign of Queen Serith Ellyn, the Fellfaere became an elite, though small, fighting force roughly equivalent to Duinnor's Kingsman Army. Training and education were rigorous, and their assignments were often difficult. Certainly they participated in many battles of note, including the Battle of Saerdulin, and the two battles against the Green Citadel. They were composed of a general fighting corps but also contained units devoted to special operations. For example, the Grey Guard was an elite unit of Fellfaere assigned to the Queen and the Palace. There were also scouting units, intelligence units, and engineering units of various sizes. It is estimated that, at its peak, the Fellfaere numbered some 70,000 soldiers, both male and female. Of course, in the early years they were made up entirely of Elifaen of Vanara. Over time, however, Elifaen from other Realms were permitted to join as were Men. Indeed, by the late Second Age, more than half of all Fellfaere were actually Men of Vanara.
See Also:
Glossary (Gray Guard, Scribblers)

Felthain   Firstborn Elifaen of the House of Mulberry. Felthain was granted the throne of Altoria after Queen Therona was deposed in the late First Age.
See Also:
Biographical Sketches (Felthain)

Fetch   A sweet and potent liquor distilled from a blend of barley and other malt grains, and blended with fruit, honey, and spices. It was peculiar to the region of County Barley, and was a specialty of that region. Sometimes it was called "Barley Water."

Finniar   One of the Nowhereans, a blacksmith.

Finteri   see Tallin, Finteri

Firefeast   It was a festival of summer, with bonfires, parades, feasts, and other celebrations. It was one of the most popular annual celebrations in the Eastlands, but enjoyed similar popularity elsewhere in the world, mostly in rural areas. Firefeast took place on Midsummer's Eve and throughout Midsummer's Day (and sometimes lasted much longer), and so it coincided with the Summer Solstice.

Firestick   Sometimes called a firetip or a match, it was a small wooden dowel, often of oilwood, the end of which is dipped in a phosphorus/sulfur paste and allowed to dry. When scratched or struck against an abrasive surface, the phosphorus tip ignited, which in turn set the stick ablaze. Firesticks were expensive, prone to failing (especially if they got wet), and somewhat dangerous. However, they did lead to a great deal of experimentation among alchemists and are thought to be the precursors of the more reliable flares of the late Second Age that burned hotter, longer, and gave off a great deal of light.

Firstborn   Those Faerekind or Elifaen who witnessed the Time Before Time. Also called the First Ones. Some of these were the embodiment of the spirits of the earth, becoming the very first of the Faere. Others were offspring of the Faere, conceived of love. Those Firstborn who lost their wings became known as the Elifaen, or Fallen Ones.
See Also:
Tales of the High Houses (The Fall of the Faere)

Fisenwold   A city located on the eastern edge of the Plains of Bletharn. Fisenwold was once a city of commerce and culture, situated on one of the main east-west trade routes as well as the north-south route to Karthia on the Osterflo. Being a vital stop for the replenishment of supplies and food for trade caravans, Fisenwold grew throughout the First Age and early Second Age to become not only a city of commerce but also a cultural oasis far from the great centers of power and population. It was estimated to have had a permanent population of nearly 40,000 at the end of the First Age.

During the Dragonkind invasion of 322 S.A., the city was burned by a detachment of Dragonkind troops and its population fled northward or were killed or taken as slaves. Fisenwold and the nearby region saw many bloody skirmishes and small battles between the Fisenwold and other easterners who desperately tried to halt and counter the Dragonkind advance. It was futile. The ill-prepared and ill-trained defenders were repeatedly massacred, and their efforts did little to slow the vast hordes of Dragonkind.

After the war, the city was partially rebuilt and enjoyed a brief renaissance. The completion of the Locks of Karthia marked the beginning of its final decline as the overland route was used less often for large wagon trains or for travellers. Quickly following was a succession of natural catastrophes, including earthquake, drought, and plague. Between 300 and 700 S.A., its population had diminished to less than 2,000. By the year 820, the city was entirely abandoned and left to ruin.
See Also:
Glossary (Karthia)
Historical Sketches (Great Dragonkind Invasion)

Fivelpont   Sheriff of Barley during the late Second Age.

Flame Masters   A loose-knit guild of alchemists located in Glareth Realm which was established late in the First Age for the exchange of secrets and recipes for methods of producing fire and light, usually by the use of admixtures and chemicals. However, some Flame Masters were interested in organic and natural sources of light and heat and in crystals that enhanced light. Glowing plants, lichen, and mosses such as Peller's Carpet were of interest to these alchemists who by necessity also became herbalists. Others devoted themselves to mineral-based sources of light and flame, and they developed various methods of refining ores and minerals.

Due to the dangerous nature of their work, there were many deadly accidents. A portion of Glareth by the Sea burned when one shop burst into flames in 1100 F.A., resulting in the expulsion of the guild from the city. In 1126 F.A., another catastrophic accident took place in a coastal village many miles south of Glareth by the Sea, one which utterly destroyed the village, killing nearly all of its inhabitants. After this incident, Glareth outlawed the location of any fire-alchemy workshops within five miles of any residence.

The Flame Masters continued to suffer mortal accidents as their admixtures became more powerful and uncontrollable. By the middle of the Second Age, most of the remaining practicing members were scattered throughout the Seven Realms and many confined their activities to handling herbal tinctures and crystal enhancement of light.

Flame Masters were credited with the invention of flares and firetips (firesticks, or matches). In the latter half of Second Age, various armed forces were experimenting with explosives and rockets, but none would see common use.

As related in *The Year of the Red Door*, King Philawain's servant, called Finn, was responsible for the catastrophic explosion mentioned above. He realized what he had done and attempted suicide, but was prevented by the Judges of Griferis who transported him to Griferis to serve there. They also removed his memory of his past life upon his arrival, and Finn did not regain his memories until after the Judges had departed Griferis (when Philawain assumed control of Griferis).

Flat   A form of metal bullion, used as currency. It is small, rectangular, and thin. Usually of solid silver or gold, but sometimes copper. Flats can be easily cut or broken into smaller pieces for small purchases. During the late First and throughout most of the Second Age, flats were commonly used, especially by travelers, as it was accepted worldwide. In the latter part of the Second Age, flats were falling out of favor in preference to standard coinage, sometimes called "rounds."

Flitter   A flying squirrel and pet of Collandoth during his stay near Tulith Attis during the late Second Age.

Flyers (airmen of the Gray Guard)   The Flyers were a corps of the Vanaran Gray Guard that specialized in building and operating gliders. They used these for a variety of purposes, including to carry messages quickly from the White Palace and elsewhere. They sometimes used them to cross difficult or dangerous terrain.

The flying apparatus itself consisted of fabric which tightly covered a frame in the shape of a wing. Suspended below the wing was a swinging harness to which the flyer (pilot) was attached. The pilot operated the apparatus by shifting his weight, pulling on different lines, or by pushing or pulling against a bar. Some of the gliders, often called "wings," or "flyers," were large enough to carry a great deal of supplies or even a passenger, which were usually strapped to the back of the pilot. The fabric skin or covering was usually made of colorful linen, but some of those used in the high snowy mountains were white or light blue. The frame was most often made of spruce and ash that was glued and lashed together.

The art of flying was discovered in Vanara sometime during the late Second Age. Details of how it worked were immediately made a state secret. Methods of construction were also carefully guarded. A central base was constructed at the White Palace, and by 850 Vanara's Gray Guard was routinely operating a fledgling flying corps from there. However, Brandis Seafar, an officer in the Guard and an expert flyer, was a strong proponent for its development and further expansion. In 867, Vanara had completed the construction of a larger base and training center, complete with workshops, located in a large cavern very near to the White Palace, within easy flying distance. Also located within the underground complex were many places where experiments were carried out and new types of gliders could be built and tested. Documents discovered by Ullin Saheed Tallin detailed the construction of huge prototypes intended to carry ten men in full battle dress. He also found evidence of various weapons mounted onto gliders, including crossbows and fire pots. Meanwhile, most of the initial training for the flyers was done at secret locations outside of Linlally that offered seclusion as well as special terrain for specific types of training.
See Also:
Glossary (Gray Guard, Seafar)

Flying Rug of Zan   A magical rug made and owned by a Dragonkind named Zan during the Time Before Time. The rug could fly through the air, taking Zan wherever he wished to go. The rug gained its magical properties from portions of a Faerekind wing that was woven in with the wool. With it Zan had various adventures which eventually took him from the Dragonlands to the east coast of the world.
See Also:
Eighteen Objects of Power (The Flying Rug of Zan)

Forlandis   Forlandis was the capital city of Tracia Realm at the mouth of the Saerdulin River at Spargers Bay. It was formerly the Kingdom of Forlandis, and was founded by Elifaen early in the First Age. It remained a relatively isolated and inconsequential kingdom until the House of Alder ascended the throne in the late First Age (around 880 F.A.). Forlandis became the seat of power, which Alder quickly expanded, eventually placing all of the region around it under its rule.

Forlandis soon became a thriving port city, trading with Glareth, Colleton, Masurthia, and Altoria. Besides sea routes, it was the terminus for land routes to Vanara as well as river routes along the Saerdulin northward to the Attis region. Its economy was seriously hampered by a series of despots who insisted on heavy tributes, and by Tracia's vulnerability to typhoons that often destroyed much of the region's coastal villages and damaged ships and shipping facilities in Forlandis. Tracia developed a strong naval force, primarily to guard its trade against pirates, and Forlandis was the location of its primary bases located in Spargers Bay. The city would be rocked by the many uprisings and periods of unrest during its history, and suffered much damage during those times. During the late Second Age, it was a hotbed of corruption, political intrigue, and conspiracy under Prince Lewtrah, and from there he enacted many unpopular laws and policies that contributed the civil war that led to his downfall and the rise of the Redvest Triumvirate.

Formouth   A city on the north shore of Lake Halgaeth in the Connassan Province of Glareth Realm. It was home to the Glareth Lakemen. In the late Second Age, Formouth was the governing center of the old Eastlands Realm as it came under the regency of Glareth. The Glarethian Lakemen prided themselves, as all of Glareth did, on their boat handling abilities and seamanship, and from Formouth they governed the lake and watched over all activities that on that waterway. During the late Second Age, the Royal Family established a residence in Formouth, and it was the home of Prince Danoss, son of Ruling Prince Carbane, who was appointed governor of the Connassan Province and Overseer of the Eastlands.

Fortnight   Two weeks, or fourteen days.

Forty-Nine, The   A way of referring to the forty-nine Bloodcoins given to the Seven High Houses of the Elifaen by Aperion.
See Also:
Historical Sketches (Bloodcoins)
Tales of the High Houses

Foxdire   Also called Sigh Mortabilis, or Grave's Breath.
1. A hardy perennial plant known for its pale red or orange blossoms that grow in a frond, somewhat resembling the tail of a fox, and bearing poisonous white glutinous berries, similar in appearance to those of mistletoe. It is most often found in shady mountain lowlands or woodland dales where there is ample moisture. In the west it is known as Sigh Mortabilis, while in other parts it is commonly called Grave's Breath due to the powerful medicinal extract made from its berries.
2. A medicinal extract or tincture made from the berries of the foxdire plant, also called Sigh Mortabilis or Grave's Breath. In small amounts, carefully administered, it is used to make a patient calm or even unconscious, particularly during surgery or other painful procedures. In greater quantities, or carelessly administered, it may cause deep and prolonged unconsciousness, perhaps lasting for days, and even death. Symptoms of overdose include shallow breathing, cold skin, and complete lack of response to any external stimuli. It is one of the few substances that seriously affects the Elifaen, and they are much more sensitive to it than are Men, even in small amounts. Foxdire was used as a poison on numerous occasions as well as a method for suicide. For example, Queen Therona is thought to have taken her life using foxdire, although some say that her death was murder, not suicide. Faeanna, mother of Shevalia (Sheila Pradkin) was poisoned to death by foxdire, although she was not the intended victim of the attack. Robby Ribbon used foxdire to mimic the symptoms of death so that he could fool Caparrashee, his banshee, into taking him to the gates of the afterlife. This succeeded, and after passing through into the afterlife, Robby learned his true name from his great-grandfather.

Frizella   see Bosk, Frizella

Frosmare Castle   An old fortress within Duinnor City that was once a residence and seat of power of the Duin Nord clans, a loose confederation of Men who settled and established farms and trade centers in the region. Frosmare changed hands several times during the conflicts amongst Men, but by the beginning of the Second Age, it was being used only as a garrison for the combined forces of the so-called Ruling Lords of Duinnor. Frosmare continued to be used after the First Unknown King came to power, mainly as an armoury, but it fell into disuse soon after the King's Academy was established. Its high, imposing walls, some six stories high, and two of its four towers were still standing well into the end of the Second Age, but due to the decrepit and crumbling condition, it was sealed so that none could gain access. There are many legends concerning Frosmare, and popular stories describe the ghosts and spirits who abide there. Sometimes, it is said, shadowy figures are seen standing watch upon its towers or pacing its high walls.

Furaman (Seamus Furaman) A trader of the Old Eastlands Realm in the late Second Age. He owned and operated a trading post located in Janhaven that served all of the surrounding region of towns and villages. Originally from Masurthia, Furaman worked as a young man for a trading company scouting sources of supplies and trade goods. Seeing the lack of trading or supply centers, he established his own small trading concern in Janhaven. When his parents died, he brought his sister to Janhaven. Traveling throughout the Thunder Mountains, Tallinvale, and the Eastlands, Furaman made many astute trade agreements, and his establishment thrived and grew. He was mysteriously able to obtain hard-to-find goods, particularly nut-oil of a very high quality, and it was rumored that he was able to do so by winning the cooperation of pixies, highwaymen, or other shady characters, but he carefully guarded many details of his dealings. Furaman accepted and made payments in a variety of ways, from bartered goods and services, to coin, specie, and jewels. From time to time, he extended loans to help local craftsmen and farmers improve their own businesses. Importantly, Furaman entered into a long-term partnership with Robigor Ribbon, a grain tradesman of County Barley who had established a sundries trade-store in nearby Passdale. Ribbon and Furaman coordinated the sale and supply of trade goods, consignments, and Furaman took special note of goods needed but not easily found within the nearby region, often managing to obtain them or else brokering deals to transport such things. Thus he provided not only market essentials but also sundry other goods. This led to an economic boom both in Janhaven and in Passdale, particularly when the bridge at Passdale was rebuilt. The bridge allowed traffic and trade to cross the Bentwide without the normally exorbitant fees charged by the ferrymen of the day. Furaman built a stockade in Janhaven to house and protect his trading operation. By 870, Furaman employed over sixty workers, mostly wagon drivers, loaders, and warehouse workers, in addition to stable hands, blacksmiths, and farriers. It was because of Furaman's operation, and the ease of supply and support that it offered, that the King's Post established a permanent base in Janhaven, which in turn brought even more traffic, commerce, and employment to the community.

During the Redvest invasion of 870 S.A., the stockade became the headquarters and base of operations for refugees from County Barley and for the region's resistance movement. Furaman freely gave of his stockpiles to support these efforts.

Gaiyelneth Labret   Handmaiden, companion, and bodyguard of Queen Serith Ellyn during the late Second Age.
See Also:
Biographical Sketches (Gaiyelneth Labret)

Galafronk   Mythical monster or goblin that feeds on naughty children. Galafronks have the ability to slip between door cracks and other such gaps in order to abduct such children. The galafronks spirit them away to a haunted wood to cook them in a cauldron filled with repulsive ingredients. Galafronks were a frequent feature of folklore and nursery rhymes in the eastern parts of the world, particularly Glareth and the Eastlands. Parents were known to threaten unruly children with such tales, which often included other supernatural creatures and beasts that were attracted to eat or consume misbehaving individuals. What follows is one of the most common nursery rhymes of the Eastlands:

> *Galafronks, galafronks!*
> *Big as a house, small as a mouse,*
> *Brown and black and gray.*
> *Squeezing between the door-cracks*
> *Up between the floor-cracks*
> *As thin and flat as smoke are they!*
>
> *With iron-strong arms,*
> *And saucer-plate eyes*
> *They mumble their charms*
> *Through teeth like scythes*
> *To get you they come, rum duma-dums!*
> *Stomping their trollfeet,*
> *Like thunder, like drums.*
>
> *Galafronks, galafronks, shadows and dust!*
> *Galafronks, galafronks, gristle and rust!*
> *Rude little girls they love to boil*
> *With beetles and spiders and bugs.*
> *And bad little boys they like to broil*
> *With maggots and leeches and slugs!*

Galinot A loose-knit confederation of various clans of Men, united under various warlords during the late Second Age. They claimed as their territory those lands in the Thunder Mountains that were west and northwest of Janhaven. The Galinots were bitter rivals of the Damar, continuously vying for control over the western mountain passes, resulting in frequent raids and skirmishes. In general, they sought to avoid confrontation or provocations that would attract the ire of Duinnor, and sometimes they even cooperated with various Realms. However, the Galinot people tended to be more interested in their farms, families, and trades than conquest or conflict, and they resisted the kinds of oppression that the Damar people were subjected to.

Gardask A land of grassy steppe, north of the Osterflo River. The inhabitants are somewhat nomadic herders, loosely banded together along clan and family lines. These people are fiercely independent and swear no allegiance to Duinnor, Vanara, or any other realm. The Gardask is known for its harsh winter conditions and its short summers. There were many attempts to explore the region. It was rumored that Gardask was where Katrina took her people when they abandoned their territories in the Carthanes, and several expeditions were later mounted in an effort to locate her or her people and the Bloodcoins that had been in her possession.
See Also:
Glossary (Northern Expeditions)

Gardin Firstborn Elifaen of the House of Beech. He established a small domain on the northwestern coasts of the world which would grow to become Glareth Realm. He was the first so-called "Sea King" due to the heavy emphasis his domain placed on trade, fisheries, and maritime industries.
See Also:
Biographical Sketches (Gardin)

Garlan   Soldier of the Seventh Guard of Vanara, the Queen's guard.

Garmitor   A mountain located in the Blue Mountains near the badlands south of Vanara. Mount Garmitor was the scene of a prolonged battle in the year 856 S.A. The battle came about when a large Dragonkind army sought to wrest the mountain from forces of Vanara and Duinnor, aiming to gain a strategic foothold in the Blue Mountains so that the desert route from Kajarahn to the Green Citadel could be better protected. Although the northern forces were garrisoned and held strong positions, the Dragonkind attack was well-planned and coordinated. Many of the keeps built on its slopes changed hands several times during two weeks of intense and almost constant fighting before the exhausted Dragonkind gave up the fight and retreated. Among those involved in this battle were Ullin Saheed Tallin and Kurk Thrubold.
See Also:
Glossary (Thrubold)
Biographical Sketches (Ullin Saheed Tallin)

Garond   Kingsman, Sergeant of Engineering Company Five, of the Fourth Army of Duinnor. He was a master of the heavy ballista and was instrumental in winning the battle between the Kingsmen and the Wickerman monster during the Wickerman Rebellion of 870 S.A.

Garthorn Pass   (Or Garthorn Slopes) A narrow pass in the Mirse region of southern Vanara between the Blue and Tulivana Mountains. The pass is a natural route through the mountains from the Dragonlands and was thus the target of frequent assaults. To the southwest of the pass is Darlang Hill, which was fortified by Vanara but inconsistently manned. Throughout the region there were other keeps and fortifications to guard the pass, some dating back to the middle First Age. In spite of all this, it was through the Mirse and Garthorn Pass that two large Dragonkind armies broke through, the first during the Dragonkind Invasion of 322 S.A., which turned east across the Bletharn Plains. In the year 506 S.A., another, smaller army broke through and then marched northward up the Bletharn Plains toward Duinnor, but was swallowed and destroyed when they inadvertently marched into Nasakeeria.

Garvin   Surname of a man and his wife who lived in Passdale during the late Second Age.

Geever   A Boskman who was wounded in a skirmish with marauders that rode into Barley County in the year 870 S.A. Later, when the Redvests invaded the Eastlands, Geever was taken prisoner and used as forces labor along with many other captured people of Barley and Passdale.

Gina   (Gina Clingdon) A girl of County Barley, daughter of the blacksmith of Passdale during the late Second Age.

Giyth   A small town along the road from Formouth to Glareth by the Sea. A parchment-producing village which during the late Second Age expanded into producing paper stock made of wood fibers.

Gladsten   Farmer of County Barley who, with his wife, was expelled from the county after a series of incidents, culminating with his refusal to render assistance to Sheila Pradkin after she was attacked by her uncle, Steggan. The Gladstens eventually made their way to Duinnor City where they became a criminal enterprise that specialized in assault, theft, and murder. Gladsten was often employed by Lord Banis to carry out various nefarious, and usually violent, assignments. He and his wife were eventually arrested during a botched attempt to murder Collandoth, Billy Bosk, Ibin Brinnin, and Sheila Pradkin.

Glareth   One of the Seven Realms, located in the northeast along the coast, east of the Carthanes and north of the Eastlands Realm. Its chief city was Glareth by the Sea. Renowned for its maritime trades, it was closely allied with Vanara and had strong trade ties to Duinnor. It had its beginnings when King Gardin of the House of Beech established his kingdom in Glareth by the Sea and was made king in 550 F.A. A proud and independent Elifaen people, they slowly increased their territory and maritime power under the reign of subsequent kings, called the Sea Kings of Glareth. Its last king, King Thalamir, abdicated full rights of kingship under pressure from Duinnor in the year 362 S.A., giving the throne to his daughter Megan to serve as Ruling Princess. Her son Carbane ascended the throne after she tired of the role. While many of its people are of Elifaen descent, by the late Second Age, Men were in the majority, and enjoyed full rights of citizenship. Marriages between Men and Elifaen were quite common in Glareth.

Glarethians were involved in several important events throughout history. Many of the supporters who assisted Serith Ellyn to overthrow Parthais came from Glareth, as well as much of the arms and financing for her effort. Glareth, too, raised a large army to join with Vanara and Duinnor to repulse the Dragonkind invasion that took place in 322 S.A., engaging the enemy at the Battle of Saerdulin as well as being instrumental in liberating Forlandis. With the support of their navy, Glarethians marched through Tracia on into Masurthia to rid those lands of pockets of Dragonkind fighters.

During the late First Age and throughout the Second Age, trade between Duinnor and Glareth became an important part of each of the two Realm's economies, with the Osterflo River serving as the primary trade route between the two. When the Locks of Karthia were completed, making the Osterflo safer and faster for heavily laden boats and barges, Glareth enjoyed a boom in its economy, virtually abandoning many of the long and difficult overland routes through the Eastlands.

Glareth was one of the leading manufacturers of linen and paper, but by the late Second Age was beginning to mass produce inexpensive but good-quality paper based on a blend of cotton and wood fibers. Chief among Glareth's exports were fish products, wine, paper, agricultural produce, finished steel products and weapons, and textile products. Their shipyards also provided boats and ships of all kinds and sizes, including transports and merchant vessels, fishing boats, and warships, and examples of all of these were commissioned and purchased by other realms. Indeed, it was Glareth's maritime and shipbuilding prowess that made it both prosperous and powerful, even though the realm was never inclined to carry out conquest.

Shortly after the death of King Inrick II of the Eastlands Realm, and with the backing of Duinnor, Glareth took over the administration of the Eastlands Realm. This was much to the relief of many Eastlanders who despised the corruption of Inrick's reign. Almost immediately, Glareth became embroiled in a series of border disputes with Tracia Realm, which sought to annex lands formerly part of the Eastlands. These disputes were thought to be ended when Prince Lewtrah of Tracia conceded to boundaries declared by Glareth in exchange for favorable trade terms. This agreement would stand and Tracia and Glareth would enjoy peaceful relations in spite of Prince Lewtrah's inept reign. During the Redvest Revolt, however, Prince Lewtrah quickly lost control of his Realm as it fell into civil war. Lewtrah held out until 853 S.A., when Forlandis came under siege by Redvest forces. Glareth, honoring a pact between the two Ruling Houses to come to one another's aid, rescued Prince Lewtrah in a daring raid. With Lewtrah gone to Glareth, his brother, Prince Lantos, continued to fight on, but would also be forced to flee Tracia to Glareth.

These events ended trade between Tracia and Glareth, as Glareth became a welcoming home for Tracian exiles and refugees fleeing the despotism of the Redvests. However, with its strong naval force and robust trade ships, Glareth continued its maritime trade by sending ships around Tracia to Masurthia and Altoria. Eventually, and as a result of the Redvest invasion of the Eastlands, Glareth sailed and marched against Tracia. They first liberated the Eastlands, and then invaded and quickly conquered Tracia.

Glowing Stone of Bazradur   The fabled stone located in a tall tower of Calamandor (the Green Citadel). It glowed brightly at night. Legend had it that as long as Calamandor preserved the stone, no attack against it would be successful. It was broken destroyed in an earthquake, and subsequently was sacked twice by Northmen.
See Also:
Eighteen Objects of Power (The Glowing Stone of Bazradur)

Golden Mantle   The mantle that completely covers the Unknown King of Duinnor, shining so brightly that one cannot look upon the King without the greatest discomfort, much less distinguish any features of the King.
See Also:
Eighteen Objects of Power (The Golden Mantle of Duinnor)

Goodwin   Farmer of Barley in the late Second Age

Gorcastle   A mythical place where all banished and vanquished monsters are chained and imprisoned. The first tales that mention Gorcastle date from the late First Age, sometime after the arrival of Men, and many think the Newcomers brought the legend with them. This notion is further supported by fragments of tales pertaining to their long sea voyage. According to these tales, there was a special place on one of the great city-ships where sea serpents and other such creatures were kept. The ship sank before reaching landfall, and there is little understanding as to why such dangerous creatures should be imprisoned aboard it. One theory has it that the creatures were actually bred onboard for food and precious oil, and that strong chains were required to keep them from thrashing about. Some say the city-ship was called Gorcastle, while others insist that Gorcastle was the name of the blacksmith who forged the chains. Still others speculate that Gorcastle was the location within the ship, perhaps even the forecastle itself.

Whatever the origin or meaning of the myth, the phrase "as strong as the chains of Gorcastle" was a common saying amongst Men, and it was picked up by the Elifaen to be mingled with some of their own folktales. By the late Second Age, the phrase was synonymous with "everlasting strength," or "indestructible.".

Gory Gulch   Properly called Peldown, it is a rugged ravine in the Blue Mountains. It was the site of a famous battle in the year 843 S.A. There, surviving northern forces made up of mostly Kingsmen and Vanaran Fellfaere, were retreating from the Second Siege of the Green Citadel when they were trapped and encircled by a pursuing army of Dragonkind. A messenger made it through the lines of fighting, carrying word to Vanara which immediately dispatched a hastily assembled army to go to the relief of their comrades. By the time the relief force arrived, intense fighting had claimed the lives of over half of the northern forces. However, in a sudden turn of fortune, Vanaran forces broke through from the south to their comrades. They forced the Dragonkind into a northward retreat, trapping them within the ravine. The slaughter was great, and the name Gory Gulch has since been used to describe the place.

Grantham Farby   Son of Blain Farby of Duinnor in the late Second Age. Later companion and friend to Sheila Pradkin, Billy, and Ibin.
See Also:
Biographical Sketches (Grantham Farby)

Gray Guard   The elite household guard of Queen Serith Ellyn, a largely independent branch of the Fellfaere. At first they served merely as the Palace Guard, but they soon were given additional duties and their numbers grew accordingly. They reported directly to the Queen's Chancellor. It is believed that some of their activities were highly clandestine in nature, perhaps involving spy craft or covert reconnaissance activities. They were known to operate special units in and around Shatuum as well as in the mountains bordering the Dragonlands, but they were also given assignments and missions throughout the world. They provided security for the royal treasures, including the Queen's Bloodcoins, and performed both espionage and counterespionage operations as well as a number of special investigations.

Notably, and especially under Lord Brandis Seafar, they developed methods of flying using gliders, with extensive flight operations based from the Palace. Flight missions around Linlally were mainly in the role a messenger service, however it is thought that they were also developing methods of moving men and supplies by air, including light assault units. Of the Grey Guard, the flyers are but one elite unit, made up entirely of volunteers. One of the ironies of the flying corps is that most, if not all, of its members are Men, as fear of heights is very common among the Elifaen.

Members of the Gray Guard made up the core of the Scribblers, a special intelligence-gathering group that made careful use of True Ink.

Many details concerning their members and the nature of their missions remained secret, but it is known that during the late Second Age, when Queen Serith Ellyn traveled to Glareth, about 100 members of the Gray Guard accompanied her party. It was never disclosed how many total members the Gray Guard truly consisted of, and officially it was never declared to have more than 1,300. However, ample evidence exists, indirectly, that their true numbers were more than three times greater at the end of the Second Age. It is thought that many members of the Fellfaere were in reality members of the Gray Guard.
See Also:
Glossary (Flyers, Scribblers, Seafar, True Ink)

Graybark   The location of an estate in Vanara that was forced in to a lease to Duinnor in the late Second Age. It is likely that Graybark would have been foreclosed upon by Bailorg had his plans not been disrupted by the death of Bailorg and the arrest of his partners, Norogus and Harmalway.

Greardon   Family of Passdale in the late Second Age that operated a flour mill. Alfred Greardon was instrumental in bringing a public school to Barley, and he later became the mayor of Passdale. He was killed in an accident that occurred at his family's mill.

Great Bell   A great iron bell made by Heneil and placed within a special chamber of Tulith Attis supposedly imbued with magical qualities. It was this bell that Robby Ribbon rang in 870 of the Second Age, which marked the beginning of his quest for Kingship.
See Also:
Eighteen Objects of Power (The Great Bell of Tulith Attis)

Great Dragonkind Invasion   The devastating invasion and war that took place in 322 of the Second Age. Only the lands of Duinnor and Glareth were spared from intrusions and attacks.
See Also:
Historical Sketches (Great Dragonkind Invasion)

Great Stone   A square block of marble some 120 feet in height, width, and length. It was quarried during the Time Before Time by Dragonkind King Kalzar. The Great Stone precipitated events that led to the Fall of the Faere.

It was said that Alonair, the Faerekind sculptor, promised to make a wondrous carving if a stone of sufficient size was prepared by Kalzar and moved into place within Kalzar's city. Kalzar undertook the challenge and, as a result, enslaved nearly all of the inhabitants of his empire in support of the project. However, the task proved too much. Having succeeded, after much difficulty, in quarrying the stone from a mountain in the western reaches of the Dragonlands, the greatest difficulty was encountered when attempting to move it across the desert some 300 miles to Kalzar's city. Although a way ahead of the stone was cleared, it persisted in sinking into sands, and its weight made even the slightest upward incline nearly impossible to scale. Kalzar threw more and more slaves at the project, working night and day under the most harsh conditions. Nearly every horse that could be found was put into the harness. Every means to ease the way, from wheels to sledges to slides, was attempted. But it was a task that proved too much for the Dragonkind laborers. According to most stories, Kalzar then claimed that the challenge of the stone was an intentional ploy meant to weaken and destroy his empire. He gave up his efforts to move the stone, reformed his armies, and invaded the northern lands to take revenge upon the Faerekind. It was this act which directly led to reprisals by the Faerekind and, ultimately, the Sundering of the Faere and the Scathing.

Many subsequent rulers of the Dragonkind have sought to take up where Kalzar left off and move the stone. Each time, however, it has proven beyond the engineering capabilities of the Dragonkind.

However, during the last days of the Second Age, the Great Stone was successfully moved by trolls under the direction of Thunderfoot and placed at the center of the artificial lake at Darini. At this location, Alonair carved of it a great and mysterious tree, somewhat in the form of a spreading oak or elm, which drew up water from the lake and released it into the air as mist or rain. The chips and leavings from Alonair's work were later used by the Nasakeerians and others to form a mosaic floor for the vestibule of the new Great Library that they built.
See Also:
Tales of the High Houses (The Fall of the Faere)

Greendale   (Marcus Greendale) The Librarian of Vanara, in charge of the great library located at the Ministers Hall in Linlally.

Greenfar   An isolated town on the outskirts of Forest Islindia, shielded from the world and under the protection of the King of the Wood (Islindia's father). Greenfar was the location of the legendary Ice Tree. The people of Greenfar had very little to do with the happenings of the world. However, it was a significant place to Robby Ribbon's quest, both during his journey to Griferis and afterwards.
See Also:
Eighteen Objects of Power (The Ice Tree of Greenfar)

Greensward Hills   The north-south line of rough hills bordering western Tallinvale. They are foothills of the Thunder Mountains.

Griferis   A floating palatial estate that hovered over the Crack Between Worlds along the western border of the known world. It is known in legend as a place of judgment, where future kings and queens may be judged of their fitness to rule. When Robby Ribbon completed his trials there, he took control of Griferis and made himself into King Philawain. He then used it as his base from which he would later accomplish his greatest deeds.
See Also:
Historical Sketches (Griferis)

Grigferith Vale   A term often, but incorrectly, used to refer to Griferis, invoking many myths and folktales about an awful valley of various terrors. It most likely sprang from actual descriptions of

Shatuum, which is located nearby to Griferis.
See Also:
Historical Sketches (Griferis)

Grisland Island   A rocky, almost barren island off the coast of Tracia. Between it and the mainland is the treacherous Grisland Strait. The island is sparsely treed and has very little fresh water. Several attempts to settle the island were made, mainly by fishermen, but island life was difficult and harsh. The island is often battered by storms, and its rocky coastline is surrounded by strong currents, particularly along the Grisland Strait.

In the early part of the Second Age, with much effort and expense, Tracia constructed docks and several lighthouses along its coast and established a small garrison to maintain and service those facilities. Later, a prison was constructed on Grisland Island to house convicts whose labor was used to maintain the docks. Amongst its most notable inmates was the family of deposed King Kapol and many of his followers who were defeated during the failed Pinewood Uprising.

Grisland Strait   A strait off the coast of Tracia between the mainland and Grisland Island. It is generally avoided by larger vessels due to its narrow and somewhat shallow channel, susceptible to erratic and dangerous tidal currents, and its opposing shores are strewn with treacherous rocks. It was the site of a naval battle between remnants of the Tracian Royal Navy and the Redvest Navy of the Triumvirate.
See Also:
Historical Sketches (Battle of Grisland Strait)

Grisland Strait, Battle of   A naval engagement that took place in the Grisland Strait between the Tracian Royal Navy (loyal to Prince Lantos) and naval forces of the Triumvirate in the year 856 S.A.. It followed only a few days after the rescue of Loyalist forces fleeing from their defeat at the Battle of the Marshlands. The costly battle raged for several hours within the confining and treacherous waters of the Strait. It was both a tactical and strategic victory for the Loyalists, as all of the Triumvirate ships were sunk or destroyed, while many of the Loyalist ships escaped, bearing away members of the royal family and many other loyalist forces to Glareth. The action effectively destroyed the Triumvirate navy as a fighting force, and the Loyalist ships that escaped eventually formed an important part of the Glareth-led fleet that would later strike back and retake Tracia.
See Also:
Historical Sketches (Battle of Grisland Strait, Battle of the Marshlands)

Grub   A term used by some Dragonkind to describe members of the upper class of their people, the Alziekfria, who have clearer complexions free from the debilitating scabs and scales that plagued the lower classes, due to the fact that the curative darakal elixir was more frequently provided to the upper classes.
See Also:
Glossary (Darakal)

Gurasa   A Dragonkind general of the late Second Age said to possess the greatest military mind since Kalzar the Great. His career was short but, until his final battle, was met with success after success. He was the father of Micerea.
See Also:
Biographical Sketches (Gurasa)

Halassir   Vision King, the Altorian name given to the Unknown King of Duinnor. It stems from the way in which those who look directly upon the Unknown King of Duinnor are filled with disturbing visions.

Halethiris   The original forest realm of the Faere that was considered the traditional center of Faerum, established during the Time Before Time, with its fabulous city of marvelous towers and glass-domed houses, many of which were supported in the branches of the colossal trees that grew there (some over five hundred feet tall). After the Fall, the Elifaen eventually repopulated Halethiris, but had not the ability to create the structures that once stood there. Power slowly shifted west to Vanara, and many tragedies befell Halethiris until its destruction by Secundur and his followers. The heart of the region became an impenetrable forest, called Islindia, after the Faere Princess who lived in those parts and who roamed its blighted and melancholy ruins. Over time, Forest Islindia became a forbidden land, so that few who ventured into the place were ever seen again, or else they emerged with a deep melancholia that often drove them to madness. After the world was remade, it was found that Halethiris was no longer blighted, but new trees were thriving where once were blighted and barren hills and vales. However, as Ullin Saheed Tallin learned, there was no longer any sign of the presence of Islindia or her father, King Ilex, who once ruled the realm, and nor did he find any evidence of habitation.
See Also:
Glossary (Ilex, Islindia)

Halfis   Tallest mountain in the Carthane mountain range located in the northwestern region of the Carthanes. Upon its summit was one of the Seven Towers. The summit is snow-covered all year long, there are no roads to its top, and only a few climbers have successfully reached the base of the tower due to sheer cliffs of ice, high winds, and frequent stormy conditions.

Halgaeth   A large freshwater lake or inland sea located in southern Glareth and bordering the old Eastlands Realm. It is the headwaters of the Bentwide and Saerdulin rivers. On its northeastern shore was the Glarethian province of Connassa with the city of Formouth on Halgaeth's northern shores. While most of Lake Halgaeth was considered to be within the Eastlands Realm, its northern shores were traditionally considered Glarethian lands, particularly the lands to the east of the lake bordered by Forest Mistwarren. However, since Glareth, through its Lakemen, controlled the lake and its shores, Halgaeth itself was always considered the domain of Glareth. When Glareth took over stewardship of the Eastlands in the middle Second Age, the territorial distinction became moot.

Halgaeth is fed by a few small rivers and innumerable tiny streams, mainly along its northern and eastern shores. The lake is a source of fish and mussels to the region and had several small fishing villages located along its shores. As well, it was often used for the transport of heavy goods, such as timber or stone, permitting traders to avoid the long tedious land routes around the lake. For this purpose, several elaborate landings or quays were constructed in the early Second Age by Glareth. Surthquay on the southwestern shore was particularly elaborate and large enough to accommodate several large boats and barges on either side of its quay. Two beacons on the end of the quay were fashioned in the likeness of outstretched and uplifted arms holding bowls that served as braziers in which fires could be lit, marking the landing for night-time use.

When Heneil's Wall was constructed, the water level of the lake rose several yards and covered the entire quay, leaving only the hands holding the braziers exposed. When Heneil's Wall collapsed in the late Second Age, releasing the lake waters to once again pour down the Saerdulin Falls, Halgaeth's water level quickly fell, exposing the old landing and permitting it to be used. In a similar fashion, all around the lake, the remains of ancient buildings and other shore structures were exposed, including many old docks in Formouth.

Sometime during the Second Age, reports began circulating among the fisherfolk of the lake concerning a giant eel or serpent which they called Slimeback. It purportedly made occasional attacks on fishing vessels and trade boats, tearing them to bits with its long toothed snout and by thrashing is huge bulk against the boats, sometimes (it was said), rising up partially out of the water to crash down upon the hapless. Slimeback became one of the legends to which disappearances were often attributed that could not be accounted for otherwise. However, due to its geography, the relative shallowness of the lake, and the regional weather conditions, sudden storms are fairly common, resulting in destructive high winds and waves that likely explain the disappearances and mishaps. The hardy fisherfolk, however, said that those were just the conditions that Slimeback favored for its attacks on boats. Indeed, it was just after such a storm that Falgo's boat encountered the beast, according to *The Year of the Red Door*, which destroyed the boat and ate Falgo.

Hammer   A term sometimes given to the legendary bell in Tulith Attis, "Tulith Hammer," also called the "great hammer" or the "Great Bell.".

Hanton Hall   A famous museum and art gallery located in Duinnor City. Established by the Fourth Unknown King, it was used as a location for holding Treasures of the Crown. Later expanded, it became a place where artists and artisans from all over the world came to study and to display their works. In its permanent collections are many works of art, including sculpture, painting, and tapestries. Notably, it holds many artifacts taken from the Green Citadel during the First Siege, several tapestries once belonging to the House of Fairmyrtle, and a vast collection of paintings.

Prior to 845 S.A., admittance was gained only by invitation of the King. Such invitations were small tokens of esteem distributed most commonly among the notable and powerful of Duinnor. However, a group of wealthy lords and ladies convinced the King to open its doors to the public for the "general enlightenment" of the people. This was done, and a small entrance fee was charged. Hanton Hall quickly became one of the most popular attractions in Duinnor, receiving visitors and visiting collections from all over the world.

It has been speculated that within the Hall's vaults were treasures never shown to the public, such as those Bloodcoins reportedly obtained by the Third Unknown King, a menagerie of beasts and fiends preserved in great jars or by taxidermy, and many other disturbing relics. Curators at Hanton Hall consistently denied such rumors, and insisted that the catalog of its collections contained no secrets and was open for public inspection.

Harbinger   A term used in legends to describe the mysterious ringer of the bell at Tulith Attis. It may have come from the original intent of the bell, which was to forewarn the defenders of Tulith Attis to an attack into the fortress from the river entrance.

Harmalway   One of the two proprietors of Norogus and Harmalway, a lending house in Duinnor. They were one of the firms in Duinnor that handled leases and liens on Vanaran properties. Two of its most notable patrons were Lord Banis and Bailorg. Norogus and Harmalway were suspected, and eventually arrested, for their involvement in many nefarious activities, including blackmail, fraud, theft, and embezzlement.

Hathrain   An Elifaen of the Masurthian House of Fairrose, a Fellfaere who became a servant of King Philawain of Griferis. He delivered Pyros's ruby Bloodcoins to Tower Halfis.

Haven Hill   A name for Tulith Attis used mostly in the region of County Barley.

Hazleton   A village in the Eastlands.

Heartflowers   A flower of the middle plains.

Hemlock (House of Hemlock) One of the Houses of the Faerekind. The members of that house were most closely associated with the lineage of Alonair, the Elifaen sculptor, but fell into decline during the Second Age. It is said that the House of Hemlock was in some way involved in the murder of Cupeldain. The lake nearby to its lands was where Cupeldain and his wife along with many others were drowned. However, many local accounts dispute Hemlock's involvement in the murders, and have it that the House of Hemlock was only one of the many houses involved in the feud that Cupeldain sought to resolve. Regardless, by the late Second Age, the House of Hemlock had lost its standing and was little known or regarded outside its lands.
See Also:
Glossary (Borwain, Threshmere)

Heneil Legendary warrior, builder, son of Silmain (first king of the Elifaen), husband to Lyrium of the House of Fairfir and twin brother of Pellen. Heneil assisted in the rebuilding of Linlally during the First and Second Ages. He also rebuilt and enhanced the fortress of Tulith Attis. He formed an alliance with Men and helped put down the Pinewood Uprising. Heneil was murdered by his brother Pellen at Tulith Attis when it was besieged by the Dragonkind during the Great Dragonkind Invasion.
See Also:
Tales of the High Houses (The House of Fairfir)

Heneil's Wall   In the Ancient Speech, "te Lamath Heneileth." The dam built at Lake Halgaeth at Saerdulin Falls to stem the flow of water into the Saerdulin. This was done by Heneil as a means of preventing heavy war-boats from approaching Tulith Attis from the south on the Saerdulin. As a result of this work, the lake's waters rose and spilled over in a different direction and essentially created the River Bentwide, which before had been a tributary stream of the Saerdulin. This remained as such until the year 870 of the Second Age when the dam collapsed catastrophically and the waters retook the old course of the Saerdulin past Tulith Attis and the Bentwide became a mere stream once more.

Herbert   Also known as Herbert the Blue, he was an Elder of Nowhere, appointed as sheriff of that place. He was killed at Tallinvale during the Redvest siege.

High Chamber   The place where the Unknown Kings of Duinnor resided, located in the uppermost floor of the High Tower of the King's Palace in Duinnor City. Since its construction, the High Chamber has been the Unknown Kings' residence, by all accounts a modestly furnished place. Its actual contents and nature remained a closely guarded secret, but it was thought to have only two or three rooms, in addition to its large main reception room. There was only one door leading into the High Chamber, and the room was divided by a curtain so that any who entered could not see to its far side.

It was to the High Chamber that the King sometimes summoned his ministers, lords, or others by use of his Avatar or his Kingsmen. Over the years, many who were summoned and returned related that their experience within the High Chambers as an uncanny and sometimes painful encounter with the King. Filling the room with the light of his Golden Mantle, the King could not be looked upon without the severest pain. During such interviews, the King seldom, if ever, spoke aloud, but spoke directly into the minds of those present before him. Thus, it is said that he had the ability to search through the hearts of his subjects while his Avatar floated nearby.

During the reign of the First through Fifth Kings, the High Chamber was always a place of coming and going. And, whereas previous Unknown Kings often went forth into the City upon the royal sedan chair, along with his Avatar, the Sixth Unknown King seldom left the High Chamber. Only on the Day of Spring, when required to renew his Kingship, did the Sixth Unknown King go forth to the

Temple of Beras to renew his Kingship and to begin a new Royal Year with a new Avatar.

Under the Third Unknown King, the position of First Lord of the High Chamber was established to serve, in essence, as chancellor or head of state charged with the task of overseeing Duinnor Realm and its interests abroad with the King's guidance and having the King's authority. The title was at first ceremoniously confirmed by the courts of Duinnor, but no person nominated by the King was ever declined. The Sixth Unknown King declared the First Lord of the High Chamber to be a lifelong appointment, and his choice of First Lord was not to be challenged or confirmed. By the late Second Age, with Lord Banis installed as First Lord of the High Chamber (and the only Elifaen ever to be First Lord), a summons to the High Chamber was as often as not a prison sentence, or worse, since it was not uncommon that those summoned would not be seen again for a long time, if ever. Also under Lord Banis, the balconies and windows of the High Chamber became a roosting place for black eagles, such as those that served Secundur, and their coming and going was watched with much consternation by the people of Duinnor.

High Houses of the Elifaen   The seven High Houses were those that received the Forty-Nine Keys to the Nimbus Illuminas, otherwise called the Bloodcoins, or simply the Forty-Nine. They consisted of Fairlinden, Fairwillow, Fairfir, Fairmaple, Faircedar, Fairmyrtle, and Fairbirch. Each of these Houses was established during the Time of Strife, and each was given Seven of the Forty-Nine Keys. "High House" was only a customary term, as there was never any real agreement or declaration that these Houses had any greater status or power than other Elifaen groups or clans.

Each of the Forty-Nine Keys (or Bloodcoins) were made of discs of heavy red gold approximately three inches in diameter and nearly a quarter of an inch thick, and each encircled a gemstone within its center. Seven different gemstones were used: amber, amethyst, diamond, emerald, ruby, sapphire, and topaz. The manner of distribution to the High Houses was as follows:

> House of Fairlinden entrusted with Sapphire Bloodcoins.
> House of Fairbirch, entrusted with Emerald Bloodcoins.
> House of Faircedar, entrusted with Amethyst Bloodcoins.
> House of Fairmaple, entrusted with Topaz Bloodcoins.
> House of Fairwillow entrusted with Diamond Bloodcoins.
> House of Fairmyrtle, entrusted with Ruby Bloodcoins.
> House of Fairfir, entrusted with Amber Bloodcoins.

When Aperion gave the Forty-Nine to the Seven High Houses, he also showed them in a vision how the Forty-Nine were to be used to open a way (called the Nimbus Illuminas) which would permit those Elifaen remaining in the world to go into Aperion's heavenly abode. However, Aperion warned them that it should be done soon, as he foresaw misfortune and continued strife if they tarried too long upon the earth. They accepted the Forty-Nine, but failed to act soon enough to avoid his prophecy.

During the early First Age, there were two failed attempts to bring about an agreement among the Seven High Houses to use the Forty-Nine Bloodcoins to open the Nimbus Illuminas. After the second failure to do so, the Bloodcoins were redistributed so that each of the Seven High Houses would possess one Bloodcoin of each of the seven types of jewel (that is, one Bloodcoin of each High House).

Eventually, most of the Forty-Nine Bloodcoins would be lost, and by the middle of the Second Age, all of the High Houses except that of Fairlinden had either died out or else disappeared. Only the House of Fairlinden would still possess its seven Bloodcoins, passed from Cupeldain to Parthais and then to Serith Ellyn when she took the Vanaran throne from Parthais.

See Also:
Historical Sketches (Bloodcoins)
Tales of the High Houses (all sections)

Highleaf   A House of Men of Duinnor established in the early-middle Second Age. Highleafs during this time were some of the chief financiers of trade firms, and operated mines and metalworks. They accrued much wealth and in 760 Clance Highleaf financed major improvements to the Locks of Karthia in exchange for certain fee concessions for its use given to its trade companies. The improvements were accomplished, which involved improving the lock gates as well as the establishment of small service settlements and inns along the route. So successful were these that traffic was more than doubled, owing to the faster and more reliable gates. In recognition of this accomplishment, Clance Highleaf was made a Lord of the Realm, with inherited rights given to his family.

In 780 S.A., Lord Highleaf purchased considerable acreage within Duinnor City and built his new estate, called Wysteria Place. There, his son built the grand Starlight Hall, with its distinctive domed towers. He and his wife died of fever, and the estate was inherited by their daughters, Victoria and Elyna, who were both quite young. Collandoth, who was a friend of the family, took it upon himself to guard the girl's fortune from greedy relatives, and it was due to his work that enough of it was preserved so that the estate could be retained under the sisters' ownership. When Lady Elyna married, she asked that her portion of the estate be sold to her sister, Victoria, so that she could invest in her husband's mining concerns. This was done, and the estate became the sole property of Lady Victoria, who preferred to be known as Lady Highleaf. Older than Elyna by nearly twelve years, Lady Highleaf never married, although she had several mildly scandalous affairs. Having also made astute investments, she was very wealthy, and she used her wealth to remodel and restore Starlight Hall, turning it into one of the most elegant and palaces in Duinnor, a site of many lavish balls and celebrations.

During the final weeks of the Second Age, Lady Highleaf befriended Sheila Pradkin and her friends, giving them much support in their cause.

Hoard of Tulith Attis   This refers to a great treasure that was part of the spoils taken from Tulith Attis after it fell to the Dragonkind during the Great Dragonkind Invasion. This included numerous items, filling two large wagons, and was taken by Bailorg from Tulith Attis when it fell. Items included elaborate jewelry, tiaras, goblets, musical instruments, lavish ceremonial costumes, weapons, armor, and headgear, many chests of silver and gold and loose gems, along with an assortment of plates, tureens, vases, decanters, trays, and candlesticks.

Accompanied by an armed Dragonkind escort, Bailorg moved this treasure through the Thunder Mountains using slaves to pull the wagons. Then, as his pursuers closed in, his Dragonkind escort fled and his slaves revolted. Enraged, Bailorg laid a curse upon them, then he, too, fled the scene. Shortly thereafter, the former slaves and the loot were discovered by Navis and Esildre. These two laid two more curses on the slaves.

The curses were as follows:.

By Bailorg: They would not find their way out of those lands until pigs grew in trees.

By Navis: They would be as a little people until the value of the Hoard was increased a thousand times and returned to its rightful heir.

By Esildre: They would know long life so that they would suffer the fullness of their punishment.

Also, perhaps feeling some sympathy for their plight, Esildre also gave them a blessing, the means of moving quickly from place to place "without hindrance" and "with quickness and in a twinkling." This blessing she likely gave so that they could avoid being devoured by beasts. As a result, they later learned to "pop" almost instantaneously from place to place.

The people who were cursed became the Nowhereans. They took the treasure, calling it The

Hoard, and safeguarded it until the late Second Age. They sought through various means, including thievery, to increase the quantity of items in the Hoard and thus its value. Eventually, Robby Ribbon sought to assign the Hoard to a distant heir of the House of Fairfir, which was Ullin Saheed Tallin of the House of Fairoak (grandson, five generations removed, of Myrium, the sister of Lyrium). But Ullin refused to accept it. Instead, he insisted that the Nowhereans would remain as they were until they had proven themselves in the world by going to the aid of Tallinvale, saying "Let your stature then be measured not by the height of your brow, but by the summit of your valor." Meanwhile, all of the Hoard that had been accumulated beyond the original treasure was released for use by the Nowhereans.

Bailorg's curse was removed when they learned how to raise pigs on platforms built in the treetops, which took a few months to accomplish. Then they not only went to the aid of Tallinvale, but they also committed themselves to assisting Robby, who had become King Philawain. As a result, they no longer felt themselves to be "a little people," and, indeed, one of them (Eldwin) did resume his original size.

The fate of the Hoard taken from Tulith Attis remains uncertain. As far as we can determine, Ullin never returned to Nowhere or sought to recover it.
See also:
Glossary (Nowhere)
Historical Sketches (The Great Dragonkind Invasion)

Ibin See Brinnin, Ibin

Ice Tree of Greenfar An uncanny tree of ice that is peculiar to the town of Greenfar.
See Also:
Eighteen Objects of Power (The Ice Tree of Greenfar)

Iceking One of the buckmarl stags of Uncle Solstice.

Ilex King of Halethiris during the Time of Strife and the early part of the First Age. A Firstborn Elifaen, Ilex and the Faerekind of Forest Halethiris did not participate with those who warred upon the Dragonkind. However, when Aperion called away all the faithful, Ilex and most of his people refused to depart since they were too much attached to their woods and streams.

During the Age of Strife, Ilex saw his kingdom fall rapidly into decline. He also watched as Silmain and, later, Cupeldain, expanded Vanaran territories eastward across the Iridelin toward his own lands. Fearing that Vanara would lay claim to Halethiris, Ilex sought to have enchantments and spells laid upon the forest to protect it, and he brought conjurers there to do so. Needing a maiden who was pure of body and heart, his daughter agreed to be the subject of the spells. However, the only effect the spells had was to give Islindia the power to temporarily bring about the past through her dreams. Not long afterwards, Islindia became the object of Secundur's desire, and the shadowy figure captured Islindia, murdered her lover, and then sought to convince her to be his concubine. She refused. At last, King Ilex and Islindia's brother, Renorlian, managed to rescue Islindia. Infuriated, Secundur caused a severe blight to fall upon the forest. In a second attempt to save his forest, Ilex sought to halt time and restore the past using spells of his own devising. He did his conjuring at a moment when Islindia dreamed her dream of remembrance, but, again, the spells went awry. Instead of giving life back to the past, Islindia was given back her wings. Thus unable to halt Secundur's blight, Ilex and his daughter watched as their people faded away and as their forest rapidly withered.

Secundur spared Ilex and Islindia from his curse so that they might witness the downfall of Halethiris. Unwilling to depart, Ilex and his daughter remained within the forlorn and stricken forest as the only survivors of their people. Over time, Ilex lost much of his human form, appearing afterwards to have a body made up of various plants, a brooding and malicious creature. Later known as King of the Wood, he ever watched over the stunted lands where his great forest once was, and guarded it against intruders who were seldom allowed to escape once they enter his land. His daughter Islindia interceded, however, on the behalf of others, and Ilex reluctantly agreed to his daughter's wishes. Thus he granted Lyrium and her people a refuge and hiding place withing the forest as well as occasional use of his magical carriage. Later, Robby Ribbon's party would also be granted safety within and safe passage through the forest.

See Also:
Eighteen Objects of Power (Carriage of Ilex)
Glossary (Islindia, Halethiris)
Tales of the High Houses (House of Fairfir)

Iridelin   The great river that flows from Vanara southward along the eastern slopes of the Tulivana Mountains to the sea. It was an important trade route between Vanara and Altoria. Its headwaters are at the Falls of Tiandari in Linlally, and it normally flows high enough for substantial traffic to move along it in the form of boats and barges conducting trade between Linlally and Draymoor. Many stretches had towing roads built along its banks so that teams of horses could draw boats upstream. There are a few places along it that are too swift or shallow for heavy boats, with shoals and rapids through narrow canyons, but these were flanked upstream and downstream by towns and villages where boats could disembark their cargos for transport overland the short distance to the next stretch of navigable water.

The river passes out of Vanara and into Altoria at Gander Falls and widens sufficiently for sailboats to make the upstream voyage. Near the coast, the river joins into, and is fed by, a vast marshland called the Hinderlands, continuing past the Altorian city of Draymoor to empty into the Craggy Sea.

In Vanara, the river marked the ancient boundary of old Vanara from those eastern territories bordered by Halethiris and that were annexed by Silmain early in the First Age. In the First Age, the river became infested with river demons and demon-serpents. These were mostly eradicated by various means with little difficulty. However, one demon-serpent was captured by Parthais and taken to Linlally. Later, it was transported to the east, and placed into the lake where Cupeldain and Loura were drowned, and where Parthais executed many in the same manner in retribution for the murders.

Ishtorgus   A Melnari of the Second Age, sometimes called Ishtorgus the Mariner. He was an advisor of King Thalamir of Glareth, the last of the Sea Kings.

See Also:
Historical Sketches (The Melnari and Their Familiars)

Islindia   Also known as the Lady of the Wood, Queen of the Wood, and the Princess of Sorrows. Islindia was Princess of Halethiris during the Age of Strife and the early First Age. Through an enchantment intended by her father, King Ilex, to restore Halethiris to the glory of the Time Before Time, Islindia was inadvertently given the power to bring about the past for one day each month. This ability brought her to Secundur's attention, who became infatuated by her beauty. Secundur captured Islindia and tried to force her to become his concubine, but she resisted. In an effort to punish her, he murdered her lover which served to make her even more resolute in her refusals. Still, Secundur continued to entreat her to be his, but she despised him and rebuffed him. She was rescued by her kin, but Secundur destroyed Halethiris with a withering blight. Only she, her father, King Ilex, and her uncle, Solstice, survived the blight Secundur put upon the forest. It is said that Islindia and her father were cursed to remain in the ruins of that place until the world was remade, at which time their spirits could be free.

In a second attempt to save his forest, King Ilex again tried to conjure time, but the spell once again went awry. Instead of making time reverse, Islindia's wings were restored to her. Even though she thus regained the ability to fly, she seldom did so. Instead, she chose to fly only during those days and nights when her dreams brought forth the gloried past of Halethiris, a period when she could fly once more in fellowship with her lost Faerekind kin. Sometimes Esildre would put off conjuring forth Halethiris for weeks. In this way, she could bring forth Halethiris on the very last day remaining for the month and continue for yet another day as the first day of the new month arrived.

With the decline and ruination of her forest, her father lost much of his human form, appearing afterwards to have a body made up of various plants. Later known as King of the Wood, he ever watches over the place, guarding against intruders, who seldom escape the place once they enter it. Islindia, too, constantly roamed the blighted forest, beset with grief for what was lost, and awaited the next time when she could bring forth the past.

It is known that, with her father's permission, Islindia gave refuge to Lady Lyrium and, later, Lyrium's daughters and many of their surviving people, all watchful and wary of being discovered by Duinnor or others. Islindia insisted that Lyrium and her people abide only within the northernmost reaches of Halethiris, and forbade them from exploring other parts. It is also known that Islindia allowed the use of the marvelous Carriage of Ilex by Lyrium and her daughters on at least four occasions. She also gave safe passage, rest, and recuperation to Robby Ribbon and his company, and did much to lift the hex of Secundur from Ullin, infected as he was via Esildre. Among the entities of the past brought back into being were a group of winged horses, and from time to time she lent these mounts to others. For example, Islindia dispatched her flying horses to render assistance to Micerea and to Ullin, and, on behalf of King Philawain, to many others as a way of transporting them to Griferis. The flying horses would also be lent to Lyrium and her daughters, to take them to Duinnor, and would be used by seven special riders sent by Philawain to carry sets of Bloodcoins to the Seven Towers in order to remake the world. Islindia has not been seen since those last days of the Second Age.

See Also:
Eighteen Objects of Power (The Carriage of Ilex)
Glossary (Ayreltide, Ilex, Halethiris)

Janhaven A trading town in the western parts of the Eastlands Realm in County Woodland at the foothills of the Thunder Mountains, situated along a route to Duinnor and also on the north-south trade route with Tallinvale. In the late Second Age, its fortunes were increased when Seamus Furaman located a trading company there and steadily expanded his business operations throughout the region. An important Post Station was also established, serving Janhaven, Tallinvale, Passdale, County Barley, and many hamlets in the Carthanes and around Lake Halgaeth.

In the late Second Age, when Triumvirate Redvests invaded the Eastlands and nearby County Barley, many refugees from the invaded lands fled to Janhaven where they organized a large resistance group. Although the Redvests made several attempts to take the town, they never succeeded against the coalition of fighters and defenders operating out of Janhaven.

See Also:
Glossary (Furaman)

Jarn Councilman of Passdale in the late Second Age.

Jatarak the Ogre A giant of the First Age that occupied the southern Tulivana Mountains and was eventually tracked and killed by Navis of the House of Elmwood. It is said that Jatarak was twice the height of a normal person, with the strength of twenty men. He had three eyes and two short horns, and he ate any Dragonkind that wandered into those mountains. The Dragonkind's efforts to hunt and kill him were unsuccessful, and so they abandoned the lands that Jatarak occupied. Without Dragonkind to eat, Jatarak quickly depleted the mountains of all game. Since the ogre could not abide the heat of the deserts, he did not venture west to hunt Dragonkind. Instead, he climbed over the mountains and went eastward, wading through the swampy Hinderlands and into Altoria. There, in 917-918 of the First Age, Jatarak rampaged by marauding, killing and eating livestock, humans, and any living creature he could find. His appetite seemed boundless, and none could stand against him. Queen Therona sent an army against him, but Jatarak was cunning and he evaded her soldiers after inflicting many casualties. At last, Queen Therona of Altoria sent forth a call to any willing warriors, bidding them come to Altoria and rid the lands of the ogre. Many responded, arriving from all over the world, and amongst them was Navis of the House of Elmwood.

Navis and the other warriors were soon on the trail of Jatarak. They chased him back to the Iridelin, which he swam across. Stripping down to only their loincloths and swords, the warriors did the same. Into the Hinderlands Jatarak fled, with forty Elifaen behind him. The Hinderlands were marshy and foggy, and Jatarak disappeared in the mists only to come at his pursuers from a different direction, repeatedly catching them off-guard and killing many before disappearing back into the fog. Yet the remaining Elifaen continued after him, crossing the Hinderlands and into the shadows of the Tulivana Mountains, where a great volcano was erupting with fire and ash and flowing lava. Jatarak turned once more, this time killing all of his pursuers but Navis of Elmwood, who fought so viciously that Jatarak fled all the faster. Into the burning mountains and onto the slopes of the fiery volcano they went until at last Jatarak came to a crevasse filled with fire. The ogre climbed down into the place (later known as the Crevasse of Fire) flinging rocks up at Navis as he followed. At the bottom, beside a river of molten fire, Jatarak turned once more to face Navis. They fought, Navis with his sword and Jatarak with his club. Jatarak was the larger of the two, and he was so strong that when he struck at Navis, his club shattered rock. But Navis was quick and clever. He dodged Jatarak's blows, and he struck with his sword until at last Jatarak stumbled. Navis then ran his sword through Jatarak's heart.

Navis cut off the head of Jatarak as a trophy and pushed the ogre's body into the river of fire. It is said that the dragon who made the fire and the volcano with his hungry bile ate Jatarak and was satiated. Thus, when Navis emerged from the mountains and recrossed the Hinderlands, already the violence of the eruption had eased and would soon be gone entirely.

Altoria hailed Navis as a great hero, and Queen Therona presented him with a specially made breastplate that was embossed with the likeness of a spreading elm tree, in honor of the House of Elmwood, which he wore thereafter at every suitable occasion.
See Also:
Glossary (Crevasse of Fire, Elmwood, Navis)

Jawrock   A standard-issue food ration that was a common part of every Kingsman's kit, and it was often found in the ration kits of other soldiers, particularly the Vanaran military.   It was a hard, light-brown bar or chunk, somewhat sticky, and was notoriously hard to chew and swallow. The recipe for Jawrock was a closely guarded Duinnor secret, and it was produced for Kingsmen by the Menicamp family of Duinnor for over two hundred years.   Although the exact ingredients and proportions are unknown, it contains dried berries, nuts, sugar, salt, and tallow. It is also thought that finely ground dried and cured meat is part of the mix, although what kind of meat is not known.

Jawrock was traditionally molded into small blocks which were individually packed in parchment, sealed with wax. It was long lasting, durable, and provided fair nutrition. Its taste and texture and density were derided by Kingsmen, and was the inspiration for many jokes. To have nothing but jawrock to eat was fairly common for those deployed in desert campaigns or on far-flung missions. It was usually consumed right from its packaging, as it required no cooking, but it was often boiled or soaked in water to make a sort of soup.

Although intended as food, Kingsmen found other uses for jawrock. With its high tallow content, they sometimes used it to oil their clothing against the elements. It was frequently used to grease the blades of their weapons against corrosion.

Jimbo   A resident of Nowhere in the late Second Age.

Kahryna   Daughter of Cassandra and Dasler of the House of Fairoak. She became the wife of Danig Tallin, a Man of the Eastlands. By him she bore two sons and a daughter, Dalvenpar, Aram, and Mirabella.

In 966 F.A., brush fires were set nearby to Fairoak lands in an effort to flush out Dragonkind infiltrators. The fires quickly got out of control and set off a devastating forest fire that destroyed much of the Fairoak lands. Lost were all of the Fairoak buildings, its vineyards and orchards, and all of its woods. Although the Fairoaks would try very hard to replant and rebuild, they battled not only erosion from heavy rains and snows, but also continued incursions of Dragonkind raiders. The Fairoaks continued this effort well into the Second Age, although much diminished in power and wealth. At last, in debt and impoverished, the Fairoaks were forced to lease their lands to Duinnor in order to pay their creditors. They removed to a modest but charming estate northeast of Linlally.

It was in Linlally that Kahryna met the dashing Danig Tallin, a Kingsman and the son of Lord Tallin of the Eastlands. They fell in love and were married and soon had three children. When Lord and Lady Tallin died, and Danig became the new Lord Tallin, he eventually removed his family from Vanara to settle in his newly-built fortified town in the Eastlands valley of Tallinvale, where his family lands were.

Kahryna and Danig lost their first son, Dalvenpar, in 837 S.A., on the bloody retreat from the first siege of the Green Citadel. It was a terrible blow to her and her husband. Their second son, Aram, would later be killed as well, and the grief proved too much for Kahryna. Although Elifaen, she died in 845 S.A., apparently from grief, two days after hearing the news of Aram's death. For reasons that remain murky, Kahryna in her dying grief placed a curse on her husband so that none of his memories would ever fade from mind. As a result of this, Danig Tallin was driven into a state of near-madness, grief, and despair until he learned somewhat to cope with the incessant memories associated with or prompted by every moment. However, in some ways, this proved to be a great benefit to Lord Tallin and, in turn, his people, as he was able to clearly recall and manage information. Thus he well-managed Tallinvale, including its defense when it was besieged by Tracian armies in the year 871 S.A.

Kajarahn (Alaberbra)   An ancient city of the Dragonlands, located in the far northwest of the deserts. Originally called Alaberbra, it was officially renamed Kajarahn, the Free City, following the devastating attacks of witches and demons that decimated the city during the early Second Age.
See Also:
Historical Sketches (Kajarahn)

Kalbrith   A small town on the Saerdulin, once an important waypoint for traffic moving on and alongside the river. It was part of the Eastlands Realm but Tracia claimed it as part of that realm. The population of the town was divided over the issue, depending on the interests of particular people and groups. In the late Second Age, Kalbrith was taken by Tracia and put under military control, and would be used as an outpost and garrison town. From 869 SA, it became as an important supply point and assembly area for the Redvest army as it prepared for its invasion of the west in 870 S.A. To further their aims, the Redvests established large labor camps, and it was here that untold thousands of Tracians were taken, mostly people from Loyalist regions, a virtual death sentence due to the harsh conditions and lack of food. From Kalbrith, these laborers were assigned to various army groups, further west, to be put to work building roads and shelters for the armies, to pull wagons, and to cut and supply wood for campfires. Well over half of these laborers were women and children. Starvation and disease were rampant, and many were left to die when they could no longer work.

Kalzar   The first King of the Dragonkind and the founder of the nation of Drakyr during the Time Before Time. He established a dynasty that lasted well into the late First Age and was later reestablished in the Second Age.

Not much is known about Kalzar's early years, except that he was a tribal leader or "Soltani" of a powerful nomad tribe located in the southeastern regions of the Dragonlands. He eventually overthrew and conquered the entirety of the Dragonlands, and ruled from a magnificent palace in the city of Tyrsharat. From there, he consolidated and increased his power and wealth, embarking on many building projects throughout the Dragonlands. It was under Kalzar that the first calendars were created (although not very well understood), and the first examples of Dragonkind writing became widespread. Under Kalzar schools were established to train builders and engineers for the construction of his monuments and other structures. Evidently, he was quite young and vigorous when his rule began, perhaps no more than twenty, and he seemed immune to the desert sickness that plagued his people. He seemed to have little interest in the lands to the north, although it is known that the Dragonkind harvested vast forests of for lumber along the southern slopes of the Blue Mountains. It is thought that he was well into his forties when he learned of Alonair and his sculptures and, as a result, sent emissaries to Alonair to make sculpture for Tyrsharat.

Alonair the Faere promised to Kalzar that if he moved a Great Stone to his city, it would be carved into a wondrous thing to behold. Alonair never said what the carving would be, but Kalzar accepted the challenge. However, the undertaking was too much, for the stone proved too large to move across the deserts. Incited by Secundur, Kalzar attacked the Faerekind lands of the north, which in turn provoked a massive counterattack by Cupeldain and others. It was this that prompted Aperion to call the Faerekind away from the earth and those who refused to go were Scathed of their wings and became the Elifaen.

The attack of Cupeldain, however, practically obliterated Kalzar's domain and his people. For many years, as the Elifaen struggled to survive, so did the Dragonkind, who entered a long period of anarchy and decline, with many of Kalzar's accomplishments falling into ruin. Northern lore has it that Kalzar was killed by Cupeldain, but Dragonkind legend maintains that Kalzar survived. According to Dragonkind lore, Kalzar died at the age of 86, an age rarely attained by any Dragonkind.
See Also:
Tales of the High Houses (The Fall of the Faere)

Kapol   King of Tracia, Lord of the House of Alder, and the last king to rule Tracia, son of an Elifaen father and mortal mother.

Kapol was only sixteen when he inherited the throne from his father. Two years later, he would confiscate the Bloodcoins of the House of Fairmyrtle and thereafter enter into a campaign to persecute all who opposed him or his right to own the Bloodcoins, whether Elifaen or Men. He was particularly suspicious of Men who served the House of Fairmyrtle as well as of the woodland Elifaen who constantly agitated for war against Men, and he was careful to maintain cordial relations with the Pinewood House. His reign was plagued by one debacle after another.

Although Kapol moved the Bloodcoins from secret location to secret location, in 266 S.A., they were stolen. This occurred after he had rebuked Queen Serith Ellyn for continually asking that they be sent to Vanara for safety. When word spread concerning the theft Bloodcoins, several Realms, including Vanara and Glareth, recalled their ambassadors in protest and put a halt to any trade with Tracia.

It was an aging Kapol who later disastrously supported the Pinewood Uprising. The uprising was defeated, Kapol's House was abolished, and his family was exiled to Grisland Island while he himself was imprisoned in Forlandis. He died in prison, and was possibly murdered.

Karkarando   A land to the far west and south within the Dragonlands. It borders the western mountains and the Craggy Sea. In the early epochs of the Dragonkind history, it was the chief source of food crops, vegetables and fruit, mainly, all of which were almost entirely replaced with darakal cultivation by the beginning of the Second Age.
See Also:
Glossary (Darakal)
Historical Sketches (Karkarando)

Karthia   A small region surrounding the lake of the same name which is a large basin of the River Osterflo. The mountains of Karthia are renown for the clarity of the rubies and for other minerals. The region was also an important trading and supply stop on the Osterflo River that flows from Duinnor to Glareth. In the Second Age, the Kings of Duinnor built a sophisticated system of locks and canals so that boats could pass around the dangerous falls and shoals on the lake's eastern and western bounds. Karthia thus became an important trading and shipping community, situated on the Osterflo roughly halfway between Duinnor and Glareth.
See Also:
Glossary (Locks of Karthia)

Katrina   A Firstborn of the Faere and leader of the House of Fairmaple.
See Also:
Tales of the High Houses (House of Fairmaple)

Kecker   A Kingsman general of the late Second Age. Kecker was the official liaison between Duinnor's Foreign Ministry and the Kingsman Army, a role long established to foster cooperation between the two organizations. However, it became increasingly apparent that not only was Kecker somewhat lax in his duties, but that certain information that passed through his office between the Ministry and Kingsmen was finding its way into the ranks of the Duinnor Regulars. It was even suspected that Kecker was on the payroll of Lord Banis. This was confirmed after Banis's death when records describing Kecker's involvement with Banis were discovered.

Khanhar Pass   A broad gap in the northern Dragonlands at the base of the Blue Mountains, located north of Calamandor (the Green Citadel). Roughly twenty miles wide from east to west, and running some thirty miles north and south, Khanhar Pass is relatively flat and wide. Due to its location on the border between the Dragonlands and Vanara, it was a strategic route for the crossing of armies back and forth. For this reason, many attempts were made to secure the pass, but with little long-term success. In the year 779 of the Second Age, the Dragonkind made an all-out attempt to establish fortifications and keeps all through the pass, served by a major fortress centrally located within the pass. However, the task was beset with difficulties. There is no water within forty miles, no wild food or forage, and the climate varies from intolerably hot to bitterly cold. The resultant logistical costs of supporting a workforce and the required army to occupy the pass were too high to sustain. When the combined armies of Vanara and Duinnor attacked in the year 781, the Dragonkind were driven out of the pass. In turn, the Northmen attempted to do what the Dragonkind had failed to do, by occupying, rebuilding, and improving the fortifications within the pass. However, they met with the same difficulties as had the Dragonkind.

Between 781 and 786, Khanhar Pass changed hands several times amid bitter fighting until, when the Dragonkind were once again ousted in 787, the Vanarans decided not to reoccupy the pass. The Dragonkind would not attempt to retake it.

Some years later, during the two invasions against the Green Citadel, Khanhar Pass was used by

the invading armies as their entrance into the Dragonlands. Each time, too, it was their point of retreat. It was at Khanhar Pass that, during the first retreat from the Green Citadel, a massacre of retreating Vanarans and Kingsmen took place, when they were surrounded and cut off by a large army of Dragonkind. During the second invasion nearly a decade later, the same fate befell the retreating invaders. Many made it through Khanhar Pass, only to be trapped and slaughtered at Peldown, later to be called the Gory Gulch.
See also:
Biographical Sketches (Danig Tallin)

King's Post   A mail and letter delivery system developed and operated under the auspices of the Kingsmen Army of Duinnor. It served all of the Seven Realms for both private letters and for official dispatches.
See Also:
Historical Sketches (Kingsmen)

Kingmaker   A name referring to Begrimlin, a Firstborn Elifaen. He was renowned for his ability to bring feuding parties to treaty, though he found little success when it came to bringing peace between his people and the Dragonkind. In the latter part of the First Age and into the Second Age, he was active in many realms.
See Also:
Glossary (Begrimlin)

Kingsmen   The elite army of Duinnor, founded and supported by the Unknown Kings. Originally, this organization was tasked with palace duties centered on the security of the Unknown Kings. However, it grew to become one of the most powerful and professional armies in the world, almost entirely displacing the Duinnor Regular Army in the most important military roles, rivaling even the Fellfaere of Vanara in its feats.
See Also:
Historical Sketches (Kingsmen)

Kluker Klag   The name given to certain southwestern tribes of men, the Cuwali, and to their lands in the Bletharn Plains.
See Also:
Glossary (Cuwali)

Knarley Knob   A high barren-top hill west of Barley.

Kudzu   A fast-growing vine which during the late Second Age was spread by followers of Wokan and used by the so-called Wickerman army to make their wicker armor. If not constantly cut back, it grew voraciously, smothering forests, buildings, and croplands, forming dense blankets over vast areas of land.

Kundorlu   In the Dragonkind Speech, teacher, or special mentor. The kundorlu of the upper castes were often also priests, mystics, or scholars in their own right and those of the lower castes acolytes and students of the great schools.

Ladentree   A major trade city in southwest Vanara, and Vanara's second-most populous city. Ladentree is thought by some to have been the oldest settled area of Vanara, with recollections of the Elifaen describing the region of dense forests, swift rivers, and fertile valleys. Ladentree was initially an agricultural center, surrounded by orchards of apple, pear, and nut trees. In the early First Age, the dominant people were of the House of Fairoak, but by the late Second Age virtually no Fairoaks remained. Its relative proximity to Kajarahn, the free city of the Dragonlands, gave it almost exclusive access for trade with the Dragonlands, and its relationship to Kajarahn deepened over the Second Age. Ladentree provided lumber, grain, fruit, finished goods, and some metals and received in kind from the Dragonlands textiles, minerals, gemstones, and pottery. Ladentree was also one of the main ways that agents and provocateurs could easily travel into the Dragonlands in the guise of traders.

By the end of the Second Age, it had a population of around 50,000, excluding a large garrison of Fellfaere and Kingsman military units. Large groups of mercenary guards were also based there, hired by traders to help safeguard their caravans through the rough and lawless mountains along the route to Kajarahn. From time to time during its history, Ladentree and the region surrounded it came under attack from marauders, renegades, bands of mercenaries, and rebel Dragonkind. It formed its own militias but was unable to secure itself from such attacks until the Second Age, when permanent detachments of Fellfaere and Kingsmen were assigned to the area.

Lady Luna   A name sometimes given to the moon. In legend, Lady Moon was wife to Sir sun. Another name for Lady Moon.
See Also:
Biographical Sketches (Sir Sun and Lady Moon)

Lady Moon   A name sometimes given to the moon. In legend, Lady Moon (or sometimes Lady Luna) was wife to Sir sun. Another name for Lady Moon.
See Also:
Biographical Sketches (Sir Sun and Lady Moon)

Laeleth   Legendary daughter of Aperion, who returned to the world to seek out her lover, Celefar, who was left behind after the Fall.

Legends have it that Laeleth's wings were broken when she fell to earth upon her return, and wandered for many years in search of Celefar. It was Laeleth who gifted Swyncraff to Cupeldain. After delivering the Swyncraff to Cupeldain, Laeleth and Celefar were never seen again.
See Also:
Glossary (Swyncraff)

Laird   Title given to landowners, particularly those of the lesser houses with substantial properties and estates. It is sometimes used interchangeably with "lord."

Lafkin   A man of Duinnor, who served in various militaries, suffered injustices, and became a renegade of the deserts. He was rescued by King Philawain and became the chief military officer of Griferis. Lafkin also delivered Ormace's emerald Bloodcoins to Tower Zurlamont.

Lakemen   Men of Lake Halgaeth, renowned for their boating skills, loyal to the Prince Danoss of Glareth, who maintained a residence and base of operations at Formouth. Lakemen plied Lake Halgaeth with their sailboats and other craft and were expert in the ways of the lake. The Lakemen considered Halgaeth their own domain, and not only do they fish in it and ferry trade upon it, but under Prince Danoss were organized into military units for the lake's defense and protection. Thus they were similar in some ways to a lake-bound navy and in other ways to marines. Some units of Lakemen were charged with patrols and policing, while others specialized in military transport.

Lamath Heneileth   The ancient name for Heneil's Wall, the dam at the headwaters of the Saerdulin at Lake Halgaeth built by Heneil as part of his defensive strategy for Tulith Attis. Heneil constructed the dam in order to prevent large boats from reaching the fortress, the kind that would typically transport enemy troops. Thus the Saerdulin was reduced to a trickle that could only take shallow-draft boats.

As the lake Halgaeth's water level rose, it spilled over at a different place to form the Bentwide River, previously only a stream.

In the Year 870 of the Second Age, when the Great Bell of Tulith Attis was rung, Heneil's Wall collapsed, sending a torrent of water along the old river course past the fortress. As a result, the lake quickly settled back to its ancient levels while the Bentwide became a tributary stream once more.

Lantos   Prince of Tracia of the House of Bayberry, who, with his older brother Lewtrah, ruled Tracia immediately prior to the revolution and overthrow by the Triumvirate. By comparison to his brother, Lantos was more sympathetic to the people of Tracia and their needs, was more intellectual and attentive to matters of state, and was a keen military leader.
See Also:
Biographical Sketches (Lantos)

Leander   Given name of Leander Fascomb, Post Rider of Duinnor. Also the given name of Leander Tallin, who died at Tulith Attis.

Leases of Forfeiture   Leases of Forfeiture is the general name given to the Duinnor system of acquiring lands and properties in other realms, usually in the guise of economic assistance, but was just as often used as a way of threatening any who might appear disloyal to Duinnor.
See Also:
Essays & Explanations (Leases of Forfeiture)

Leeriver   A local name for the area just south of Passdale on the west bank of the Bentwide during the late Second Age while it was still a river (before the collapse of Heneil's Wall).

Legthar   One of the Elders of Nowhere in the late Second Age.

Lerse   A tributary of the River Saerdulin located south of Tallinvale and north of the Fengal River. The Lerse marks the old boundary of the territory west of the Saerdulin that was disputed by the old Eastlands Realm and Tracia Realm during the Second Age. In the late Second Age, a twenty-mile line of keeps and small posts were constructed by Lord Tallin north of the Lerse running east and west to guard Tallinvale against Tracian intrusions. Sometimes called the Tallinvale Line, these marked the border of lands claimed by the House of Tallin and Fairoak.

Where the Lerse flows into the Saerdulin was the site of the Battle of Saerdulin, as the Dragonkind invaders of 322 S.A. made a stand between its southern banks and the western banks of the Saerdulin, thinking the two rivers would protect their flanks. In spite of this, the Dragonkind were utterly defeated.
See Also:
Glossary (Saerdulin, Battle of)
Historical Sketches (Great Dragonkind Invasion)

Lewtrah   The unpopular Ruling Prince of Tracia Realm immediately prior to being ousted and forced to flee Tracia by the Redvest Triumvirate.
See Also:
Biographical Sketches (Lantos)

Limbo   Boy of Nowhere during the late Second Age.

Linlally   The ruling city of Vanara. Founded and built by Cupeldain, it was enhanced by the carvings and statues of Alonair. It was originally the name only for the palace that Cupeldain built atop the Falls of Tiandari, but later became the name for the larger city that grew up around and below the palace along the banks of the Iridelin River. In the latter Second Age, Duinnor commonly stationed armies there, ostensibly for defense purposes since Linlally is the closest major city to the Dragonlands. Also by that time, the city had grown in size and sophistication. Its streets were paved, with fine bridges crisscrossing the river, and splendid buildings, palaces, and markets. It was a bustling city of trade, culture, education, court, and government. By the end of the Second Age, its inhabitants numbered around 200,000 in the city-proper, with almost as many people living and working nearby in the region nearby along the Iridelin.

Lizard   A derogatory term for a Dragonkind person.

Lochton   A town nearby to the estates of the House of Hemlock located on the western shore of a small lake in the easternmost reaches of Vanara's frontier, just west of Forest Islindia. It was in this lake that Cupeldain and his wife (along with their traveling companions, including Shevalia and Bychanter) were drowned by one of the Elifaen clans of the region who were engaged in a bloody feud which Cupeldain hoped to resolve. When Parthais came and put down the feud, he executed several men and women from both sides of the feud by having them likewise drowned in the lake. It is said that Parthais also released a demon or water serpent into the lake to feed upon the spirits of the dead. Thus, the lake was thereafter considered haunted, and the people who live nearby have ever since reported sightings of apparitions and ghosts floating about or just underneath the lake's surface. It is of note that all fish disappeared from the lake around this time, although its shores teemed with wildlife.
See Also:
Glossary (Hemlock)

Locks of Karthia   A series of locks and canals constructed along the Osterflo River in Karthia region where the natural course of the river is filled with rapids and dangerous boulders as it passes through the Carthanes. Previous to the construction of the locks, traders and travellers had to disembark from the river and follow roads beyond the river's obstacles for some fifty miles before reembarking, making the river route between Glareth and Duinnor costly and slow.

Although the building project had been proposed as early as the late First Age, no workable plans or financing were deemed feasible until the early Second Age, and many engineering challenges had not been resolved. However, several careful surveys were conducted by a consortium of Duinnor aristocrats and officials. The idea gained renewed interest under the reign of the First Unknown King, who ordered enhanced surveys and organized the construction of elaborate models. By the time the Fifth Unknown King came to power, plans had been more or less finalized, and construction was finally begun in 320 S.A.

As expected, it proved to be a difficult and dangerous project, engaging thousands of workers for over 40 years. To build and operate the locks, many technological innovations were made, including large screws and gears made of iron and steel, various pumping systems, and many massive cranes, winches, and derricks. Armies of workers representing a span of disciplines and expertise were involved, including machine engineers, metalworkers, miners, stonecutters, woodworkers, boatbuilders, bargemen, teamsters. The logistics to support such a vast workforce for so long was itself an epic undertaking. It was not only the largest civil engineering project ever undertaken, but was also the most expensive, with Duinnor bearing the lion's share of the construction costs. Over 40,000 workers were employed during its construction, and it was built under the direct supervision of Kingsman engineers. It was dangerous, with various accidents and calamities that killed or maimed thousands. There were major delays and technical setbacks, particularly with the design and strength of the lock gates. Dredging of diversionary channels was necessary, as was the construction and use of cofferdams. The pumping systems were at first inadequate, and there were frequent failures with the derricks used to drive pilings and the cranes used to lift stone and machinery into place. The weather also played a role over the years, with several powerful blizzards and frigid temperatures creating icy conditions that made progress impossible. Three times, massive spring floods inundated the region and caused severe damage and many casualties.

The locks were finally operational by 360 SA. The first locks and canals were plagued by breakdowns and mishaps, but remained more or less in working order. Some of the iron used in the gates had to be repeatedly replaced, for example. One of the drawbacks of the initial design and construction was the very narrow locks and canals that permitted only small trade boats and barges to pass through, or, once within a lock, did not allow vessels adequate room to pass one another. The system was also prone to over flooding, especially during the spring, and the lock gate mechanisms tended to jam or freeze during winter. To remedy these issues, a major renovation was almost immediately under consideration, and, in 620 SA, major rebuilding of the locks and canals was begun. Locks and channels were widened, newly designed mechanical lock gates, pumps, canal roads, and towpaths were built. This work was done incrementally over the next 80 years. But by the year 710, much larger boats and barges were passing through Karthia, and at a much faster rate. For the first time, the Osterflo route to and from Duinnor and Glareth became routine, reliable, and profitable for bulk cargo. Karthia, the town, grew in size, as did the many small villages along the canals and approaches. Passenger lines that ferried travelers up and down the river were also established, along with King's Post stations. Thus, a bustling and vibrant river economy was established, yielding much wealth and revenue.

Once the locks were completed, trade and travel between Glareth and Duinnor boomed. Heavy goods, such as metal, lumber, and minerals flowed both ways. At first, fees were charged based on the size of each vessel that used the passage, but later on fees varied according to various criteria, including type of craft, cargo value, and passengers. The Osterflo route not only benefited Duinnor and Glareth directly, but greatly enhanced trade with coastal regions of the eastern world since goods could more easily and more cheaply be shipped to and from Glareth rather than traveling the long and tedious overland routes through the Carthanes. In the Eastlands, Colleton suffered as it was no longer the terminus for a great deal of overland trade, but became more or less a service port. Duinnor's trade passing through Altoria, bound for the east, was much reduced as well, and Vanara took advantage of this to negotiate favorable shipping costs for its own commerce moving to and through Altoria along its roads and through its port at Draymoor. Thus many interior towns and cities along the old overland routes declined, and some were completely abandoned, while others nearer to the waterways saw an increase in trade and economic activity, especially in and around Glareth.
See Also:
Glossary (Karthia)

Loringard A high pass on the road from the Eastlands to Duinnor in the Carthane Mountains. This route is somewhat treacherous due to the precarious heights and terrain and the many falls and streams that cross it, often washing out the path. It is favored by Post Riders during the summer months because it is a more direct way to and from Duinnor and the Eastlands than other routes farther north or south. However, the pass, actually a small vale high up among towering peaks, is usually snowbound by early autumn and is often impassable until late spring. It is also quite vulnerable to avalanche.

Loura Wife of Cupeldain, mother of Parthais. She never spoke, but she was able to communicate with others through her expressions and perhaps with some form of telepathy. She was assassinated, along with Cupeldain and many others, in 920 of the First Age during a trip to finalize peace between feuding clans of Elifaen.
See Also:

Lowbough   A town in the Eastlands known for its textiles.

Lucinda   Daughter of Chantay and Galanas of the House of Faircedar.
See Also:
Tales of the High Houses (The House of Faircedar)

Luna's Lantern   A magical lamp of Glareth by the Sea that once guided sailors safely to port.
See Also:
Eighteen Objects of Power (Luna's Lantern)

Lyrium   A Firstborn Faere who, with her sister Myrium, was the founder of the House of Fairfir. Lyrium wed Heneil, son of Silmain, and had twin daughters, Belmira and Elmira.

In the Time of Strife, Lyrium became renown for her gift of Sight, which enabled her to foresee portents of things to come. Using this skill, she was able to help her people overcome many of the difficulties that the Elifaen faced after the Fall. She was among the seven who received Bloodcoins from Aperion, hers being of gold and amber. Unlike other Elifaen, who lost their First Tongue rapidly and most of their corresponding "supernatural" skills, Lyrium's Sight would only very slowly decline. She would eventually have to resort to various rituals to summon her ability, but it never wholly left her, even though what she Saw became increasingly difficult for her to make sense of. With her Sight, she was able to acquire Ethliad the Sword and the Ring of Hearing, and she predicted the fall of Tulith Attis as well as the coming of King Philawain.

During the siege of Tulith Attis, she entrusted her Bloodcoins to Faeanna, her bodyguard, to be smuggled away, but Faeanna and the Bloodcoins would become lost. Lyrium herself survived Tulith Attis, but was forced to flee and go into hiding. Hundreds of years later, she briefly emerged from hiding in order to meet Robby Ribbon to affirm his quest and to offer her support. However, there was little she could do to sway events one way or the other during Robby's quest. She at last departed the world when it was remade.
See Also:
Tales of the High Houses (The House of Fairfir)

Maggie (Maggie Shawmill)   Girl of Barley in the late Second Age.

Makeig (Martin Makeig)   Colorful Loyalist naval captain of Tracia. He was in command of the warship Golden Swallow at the Battle of Grisland Strait, and his cunning and bravery enabled the ship bearing Prince Lantos to escape, although the Golden Swallow was destroyed during the action. Makeig and many of his crew survived the battle by abandoning their ship at the last moment and swimming ashore. Led by Makeig, the crew of the Golden Swallow then fled northward through Tracia, seeking to escape to Glareth. They were almost constantly pursued by Redvests, and many more crewmen were lost during this trek than were lost in battle. At last, Makeig and his remaining men turned westward and crossed the Saerdulin to enter the Thunder Mountains.

Makeig and his men arrived in Hill Town in the spring of 857, where they settled. Makeig found the place disorganized, squalid, and harassed by warlord mercenaries, particularly the Damar, and he quickly put himself in charge of things. So desperate the inhabitants were for food and basic needs that Makeig formed the Thunder Mountain Band, a loose-knit group of highwaymen made up mostly of members if his crew. Eventually, he sought to cast off that way of life by promoting trade, farming, and commerce among his people. When Hill Town became embroiled in the war between Tracian Redvests and Tallinvale, Makeig was instrumental in assisting Eastlands refugees, and he took part in many battles and skirmishes against the Redvests in and around the region of Janhaven and Passdale.
See Also:

Makewine   Elder of Nowhere.

Mar Henith   The Redvest general and former Kingsman who defeated Prince Lantos at the Battle of the Marshlands and who later oversaw the siege of Tallinvale in the late Second Age.

Mar Henith was born in 817 S.A., the only son of Lord Emard of the mortal House of Gull, in Tracia Realm. Upon his father's retirement from serving as a Kingsman, Mar Henith became a Kingsman in his father's place. At the Academy, Mar Henith performed well, and was particularly adept at engineering. Because of this, he was assigned to the famed 3rd Engineer Battalion of the Kingsman First Army. He served with distinction during the Second Siege of the Green Citadel, where he supervised the building of siege towers and large trebuchets. After the sack of the city, his battalion was amongst the first to be withdrawn, and its members suffered the fewest casualties during the retreat since they traveled a different route than the main army. A few weeks after the battle, Mar Henith (along with nearly all Tracians serving as Kingsmen) abruptly resigned his commission and returned to Tracia. Since certain legal conditions had to be met in order to resign from the Kingsmen, and since (like many other Tracians), Mar Henith never attempted to meet those requirements, he was designated by Duinnor a deserter and a traitor by Royal Decree.

The House of Gull was a staunch supporter of the Triumvirate, and upon Mar Henith's return to Tracia he was given the rank of general in the Redvest Army and immediately put in charge of fighting Loyalist forces in Tracia. Under his command, Redvest forces successfully took Weatherlee and Sorghwall. Henith was then recalled to Forlandis to oversee certain aspects of securing that city.

General Mar Henith, whose forces had not yet known defeat, was sent against Prince Lantos in 856, and he commanded the Redvests at the Battle of the Marshlands. There, Mar Henith successfully cut off the Loyalists from receiving provisions by land and forced a battle that lasted four days and nights, with much of the fighting taking place in the swamps and marshes. Prince Lantos was forced to concede the field, as it were. Lantos then led a rearguard action against Mar Henith's pursuing Redvests that allowed many of his Loyalist soldiers to escape by boats through the marshes to the sea. There, they were picked up by ships bound for Glareth. Mar Henith, seeking to capture rather than kill Prince Lantos, continually sought to surround the Prince. But, in a daring move, Loyalist Naval forces send a contingent of marines assisted by local Tracian boatmen into the marshes by night and rescued the Prince and his remaining men. They would be taken aboard the Barge Royale, soon to be engaged in a naval battle at Grisland Strait. However, the Battle of Marshlands is considered a victory for the Redvest Triumvirate, and for General Mar Henith, since it effectively eradicated organized resistance to the Triumvirate on Tracian soil.

Mar Henith was hailed by the Redvests as a hero, and soon all of Tracia was under the complete domination of the Triumvirate. Some years later, when the Triumvirate planned their invasion of Masurthia, Mar Henith warned against leaving Tallinvale on their northern flank, and he requested an army be given him that was sufficiently large to invade Tallinvale and overwhelm Tallin City. However, the Triumvirate did not fully heed Mar Henith. Instead, they sent Mar Henith to assist in the organization of the massing armies that were to go westward while they sent an inexperienced general with an inadequate force against Tallinvale. The results, as Mar Henith had predicted, were disastrous. The Redvest army sent against Tallinvale was cut to pieces and routed by Tallinvale. Enraged and embarrassed, the Triumvirate reversed themselves and ordered Mar Henith to lead a new and offensive to conquer and destroy Tallinvale. However, in a dramatic turn of events, his forces were utterly defeated at Tallinvale and Mar Henith was among the thousands of Tracian soldiers that died in the fighting.
See Also:

Historical Sketches (Battle of the Marshlands, Battle of Grisland Strait)

Mariglia   A mountain witch that attacked and wounded Faslor but was then killed by one of his companions, a Kingsman who would become the great grandfather of General Capstor who served in Vanara in the late Second Age.

Marren   A village in western Glareth, west of Lake Halgaeth. Although primarily a farming community during the late Second Age, it also produced a high-quality wool that was unusually soft. Also, there was a family of minstrels from the region that traveled extensively throughout the Seven Realms.

Marshlands, Battle of the   A battle that took place in the swamps and marshes of Tracia between Triumvirate forces and the retreating Loyalist forces under Prince Lantos. It is remarkable for the fact that Lantos was able to hold off a far superior force in a careful rearguard action while his people (many civilians as well as soldiers) were rescued by a massive effort of local boatmen and taken to awaiting Loyalist ships that would carry them away to Glareth.

The battle marked the last vestige of organized resistance on the part of Loyalist land forces in Tracia (until many years later), and it was the prelude to the naval action at the Battle of Grisland Strait.
See Also:
Historical Sketches (The Battle of the Marshlands, The Battle of Grisland Strait)

Masarro   A river on the southern coast in the frontier between Masurthia and Tracia Realms. The territory on both sides of the Masarro was in dispute for many years. During the late Second Age, the mouth of the Masarro was the location of a clandestine base for the Loyalist Tracian Navy after the takeover of Forlandis by the Redvest Triumvirate.
See Also:
Biographical Sketches (Martin Makeig)

Masurthia   One of the Seven Realms, located on the southern coast of the world between Altoria and Tracia. Masurthia was formed of territories that came under the rule of the Kingdom of Solsorna during the First Age. Later, it would go to war with Altoria in a bid to secure lands and trade routes. The war would end when Parthais marched from Vanara and overwhelmed both Altoria and Masurthia with his armies. He then enforced a peace between the two. Parthais would negotiate a settlement to land disputes and would put the western border of Masurthia along the River Wachee, where it would remain.

Solsorna was Masurthia's only city of consequence, its capital under various Kings and Ruling Princes. Its fortunes would wax and wane and it would never achieve the wealth or power of other Realms.

Megrinor   The great mountains of Vanara, stretching from Shatuum to the Dragonlands. Among the notable peaks of the range is the great Mount Cassos. Also within this range is the fabled Mount Algamori. The Blue Mountains is a lesser range bordering directly upon the northern Dragonlands; it joins the Megrinor range to the Tulivana mountain range along the eastern borders of the Dragonkind. These three ranges form a box around the western, northern, and eastern boundaries of the Dragonlands, with the Craggy Sea to the south.

Melnari   A very small and peculiar group of males who were mystics. Only six were known to have

lived at various times from the early Second Age until the end of that age. Most notable among them was Collandoth (Ashlord). Others were Ishtorgus, Tolimay, Raynor, Barian, and Micharam. Some served as advisors and tutors of kings and queens.
See Also:
Historical Sketches (The Melnari and Their Familiars)

Mena A Firstborn of the Faerekind, wife of Parthais, mother of Thurdun and Serith Ellyn. Mena was born of the spirit of the forest, with very dark green hair, brown skin like pine bark, and eyes the color of forest bluebells. She was of the region south of old Vanara, in the area that was to become the Dragonlands much later. She and Parthais fell in love and had two children, Thurdun and Serith Ellyn, both born during the Time Before Time. For a long while, the family was very close-knit, never far from one another, enjoying all of the joys of life together throughout the early days of the world. When Morgasir was destroyed with his dragons and monsters, and thus the Dragonkind people emerged, Mena was among the first to see and report of their existence. It was thought that she was one of those who sought the destruction of the Dragonkind by helping to make the Crack Between Worlds, cutting of the southwestern lands from water and rain. She was dismayed, however, at the results, apparently not expecting things to go as they did. There is little known about her between then and the Fall of the Faere, but according to comments made by Thurdun, she encouraged her children to keep watch over and explore the Dragonlands. It was Mena who first alerted the Faerekind concerning the approaching armies of Kalzar, and with the rest of her family she took up arms against them and was Scathed of her wings.

During the First Age, she became increasingly disenchanted with life and the ceaseless struggles against the Dragonkind, although she fought alongside the rest of her family under Cupeldain's leadership. She was killed in the same battle that took the life of King Silmain, which further increased the tensions between the House of Fairlinden and Ormace's House of Fairbirch. It is thought that her death rendered Parthais even more prone to fits of spite and anger than ever before, though he was held in check by his father. Just prior to the battle in which she was killed, she foresaw that Serith Ellyn would come to rule Vanara and that Serith Ellyn would, in turn, come to serve a great king. Serith Ellyn was never told of this prediction, which eventually came to pass, but it caused much consternation among the leading Faerekind, and especially in Parthais. The prophecy may have contributed to his paranoia and his mistrust of Serith Ellyn, leading him to send her into exile.
See Also:
Biographical Sketches (Parthais)
Glossary (Serith Ellyn)
Tales of the High Houses (Fall of the Faere, Last Book of Nimwill, House of Fairlinden)

Micerea Dragonkind woman, dreamwalker, conspirator, and instructor to Robby Ribbon. Her father was Gurasa, the great Dragonkind general. To her acquaintances, she seemed lazy and dim-witted, preferring luxury above all. That was a ruse devised by her father. She was secretly trained by her father in the history and lore of the Dragonkind as well as of the northern lands. Gurasa also trained Micerea in the use of sword and lance, and she was an expert rider. Gurasa often used Micerea as a courier, going throughout the Dragonlands to deliver dispatches to his fellow conspirators. It was during one of these assignments that she met Ullin Saheed Tallin. Later, when Gurasa discovered that Micerea was a dreamwalker, he arranged for her to be tutored in that art, and she would eventually use dreamwalking to carry out various missions.

Micerea would be instrumental in bringing about the rise of King Philawain and the remaking of the world at the end of the Second Age. She served Philawain not only as an instructor, but also as a messenger, courier, and spy. At the end of the Second Age, after the world was remade, Micerea and Ullin would marry and they elected to remain on the earth, settling in the newly recovered city of Darini in the former Dragonlands. Together, the two bore a daughter, called Mira.

Micharam   Known as Micharam the Poet, a Melnari fond of forests and wild places, perhaps with the ability to speak with insects. He was famous for his poetry, which was sometimes quite lewd or insulting.
See Also:
Historical Sketches (The Melnari and Their Familiars)

Middlemount   A high plateau between Duinnor and the Carthanes located north of the Bletharn Plain and south of the River Osterflo. It is an area about 400 miles across from east to west and around 100 miles from north to south, roughly in the shape of an oval. Its rim is characterized by many escarpments, and its broad relatively flat top is from 300 to 500 feet above the surrounding regions. It is rocky, has very few trees, has only a few sources of water, and it is windswept and relatively barren save for grasses and moss in abundance. From early autumn through late spring, it is usually covered with snow and ice. There are only a few trails across it, entirely unsuitable for heavy traffic, so most travelers that make the passage across it are on foot, horseback, or have relatively light carts and wagons.

Midsummer   The day of the summer solstice, and one of the days of the year not counted as a month day, usually falling three weeks into Sixthmonth. Midsummer's Day is often celebrated with festivals, bonfires, feasting and music. In the Eastlands and a few other parts, such celebrations are called Firefeasts.

Midwinter   The day of the winter solstice, and one of the days of the year not counted as a month day, usually falling three weeks into Twelfthmonth. According to some ancient calendars, Midwinter's was the last night of the year and was a night of celebration, gift-giving, and feasts. In the Second Age, the New Duinnor Calendar supplanted the older ones, and put the last day of the year some ten days after Midwinter's Day. Regardless, Midwinter's remained an important day of celebration, retaining many of the old traditions well into the late Second Age, and is still considered by many to be the natural and spiritual end of the year.

Miladora   One of the Elders of Nowhere.

Millithorpe   One of the Elders of Nowhere.

Millsin Fork   A small village in the eastern Carthane Mountains. It is the source of flint and lime.

Mimblewan   A town near the coast of the Eastlands Realm that produced glass jugs and other wares.

Minion Gap   A place north of Forest Islindia between Duinnor and Vanara. Travelers from Edgewold town go that way around Islindia to Vanara rather than risk entering the forest. Near Minion Gap are the ruins of several ancient structures, including various henges. It is thought that these were constructed during the Time Before Time or the Age of Strife, perhaps for ceremonial purposes. By the First Age, all were in a state of ruin. It was at one of these henges, near Minion Gap, that Lyrium acquired the Ring of Hearing.
See Also:
Eighteen Objects of Power (Ring of Hearing)
Glossary (Tarsus Maklaran)
Tales of the High Houses (House of Fairfir)

Mintar   One of the Wanderers, a star that moves across the night sky along its own path, progressing very gradually from night to night at a predictable rate, as do most Wanderers.

Mirabella (see Ribbon, Mirabella)

Mirse   A region in Vanara along the eastern end of the Blue Mountains where it meets the Tulivana Mountains, often called The Mirse. It is a broad valley bordered on the east by a bend in the River Iridelin. On its southwestern side are few natural barriers into the Dragonlands and thus has been overrun many times by incursions by the Dragonkind and is considered one of the strategic gateways into the Northlands. In the Second Age, it was twice the invasion route used by Dragonkind forces, most notably during the Great Invasion of 322. After that invasion and the second, lesser invasion that took place in 506 S.A., the southern regions of The Mirse, particularly in and around Darlang Hill, were more heavily fortified by Vanarans. However, by the late Second Age, the region was once again patrolled by sparse units of Fellfaere and Kingsmen and local militia groups bore the heaviest responsibilities for safeguarding the Mirse against attack.

Missenflo   The river that flows along the western edge of the Thunder Mountains and eastern edge of the Plains of Bletharn. It flows southward through the Kingdom of Sudamoor into Lake Adin.

Mistletoe   A parasitic plant that lives within the branches of trees, particularly hardwoods such as oak. Mistletoe, which remains green year-round, is said to have peculiar and mysterious properties. It is generally considered poisonous, but some herbalists and alchemists use it to make various extracts and potions.

Mistwarren   A dense forest on the eastern shores of Lake Halgaeth, stretching from Formouth to the region near County Barley, where it is called the Boggy Wood. The forest once stretched nearly to the eastern coast, but was much reduced by Newcomers.

In the First Age, Forest Mistwarren was populated by various Elifaen clans that seldom had dealings with others of their kind. It was these who first spread news of the Newcomers when they began landing on the eastern shores. The Newcomers (Men) set about clearing swaths of the forest for their settlements and their fields, to the dismay of many Elifaen. Most of the Elifaen inhabitants retreated from the Newcomers but some ventured out to greet and befriend the settlers. Needless to say, the tension between the forest Elifaen and the Newcomers sometimes resulted in violent confrontations, and it was not uncommon during the late First Age for there to be frequent raiding parties on Newcomer villages. However, the rapid expansion of the settlers and their farms pushed back the Elifaen. By the middle of the Second Age, only small isolated pockets of Elifaen remained within the forest.

During the Great Invasion of 322 S.A., some of the Mistwarren Elifaen joined with the defenders of Tulith Attis, while others acted as scouts for the armies of Glareth. By the late Second Age, no known villages of Elifaen remained in the forest, though legends and lore has it that some Elifaen who never had dealings with the world outside of the forest still dwelled there, variously entertaining and waylaying those who hunt or travel within their lands. Most people of the Eastlands considered the forest as a place of fearful enchantments and very few ventured into it.

Moonbeam   One of the stags of Uncle Solstice.

Morgasir   One of the Firstborn of the Faere. It was Morgasir who first delved into the dark secrets of the world and conjured demons, witches, and dragons, which he commanded. His works threatened to undo the intent of Beras, and so Morgasir was destroyed in a great battle between the two, resulting in the destruction of Morgasir's domain. It is thought by some that the remnants of those lands after Morgasir's destruction formed the crags and rocks that litter the Craggy Sea. However, some of his offspring survived to make terror and mischief in the world and to perpetuate his evil. Secundur was one of Morgasir's followers who escaped the destruction that came upon Morgasir. According to legend, the Dragonkind were created to serve the dragons of Morgasir, but were freed from bondage when Morgasir and most of his dragons were destroyed. Eventually, the Dragonkind came to associate themselves as offspring of the ancient dragons, and as heir to their power.

Mossweren Heights   A region south of Duinnor City and west of Nasakeeria, north of Minion Gap.

Mulberry (House of Mulberry)   One of the chief Elifaen Houses of Altoria, the House of Mulberry was established by Felthain, a Firstborn, during the reign of Silmain. Felthain became King of Altoria after Therona was dethroned.
See Also:
Biographical Sketches (Felthain)
Tales of the High Houses (House of Fairwillow)

Mulberry Race   The Mulberry Race, or simply "Mulberry," was a long-distance horse race from Duinnor City to Draymoor and back, some 4, 000 miles. The first Mulberry was held in the year 206 S.A. and was sponsored by the Altorian Royal House of Mulberry. It would take place every ten years until the year 800, when it became an annual event. The route of the race and the racing rules changed very little over the years. Each entrant, usually sponsored by a wealthy horse owner, consisted of a single horse and rider. The race route was from Duinnor City to Airemoor, then to Linlally. From Linlally riders traveled south along the River Iridelin to Draymoor. All riders were required to stop at specified waypoints along the route so that a travel log, which they were required to carry, could be updated and certified by race officials.

By the mid-800s, each race averaged about 300 entrants, of which less than fifty would successfully complete the race. Accidents, serious injuries, and even deaths were common, especially during the early years before improvements were made to roads and before the communities along the way were well-enough established to provide aid and assistance.

The Mulberry Race did as Felthain hoped, and brought greater attention to the roads, bridges, towns, and villages along the route. Spectators were encouraged to attend all along the way, to watch and cheer on the participants. Passenger traffic along the Iridelin increased, as did the number of inns and accommodations along the way, with the related increase in services and supplies needed by spectators and participants alike. Roads and bridges were quickly improved and better maintained, which made the route much better for trade and commerce.

Although the winners were declared in Duinnor City (upon their return), there was much ceremony and celebration in Draymoor, too. The race schedule stipulated that two weeks of rest be given after the first horseman arrived in Draymoor, and this period was one of galas, concerts, balls, and dances, with the Royal Palace of Draymoor at the center of the city-wide festivities.

The record time was established in 821, by Basley Crasson riding a horse named Tenderhoof and completing the route in 109 days, 12 ½ hours. Tenderhoof was one of the tall, sure-footed, stalwart breed called "Majestic," raised by the Thrubolds of Duinnor. These horses were renowned for their endurance and gentle dispositions. Soon after this win, Thrubold horses dominated among the Mulberry winners.
See Also:
Glossary (Anerath)

Myrium   Twin Sister of Lyrium and wife of Pellen.   She had one child, a son named Dalcadian. Pellen murdered Myrium during his plot to steal Lyrium's Bloodcoins.
See Also:
Tales of the High Houses (House of Fairfir)

Narrows   A narrow gap in the Thunder Mountains located on the road between Janhaven and Passdale of less than a half-mile in length. The path through the gap was probably deepened as a result of thousands of years of traffic. During the Redvest invasion of 870, the Narrows was the location of an important strongpoint and roadblock erected by refugee fighters based in Janhaven, its purpose being to prevent the Redvests from using the road to attack Janhaven.

Nasakeeria   A so-called forbidden land that was protected and isolated by a ring of fire, called Aperion's Fire, which incinerated any humans that sought to cross its border. Nasakeeria was within Duinnor Realm, on the northern borders of the Plains of Bletharn southwest of the Middlemount.

In the late Second Age, it was revealed that people who lived within Nasakeeria were descendants of the Dragonkind who, in terror of Kalzar, abandoned Darini, their city in the desert lands, and secretly migrated far to the north to a place that Aperion gave them to live in peace, This place, called Nasakeeria, was protected from attack by Aperion's Fire until such a time when the people could return to their desert home.

Away from the deserts, and away from the sickness common to the desert regions, the people of Nasakeeria established small towns and farms, maintaining a tradition of watching and waiting. Eventually, due to events brought about by King Philawain, the people of Nasakeeria were able to migrate back into the Dragonlands where they reoccupied and restored the abandoned city of Darini.
See Also:
Eighteen Objects of Power (Nasakeeria's Ring of Fire)
Glossary (Aperion's Fire, Darini)

Navis   A Firstborn of the House of Elmwood, son of Banis, who with his siblings, Atlana and Esildre, was born during the Time Before Time. As did his siblings and his father, Navis refused to go with Aperion and was Scathed of his wings. Navis was a renown warrior and had many adventures. He fought many battles under Silmain, Cupeldain, and Parthais. When a great monster, Jatarak the Ogre, appeared in the region of Altoria during the First Age, Navis pursued him into the Crevasse of Fire and slew him. In the Second Age, Navis single-handedly fought and slew an entire legion of Dragonkind at the Battle of Saerdulin. He and his sister Esildre later became students of Raynor the Wise. After Esildre went to Shatuum, Navis traveled there seeking to free her, but he never returned. It was later discovered that he and the other members of his party were murdered by Bailorg, who acted on instructions from Banis, Navis's own father.
See Also:
Biographical Sketches (Esildre)
Glossary (Atlana, Banis, Crevasse of Fire, Jatarak the Ogre, Saerdulin)

New Passbarley Bridge   The name given to the bridge across the Bentwide River that was rebuilt in the late Second Age at Passdale. It was the third bridge to be located at that site. The first bridge was washed away when the waters of the Bentwide rose after the construction of Heneil's Wall, which redirected the waters of Lake Halgaeth into the Bentwide. Heneil built a new bridge to serve traders coming and going from Attis. This second bridge was later destroyed in order to slow the approaching Dragonkind in 322 S.A. The Dragonkind hastily rebuilt it, but after the battle it was left to rot and ruin, with only the two stone support piers (those erected by Heneil) remaining. In the late Second Age, Robigor Ribbon and others of Passdale and County Barley built a new span across the Bentwide, making use of the old piers. It consisted of a deck partially supported by thick cables and chains that hung from Heneil's original support towers. It, too, would be destroyed, this time when an invading army of Tracian Redvests entered the region and threatened Passdale.

Newstone Ferry   A Bentwide crossing south of Passdale.

Nightar   A prince of Nasakeeria in the late Second Age

Nimbo   Boy of Nowhere.

Nimbus Illuminas   The Rainbow of Aperion, sometimes also called the Bridge of Light. For centuries, no one knew exactly what the Nimbus Illuminas actually was, only that the Forty-Nine Keys (or Bloodcoins) Aperion gave to the Seven High Houses were keys to be used to open the Nimbus Illuminas. It would serve, it was thought, as a way for the Elifaen to leave the earth and rejoin the Faerekind in Aperion's heavenly abode. Although there was speculation that the Seven Towers had something to do with it, and there were many attempts to scale the towers and investigate. It was not until King Philawain settled the matter, using the towers as intended, and all of the Bloodcoins, too, bringing about the remaking of the world.
See Also:
Glossary (Bloodcoins, Seven Towers)

Nimwill   A Firstborn Elifaen who was the scribe and court chronicler of Parthais during his reign as King of Vanara. As such, Nimwill attended and personally recorded many events that took place within the Royal Court, and he also traveled with Parthais to record various exploits and experiences. Nimwill was with Parthais when he executed those accused of murdering Cupeldain, and he was also with the king during his many campaigns in the Dragonlands as well as other parts of the world. He was at the Battle of Tamkal Plain when King Parthais slew King Salkasin, and he was in Masurthia when Parthais forced King Barindon and Queen Therona to make peace. Nimwill also accompanied King Parthais to see the legendary place called Griferis.

After Parthais exiled his son and daughter (Thurdun and Serith Ellyn), and grew more and more tyrannical, Nimwill continued to serve him. However, during the Purge of Scholars, and without the knowledge of Parthais, Nimwill secretly assisted many scholars by helping them to escape Vanara, often to other realms, and saving many books and scrolls from destruction. It was a dangerous, being at once the official chronicler of Linlally's royal court while acting against the will of his king. Meanwhile, he worked tirelessly to transcribe materials written in the various old scripts into the so-called New Writing that Parthais sought to impose upon Vanara. It is thanks to Nimwill's efforts that Vanara was able to retain as much literature as it did, although many of the originals from which he worked were destroyed before he could smuggle them away.

When Serith Ellyn overthrew her father, Nimwill continued as her chief scribe for a time. He oversaw the restoration of many hidden manuscripts to Vanara and the organization of several libraries and archives within Linlally, most notably the one at the Hall of Ministers. He retired in the year 202 of the Second Age, giving over his duties to Orinus.

In the year 275 S.A., Nimwill traveled east, intending to go to Glareth to make copies of manuscripts sent there during the Purge of Scholars. He passed through Attis and visited with Lyrium and Heneil for a brief time before continuing on to Glareth, but he never arrived. No one knows what happened to him, and no trace was ever found of the party he was traveling with. Some speculate that they were killed or captured by Pinewood rebels, while others insist that King Inrick of Colleton imprisoned him. Still other legends have it that Nimwill's party became lost within Forest Mistwarren and never emerged. Since he was Elifaen, some speculate that he may still be alive somewhere in the world.
See Also:
Biographical Sketches (Parthais)
Essays and Explanations (Literacy and Education)
Glossary (Mistwarren)
Tales of the High Houses (Last Book of Nimwill)

Nokershire   A coastal village in Glareth Realm.

Noringtown A suburb of Duinnor.

Norogus One of the two proprietors of Norogus and Harmalway, a lending house in Duinnor. They were one of the firms in Duinnor that handled leases and liens on Vanaran properties. Two of its most notable patrons were Lord Banis and Bailorg. Norogus and Harmalway were suspected, and eventually arrested, for their involvement in many nefarious activities, including blackmail, fraud, theft, and embezzlement.

Northern Expeditions   The general term referring to various expeditions into the Northern Wastelands, Endeweir, and along the northeast coastal regions north of Glareth Realm.

Interest in the regions north of the Osterflo waxed and waned throughout the First Age, with only a few tenuous forays by hunters, trappers, and adventurers. However, when it was reported that Katrina's people of the House of Fairmaple had disappeared from the Carthanes, and that it was rumored they had migrated to the far north, interest was rekindled.

The first major expedition was sent by Glareth with the dual purpose of mapping the northeast coastlines and to seek out any suitable rivers that could be navigated into the interior. Four ships set out in the spring of 196 S.A.. Two of the ships were lost in storms, and the other two returned late in the year, having nearly become trapped by sea ice. Several rivers had been discovered along 300 miles of rocky coastline, but all were shallow, white-water rivers cascading over falls and through narrow canyons, too treacherous or arduous to allow easy access and exploration of the interior. Over the next two hundred years, Glareth would continue to send forth expeditions, and would slowly establish settlements along the northern coasts. But an easy passage by water into the interior was never found, nor were any hints of Katrina's fate discovered.

When the First Unknown King came to power, one of his first acts was to commission Duinnor's own expedition, likely in the hopes of locating Katrina's people and, more importantly, obtaining her Seven Bloodcoins. Duinnor's first major expedition crossed the Osterflo in the year 233 S.A., but it never returned. Over thirty years later, the Third Unknown King sent a second and larger expedition into the north. Of roughly two hundred men, nearly half managed to return six years later, reporting that most of their casualties were the result of lack of food, extreme cold, and wolves. Fully six months of each year, on average, were spent in winter camps, the land being so hostile and cold, with snow as much as twenty feet deep, that movement from mid-autumn to late spring was impossible. In the warmer months, the land remained barren, with few trees, many bogs and lakes. According to their reckoning, they claimed only to have penetrated two hundred miles north of the Osterflo.

Duinnor's next expedition departed the Osterflo in 285 S.A., intent on tracing a northward route just west of the foothills of the northern Carthanes. This expedition returned in 288, having lost only seven out of the sixty that had started out. They reported finding the ruins of several very old villages, but the only living things they encountered were birds, bears, wolves, deer, and smaller mammals such as rabbits, foxes, and otter. They also reported seeing to the west and north a vast icy plain, whilst to the east the Carthanes remained snow-covered year-round almost to their base.

A new expedition was almost immediately planned. This one would establish several depots with caches of food, fuel, blankets, sleds, and other needed supplies. Within five years, this was done, with the northernmost depot carefully located some two hundred miles almost due north of Blueshoals on the Osterflo. These expeditions prepared careful maps during their excursions. The final expedition crossed the Osterflo at Blueshoals in the early winter of 413, a group of thirty Kingsmen, all veterans of previous expeditions. Their intent was to travel swiftly and lightly, using skis and buckmarl-drawn sleds. They made it to the northernmost depot within two months with little difficulty, where they remained for the remainder of the winter. Spring came, and the ground remained covered with ice and snow, but stretched out northward beyond sight with very few hills or other features. The party dispatched a group to return as messengers to relay their progress to the King, then they loaded their sleds and sledges with all of the supplies they could transport, and set out to penetrate further north.

Officially, they would never be heard from again. Unofficially, rumors spread that three men made it back to Duinnor, but they were sworn to secrecy concerning what they saw and experienced. Further adding to the mystery, these three men, so the rumors went, were each separately reassigned to Kingsman units in the Blue Mountains, and each died in different skirmishes there. The families of these men and others lost on the expedition, petitioned the King, and later the courts, for news of their loved-ones, but the King made no response and the courts were barred by the King from investigating. No documents pertaining to this matter have ever been located. As far as is known, Duinnor sponsored no further expeditions. It is reasoned by some that the King accomplished his goal and had gained the Bloodcoins of Katrina. Whether he acquired his Bloodcoins in this manner or not, Katrina's Bloodcoins were in fact part of the collection that the Sixth Unknown King had in his possession when he was overthrown by Philawain.

Northlands A term used by the Dragonkind to describe the regions to the east and north of the Dragonlands.

Northmen A term used by the Dragonkind to refer to Men and Elifaen.

Northmetal Northmetal is a magnetic ore (or lodestone) which is relatively rare. When a small bit is shaped and hammered into a thin, flat blade and balanced on a pin, one end of the blade always points northward. The use of northmetal devices was becoming common by the middle of the Second Age, particularly by sailors.

The use of northmetal for this purpose was well understood by the Dragonkind, who routinely used it to help guide their caravans more precisely during daylight hours or during dust storms when stars could not be seen. Because their routes and waymarkers were often obscured by sand, their use of such northmetal devices saved many caravans from losing their way. The Dragonkind were also the first to discover locations where the magnetic needle varied when compared to celestial objects, and some of their maps noted these places and the amount of deviation from "true" or celestial north.

By the end of the Second Age, "compasses" were being used on Glarethian and Altorian ships and it was commonly used by surveyors, mapmakers, and militaries. Incredibly, in spite of its value, no real effort was made to mass produce compasses or distribute them to armed forces.

Nowhere The land of the Nowhereans, a diminutive people sometimes called Pixies in a derogatory manner. It was located in the western Thunder Mountains.

The people of Nowhere were former slaves who had been in service to Bailorg during the Great Invasion. They were trapped within their lands by a curse of Bailorg when they revolted against him. Later, they were made small by being cursed by Navis of Elmwood, and they were given long life and the ability to instantly from place to place by Esildre.

The land of Nowhere itself is a small hilly forest surrounded by mountains to the north, east, and south. To the west it is bounded by a deep gorge. Although tiny in land-area, no more than 60 miles in circumference, it provided ample soil, water, fish and game, and good land for small farms.
See Also:
Biographical Sketches (Esildre)
Glossary (Bailorg, Hoard, Picathia)
Historical Sketches (Great Dragonkind Invasion)

Oilwood   An aromatic, resinous wood that is taken from the stumps of trees, particularly pine and other conifers. The wood is often traded in small wax-sealed blocks for use as matchsticks. It is sometimes called "lighter wood" or "fat lighter." It is easily lit by a small flame and burns bright and hot. In the late Second Age, chemical paste was developed which, when applied to the tip of an oilwood stick and allowed to dry, permitted one to light the oilwood merely by scratching the stick onto a rough surface, such as a rock. These were called "firesticks," and became the basis for bright handheld flares. Eventually, as the alchemical paste became more reliable and hotter, oilwood was no longer required to make firesticks and was slowly replaced by ordinary wood. At the same time, the alchemists perfected the paste itself so that flares became brighter and hotter with fewer flames.
Use of oilwood declined in general, especially as a trade good, although it continued to be gathered and used locally for personal and household use.

Oldgate   A place marked by a pair of stone pillars located at the Old East Road, near Tulith Attis. The pillars were once the entrance to the settlement of Attis, which was destroyed during the siege of Tulith Attis. Although Attis would never be rebuilt, the stone pillars remained standing for hundreds of years.

Oracle   A person who is consulted concerning the future, or a declaration or prophecy given by a holy person, particularly in response to a query or adjuration. These are often done in a near-delirious state of mad raving ecstasy. The most famous oracle was that of the Temple of Beras, who had a mysterious relationship with the Unknown Kings of Duinnor who went to the Temple each year to renew their Kingship. The renewal ceremonies within were secretive, and no one but the monks of the Temple, the Oracle of Beras, and the Unknown King were privy to what took place during such ceremonies. King Philawain (Robby Ribbon) discovered that the reason for the Beras Oracle's odd behavior was that he was continually in a state of dreamwalking, even while awake and communicating with others around him.

Ormace   Founder of the High House of Fairbirch. It was Ormace who infamously forced the other High Houses to redistribute their Bloodcoins so that none would have seven Bloodcoins of the same type (that is, of the same type of gemstone).
See Also:
Tales of the High Houses (The House of Fairbirch)

Osterflo   The long river that flows from northern Duinnor eastward to empty into Salfin Bay at Glareth by the Sea. It was originally called the "duin nord," or north river, and is the basis for Duinnor's name. The name Osterflo, however, was the old Glarethian name of the river and came into standard use by the middle of the First Age.

The Osterflo was an important but treacherous trade route prior to the construction of the Locks of Karthia, a set of locks and canals that permitted boats to avoid the series of waterfalls and shoals along the Osterflo near the Carthane Mountains near Karthia (roughly midway between Duinnor and Glareth). After the construction of the Locks, the Osterflo became the primary northern trade route between east and west.
See Also:
Glossary (Karthia, Locks of Karthia)

Overlord   A title sometimes given to the Unknown King of Duinnor, also called the King of Kings, since he was sovereign over all other rulers.

Packlin   A Boskland farmer.

Palos   One of Lucinda's two sons.
See Also:
Tales of the High Houses (The House of Faircedar)

Paltera   A mountain witch who occupied a territory in the western slopes of the Thunder Mountains near the Missenflo River. She attacked Robby Ribbon's party, as related in *The Year of the Red Door*, nearly capturing Ibin Brinnin. However, Collandoth managed to kill her. He then tracked down her lair, where many of her offspring (sired by Valkose the Demon) incubated. Collandoth destroyed the offspring, then engaged in a battle with Valkose.
See Also:
Glossary (Valkose the Demon)

Pargolis   A Redvest officer under General Vidican's command.   He was one of the Redvests chosen to reconnoiter County Barley and Passdale as a part of the Redvest invasion plans.   As a result of his lurid behavior, he was confronted by Ullin at Colleton, and the two engaged in a serious fight, with Ullin barely escaping.   Later, during the occupation of County Barley by the Redvests, Pargolis captured Raenelle Bosk and raped her repeatedly.   She eventually killed him.

Parthais   The third King of Vanara who ascended the throne after the death of this father Cupeldain. Parthais became a despot and was eventually overthrown by his daughter, Serith Ellyn, who then became Queen of Vanara.
See Also:
Biographical Sketches (Parthais)
Tales of the High Houses (Last Book of Nimwill, House of Fairlinden)

Passdale   A town in County Barley of the Eastlands Realm on the banks of the Bentwide River. It was located on the site of a small settlement known as Dalefath, which was destroyed in the Dragonkind Invasion of 322 S.A.

Peldown   The proper name for Gory Gulch, but after the battle that took place there in the late Second Age, Peldown was used less often.
See Also:
Glossary (Gory Gulch)

Pellen   Twin brother of Heneil, husband of Myrium.   Traitor of Tulith Attis.   Called Throgallus by Secundur.
See Also:
Biographical Sketches (Pellen)
Tales of the High Houses (House of Fairfir)

Peller's Carpet   A moss that grows underneath moist rocky outcrops. It has the peculiar property of glowing in the dark and is sometimes used on garden paths. It is said to have certain medicinal properties and, when properly prepared, it could be added to smoking mixtures as a mild intoxicant.

Peninflo   The proper and ancient name of the river Bentwide and the small valley in Barley through which it flows.

Picathia   The land from which Nowhereans claimed to have originated. They were enslaved by the Dragonkind and made to serve them during the Dragonkind Invasion of 322 S.A. Picathia itself was believed to have been somewhere in the northern lands of Altoria, although there are no reliable records of such a land or people. Wherever Picathia was, all of the people were taken from their

homeland and forced with the Dragonkind army to Tulith Attis under an Elifaen overseer and traitor named Bailorg. Most did not survive the journey east, due to the extreme conditions of the weather, lack of food, and harsh treatment. After the fall of Tulith Attis, the surviving Picathians were forced by Bailorg to push and pull two very large wagons of spoils westward into the Thunder Mountains. Before they made it out of the mountains, the Picathians revolted against Bailorg when his guards deserted him. As a result of their revolt, they were cursed by Bailorg, Navis, and Esildre, which forced them to remain within the region, which became known as Nowhere.   Later, they would identify themselves as Nowhereans.
See Also:
Biographical Sketches (Bailorg, Esildre)
Glossary (Hoard, Nowhere)
Historical Sketches (The Great Dragonkind Invasion)

Pinewood Uprising   Although it began as an anti-Men uprising fomented by woodland Elifaen of the Eastlands and Tracia, it transformed into a confusing civil war between various alliances of Men and Elifaen. It began in 278 S.A. and was of such violence that it threatened to lead to widespread war between the Seven Realms. It came about as a reaction to the increasing encroachment of Men into the forest territories of the east, particularly in the Eastlands and in Tracia. The woodland Elifaen of the region resented the way Men cut forests for fields and took lands that they claimed were traditionally Elifaen lands. From at least the beginning of the Second Age, there was sporadic violence against Mortal settlements, mainly theft of cattle and destruction of crops, but it was unorganized and of little consequence regionally. In turn, however, Men blamed the Elifaen of the region for spreading disease (to which the Elifaen were immune), and after the plague of 270 S.A., some Men began conducting raids into the forest, deliberately cutting groves of what they believed were trees sacred to the Elifaen. Soon thereafter, there was unrest throughout the east as tensions increased.

Although Heneil and others in the Attis region of the east formed cordial relations with Men, rifts quickly spread elsewhere between the Elifaen. In northern Tracia, a band of Elifaen united under the leadership of the House of Pinewood began raiding both Men and Elifaen villages, burning them to the ground and killing many. The uprising then spread rapidly, pitting village against village, and bringing violence throughout the east. Heneil, seeking to protect his region of Attis, made a pact with Men and began leading counterstrikes against Pinewood. Glareth soon came to the aid of Attis and the Eastlands, while King Kapol of Tracia backed Pinewood (although many in Tracia opposed both Kapol and Pinewood), turning the uprising into a wider civil war. However, all other realms quickly came to the aid of Glareth and the Eastlands. Within four years, Pinewood and Kapol were defeated, and their Houses abolished. Various leaders of Pinewood were arrested for their crimes, but many were murdered in retribution before they were put on trial. Kapol was deposed, and he died in prison under suspicious circumstances, while his family was sent into permanent exile on Grisland Island.

In the years that followed, the number of Elifaen in Tracia would rapidly decline until, by the late Second Age, no Elifaen were reported on the official census.
See Also:
Glossary (Kapol)

Pixies   A derogatory name given to the little people who dwell in the western Thunder Mountains. The name comes of the reputation for mischief and thievery that those people were known for.
See Also:
Glossary (Nowhere, Picathia)

Prefect   A high official, usually of a city, somewhat akin to a high-ranking clerk but with the powers of a judge. This is not to be confused with the Prelect of Duinnor, whose duty it is to announce official proclamations and decrees, both those of a public nature concerning all persons, as well as those pertaining to only a few. In the late Second Age, it was the Prefect of Duinnor that issued and recorded travel passes and placed conditions on Elifaen who traveled throughout the Seven Realms in accordance with laws and policies enacted by the King. The Prefect of Duinnor had no power of enforcement other than to report any lapse or irregularity to the Kingsmen or to the various ministries as each situation warranted.

Prerogatives of the Realms A system of laws and conditions between Duinnor and other Realms which outlined what powers would be retained by each realm's Ruling Prince and what powers would be reserved to Duinnor. These varied with each Realm and were never fully implemented in Vanara.
See Also:
Essays & Explanations (Prerogatives of the Realms)

Prideling One of the buckmarl stags of Uncle Solstice.

Punk A type of tinder used to catch a spark from a flint and steel making fire. It is made of the dry, rotted, almost powdery wood found within old logs, often called punkwood.

Purge of Scholars An effort by Parthais to control writing and information, which led to the flight of many scholars from Vanara and the loss of many manuscripts.
See Also:
Essays & Explanations (Literacy and Education)

Pyros Firstborn Elifaen and founder of the High House of Fairmyrtle who was entrusted with Ruby Bloodcoins from Aperion.
See Also:
Tales of the High Houses (The House of Fairmyrtle)

Queen of the Night A name sometimes given to the moon. In legend, Lady Moon (or sometimes Lady Luna) was wife to Sir sun. Another name for Lady Moon.
See Also:
Biographical Sketches (Sir Sun and Lady Moon)

Queen of the Wood This title refers to Islindia, daughter of Ilex
See also:
Glossary (Islindia)

Queen's Academy The Queen's Academy was a school located in Linlally established by Queen Serith Ellyn in the early years of her reign. It did not have a specific focus, nor was it purely devoted to those who would serve Vanara, but was open to all. The Queen made generous annual gifts and grants both to the school itself, but also to individuals to pay for their education, to house and feed them, and to support their families. Serith Ellyn understood the need for a literate citizenry, and she created many schools for children from which the Academy drew many of its students. The Academy grew over time and its curriculum including virtually every subject, including language and writing arts, music, painting and sculpture, history, agriculture, alchemy, engineering, medicine, metallurgy, geography and surveying, legal systems and law enforcement. Eventually, all Fellfaere recruits were required to complete some courses at the Academy. In addition, many facilities were devoted to research and testing. These included those devoted to optics, plant propagation, astronomy, and (in the late Second Age) the new field of aeronautics.

The Academy paid its instructors and scholars handsomely, and it also established ongoing programs of cooperation with other schools, even those as far away as Duinnor and Glareth.

Special care was taken to attract scholars and teachers from other Realms on a permanent or visiting basis.
See Also:
Essays and Explanations (Literacy and Education)

Radasa   A Dragonkind, the son of Emal, who was a successful trader of Kajarahn during the last years of the Second Age. He learned the business and inherited his father's talent and integrity, although he was quite precocious as a youngster. Radasa was with his father when Gurasa's representative (Tareef) delivered Gurasa's battle standard to be delivered to Tallinvale. Later, after his father died and Radasa took over the family business, he became one of the most successful traders in Kajarahn, although, due to his generosity, he never accumulated much wealth. He married and had three daughters, and the family often traveled together on Radasa's business.   However, this proved fateful. On one such journey, they were captured by renegades and sold into captivity, the new captors being wraiths from Shatuum who regularly brought slaves to Shatuum to be violated and converted into monstrous beings. But they were rescued by King Philawain (with the help of Micerea and Finn), and the entire family entered into service at Griferis.

Raenelle, see Bosk, Raenelle

Raskin   Mysterious Elifaen assistant to Uncle Solstice.

Raynor   A Melnari, known as Raynor the Wise. He was a renowned tutor and educator with many notable students, including Navis and Esildre of the House of Elmwood. He was a close associate of Collandoth.
See Also:
Historical Sketches (The Melnari and Their Familiars)

Red Feather of Callowain   A large feather capable of foretelling the weather.
See Also:
Eighteen Objects of Power (The Red Feather of Callowain)

Redvests   A name for the soldiers of the Triumvirate of Tracia due to their reddish surcoats, capes, and tunics. Officers and elite members wore red trimmed in white or yellow-gold. The ordinary soldiers or lower ranks wore clothing that was fairly simple, generally of a duller red hue.

Redwater Gorge   Also called Redwater Gulch, a deep and narrow gorge in the western Carthane Mountain range which borders the land of Nowhere.

Regent   Regents, in general, were those persons placed in charge of certain matters in lieu of the actual king or governor. For example, in Vanara, the Chancellor is second in power and importance to the Queen, serving as the administrative governor of Vanara and overseeing all military and civil branches of government. As well, the Vanaran Chancellor is also the Chief Judge of the Realm, supervising the courts of other judges or acting as a judge himself from time to time. When, during the late Second Age, Queen Serith Ellyn traveled to Glareth, the Chancellor was Regent of the Queen and ruled Vanara in her absence.
Elsewhere, when the Eastlands failed and King Inrick was deposed, and no suitable Ruling Prince could be found, Duinnor made Glareth's Ruling Prince Regent of the Eastlands. Eventually, the duties fell to Prince Danoss, son of Ruling Prince Carbane. However, the regency of the old Eastlands realms

was beset with problems ranging from the failure of Duinnor to provide support, lack of resources for developing and maintaining ports, roads, and bridges, and a small, mostly rural population. Through various intrigues carried out by Tracia, Glareth's control over the Eastlands was weakened, particularly in the south, where the border between Tracia and the Eastlands were constantly disputed.

Renewing An annual ceremony or ritual common in the Eastlands wherein the people gave their oath of fidelity to the King of Duinnor. Although the practice varied from place to place, it most often occurred in the autumn of the year after harvest when the annual census was taken. Thus, it was often associated with harvest festivals and rites. The actual term "Renewing" comes from a law that required that all listed on the census roles make or renew their oath to the Unknown King of Duinnor.

Renorlian Son of King Ilex of Halethiris Forest, brother to Islindia. Little is known about Renorlian except that he helped his father rescue Islindia when she was taken by Secundur. He died, along with almost everything else, when Secundur laid a withering blight upon Halethiris.
See Also:
Glossary (Halethiris, Ilex, Islindia)

Ribbon, Balfast A farmer in County Barley of the Eastlands. When his son and daughter-in-law died of fever, Balfast took in his grandson Robigor and raised him as his own.
It was Balfast Ribbon who gave Robby Ribbon his true and secret name.

Ribbon, Mirabella (nee Tallin) Elifaen daughter of Lord Danig Tallin and Kahryna of the House of Fairoak, wife of Robigor Ribbon and mother of Robby. She fought alongside her brother, Aram, at the second siege of the Green Citadel and at Gory Gulch. Aram was killed at Gory Gulch, but Mirabella survived. She later became a close friend to Frizella Bosk. She married a man of County Barley, Robigor Ribbon, and had a son, Robby, and established a home in Passdale. There, under the guidance of her friend Frizella, Mirabella learned how to do all the things that a domestic life required, things that would have seemed quite menial to her immediate family. She learned to keep house, cook, sew, and tend the family business (a sundries shop). And she became an important and respected community member, always ready to lend her help to others. She and her family lived in Passdale until the Tracian Redvest Invasion of 870 S.A. when she was forced to flee. Mirabella then became the leader of a resistance force made up of a coalition of refugees, other inhabitants of the region, and Hill Town Tracians (who were opposed to the Redvests). Mirabella was killed during a mission to assassinate an enemy dreamwalker. Much of her story was related within *The Year of the Red Door* and need not be repeated here.

Ribbon, Robby Son of Robigor and Mirabella Ribbon. Robby inadvertently rang the Great Bell of Tulith Attis while trying to escape wolves. Among those who learned of the incident, he became known as The Bellringer.
He would eventually become the Seventh Unknown King, and would reveal his true name as he abdicated to Queen Shevalia. As King Philawain, he became ruler, at least for a short time, over all Seven Realms, the Dragonlands, Griferis, and the Realm of Dreams. His work would bring about the end of the Second Age, the opening of the Nimbus Illuminas, and the willing departure from the earth of most of the population of the world, thus remaking the world. The written work of *The Year of the Red Door* is a sweeping account centered on Robby Ribbon's quest and his rise to power.

Ribbon, Robigor   Tradesman of Passdale, County Barley, in the Eastlands. Twice Mayor of Passdale, he was responsible for the rebuilding of the bridge across the Bentwide located in Passdale and for increasing trade and commerce in the region by his dealings with various traders, farmers, and merchantmen. He was Robby Ribbon's father and husband to Mirabella Tallin of the House of Fairoak. Within *The Year of the Red Door* are many stories and anecdotes concerning Robigor. Among other things, these had to do with his role as a leader in Passdale, his problematic relationship with Lord Tallin, and his effort to bring word of the Redvest Invasion to Glareth. When the world was remade, Robigor was transformed so that he could join his beloved wife, Mirabella.

Ring of Hearing   A magical ring that enabled its wearer to know the thoughts of those present. It was created by a sorcerer known as Xilos and was used by Tarsus Maklaran to gain great power in Duinnor. The ring was later acquired by Lyrium and, centuries later, it was destroyed by Robby Ribbon.
See Also:
Eighteen Objects of Power (The Ring of Hearing)
Glossary (Tarsus Maklaran, Xilos)
Tales of the High Houses (The House of Fairfir)

Rinspoon   Tale teller of Hill Town.

Rivertree   Tavern near Passdale.

Robby (see Ribbon, Robby)

Robigor (see Ribbon, Robigor)

Rose, Lantin   One of the Hill Town people, a member of the Thunder Mountain gang, and purser to Captain Martin Makeig.

Saerdulin   A major river of the east, running from its headwaters, Lake Halgaeth, through the old Eastlands Realm into Tracia and then to the sea. Just south of Lake Halgaeth, it flows past Tulith Attis, where there was once a landing. Further downstream, Kalbrith was located on its banks. Forlandis, in Tracia, was located at the mouth of the Saerdulin where it empties into Spargers Bay. Heneil built a dam at Lake Halgaeth and most of the water was redirected into the Bentwide for centuries.

   The Saerdulin was an important waterway for trade goods. Due to its depth and the fact that it had no shoals or rapids south of the Bentwide, large and heavily encumbered vessels could navigate it. From Forlandis to Kalbrith, it was wide enough for sailing vessels. Several factors contributed to it falling out of use for trade navigation, including the destruction of so many river settlements by the Dragonkind (during the Great Invasion), civil unrest, and the shifting of trade routes northward and southward when more reliable coastal routes and vessels became widely used. In the Second Age, when corruption under Prince Lewtrah was widespread, various fees, taxes, and restrictions were constantly changing, driving many barge companies out of business. By the time the Triumvirate came to power, there was very little regular boat traffic anywhere along the Saerdulin north of Forlandis.

Saerdulin, Battle of   Sometimes included in descriptions of the Battle of Tulith Attis, this battle took place a week or a fortnight after Tulith Attis was sacked (sources disagree), and took place on the western bank of the Saerdulin at the confluence of the River Lerse, with the south bank of the River

Lerse on the northern flank of the Dragonkind forces. The Dragonkind, thinking that the two rivers protected their flanks, sought to force the combined armies of Glareth, Vanara, and Duinnor into a frontal assault against their more advantageous defensive position. However, sufficient forces under the leadership of Navis and Esildre of Elmwood managed to swim the Saerdulin and Lerse Rivers under cover of darkness. They then attacked the Dragonkind's unprotected rear flanks, wreaking havoc and panic. The carefully timed rear assault weakened and disorganized the Dragonkind forces, allowing the simultaneous frontal assault to succeed. As a result, the Dragonkind forces were decimated, and only a handful of the invaders managed to escape the carnage.
See Also:
Historical Sketches (Great Dragonkind Invasion)

Sagwist Man of Passdale who was the keeper of the Common House.

Saheed A given name among Men, particularly of the Tallin and Markal lineages.

Saliley Vintner family of northern Barley renowned for their light sweet wine. In the late Second Age, Saliley wine was transported far and wide and was among the first wines of the region to be sold in glass bottles in addition to jars and casks.

Salkasin King of the Dragonkind from 960 until 970 F.A.. He was killed by King Parthais of Vanara at the Battle of Tamkal Plain.

Salkasin was the son of the powerful warlord, Tikalaman, who warred with the kings of the Dragonkind until they were defeated. Tikalaman made himself king, and upon his death, Salkasin inherited the throne and his father's powerful army. Salkasin's ambitions were not limited to control of the Dragonlands, and he worked to build the military strength of his armies. In 968 F.A., he began a project of building a line of defenses across the northern borders of the deserts, which immediately came under attack by Vanaran Fellfaere. Seeking to deal a crippling blow to Parthais, Salkasin personally led a large army north and east to outflank the Vanarans. However, Parthais learned of his plan, and was waiting for Salkasin with his own army at Tamkal Plain. During the battle, Parthais and Salkasin fought each other, and Parthais slew Salkasin and routed the Dragonkind.

After the death of Salkasin, the Dragonlands once again fell into turmoil as various warlords and generals vied for the throne, thus continuing the Age of the Warlord Kings, which would last until Xurnon I came to power around 205 of the Second Age.

Salzadur One of the kings of the Dragonkind in the Second Age, father to Belsalza who succeeded him to the throne. Salzadur was the tribal leader of the Kalazin tribes of southern Dragonlands, a rich and powerful people. He led armies against his neighbors, conquering them, but he showed leniency to any who would agree to the law of his tribe. He claimed direct lineage from Kalzar the Great, and as his power grew, he turned his eyes upon the throne in Tyrsharat, where a series of corrupt and weak kings had sat for generations. In 819 S.A., he declared himself rightful King of the Dragonkind, and rode to Tyrsharat with his army to take the throne. The city welcomed him and there was little bloodshed as he assumed rule. All this was accomplished before he was thirty-five years of age.

After assuming the throne, he reformed the administration of the Dragonlands, tirelessly working to unite the many feuding factions within the Dragonkind courts and armies. He gained renown as a just and tolerant but firm ruler, and his rewards were as lavish as his punishments were cruel. Salzadur resurrected many ancient traditions of the Kalzar House and gave a renewed sense of the pomp and authority of the Imperial House. He used his popularity to reform many of the legal systems of the land, instituting a system of earned advancement in both the civil court positions and in the armies (rather than the previous system of bribes and tribal inheritance). He also made overtures with

Vanara and Duinnor for peaceful settlements of dispute, and re-established a long-lasting accord between Tyrsharat and Kajarahn, confirming Kajarahn's status as a free and independent city. One of his last acts as king was to win an agricultural trade agreement with Vanara so that the Dragonkind would receive trees and other crop-plants in exchange for minerals and fabric. He fell ill and died at the age of sixty-one to be succeeded by his son, Belsalza, who would reverse many of Salzadur's reforms and policies.

Sapirday　The luxurious royal palace in the Dragonkind city of Tyrsharat. It was built by Kalzar and expanded by many subsequent kings. Over thousands of years, it would fall into ruin, be destroyed by fire and by earthquake, was rebuilt, remodeled, and then allowed to fall in to disrepair once more. When Salzadur became king of the Dragonkind, he at once set to work restoring it. Under him, Sapirday exceeded all other palaces of the Dragonlands in size, grandeur, and elegance. Its courtyards and gardens were the luxurious, and featured many fountains and pools. Sapirday was lavishly decorated with the finest tapestries and curtains, tilework, furnishings, lamps, intricately carved doors and windows. Besides the King's wing and the throne rooms, it had over 200 guest rooms, 20 kitchens, 50 bathes, and 10 large and spacious dining halls and its own temple. It also housed the courts and bureaus of many of the governing ministers and advisors. Its staff, excluding guards and ministerial staff, numbered over 2,000. Situated on and around a broad hill, the palace dominated the city's skyline with its many tall and elegant towers and walls.

Sarkul al denar barath　A proverb of the Dragonkind, meaning "forward the stone inches," and stemmed from the history of the Great Stone. It means, roughly, that an impossible task slowly gets done, or that, somehow, things will work out. But it also was an expression of fatalism and futility, given the belief that any attempt to move the Great Stone was doomed to failure. By the Second Age, the latter usage was the more common one among the Dragonkind, and the previous, slightly more optimistic (or determined) meaning was seldom thought of.

Scathing　The process through which all Elifaen born after the Fall acquired the scars that mark their kind. In cases where both parents are Elifaen, Scathing took place within the womb before birth, but many did not survive the ordeal and were stillborn. In cases where the mother alone was Elifaen, Scathing could happen at any age of life, but most often it was during youth. Whenever it occurred, it was accompanied by severe delirium and pain. Such was the madness of mind and pain of body, that suicide was not uncommon, while many others simply ceased to live. Those that did survive became immortal, and fully Elifaen with the inherited scars common to all their forebears.
See Also:
Essays & Explanations (Being Elifaen, Concerning Elifaen Inheritance, Scathing, and Immortality)

Scribblers　The Scribblers were a highly secret group of Vanara's Grey Guard that specialized in the use of True Ink for the purpose of gathering information. They were established and supervised by Brandis Seafar in late 868 or early 869, and had their center of operations in a highly restricted area of the White Palace in Linlally.
See Also:
Eighteen Objects of Power (True Ink)
Historical Sketches (True Ink and the Scribblers)

Seafar　A House of Men who originally settled in the northern coastal regions of Tracia but later settled mostly around the Bransondale region. They eventually resettled in Vanara and rose to great prominence as the most powerful House of Men in that Realm.

Tritian Seafar first came to the attention of the House of Fairmyrtle as a skilled farmer, and his family would serve Fairmyrtle until it was dissolved with the death of Nianan. Fairmyrtle lands were broken up, and Devan Seafar managed to secure a substantial portion of them for the remaining Elifaen of Fairmyrtle and for his own people. When the Great Invasion of 322 took place, their lands were overrun by Dragonkind, and the Seafars with their Elifaen allies became guerilla fighters that harried the enemy as they moved up and down the Saerdulin. They joined with Serith Ellyn's armies at the Battle of Saerdulin and, afterwards, directed much of their efforts to hunt surviving Dragonkind, acting as scouts and skirmishers. When the fighting was over, Seafars came under attack by certain Glarethian Elifaen as blame for the massacre at Tulith Attis shifted from party to party. However, Queen Serith Ellyn was aware of the connection between Seafars and the House of Fairmyrtle, and their zealous fighting style won them over to the Vanarans. In later years, Serith Ellyn invited many Men to settle in Vanara, and most of the Seafars migrated.

In Vanara, the House of Seafar would have a pivotal role in resurrecting trade routes, establishing boating and barge communities along the Iridelin and securing lucrative trade agreements with Altoria and the other southern realms. They also served in various military capacities and as administrators. In 796 S.A., Serith Ellyn elevated Hamish Seafar to a Lord of the Realm, the first mortal to have such a title. Hamish Seafar served the Queen as her ambassador to Duinnor, and he sought to thwart Duinnor's growing involvement in Vanaran affairs. His son, Rolland Seafar, was confirmed as Chancellor of the Queen in 829 S.A. Although the position was not hereditary, Seafars would repeatedly be confirmed in that office to serve in that capacity throughout the remainder of the Second Age.

Of note as well, before he became Chancellor in 865 S.A (and at the age of thirty-four the youngest to have that title), Brandis Seafar was a member of the Queen's Gray Guard, an avid explorer and mountaineer, and an expert flyer. It was Brandis Seafar who saw the importance of developing Vanara's flying corps beyond a messenger service. As a young officer, he urged his father and the Queen to direct resources into improving the gliders, equipment, and training for the corps, and making them an integral part of the Gray Guard. Due to his initiatives and work, by the time Brandis Seafar became Chancellor, a vast construction project was newly completed on the northern cliffs nearby to Linlally that consisted of a huge artificial cave to act as a center of flight operations, workshops, and a training base. It was rumored also that Brandis Seafar secretly made diplomatic overtures to disgruntled elements within the Dragonkind elite in order to encourage and foster insurrection and sedition against the Emperor. Some even suggest that Brandis was part of a broader conspiracy involving high-ranking leaders of Duinnor and Glareth, though no evidence has ever been put forward to support such claims. However, it was common knowledge that under Brandis Seafar, several attempts were made to establish garrisons between Ladentree and Kajarahn to patrol and assist against robbers and renegades, and some point to these efforts as evidence of a deeper purpose. These garrisons were the subject of consternation among the Dragonkind, who feared they were intended to be used as advance bases for military operations against the Free City.

Under Brandis Seafar, special observation garrisons around Shatuum were strengthened and reinforced, a system of regular relief and resupply was established. He also oversaw and supervised a growing intelligence-gathering network, and helped establish procedures for the use and security of True Ink. As well, he launched many clandestine missions into the Dragonlands, some of which were in support of Dragonkind in opposition to the royal power in Tyrsharat.

Brandis Seafar and Gaiyelneth Lebret fell in love with one another, but due to their duties (she was the handmaiden and bodyguard of Queen Serith Ellyn), had little chance to deepen their relationship until after the world was remade. When that happened, the two elected to remain in the world and lived in Linlally for many years.

Secundur One of the Firstborn. He was believed to be a follower of Morgasir, but escaped the destruction that befell his teacher. Known as the Lord of Shadow because light was very painful to him. Ever the provocateur of discord among people, he was held responsible for many of the world's woes, including the perpetual strife between the Dragonkind and the peoples of the northern lands. It is said that he provoked Kalzar to attack the north, and later provoked Cupeldain to retaliate. He also frequented Vanara, and spoke lies and rumors to Ormace and others when Cupeldain sought to have the Forty-Nine gathered. Later, King Parthais granted to Secundur a remote region of northwestern Vanara, bordering Duinnor's southwestern territories, which was later known as Shatuum. There, Secundur slowly gathered his might, breeding foul creatures and hatching dark plots against other lands. King Philawain eventually saw to Secundur's demise, shortly before the world was remade.

Seleesa   Maiden of Nasakeeria, said to have been a witch or sorceress with the power to change her form into that of a fox. It was prophesied that she also held the power to restore trickling waters to full flow, but she did not know what that meant, or where this would take place, until she, along with the people of Nasakeeria, migrated back to their ancestral city of Darini in the Dragonlands. There, Seleesa found the key to the blockage of water that had supplied the city in the ancient past. She was able to direct her people how to clear the blockage, and almost immediately clean fresh water poured abundantly through the city's water channels and replenished its long-dry pools, wells, and its large central lake.
See Also:
Glossary (Darini, Nasakeeria)

Seltin   Grandson of Eldwin, an Elder of Nowhere.

Serith Ellyn   Firstborn Elifaen, Queen of Vanara, daughter of Parthais and Mena of the House of Fairlinden. Serith means "most high." She and her brother Thurdun were exiled by King Parthais, and they were later the targets of his agents, whose orders were to hunt them down and kill them both. Parthais was no less cruel to his own people who pleaded for deliverance from his tyranny. Serith Ellyn secretly raised an army and managed to position it well within Vanara without being detected. In a bold and swift night attack, she led her army into Linlally and stormed the White Palace, where she slew her father. The beginning of the Second Age began at the start of her reign.

Serith Ellyn and her brother Thurdun were both Firstborn. During the Time Before Time, their mother Mena became increasingly wary of the Dragonkind, and she advised her children to do as she did and fly over the Dragonlands to watch various places and happenings. Cupeldain and Parthais were against this, so the siblings, almost always in company with each other, conducted their explorations secretly. In this manner, they were the first to discover a recently abandoned city in the western reaches of the Dragonlands, later identified as Darini (whence the Nasakeerians came). They also saw for themselves the trouble and terrible sacrifices that the Dragonkind were suffering in their endeavor to move the Great Stone.

Later, after the Fall of the Faere, Serith Ellyn struggled, as did all Elifaen. But she became a fierce warrior, adept in planning and leadership. She understood how to make the most of the talents and skills possessed by others, and, unlike her father, how to forge meaningful pacts and coalitions within Vanara. These skills worked to her advantage when Parthais exiled her, allowing her to garner and organize much support.

It is known that, during her exile, she traveled to and entered Griferis. However, she never recorded any of her experiences there, nor would she speak in any detail of what she endured within Griferis. But it was after her emergence that she exhibited her leadership skills when assembling and leading the forces that would return her to Vanara. She further demonstrated her leadership throughout her reign as Queen of Vanara.

In the Second Age, as Duinnor grew in power and influence, she worked diligently to maintain Vanara's independence and sovereignty. She never conceded her station as Queen of Vanara and was never forced to comply with Duinnor's law as it was imposed on other Realms. She fought against the practice of leasing Vanaran lands to Duinnor, and she encouraged increased self-sufficiency through expanded trade with other Realms. During the Great Dragonkind Invasion, she lead a huge force against the invaders, culminating at the Battle of Saerdulin. In the strife and near-civil war that resulted, she firmly quelled many minor revolts and feuds that arose between various factions of Men and Elifaen. Thereafter, she continued to work to safeguard Vanara against both the Dragonkind and Duinnor's encroaching sway.

During the Year of the Red Door, owing to various issues, she decided to travel to Glareth. Her main intention was to secretly deliver her Bloodcoins to the safekeeping of Prince Carbane, feeling that Duinnor might find a way to take them from her if she did not hide them well out of Vanara. Along the way, she discovered for herself the various obstacles and problems that Vanarans faced while traveling. While on her way to Glareth, she met Robby Ribbon. Learning that he was The Bellringer, she immediately sensed that he indeed might be the foretold king that would change the world. Upon further consideration, she did not give her Bloodcoins over to Glareth, but was eventually convinced to hand them over to King Philawain (Robby Ribbon).

See Also:
Tales of the High Houses (Last Book of Nimwill, House of Fairlinden)

Seven Towers Seven very tall towers of mysterious origin that were scattered throughout the world. They appeared around the beginning of the First Age of the world. Each tower was alike in form and height, a smooth gracefully-waisted column of stone rising some 980 feet from its base. Each tower was positioned at the top of one of seven mountains scattered across the world. And each was topped with what appeared to be a glass or crystal dome of some kind, and each of a different color: white, yellow, blue, red, purple, green, and orange. Many believed (correctly) that they had something to do with the Forty-Nine Keys of the Nimbus Illuminas, which are of similar hues.

The method of construction, and those who constructed the towers, remains a mystery, as do the secrets of exactly how they used the Bloodcoins to bring about a remaking of the world. Many theories abound, but most include the idea that a race of builders descended from the heavens and simultaneously made all of the towers under the direction of Aperion. Although many attempts were made to penetrate the towers, or to scale them, none succeeded until King Philawain's seven emissaries were sent, one to each tower, bearing a corresponding set of Bloodcoins.

Each tower acquired the name of the mountaintop upon which it was constructed:
The white Tower Vendril, northwest of Duinnor, for the Diamond Bloodcoins (Therona).
The red Tower Halfis, in the Carthanes, for the Ruby Bloodcoins (Pyros).
The yellow Tower Sirrian, in Tracia Realm, for the Amber Bloodcoins (Lyrium).
The blue Tower Medios, in Vanara Realm, for the Sapphire Bloodcoins (Cupeldain).
The purple Tower Altor, located in Altoria, for the Amethyst Bloodcoins (Chantay).
The orange Tower Ulaman, in Glareth Realm, for the Topaz Bloodcoins (Katrina).
The green Tower Zurlamont, in the Dragonlands, for the Emerald Bloodcoins (Ormace).

Philawain either correctly surmised (or had privileged information that we know nothing about) that the only way that the Bloodcoins could be delivered to the Towers was by traversing through the air, since none of them could be scaled, and there were no doors or internal passages to allow and ascent. In his notes, Ullin Saheed Tallin later expressed the opinion that when the Bloodcoins were originally delivered by Aperion, it was at a time during which it was very possible for the Elifaen to change their ways and attitudes. Perhaps it was hoped by Aperion that the Elifaen would thus recover themselves from their plight, regain the use of the First Tongue, and thereby regain their ability to fly, demonstrating a readiness and desire to leave behind violence and hate. This is why Aperion warned them to act soon. But they did not.

Ullin went on to speculate that the purpose of the Unknown Kings was always to do for the Elifaen that which their leaders could not bring themselves to do on their own, that is, to gather together the Bloodcoins and to find a way to use them as intended.   But here, again, the Unknown Kings failed by their own lust for power and by the machinations of Secundur.   Furthermore, Ullin suggested, Aperion knew this would happen, and put into play a last chance for a Last King to do what all others failed to do.

To accomplish this, King Philawain arranged with Islindia for the use of seven flying horses to transport riders bearing the original sets of Bloodcoins to the Seven Towers.   The Year of the Red Door does not detail his negotiations with her, nor does it say how those who delivered the Bloodcoins were selected.   The tale makes it clear, however, that the journey was arduous and the delivery onto the very top of each Tower was dangerous.   Upon the delivery of each rider to a tower, the flying horse had to immediately depart, abandoning their riders in order to return to Islindia's forest before her dream, which sustained their corporeal existence, faded.   This they did, but at great peril to each rider, all of whom had difficulty leaving their mounts and finding a footing on the top of the towers.   Indeed, only Lafkin and Alzeeran, who were not Elifaen, were the only ones that did not suffer terrible pain during the dangerous delivery, including profuse bleeding from their scars. Winnefras, due to the insolence of her mount (Shartide) was almost killed, and indeed both her legs were broken during her "landing" on Tower Ulaman.   Hathrain, Thurdun, Tyrillick, and Unther suffered less than Winnefras, but all were quickly healed of their wounds and pain when they encountered the towers' mysterious attendants.   Afterwards, when the Bloodcoins were delivered, they were mysteriously and seemingly instantaneously transported into King Philawain's presence at Duinnor.
See Also:
Glossary (Nimbus Illuminas, Alzeeran, Lafkin, Hathrain, Thurdun, Tyrillick, Unther, Winnefras, Shartide)
Historical Sketches (Bloodcoins)
Tales of the High Houses (All Sections)

Shadowbane   A rare and mysterious tree of the Time Before Time. It is said that light passed through its leaves so that it did not provide shade and, at night, the leaves glowed with a soft light, dispelling any shadow (hence its name). Its wood was used to form magic staffs of early conjurers, the most famous rod being Swyncraff.
See Also:
Eighteen Objects of Power (Swyncraff)

Sharlofiorn   Estate of southeastern Tracia. In the late Second Age, Prince Lantos held the title of Duke of Sharlofiorn.

Shartide   Ill-mannered and complaining flying horse of Islindia, cousin of Ayreltide.   He was the horse assigned to carry Winnefras to Tower Ulaman so that she could deliver a set of Bloodcoins. But, being impatient and cantankerous, he literally dumped her off his back to fall onto the tower, which nearly killed her.

Shatuum   This was the forbidden land on the borders of Vanara and Duinnor along the western edge of the world adjacent to Mount Algamori. It was a large region ruled by Secundur, where he created many vile and perverted creatures and assembled his armies. The region was given over to Secundur's control by Parthais in an effort to make a barrier that would prevent anyone from ascending Mount Algamori and reach Griferis.
See Also:
Glossary (Secundur)
Tales of the High Houses (The Last Book of Nimwill)

Sheila (Sheila Pradkin)   Girl of County Barley, ward of Steggan Pradkin, her uncle. Her proper name was Shevalia of Waterstone, named for her grandmother, and she was the daughter of Lord Waterstone and his wife, Faeanna. However, Faeanna died when Sheila was very young, and her father sent her away for her safety, putting her under the care of Steggan Pradkin, his half-brother. Steggan turned out to be untrustworthy, a drunkard with a propensity for violence and laziness. He squandered the allowance Waterstone had advanced to him, mostly on drink.

Thus, Sheila suffered many hardships, poverty, abuse, and neglect. Without family or friends to speak of, she was forced to fend for herself, hunting, fishing, and scavenging for food and clothing, and was for many years a nuisance, bully, and minor rogue. Many called her the Wild Girl of the Woods. There were several attempts by citizens of Passdale and Barley to intercede on her behalf, most of which were rebuffed by Steggan, some of which Sheila herself resisted or even scorned at. However, she was somewhat befriended by Frizella Bosk, who taught Sheila much. She eventually met and fell in love with Robby Ribbon, and their relationship changed her life and her attitude toward many things. Robby began her education by teaching her the fundamentals of reading, writing, and arithmetic, and he read to her from books that he owned or borrowed. Eventually, she would find herself under the tutelage of Collandoth (Ashlord).

She accompanied Robby Ribbon on his quest for kingship, and endured many hardships. In Duinnor, she was Scathed, which revealed that she was Elifaen. She would marry King Philawain, who was actually Robby Ribbon, and after Philawain abdicated to her, she ruled Duinnor as Queen until the world was remade. Much of her life, her adventures and trials, and her fate are related within the pages of *The Year of the Red Door.*

Shevalia   Firstborn Elifaen, daughter of Desira who was sister to Tiryna (wife of Banis). It is not known who her father was, but some believe that she was the love child of Desira and Banis. Shevalia was quite beautiful, with golden eyes, light brown hair, and, like her mother, pleasing in form. When she appeared in Silmain's court with Desira, the two ladies were ever the objects of jealousy. Shevalia's interests were in forests and plants rather than court intrigues, and when she traveled to Fairmaple lands, she met and married an Elifaen by the name of Bychanter. They had a daughter named Faeanna and settled in Linlally. There, she became a friend of Loura, Cupeldain's wife, and of Lyrium. When Cupeldain and Loura traveled to eastern Vanara on a peace mission to feuding Elifaen clans, Shevalia and Bychanter went along with them, but Faeanna, who was by now serving as Lyrium's maid and bodyguard, remained in Linlally. When Cupeldain's party was attacked and captured, Shevalia and Bychanter were both murdered, along with Cupeldain and Loura and most of those who traveled with them. They were weighed with heavy stones and chains, it is told, and cast into a lake. It is said that Shevalia's spirit still haunts the forest lake, along with the spirits of all those who were drowned there.

Silmain   The Elifaen who united many Vanaran clans and some woodland tribes, after Aperion's host departed. He declared himself "King of the Faere" and attempted to join all of the Elifaen together. It was Silmain who first attempted to have all of the Forty-Nine Keys of the Nimbus Illuminas brought together, but he was defeated in that effort. Silmain had two sons, the twins Heneil and Pellen, who both refused Silmain's throne when he died.

Silthrin   The "ring of blades," also called Simplus Habilis, or Hand-of-Thorn, a dense hedge of thorny vine-like brush that surrounded Forest Islindia and thwarted entrance or escape from that forest. Silthrin plants grew as tall as many trees, with branches that fell back upon themselves and upon the ground in a tangled thicket. The thorns of the Silthrin were razor sharp and, as if to increase their menacing appearance, they were grouped in clusters of five slender fingers, the curved nail of each being the actual thorn, in a shape eerily similar to a hand.

Sir Sun   A name sometimes given to the sun. In legend, Sir Sun was the husband of Lady Moon.
See Also:
Biographical Sketches (Sir Sun and Lady Moon)

Slimeback   The name given to the legendary water-monster of Lake Halgaeth. It was reputed to be a giant serpent-like creature, by some accounts over sixty feet in length, with a long snout and rows of razor-sharp teeth. It had oily, leathery skin, hence its name. The first written accounts that mention the creature date from the late First Age, but countless tales and lore have sprung up since then. There are few eyewitness accounts, and most of those are suspect. But local fishermen insisted that Slimeback was the cause of many disappearances and accidents on the lake. However, Lake Halgaeth was famous for its sudden storms which created violent waves, and tales of Slimeback are thought by most to be a way of explaining away the tragic loss of so many otherwise experienced and lake-wise boatmen. Still, there were several instances of empty boats found adrift with damage that no storm could cause. As well, there is a passage within *The Year of the Red Door* that relates how the traitor Falgo was killed by just such a creature that the legends and lore describes.

Slobberfang   Also called Wolftooth, a feverish ailment resulting from being bitten by wild animals. It is particularly associated with wolves.

Solsorna   The capital city of Masurthia, located on the Bay of Famatir, formerly the Kingdom of Solsorna. Solsorna was originally settled and established by coastal Elifaen in the First Age and had little to do with other Elifaen. They had not participated in the conflict against the Dragonkind, which led to the Scathing, but would not give up their lands or waters.

Southernmost Masurthia is a hot, temperate land with a coastline of marshes and estuaries. The people lived by fishing and gathering nuts and farming vegetables and corn. Until the founding of Solsorna, they lived primarily in scattered coastal villages within easy sailing of each other in their skiffs. Eventually, several trade routes would open between Vanara, Altoria, and Tracia, passing through Masurthian territories, and these brought new products and wealth to the region. Around 400 F.A., the House of Sumac was established of Elifaen living near the mouth of the Talkana River, and from that House the Kingdom of Solsorna would be founded. Solsorna would grow in power and might, and the House of Sumac steadily expanded its reach. In 931 F.A., both Altoria and Masurthia were engaged in efforts to seize lands along the Wachee River. Each wished also to exert control on the overland trade routes between Vanara and Tracia. Armed skirmishes quickly led to war. Within a month, conflict had disrupted important trade along the route used by Vanara and essentially closed the ports of Draymoor and Solsorna, effectively isolated Vanara from Tracia as well as the sea routes to the Eastlands and Glareth.

The Vanaran economy reeled as its exports piled up, unable to reach faraway markets. As a result, Parthais led a large army that outnumbered the combined armies of the combatants, and he took the entire Wachee River valley by force. He then threatened both warring realms with invasion and destruction unless they brought hostilities to an end. In the settlement that he brokered, all lands to the west of the Wachee became Altorian, whilst those to the east became Masurthian lands. The peace agreement stipulated that the House of Sumac would be recognized as sovereign of the Kingdom of Solsorna, and the lands of Masurthia would be its Realm, but Vanaran recognition of Masurthia would be contingent on Vanaran traders being permitted freedom of travel on all roads through Masurthian territories without tax or toll. King Barindon of the House of Sumac reluctantly agreed, although it would deprive him of levies that he wished to enforce along the trade routes. The agreement also stipulated that Altoria and Masurthia compensate Vanara for lost trade and for the costs incurred by the Vanaran incursion. This was mostly done by removing all tariffs and port fees imposed on

Vanaran traders and their goods. However, over the following years, Parthais continually increased the amount due to Vanara under the settlement, which the other parties resented.

King Barindon exploited every opportunity to tax trade passing through his realm, especially on goods bound for Vanara. At the same time, he lavished spending on Solsorna, building docks and shipyards. He signed agreements with particular Tracian and Glarethian traders so that Solsorna would become a vital free port of call for their ships. Soon goods that previously passed through Altoria came instead through Solsorna, to be taken overland to Vanara. Supporting industries, naval stores, wagon-making, coopers, taverns, and inns soon sprang up in Solsorna and all along the roads passing through Masurthia. However, Barindon's schemes were ultimately ruinous as his appetite for wealth spread corruption and bribery and only bolstered smuggling and piracy.

By the late First Age, Masurthia had reached its zenith and was already well in decline when the great Dragonkind Invasion of the Second Age took place and Masurthia was overrun. Solsorna was besieged, and though it did not fall, it suffered great loss of life and destruction and continued to be isolated until the Dragonkind were driven out. Afterwards, as Solsorna and Masurthia struggled to recover, a series of earthquakes, plagues, tsunamis, and typhoons battered the region. By 870 S.A., Solsorna's population was less than half of what it was but two centuries earlier.

Soltani Pass   In the western plains, a vale between two opposing heights south of the town of Edgewold. In the Second Age, a battle took place there between an army of Kingsmen and an army of Wickermen.
See Also:
Historical Sketches (Battle of Soltani Pass)

Sorrowcups   Small purple cup-like blossoms similar to violets.

Snowbutter   Like jawrock, the recipe for preparing snowbutter was a closely guarded secret. And like jawrock, one might not want to know how it was made. Snowbutter was not meant to be tasty, but to supply needed calories to soldiers on patrol in the frigid seasons and climes. Like jawrock, it was also made by the Menicomp family, but other producers made their own versions. The Menicomp version was preferred by many because it was wrapped in parchment upon which was printed short witty stories, crossword puzzles, or various items to distract one from the tedium of military service. Unlike jawrock, because some of the ingredients spoiled easily, and for the purpose that snowbutter was intended, jawrock had to be kept at very low temperatures, preferably frozen. The Menicomp prepared and stored their version of snow butter in specially designed ice-caves located just north of Chirath, Duinnor, near Mount Vendril, and they shipped it within ice-packed containers. In the late Second Age, they set up manufacturing in Vanara to save on shipping costs. Like jawrock, it was often eaten raw or heated in water for a hot soupy drink.

Spargers Bay   A bay located at the mouth of the River Saerdulin, and the site of some of the earliest settling places of Men when they first came to the shores. It is also the location of Forlandis, the capital and largest city of Tracia.

Spritsul   A surname amongst Men who settled in Glareth Realm. Most notable amongst them was Lady Carylla Spritsul, who married Metlar Tallin. The lineage would decline rapidly throughout the Second Age, becoming little known outside of Glareth. Another person of this lineage was Tyrin Spritsul, a mercenary who fell in love with Esildre. He later befriended Robby Ribbon and together the two made a daring escape from Wickermen who had captured them. Tyrin later died from wounds received during the Battle of Tallinvale.
See Also:
Biographical Sketches (Tyrin Spritsul)

Starhart   Surname of husband and wife, Bob and Lally. Bob Starhart was a Post Rider of County Woodland (Janhaven) and County Barley. In the year 870 of the Second Age, he went missing while out on his route and was never seen again.

Starlerf   Poet of the First Age. Little is known about Starlerf, but he apparently lived in a region called Everis, which some think was located in lands that would later become part of Masurthia. However, several volumes of poems are attributed to Starlerf, who copied them by hand in several scripts, including the New Writing that was developed in Vanara during the First Age. Most of his poetry pertains to idyllic themes of forest and field, but some recount tales of the Time Before Time, leading many to believe that he was a Firstborn.

Starshine   A buckmarl stag of Uncle Solstice.

Stavin   Garnor and Dorcilla, man and wife of Greenfar.

Stayborn   River in Vanara, minor tributary to the Iridelin.

Steggan   Steggan Pradkin, the half-uncle and guardian of Sheila Pradkin. Steggan was the illegitimate son of Lord Sartis Waterstone and half-brother to Waterstone's legitimate son, Harmon. Harmon would go on to become the new Lord Waterstone at his father's death. Steggan was left with a legacy from his father, but it was almost immediately squandered. As a result, Steggan was forced to work as a laborer. He was a tenant laborer on an estate near Sorghwall when he was given charge of Lord Waterstone's daughter, Shevalia.

He was a lazy and mean-spirited man, often drunk, often violent. As related in *The Year of the Red Door*, he proved both unreliable and vile, abusing his wife until she ran away, then, later, sexually assaulting Shevalia. He was approached by Bailorg, who supplied him with money as payment for certain errands, but Steggan squandered this money on drink and did not perform the errands. Realizing the mistake, and the mortal consequences when Bailorg learned of the treachery, Steggan broke open the box of Bloodcoins given for Shevalia to keep. Not knowing what the Bloodcoins were, thinking they were merely ancient Faere coins, Steggan took them and used them to complete the errands he had promised. The coins were given by him as payment for dispatches to be posted on behalf of Bailorg, and they wound up in the possession of the wife of a Post Rider. She would, in turn, exchange them at Robigor Ribbon's store in Passdale. Meanwhile, Bailorg learned of Steggan's treachery and tortured Steggan into confessing what he had done, although he left out certain critical details owing to his state of drunkenness. Bailorg, infuriated, hung Steggan by chains from the rafters of Steggan's home. Much of this was eventually pieced together by Collandoth (Ashlord), but he did not understand that the "coins" involved were Bloodcoins until much later.
See Also:
Glossary (Bailorg, Sheila Pradkin, Shevalia)

Stingorn   A carnival man known for his Conundrum Box, a trick box that only he could open. He would offer a wager to any who could open the box and obtain the coins that he and the contestant had placed within. By devious means, he permitted the Conundrum Box to be opened frequently enough to encourage people to try their hand at it, but not enough to lose many wagers himself. At the Fall Festival of County Barley in 870 SA, Stingorn was hired by Bailorg in an effort to identify the person who rang the Great Bell, thinking that a person who could open the Conundrum Box with ease would be The Bellringer. Although Robby did open the box, Bailorg and Stingorn were made to suspect Billy Bosk instead, as related within *The Year of the Red Door*.

Storm Bag   A bag or pouch in which were kept magical tiles that could be used to conjure a variety of weather conditions.
See Also:
Eighteen Objects of Power (The Storm Bag)

Sudamoor   A small kingdom, independent from the Seven Realms, situated to the southeast of the Plains of Bletharn, against the northern shores of Lake Adin. Very little is known about the region, and it never sent ambassadors or trade delegations to the other realms. For all intents and purposes, it was always ignored by the outside world.
See Also:
Eighteen Objects of Power (The Cornucopia of Sudamoor)

Sun King   A reference to the king and ruler of the Dragonkind.

Sundering   Also called The Fall, or The First Scathing.

Surthquay   An ancient boat landing on Lake Halgaeth. It has two distinctive braziers at the end of the quay, carved in the likeness of arms up-stretched, with a bowl (the brazier) in each hand.

Surthquay was built in the First Age to serve as a landing for trade boats bearing goods. It was perhaps the earliest of many such docks and quays and camping sites built by Glarethians and others who used Lake Halgaeth for trade and commerce. However, when Heneil erected a dam on the Falls of Saerdulin, the waters of Lake Halgaeth steadily rose, covering over all of Surthquay but its two uplifted arms. Before the structure could be heightened and rebuilt, Tulith Attis came under attack by invading Dragonkind. Surthquay remained underwater until the late Second Age when Heneil's Wall at last collapsed, freeing the waters of Lake Halgaeth to flow back into the River Saerdulin. This lowered the lake's water to its old level, revealing the entire quay.

Sweedmiller   Elder of Nowhere.

Sword of Chaldron   The Sword of Chaldron is an apparition that appears in the night sky at intervals of several centuries, a long swath of pale blue light. It is so named because that constellation is where it first appeared according to Dragonkind lore. The Elifaen call it Aperion's Scythe, and both peoples have similar stories of how, during past appearances, great houses fell and kingdoms came to ruin. As well, both the Dragonkind and the Elifaen consider the Sword of Chaldron a harbinger and omen of great changes soon to come about in the world. Men have no such legends or tales of it, though through their association with the Elifaen they, too, look upon the heavenly marvel as a sign of woe.

By the late Second Age, it was well understood that the Sword of Chaldron and other similar apparitions were some sort of celestial bodies and are now considered among the Wanderers. Unlike most Wanderers, Chaldron and other objects akin to it disappear for years, and sometimes centuries, before returning. These are called "comets."

The Sword of Chaldron, or a similar celestial apparition, reappeared in the sky during the final days of the Year of the Red Door.

Swyncraff   A magical staff or rod that obeyed its master by remaining in any shape as long as its owner desired. It could be as hard as steel or as supple as rope. Legend holds that it belonged to Laeleth who gave it to Cupeldain, and it is thought to have been made of the wood of a shadowbane tree.
See Also:
Eighteen Objects of Power (Swyncraff)
Glossary (Shadowbane)

Sylphaen   Children of mortal Man and female Elifaen. These children inherit the characteristics of the Elifaen. It is thought the word stems from a phrase of the Ancient Tongue "sylph faen," or "airy one who has fallen" (literally "airy one who fell").

Sylphmar   Children of mortal women sired by Elifaen. These children do not inherit the characteristics of the Elifaen (only those born of female Elifaen do). It is thought that the word is derived from a phrase of the Ancient Tongue "sylph mort a mar" or "airy one but mortal of the sea," with sylph indicating some Faerekind lineage. Compare to "Sylphaen."

Talkana   A river that flows from Lake Adin and empties into the sea at the Bay of Famatir in Masurthia. Its flow varies greatly with seasonal rain and snowmelt, and long stretches of it are often only a few inches deep. It deepens considerably as it nears the coast, with the last seventy-five miles or so being navigable by small boats and barges.

Tallin   One of the most powerful lineages of Men. They established a domain in the Eastlands, in a valley called Tallinvale. In the late Second Age, the House of Tallin and the House of Fairoak would join, through the marriage of Danig Tallin and Kahryna of Fairoak. They would have three children, Aram, Dalvenpar, and Mirabella.
See Also:
Biographical Sketches (Danig Saheed Tallin)

Tallin, Aram Saheed   (Aram Saheed Tallin) Son of Danig Tallin and Kahryna of Fairoak. Aram was their middle child, being younger than his brother and older than his sister (Dalvenpar and Mirabella). Aram Saheed wed Sharyn Northstar (of a house of Men) was father to Ullin Saheed. Aram became a Kingsman after his older brother's death, but was himself killed at Gory Gulch.

Tallin, Dalvenpar   (Dalvenpar Tallin) Eldest son of Danig Tallin and Kahryna of the House of Fairoak. He befriended Gurasa during that Dragonkind's travels and became something of a guide and protector of Gurasa. Years later, Dalvenpar became a Kingsman, destined to fight against the Dragonkind and to participate in the disastrous First Siege of the Green Citadel. Dalvenpar was among the thousands who died during the bloody retreat from the Dragonlands. As it happened, his body was found by Gurasa, who was grief-stricken by the loss of his friend.
See Also:
Biographical Sketches (Gurasa)

Tallin, Danig Saheed   (Danig Saheed Tallin) In the late Second Age, the Lord of Tallinvale. Father of Dalvenpar, Aram, and Mirabella. Grandfather of Robby Ribbon.
See Also:
Biographical Sketches (Danig Tallin, Gurasa);
Glossary (Tallinvale, Battle of)

Tallin, Finteri   Daughter of Arlam Tallin, and descendant of Men who first landed on the shores of the world. She wed Dalcadian, son of Myrium and Pellen (brother of Heneil), and bore a son named Metlar who inherited her titles, and since he was not Elifaen, he took her maiden surname. Thus the Tallin lineage became related to Silmain as well as to the House of Fairfir. It was this lineage that Robby Ribbon cited when he delivered the Hoard of Nowhere to Ullin Saheed Tallin, thus fulfilling one of the conditions of the curses laid on the people of Nowhere.

Tallin, Mirabella   see Ribbon, Mirabella

Tallin, Ullin Saheed   Kingsman and veteran of many desert campaigns and adventures in the late Second Age.. He was the grandson of Lord Danig Tallin, son of Aram and Sharyn Tallin, and Mirabella's nephew. He was an important ally, guide, and friend to Robby Ribbon, and he was instrumental in the success of Ribbon's quest. Ullin later founded the Great Library of Darini, from which he led many expeditions to recover books and documents from across the world. It is because of his work that this Reader's Companion was made possible.
See Also:
Introduction
Biographical Sketches (Ullin Saheed Tallin)

Tallinvale   A small but fertile valley along the eastern foothills of the Thunder Mountains in southwestern Eastlands. It is situated just north of territory in dispute, claimed both by Tracia and by the Eastlands. Tallin City, the ancient home of the family that gives its name to the region, is a prosperous and thriving center of agriculture and commerce, due chiefly to the guardianship of Lord Danig Tallin. Tallin City and Tallinvale are often used interchangeably.

Tallinvale, Battle of   Sometimes referred to as the First and Second Battles of Tallinvale, essentially meaning the "first" major assault (which was repelled) and the "second" major assault (likewise repelled).

This was an attempt in 871 S.A. by the Redvest Triumvirate of Tracia to eliminate Tallinvale as a stronghold in the Eastlands. As the Redvests swept through the Eastlands, they began gathering the bulk of their armed forces to the west of the Saerdulin for their planned assault against Duinnor. However, Tallinvale, to the north, was poised as a powerful force that could threaten their vulnerable flanks and supply lines. Lord Tallin knew the strategic importance of his doman, and he began preparations well ahead of the Redvest offensive against Tallinvale. He ordered the withdrawal of as much of the population as possible to within the city walls and the destruction or removal of anything that would be of material help to the enemy. He also accelerated arms production, training, and recruitment. He was also motivated to delay, or if possible spoil, the Triumvirate's invasion against Duinnor, or at least give his grandson, Robby Ribbon, time to warn Duinnor and to accomplish his quest.

As this situation and the fighting are well-described within *The Year of the Red Door*, we will not burden you with details here. In brief, then, after isolating Tallin City, the Redvests gradually prepared for two assault vectors, one from the south, mainly to serve as a diversion, and the main assault against the north walls of the city. Mar Henith launched these as night actions, hoping that darkness would help cover the movements of his troops. The northern assault vector was demolished and destroyed by Tallinvale with the help of trolls. Even though the bulk of the Redvest army was in disarray (with Mar Henith killed), the Redvests consolidated quickly against the southern walls. This assault was begun just as a Kingsman army arrived, and the Redvests were decisively defeated. Suffice it to say that the siege and battles were extremely costly, but under Danig Tallin's leadership, and with the help of trolls and the Kingsmen, the determined and skillful people of Tallinvale ultimately and utterly defeated the Redvests around Tallinvale. Yet all of this wrought severe devastation to the lands in and around Tallinvale, and Tallin City itself suffered severe damage. Casualties were very high.
See Also:
Glossary (Cartu, Eldwin, Herbert, Mar Henith, Brennig)
Biographical Sketches (Artais Teracue, Danig Tallin, Esildre, Tyrin Spritsul)
Historical Sketches (Triumvirate)

Tallinvale Line   A series of keeps and small fortified outposts located in the southernmost region of Tallinvale, some few miles north of the River Lerse.

Tallmaple   One of the ancient houses of the Faerekind. Most notable of that House was Tyrillick, who served Lyrium as captain of her household guard. For many years, it was assumed that he had died at Tulith Attis when it was overwhelmed by the Dragonkind. However, it was later discovered that he had escaped that fate, but had many adventures until he rejoined the remnants of the House of Fairfir to continue service with them.

Tameron   A constellation, also called the Seven Princesses, the Seven Maidens, or the Thimble Pot. It is made up of several stars very closely clustered together within a pale bluish haze.

Tamkal Plain   A flat desert expanse in the northeast of the Dragonlands, between the Nalamain Hills and Almedian. It was the site of a famous battle of the First Age.
See Also:
Glossary (Tamkal Plain, Battle of)

Tamkal Plain, Battle of   A famous battle that took place in the First Age, sometimes called the Battle of the Kings. It came about after King Salkasin of the Dragonkind sought to establish a line of keeps and fortresses along the northern borders of the Dragonlands. Vanara, fearing that these would be used to protect an invading army, began a campaign to disrupt their construction and to destroy those already completed. King Salkasin led a large army north and east, seeking to swing around the Nalamain Hills to outflank the Elifaen. However, learning of this, King Parthais of Vanara led his own army into position ahead of the Dragonkind and met them on the Tamkal Plain within sight of the Nalamain Hills. It was a short but intense battle, and the only time when kings of the Dragonkind and Vanara would personally face one another. Parthais won the contest, killing Salkasin and beheading him while his troops routed the rest of the Dragonkind. This decisive battle resulted in many years of relative peace during which the Dragonkind engaged in a series of internal power struggles. With the death of King Salkasin, the lineage of Kalzar would be broken until the Second Age when it would be revived by Salzadur.

Tarsus Maklaran   A man of Duinnor who rose to almost unrivaled power in the early Second Age. He acquired a Ring of Hearing, enabling him to know the thoughts of others. He then used it to increase and secure his power and dominance over other lords of Duinnor. He would eventually die from wounds received from a wolf attack, and would lose the ring, which would be found by Lyrium.
See Also:
Tales of the High Houses (House of Fairfir)

Tavin   One of Lucinda's two sons (House of Faircedar)
See Also:
Tales of the High Houses (The House of Faircedar)

Teracue, Artais   General of the Kingsman Fourth Army in the late Second Age, notable for his victory over the Wickermen at the Battle of Soltani Pass and for his relief of Tallinvale when it was besieged by Redvests.
See Also:
Biographical Sketches (Artais Teracue)
Historical Sketches (Battle of Soltani Pass)

Thalamir   The last Sea King of Glareth, of the Elifaen House of Beech, who was instrumental in bringing about the wealth and power that Glareth would enjoy during the latter part of the Second Age after his reign ended.
    Son of King Samis, and grandson of King Gardin, he was born in the year 1056 of the First Age. When King Samis ordered Glarethian troops to assist Queen Serith Ellyn and help her take the throne

from Parthais, Thalamir was appointed to command those forces. However, King Samis proved an ineffectual king, prone to forgetfulness, and some say that he suffered a distracted mind which worsened with age. So Prince Thalamir increasingly assumed many duties that would have normally been performed by the King. It was Prince Thalamir who saw to it that Glareth maintained its government and sought to increase its maritime power.

Thalamir was a keen military thinker, and when the Great Dragonkind Invasion took place, he led the Glarethian forces that (alongside forces from Vanara and Duinnor) defeated the Dragonkind at the Battle of Saerdulin. Not long afterwards, in 323 SA, King Samis abdicated to Thalamir.

Thalamir immediately instituted an even greater program of shipbuilding that would increase the trading power of Glareth. He also made laws protecting the rights of all Glareth citizens, regardless of rank or race, and began an ambitious campaign to increase Glareth's agricultural and industrial potential. However, he would be remembered for his defiance of Duinnor, refusing to pay tribute or enforcing tax gathering for Duinnor. Duinnor eventually won the squabble by blockading all trade from Glareth along the Osterflo River. Duinnor also threatened to exact an agreement from Tracia, Masurthia, and Altoria to ban Glarethian ships from their harbors (a threat which never materialized). As the years went by, and the dispute heated, a series of crop failures and plagues struck Glareth and the Eastlands. Fearing that his people would starve unless trade resumed along the Osterflo, Thalamir agreed to abdicate on the condition that his lineage would rule Glareth as hereditary Ruling Princes. Duinnor, also hurting from the trade disputes, agreed. One of the important concessions that Thalamir won from Duinnor was a provision that no one in service to Glareth would be required to serve as Kingsman.

Thalamir's last year as King was the year 362 S.A., and though he had the right to continue as Ruling Prince, he fully abdicated to his daughter, Princess Megan. Thalamir lived to witness the completion of the Locks of Karthia, which bolstered the Glareth economy. He also acted as unofficial ambassador to Vanara, and he brought about many treaties between the two Realms that would bring them closer together as the age progressed. He returned to Glareth and died in 369 S.A. It is worth noting that the agreement exacted of Thalamir for his abdication was rapidly adopted, with variations, throughout the other Realms as Duinnor exerted its power over them.
See Also:
Essays and Explanations (Prerogatives of the Realms)
Historical Sketches (Glareth)

Therepolon   One of the Wanderers, a star that glows bright yellow and moves across the night sky along its own path.

Therona   Former Queen of Altoria, of the High House of Fairwillow. She was given by Aperion seven diamond Bloodcoins, but she was adamantly against using them for their intended purpose. She was forced to abdicate when she could (or would) not account for the whereabouts of her Seven Bloodcoins. She later died in exile, probably by her own hand.
See Also:
Biographical Sketches (House of Mulberry)
Tales of the High Houses (House of Fairwillow)

Thistledown   The location of an estate in Vanara that was forced in to a lease to Duinnor, and would have likely been foreclosed upon by Bailorg had their efforts not been disrupted by the death of Bailorg and the arrest of his partners, Norogus and Harmalway.

Threshmere   Lord of the House of Hemlock during the late Second Age. He was born of an Elifaen father and mortal mother. His own wife died shortly after giving childbirth to his only son. According to people of the region, and Threshmere himself, his son was killed when attacked by a lion. Another boy was seriously maimed by the same lion, and this boy would later become Threshmere's ward.

During the late Second Age, Lord Threshmere of this House entered into a dispute with Duinnor, which moved to impose sanctions on Hemlock for failure to provide Threshmere's son to serve the King. Threshmere reported that his son had died as a child and there were no other heirs. During this time, Robby Ribbon and his company encountered Threshmere when they accompanied a Post Rider to serve a new Summons to Hemlock. There they met Threshmere's young ward, named Borwain, who served Threshmere as something of a secretary. Borwain, disabled from youth and on crutches, was noted to have unusual and uncanny powers of artistry. His completed drawings and paintings seemed to be animated, with motion and changes taking place on the canvas in front as one viewed them. This led some to suspect that he had a gift similar to that of Alonair (whose sculptures seemed animate) and was therefore Threshmere's actual son. After Lord Threshmere and Borwain went to Griferis to serve King Philawain, Threshmere admitted this was so. The lies he had told Duinnor about the death of his son was part of a ruse to prevent Borwain from being forced into a humiliating circumstance, being clearly physically unfit for the requirements of becoming a Kingsman. It was while at Griferis that Borwain produced many drawings and paintings depicting life at Griferis as well as portions of King Philawain's story.

See Also:
Glossary (House of Hemlock)

Thrubold   One of the oldest families of Men in Duinnor, and renown breeders of fine and powerful horses. Family lore has it that during the Purge of Scholars, one of the refugees from Vanara who migrated to Duinnor met a Mortal woman and they married. The Thrubolds established themselves along the north banks of the River Whitefall, and by the early Second Age they held extensive lands for farming and ranching. By the middle Second Age, the Thrubold name was well known in Duinnor for the horses they raised. One of the breeds the Thrubolds were especially proud of were tall, swift horses, as sure-footed as any, and possessed of unparalleled endurance. By the late Second Age, this breed, called Majestic, dominated the annual Mulberry Race, a long-distance competition from Duinnor City to Draymoor and back. From 800 S.A., when the Mulberry was first held, until 870, Majestics took the First Prize twenty times, and placed another thirty times within the top three contenders. Needless to say, horses of the Thrubolds' Majestic line were highly desired by the wealthy. By the late Second Age, the Thrubold Stables were not only supplying such refined and capable horses to the wealthy, but were also providing large herds to Duinnor for its military.

Thrubold, Kurk   Kingsman of the Thrubold family who served with distinction at the Battle of Garmitor (856 S.A.) and was severely wounded. He would have died on the battlefield but for the bravery of Ullin Saheed Tallin who saved his life (In gratitude, Ullin would later receive a horse as a gift from the Thrubold family, called Anerath.) Unable to continue serving as a soldier, Thrubold was ordered back to Vanara where he was assigned less strenuous duties with the Constabulary until he was fully healed. However, he quickly earned a reputation for solving difficult criminal cases and was retained. He eventually became a captain and was instrumental in the dismantling of Lord Banis's network of criminal enterprises.

Thunder Mountains   A mountain range between the Eastlands and the middle Plains of Bletharn, south of the Carthanes and stretching into the foothills within Tracia and Masurthia. The Thunder Mountains are named for the noise once made by its most feared inhabitants, the trolls.

Thurdun   Son of Parthais, brother of Queen Serith Ellyn of the House of Fairlinden. Among those that King Philawain sent to deliver Bloodcoins to the Seven Towers, Thurdun who delivered

Cupeldain's (Serith Ellyn's) sapphire Bloodcoins to Tower Medios, would be the only one who had actually been alive when the Bloodcoins had been originally given by Aperion.   Perhaps that is why King Philawain recruited him.
See Also:
Tales of the High Houses (House of Fairlinden)

Tiandari, Falls of   Five sheer-drop waterfalls emanating from the high mountain lake situated on the mountaintop above Linlally and the headwaters of the River Iridelin. The natural lake is fed by meltwater from a glacier that stretches all the way upward to Mount Cassos. On this lake is where Cupeldain and others built the White Palace which would become the royal residence for Vanaran rulers. The lake, which is almost circular, was eventually bounded by thick walls but gates were put into the walls so that the falls, which consisted of five separate streams close together, could be blocked from time to time. This was often done for ceremonial purposes. The five falls are often called the Falls of Tiandari, or the Children of Tiandari, the latter referring to the fact that the lake itself is called Tiandari. The falls, which are normally rather thin, cascade straight downward to a large pool some 1,600 feet below. From there the water spills into a winding whitewater river that flows over lesser falls and shoals, through the city of Linlally. Eventually, just outside of Linlally, the flow joins with other streams and rivers to form the great Iridelin. In the late Second Age, this area was remodeled so that a large platform jutted out over the falls from which Flyers would launch themselves into flight.

The summit of the falls, which could be seen from the city below, was a traditional place of execution. The condemned was chained to a large rock and then the rock was tipped over the side of the wall above the central fall which would drag the condemned over the side to plummet into the pool below. In the year 871 of the Second Age, this was the fate of Captain Faradan, who led the deadly attack on the White Palace and was captured. He was quickly tried and condemned. In the absence of Queen Serith Ellyn, Lord Brandis Seafar conducted the execution and personally "tipped" the rock to which Faradan was chained.

Tilderry   A textile town in the Eastlands just south of the confluence of the Bentwide and Saerdulin rivers.

Timbo   Boy of Nowhere.

Tiryna   Firstborn of the Faerekind, and sister to Desira. Tiryna wed Banis and had three children, Atlana, Navis, and Esildre. She departed with Aperion.

Tobin   Field foreman of Boskland.

Tolimay   A Melnari, sometimes called Tolimay the Angry.
See also:
Historical Sketches (The Melnari and Their Familiars)

Toliss   A Prince of Duinnor, unrelated to the King, in the Second Age. During the late Second Age, he expanded the King's Post, using Kingsmen as couriers throughout the Seven Realms. Toliss, a Kingsman himself and a former Post Rider, was keen to establish rapid and normal lines of communications throughout the Realms for official Duinnor business but also for general use by all people. He persuaded the King to subsidize the Post with greater resources to establish additional Post Stations, riders, and equipment. He also persuaded the King that fees for sending letters should be kept to a minimum in order to encourage trade correspondence. Toliss successfully defended the use of Kingsmen rather than civilians as long-distance Post Riders, arguing that highwaymen would think twice before robbing or attacking a Kingsman and that, if attacked, Kingsmen were better trained to defend themselves and the post they carried. However, Toliss agreed that local Post Stations should be manned with delivery riders who were recruited from local men for short local routes. Long distance deliveries between Post Stations would always be performed by Kingsmen, though.

Several attempts were made by various lords of Duinnor to take over the King's Post, most notably in 861 S.A., when Lord Banis established a separate delivery corps within the ranks of the Duinnor Regular Army. However, inept management, graft, and numerous incidents of lost dispatches resulted in even the Regulars using the King's Post for reliable deliveries. By 870 S.A., the aging Toliss was still managing the King's Post, but had by then delegated much decision-making to others. It had become arguably the largest civil service, employing as many as 12,000 regular postal servants, post riders, and station-keepers. There were King's Post stations located in virtually every county and shire throughout the Seven Realms, including Vanara and Tracia. In addition to normal delivery duties, Post Riders were required to submit regular reports on a variety of topics, including the condition of roads and bridges, bandits, the effect of weather on travel, local changes in leadership or regional troubles. From time to time, they were required to make specific inquiries on behalf of the King or the Kingsman high generals. Some Post Riders, such as Ullin Saheed Tallin, were assigned special post duties that required them to perform services under the direction of specific people (in his case, Ullin reported directly to Collandoth).

Tonifor   Boskman, cousin to Billy Bosk on his father's side.

Toolant   Former advisor to Prince Lewtrah and the court of Tracia before it was overthrown by the Redvest Triumvirate. He was often called Toolant the Red for his bright red hair and beard. Toolant inveigled himself into a variety of courts and eventually found a position of advisor to Lord Tallin. This was a ruse, however, as Tallin knew that Toolant was a spy and agent of Tracia. Toolant was used, therefore, to send false and misleading information to the Triumvirate, and by devious means to garner information concerning the Damar's alliance with Tracia. Eventually Tallin arranged for Toolant to be framed for treason against Tracia while in Damar City, and Toolant was beheaded by the Damar.

Torch of Solstice   A legendary torch carried by Solstice, brother of King Ilex. It is said that wherever he goes, the torch goes with him, and that its light never fades. Some say that it is this torch that gives Solstice his ability to spread good cheer and good fellowship wherever he goes.
See Also:
Eighteen Objects of Power (Torch of Solstice)

Torman   Livery and stable operator in Passdale. He partnered with a master blacksmith named Clingdon who made horseshoes and other equipment needed by his farriers and saddlers.

Torridge   Elder of Nowhere.

Tracia   One of the Seven Realms, located to the southeast of the world along the coasts where Men first settled. Its chief city is Forlandis. Tracia was ruled by a lineage of Kings until King Kapol was deposed for his involvement with the Pinewood Uprising in the Second Age. Prince Dulmian of the House of Bayberry was then named king, and later would be relegated to Ruling Prince. His lineage ruled until the Triumvirate Redvest uprising in the late Second Age, and his heirs, the Princes Lewtrah and Lantos, fled to Glareth.
See Also:
Biographical Sketches (Lantos, Martin Makeig)
Glossary (Kapol, Pinewood, Lewtrah, Seafar, Waterstone)
Historical Sketches (Triumvirate)

Trebuchet   A type of ballistic engine of war used to hurl missiles at the enemy. Trebuchets make use of counterbalance weights to move a throwing arm (similar to the throwing arm of a catapult) to which a sling holding the projectile is attached. Trebuchets can be quite large and can hurl enormous missiles a great distance with accuracy. During the Battle of Tallinvale, large trebuchets were employed by the Tracian Redvests against the defenders, some nearly five stories tall. Tallinvale defenders also used trebuchets, though not as large. Large stones usually served as missiles, although baskets of flaming oil, or other projectiles might also be thrown. At the First Siege of the Green Citadel, the besiegers hurled the bodies of slain Dragonkind over the walls of the city, copying (it is said) the actions of the Dragonkind at the siege of Tulith Attis.

In the Second Age, small trebuchets were developed for naval use, employing tanks or barrels of water as counterweights so that they could be lightened when not needed. They were not very effective due to the unsteady rocking motion of ships and because of restrictions imposed by rigging and sails. Only very small ones were deemed useful, mainly during close-quarter battles to provide plunging fire prior to boarding actions. There remained a general naval preference for catapults and ballistae over trebuchets. The most notable exception came in the form of special large barges, specifically constructed as trebuchet platforms. These were developed by Glareth and were intended for use in riverine or coastal regions during attacks on ports or enemy fortifications ashore. They were made to be firmly anchored after being towed into place by service ships crewed with specialists. When Prince Carbane led his armada against Tracia in 871 S.A., he was known to have nine of these vessels in his fleet.

Triumvirate   The trio of dictators that overthrew Tracia in the late Second Age.
See Also:
Historical Sketches (Triumvirate)

Trolls   A crude race that populated the Thunder Mountains and whose noise while walking or moving rocks gave the mountains their name. The trolls were large, heavy, stone-like creatures, squarish of form and of a brutish disposition. They lived by eating rocks and sometimes other large creatures. They were capable of making stone and iron implements, sometimes by simply shaping with their hands and sometimes by rubbing stones together to generate heat that was so intense that glass was sometimes formed as a result. They excelled at stacking stones to make strong bridges and huts. They dwelled mainly in the eastern mountains and were rarely encountered elsewhere. The trolls inhabited the Thunder Mountains well before Men came to the eastern shores.

Trolls tended to shun daylight, and they worked, hunted, and foraged mainly at night. Crude and dim-witted, trolls were known for being ungovernable by any but their own king, whom legends call Thunderfoot. Yet they were strong and knew little physical pain, were immune to fire and did not require air to breathe. When they set upon a course of action, they stubbornly stuck to it regardless of reason. There are many stories about the selfishness and stupidity of trolls and of various heroes outwitting them to steal their treasure or to cross their guarded bridges and mountain roadways.

It was thought by some that they were the mal-conceived beings of Morgasir the Vile, tutor of Secundur. They were, in fact, creations of Alonair the Sculptor, who banished them to the Thunder Mountains for their crudeness. But Alonair gave them their king, Thunderfoot, to rule over them. Regardless, they abruptly disappeared late in the Second Age, leaving their mountain caves and homes abandoned.

It was later revealed that Alonair and Lord Tallin coerced the trolls into building the fortifications of Tallinvale, including the building of its defensive walls, tunnels, canals, and an underground lake covered by a roof field held up by the trolls. To disguise the lake, earth and soil were put atop the roof so that crops could be planted. During the siege of Tallinvale, a secret word was given to the trolls at an opportune moment, and, following their orders, they dropped their arms and collapsed the ground beneath the invading Redvests.

Later the same year, Robby Ribbon would use the trolls to perform two special tasks. One was to deliver the population of Nasakeeria out of that land and return them to the Dragonlands so that they could reoccupy Darini, the city of their origin. The second task was to push mountains of rock into the Crack Between the Worlds, damming up its waters to overflow and inundate much of the Dragonlands in order to wash the lands clean (of the dust which caused the desert sickness) and to begin its restoration to fertile land. After this final mission, all trolls returned to the earth, for which they longed, becoming once again mere stones.
See Also:
Biographical Sketches (Alonair)

True Ink A magical ink that fades and becomes invisible if what is written with it is false. True Ink was discovered by Vanarans and its making was a closely held state secret.
See Also:
Eighteen Objects of Power (True Ink)
Historical Sketches (True Ink and the Scribblers)

Tulith A word derived from the Ancient Speech that means "high place," or "place of watching." It is generally used to mean a kind of tower or high keep, such as Tulith Morgair, but can sometimes denote an overlooking fortress such as Tulith Attis.

Tulith Attis A fortress in County Barley, of the Eastlands. It was the site of a siege and subsequent massacre during the Great Dragonkind Invasion, and events there precipitated much discord between Men and Elifaen.

Tulith Attis, meaning High Place of Attis (Tulith, "high place" or "place of watching"), is thought to have been named for the original builder, Attis, and the name of the town over which the fortress loomed. Tulith Attis grew from a simple keep to a powerful fortress overlooking the town of Attis and the bridge over the River Saerdulin south of Lake Halgaeth in the Eastlands Realm. It was the site of a major battle when the Dragonkind invaded in 322 S.A. Although Heneil had refortified the place, and laid spells and traps against forewarned treachery, the fortress fell anyway, supposedly when some trusted person betrayed the defenders who were then massacred. Laid waste by the Dragonkind, the fortress and the region immediately surrounding was abandoned and left to ruin. However, it was within the fortress that the Great Bell was placed, designed to be triggered by invaders and to spread dire warning across the world. The Bell was not rung during the siege of Tulith Attis and it remained silent for centuries until it was rung by Robby Ribbon of Passdale.
See Also:
Tales of the High Houses (House of Fairfir)

Tulith Morgair A small beacon tower or keep on the west side of the Thunder Mountains. It is situated at the cliff end of a shoulder of a mountain that juts westward and overlooks a ford of the River Missenflo along the old road to Fisenwold. It was built by Danthis of Duinnor in the early Second Age as a part of a line of keeps and watchtowers that were to guard the trade routes to Duinnor. A battle took place below it along the banks of the Missenflo when a small loose knit army of men and Elifaen tried in vain to stop the eastward march of Dragonkind during the invasion of 322 S.A. The keep was abandoned and soon fell into disuse and ruin. By the late years of the Second Age, it was all but forgotten.

Tulivana (The Tulivanas) A virtually impenetrable mountain range running north and south from Vanara to the sea and to the west of Altoria. To the south, it rises up from the sea to the west of the

Hinderlands. In the north, they bend westward into the Blue Mountains and the Megrinor Mountains. Along its eastern feet runs the Iridelin River, from Vanara to Altoria, feeding the Hinderland marshes before emptying into the Craggy Sea. This is where the Tulivanas break into the sea, and form the Craggy Sea's most notable rocky formations, with its thousands of rocky islands and reefs. To the west of the Tulivana range are the deserts of the Dragonkind. From north to south, its slopes are sharp and rugged, with frequent earthquakes and avalanches and a few volcanoes. With its narrow and easily defended passes, the Tulivana Mountains make a natural strategic barrier against Dragonkind incursions. There have been only a few times in history when the Dragonkind managed to break through in large numbers, including the Great Invasion that took place in the early Second Age.

Along the western slopes of the Tulivana, particularly at lower altitudes in the southern part of the range, are the Dragonkind's most valuable arable lands outside of Karkarando. Although there are no great rivers, there are numerous small springs and seasonal streams. Most of the grain, cattle, and horses produced in the Dragonlands come from the many small farms located there. It was once a source of lumber, but changing environmental conditions, erosion, and over-harvesting almost entirely denuded the region of trees by the middle of the First Age. From time to time, daring Dragonkind have passed over the mountains to harvest trees on the eastern slopes, but this became increasingly rare as Altorian patrols became more numerous.

Tulleg See Glossary (Kranneg)

Turnbuckle (House of Turnbuckle) A lesser house of Men in Tracia, dissolved in 840 S.A. when the last of that line died. Turnbuckles traced their lineage to the original ships that brought Men to the world. Though never powerful, they were embroiled in many conflicts. Their lands bordered those of the House of Fairmyrtle and they were considered allies to Fairmyrtle. During the Pinewood Uprising, the Turnbuckles suffered attack because they would not support the uprising. Later, when King Kapol took the Bloodcoins of Fairmyrtle, Lord Turnbuckle sought unsuccessfully to intervene to have them sent to Vanara. During the Great Invasion of 322 S.A., the Turnbuckles abandoned their estate for a time, becoming guerilla fighters on the run from the Dragonkind invaders. After the war, the House fell into steady decline, never recovering lands or wealth lost to them during the invasion and the years of conflict that plagued Tracia in the aftermath of the invasion. When the House of Turnbuckle was dissolved, most of its people migrated to Glareth or to the Eastlands. Some remained, taking up employment at other estates within Tracia.

Twobanks A local name for the area of Barley, originally meaning all the land between the old course of the Rivers Saerdulin and Bentwide, but more later referring the people who occupy Barley and Passdale. The Mayor of Twobanks was an unofficial title given to Robigor Ribbon, who was the first Barleyman ever to become mayor of Passdale.

Tyrillick An Elifaen of the House of Tallmaple. He was captain of Lyrium's household guard and presumably died with her when Tulith Attis fell to the Dragonkind. However, it was later discovered that he had escaped that fate, but had many adventures until he rejoined the remnants of the House of Fairfir to continue service with them. It was Tyrillick who delivered Lyrium's invitation to meet her at Tallinvale. Tyrillick also would be one of the couriers King Philawain would send to deliver Bloodcoins to the Seven Towers, a necessary step for opening the Nimbus Illuminas and remaking the world. Tyrillick delivered Lyrium's set of amber Bloodcoins to Tower Sirrian.

Tyrin (Tyrin Spritsul) A mercenary of the late Second Age.
See Also:
Biographical Sketches (Tyrin Spritsul)

Tyrsharat   The capital city of Drakyr, from where the kings of the Dragonkind rule. It was the most ancient of the desert cities, built by Kalzar before the First Age at a location where there were many wells and oases. Also sometimes called the Golden City because of the gold-plated roofs and domes that reflected the sun. It was the largest city of the Dragonlands and was the center of power for government and commerce. At the time of Salzadur's census, it was found to have almost a million inhabitants (which included slaves) within its vast walls. It was a center of textile production, metalworking, and many luxury items (perfumes, jewelry, etc.). Nearly all of the powerful people of the Dragonlands had palaces there. Due to abundant and reliable sources of water from its many wells, there were many gardens within the city, ranging from the most lavish within and around palaces and courts, to small garden plots within even the poorest quarters.

Uden   One of the First Men, known as Uden of Selacia, who chronicled some of the events of the early Second Age. He witnessed the reconstruction of Tulith Attis during the time of Heneil, but was not alive when the fortress fell to the Dragonkind.

Ullin   Derived from Ullinessin, a name among Men, particularly among the great houses of those who trace their lineage to the arrival of Men.

Ullin Saheed Tallin   see Tallin, Ullin Saheed

Umston   Small town of the Eastlands Realm.

Undertree   A small town near the western edge of Tallinvale, just outside of the valley proper, within the foothills of the Thunder Mountains.

Unerring Arrow of Kalsabahyood   A magical arrow that never missed its mark.
See Also:
Eighteen Objects of Power (Unerring Arrow of Kalsabahyood)

Unther   An Elifaen of the Glareth House of Seafoam, a Fellfaere who became a servant of King Philawain of Griferis. He delivered Therona's diamond Bloodcoins to Tower Vendril.

Valkose   An unruly and powerful demon of the Time Before Time who came to serve Secundur. Valkose may have been the only creature made by Morgasir to have escaped the destruction brought by Beras upon Morgasir and his followers. There are no stories that account for what happened to Valkose or where he went, but it seems he, like dragons, dwelled deep beneath the earth within hidden lairs and tunnels and dark caverns. How he came into Secundur's service is also unknown, nor is it certain that he was ever a true servant rather than merely a sympathetic associate. However, it is fairly clear that he had some abode within Shatuum as it was with Shatuum's witches that he spawned the Captains of Shatuum. And Valkose apparently traveled swiftly and far from Shatuum, through deep passages within the earth, to have wickedness with other witches, such as Paltera, the witch of the western Carthanes.

Collandoth uncovered Valkose's existence when he found and destroyed the lair of Paltera, and it is from his encounter with Valkose that we have our only description of the creature, which is somewhat vague. But from that and a few other clues, we speculate that Valkose was a male demon of powerful stature, perhaps fifteen or sixteen feet tall. In normal guise, he was muscular, with very dark red skin, a large head with (we believe) horns similar to those of a ram. His eyes burned fiery red. He breathed out super-heated air and was able to vomit a blast of directed fire. His voice could vary from soft to harsh, full of mocking insults. According to Collandoth, Valkose knew how to look within his foes and find their foibles, their shames, their failures, and their fears. Valkose exploited that knowledge through taunts, accusations, and terrible statements that warped and bent the truth and deeply disturbed the mind and heart. Thus was Valkose not only terrible in physical aspect, but he was vile and evil of intellect and spirit, too. He used words as powerfully and as harmfully as he used his deadly breath. At no point does Collandoth mention or indicate that Valkose used any weapons other than his strength, his fire, and his words, no sword or whip or spear nor any club. Yet he was able to smash rocks asunder with his voice and his breath. Collandoth fought with his staff and sword, and with every deadly stroke that Collandoth gave the creature, Valkose merely slothed off his outer skin to reveal an even more fearful creature beneath, ever increasing in loathsomeness and ever more dreadful. As Collandoth himself related, Valkose was the stronger by far, and it was not within Collandoth's power to be victorious. Valkose knew this, and as Collandoth retreated, ever more wounded and weakened, Valkose only seemed to grow stronger and fiercer until at last Collandoth was utterly annihilated, a victim of his own hubris as much as Valkose. We know from Collandoth's tale that Valkose emerged into the world only to be met by Aperion, who was awaiting this. So Collandoth's task was merely to draw Valkose forth into the light, forth from the dark recesses of evil, and to deliver Valkose unto Aperion's sword of justice. And so Valkose entered battle with Aperion, of which we know very little, except that Valkose was vanquished, reduced to a fearful tatter which fled home to Shatuum, chased all the way by the pursuing Aperion. Fortunately for the world, Collandoth was reanimated and reformed and given back to the task of helping Robby Ribbon.

We have scoured all of the books we have been able to find, and we have talked to many people. We have sought opinions and speculation. But we cannot say why Aperion, who came so far from his heavenly abode to face the demon, then chose to spare Valkose, or why he allowed Valkose to reach Shatuum. We do know, however, that the witches of that place shredded apart the spirit of Valkose to give the Captains of Shatuum more power. "Of the voice of Valkose, they made the crack that would come from their whips, and of his breath they filled their whips with fire. And a portion of the potion they gave to Throgallus, to reign over the Captains, second only to Secundur." So says *The Year of the Red Door*. So we can only speculate. Perhaps Aperion knew that only the power of Valkose, expressed through those whips and the will of Throgallus, could hold the legions of Shatuum in check long enough to permit Robby the time to complete his quest. For without those implements of terror, how else could that teeming flood of monsters have been restrained during those last momentous days?

Valley of Dreams   A valley in northern Vanara where is located the Temple of Beleron, an important place of meditation and contemplation.

Vanara   One of the Seven Realms and the most ancient of all, believed to be among the first places where the Faerekind of the world lived. It was in Vanara that the Faerekind built their first cities, before the Fall. It lay to the south of Duinnor and just north of the Dragonlands, separated by a rugged range of mountains from the deserts. Forested, fertile and green, Vanara was ever the target of attack by Dragonkind, and it was the place from which most northern assaults into Dragonlands were made.

After the Fall, and when the Elifaen began to reassert themselves in the world, Vanara was united under Silmain. Upon his death, Cupeldain of the House of Fairlinden became king. After Cupeldain's death, his son Parthais ruled, followed by the daughter of Parthais, Serith Ellyn, who ruled until the end of the Second Age.

Vanara and its people were central to all of the major events of the world. Thus, virtually all of history is in some way or other connected to or a result of Vanara as the place where all of the troubles of the world had their ultimate beginnings.
See Also
Tales of the High Houses

Vendril   A high snow-capped mountain northwest of Duinnor. It is the source of unusually pure silver ore. Gemstones are also found there, including rubies and sapphires. It is also the location of one of the Seven Towers of the same name bearing a light-colored top of white or clear sparkling glass.

Veritask   A legendary advisor and soothsayer to Aperion who foretold the coming of strife among the Faerekind. Legend had it that he would return to "look upon the world" when the time was growing ripe for it to be remade. In the late Second Age, this name was given to a bright reddish star that suddenly appeared in the west and was seen in Vanara and Duinnor. It was first observed on Midwinter's Day in the Year 869 and remained visible until Midsummer's Day of 870.

Vidican (Branthis Vidican)   Tracian Redvest general who led an army into the Eastlands during the late Second Age and captured County Barley and Passdale. He was assassinated by Mirabella Ribbon.

Vinkasinea   A witch of the ancient world. She persisted until the Second Age and re-emerged during the Second Demon War. She briefly captured Collandoth, but he was rescued by one of his companions of the Nine Banes, who killed her.

Wachee   The river that forms much of the border between Altoria and Masurthia. The region was the site of an intense border dispute that led to war between the two Realms during the First Age. When Vanaran trade was disrupted, Parthais led a large Vanaran army into the region and by force put an end to the dispute. Parthais forced the warring realms to make peace and to agree that the Wachee would forever be the border between the two. He also secured pacts from each of the two warring realms that any future disputes over Wachee lands were to be settled by Vanara. Parthais also made it clear that if any future disputes disrupted trade in any way, both Altoria and Masurthia would be annexed by Vanara and its people subject to heavy tribute.

It is said that during the Time Before Time, the Wachee was wild and swift, but it slowly lost much of its power, and began winding more slowly to the sea. It has numerous small tributaries, and the land surrounding is fertile, with large areas of dense forest. Near the coast, the land around the Wachee becomes marshy and swampy, with many fishing villages in the region.

Wanderers   The Wanderers are a group of celestial bodies that slowly progress across the backdrop of stars in regular and predictable ways. Most are starlike in appearance, but with more distinct hues (such as yellow or blue). Some are very bright, while others are quite dim. Most appear in the sky for a season or two, the time of their rising and setting progressing regularly over the years, so that one that appeared during the winter might in decades to come be in the summer sky. Some of the Wanderers are quite different in appearance, often fuzzy and sometimes with long trailing or leading swaths of light. The Sword of Chaldron is one famous example. Some Wanderers come and go at long intervals, sometimes only visible for a few short days or weeks before receding out of view for many years. This group of Wanderers are called "comets" or sometimes "hairy stars" due to their trailing "mane" or fuzzy appearance.

The Wanderers are the stuff of legend and myth. Nearly every region has its own tales concerning them. In Altoria, it is said that they are Faerekind assigned to watch the world. In Vanara, they are said to be Faerekind that somehow became lost when Aperion and his host left the world, and that they continue to seek a path to join them. In Glareth and the Eastlands, some are associated with watery spirits, as they are seen to rise from the watery horizons of the Great Sea. In the Dragonlands, legends say that some of them are dragons thrown by their tails by Beras away from the world. Others are said to be the oases of the dead.

Watcher A term sometimes given to those who delve into the mysterious and mystical. Sometimes it only means one who is an agent of another, or one who is commissioned to observe events and discern the meaning of those events and other signs. Collandoth was often called "The Watcher," but so were many others, including Men, Elifaen, and even Dragonkind.

Waterstone A House of Men, of the Weatherlee estates in Tracia. In the late Second Age, Lord Waterstone was a staunch Royalist, although a critic of Prince Lewtrah and an advocate for reform, and he actively opposed the Triumvirate's violent rise to power. It was rumored, and later confirmed, that his wife, whose name was Faeanna, was Elifaen. When she was killed in a bungled attempt to assassinate him, Waterstone redoubled his efforts to oppose the Triumvirate. Soon, he would report that his small daughter, Shevalia, had died of fever, and Waterstone thereafter turned his grief into a zealous campaign of support for Prince Lantos, who was having a difficult time raising supplies and men to oppose the Redvests. Waterstone was captured by Redvests and sentenced to hang, but he died in prison before the sentence could be carried out. All of the Waterstone holdings were confiscated, the title and name dissolved by Triumvirate decree, and the name of the region was changed from Weatherlee to Roanshire.

It was later discovered that Waterstone's daughter had not died, but had been smuggled away to the Eastlands to remain in hiding. Her name was Shevalia, known in County Barley as Sheila Pradkin. Her murdered mother was in truth Faeanna, who was given Lyrium's seven Bloodcoins to smuggle away from Tulith Attis before it fell to the Dragonkind and then to safeguard them until she and Lyrium could meet again. However, Faeanna and Lyrium failed to locate each other afterwards. Faeanna had confided all this to Lord Waterstone, and when, of desperation, he sent his daughter away from Tracia, he sent the Bloodcoins with her. But the coins, like Shevalia herself, would become orphaned and lost until recovered, quite by happenstance, by Robby Ribbon.

Wayfind One of the buckmarl stags of Uncle Solstice.

Wayford Common A large flat field to the west of Passdale where the people of the region often had their fairs and festivals.

Wayregyle Region to the northwest of the Carthane Mountains where a type of hardy olives were grown for oil and food.

Weatherlee Name of estates and minor principality of Tracia belonging to the House of Waterstone (a House of Men). The area later became known simply as Waterstone. When the Tracian Triumvirate abolished the House of Waterstone, its name was changed by decree to Roanshire.

Weepingbrook Small stream in Barley that was considered haunted. Legend tells that during the fall of Tulith Attis, women fleeing from the slaughter came upon their dead spouses lying about the banks of the stream. There, they wept and swore terrible oaths of vengeance and anguish, and were turned to stone by their anger. It is said that much of their ire was directed against Duinnor since forces of that Realm did not come (or had not arrived) in time to save them.

Westerman A term used to refer to Men living or from the western parts of the world, particularly Duinnor and Vanara.

Westerspeech A name sometimes given for the dialects spoken in the western realms during the Second Age, one which was derived from the Ancient Tongue.

Westlands   A term generally referring to Altoria, Duinnor, and Vanara, but may be used to refer to any area west of the Great Bletharn Plains.

Westlawn   Town in the western edge of the Plains of Bletharn. It was overtaken by devotees of the cult of Wokan, called Wickermen, and entered into a feud with the neighboring town of Edgewold. The resulting hostilities led to a major battle involving armies from both places and, joining with the Edgewold fighters, Kingsman forces of Duinnor. It was at Westlawn that the Wickermen created a monster from the choking vines that they propagated.
See Also:
Historical Sketches (Battle of Soltani Pass)

Westleaf   A type of aromatic smoking herb or tobacco that is mildly intoxicating.

Weylan (Chrisafer Weylan)   Tallinvale Captain of the Northern Gate and childhood friend of Ullin Saheed Tallin.

Wickerlands   Those areas in the west that were under the possession of the Wickermen of the town of Westlawn during the Second Age.

Wickermen   In the late Second Age, these were worshipers of Wokan, spirit of the grasping vine, which is a form of kudzu. The Wickermen made woven armor from the vine and planted it throughout the fields of their enemies. Their center was located at Westlawn and from there they launched a campaign against neighboring Edgewold that eventually resulted in the Battle of Soltani Pass where the Wickermen army was defeated and, shortly after, led to the capture of Westlawn and the destruction of their cult.
See Also:
Historical Sketches (Battle of Soltani Pass)

Winborn, Sam   Farmer of Barley in the late Second Age

Windard   Head butler and keeper of Tallin Hall in the late Second Age.

Winnefras   An Elifaen of the Altorian House of Sandspur, a Fellfaere who became a servant of King Philawain of Griferis. She delivered Katrina's topaz Bloodcoins to Tower Ulaman.

Winterford   Young man of Martin Makeig's Hill Town people. Winterford was an officer under Makeig aboard the Golden Swallow. He was aboard during the Battle of Grisland Strait and was with Makeig's surviving group after the loss of their ship and during their subsequent escape from Tracia. He and his fellow shipmates eventually settled in Hill Town, in the Thunder Mountains.

Wokan   Dark spirit of the grasping vine. Wokan was worshiped in various places, but its most notable adherents were those of the Wickerman rebellion who took over the town and region of Westlawn in the west. There, a mysterious sorcerer named Bunar invoked Wokan to infest neighboring fields with a vine known as "kudzu." In Wokan's name, Bunar conjured a monster made of the flesh of men and tendrils of the vine. The monster almost immediately killed its creator. Just a little while later, it rampaged through Westlawn, broke free of the town, but then came under attack by Kingsmen and was destroyed by fire.

Wolftooth   Also called Slobberfang, a feverish ailment resulting from being bitten by wild animals, particularly wolves.

Xilos   A reclusive sorcerer who lived in the mountainous region of Vanara south of Islindia. He fashioned many objects of power and magic, including the Red Feather of Callowain, Luna's Lantern of Glareth by the Sea, the Ring of Hearing, the Storm Bag, and other objects. It is said that he fashioned the sword Ethliad and gave it that name in honor of his tutor. In the early Second Age, Xilos was murdered by Tarsus of Duinnor in a dispute over the Ring of Hearing.
See Also:
Eighteen Objects of Power (Ring of Hearing, Red Feather of Callowain, Luna's Lantern, The Storm Bag, Ethliad, the Sword)
Tales of the High Houses (House of Fairfir)

Yarmon   A trusted carriage driver and native of Duinnor City. Collandoth hired him to drive Sheila about Duinnor City. Because of his knowledge of the city and the people there, he was also able to perform discrete inquiries on Sheila's behalf.

Zurlamont   A low mountain located in the southernmost region of Karkarando in the Dragonlands, not far from the coast. Upon its summit is the Tower Zurlamont, one of the Seven Towers of mysterious origin and purpose.

General Chronology of the World
Through 868 Second Age

This is a general chronology of events. Some are legendary or mythical, others are historical, and yet others are personal events. All pertain to or contributed, directly or indirectly, to the culmination of the Second Age. As for those events that took place in the final years of the Second Age, we only listed a very few because details of those years are somewhat covered within The Year of the Red Door. We only list here events that occurred in years through 868 of the Second Age because the most pertinent events of the final years of the Second Age are recounted within the text of The Year of the Red Door. We generally do not give precise dates (such as months or day) due to the many discrepancies in our materials and the variety of calendars used across the ages.
See Also:
Essays and Explanations (Calendars and Timekeeping)

The Time Before Time

No one knows how long the Time Before Time lasted. As its name implies, time was somewhat meaningless during this period. Certainly, its passing was not recorded, or else such records have not survived. Some scholars speculate that this period was well over 200,000 years long, while others argue that its length was inconceivably long and cannot be measured or stated sensibly. Be that as it may, legends and myths concerning the Time Before Time do indeed survive. It is from those stories that the salient aspects and events of the period are here assembled into some meaningful if not somewhat arbitrary order. Therefore, we use numbered "events" rather than "years" for those entries pertaining to the Time Before Time and the Age of Strife.

Time Before Time, I
The Earth and Stars are made by Beras. He makes Lady Moon and her husband Sir Sun to shine upon the world. There is no daytime and no nighttime as, hand in happy hand, Lady Moon and Sir Sun and all the Stars that are their companions walk the sky and look upon the works of Beras.

Time Before Time, II
The Faerekind (Firstborn) come into the world. Of the various spirits of creation, they are made into flesh. They know not sickness, hunger, or death, and are given wings so that they may rejoice in all of the places of the world, the earth, the waters, the forests, and the sky.

Time Before Time, III
Aperion comes into the world to guide his people. He is the last of the Firstborn to come into the world without conception and is made of the spirit of the Faere.

Time Before Time, IV
Morgasir, a Firstborn Faere, creates Dragons in the south of the world, and makes many other foul creatures. To serve the Dragons, he makes the Drakyr, a race of slaves that will later be known as the Dragonkind.

Time Before Time, V
Morgasir is destroyed by Beras along with most of his creations. However, many escape, including Secundur, his pupil, and a number of dragons, demons, witches, and other dark creatures. Also spared are the Drakyr, who are now freed of their bondage but must now fend for themselves.

Time Before Time, VI
The Faerekind rejoice in the things of the world and in fellowship with one another. Some form strong attachments to each other and from these unions are conceived new Faerekind.

Time Before Time, VII
Some of the Drakyr, calling themselves the Dragon Peoples, or Dragonkind, occupy the lands of the south and begin to flourish.

Time Before Time, VIII
Secundur incites the Faerekind against the Dragonkind. Some of the Faerekind lay blight to the southern lands, diverting rains and rivers, and turning the southern regions into desert.

Time Before Time, IX
The Dragonkind send emissaries to the north, but they are rebuffed by the Faerekind. As punishment for their rudeness, and to make his people mindful of mortal time, Aperion separates Night from Day, causing Sir Sun and Lady Moon to part company and begin their ceaseless wandering across the sky and around the world.

The Age of Strife

Generally speaking, scholars consider the Age of Strife to be part of the Time Before Time since there survived no calendars of the period. However, scholars of the Dragonkind more commonly refer to this period as the Age of Strife, and there is evidence that they began making calendars during this period or perhaps even before. However, just as with the Time Before Time, it is not known how long this period lasted, for the only records of the period were kept by the Dragonkind and are fragmented. None of the original Dragonkind records of this period survive (although some are referred to in later Dragonkind writings). The Elifaen did not develop writing or record-keeping until near the end of this period. But it can be estimated that the Time of Strife lasted for at least seven thousand and perhaps as many as twenty-five thousand years. As with the Time Before Time, we use numbered "events" rather than "years" for these entries.

Age of Strife, I
Secundur continues to incite the Dragonkind and the Faerekind against one another by his whisperings and accusations.

Age of Strife, II
Cupeldain, Silmain, and others of the Firstborn build the first city, called Linlally, in the region that would later be called Vanara. It has gardens and a grand palace in the center of a high mountain lake from which flow the five Falls of Tiandari.

Age of Strife, III
The Dragonkind continue to struggle for survival within the harsh deserts. Countless generations live and die as they slowly form tribes. They fare best in the far southern reaches near to the coast where they can fish for food and cultivate meager crops in the few river basins that still run with fresh water.

Age of Strife, IV
The Faerekind known as Alonair makes fabulous stone likenesses that amaze all who see them by their lifelike quality. Many of these grace Linlally.

Age of Strife, V
Some of the Dragonkind discover oases within the parched deserts farther north and begin establishing small settlements around them. They also discover minerals and other resources to use as trade goods with the southern tribes. Small settlements begin growing to become cities.

Age of Strife, VI
The Elifaen of Forest Halethiris build the first of their beautiful glass-domed structures within the branches of their massive trees. Within these structures are brought birds and animals of the forest floor to play and converse with the forest Elifaen. Streams are even coaxed to travel uphill, some winding around the trunks of the gargantuan trees to spill out over the domes in fabulous fountains of shimmering spray.

Age of Strife, VII
In the Dragonlands, food production increases and tribal warlords vie with one another for power and control over crops and trade. The most powerful of these, Kalzar, subjugates most of the other tribes and builds his desert city, Tyrsharat. Elsewhere in the northern deserts, other towns and cities begin to grow and flourish, particularly in those places where the Dragonkind have learned to carefully manage limited water resources.

Age of Strife, VIII
Cupeldain and Loura meet for the first time and fall in love.

Age of Strife, IX
Kalzar and his followers have conquered virtually all of the Dragonlands, and he makes himself King of the Dragonkind.

Age of Strife, X
Alonair the Sculptor continues to grace the northern city of Linlally with marvelous statues and carvings. Hearing of them, Elifaen travel from afar to see them and to see Cupeldain's beautiful city with its castle atop the great Falls of Tiandari.

Age of Strife, XI
Kalzar, the King of the Dragonkind, hears of Alonair's skill and applies to him to fashion some sculpture to adorn his desert city. Alonair agrees, but only if Kalzar provides a massive stone for the carving. It is to be placed in the center of the desert city, but must be cut from solid granite from far away in the western mountains. It is to be "nine times the height of Kalzar and the same in its width and breadth." That is, a cube of granite 80 cubits high, wide, and long (about 120 feet). Kalzar, his pride swollen by the whispers of Secundur, agrees to the impossible task, and decides to wrest the Great Stone needed by Alonair from the mountains and bring it to his city. Alonair promises to make a wondrous carving of it, once it is in its place.

Age of Strife, XII

Kalzar immediately sets to work assembling the huge force needed to quarry the stone and to transport it across the deserts. The challenge is fraught with dangers and setbacks, and after a dozen years it is at last cut and freed from the mountain quarry. However, moving it across the desert proves nearly impossible. Kalzar continues to sacrifice great numbers of his people and the wealth and resources of his empire to move it. After years of struggle, Kalzar all but gives up.

Age of Strife, XIII

Secundur tells Kalzar that the challenge of the Great Stone was a ploy intended to humiliate him and to tax his empire. He incites Kalzar to lead a Dragonkind army against the Faerekind lands of the north. Aperion advises the Faerekind to give way before them, but many will not give up the things they made, or the mountain forests they love. When the invading army comes, they lay waste vast regions and kill many Faerekind as they drive through the mountains of Vanara.

Age of Strife, XIV

In retaliation for the destruction of their things and for the death of many of their brothers and sisters, the Faerekind, prompted by the whisperings of Secundur and led by Cupeldain, attack the invaders, driving them back. Cupeldain presses the attack into the Dragonlands and destroys much of the southern lands, killing thousands of Dragonkind wherever they are found. At the hands of Cupeldain and the legions of Faerekind who follow him, the young, the old, and the helpless of the Dragonkind receive the same treatment as the soldiers of Kalzar, and none that the Faerekind come upon are spared.

Age of Strife, XV

In response to the bloodshed, Aperion puts a halt to the fighting by forcing all of the Faerekind, those who were fighting the Dragonkind, and those who would not fight, to return to the north and gather upon the plains before him. Aperion gives the Faerekind a choice: to leave the world with him, or to remain upon the earth. Those who depart the world with Aperion fly away into the sky and heavens to a place that has been prepared for them in the stars. Those who elect to stay upon the earth are stripped of their wings. This event is variously referred to as "The Fall," "The Departing," and "The First Scathing." Those that are stripped of their wings come to be called the Elifaen, or Fallen Ones.

Age of Strife, XVI

Kalzar, the first King of the Dragonkind, dies. His throne goes to his son, Diamases, but he lacks the support of many desert tribes and the empire that Kalzar built begins to falter.

Age of Strife, XVII

Laeleth, daughter of Aperion, returns to the world, against her father's wishes, to find her former lover, Celefar, who remained in the world. She has lost her wings in the effort, and, broken and bent by the great fall from the heavens, she wanders the world in search of Celefar.

Age of Strife, XVIII

The first record of the seasons, including the passing of one year to the next, is made by the Elifaen, using an early form of cuneiform writing similar to that which had been in use by the Dragonkind.

Age of Strife, XIX

For many years, the Elifaen struggle, learning to live as the lowly creatures of the earth, without wings to lift them into the air. Many do not survive. Although they do not sicken, nor do they grow old, they now know weariness, hunger and pain, and death by violence or accident. For the first time, Elifaen hunt and eat flesh. During this period, some even turn to eating their own kind. Many take their own lives while others waste away, idle and filled with melancholia, turning into miserable wraiths until, after uncounted seasons, they turn to dust.

Age of Strife, XX

Diamases dies. The Dragonkind empire that Kalzar built fractures, and a series of kings and warlords will come and go. They launch sporadic attacks against the north, seeking land, but none meet with success.

Age of Strife, XXI

The First Tongue already begins to fade and the ability to communion with the living things of the world, and with the earth and waters, the forests and mountains, also diminishes. For most, this takes place rapidly, and the Elifaen develop a new, cruder language in order to speak with each other. Some very few retain use of the First Tongue for a long time, even developing a way of writing for it. But they, too, over the ages that follow, are unable to fully retain the language.

Age of Strife, XXII

Some of the Fallen Ones, calling themselves Elifaen, band together. Under leaders like Cupeldain, Katrina, Pyros, and Silmain, the plight of the Elifaen eases. They quickly learn to hunt and to make fire, and they learn about planting and harvesting and other things to relieve their suffering. Metal-making is rediscovered, too, and the art of weaving cloth. They struggle to further develop their writing, but it would be many years before there is any agreement among the different groups and clans scattered over the world. Still, the Elifaen build new cities and rebuild some of the old ones, and they create in them places of learning. Halethiris, once the center of Faerum, is also repopulated, and its tree-houses, topped with domes of gold-framed glass, located in the branches of the gargantuan trees of Halethiris Forest are reoccupied and somewhat restored. Meanwhile, Linlally, the primary city of Vanara, is rebuilt by Cupeldain and begins to flourish. Other settlements are established and begin to grow, such as Glareth by the Sea, Forlandis, and Colleton in the east, and Solsorna and Draymoor in the south.

Age of Strife, XXIII

The Elifaen begin organizing clans or "houses" and name them for trees or other plants. Cupeldain calls his clan the House of Fairlinden. Others follow suit, with the twins Lyrium and Myrium jointly establishing the House of Fairfir. Five other houses will be those of Fairmyrtle, Fairmaple, Fairwillow, Faircedar, and Fairbirch. Over time, these will be the Seven High Houses of the Elifaen. But as strife continues and loyalties and alliances shift, more houses will be established.

Age of Strife, XXIV

Many Elifaen grow discontent and resentful of Cupeldain and Silmain who represent to them the excesses that led to their Scathing. Squabbles erupt over position, power, and land. Strife abounds as there are frequent feuds and bloodshed amongst the Elifaen. Secundur continually roams the world, nurturing discord, planting weeds of mistrust, and delving into crafts taught to him by Morgasir.

The First Age

By the First Age, a variety of general systems of counting years were in use, and by the end of the First Age they were fairly reliable.   However, scholars have always debated the years for the earliest events listed here, particularly for those that happened before Silmain became King.

First Age, Year 1
Aperion returns to the earth to offer the Elifaen a way of departing. He presents them with the mysterious Nimbus Illuminas, consisting of forty-nine parts fashioned of seven kinds of precious and semiprecious stones: Diamond, Emerald, Ruby, Sapphire, Amber, Amethyst, and Topaz. These are called the Forty-Nine Keys, but because of their appearance, they will later be called the Forty-Nine Bloodcoins. He gives each of the Seven High Houses one set of seven, and, through a vision, he entrusts the instructions for their use to the head of each High House. Over time, those instructions, along with most of the Forty-Nine, will be lost, and only a few of the original Seven High Houses will remain in the world.

Within the year after the giving of the Forty-Nine to the Seven High Houses, six towers mysteriously appear throughout the world. The towers are alike in form and height, smooth, gracefully-waisted columns of stone rising up to 980 feet from the tops of six separate mountains. Each is topped is different, however, with what appears to be a glass dome of some kind, and each dome is of a different color: white, yellow, blue, red, purple, and orange. It is thought by most to have something to do with the Nimbus Illuminas and the Forty-Nine Keys or Bloodcoins due to those colors, but the missing tower of green seemed to counter that theory. It would not be until late in the First Age that the existence of the seventh tower is confirmed, located in a far southwestern region of the Dragonlands known as Karkarando.

The method of construction, and those who constructed the towers, remains a mystery, as does their actual purpose. Many theories abound, but most include the idea that a race of builders descended from the heavens and simultaneously made all of the towers. Although many attempts have been made to penetrate the towers, or to scale them, none have succeeded.

They each acquired the name of the mountaintop upon which they were constructed. Here are their names and locations:

> The white Tower Vendril, northwest of Duinnor.
> The red Tower Halfis, in the Carthanes.
> The yellow Tower Sirrian, in Tracia Realm.
> The blue Tower Medios, in Vanara Realm.
> The purple Tower Altor, located in Altoria.
> The orange Tower Ulaman, in Glareth Realm.
> The green Tower Zurlamont, in the Dragonlands.

First Age, Years 1 through 142
During this time, divisions continue to plague the Elifaen. Many wish to lay claim to the Forty-Nine Bloodcoins. Each of the Seven High Houses splinters as more Elifaen establish their own separate

lineages, and as discord continues, resulting in additional Houses being established. These include Fairholly, Fairoak, Hemlock, Pinewood, Elmwood, Persimmon, and Beech, among many others.

First Age, Year 143
Silmain of Vanara seeks to wrest control over all of the Elifaen. He declares himself King of the Faere, much to the dismay of the Elifaen of other realms. Backed by several Houses, including Cupeldain's powerful House of Fairlinden, Silmain establishes himself in Linlally of Vanara. He assembles a great army to attack and destroy the Dragonkind who still harry Vanara's southern flanks.

First Age, Year 168
Silmain leads his army of Fellfaere (as Elifaen warriors are called) southward in an effort to destroy the centers of Dragonkind power. Instead, the Elifaen become mired in a long war with few decisive victories. Many Elifaen are lost in battles and skirmishes, while many others are captured and taken into servitude by the Dragonkind.

First Age, Year 302
Silmain, disheartened by the failures of the wars and facing growing discontent at home, calls a great council of all the High Houses in order to bring the Bloodcoins together, open the Nimbus Illuminas, and make a way for the Elifaen to depart the world. Cupeldain is against this and pleads for continued war to reclaim the desert lands for the Elifaen, and he openly desires the utter destruction of the Dragonkind. Others, though uninterested in the wars against the Dragonkind, but having no desire to leave the earth or to abandon their rivers and forests, also oppose Silmain's plan. The debate stretches over a period of twelve years, and slowly Silmain loses his case for departure.

First Age, Year 314
After twelve years of debate over the Nimbus Illuminas, negotiations among the Elifaen completely break down. During these years, the Dragonkind rebuild their forces and pose new threats to the northern lands. At last, Silmain is forced to support a plan for renewed war which would last, on and off, for more than a century and a half.

First Age, Year 319
Silmain seizes the rich and fertile lands to the east of Vanara, across the River Iridelin, that are populated by many Elifaen who resist Vanara's authority. His unsuccessful bid to have the Nimbus Illuminas used to open a way for his people's departure has seriously diminished his political power and influence among the Elifaen, and the seizure of the eastern lands is his method of forcing cooperation and compliance with his rule.

Vanara is now fighting a defensive war along its southern borders as Dragonkind raids increase in frequency and drive deeper and deeper into Vanara with each passing year. Silmain knows that Vanara cannot defend against the Dragonkind without help, much less carry out an offensive campaign. He also knows that his own kind will not support any peace efforts to bring about truce, even if the Dragonkind could be enticed to parley.

First Age, Year 320
In the newly seized territories east of the River Iridelin, a coalition of woodland Elifaen raise an army to resist Silmain's efforts to bring them under Vanaran rule. Silmain responds by sending an overwhelming force across the Iridelin to quash any resistance. This takes two years to accomplish, during which there are many bloody battles and many more reprisals that spark feuds among the

Elifaen of the region. In the end, Silmain succeeds, and the "lands across the river" fall under Vanaran rule from the Iridelin to the western boughs of the old forest of Halethiris (later to be called Forest Islindia).

First Age, Year 382
The Vanarans, having driven the Dragonkind back across the Blue Mountains, now seek to press the advantage, and they destroy many settlements and garrison towns in the nearby desert. However, the Dragonkind do not go easily, and the effort of the Elifaen to retain captured desert lands is costly in blood and treasure.

First Age, Year 425
The Dragonkind learn to draw the Elifaen deeper into the desert, yielding territory while inflicting high casualties on the Elifaen, then diverting forces to harry and cut off supply routes from the north. Over the next fifty years, even though the Dragonkind are somewhat disorganized and inconsistent, the fortunes of war generally favor them as the Elifaen are continually tempted to fight ill-advised battles.

First Age, Year 454
Silmain leads a small army into the Mirse region of Vanara to fend off a Dragonkind incursion. After heavy fighting, Silmain's army surrounds the Dragonkind, but Silmain realizes that his army is too small to contain them. Feigning that he has a greater force than he does, Silmain offers a truce to permit the Dragonkind to retreat through their lines and back to their desert homes without harassment. However, Vanaran reinforcements arrive just as the Dragonkind reach the Nalamain Hills, and Silmain breaks his promise and attacks. It is a fierce battle, during which Silmain loses Ethliad, his sword, and is killed. In the confusion, the sword is not recovered, and it is presumed to have been carried away by escaping Dragonkind.

Silmain's death is viewed as a calamity and is followed by a period of division and strife among the Elifaen. Vanara rapidly declines in power as various Elifaen factions seek to break away from Vanaran rule. Silmain's sons, Heneil and Pellen, are offered the throne by a coalition of Vanaran Elifaen, but they decline. Cupeldain, fearing violence, recalls his army from the Dragonlands to face threats at home. Meanwhile, the Dragonkind, due to tribal squabbles and a series of power-struggles, fail to take advantage of the Elifaen conflicts.

First Age, Year 475
Kalzar's dynasty is renewed as his descendant, Tajahnaman, rises to power in the southern Dragonlands. Although he is only in his early twenties, he proves to be a charismatic leader, and he builds a powerful army. His armies crush opposition within the Dragonlands, and extend his rule northward. In the southern regions of the Dragonlands, Tajahnaman quickly takes control of the important waterways and agricultural activities. He reorganizes the trade guild system and reconstitutes the priesthood under his direct authority. By the Year 475, he is twenty-eight years old and has instituted a new system of provinces, each controlled by a semi-autonomous city-state, and his empire stretches throughout the desert lands south of the Blue Mountains and west of the Tulivana Mountains.

First Age, Year 483
Tajahnaman leads an invasion against the north, seeking to wrest control of key passes within the Blue Mountains that border Vanara. However, this serves to re-unite the Elifaen and the Dragonkind are easily turned back.

First Age, Year 486
Cupeldain becomes King of the Elifaen. He is quickly embroiled in a series of internal conflicts, and there are several unsuccessful attempts upon his life.

First Age, Year 489
Tajahnaman leads a second invasion into the Northlands. Cupeldain has not yet had time to consolidate his power, and the Dragonkind break through the important passes of the Blue Mountains to lay waste areas of Vanara. After bitter fighting, Tajahnaman is stopped only a few miles south of Linlally and is forced back. The Elifaen are unable to press the Dragonkind retreat, yet Tajahnaman is weakened. For many years thereafter, Tajahnaman devotes the efforts of his empire toward moving the Great Stone, but with little progress.

First Age, Year 491
In the Dragonlands, the medicine called darakal is refined for the first time. It is made from a rare herb grown in the more hospitable river valleys of the southern Dragonlands in a region called Karkarando nearby to the sea. In small quantities, taken at wide intervals, darakal provides relief from the sickness that normally shortens the lives of the Dragonkind. It is soon discovered that a more refined version, taken at frequent intervals, almost completely rids one of the scales and other illnesses associated with living in the deserts. Tajahnaman quickly moves to secure monopolies on the cultivation of the herb and on the refining of darakal.

First Age, Year 494
Tajahnaman dies and his son, Churadu, assumes power. In an effort to seal his rule, Churadu establishes the Priesthood of the Dragon, converting the previous loose-knit dragon worshipers into a cohesive religious order, declaring himself to be the direct representative of the Dragon Father and the religion's High Priest. Backed by the Dragon Throne, and protected by an elite force of the Emperor's soldiers, the Priesthood is placed in charge of the distribution of darakal. Those not authorized by the Priesthood or who are not gifted directly by the throne, and who are found in possession of darakal, or of cultivating the herb without authority, face execution. In spite of those efforts, a black market that trades in the herb comes into existence, and efforts of the Throne to stamp it out meet with only limited success.

First Age, Year 496
Churadu imposes a class system in the Dragonlands. Those favored by the Throne are provided with darakal more frequently than those less favored. While this system limits any widespread benefit from darakal that the Dragonkind population may gain, it serves to further solidify the power of the Kalzar Dynasty.

First Age, Year 510
Duinnor is established north of Vanara. It is primarily an agricultural region and enjoys relative peace, being far from the wars to the south. It is ruled by a group of lords who share power and authority.

First Age, Year 552
Linlally grows and prospers under Cupeldain in spite of continued wars and disputes with the Dragonkind.

First Age, Year 620
The coastal region of Altoria, under the rule of Queen Therona of the House of Fairwillow, grows and becomes an important ally to Vanara. It lies at the southernmost portion of the Elifaen world, located along the southern Iridelin to the coastlines just east of the treacherous Craggy Sea. This area of the sea is covered by thousands of square miles of shallow shoals, jagged rocks, and sharp reefs beaten by tides and waves and churning currents. Boats attempting to cross it are shattered, and many Dragonkind and Elifaen alike are killed attempting its navigation.
Altoria's armed forces, though few in number, are easily able to contain Dragonkind forays through the Hinderlands, a vast land of marsh and swamp at the foot of the Tulivana Mountains that stretch north and south and acts as an additional barrier between the deserts and the green lands to the east of the mountains. Altoria has robust fishing, shipbuilding, and other maritime industries, but it poses no threat to the Dragonkind, nor vice versa, due to the unnavigable Craggy Sea that lies offshore between the two enemies.

First Age, Year 685
Aldiantur, Churadu's descendant and the present King of the Dragonkind, is murdered while attending a religious ceremony. This sparks a series of civil wars amongst the various claimants to the throne, bringing the Kalzar Dynasty to an end. Ralaram, a warlord from the southeastern Dragonlands, successfully seizes the throne. Over the course of the next many centuries, a series of kings will rule the Dragonlands until the rise of Xurnon I. The Dragon Priesthood is variously purged and reformed as each successive ruler seeks to consolidate or extend his power. As well, each successive king will use conquest and attacks upon the Northlands to further their rule, but with few long-term results.

First Age, Year 732
The Accord of Sianne is reached and effectively creates a truce between the Dragonkind and Vanara. Part of this accord establishes safe trade routes to and from the desert town of Alaberbra (later to be called Kajarahn) in the northwestern Dragonlands. This agreement benefits both sides as it helps to safeguard important trade of spices, textiles, and other commodities between Vanara and the Dragonlands.

First Age, Year 744
The tenuous Accord of Sianne is broken when a band of Elifaen raiders strike a large Dragonkind caravan making its way from Alaberbra (later to be called Kajarahn) to Calamandor (the Green Citadel). Several of the slain are members of high-ranking Dragonkind families. The perpetrators are soon revealed to Cupeldain who then seeks their capture. He succeeds in arresting four of the leaders of the raid, along with fifty of their followers. They are sentenced to death and executed by being cast from the summit of the Falls of Tiandari in Linlally. However, before others can be brought to justice, a party of Dragonkind assassins is dispatched into Vanara to carry out reprisals. They murder over a hundred Elifaen in various regions of Vanara, including seventeen Elifaen lords and High Councilors. These attacks of the Dragonkind and the Elifaen upon each other quickly lead to widespread hostilities.

First Age, Year 752
The so-called Second Dragon War commences with Cupeldain leading forces into the desert. This war would last for over two-hundred years, with few decisive victories by either side, but with a great loss of blood and treasure. This epoch establishes what some Elifaen scholars term the "normalcy of war," since it became a way of life throughout Vanara and spread to the other fledgling realms.

First Age, Year 810
Cupeldain, like his predecessor, tires of war and strife. Like Silmain before him, he calls a council to bring together all of the Forty-Nine Keys (or Bloodcoins). Members of the High Houses of the Elifaen come to Linlally from all over the world. Cupeldain's proposal is opposed by many, including the Halethiris Elifaen under King Ilex who wields considerable influence, and Secundur works behind the scenes to spread discord. However, Ormace of the House of Fairbirch is the most outspoken opponent to Cupeldain's plan, and Ormace threatens to destroy those Seven that were entrusted to him by Aperion. In an attempt to preserve peace, the Seven High Houses decide to re-divide the Forty-Nine amid fears that one House might use its Seven to depart without the consent of the others. The Forty-Nine Bloodcoins of the Nimbus Illuminas are re-divided, each House taking one of its own and one from each of the other six Houses. Cupeldain is heartbroken, but he becomes determined to end the continual feuding among his people.

First Age, Year 816
Fearing that Ormace of the House of Fairbirch may try to wrest her Bloodcoins from her, and having no confidence that Cupeldain or Heneil (son of Silmain) might come to her aid, Katrina of the House of Fairmaple leads her people away from Vanara. They go to the western slopes of the Carthane Mountains in the region of Wayregyle. There, the House of Fairmaple establish themselves, making it known that Vanarans are not welcome.

First Age, Year 821
King Ilex of Halethiris, who fears the further expansion of Vanara, attempts to resurrect the glory of his forest kingdom by bringing conjurers and witches into his court to lay enchantments and spells upon the forest. They require a maiden who is pure of body and of heart, and his daughter Islindia agrees to be their subject. Their spells fail to bring back the days of glory, but leave Islindia with the power to bring about the past temporarily into the present through her dreams and memories. It is this power that brings her to the attention of Secundur, and he quickly becomes infatuated with her beauty.

First Age, Year 823
Princess Islindia of Halethiris is kidnapped by Secundur after he murders her lover and makes the blame fall upon Islindia's brother. He strives to convince her to become his bride, but she rebuffs him. She is rescued by her brother and her father, King Ilex, and in retaliation, Secundur lays a terrible blight upon the forest that will destroy it and all its inhabitants within a season. Only King Ilex and his daughter Islindia are spared so that they may witness the destruction. In an effort to save his forest, King Ilex attempts to conjure time so that it will not pass, but his spells go awry. The forest quickly declines, and the great trees die and fall. However, the spells have unexpected results. Islindia is given back her wings that were lost in her Scathing, and the King along with all his guard are transformed into spirits of the wood. By year's end, the forest is all but destroyed, becoming a forlorn, abandoned place filled with strange and uncanny spirits and haunted by the melancholy Islindia and her father's spirit. He eventually becomes known as the King of the Wood, and she as Queen of the Wood. Over the years, many will venture into the forest to explore the place and to learn its secrets, but the few who manage to emerge are reduced to deep melancholy and madness, unable to say or express clearly what they witnessed within. Eventually the place becomes known as Forest Islindia and is considered by most a forbidden land.

First Age, Year 834
Duinnor grows in influence and power as more of the Elifaen go there seeking to escape the wars and intrigues of Vanara. They establish trade with the other lands to the east, and they make use of the Osterflo River to take their goods east to Glareth by the Sea.

First Age, Year 835

Earthquakes shake the world. They are commonly attributed to the ancient Dragons, thought to be shaking the earth from within their deep lairs far underground. Many cities and villages are destroyed in the Dragonlands, Altoria, and Masurthia. Strong quakes are felt as far north as Vanara, where some buildings fall. In the mountains to the north of Linlally, the tremors set off a vast avalanche of rock and ice. The House of Fairbirch, including its villages and castles, is completely destroyed, and Lord Ormace and all of his are people killed. No one in the valley survives, and it will be many years before any attempt is made to excavate the ruins in order to locate the Bloodcoins of Fairbirch.

First Age, Year 840

More earthquakes are felt throughout the world. A series of great waves, some over 90 feet in height, pound and inundate the coastlines of the east with waves reaching far inland. Although sparsely settled, many Elifaen villages and settlements are completely destroyed, along with vast areas of marshland.

Many scholars of Mortal History will later propose that these tumults (earthquakes followed by tsunamis) must have coincided with the mysterious cataclysms that destroyed the ancient homelands of Men and set them to roam the seas for six generations in their great City Ships.

First Age, Year 874

The first efforts are made to excavate the ruins of the House of Fairbirch the ruins of the House of Fairbirch, destroyed by avalanches thirty-nine years earlier. The undertaking will continue for eight years, hampered by winter snows and spring floods. At last, the ruins of Castle Ormace are uncovered, and the remains of Ormace and many other dead Elifaen are found. Although his treasury rooms are discovered to contain a vast fortune, his Bloodcoins are not found.

First Age, Year 880

Witches and demons come into all regions of the world, and much chaos is spread by their mischief and evil. Such is the havoc they wreak, that fighting between the Dragonkind and the Elifaen ceases as they turn their efforts against these threats. This period, lasting some twenty-five years, is sometimes referred to as the First Demon War.

First Age, Year 915

An ogre has come into Altoria and is terrorizing the population. He is Jatarak, and he is twice the size of an ordinary person and has great strength to match. He is bloodthirsty and craves all living flesh. Jatarak eats any person he finds, coming into villages and farms, eating people and livestock. Queen Therona sends her army to kill him, but he eludes them, killing many in the process until few are willing to face him. Desperate, Therona sends word to Vanara and to other lands, begging all brave warriors to come to her assistance.

First Age, Year 918

Many come to Altoria to hunt Jatarak the Ogre. Among these are Navis of the House of Elmwood. He pursues Jatarak across the River Iridelin, through the Hinderlands, and into the mountains. There, at the Crevasse of Fire, Navis and Jatarak do battle. Navis is victorious, and he brings Jatarak's head back to Altoria to show Queen Therona. The inhabitants of Altoria are jubilant, and Navis is hailed as a great hero. The Queen rewards Navis with many gifts, including a battle-worthy breastplate that her artisans have embossed with the likeness of a spreading elm tree, in honor of his House of Elmwood.

First Age, Year 920
While traveling on a mission in eastern Vanara to resolve disputes among various clans of the Elifaen, Cupeldain and his party are set upon and captured. All of Cupeldain's party is murdered by being weighed with chains and drowned in a lake. Among those murdered are Loura, Cupeldain's wife, and their friends, Shevalia and her husband Bychanter. Blame is first cast upon the House of Hemlock, in whose territory Cupeldain was slain and which was a participant in the feuds that Cupeldain sought to resolve. This incident immediately sparks intense reprisals, and violent feuds engulf the region.

Learning the news, Cupeldain's son, Parthais, immediately takes an army into the feuding territories to force an end to the feuding and to find those who murdered his parents. He executes several men and women from both sides of the feud by having them drowned in the same lake where his parents were murdered. Afterwards, he releases a demon-serpent into the lake to feed upon the spirits of the dead, both the guilty and the innocent. The incident shocks all present, but Parthais declares himself King of Vanara and warns the people of the region against any further feuds that might threaten his realm.

Lucinda of the House of Faircedar, a supporter of Hemlock, fears retribution on her people by Parthais, Cupeldain's son. She and her people leave Vanara bound for the northeast. They are welcomed by King Gardin of the Glarethian House of Beech.

First Age, Year 931
A dispute breaks out between Masurthia Realm and Altoria Realm over boundaries and tribute. Each raises an army and attacks the other, but no decisive victories take place. Trade between those realms and Vanara is soon disrupted.

First Age, Year 935
Queen Therona of Altoria does not show her Bloodcoins to her ministers as has been her tradition to do every twenty-four years. She cites the hostilities with Masurthia and the dangers of showing them publicly. At first, this raises few concerns among Altorians, who are very supportive of their queen.

First Age, Year 937-940
Parthais, the son of Cupeldain, who has not yet been confirmed as King, leads an army to the southern realms of Altoria and Masurthia and enforces peace between the two. By further threatening to break off all trade with the two feuding realms, and blockading all trade routes, Parthais forces them to settle their disputes. In the Year 940, Altoria and Masurthia will reach an accord concerning boundaries, and within two years Parthais withdraws his occupying forces.

First Age, Year 942
Parthais, son of Cupeldain, formally ascends to the throne in Vanara as King of the Elifaen. He sends agents to Glareth to provoke King Gardin of the House of Beech and Lucinda's House of Faircedar against one another.

First Age, Year 944
Parthais sends envoys to Wayregyle in an effort to convince Katrina to return with her people to Vanara. The envoys are rebuffed. Parthais will try repeatedly, but, as often as not, his envoys are turned back unceremoniously.

First Age, Year 945

In Glareth, a plot to overthrow King Gardin's House of Beech is uncovered. Several captured Vanarans say that Lucinda and her House of Faircedar are behind the plot. King Gardin discounts the claims, but, nonetheless, the people of Glareth are incited against the House of Faircedar. It is then discovered that the Vanarans who claim that Faircedar is to blame are actually members of the House of Walnut, who are closely allied to Parthais and the House of Fairlinden. However, most Glarethians are still convinced that Faircedar had a role in the failed overthrow attempt.

First Age, Year 947

King Barindon, hearing of the troubles besetting the House of Faircedar, invites Lucinda to come with her people to Masurthia. At first Lucinda is reluctant, but when seven Masurthian ships arrive to be Faircedar's transport, she agrees to go. Against the advice of King Gardin, Lucinda departs with her husband, daughter and two sons, along with many others of their household. However, many of her people choose to remain in Glareth, and they renounce all ties to Faircedar.

Lucinda's ships are beset with many problems, and only three of the seven will make it to Forlandis in Tracia. Among those lost at sea along the way are Lucinda's husband and many members of her household. Lucinda and the survivors of her people remain in Forlandis for the winter, and plan the last leg of their journey to Masurthia.

First Age, Year 948

With only three of the original ships that left Glareth, the House of Faircedar departs Forlandis bound for Masurthia. Five days later, they are hit by a typhoon. Lucinda is drowned and her daughter is killed before the three ships are driven ashore and wrecked. Many others have also died. Lucinda's two sons, Tavin and Palos, are spared, and the Bloodcoins are saved. After waiting three weeks for rescue, Tavin and Palos along with thirty others decide to strike out overland for Solsorna in Masurthia. They are never seen again, nor are their Bloodcoins.

First Age, Year 964

Renewed fighting between the Dragonkind and Vanara takes place. Each side still seeks to secure the southern Blue Mountains.

In Altoria, which has been at peace for twenty-four years, Queen Therona still refuses to show her Bloodcoins to her ministers.

First Age, Year 966

Vanarans deliberately set fire to their southern forests in an effort to flush out Dragonkind infiltrators. It is a calamity of epic proportions and forever changes the landscape of Vanara's southern mountains. Lost in the fires are hundreds of thousands of acres of vineyards, croplands, towns, and virgin forest. Infuriated, Parthais seeks to punish those responsible, leading to long, drawn-out tribunals.

First Age, Year 967

In spite of growing pressure and discontent among her ministers and people, Queen Therona still refuses to show her Bloodcoins. Three of her ministers take matters into their own hands and force their way into the Altorian Royal Vaults, only to discover that the Bloodcoins are missing. They then confront Queen Therona, who attempts to have the ministers arrested and executed for treason. Instead, the arresting guard escorts the ministers to a place of safety, then they make known the fact of the missing Bloodcoins. Within days revolt threatens to overthrow the Queen and riots take place as she is called upon to produce the Bloodcoins or to explain what happened to them. When a mob tries to storm her palace, several people are killed by the Royal Guard. At last, facing dethronement and public humiliation, she agrees to abdicate to the popular Prince Felthain of the Altorian House of Mulberry. Felthain places Therona under guard and she is exiled to a villa in northern Altoria. She refuses to say what happened to the Bloodcoins.

First Age, Year 971
The Battle of Tamkal Plain takes place. King Salkasin of the Dragonkind seeks to establish a line of keeps and fortresses along the northern borders of the Dragonlands. The Elifaen, fearing that these would be used to protect an invading army, begin a campaign to disrupt their construction and to destroy those already completed. Salkasin leads a large army north and east, aiming to go around the Nalamain Hills in order to outflank the Elifaen. Learning of this, King Parthais of Vanara leads his own army into position ahead of Salkasin's columns to meet them on the Tamkal Plain. There, Parthais and Salkasin face each other in battle and fight in personal combat, King against King. After a long, hard duel, Parthais is victorious, Salkasin is slain, and the Dragonkind are routed. Elifaen casualties are high and include many Firstborn.

First Age, Year 980
In northern Altoria, the former Queen Therona is found dead at the villa where she is exiled. She has taken Sigh Mortabilis (foxdire) that has been smuggled into the villa by her servants. She never revealed what became of the Seven Bloodcoins entrusted to her.

First Age, Year 1020
Still struggling with the loss of the First Tongue, Elifaen writing further develops and takes the form of a phonetic runic script. Parthais declares it the "New Writing," and orders that all scribes be instructed in it and all chronicles be recorded using it. The speech of this writing would later be called the Ancient Tongue and is sometimes confused with the First Tongue. The Ancient Tongue would continue to develop. As it mixes and blends with other dialects, it would later form the basis of the Common Speech that would become prevalent in the east and the language of trade throughout the Realms.

First Age, Year 1100
Various small incursions of Dragonkind occur over the next several decades, with several small bands conducting raids as far east as Tracia. They do not seem coordinated or organized from within the Dragonlands and are thought to be sundry adventuresome groups striking out of the Dragonlands on their own to obtain spoils. They have little effect, however, except to increase the general wariness of the northern and eastern realms.

First Age, Year 1126
A new mortal race appears for the first time on the far eastern coastline. They call themselves Men. The Elifaen of that region are wary of the newcomers and most retreat from the coastal areas where the new people make their settlements.

First Age, Year 1149
Elrasil the Hunter arrives in Linlally and tells Parthais of a fantastic floating castle at the edge of the world. Parthais is determined to see it for himself and departs Linlally with a large party, guided by Elrasil, to find the place.

First Age, Year 1150-53
Having recently returned from his expedition to see the floating castle told to him by Elrasil, Parthais secretly grants certain lands to Secundur. They are to the northwest of Vanara, nearby the edge of the world, and will later be called Shatuum.

After a dispute, Parthais banishes his son and daughter, Thurdun and Serith Ellyn, from Vanara. It is told that Serith Ellyn goes to the floating castle that will become known in legend as Griferis. Her brother, Thurdun, secretly builds an army-in-waiting, formed by others who are banished from Vanara, those wronged by the unjust rule of Parthais, and other sympathizers.

First Age, Year 1156
The rule of Parthais grows more unjust. In a fit of rage, he orders the execution of all Elifaen scribes who still refuse to use the New Writing and the destruction of all books, scrolls, and tablets that bear any other writing. Lost are over four hundred scribes and learned ones and untold numbers of records and written works throughout Vanara. However, many anticipate the order given by Parthais, and many thousands of manuscripts and works of writing are removed to Duinnor and to faraway Glareth by the Sea, along with a sudden migration of fleeing scribes and scholars. Duinnor and Glareth welcome these refugees, and this begins Duinnor's period of ascendancy as a place of learning and scholarship. It also marks the beginning of Duinnor's influence in the world. These events will come to be known as the Purge of Scholars. When Lord Banis, High Judge of Vanara, refuses to cooperate with Parthais, he flees Vanara with his son and two daughters, Navis, Atlana, and Esildre. They will remain in hiding at a remote castle in northern Vanara.

First Age, Year 1160
Parthais is angered by Duinnor's acceptance of Vanaran refugees, including many scholars who bring with them thousands of books and scrolls. He sends his ambassadors to Duinnor, claiming that the books and scrolls were taken from Vanara illegally, and he demands their return. Parthais also demands that all Vanarans are to be expelled by Duinnor. Parthais threatens war with Duinnor should his demands be refused. He sends similar demands and threats to Glareth by the Sea. Both Duinnor and Glareth ignore the claims and demands of Parthais. However, later this year, Duinnor begins the construction of defensive works intended to thwart Parthais should he carry out his threats. A line of these works will later become the walls that will surround Duinnor City.

First Age, Year 1260
Thurdun, constantly on the run and at the same time trying to organize an army to lead against his father, goes to Wayregyle. His aim is to remind Katrina and the House of Fairmaple of their oath to support Cupeldain's House of Fairlinden and to convince her to join with him against Parthais. However, when he arrives in Wayregyle, he finds only a few settlements of Newcomers (Men) who live among the overgrown ruins of castles and villages left behind many years earlier. Thurdun is also told that some of the mountain Elifaen have stories of how Katrina led her people away across the "northern river," (meaning the Osterflo) with the aim of crossing into the icy wastelands to make new settlements far away.

First Age, Year 1273
Serith Ellyn and her brother Thurdun return to Vanara and overthrow Parthais. Parthais is killed, and Serith Ellyn becomes Queen of Vanara. The last year during which Parthais ruled is considered the last year of the First Age of the World, by order of Queen Serith Ellyn.

The Second Age

Officially, the Second Age began on the first day of spring in the year 1273 (a month after the overthrow of Parthais by Serith Ellyn) and ended on Midwinter's Day, at which point a new year began. This would later be adjusted.
See Also:
Essays and Explanations (Calendars and Timekeeping)

Second Age, Year the First
Serith Ellyn is formally crowned Queen of the Elifaen, Ruler of Vanara, Keeper of the Winged Soul, and holder of the Seven Bloodcoins, Keys to the Nimbus Illuminas, of Cupeldain's House. She declares the beginning of a New Age, promising to her people that she will do her utmost to protect their security, to promote their prosperity, and to combat corruption withing the legal system and within markets and trade. From this point onward, the previous years will be regarded as the First Age. For a while, the present age is referred to as the New Age, but eventually is called the Second Age.

Second Age, Year 11
Lord Banis returns to Vanara and serves the court of the new Queen.

Second Age, Year 27
Men form an alliance with the Elifaen of the Kingdom of Glareth by the Sea. Vanara is excluded from the accord, but does not oppose it.

Second Age, Year 130
Trolls are discovered inhabiting the mountains east of the River Saerdulin. They build crude stone houses and make paved roadways. Little is known about them, where they came from, or how they live. They attack travelers who venture into the region. However, due to their slowness and lack of wit, few but the most incautious travelers are harmed. Thunder rumbles throughout the mountains as a result of their stone-moving activities, and soon the region is named for that sound (the Thunder Mountains).

Second Age, Year 195
A fever sweeps through the east. The Elifaen are immune to it, but many Men die, including the husband and of Byrniece of the House of Fairmyrtle. This same year, tragedy strikes the House of Fairmyrtle once again when Byrniece's son and daughter are drowned at sea.

Second Age, Year 196
In Tracia, while riding across her estate with a party of her people, a boar charges out from a thicket of trees and attacks Byrniece's horse. Byrniece is thrown from her saddle and her horse falls upon her, killing her instantly. She is survived by her granddaughter, Nianan, who is grief-stricken and will become a recluse within the manor of Fairmyrtle.

Second Age, Year 202
Nimwill, Chronicler of the Royal Court since the time of Parthais, retires. Orinus, his student, becomes Court Chronicler in his place. Nimwill will remain in Vanara for many years before setting

out to see the world. The last record of him will be in the year 357 S.A., when he is a visitor to King Thalamir's court in Glareth by the Sea.

Second Age, Year 205
Xurnon, a powerful tribal leader of the southeastern tribes of the Dragonkind, declares himself King of the Dragonkind, and marches upon Tyrsharat. His armies easily defeat the weak forces of his rival, Omaldin, who had seized the city in a bid to make himself king. After nearly a year of siege, Tyrsharat falls when the Dragon Priesthood, persecuted under Omaldin, foment revolt within the city and welcome Xurnon. Omaldin is put to death, and Xurnon assumes the throne, declaring himself king of all the desert lands. The dynasty that Xurnon establishes will rule the Dragonlands for the next five centuries.

Second Age, Year 217
The race of Men rapidly grows in numbers. Their agricultural townships spring up far and wide along the coastal lands. In the west, they are fewer in number but settle without permission wherever they wish. Their forest-clearing activities displease many Elifaen. Vanara seeks to discourage the settlements of Men by surveying lands, issuing deeds to native-born Vanarans, and declaring all non-deeded lands to be sovereign property of the Throne. In the west, certain grants are allowed to Men, but most are pushed north into Duinnor territories, where they are more or less welcomed.

Second Age, Year 225
Nianan of the House of Fairmyrtle, granddaughter of Pyros and Duiniece, dies at her estate in Tracia. She has no children and the House of Fairmyrtle is declared dissolved. Her servants attempt to smuggle out her Bloodcoins, but eighteen-year-old King Kapol of the Tracian House of Alder personally rushes to her estate with a small army. He pursues and intercepts the party of Men with the Bloodcoins, arrests them on charges of theft, and seizes the Bloodcoins for the purpose, he declares, of safekeeping. When Serith Ellyn hears of this, she sends envoys to Tracia to urge Kapol to release the arrested men and to send them and the Bloodcoins to Vanara. Kapol refuses, and he openly persecutes those supporters of Fairmyrtle still at large within Tracia, many of which are Men who had long been friends and servants of Fairmyrtle.

Second Age, Year 230
The Temple of Beras is established near Duinnor City. It is built on the crest of Mount Onuma, a low mountain overlooking the city, nearby to where the Old Kings of Duinnor have their burial grounds. Its construction begins on spring day, and is completed by Midwinter's. It becomes a mysterious center of worship and meditation. Its founders are unknown unto this day, but a mysterious relationship will exist between it and the New Kings of Duinnor. The first and each subsequent Unknown King will emerge from that place, and each spring the King of Duinnor will go to the Temple in a great precession to enact some mysterious ceremony that is thought to ensure his continued rule for the upcoming year. Upon emerging from the Temple, the King will have a new Avatar, or else the Avatar will be in a new form. It is from this point forward (the Vernal Equinox) that the Duinnor Royal Calendar marks the beginning of its New Year, named for the shape or form of the Avatar. Unless otherwise noted, the Royal Duinnor Calendar is used in this chronology henceforward.

Second Age, Year 231
The Year of the Inkwell (1st Year of the 1st Unknown King of Duinnor)
The Rule of the Unknown Kings of Duinnor Begins
On the Spring Equinox of this year, the Throne of Duinnor is established as the First Unknown King

seizes power from the group of lords (some say warlords) who jointly govern the lands of Duinnor. No one knows who he is, where he came from, or how he obtained his power or his mysterious Avatar, which is now first seen in the world in the form of an inkwell. The year will be called the Year of the Inkwell, and thus begins a tradition of naming each subsequent year after the form the Avatar takes for that year. The meaning of the shape and form of the Avatar, and the nature of its relationship to the King, remains a mystery. At any rate, each king must travel to the Temple of Beras to renew his kingship. This is done annually on the Spring Equinox, at which point the new regnal year will begin, with a new Avatar. Thus the standard year and the regnal year are offset from one another. (See About Calendars and Timekeeping)

The King is always attired from head to toe in a glowing, golden mantle. It shines very brightly of its own light, and all who look directly upon it are befuddled. If they look upon the King too long, they will fall into permanent madness.

Like all subsequent Unknown Kings, the King of Duinnor has the ability to know the hearts of any within his presence and can communicate without words if he chooses to do so. As well, the Avatar, which can move freely about Duinnor City, has the peculiar power to summon anyone the King wishes to see; none but the Melnari have it in their power to resist the summons, should they wish to do so. But the Avatar is normally accompanied by armed Palace Guards to force compliance, if necessary.

The new King immediately begins to assemble a loyal court. He also orders the construction of a vast palace with a high tower in which he will have his High Chamber. By the end of the year, the King has begun the disassembling of the previous order of rule, and through rewards and intimidation his power is extended throughout Duinnor.

Second Age, Year 235
The Year of the Blue Butterfly (5th Year of the 1st Unknown King of Duinnor)
The trading town of Attis is established by Elifaen. It is located on the northern course of the River Saerdulin not far from Lake Halgaeth which feeds the river. Trading vessels carry crops and goods to and from Attis as far south as Tracia along the Saerdulin, while its proximity to Lake Halgaeth enables boatmen to easily transport goods north and south across the lake, enabling prosperous trade with Glareth. As well, Attis lies on one of the main routes from the coastal regions to the West. As a result of its location, Attis becomes an important and prosperous community occupied mostly by Elifaen, but with many Men in the surrounding settlements.

Xurnon II assumes his father's throne in the Dragonlands. Along the western slopes of the Tulivana Mountains, where most of the wheat fields are planted, Xurnon II builds large irrigation canals to channel water for crops. In the southwest, he increases the yield of darakal crops by building a system of small interconnected reservoirs to catch rain and snowmelt runoff from the western mountains. These efforts will gradually increase the food supply in the Dragonlands, and he uses the surplus to feed additional slaves who labor in mines. With an abundant supply of coal, weapons production will increase.

Second Age, Year 244-245
The Year of the Shackle (1st Year of the 2nd Unknown King of Duinnor)
The First Unknown King suddenly dies and the Second Unknown King assumes the throne of Duinnor.

Responding to the influx of Men into Duinnor's territories, the Second Unknown King orders equal rights to be accorded to all Duinnor citizens, regardless of race. In addition, he embarks on an ambitious program of building. Walls of stone soon ring the old city of Duinnor, and an Army of King's Men (the Kingsmen) is established.

Xurnon II dies and his son, Vaza, takes the Dragonkind throne at age twenty.

Second Age, Year 250
The Year of the Trout (6th Year of the 2nd Unknown King of Duinnor)
The Seven Realms are by now formed, although their boundaries will be in flux for many years. They are Masurthia, Altoria, Vanara, Duinnor, Glareth, Eastlands, and Tracia. In the Eastlands Realm, the coastal kingdom of Colleton is the center of governance, but the town of Attis competes in power due to strong trade relations with the other Realms. As Attis grows, the King of Colleton struggles to retain power through taxation and tribute but meets with little success, and the influence of Colleton and its throne begins to wane.

Second Age, Year 262
The Year of the Blue Flower (18th Year of the 2nd Unknown King of Duinnor)
Bowing to growing concern over the encroachment of Men, Queen Serith Ellyn issues the House Edicts which outline the rules of Elifaen House Names, their inheritance, and in what circumstances House Names may be passed down to children of Men (only in the case of an Elifaen mother and matron of the House). While this serves to quell discontent amongst Vanaran Elifaen, the rules are never strictly enforced except in a few unusual cases that were brought before the Vanaran courts. However, the Edicts will serve as a model for other realms. Both Duinnor and Glareth adopt the Edicts almost without modification, although in practice Duinnor will favor Men over Elifaen. The rulers of the Realms work to reach an agreement on how the Edicts are to be applied, but they are reluctant to give up their power to apply or to enforce the Edicts. A Council of Houses is eventually formed that will be the deciding body for when and how the Edicts are to be applied in specific cases.

Vaza, King of the Dragonkind, dies. His daughter, Nebalasa, takes the throne as the first and only Queen of the Dragonkind. She is sixteen years old and will rule for twenty years. Nebalasa must cope with a rapidly increasing population of Dragonkind, the result of increased food supplies. She begins an ambitious project of organizing new armies, ordering every other male child of each household into service. At the same time, she instructs that the Priesthood of the Dragon show preferential treatment in distributing darakal to her soldiers.

Second Age, Year 266
The Year of the Starfish (22nd Year of the 2nd Unknown King of Duinnor)
The New Calendar of Duinnor is adopted on the morning of the eleventh day after the Winter Solstice, in keeping with the ancient calendars, but correcting the drift of those previous calendars. The Royal Duinnor Calendar is kept separately, still beginning on the day after the Spring Equinox. Over time, the New Calendar will replace date systems peculiar to other regions due to the growing importance of trade between realms and the overriding influence of Duinnor over such trade.

King Kapol of Tracia is under continued pressure from Serith Ellyn to send the Bloodcoins that he seized from Fairmyrtle to Vanara. In response, Kapol has them removed from Forlandis and taken to a secret location to be safeguarded.

Second Age, Year 270
The Year of the Bridle (26th Year of the 2nd Unknown King of Duinnor)
A plague that strikes the population of Men sweeps through the east. While the Elifaen are immune, one in four mortals will succumb to the incurable fever. Some cast blame on the Elifaen, and tensions rise between the races. There is sporadic violence against the Elifaen in Tracia, parts of the Eastlands, and near Glareth.

Second Age, Year 278
The Year of the Sandglass (34th Year of the 2nd Unknown King of Duinnor)
The forest-dwelling Elifaen, particularly of the east, continue to oppose the spreading of Men and the felling of forests for fields and for building materials for new towns and settlements. In the east, some of these Elifaen form into several bands under the leadership of the House of Pinewood and strike throughout the Eastlands Realm, Tracia, and Glareth. They maraud, stealing cattle, burning farms and villages, and committing occasional acts of kidnapping.

Heneil, who is living at Attis, takes charge of its defense and begins the reconstruction of the fortress that overlooks the town and the bridge that crosses the River Saerdulin.

The place where King Kapol of Tracia has hidden the Bloodcoins that he took from the House of Fairmyrtle is discovered and attacked by a large group of armed bandits. The castle is stormed, and the place is looted and burned. Soon the theft of the Bloodcoins is widely known, and this serves to bring further shame and outrage against Tracia and its monarch.

Second Age, Year 281
The Year of the Needle (37th Year of the 2nd Unknown King of Duinnor)
In the Eastlands, the Elifaen of Attis join with Men in their defense against the raids of rebellious Elifaen. This leads to a short civil war amongst the Elifaen, threatening to spread throughout all of the Realms. Glareth comes to the aid of Attis, while King Kapol of Tracia backs the House of Pinewood. However, all other Realms also back the Eastlands and Glareth by sending aid and armed forces to the Eastlands to assist. Within Tracia, resistance to Pinewood and Kapol strengthens when several clans of men, including the powerful Waterstone, join together to fight against King Kapol and Pinewood from within Tracia.

Queen Nebalasa of the Dragonkind dies. Her son, Vaza II, takes power, and continues her policies of giving the army preferential treatment in all things, including food, darakal, and status.

Second Age, Year 285
The Year of the Rabbit (41st Year of the 2nd Unknown King of Duinnor)
In Tracia, Pinewood and King Kapol are defeated, and aging King Kapol of the House of Alder is deposed. His house and the House of Pinewood are dissolved. Before the leaders of Pinewood can be put on trial, they are attacked and murdered. Prince Dulmian of the House of Bayberry is appointed to the Throne of Tracia by a council made up of the victorious leaders of Tracians, Eastlanders, Masurthians, and Glarethians. He will be recognized as the rightful ruler by Duinnor, with other realms following suit soon thereafter. As a reward for his support against Pinewood and Kapol, Dulmian elevates clan chief Waterstone to the status of Lord of the Realm and returns to his people lands that had been taken by King Kapol for Waterstone's opposition to him. Meanwhile, the former king, Kapol, dies in prison. King Dulmian, in an act of mercy, orders that Kapol's large family is to be spared from the executioner, but they are to be exiled to Grisland Island for the rest of their lives.

Second Age, Year 292
The Year of the Wheel (1st Year of the 3rd Unknown King of Duinnor)
The Second Unknown King of Duinnor dies and is replaced by the Third Unknown King. There is little disruption of power, though, and the Third Unknown King resumes the efforts of his predecessor by seeking to expand Duinnor's trading power and its armed forces. By now, it is apparent that the death of each King is brought about by the one who will take the throne.

Second Age, Year 302
The Year of the Frying Pan (10th Year of the 3rd Unknown King of Duinnor)
Duinnor advocates for all Men to be granted the same Rights of Hearing before tribunals regardless of the Realm in which they may live. Duinnor's efforts are met with little success. Eastlands, Glareth, and Tracia agree to the Accord of Duinnor in exchange for certain protections and guarantees.

Second Age, Year 308
The Year of the Abacus (1st Year of the 4th Unknown King of Duinnor)
The Fourth Unknown King assumes the throne of Duinnor. He seldom leaves his palace and is soon replaced.

Vaza II dies and his son, Xurnon III, takes power. He is intent on conquest and sharply increases the number of soldiers in his armies. Under Xurnon III, great hardship will befall his people, who suffer from chronic food shortages and are growing discontent. The population of the Dragonkind has risen during the previous generations, though darakal production has not been substantially increased. During Xurnon III's first year, the wheat crops fail, and several minor uprisings are put down as the Dragonkind grow hungry and desperate.

Second Age, Year 318
The Year of the Green Bottle (1st Year of the 5th Unknown King of Duinnor)
The Fifth Unknown King assumes the throne of Duinnor. He quickly imposes conditions on the other Realms for Duinnor's support in defense against the Dragonkind. As a result, Duinnor gains a foothold into the governing of all other Realms.

Duinnor begins the construction of the Locks of Karthia along the Osterflo River roughly halfway between Duinnor and Glareth. The locks and corresponding canal will enable boats to bypass the treacherous Karthian Falls. This project will take nearly fifty years and is paid for through various fees and tributes imposed on other Realms.

Xurnon III's reign begins to falter when the darakal crop fails. Since his armies obtain the herb in preference to all others, the ranks swell with volunteers, giving up their trades in order to obtain the precious herb. In order to keep people working in the mines and fields, Xurnon has his generals commit a certain portion of their soldiers to labor. However, his generals resist, and, fearing for his dynasty, Xurnon concedes to a massive invasion of the northern realms. Rather than attacking the powerful Vanarans, their plan is to capture swaths of eastern lands, making them colonies for exploiting the agricultural riches. However, Xurnon worries that the crop failures will prevent adequate supplies for the army. When Xurnon decides to cancel the invasion, an Elifaen appears in his court and tells Xurnon that if his armies can drive eastward, and put a wedge through the Eastlands, the Elifaen and Men of the region will be easily enslaved. The key, the mysterious Elifaen says, is to take Tulith Attis. Xurnon is still doubtful, but the Elifaen says that Tulith Attis will fall, since a high born Elifaen at Tulith Attis will help them. Although records of these meetings will survive, the identity of the Elifaen who met with Xurnon as well as the traitor at Tulith Attis will remain shrouded. Xurnon, still mistrustful, nonetheless agrees in order to save his throne from the growing unrest amongst his generals.

Second Age, Year 322
The Year of the Lamp (4th Year of the 5th Unknown King of Duinnor)
A mighty force of Dragonkind sweeps north, overrunning The Mirse. By some estimates, they number in excess of a quarter of a million soldiers and support. They cross the River Iridelin south of Forest Islindia, then split. While one portion marches eastward across the Plains of Bletharn, the bulk of the army descends upon Altoria and Masurthia. They will continue to divide, leaving adequate forces to conquer Altoria and Masurthia while permitting the rest of their army to drive eastward into Tracia. So sudden is this onslaught, and so swift are their movements, that Vanara cannot assemble an army large enough to effectively face them. The best that Vanara can do at such short notice is to harry the fast-moving Dragonkind as they enter Masurthia. While this is done, the bulk of Vanara's remaining army is engaged along the Blue Mountains by another Dragonkind army that feints invasion through the Khanhar Pass and elsewhere. Learning that the Dragonkind intend a broad pincer movement against the eastern realms, Vanara and Duinnor quickly form an alliance and agree to send additional forces eastward in pursuit across the Plains of Bletharn. Queen Serith Ellyn calls for every able-bodied fighter and hastily assembles an army of over seventy-thousand to go east. Her armies and those from Duinnor are to converge at the city of Fisenwold, near the River Missenflo and Tulith Morgair. The Vanarans arrive first and find the city sacked and the surrounding countryside strewn with the dead of Fisenwold's small army. They wait for over three weeks, but the Duinnor army does not arrive, so Serith Ellyn leads her forces on into the Thunder Mountains. Had it not been for this delay, it is likely the Vanarans would have reached Tulith Attis in time to prevent the massacre that will take place there.

Unbeknownst to the Vanarans, the Duinnor army, in its haste to reach their rendezvous, attempts to cross through Nasakeeria, but none ever emerge. A sole messenger, sent back to Duinnor before the army entered Nasakeeria, is the only survivor of those forces. When no more messengers arrive, Duinnor immediately dispatches a second smaller army, entirely on horseback, to travel swiftly around Nasakeeria and to the east. They meet and join with the Vanarans two days before arriving at Tulith Attis, where they are joined by a large army from Glareth.

Meanwhile, the Dragonkind who have pushed through the Thunder Mountains are joined at Tulith Attis by a large force that came up through Tracia. Together they lay siege to Tulith Attis while another force sacks Colleton on the coast. Tulith Attis falls when its gates are breached, and no one within the fortress is spared.

The combined armies of Vanara, Glareth, and Duinnor arrive too late to prevent the destruction of Tulith Attis and the slaughter of all who have taken refuge there, and the gruesome scene they come upon at Tulith Attis and the surrounding fields fills the arriving soldiers with horror and with the desire for vengeance. It is apparent, too, that the gates were not forced, for they stood open and undamaged, and was clearly the way the fortress was taken, immediately leading to suspicions of treachery.

Although many families of Men are victims, some blame them for conspiring with the Dragonkind, added to the already existing tensions stemming from the late arrival of the Duinnor forces (made up of mostly Men). Later, the blame for the destruction and slaughter at Tulith Attis shifts to the Elifaen. Nonetheless, the armies from the west and north pursue the Dragonkind, encircling and defeating them at the Battle of Saerdulin. But the seeds of discord are sown between Men and Elifaen.

During the invasion of the Eastlands, Inrick, King of Colleton and overlord of the Eastlands, escapes along with his army before the Dragonkind reach Colleton, abandoning his people to their fate. When the Dragonkind leave his burning city, he returns and finds nearly all of the inhabitants dead or carried away.

All of the southern and eastern realms but Glareth (that is, Tracia, Eastlands, Masurthia, and Altoria) suffer greatly from the invasion. As well, Vanara suffers great loss of life and resources and is humiliated by the failure to prevent the Dragonkind from breaking out of the desert in such force. Although Vanara itself was spared the brunt of the invasion, many areas were depopulated to supply the needed armies, leaving farms and fields untended for over a year, and workshops and trading floors idle. Glareth and Duinnor, however, are relatively unscathed, and they continue to grow in power, with Duinnor soon consolidating its rule over the other Realms of the world.

Second Age, Year 326
The Year of the Button (8th Year of the 5th Unknown King of Duinnor)
Thousands of Men migrate from the east to Vanara by invitation of Queen Serith Ellyn. Most had lost their livelihoods and possessions during the Dragonkind invasion. But Serith Ellyn had been deeply impressed by their their bravery and loyalty during the battles to expel the invaders. This effectively ends all persecution of Men in Vanara by the Elifaen, and it garners an abiding loyalty of the Men of Vanara to the Queen and her Realm. Amongst those who remove to Vanara are the survivors of the mortal House of Seafar, whose descendants will rise to hold great power in Vanara. This migration also begins the growth of the population of Men in Vanara and within a few hundred years they will be equal in number to the Elifaen.

In Duinnor, the King commands that scholars make an attempt to decipher certain old tablets, scrolls, and manuscripts. The two dozen items are delivered to the Academy, and, under guard, many scholars gather in an attempt to do as the King wishes. Some are written in peculiar runes, while others are cast into clay tablets in the form of cuneiform symbols. It is apparent that they pertain to the early Elifaen history of the First Age, or perhaps before, but none can make sense of them. Some believe they are part of the vast horde of writings that were smuggled into Duinnor during the Purge of Scholars over 400 years earlier. They have little success until a Melnari called Raynor arrives and is able to translate the writing. Most pertain to mundane events during the reign of King Silmain of Vanara, but two of the tablets contain tales relating to how Aperion summoned the High Houses of the Elifaen and gave them the Forty-Nine Bloodcoins.

Second Age, Year 331
The Year of the Quill (13th Year of the 5th Unknown King of Duinnor)
This would be the last year of the Fifth Unknown King of Duinnor. He had many notable accomplishments, including vast road-building projects and the construction of the Locks of Karthia (although he would not live to see that project completed). However, he would be remembered primarily for his failure to forestall the Dragonkind invasion or to relieve Tulith Attis before its defenders were massacred.

Second Age, Year 332
The Year of the Silver Chalice (1st Year of the 6th Unknown King of Duinnor)
The Sixth Unknown King assumes the throne of Duinnor after what is perceived as an intense battle between the old king and the challenger within the Royal Palace during a mighty storm over the city. The first year of the Sixth Unknown King begins with the Year of the Silver Chalice.

Second Age, Year 343
The Year of the Golden Ring (11th Year of the 6th Unknown King of Duinnor)
The Second Demon War begins as demons, witches, and other creatures reemerge into the world. They blight the Plains of Bletharn (southeast of Duinnor) and terrorize the Carthanes. Nearly simultaneously, a great demon appears in the Dragonlands, along with many witches that act as his followers. Seeking flesh to eat, they conduct many raids and disrupt trade and commerce between the desert provinces. Vanara is not spared, as raids take place along its northeastern frontiers and in the southern mountains.

Many of these creatures have the power to enchant and smite entire regions with spells and incantations, allowing the witches and lesser demons to easily ensnare, enslave, or devour their victims. Preferring lairs that are underground, behind waterfalls, or within lakes, they are difficult to find and kill. Like the previous Demon War, both the Dragonlands and the north are plagued by these creatures.

Second Age, Year 347
The Year of the Giant Tortoise (15th Year of the 6th Unknown King of Duinnor)
The first mention of Collandoth occurs within Duinnor annals of this year. He is named as a great witch hunter, but is, in fact, only one member of an elite company of hunters from the Duinnor region. A brief accord is reached with the Dragonkind, and these hunters are invited south to assist in the eradication of witches in those lands. Most of the company refuse, but Collandoth and eight others agree, meeting with great success, and they are indirectly accorded high honors by King Xurnon IV. During this time, Collandoth and company are sometimes called the Nine Banes of Duinnor.

Second Age, Year 354
The Year of the Firefly (22nd Year of the 6th Unknown King of Duinnor)
Having completed their mission in the deserts, the Nine Banes of Duinnor are recalled to face a final threat in the northeast forests of Vanara. Five are killed in battle before the witch is vanquished. As a result of this costly encounter, the reputation of the surviving members of the group is greatly diminished, and there is resentment on the part of the families of those who are killed. For a number of years, Collandoth is shunned by all but a few, and becomes a wanderer and, later, a Watcher, his earlier deeds mostly forgotten.

The Eastlands continue into general decline. After the Dragonkind invasion, people are reluctant to resettle the region. Once-fertile fields go unplanted, and many villages and towns are never rebuilt, while others are simply abandoned. There is also unrest and growing resentment against new taxes levied by King Inrick of Colleton and the tributes collected for Duinnor. Riots are so common in Colleton that Inrick rarely ventures forth, and his small army is hard-pressed to keep order. Meanwhile, in other parts of the Eastlands, people go hungry and many choose to migrate north to Glareth or south into Tracia.

Second Age, Year 355
The Year of the Bellows (23rd Year of the 6th Unknown King of Duinnor)
The King's Academy is founded, consolidating many training facilities within Duinnor. It is located within the confines of a large estate within Duinnor City. Its first Head Scholar is Raynor the Melnari, who organizes the instruction of cadets in academic matters such as reading, writing, mathematics, engineering, and history, subjects that the King has expressly ordered all Kingsmen to be

trained in besides their usual military training. Under Raynor, the Academy will grow into the largest and most prestigious center of learning in Duinnor.

Second Age, Year 357
The Year of the Iron-shod Chest (25th Year of the 6th Unknown King of Duinnor)
The House of Tallin is recognized by Duinnor as a Named House of Men in honor of Leander Tallin, who was killed during the defense of Tulith Attis. The honor is bestowed upon his surviving son, Ullinessin, at the same time that many Men are similarly recognized by Duinnor in an effort to quell discontent. Ullinessin is also granted extensive land holdings in what would later be known as Tallinvale. He lays the first foundations of what would become Tallin Hall, and the structure that he builds utilizes timbers carefully preserved by his forebears from one of the old city-ships that first brought Men to the world. Tallin Hall would be added upon time and again by the generations of Tallins to follow, and would eventually be surrounded by a thriving town.

Extensive lands in the Eastlands nearby to Tulith Attis are also granted to Lowry Bosk, grandson of Bilaylin the Hammer who fought and died at Tulith Attis. In exchange, Bosk and his heirs would be required to see to the defense of the region by maintaining arms for that purpose. The lands are already occupied by members of the Bosk family, and they would eventually become an Honored House, with the right to petition the Kings of Duinnor. The Bosk holdings (called Boskland) take up most of what would later be called County Barley, but would shrink over time as various parcels are sold or deeded away.

The Locks of Karthia are completed, and soon the River Osterflo will become the primary trade route between Duinnor and Glareth. As a result, both Glareth and Duinnor prosper, while Tracia and the Eastlands diminish in power, wealth, and influence.

Second Age, Year 362
The Year of the Broom (30th Year of the 6th Unknown King of Duinnor)
In the Eastlands Realm, King Inrick of Colleton dies and is replaced by his son, Inrick II. He will continue his father's levies of heavy tribute and taxation, which will further stifle trade with Colleton and with the Eastlands in general. He will also antagonize both Glareth and Tracia by demanding tariffs of Tracian ships that come to Eastlands ports or any ships bound for Tracia from Glareth.

King Thalamir of Glareth, under growing pressure from Duinnor, abdicates. However, he negotiated several important concessions, including naming his son Hereditary Ruling Prince of Glareth Realm, and the provision that none serving the Ruling Prince of Glareth would be required to serve as Kingsmen. King Thalamir's abdication will ensure the resumption of trade between Duinnor and Glareth, which badly needs the relief from a famine that threatens the realm. Indeed, many Glarethians believe that Thalamir only abdicated so that Duinnor would guarantee shipments of badly needed grain and food, a feeling that only increased his people's already strong support for the House of Beech.

Under Thalamir, Glareth has risen to become a powerful economic and military force, and its growing navy and maritime industries will continue to play an important role in history as the
Second Age progresses. Thalamir was also responsible for instituting laws to protect the rights of citizens of Glareth Realm regardless of their race or family status (that is, whether Elifaen or mortal, and whether lord or commoner). The system of feudal lords and inconsistent laws that predated Thalamir will give way to uniform codes of justice and a judicial system relatively free from

corruption. During his last years, he successfully advocated for a bicameral parliamentary system of rule under a Pact of Governance that codified the Glareth legal system.

Second Age, Year 420
The Year of the Winecork (88th Year of the 6th Unknown King of Duinnor)
In Colleton, a conflict of feuding lords erupts upon the death of King Inrick II who has no heir. This quickly spreads throughout the coastal region as people refuse to pay taxes or tribute previously forced of them by the King. Lord Barsus, nephew of the dead king, manages to gain power, declaring himself king, and proclaims that the Eastlands will no longer be subservient to Duinnor. This fuels riots and further bloodshed around Colleton, and the city is almost entirely destroyed by fire.

Late in the year, combined forces from the Attis region and from Glareth converge on Colleton to force the ouster of Lord Barsus, who is killed in the fighting. Afterwards, Lord Tallin of Tallinvale is offered guardianship over the Eastlands as a Duinnor Prince, but he declines, serving to incite resentment against the House of Tallin by Duinnor. These events lead to the failure and dissolution of the Eastlands as an autonomous realm. Glareth is granted stewardship over the Eastlands, but disputes immediately spring up between Glareth and Tracia over territories bordering Eastlands and Tracia. This begins what is called by historians, the Era of Concession. During this fifty-year period, Duinnor exerts its power and wealth to impose its law upon the other Realms. Through tribute, intrigue, and trading might, Duinnor weakens the thrones of all the other Realms. One by one, the ruling houses of these realms falter, and their thrones are removed to Duinnor. At the end of this period, only Vanara and Glareth are still ruled directly by its sovereigns, though both Realms must pay what amounts to heavy tribute to Duinnor, and must enforce Duinnor Law within their realms (with a few minor exceptions).

In Duinnor, Lord Harstaff, First Lord of the High Chamber, dies mysteriously. The King appoints Lord Banis to take his place, becoming second in power only to the King. The black eagles that would later be associated with Banis take up their normal roost on the King's Tower where his High Chamber is located.

Esildre, daughter of Lord Banis, goes to Shatuum and becomes concubine of Secundur.

Second Age, Year 470
The Year of the Rudder (138th Year of the 6th Unknown King of Duinnor)
Duinnor Law and the King's Rule are imposed by various means on all the Seven Realms. Houses of Elifaen and certain Houses of Men are required to be recognized by Duinnor. Service to Duinnor is required of each Named House. The eldest living son of each House, or the Head of Household, is required upon pain of death to serve in the King's Army. If there is no son, heavy tribute must be paid by the House, or else its lands and property may be confiscated. In exchange, the estates of the Named Houses are to be recognized and protected by Duinnor. The minimum term of service for each Kingsman is twenty-five years or until released from active duty. From the most distinguished ranks are selected the Palace Guard and members of other important units. Over time, the Kingsman ranks are opened to professional soldiers who have distinguished themselves in other armies of Duinnor. Eventually, the Kingsman forces will number over 35,000 soldiers of all disciplines and will be divided into eight armies. Duinnor will continue to form and maintain its Regular Army and other armies of lesser prestige and discipline, mainly to provide fodder for the southern wars.

Second Age, Year 483
The Year of the Loom (151st Year of the 6th Unknown King of Duinnor)
The first census of the world takes place. Ordered by Duinnor, it is to be performed each year. Each person must sign a book attesting to his name and age, as well as the names and ages of all members of his household. Other information must also be provided, such as occupation, and certain aspects of property. Every county, shire, town, and village must comply or face steep fines and tributes. In most Realms, this accounting is performed in the autumn of the year, traditionally incorporated into the harvest celebrations. Since an annual oath of loyalty to Duinnor must also be made, it is normally part of these duties and is often called "The Renewing."

Lord Banis's son, Navis, leads a small expedition to Shatuum in an effort to free his sister from Secundur. He is never seen again.

Second Age, Year 485
The Year of the Whetstone (153rd Year of the 6th Unknown King of Duinnor)
The first Leases of Forfeiture are taken by Duinnor on properties and estates in Vanara. These follow a general policy of confiscating property belonging to Houses that do not send their eldest son to serve in the Kingsmen ranks and are unable to pay the penalties for not sending an elder son or for having no elder son to send. New laws, instituted by Lord Banis, expand Forfeiture rules so that any property in any realm may be given over to Duinnor by lease, giving the King all rights to manage or dispose of the property. In order to preserve the property rights to one's land, heavy fees, called a Lease Tax, must be paid each year to Duinnor. By various means, Duinnor begins pressuring citizens of Vanara to leave their lands and properties. Strongly opposed by Queen Serith Ellyn and rulers of other realms, Duinnor threatens to withdraw military support or to levy tariffs on trade. However, Duinnor delicately manages its lease policies so that land acquisition is gradual. Many people will refuse to give Duinnor leases until forced to do so. Many of those who abandon their properties leave Vanara in an effort to reestablish themselves in other realms. Many travel to Glareth.

These practices are not supported by all in Duinnor. Some view them as contrary to basic principles of civil morality, while many conservative elements within Duinnor view the practice as undermining Vanara's ability to act as a defensive buffer against the Dragonkind.

Second Age, Year 491
The Year of the Golden Flame (159th Year of the 6th Unknown King of Duinnor)
Fearing that an influx of wealth from Vanara to Glareth may lead to powerful new alliances between arriving Elifaen and Glarethians, Duinnor imposes the Road Tax. This compels each municipality, village, town, and county outside Vanara to exact a fee upon any Vanaran Elifaen traveling through it. However, it is left to each local authority to decide the amount of the fee to be levied upon each Vanaran traveler, and Duinnor requires that only one-third of the fee may be kept by the local authority, the rest to be sent to Duinnor. As a result, very few Vanarans who are forced to leave Vanara as a result of the Duinnor leases arrive in Glareth with their wealth intact. Duinnor, acting as though to relax these requirements, makes a provision in the law that permits Elifaen to travel through Duinnor lands without fee. However, to travel from Duinnor to Glareth down the River Osterflo requires the purchase of boats and the hiring of boatmen. The fees and taxes upon these activities bring new revenues to Duinnor, and more than make up for the loss of Road Taxes collected.

Naturally, the Road Tax is extremely unpopular in Vanara. Queen Serith Ellyn is outraged by it, and sends vehement protests to Duinnor, threatening to cut off all trade and to expel all Duinnor citizens, including Duinnor military forces. At the same time Queen Serith Ellyn will secretly negotiate with

Altoria and Glareth so that the Road Tax is not fully enforced in those realms, and so that travelers from Vanara to Altoria may go unmolested down the Iridelin to Draymoor, where they may board ships to Glareth.

Vanara's protests and threats are ignored by Duinnor. The King knows that Vanara relies upon Duinnor trade and Duinnor military support against the Dragonkind.

Second Age, Year 493
The Year of the Scythe (161st Year of the 6th Unknown King of Duinnor)
Duinnor begins to place markers around the borders of Nasakeeria in an effort to warn and forbid travelers from crossing the ring of bones that so many choose to ignore. The markers are pillars of stone, standing eight feet high, each with a large carving of a skull at the top. Also, each marker is inscribed with a written warning for all to turn back. Beginning at the westernmost border of Nasakeeria, Duinnor seeks to place a marker approximately every three to five hundred yards, proceeding north and eastward. However, the project is beset with difficulties, controversy, and delays. It will be nearly sixty years before it is completed.

Second Age, Year 499
The Year of the Seashell (167th Year of the 6th Unknown King of Duinnor)
Queen Serith Ellyn, in an effort to alleviate those facing foreclosure of their estates, seeks to purchase their leases. However, she soon discovers that this procedure would drain the treasury of Vanara with little return, and it is abandoned.

Second Age, Year 505
The Year of the Hooded Cloak (173rd Year of the 6th Unknown King of Duinnor)
A Great Storm of torrential rains and high winds batters the eastern coasts of the world, destroying towns and villages in southern Glareth and all along the coast of the Eastlands. Ships docked at Colleton are pushed far inland by the storm's surge, and much of the city is inundated by water. Ishtorgus, the Melnari who was instrumental in bringing about Glareth's maritime power, is lost when the ship he is aboard is driven far out to sea and is then swallowed by a maelstrom.

Second Age, Year 506
The Year of the Broad-Rimmed Hat (174th Year of the 6th Unknown King of Duinnor)
An army of Dragonkind break through into Vanara, swinging east to avoid battle, and march swiftly northward toward Duinnor. Serith Ellyn sends a warning to Duinnor and dispatches forces in pursuit, but they trail far behind the Dragonkind. Before any opposing armies encounter each other, the Dragonkind enter the mysterious region of Nasakeeria along its southern borders where there are not yet any warning pillars. The Dragonkind army is devoured by flames as they cross the border.

Second Age, Year 548
The Year of the Horseshoe (216th Year of the 6th Unknown King of Duinnor)
The last of the stone pillars intended to serve as warning markers surrounding Nasakeeria are put in place. Nasakeeria is now encircled by such markers every few hundred yards, and completes a long and costly project.

Second Age, Year 572
The Year of the Rope (240th Year of the 6th Unknown King of Duinnor)
The Yellow Death, a pandemic, spreads through the west. It is a disabling fever, and so many fall ill

and die that trade with the east falters. Glareth, fearing it may spread to its Realm, imposes a blockade of all boats coming down the River Osterflo and seeks to quarantine itself from the rest of the world.

Second Age, Year 575
The Year of the Shovel (243rd Year of the 6th Unknown King of Duinnor)
The Yellow Death reaches all of the Realms and spreads throughout the Dragonlands. One in five of the race of Men die, and one in three of the Dragonkind, but the Elifaen are not affected. In the west, heavy snowfall and severe cold kill many who are weakened by the years of plague. In the spring, the Osterflo and other rivers flood their banks, destroying many towns and vast areas of cropland.

In the east, Glareth is severely damaged by the flooding Osterflo. The Yellow Death plagues the Eastlands and Tracia, and, in the south, Altoria and Masurthia suffer terrible losses due to the fever.

Second Age, Year 590
The Year of the Waterfall (258th Year of the 6th Unknown King of Duinnor)
Impoverished by years of famine and plague, Duinnor struggles to reassert itself. Other Realms fair no better, and have little to offer Duinnor in the way of tribute or trade. The influence of all Realms declines, and in many places the law and its enforcement are left in the hands of local authorities. Vast areas of the eastern realms are depopulated, and many towns and cities are abandoned.

Esildre escapes from Shatuum and Secundur, but not before she is cursed by Secundur. She travels first to Vanara, where she learns of the fate of her brother, but is shunned by her sister, who blames her for their brother's death, and by others due to her relationship with Secundur.

Second Age, Year 620
The Year of the Pitcher (288th Year of the 6th Unknown King of Duinnor)
The first of a series of warlords vies for power in the Thunder Mountains.

Esildre takes up residence in a remote castle in the northern territory of Vanara. She will soon acquire a reputation for hosting orgies that result in the madness and death of many of her guests. Tales of her debauchery reach far and wide and further sully her reputation.

Second Age, Year 682
The Year of the Blinding Light (alternatively called by some scholars the Year of the Lightning Bolt) (350th Year of the 6th Unknown King of Duinnor)
Small, short wars continue to spring up between the Dragonkind and those of the North. The Dragonkind twice invade Vanara, only to be repulsed by the combined forces of Vanara and Duinnor.

Esildre mysteriously expels all guests from her castle and will become a recluse, surrounded only by her blind servants, who are immune to her curse.

Second Age, Year 698
The Year of the Broken Spectacles (366th Year of the 6th Unknown King of Duinnor)
Duinnor imposes a standard of weights and measures to be used in commerce. Other realms adopt these standards fairly quickly, but retain some of their own local standards, too.

    Examples of the King's Measure:
            1 pound = 16 ounces = 1/4 stone

1 yard = 3 feet = 2 cubits
1 mile = 1/3 league = 8 furlongs

Furthermore, Duinnor insists that all trade with Duinnor be done using the King's Silver and Gold, a monetary standard:

1 Duinnor Silver is to be one King's Ounce in weight
1 Duinnor Gold is to be 1/2 King's Ounce in weight
1 Duinnor Gold coin is to be equal to 10 Duinnor Silvers
1 Duinnor Penny is to be equal to 1/100th Duinnor Gold

Duinnor also declares that any Duinnor Coin be exchanged for no less than 1 and 1/10th the equivalent weight in "foreign" metal. In trade, the additional King's Tenth is to be demanded in favor of Duinnor and provided to the King on all trade transactions, regardless of the coin or medium of exchange.

Second Age, Year 704
The Year of the Weather Vane (372nd Year of the 6th Unknown King of Duinnor)
The Dragon Empire, still weakened by the plagues of the previous centuries, struggles to reestablish control within its territories, while at the same time it conducts raids upon Vanaran lands.

Second Age, Year 723
The Year of the Washboard (391st Year of the 6th Unknown King of Duinnor)
A treaty of peace is reached between the Dragonkind and the Seven Realms, and lasts for eight months before it is shattered when an ambassador from the Dragonkind is assassinated in Vanara.

Raynor, who has been the longtime head of the King's Academy, is ousted amid accusations that he is a spy for other Realms and even the Dragonkind. The accusations are blatantly false, but Raynor loses his position. He will become a bookseller, copyist, and tutor.

Second Age, Year 734
The Year of the Hammer (402nd Year of the 6th Unknown King of Duinnor)
Renewed warfare between the Dragonkind and Vanara. Duinnor establishes a permanent military presence in Vanara.

Second Age, Year 750
The Year of the Fog (418th Year of the 6th Unknown King of Duinnor)
Danig Tallin is born in Vanara, son of Metlar Tallin and Lady Carylla (née Spritsul)

Second Age, Year 765
The Year of the Saddle (433rd Year of the 6th Unknown King of Duinnor)
The House of Fairoak is forced to lease its lands in Vanara to Duinnor. Members of its house scatter, but Lady Kahryna remains in Vanara for a time.

Second Age, Year 768
The Year of the Perfume Bottle (436th Year of the 6th Unknown King of Duinnor)
Danig Tallin attends the Kingsman Academy in Duinnor.

Second Age, Year 772
The Year of the Scorpion (440th Year of the 6th Unknown King of Duinnor)
Danig Tallin graduates from the Kingsman Academy and is assigned to the Kingsman Fourth Army.

Second Age, Year 776
The Year of the Rainbow (444th Year of the 6th Unknown King of Duinnor)
A renegade Dragonkind leads a small army through the Blue Mountains and establishes a fortified encampment near Ladentree, conducting raids and disrupting trade between Ladentree and the Free City of Kajarahn. Serith Ellyn sends her brother Thurdun to lead a small army of Fellfaere against the Dragonkind. With them go a battalion of the Kingsman Fourth Army. The siege of the Dragonkind encampment lasts a week until it is overrun by Northmen forces. Danig Tallin, fresh out of the Academy, is attached to the Kingsman Fourth as a young officer, and he distinguishes himself by engaging and killing the Dragonkind general in personal combat.

Second Age, Year 779
The Year of the Crutch (447th Year of the 6th Unknown King of Duinnor)
The Dragonkind send a large army from the Green Citadel to the Khanhar Pass and begin erecting fortifications.

Second Age, Year 781
The Year of the Burning Brazier (449th Year of the 6th Unknown King of Duinnor)
Danig Tallin and the Kingsman Fourth Army join with Fellfaere on an assault of Khanhar Pass, to prevent the Dragonkind from completing their fortification work. They are met in the Blue Mountains north of the pass and a three-week battle ensues. The Dragonkind are reinforced from the south, but the Northmen succeed in driving them back into their incomplete fortifications at Khanhar Pass. Joined by fresh armies from Vanara and Duinnor, a second battle begins, and the Dragonkind abandon the pass and retreat. The victorious Northmen resume the work of the Dragonkind, seeking to make the pass secure from future attack, but, like the Dragonkind before them, they are hampered by shortages of water and supplies. Over the next five years, the Khanhar Pass will change hands several times with neither side able to hold the pass for very long. By the year 788, the pass will be abandoned by both sides, although each will continue to send forays through it to harass the other.

Second Age, Year 785
The Year of the Dice (453rd Year of the 6th Unknown King of Duinnor)
Danig Tallin meets and marries Kahryna of the House of Fairoak. Their time together is cut short as Danig is sent back to be stationed at Khanhar Pass, which has once again been taken from the Dragonkind.

Second Age, Year 786
The Year of the Thorn Vine (454th Year of the 6th Unknown King of Duinnor)
Danig Tallin, now a general of the Kingsman Fourth Army, must defend Khanhar Pass with few men and dwindling supplies against a well-equipped force of Dragonkind. He is forced to withdraw all of his soldiers from the various outlying keeps and fortifications to the central fortress at the center of the pass. However, he is well-prepared, and by using cleverly constructed outer works, and by strictly rationing his supplies, he wears down the Dragonkind who are never able to breach his defenses. After a six-week siege, the Dragonkind, exhausted, frustrated, and facing shortages of food and water, withdraw. Danig is hailed as a great general.

Second Age, Year 787
The Year of the Lady's Fan (455th Year of the 6th Unknown King of Duinnor)
Danig Tallin is recalled to Duinnor, where he is given a hero's welcome. He and his wife are feted and celebrated, and the King, in a rare public ceremony, bestows Tallin with the Ring of Valor. Within a few weeks of their stay, they learn that it has been decided to abandon Khanhar Pass, which infuriates and disappoints Tallin. He is given an assignment to advise the Fourth Army's training battalion, and he and Kahryna will stay in Duinnor for a year while he does so.

Second Age, Year 789
The Year of the Dark Window (457th Year of the 6th Unknown King of Duinnor)
Danig is reassigned back to Vanara and is put in charge of overseeing the security of Ladentree. Since his parents and his wife live in Linlally, he will travel extensively back and forth from Ladentree, Linlally, and Duinnor.

Second Age, Year 790
The Year of the Blue Jay (458th Year of the 6th Unknown King of Duinnor)
Dalvenpar Tallin is born.

Second Age, Year 791
The Year of the Lady's Comb (459th Year of the 6th Unknown King of Duinnor)
Aram Tallin is born

Second Age, Year 793
The Year of the Spoon (461st Year of the 6th Unknown King of Duinnor)
Lord and Lady Tallin of Vanara die of fever while their son Danig is away in Duinnor. Upon his return to Vanara, he is confirmed as Lord and Liege of Tallinvale.

Mirabella Tallin is born

Second Age, Year 795
Year of the Carved Horse (463rd Year of the 6th Unknown King of Duinnor)
Gurasa is born in the Dragonlands.

Second Age, Year 800
The Year of the Millstone (468th Year of the 6th Unknown King of Duinnor)
Having given more than the usual twenty-five years of service as Kingsman, Lord Tallin is granted a discharge with the rank of general. He departs the west with his family and takes them to Glareth while he sees to the restoration and remodeling of Tallin Manor in what is now known as Tallinvale.

Second Age, Year 801
The Year of the Fireplace (469th Year of the 6th Unknown King of Duinnor)
The trolls that occupy the eastern Thunder Mountains completely disappear, as if overnight.

The walls of what is later known as Tallin City, in Tallinvale, mysteriously appear this year. Danig Tallin will never say how they came to be constructed. During the next two years, he works feverishly to complete the defense works of the walls and to coax people to come and settle in the town and region. By offering generous leases and numerous titles to property within Tallinvale, he entices many tradespeople and skilled craftsmen from Glareth and elsewhere, in addition to farmers and laborers. He establishes a civil government made up of counselors and a mayor who are all elected, a fair taxation system to support the government and schools, and to maintain infrastructure such as roads and bridges. During the next few years, the valley fills with farms and villages. The population of the region, including Tallin City, rapidly grows, and the citizens of Tallinvale will become some of the most prosperous people in the Eastlands Realm.

Second Age, Year 803
The Year of the Dragonfly (471st Year of the 6th Unknown King of Duinnor)
Lord Tallin brings his family to live in Tallinvale. The renovation and expansion of Tallin Hall, their new home, is nearly complete. Lord Tallin will soon organize a defensive force for Tallinvale and for Tallin City, as the new walled town surrounding Tallin Hall is called. Under his leadership, the town and surrounding valley will rapidly grow and prosper.

Second Age, Year 805
The Year of the Baby Rattler (473rd Year of the 6th Unknown King of Duinnor)
A new treaty with the Dragonkind is reached.

Second Age, Year 806
The Year of the Looking Glass (474th Year of the 6th Unknown King of Duinnor)
The growing discontent with the King's Tenth results in a reduction of the trade and tax rates, and other tributes to 1/100th and is thereafter called the "King's Own Penny," or kingspenny. Enforcement and collection of these taxes will continue to vex Duinnor due to the complexities of trade agreements, special favors granted by the Crown, and the logistics of transporting the collectors and the treasure they collect across vast distances. The collectors require armed escorts for protection, and these escorts, usually Kingsmen, often serve as intimidation in order to enforce tax collection.

Second Age, Year 807
The Year of the Scare Crow (475th Year of the 6th Unknown King of Duinnor)
Collandoth travels to Tyrsharat in the Dragonlands on the behalf of Duinnor and Vanara, where he will seek to negotiate certain trade accords. His previous experience within the Dragonlands and his reputation as one of the Nine Banes opens many doors to him, but he is treated with suspicion. However, he chances to meet a young Dragonkind boy named Gurasa. Gurasa, enthusiastic to learn all that Collandoth can tell him about the Northlands, impresses the Melnari with his intellect, curiosity, charm, and kindly nature. When Collandoth departs to return to the north, he reluctantly agrees to take Gurasa along with him. However, fearing the boy would be persecuted for being a Dragonkind, Collandoth arranges a convincing disguise for the boy. Their first stop is Linlally.

Second Age, Year 808
The Year of the Plough (476th Year of the 6th Unknown King of Duinnor)
With Collandoth acting as his guide and guardian, Gurasa travels throughout Vanara before setting out for Duinnor.

Second Age, Year 809
The Year of the Glass Ax (477th Year of the 6th Unknown King of Duinnor)
Lord Tallin travels to Duinnor to carry a proper accounting of the tribute and treasure taken from Tallinvale and the surrounding regions. He shows that Duinnor's tax men have been engaged in embezzlement and begins a process by which many others will bring proof of the Treasury Minister's incompetence. Tallin has brought with him his son, Dalvenpar, and together they visit the Temple of Beras. While Tallin meets with various monks on private business, his son Dalvenpar meets Gurasa, who is in company with Collandoth. Gurasa accompanies the Tallins back to Duinnor for sightseeing,

and the three quickly become friends. Together they will travel east, first to Glareth by the Sea and then on to Tallinvale, where Gurasa will stay for several months as a guest of Tallin Hall. During this time, he and Dalvenpar Tallin become close friends, with the older Dalvenpar acting as Gurasa's brotherly protector and teacher.

Second Age, Year 811
The Year of the Melon Slice (479th Year of the 6th Unknown King of Duinnor)
Dalvenpar Tallin and Gurasa travel to Glareth by the Sea. There, Gurasa meets Aram Tallin, who is a student at the Glareth Academy. They also meet Sharyn Northstar, a very young girl, the daughter of Aram's sailing instructor.

Second Age, Year 812
The Year of the Hornet (480th Year of the 6th Unknown King of Duinnor)
After traveling extensively throughout the Seven Realms, usually in disguise to avoid harassment, Gurasa returns to the Dragonlands. He promptly has a special ring made and sends it to his friend Dalvenpar. Gurasa continues his travels within the Dragonlands until he is beset with family problems that require him to enlist in the Dragonkind army. Though slight of frame, his intellect and cunning enable him to excel in tactics and leadership.

Dalvenpar Tallin receives the ring from Gurasa. He wears it proudly as he, his brother, and his sister sit for a portrait. Soon after, he departs Tallinvale for Duinnor to become a Kingsman.

Second Age, Year 817
The Year of the Dewy Spider Web (485th Year of the 6th Unknown King of Duinnor)
Aram Tallin travels back to Glareth on business and visits his old sailing instructor, Miles Northstar. He becomes reacquainted with his daughter, Sharyn, now 14 years old, and they fall in love.

Second Age, Year 818
The Year of the Shepard's Flute (486th Year of the 6th Unknown King of Duinnor)
Robigor Ribbon is born to Hannis and Beatrice Ribbon of County Barley in the Eastlands.

Second Age, Year 820
The Year of the Milk Stool (488th Year of the 6th Unknown King of Duinnor)
Aram Tallin weds Sharyn of the Glarethian House of Northstar (a house of Men). The two take up residence at the Tallin estate in Tallinvale.

In the Eastlands, many succumb to fever. Among those who are stricken are Hannis and Beatrice Ribbon, but their young son, Robigor, survives to be raised by his grandfather, Balfast.

Second Age, Year 821
The Year of the Bellows (489th Year of the 6th Unknown King of Duinnor)
Renewed hostilities break out between Vanara and the Dragonlands. Several villages in the southern Vanaran hills are attacked and destroyed, its people killed or taken away as slaves into the deserts. Trade with the Free City of Kajarahn (formerly known as Alaberbra) is disrupted.

Second Age, Year 827
The Year of the River Stone (495th Year of the 6th Unknown King of Duinnor)
Vanara is forced by Duinnor to participate in an ambitious invasion of the Dragonlands. Six armies cross the southern mountains into the desert and march on the Green Citadel, which is believed to be

the base from which the Dragonkind organize and launch attacks on the north. The invading forces are composed of Fellfaere, Kingsmen, and Duinnor Regulars, and small units from other Realms. This will be the first of two bloody and costly campaigns against the city. The northern forces lay siege and launch ferocious attacks which soon breach the city's defenses, and a fury of fighting and destruction takes place within the city. There is much looting, including by the city's own people, and atrocities are committed by both sides. After the city is successfully overwhelmed and sacked by northern forces, they are harried on their retreat by newly arrived and reorganized Dragonkind armies, and there are thousands of casualties. In the aftermath, the retreat would come to be called the Road of Dry Blood. Among its casualties is Dalvenpar Tallin.

Gurasa, who has become a great and powerful general of the Dragonkind, is made a scapegoat for the disaster and he is put on trial for his failure to prevent the sacking of the Green Citadel. After a long drawn-out trial, lasting almost two years, he will be vindicated, but his career is ended and he is a broken man, shunned by many of his former colleagues.

Second Age, Year 829
The Year of the Battering Ram (497th Year of the 6th Unknown King of Duinnor)
Gurasa, now officially vindicated of any failure to prevent the sack of the Green Citadel, is awarded an honored retirement and is removed from service to King Belsalza. Although very popular with the Dragonkind people, Gurasa is thus shunned by those in favor with Belsalza, and his forced retirement ends his military career. He returns to his home in the desert town of Almedian, where he is received as a hero.

Second Age, Year 833
The Year of the Harp (501st Year of the 6th Unknown King of Duinnor)
The King's collectors (tax men) do not go forth from Duinnor due to failures on the part of Duinnor's ruling class to agree upon how the taxes and tributes are to be assessed. The King is asked to intervene, but he does not act. Meanwhile, tributes and taxes collected by local magistrates all over the Seven Realms remain in their collection places for the first time in memory.

Second Age, Year 836
The Year of the Snowflake (504th Year of the 6th Unknown King of Duinnor)
Ullin Saheed Tallin is born, son of Aram and Sharyn Tallin of Tallinvale.

Second Age, Year 839
The Year of the Rotten Meat (507th Year of the 6th Unknown King of Duinnor)
After resisting the King's Summons for several years, Aram Tallin departs Tallinvale to become a Kingsman in his brother's place. He is followed some weeks later by his sister, Mirabella. She stays in Duinnor during Aram's training and undertakes private studies of her own and is tutored in history, the art of war, and the use of the bow and sword.

In the Dragonlands, Gurasa's wife bears him a daughter, called Micerea. Later in the year, a fever sweeps through the village of Almedian. Micerea is spared, but her mother is severely weakened, and all of her three older brothers die. Gurasa, who never falls ill, is nonetheless stricken with grief and depression.

Second Age, Year 841
The Year of the Cricket (509th Year of the 6th Unknown King of Duinnor)
Since Aram Tallin is already well-educated, he only has to complete the military portion of the

training at the King's Academy in Duinnor. When he graduates, he is ordered south to Vanara. Mirabella goes with him.

Second Age, Year 843
The Year of the Thimble (511th Year of the 6th Unknown King of Duinnor)
For the second time, a conquest of the Green Citadel takes place by forces from the Seven Realms. Although the Dragonkind stronghold is barely recovered from the first siege, the Seven Realms fare no better than before. The campaign lasts three years until the city falls. After its plunder, the forces of the north withdraw. They are unmolested until they reach Khanhar Pass, where they are then pursued by a large force of Dragonkind. Fighting a bitter rearguard action through the mountains, the retreating Northmen are bottled up within several canyons where the Dragonkind unleash a series of well-laid ambushes. At one such place, later to be called Gory Gulch, terrible fighting takes place for two days as a beleaguered unit of Kingsmen attempts to fight its way through Dragonkind fighters. Had it not been for a rescue force sent by Vanara, all would have been lost. As it was, three in five Kingsmen are killed, including Aram Tallin. Two days after the remaining Kingsmen survivors are rescued (among which is Aram Tallin's sister, Mirabella), Vanaran forces trap a force of 2,000 Dragonkind in the same place, and a second battle begins. None of the Dragonkind survive.

Gurasa, living in Almedian, hears of the conflict but is not called to duty. He expressly forbids any of his people to join in the defense of the Green Citadel or in the pursuit of the retreating Northmen. As news reaches him of the sack of the Green Citadel and of the subsequent fighting in the Blue Mountains, he sinks deeper in to depression.

Second Age, Year 844
The Year of the Arrow (512th Year of the 6th Unknown King of Duinnor)
Mirabella Tallin returns from the wars with news of her brother's death. Kahryna Tallin dies of grief two days later. Aram's wife Sharyn and her son, Ullin Saheed, depart soon after for Glareth to live with her people.

In the Dragonlands, Gurasa keeps to himself. He dotes on his daughter as his wife grows weaker from a series of illnesses.

Second Age, Year 845
The Year of the Boiling Basin (513th Year of the 6th Unknown King of Duinnor)
Mirabella Tallin, as she did before she ran away with Aram, continues to rebuff potential suitors, and she resists her father's attempts to find a husband for her.

Second Age, Year 846
The Year of the Scales (514th Year of the 6th Unknown King of Duinnor)
In Glareth, Sharyn Tallin reluctantly permits her son, Ullin Saheed Tallin (age 10) to return to Tallinvale. Ullin has been miserable and unhappy in Glareth, and it is her hope that he will be happier with his father's relatives. In Tallinvale, he is received somewhat coolly by his grandfather, Lord Tallin. However, Mirabella dotes on Ullin, he being one of the few people with whom she is willing to keep company. She continues to be reclusive, rebuffing visitors and suitors, and is rarely seen outside of Tallin Hall.

Several attempts are made to scale Tower Vendril in northeastern Duinnor Realm by driving spikes into the tower wall and, by a system of ropes, climbing up its side. However, the first climber dies when a spike gives way and he falls to his death. A month later, a second climber attempts to complete what the first had begun, but he freezes to death when a sudden blizzard sweeps through the region. His body remains dangling on his ropes while his remains are consumed by carrion. For many years, his skeleton can be seen, not even halfway up the tower, and bits of bone and skull rain down periodically as the clothes and ropes holding the corpse together slowly rot away. Those living in the region are outraged at the defacement of what they have come to think of as their own tower, and they put a stop to any further climbing attempts on Tower Vendril.

Second Age, Year 847
The Year of the Ship's Anchor (515th Year of the 6th Unknown King of Duinnor)
Robigor Ribbon, country trader and businessman of County Barley, has purchased a property in Passdale that he intends to make into a sundries shop, renovating the upstairs to make it a suitable home. He takes a shipment of grain to Tallinvale for his friend Garend Bosk. The grain was purchased by Lord Tallin, and Robigor goes to Tallin Hall to receive payment. During the visit, he meets Mirabella Tallin for the first time.

Second Age, Year 848
The Year of the Coral Snake (516th Year of the 6th Unknown King of Duinnor)
Robigor Ribbon weds Mirabella, and they move to Passdale in the County Barley to set up house and to do business in the sundries trade.

Second Age, Year 849
The Year of the Silent Drum (517th Year of the 6th Unknown King of Duinnor)
Robby Ribbon is born to Robigor and Mirabella Ribbon of Passdale.

Second Age, Year 850
The Year of the Tankard (518th Year of the 6th Unknown King of Duinnor)
A daughter is born to Lord and Lady Waterstone, of Tracia Realm, whom they name Shevalia, after Lady Waterstone's deceased mother.

In the Dragonlands, Gurasa's wife dies. His only consolation is his young daughter, upon whom he lavishes his love and affection. He also begins sharing with her his knowledge of the Northlands, telling her stories of his travels and adventures, and he begins secretly training her to ride and to fight with sword and dagger.

Second Age, Year 851
The Year of the Basket (519th Year of the 6th Unknown King of Duinnor)
Frizella Starfind, friend to Mirabella, weds Garend Bosk, a member of the powerful Bosk family, and friend to Robigor Ribbon. Garend Bosk is also Sheriff of Barley. Within the year, they will have a daughter, named Raenelle.

Second Age, Year 852
The Year of the Honeysuckle Vine (520th Year of the 6th Unknown King of Duinnor)
In Tracia, there is widespread unrest as groups of disgruntled lords and factions of the Royal Army seek to break away from Ruling Prince Lewtrah's corrupt rule. Those loyal to the Ruling Prince and his brother, Prince Lantos, are targeted by various intrigues and even outright violence. Lord Waterstone, who is a sharp critic of Lewtrah but nonetheless supports the monarchy, is not spared as his wife is murdered by poison in a bungled attempt to kill him. His daughter, Shevalia, is unharmed.

Bilaylin Bosk is born to Garend and Frizella Bosk. He is named for one of their famous forebears, Bilaylin the Hammer, who died while fighting at Tulith Attis. The boy will be called Billy.

Second Age, Year 853
The Year of the Candle (521st Year of the 6th Unknown King of Duinnor)
Unrest in Tracia breaks out into civil war. Ruling Prince Lewtrah, who is unpopular with the people, is driven from the city and flees to Glareth. Various factions loyal to the Tracian throne fight on, particularly the Prince's brother, Prince Lantos. Antiroyalist forces unite under a triumvirate made up of noblemen Dargos Sagrin, Garg Bonovanti, and former general of the army Usler Vasos. Already, they control most of Tracia, and their followers, in their red surcoats and tunics, quickly overrun the Realm, imposing harsh laws and exacting high tributes. Prince Lantos fights on, but is poorly equipped and has few resources to call upon. Duinnor makes no move to send aid, though Glareth does in the way of naval support to evacuate Prince Lewtrah and his family.

Ullin Saheed Tallin departs for Duinnor to become a Kingsman. This act disappoints his grandfather, Lord Tallin, though it saves Tallinvale from paying the required "tribute in lieu of service." Due to his excellent education in Tallinvale, he will excel in every subject at the King's Academy.

In the Dragonlands, Gurasa and his daughter Micerea travel extensively, going to the Green Citadel, to Kajarahn, and to Tyrsharat. During these travels, he brings Micerea more into his confidence. He encourages her to appear silly and spoiled while in public in order to hide her true strength and her skills.

Second Age, Year 854
The Year of the Lion (522st Year of the 6th Unknown King of Duinnor)
Robby Ribbon falls seriously ill. His symptoms are unusual, and he becomes delirious, racked with chills and fever, and his parents despair. Mirabella sends for her friend, Frizella, who knows folk medicine, but there is little that Frizella can do. Helpless, Robby's parents watch as the boy wastes away. However, two mysterious strangers appear at the door and ask to see the lad. They are Elmira and Belmira, daughters of Lyrium. They stay only for a few hours, speaking to Robby and debating with each other as to whether he should live or not. But they, too, realize that they have no power to influence his condition one way or the other. Yet, the lad seems to respond to their presence, and, in an effort to comfort him, the two sisters softly sing to him. His fever breaks, and the sisters depart as mysteriously as they had appeared as the boy falls into a recuperative sleep.

Within the constellation of Behemoth, the star that is its eye suddenly brightens. Normally dull orange in color, it burns with a blue-white light as bright as the half-moon. Across the world, astrologers search their charts and ponder its meaning. In the far southern reaches of the Dragonlands, the slaves who are made to work the fields of darakal view it as an omen that their liberation is soon to come. After seven days, the star quickly fades until it is a dim glowing remnant of bluish haze.

Steggan Pradkin arrives in County Barley from Tracia after having acquired a farm there. He brings with him his wife and a four-year-old girl whom he calls Sheila, saying that she is his niece and ward.

Second Age, Year 855
The Year of the Hangman's Noose (523rd year of the 6th Unknown King of Duinnor)
Ullin Saheed Tallin graduates with honors from the King's Academy in Duinnor, having completed his initial training almost two years earlier than most. He is sent to Vanara to serve in the desert.

Second Age, Year 856
The Year of the Snuff Box (524th Year of the 6th Unknown King of Duinnor)
A winter fever sweeps across the Eastlands. Robigor Ribbon and many others fall ill. He recovers, but others do not fare as well. By the end of winter, one in every ten people in County Barley, and every member of some families, is dead from the disease. Among the dead are several members of the Bosk family, including Harrald Bosk's two oldest sons, his wife, and his daughter. His youngest son, Garend Bosk, does not become sick, and neither does his wife or his children.

In Tracia, Prince Lantos' land forces are defeated at the Battle of the Marshlands. His navy, which has remained loyal to the throne throughout the civil war, has by now been deprived of supplies and men, but manages to rescue the Prince. Triumvirate naval forces pursue the Prince into Grisland Strait, where a fierce naval engagement ensues. The Prince escapes, owing to the brave and cunning actions of the Golden Swallow, commanded by Captain Martin Makeig, who turns his ship into the Triumvirate pursuers. The Triumvirate ships are all destroyed in the engagement, permitting the Prince to sail away unscathed. Elsewhere, Triumvirate ships and dockyards are sunk and burned by raiding corvettes, and all Loyalist craft are scuttled and burned to avoid their capture. Although defeated at Grisland Strait, the battle effectively seals the Triumvirate's control over all of Tracia. During the following years, the Red Trio, as they are called, will consolidate their power, turning the Realm into a virtual thralldom under their rule. Few estates remain intact as they are taken over by those favored by the Triumvirate. Crop failures and isolation from trade hamper Tracia's new rulers, who gradually move to increase their military forces.

Fresh from the Academy and eager to prove himself, Ullin takes part in the Battle of Garmitor against the Dragonkind, where he leads a platoon of Kingsmen who act as scouts and observers. His platoon bears the brunt of a night attack and Ullin is wounded along with many of his men. However, they hold their position and repulse the enemy until friendly reinforcements arrive, thereby thwarting a flanking move on the part of the Dragonkind. After the battle, he is cited for bravery and leadership and earns a field promotion to lieutenant commander. His eye for detail and his cunning tactics bring him to the notice of his superiors, and he is sent back to Duinnor for further training in as an engineer and mapmaker while he recuperates from his wounds.

Second Age, Year 857
The Year of the Icicle (525th Year of the 6th Unknown King of Duinnor)
Steggan Pradkin takes Sheila to Passdale in his wagon so that he can do business with Robigor Ribbon. He ties her feet so that she cannot escape from the wagon. At the Ribbons' store, Sheila meets Robby for the first time when Robby frees Sheila from the rope that Steggan tied her up with and gives her an apple.

Second Age, Year 858
The Year of the Pine Cone (526th Year of the 6th Unknown King of Duinnor)
Under pressure from the local schoolmaster, Steggan Pradkin tries to force Sheila to attend school. Sheila rebels and receives a severe beating from Steggan and runs away from home, only to be caught stealing eggs from the Gladstens' nearby farm. This prompts a visit by the Sheriff of Barley, who is Mr. Bosk, and a visit by his wife, Frizella.

Ullin Saheed Tallin is sent on a long assignment to the old Eastlands Realm to make improvements to the out-of-date maps. He stays for several months in Passdale with the family of his aunt, Mirabella. As he roams around Barley surveying and making his maps, Sheila Pradkin dogs him, mercilessly pelting him with clots of dirt, and taunting him with names. Ullin retaliates by throwing her into the river, where she finds a basket of soap and other gifts he has left for her.

Second Age, Year 859
The Year of the Longbow (527th Year of the 6th Unknown King of Duinnor)
In the Eastlands, Harrald Bosk, the Laird of Boskland, dies and his son, Garend, becomes the new laird. Among the old laird's accomplishments is the increased productivity of his estate. As well, Harrald Bosk worked with Alfred Greardon of Passdale (who would later become mayor of that town) to bring a school to the county and to find a suitable schoolmaster. When this was done, he prohibited the further use of children as workers anywhere on his estate without them first being able to read and write and perform basic arithmetic to the satisfaction of the schoolmaster, thus forcing parents to send their children to school. He claimed that this was to protect children from accident and injury before they were strong enough to work, and also to ensure that in future years those children would be better workers, craftsmen, and foremen. There was stiff resistance to this, since many children were needed as apprentices from an early age, and Garend Bosk, when he becomes laird, will continue seeking solutions to this conundrum over the next many years.

With the help of his friend Robigor Ribbon, Garend has already increased the wealth of his lands and his people by shipping crops and trade goods far and wide, down the Saerdulin, north to Glareth, and west through Janhaven to other regions. Garend has worked tirelessly since childhood for his estate, unafraid of working fields, repairing buildings and bridges, or whatever is required to see a task done. By the time he becomes Laird and receives the seal of his House, he is already a respected man of County Barley, having twice served as its sheriff. One of his first acts is to declare that all his tenants are to be given a greater share of the fruits of their labors, and he begins a system of paying them an annual wage in silver, and he halts the practice of collecting rent from those workers who live on his lands.

Having shown a great talent for mapmaking and other engineering arts, Ullin Saheed Tallin is recalled by Duinnor to serve again in Vanara on the southern frontier between Vanara and the Dragonlands. He is favored by members of the Duinnor High Command in Vanara and promoted to commander. With the promotion come several important assignments in the Dragonlands.

This summer, Sheila learns to fish, taught by a vagabond old man. Taking inspiration from this, she will also learn to hunt. She thus assures herself of food and begins to become healthier and stronger than before.

Second Age, Year 860
The Year of the Buckmarl (528th Year of the 6th Unknown King of Duinnor)
Mr. Broadweed, the local schoolmaster in County Barley, makes a renewed effort to convince Steggan to allow Sheila to come to his school. He tells Steggan that he will not have to pay for any books or such, but that Sheila must attend regularly. After a long argument with Sheila, she reluctantly agrees to attend, but only does so for a few days, unable to bear the taunts of the other children who make her feel ignorant and scorn her for her manners and behavior. She does not return, and Steggan is more than happy for her to work his farm and to bring meat to his table through her fishing and hunting.

Second Age, Year 861
The Year of the Bronze Helmet (529th Year of the 6th Unknown King of Duinnor)
Mr. Broadweed visits Steggan again and tries to convince him to force Sheila to go to school. Broadweed and Steggan have a heated argument about Sheila's well-being. Mr. Broadweed goes away,

having been told by Steggan that Sheila will not return to his school as she is too much needed on the farm. In spite of this, she often sneaks away to watch the school ground, or to peer into the windows during lessons.

Second Age, Year 862
The Year of the Broken Sword (530th Year of the 6th Unknown King of Duinnor)
Ullin Saheed, while on assignment in the Dragonlands, meets Micerea, daughter of Gurasa.

Second Age, Year 863
The Year of the Clothes Pin (531st Year of the 6th Unknown King of Duinnor)
Ullin Saheed returns to Vanara from a long assignment in the Dragonlands. He is near death, sick from exposure, dehydration, and exhaustion. While recovering in hospital, he meets Collandoth who convinces him to apply to the King's Post as a special courier. Collandoth will unofficially be his direct superior (though Collandoth holds no rank). Collandoth and his secret colleagues use Ullin Saheed as a courier for their clandestine dispatches.

By now, Sheila Pradkin is visiting Frizella Bosk from time to time. Her visits will grow more frequent as Mrs. Bosk takes a liking to Sheila. Sheila brings herbs that she finds in the woods to Mrs. Bosk, and also game from time to time. In turn, Mrs. Bosk teaches Sheila somewhat of plant lore and remedies. However, Sheila's visits are infrequent and often short since she is wary of Mrs. Bosk's daughter, Raenelle. Nevertheless, she will look to Mrs. Bosk for companionship from time to time. It will be Mrs. Bosk who will explain to Sheila the womanly changes that are taking place in her.

Second Age, Year 864
The Year of the Blue Shirt (532nd Year of the 6th Unknown King of Duinnor)
Collandoth and Ullin Saheed travel to the Eastlands. Collandoth takes up residence near Tulith Attis, while Ullin Saheed travels on to Glareth by the Sea to visit his mother, who resides there.

Second Age, Year 865
The Year of the Bread Loaf (533rd Year of the 6th Unknown King of Duinnor)
Ullin Saheed returns to Duinnor. He will continually travel to and from the west and the Eastlands for several years, carrying dispatches sent to and from Duinnor, Vanara, and Glareth by the Sea.

In Glareth by the Sea, exiled Prince Lewtrah dies suddenly. His death is something of a relief to Prince Carbane as well as many Tracian exiles, as he was never popular and was blamed for many of the woes that resulted in their exile. Prince Lantos, Lewtrah's younger brother, is declared the Ruling Prince in Exile by Glareth. Young, handsome, and dashing, his popularity with the Tracian people is immense. Upon hearing the news, there are several failed attempts to assassinate the Red Trio in Tracia, and several Tracian Generals are implicated. This only brings about widespread purges, and many people are imprisoned or executed. Others flee into the Eastlands, Masurthia, or to Glareth by the Sea.

Sheila Pradkin continues to suffer from her uncle's mistreatment. She spends more and more time away from the farm hunting, fishing, or even working the fields with other laborers in Boskland and elsewhere. From time to time, she receives beatings from Steggan, and more than once she fends off drunken assaults upon her.

Gurasa discovers that his daughter Micerea has the ability to dreamwalk, and he arranges a tutor for her.

Second Age, Year 866
The Year of the Pine Sapling (534th Year of the 6th Unknown King of Duinnor)
Robby Ribbon is thrown from his horse while riding nearby to Tulith Attis with his friend Billy Bosk. This happens just as he and Billy come upon the old barrows near the fortress. Robby is not seriously injured, but they spend the rest of the day trying to round up the errant horse. They will never learn what spooked the horse, but since they are forbidden to go there, the misadventure remains their secret.

Second Age, Year 867
The Year of the Battle Lance (535th Year of the 6th Unknown King of Duinnor)
Although Sheila and Robby have encountered each other before, mainly at Boskland, they will form a friendship this year. Robby will strive to teach Sheila to read and write, while Sheila tried to show Robby how to fish. By Midwinter's Day, they will be romantically involved, though it will be a problematic relationship. Sheila will insist that their relationship is to be kept a secret from all. However, over the next two and a half years, it will become more difficult to hide their relationship as they are more often seen together.

Second Age, Year 868
The Year of the Spark (536th Year of the 6th Unknown King of Duinnor)
Micerea is now an active part of Gurasa's conspiracy to bring about some manner of peace between their people and Vanara. He continues to use her as a messenger, but begins to instruct her on the lore of the north pertaining to prophecies that the next king of Duinnor will come from a Joined House. He suspects this will be that of Tallin and Fairoak, and, knowing about Ullin and Micerea's longing for him, he sends her out to look for him and to keep watch on him through dreamwalking. She locates Ullin in Vanara and keeps track of him as he travels from there to Duinnor. She will accompany Ullin, and visit his dreams, as often as she can. But, at her father's request, she does not reveal to Ullin that she is not merely a dream.

Historical Sketches and Tales

Some of the following sketches and summaries were specially prepared by our team for this Reader's Companion, while others contain "tales" based on commonly held views and beliefs of the past ages of the world. Generally, these sketches have been deemed too lengthy to include in the Glossary Section of this Companion. Some of these entries are based on direct eyewitness accounts, while others rely on information and materials produced prior to the end of the Second Age. As well, some information here was widely known (or believed), while some of this information only came to light years later as various documents were uncovered.

Our goal is to give you a flavor of things rather than a comprehensive history. Not only did history obviously shape the outcome of the Year of the Red Door, but it also shaped and channeled what people thought and felt about their past and about the circumstances of their lifetimes. Truth, misconception, lore, legend, and myth all shaped their stories, music, poetry, and art as much as it did their great cities, governments, armies, and conflicts.

****

A Brief History of Men

Although most of the history of Men prior to their coming to the shores of the world was lost, certain tales have been passed down that give a general outline of the events leading up to their arrival. Most of these accounts state that another world once existed far to the east across the Great Sea and was the home of Men. They were long established there, having been created by Beras to populate those lands and to have in those lands homes and farms and cities. It is not known nor speculated by the tellers of these legends how long Men abided in that land, variously called Ur or Atlantis or Panabode. However, it is certain that their race was long established before catastrophe struck.

Various accounts relate that the lands began to shake violently and sink slowly away, that volcanoes sprang up across the land, and that the sea began encroaching steadily upon the coastal regions, slowly inundating towns and cities. Typhoons repeatedly battered the lands, too, causing great loss of life and destruction. It is told that Men began building floating cities to escape the rising waters, complete with small farms and all those things that a city needs. However, no sooner than these cities were built than the sea began rising all the faster as the remaining lands continued to sink away. In the last years, a great shipbuilding effort was made, laying waste to vast forests. It is said that these massive structures were built of wood, copper, and stone, and that each large city was made of interlocking blocks that allowed the sections to move up and down somewhat.

At last, the end came in a series of violent explosions of fire, likely volcanic eruptions, that engulfed the remaining lands before the land altogether subsided beneath waves and noxious fumes. The only survivors were those who already lived upon the city-ships or who managed to take to smaller ships or boats. All told, a dozen city-ships survived the catastrophe, and, by some accounts, they held over forty thousand souls. Knowing that their survival rested upon cooperation and a quick escape from the smoking waters, they quickly organized themselves into a fleet for a voyage away from those doomed waters. Each ship, the largest of which was said to be a furlong wide and over twice as long, erected high, strong towers to act as masts for the hoisting of sails. Systems were devised for rudimental steering and for pumping out seawater, for collecting and storing rainwater for drinking, as well as for growing small crops to supplement the fisheries that developed.

Life aboard was hard. Often there were shortages of food and water. The ships needed constant maintenance and repair, and the materials needed were in short supply. It said that every few years, the seafarers would come upon small islands and that if there were any trees to be had, all were harvested, as well as anything else of use, including animals, birds. After a long while, most subsisted on fish and products made from creatures of the sea. Sometimes special forms of kelp were harvested to make fabric or rope. Many ferocious sea monsters were encountered, and sharks continually infested the waters surrounding the ships. Disease, particularly scurvy, was common. But disputes were few, since their numbers were dwindling and all needed the help of all others in order to survive.

It was claimed that from the time the last Men watched their homeland sink away until the time of their first sighting of the western world was a span of six generations. During this time, much of their history was forgotten, and many previous customs were lost. Only a few examples of their writing remained, mostly bits of words and phrases carved into the timbers of their ships. Knowing no other existence but that of the sea, the people aboard these vessels steadily but slowly sailed westward. Disease and privation took their toll, as did violent storms that stirred crushing waves and devastating winds. Of the twelve city-ships, four were lost within a generation to storms. Two more were abandoned when they became damaged by fire. Another was abandoned when it struck a reef and could not be dislodged, and as much of its timbers and materials were salvaged for use on the remaining five city-ships. By the time the fourth generation was dying away, and the fifth was having young of their own, all five of the great ships were slowly sinking. Only constant pumping and bailing kept them afloat, their timbers rotted, their sails all but gone. When the first sightings of land were made, fewer than twelve thousand souls remained aboard them.

It is recorded by Elifaen chroniclers that Men first came to the shores of the world in the year 1126 of the First Age along the coast of what would later become the Eastlands Realm. During the first year, most of the Newcomers (as they were called by the Elifaen) did not realize that the lands were already occupied, as the wary Elifaen who watched them kept themselves hidden. But the new arrivals immediately set to work clearing and cutting timber for homes, set about hunting and fishing and gathering food from the forests. They brought from their ships iron and other metals, and they took as much timber from the grounded ships as possible.

It was not long, however, before they realized they were being watched. They glimpsed the handsome Elifaen upon their buckmarls and heard the haunting strains of their singing in the woods on moonlit nights. As the first years passed, and they continued to establish themselves, stories began circulating about the strange and beautiful creatures. Hunters told how their prey was inexplicably startled before their arrow could be loosed. Children who became lost in the woods miraculously reappeared, claiming that they were fed and protected by fairies who rode deer. Another tale recounted how one village was facing starvation due to an early frost that destroyed their meager crop, but mysterious strangers appeared, a young man and young woman, and showed them where they could gather enough nuts to survive.

But, for the most part, the Elifaen remained aloof, choosing to keep their distance and to retreat from the settlements of the Newcomers, though they kept vigilant watch over all their activities. At first, they were afraid that these were members of the Dragonkind, so dirty and squalid their lives seemed. But the Elifaen were amazed at the hard work of the Newcomers, their determination to survive, and their short, vulnerable lives. Then, a band of renegade Dragonkind swept through the eastern lands and attacked the villages and towns of Men before the Elifaen could stop them. This was when the Elifaen came to truly fear and respect the Newcomers, for they saw how bravely they fought to save their friends and families, how they quickly forged arms and made for their defense. It was in those days that some of the Elifaen first openly approached Men and formed the earliest alliances with them. They taught the Newcomers about their own people, and took some of their leaders to Glareth by the Sea to see that kingdom, and even to far away Duinnor and to Vanara to meet King Parthais. This was the beginning of the spread of Men throughout the lands of the earth, and the making of their new history with the Elifaen.

Shortly after King Parthais of Vanara was removed and his daughter, Serith Ellyn, became Queen, populations of Men had grown dramatically, and they lived in every part of the world. Tensions began to rise between the Elifaen of the eastern forests who resented how the Newcomers continually cleared trees for farms and for lumber. And it was feared that Men would soon outnumber the Elifaen in those parts, for they had many children and the Elifaen, though immortal, had very few. Yet many of the Elifaen were fascinated by Men. They admired their adventurous spirit, their love of song and good fellowship, and their tenacious, if short-lived, strength. The Elifaen were continually amazed, though, by how delicate Men were, how slight wounds bring about death, how sickness and starvation may quickly kill them, and how they grow old to have gray hair (or none at all), wrinkles, shallow voices, and poor eyesight. In spite of these flaws, some of the Elifaen suspected that Men enjoy lives more fully than they did, for Men did not seem so prone to melancholy as did the Elifaen. And many Elifaen took up company with Men, and some had husbands or wives who were Newcomers. A few of the Elifaen began to suspect that their own fate might somehow rest in the hands of these new and mysterious people.

By the end of the Second Age, Men outnumbered Elifaen in almost every region, due primarily to their much higher birthrate. In some regions, it was rare to find any Elifaen at all, such as Tracia and the old Eastlands Realm. In Duinnor, according to the census of 869, Elifaen made up only about 20% of all residents. The same was more or less true in Altoria and Masurthia (their census records are somewhat disputed). Vanara was almost evenly divided between Men and Elifaen, and Glareth's proportion of Men was around 60% of the population.

However, Men enjoyed a larger proportion of wealth, it seems. Land ownership in acres by Men (at least that which was assessed by Duinnor) was significantly higher than for Elifaen in all regions except Vanara. Shops, smithies, factories, mining, and other commercial or industrial concerns were almost exclusively owned and operated by Men in every Realm, even in Vanara. However, in the educational arena, in medicine, alchemy, and other technical arts, Elifaen dominated, likely due to the fact that their long lives allowed them to acquire and apply their knowledge and skills, such that their expertise was rarely disputed. Indeed, many Elifaen had long-term employment under Men, as their expertise and skills—sometimes garnered over centuries—were highly valued. Thus, many Elifaen served Men as foremen, supervisors, advisors, skilled workers, and in all sorts of capacities.

Over the course of centuries, the relationships between the Elifaen and Men varied for many reasons. Resentments, suspicions, power struggles, and even superstition ebbed and flowed, driving tensions and conflicts. The uniform threat of the Dragonkind went far to unite the two races, but even on the field of battle there was cause for tension. In the early years, Men simply did not understand how durable the Elifaen were, how rapidly they healed of wounds, and how invulnerable to sickness they were. Casualty rates in war were always higher with Men, plagues and pandemics did not affect the Elifaen, either. Hunger, thirst, and the vicissitudes of temperature did not seem to affect the Elifaen as much. When tensions ran high, when there were disagreements, Men often resorted to complaining that the Elifaen took advantage of Men's numbers to throw them into hopeless battles they could not win. With only a few exceptions, Men generally refused to serve under the leadership of Elifaen officers.

Blame was sometimes cast on the Elifaen for spreading disease, especially in the Eastlands and Tracia. And sometimes Men accused the Elifaen of casting magic spells and performing all sorts of witchcraft to harm crops and livestock, to make storms, or to bring drought.

Many Elifaen feared the growing numbers of Men and their propensity for cutting forests and clearing fields. Men had an early reputation for being unwise, uncouth, and uncivil, for drunkenness and riotous behavior. The fact that poverty among Men was rife, especially in the early Second Age, seemed proof enough to many Elifaen of the ignorance and crude thinking of all Men.

And of course, the established structures of power—the kingdoms, principalities, and estates of the Elifaen—often did not suit the aims and ambitions of Men.

Among the most consistent issues that seemed to affect relations were the combined effect of the Elifaen's long lifespan and low birth-rate compared to Men. Since it came to be understood that Elifaen could only be born to Elifaen women, some Elifaen regions went so far as to outlaw the marriage (or relations) of any Elifaen male with any Mortal female, because that would not result in an increase in the Elifaen population. But Elifaen women were highly sought after by Mortal males, the offspring of which would ensure their lineage. Never mind that such unions only rarely brought many children. Mortal females were thus in competition with their Elifaen counterparts who never grew old, and never lost their beauty, and never suffered the normal diseases or ailments of Men. In some areas, rumors took hold that children born of mix marriages were destined to be dwarves, pixies, imps, or other such malevolent creatures.

And so when conflicts arose, especially when fueled by multiple factors, violence exploded and atrocities were committed. The Pinewood Rebellion was probably the most notable of these conflicts, but the years after the fall of Tulith Attis also saw episodes of violence, most often in the form of minor feuds.

Relationships therefore remained uneasy throughout the Second Age. More thoughtful leaders, such as those in Glareth and Vanara, worked hard to accommodate and integrate both races into civic and government affairs, and to remove social boundaries between groups. Ironically, it was Duinnor Law, particularly its code of justice, that served as a model for Vanara and Glareth (as well as other Realms), even though Duinnor often undermined and corrupted its own application of law. But officially, anyway, members of both races had equal access to justice, were equal in civic affairs, and in law. Not until the Sixth King of Duinnor implemented travel restrictions on Elifaen, to be enforced by Men, was there a legal instrument for pitting members of one Race against another. Indeed, one of the first acts of Queen Shevalia was to revoke all travel restrictions, road tolls, and all discriminations against Elifaen (even though the world was remade well before any of her edicts could be codified and passed into law).

But when the world was remade, all things changed. For the first time, all people, regardless of race, were given control over their fate, could choose to remain in the world or to depart it. Those Elifaen who remained began to age, albeit slowly, and those Men who remained did not age as quickly as before. That is, lifespan became long but more or less the same between the two races. (It should be noted that the Elifaen who remained in the world were healed of their inherited scars and no longer carried any such blemish.)

Today, the differences between Men, Elifaen, and Dragonkind are in name only, if ever those names are invoked at all, and the memory of those past tensions and conflicts that existed before has now faded away.

****

Altoria

One of the smaller realms to the south at the edge of the world where the sea begins. To its east is Masurthia, to the north is the Great Bletharn Plain, and to the west is the Hinderland (or Hinderlands), a vast area of marshlands and bogs bordered by the impenetrable Tulivana Mountains. The Hinderland, aptly named, prevents the Dragonkind from crossing over to the east from their deserts. Altoria is further protected from the Dragonkind by the treacherous Craggy Sea to the west.

The realm is named for Mount Altor, upon which stands one of the mysterious Seven Towers, one that is topped with a purple dome. It was settled by various Elifaen tribes, many of which sought to separate themselves from the conflicts in Vanara. Foremost amongst these was Queen Therona's House of Fairwillow, who established her rule over Altoria during the Time of Strife. During the First Age, Altoria became prosperous due to its fertile agricultural lands, its fisheries and maritime industries, and its textile trades. Altoria and Vanara developed important trade relations using the

River Iridelin to transport goods north and south. It continued to develop and increase its trading might by sending and receiving goods overland to Duinnor and by ship to the other coastal realms of the world. Chief amongst its exports were olive oil, coffee, tea, and linen. It imported almost all of its steel and metals, having few productive mines. Under Queen Therona, its chief city, Draymoor, grew and prospered. As the relationship between Altoria and Vanara grew closer, Altoria would send troops to support Vanara in several campaigns against the Dragonkind.

Although the Craggy Sea, the Tulivana Mountains, and the Hinderland served as natural barriers to Dragonkind incursions, there were several instances when large Dragonkind forces managed to break through into Altoria. Most often, these were easily turned back or defeated by the small Altorian army. However, late in the First Age, a small army managed to strike deep into Altoria. They were quickly cut off from returning to their own lands and began a five-year trek eastward, raiding and pillaging as they went. They passed through Masurthia and into Tracia, then turned northward into the Eastlands. By the time they made it into northern Eastlands, their numbers had dwindled to only less than a thousand hardened raiders who attacked and laid waste to many settlements of Newcomers. The Newcomers (Men) quickly organized themselves and fought back, successfully defeating and breaking up the Dragonkind forces.

As a result of this incursion, Queen Therona increased her armies and their vigilance upon the Hinderlands.

In 918 of the First Age, Altoria was the victim of attacks by Jatarak the Ogre. He was driven into the Tulivana Mountains and eventually killed by Navis of the House of Elmwood.

During this period, both Masurthia and Altoria sought to increase their territories between the River Egochee and the River Wachee, a rich agricultural region. Both Masurthia and Altoria claimed those lands, although most of its inhabitants were Altorian. In 931 F.A., Masurthia provoked violence in the area by hiring mercenaries to burn one of their own villages and casting blame on Altoria. Using this as a pretense, Masurthia then sent an army into the region to seize lands along the western banks of the Wachee. Altoria responded by sending its own army across the Egochee and soon the two realms were engaged in many battles ranging throughout the disputed region. Late in the year, Masurthia sent a strong naval force up the Iridelin to raid Draymoor with the goal of burning and destroying docks and warehouses. Although not really successful, the raid caused damage enough and served to effectively end trade with Vanara for both warring sides. Altoria, with her docks in disarray, sent strong forces to close and patrol the overland trade routes used by Masurthia to send its goods to Vanara. Altoria also sent a retaliatory naval force to harass and raid Masurthian coastal towns and villages.

Since Vanara depended on the land routes for much of its trade with Masurthia and Tracia, and with more difficulties with disrupted shipping, King Parthais of Vanara intervened. Without warning, he led a large army into the region, through Altoria and then on to Masurthia, and effectively seized all of the disputed lands. Neither Altoria nor Masurthia were a match for Parthais and his Fellfaere, and were forced to concede to a truce dictated by Parthais as he threatened each side with conquest unless they reached an accord with each other and with new trade terms favorable to Vanara. At last in 940 F.A., Altoria and Masurthia signed a treaty defining the border between the two realms as the River Wachee, with free access to the river granted to both sides.

During this conflict, Queen Therona did not publicly show her Bloodcoins as was her normal practice, claiming that hostilities made doing so too risky. After the fighting had ended, however, she still did not show them when the next time arrived for doing so, and it was revealed that she no longer had possession of the Bloodcoins. This revelation led to widespread protests and riots, as all Altorians had been made to believe that the Bloodcoins were a sign from Aperion of their sovereignty. Queen Therona was deposed in 967 F.A. and was replaced by Prince Felthain of the House of Mulberry. Therona was exiled and would later commit suicide, but she never revealed what happened to her Bloodcoins.

In 322 of the Second Age, Altoria was attacked and virtually overrun by the Great Dragonkind Invasion of that year. Draymoor was attacked and severely damaged, but its people managed to hang on to the city while the rest of Altoria was pillaged and looted. During this time, nearly the all of Altoria's armed forces outside of Draymoor were slain, with remnants retreating into Masurthia before the invaders. Such was the devastation wrought upon Altoria and Masurthia that they did not recover for many generations. Fully one-half of Altoria's population was slain, its farms and villages were nearly all destroyed, and even after the Dragonkind were defeated, famine and disease continued to take its toll. Under Ruling Prince Gerald, an Elifaen of the House of Mulberry, Altoria would struggle to recover. At the same time, the people grew wary of Vanara, having been unable to contain the Dragonkind as before, and their ties with Vanara weakened. Indeed, Altoria embarked on a long-term project of a vast defensive system and fortifications, particularly in the Hinderlands. Meanwhile, Duinnor, which was generous with its financial aid, became a more important ally to Altoria in spite of the distance between the two realms.

See Also:
Biographical Sketches (Felthain)
Historical Sketches (The Great Dragonkind Invasion)
Tales of the High Houses (Therona)

****

Bloodcoins

The common name for the Forty-Nine Keys to the Nimbus Illuminas, often called simply the Forty-Nine. They were discs of heavy red gold, approximately three inches in diameter and nearly a quarter of an inch thick, and each encircled a gemstone within its center. Seven different gemstones were used: amber, amethyst, diamond, emerald, ruby, sapphire, and topaz. The surfaces of the metal surrounding each gemstone had decorative patterns engraved and in relief.

These forty-nine objects were given to seven leaders of the Elifaen by Aperion along, as the tales go, instructions for how they could be used to open a way for the Elifaen to depart the earth and reconcile with the Faerekind that had already departed. This the Elifaen failed to do, and during the subsequent centuries many sets would become lost. At last, King Philawain managed to gather them all and use them to remake the world.

There are various theories as to how they came to be called Bloodcoins. One stems from a legend pertaining to Chantay and her daughter Lucinda, that when Chantay was driven mad by the Seven given to her by Aperion, Lucinda cut off her mother's head and Chantay's blood covered the objects of the dispute. Others say that they are called Bloodcoins because they were given to the seven greatest "blood houses" or bloodlines of the Elifaen. Another explanation stems from the superstition that any Mortal who possesses any Faere coin of any kind will meet with bad luck or death (But there is no indication that this belief existed at all until sometime during the latter part of the Second Age.).

Most tales and legends state that during the Time of Strife, after the earthly Elifaen had lost their wings and were struggling to survive, Aperion took pity on their plight. But he was doubtful that those who remained upon the earth were trustworthy or had learned their lessons, so he devised a method of testing them. Should they pass the test, the Elifaen would be able to break their earthly bonds and return to his fold by leaving the world, thus regaining their status as Faerekind. So he fashioned the Forty-Nine.

Then Aperion summoned the leaders of the Elifaen to the summit of Mount Cassos, giving them the means to come instantly before him should they desire to hear his words. This summons, some legends say, was not in the form of a demand, but one of powerful urging. Some legends say that he expected only one leader to come, Lyrium of the House of Fairfir, yet he was pleased that the others came, too. Other legends say that Secundur knew of Aperion's plan and that it was he who urged the others to respond to Aperion's summons, knowing that their hatred of the Dragonkind would thwart Aperion's hopes and plans. Those legends have it that Secundur knew that he could not corrupt Lyrium, but that if a group came before Aperion, the chance for discord was greater.

Of all the Elifaen Houses, only seven responded. These would come to be called the Seven High Houses: Fairlinden, Fairwillow, Fairfir, Fairmaple, Faircedar, Fairmyrtle, and Fairbirch. To each High House, Aperion gave seven of the Forty-Nine. During the First Age, they would be redistributed, but the original manner of distribution by Aperion was as follows:

Cupeldain's House of Fairlinden, entrusted with blue Sapphire Bloodcoins

Ormace's House of Fairbirch, entrusted with green Emerald Bloodcoins

Chantay's House of Faircedar, entrusted with purple Amethyst Bloodcoins

Katrina's House of Fairmaple, entrusted with orange Topaz Bloodcoins

Therona's House of Fairwillow, entrusted with white Diamond Bloodcoins

Pyros's House of Fairmyrtle, entrusted with red Ruby Bloodcoins

Lyrium's House of Fairfir, entrusted with golden Amber Bloodcoins

When Aperion gave the Forty-Nine to the High Houses, he also showed them in a vision how the Forty-Nine were to be used to open a way (which Aperion called the Nimbus Illuminas) for the Elifaen to depart the earth and come to go into Aperion's heavenly abode. However, Aperion warned them that it should be done soon, as he foresaw misfortune and continued strife if they tarried too long. They accepted the Forty-Nine, but failed to act soon enough to avoid his prophecy. It was not long before discord and treachery sprang up within and amongst the Houses, and the Forty-Nine came to be called Bloodcoins.

During the First Age, there were two failed attempts to bring about an agreement among the Seven High Houses to use the Forty-Nine Bloodcoins and to open the Nimbus Illuminas. First was Silmain's effort. Cupeldain tried, too, during his reign, but also failed to gain consensus. Indeed, such was the sentiment against Cupeldain's plan that Bloodcoins were redistributed so that each of the Seven High Houses would possess one Bloodcoin of each of the seven types of jewel (that is, one Bloodcoin of each High House). Ostensibly, this was so that no House could use their given Bloodcoins without the consent of all others.

Eventually, most of the Forty-Nine Bloodcoins would be lost, and by the early Second Age, all of the High Houses except that of Fairlinden would either have died out or disappeared from the world. Only the House of Fairlinden would still possess its collection of seven Bloodcoins, passed from Cupeldain to his son Parthais and then to Serith Ellyn, daughter of Parthais, when she took the Vanaran throne as Queen.

However, during the middle Second Age, it became known that the Fifth Unknown King of Duinnor had somehow acquired two or possibly three sets of the Bloodcoins, and it was assumed that much of his will was directed at obtaining the rest of them. When the Fifth Unknown King was replaced by the Sixth, it was thought that he carried on his predecessor's efforts and that he may have obtained a fourth set. Indeed, when King Philawain came to power as the final King of Duinnor, it was discovered that the previous Unknown Kings had managed to gather five sets of Bloodcoins.

Philawain knew how they were to be used. Obtaining the final two sets, he reunited each like coins into their original sets. Then he dispatched couriers, riding upon Islindia's flying horses, to

each of the Seven Towers that corresponded in color to each set of Bloodcoins. There, the coins were delivered, fulfilling an essential condition for the remaking of the world.
See Also:
Tales of the High Houses

✳✳

Duinnor

Duinnor was a northwestern Realm, taking its name from the ancient name for the river that flows along its northern bounds. Among the smallest of the Realms in land area, it was nonetheless highly populated, and, as the ruling realm of the Unknown Kings, it was the most powerful of all the realms. Its chief city was Duinnor City.

Duinnor's early history is somewhat vague. Vanaran records dating from the early First Age mention the region as the land of the north river (Duin Nord), bordering lands to the southwest that were controlled by Katrina's House of Fairmaple (until they abandoned those lands for the Carthane region). Its southern borders varied throughout history, but generally encompassed Averstone, Minion Gap, and, reaching around Forest Islindia, the regions surrounding the Farduin River, Edgewold and Westlawn. Nasakeeria was on its eastern border. Northward it reached the Osterflo at the confluence of the River Whitefall, and westward to Chiroth and Mount Vendril.

In the early First Age, this area was considered by many to be an unorganized, lawless region of somewhat rebellious Faerekind who did not wish to submit to Vanaran authority. It is speculated that while Katrina held sway in the region, many other groups settled to somewhat enjoy her protection. The land was fertile and rich in natural resources, including iron, tin, silver, and precious gems. Throughout the middle First Age, and well after Katrina departed the region, commerce and trade became increasingly important, with Duinnor supplying finished iron goods, steel, grain, and lumber as well as other commodities. From Duinnor, goods were being routinely transported by the River Osterflo to Glareth and by roads to the Eastlands, and Vanara. What would become Duinnor City was founded at the nexus of trade routes and the place where many raw materials were refined or made into various products. Grain, including wheat, rye, barley, and oats were important crops, along with vegetables, nuts, and flax. Cattle and horses were raised, along with sheep, goats, pigs, chickens, and geese. Regionally, fish was abundant in the rivers and streams.

As mentioned, routes were established to reach and connect with every other region, and Duinnor's goods were always in ample supply by road and river.

By the middle of the First Age, Duinnor City was the center of economic activity, and its wealth grew considerably. Ruled by a council of elders, and later Lords, the town enjoyed safety from the wars and conflicts elsewhere and was not vulnerable to natural disasters that frequented other parts, except for the occasional blizzard or flood.

Upon the arrival of Men, and ever in need of labor and skills, the Elifaen of Duinnor quickly accepted members of the new race, and within only a few generations, Men had established their dominance. By 1100 F.A., Duinnor was already quite powerful, with a growing central city, coordinated policing forces, and active cultural centers. It had an unusual system of government, whereby a council of twelve to twenty Ruling Lords jointly agreed upon how the region was to be run, deciding matters of law and trade agreements, and providing armed forces to protect its trade routes. These lords answered to their own people, at least to some degree, who sometimes ousted one in favor of a new leader. Over time, as the power of various lords waxed and waned, more of the lords that governed were Men, and by the end of the First Age, no Elifaen was serving as a Ruling Lord. From time to time, one of the lords would be named Honorary King for a period of twenty years. Usually this title was given only as a way of honoring some particular person, and did not bring with it much power. Although they were often competitors in commerce and politics, the lords managed to effectively govern Duinnor until their overthrow by the First Unknown King in the early Second Age. By that time, they had established a codified system of law, various public works bureaus, and a system of policing, and even a small army.

During the Purge of Scholars (1150-1165 F.A.), many Vanaran scholars migrated to Duinnor, along with a wealth of books and manuscripts. Duinnor welcomed them, and soon put the scholars to use as teachers, schoolmasters, alchemists, and in other academic trades. To this end, Duinnor collected taxes and fees to pay for the establishment of schools and centers of learning, being one of the earliest realms to do so. King Parthais of Vanara considered this migration and Duinnor's welcoming policies an affront to his authority, and he demanded the return of the Vanaran scholars and the wealth of literature they took with them to Duinnor. When Duinnor ignored his demands, Parthais threatened war unless Duinnor expelled the Vanaran refugees and relinquished any property those refugees had brought to Duinnor. Duinnor's response was to strengthen its fortifications, and build new walls around its city, and to increase the size and capabilities of its armed forces. So it was that the tension and intrigue between the two realms, and with increasing threats from Vanara, Duinnor rapidly became a considerable military power, one strong enough to deter any but the most massive hostile action on the part of Vanara. But Duinnor's leaders knew that the Dragonkind also watched from afar, and that Vanara had to defend its southern borders. So, with greater confidence, Duinnor continued to defy Vanara.

War between Vanara and Duinnor never came. But Vanaran dissidents, not only scholars, steadily trickled to Duinnor. Some of these were Vanarans that had been mistreated by Parthais, others were fugitives seeking to escape the insecurities of Parthais's erratic purges. Still others came to Duinnor simply to seek a more peaceful home. Eventually, Serith Ellyn, the rebel daughter of Parthais, arrived. She quickly gained much support from not only the diaspora but also from Duinnor generally, as her opposition to her father served Duinnor's interests. It was in Duinnor that Serith Ellyn and her brother Thurdun gathered the army that would successfully march against and overthrow Parthais.

With such power, Duinnor was soon imposing its will on the nearby mountains and valleys, expanding its rule and declaring its sovereignty over wider areas, exploiting and developing the region's rich natural resources, mining iron and precious minerals, and developing vast plantations. By the beginning of the Second Age, the population of Men well exceeded that of the Elifaen, and it was they who were firmly in control of Duinnor.

In 231 S.A., the First Unknown King overthrew the Ruling Lords and seized power in Duinnor City and over all of Duinnor. It is not fully understood how this was accomplished, although the Ruling Lords conceded to the takeover without violence. It occurred at a time when the cooperation between lords was at a low point, during which violence and feuds were becoming more common. One lord in particular, Tarsus, had contributed much to Duinnor's troubles by his aggressive efforts to undermine his rivals. Even after his death, turmoil did not subside. Trade negotiations with other Realms had languished, leaving the people with no buyers for their products. The roads were allowed to deteriorate, policing became unreliable, and productivity was decreasing. In short, the people were generally dismayed by the sudden change, but hopeful that the new king and their new kingdom would resolve so many problems ordinary people faced.

Indeed, the Unknown King, with his mystical aura and power, rapidly made changes, including legal reforms, in the structure of governing, assigning ministers and overseers to carry out his edicts and to solve (or resolve) problems.

Since then, Duinnor's military and economic power steadily increased through the reign of successive Unknown Kings. By the middle of the Second Age, Duinnor had gained hegemony over the other Realms of the world and was imposing (or striving to impose) its will and governance everywhere. The Unknown Kings forced the rulers of the other Realms into allegiance to Duinnor, and forced the abdication of the Kings of the other realms, relegating them to Ruling Princes. Only Vanara was able to resist Duinnor, retaining its Queen, Serith Ellyn (although Vanara was forced by various means and concessions to agree to Duinnor's supremacy). By exerting its might, Duinnor thus consolidated the Seven Realms under its rule, enforcing Duinnor's laws, system of currency, standards of weights and measure, and even its calendar (the "King's Law") in other lands.

Over time, the accomplishments of Duinnor were matched only by the increasing despotism of the Unknown Kings. Their actions were inconsistent, sometimes putting forth great reforms, initiating and carrying out great public projects, while at other times seemingly entirely disinterested in the internal affairs of Duinnor, allowing ministers to accumulate and exert more and more power. Little was done to fairly resolve relationships with Vanara, especially, and Duinnor repeatedly paid dearly in blood and treasure for various wars with the Dragonkind. Meanwhile, although asserting its rights to do so, it did not enforce its own laws and policies in places like Tracia, Masurthia, and the Eastlands, leaving matters to deteriorate. At last, Tracia revolted. Its corrupt Ruling Prince, ostensibly supported by Duinnor, was overthrown by an even more corrupt and despotic dictatorship as civil war swept Tracia and threatened to engulf other realms. Yet Duinnor did nothing to prevent these events, nor did it respond when Tracia threw off the King's Law and began its plan of conquest over its neighboring Realms. Even after news of Tracia's invasion of the Eastlands reached Duinnor, the King did little or nothing, even though appeals were made.

The influence and interference of Shatuum were reasons often given for the decline and disinterest of Duinnor's rulers. It was made clear by documents discovered by the Kingsman Constabulary that Lord Banis had made a deal with Secundur for the use of his black eagles. These creatures were used by Banis, and by the Unknown King, to spy in various ways, but the creatures always flew to Secundur to relay what they had reported. The Banis documents, most in his own writing, reveal that Banis knew that the eagles were passing along information to Secundur. It was also discovered that Banis tried to influence the Unknown King to assign many matters of state to those approved of or working for Banis. What is unclear is whether Banis himself was directly influenced by Secundur. But had it not been Banis's sudden death and, shortly thereafter, the arrival of King Philawain, it seems clear that Banis would have taken over the entire judiciary system, and likely all policing forces. Banis himself was much despised by most of Duinnor, and there were several attempts on his life. And although some judges and investigators tried to implicate Banis in many nefarious activities, none succeeded. As well, the Kingsman Army actively opposed many policies put in place by Banis and had to continually work to prevent Banis from interfering in military matters.

Thus, at the end of the Second Age, Duinnor was primed for revolt, just as in the days when the First Unknown King came to power.

See Also:
Essays and Explanations (Leases of Forfeiture)
Glossary (Banis)

****

The Eastlands

Also called "Eastland," "Eastlands Realm," or "the Old Eastlands Realm." Although its boundaries varied, and were often in dispute, generally it covered the area from Calletshire in the north to the region between Bessinton and Bransondale in the south. From the sea, it reached westward well into the Thunder Mountains.

The Eastlands was among the last places to be settled by the Elifaen, and throughout most of history, well into the First Age, it was mostly forested lands with a few areas of cultivation. Its population was fairly sparse. Various rulers vied for power, and most selected the port town (later city) of Colleton as the center of their rule. By the end of the First Age, it was ruled by King Inrick I, and was recognized by the other realms and rulers of the world.

After the Seven Realms were firmly established in the Second Age, it suffered many misfortunes, including droughts, floods, plagues, and invasion. Its capital was at Colleton on the coast, an important trading port. However, in spite of the rich natural resources of the lands, the inept rule of its kings prevented the Eastlands from becoming very strong.

During the early Second Age, the town of Attis grew in wealth and power, and the kings of Colleton sought to weaken the town by levying heavy tributes. Compliance was inconsistent, at best. Attis nonetheless rapidly became an important crossroads in overland trade, located along both the north-south and east-west routes to and from other realms. Its power grew to rival, if not exceed, that of Colleton.

The Dragonkind invasion of 322 S.A. resulted in the destruction of nearly all of the towns in the Eastlands, including Colleton and Attis. After the Dragonkind were defeated and driven out, much of the Eastlands remained unsettled, and King Inrick's rule was confused and corrupt. In 420 S.A., at the death of Inrick the Second (who had been as inept and corrupt as his father), an uprising in Colleton resulted in the city being burned once more. The uprising was quelled by combined forces from the Attis region and from Glareth. Since no one could be enticed to the throne, the ruling family was dissolved, and the Eastlands came under the guardianship of Glareth. Colleton would never regain its previous status. Attis would remain unoccupied thenceforth. East of the River Saerdulin, settlements and farms only very slowly re-established. Boskland, located between the Saerdulin and Bentwide rivers, was notably one of the first successful farming estates. West of the Rivers Saerdulin and Bentwide, Tallinvale and Tallin City grew and prospered under the management of Lord Danig Tallin. Smaller communities in western Eastlands also began to thrive in the late Second Age, including Janhaven and Passdale.

From its inception, the border regions of the Eastlands were constantly in dispute, with much disagreement as to the exact locations of the borders with Tracia and with Glareth. During the late Second Age, and under the regency of Glareth, the northern borders were firmly established. However, to the south, Tracia slowly encroached northward, effectively wresting control of territory once understood to be part of the Eastlands. To the west, beyond Janhaven and Tallinvale, warlords established themselves, primarily in the Thunder Mountains and northward into the Carthanes. Their power waxed and waned, and much of their efforts were against competing warlords. By the late second age, the Damar warlords were in control of the western Thunder Mountains.

****

Great Dragonkind Invasion

Also called the Great Invasion, or the Invasion of 322. It was the largest, most devastating invasion of Dragonkind in history, which took place mainly in the year 322 of the Second Age.

It is not known precisely why such a large offensive took place, nor the goal. Centuries afterwards, manuscripts would be uncovered that suggest that Dragonkind King Xurnon III intended to capture eastern lands for colonization. The veracity of the manuscripts remains in question, and the implausible explanation for the invasion is dismissed by most scholars. To target the Eastlands and Tracia made no sense, scholars say, when nearby Altoria and Masurthia, realms the Dragonkind would have to conquer on their way east, would have sufficed for a massive territorial expansion. Some suggest that Xurnon's generals were overly ambitious, and there is reason to suspect that the deep incursion into the Eastlands was planned from the beginning, influenced perhaps by the promise of untold riches. Certain Dragonkind documents (the authenticity of which have been disputed) indicate that at least one Elifaen called Bailorg, and perhaps a few Men, served the Dragonkind in some capacity, probably as advisors or spies who provided valuable military intelligence concerning the north and eastern Realms. It is also known that once the Dragonkind reached Fisenwold, they were accompanied by thousands of prisoners used as laborers, some of which were under the command of Bailorg. These non-Dragonkind operatives would perhaps explain how the Dragonkind were able to surprise and overwhelm its opponents. So while the rationale for the invasion remains steeped in speculation, certain facts are undisputed.

In the last month of 321 S.A., an army of Dragonkind made a sudden attack into the Blue Mountains, driving through the surprised and unprepared Vanaran forces toward Peldown (a place later to be called Gory Gulch). The Dragonkind moved slowly but methodically and did not seem intent on holding positions, but were nonetheless determined to engage Vanaran forces. Vanaran scouts reported road-making activities were taking place behind the Dragonkind, apparently in preparation for a larger army to follow. Several Vanaran battalions were therefore called away from the Mirse region, while additional forces were dispatched from Linlally to face the threat. All this took place over the course of the last two weeks of 321 S.A. This operation action was only a feint, as it turned out.

Six additional Dragonkind armies were massed and waiting just south of the Nalamain Hills. When the first army succeeded in drawing off Vanaran forces from the Mirse region, these went on the march, driving swiftly into the Mirse. One army turned north and east, engaging Vanaran forces from their rear. Thus engaged on two fronts, the Vanarans did not receive word until much later of the existence of the five other Dragonkind armies that were rapidly crossing the Iridelin. On the other side, they moved out into the Plains of Bletharn and split once more. One army marched south into Altoria while the other three marched across the Plains of Bletharn. Although the figures are constantly in dispute, it seems that the total strength of the five armies was well over four hundred thousand soldiers, with perhaps as many as seven hundred thousand, not including slaves. Many more slaves along with food and supplies were captured as the armies advanced.

Those Dragonkind that held back the Vanarans were fewer in numbers, but were made up of crack soldiers possessing clear intelligence concerning Vanaran dispositions, strength, and they had specially prepared maps detailing mountain passes, river crossings, and other strategic and tactical locations. Some of these maps and documents were captured, leading to much speculation as to how such information was obtained by the Dragonkind. One such map bore inscriptions that were clearly written in a Vanaran script.

In the south, the Altorians quickly detected the invading army and mustered for its defense. However, the Dragonkind, moving quickly on foot and horseback, soon overwhelmed the small ill-prepared Altorians, sacking and destroying towns and villages as they went. A large force, perhaps an entire army, was sent against Draymoor as the remainder of the Dragonkind turned eastward and marched into Masurthia. As the surviving Altorians retreated into Masurthia, they exacted heavy casualties upon the Dragonkind, but they could not halt the advance. Meanwhile, Masurthians were forewarned and gathered to face the invaders. Over the following month, they would slow the Dragonkind, but could not stop them from sacking Solsorna. Yet the fighting resulted in a much-diminished Dragonkind army that moved into southern Tracia and laid siege to Forlandis.

Meanwhile, the other Dragonkind armies quickly crossed the Plains of Bletharn and fell upon the city of Fisenwold, which held out for two weeks of desperate fighting. After the city fell, and with little further resistance, the Dragonkind moved into and through the Thunder Mountains just as a winter storm struck the region. Their advance was hampered by snow and freezing rain, and many Dragonkind died of exposure. There would be rumors, for years to come, that they engaged in acts of cannibalism, turning on their slaves and even some of their own comrades.

During these weeks, the Vanarans quickly gathered to their defense and engaged in intense fighting against the two Dragonkind armies in their lands. One of the invading armies was pushing north and west from the Mirse, and the other was by now farther west, approaching the region of Ladentree and the River Strayborn. But these armies were not coordinated with each other, and made no effort to link up. Facing the withering onslaught of the Vanaran Fellfaere that now massed against them, the Dragonkind quickly faltered, having virtually no supplies, no supporting columns, nor any reserves. But they refused to retreat in spite of their hopeless losses. Queen Serith Ellyn, at the front of the fighting, realized that something else was afoot. She was soon confirmed in this view by reliable reports of the large Dragonkind forces now moving south and east. Word was immediately dispatched to Duinnor. Once the Queen was convinced that the Vanaran incursion was only a diversion in strength, and that no credible threat to Vanara itself was imminent, she led an army eastward in pursuit of the Dragonkind, hoping that those invading Altoria could be dealt with by that realm. The Queen soon had word that Duinnor was dispatching an army eastward as well, and the two would converge on Fisenwold.

When the Vanaran army reached Fisenwold, they found it sacked, and the surrounding region littered with dead. Serith Ellyn dispatched several small parties of Fellfaere to Glareth with warnings while she sent others to trail the Dragonkind. At Fisenwold she encamped her army, impatiently awaiting the arrival of Duinnor's army, as was agreed.

Unbeknownst to Serith Ellyn, the first Duinnor army was by then already annihilated when they brazenly marched into Nasakeeria, seeking, it was later thought, to cut a day or two from their march. When Duinnor received word of this, from the lone survivor (a messenger sent back to Duinnor with dispatches), the King was furious and sent out a second army, almost entirely on horseback, to rendezvous with Serith Ellyn. By some accounts, it was the largest gathering of mounted soldiers that had ever ridden together, numbering some 6,000 riders.

Meanwhile, as Serith Ellyn's forces waited, the Dragonkind advanced on Tulith Attis and began their siege. By then, the southern Dragonkind army had swung northward from Forlandis along the Saerdulin and joined those who came through the Thunder Mountains. Tulith Attis, well forewarned, had gathered as many fighters as could be mustered, by some accounts some 30,000 strong, along with many women and children. Although bravely defended, Heneil's forces at Tulith Attis were outnumbered and outmatched. Its defenses, though strong, were not capable of resisting the powerful war machines that the Dragonkind constructed and massed. Tulith Attis was a relatively small fortress, with strong shelters for only a small garrison. But it was so overcrowded that the missiles shot by the besieger's trebuchets and catapults had a devastating effect upon the defenders. According to the few accounts (mostly from Dragonkind sources), no terms of surrender were offered or asked for. By all accounts, the defenders knew that allies were on their way, and they fought all the harder to hold out. However, after two weeks, Tulith Attis was betrayed by Pellen, brother of Heneil, who saw to it that the gates were opened to the Dragonkind. A massacre ensued Of those still within the fortress (some had already made an escape), only Lyrium survived. (But because she was afraid of Pellen, she remained in hiding and it was not generally known that she survived until centuries later.) It was later estimated that over 20,000 men, women, and children were slain.

The Dragonkind lingered another week, looting and pillaging, before they received reports of several armies converging on them. Besides treasure and such valuables, they were keenly interested in gathering all of the steel and iron that they could, since these were almost as valuable to them as gold. So much such cumbersome metal was taken that the Dragonkind, and under pressure to move quickly, they would soon discard most of their burden by hiding the metal in a vast secret barrow.

The approaching armies were made up of Glarethians marching from the north and the combined might of Vanara and Duinnor coming from the west. Together, these three armies converged on Tulith Attis (a smaller, separate Glarethian force marched to Colleton to relieve it). When the armies neared Tulith Attis, they at first thought the place to be on fire with pitch, so thick were the black clouds of vultures that covered the place. What they found filled them with shock, anger, and resolve. Not a single person was found alive. The town of Attis was completely obliterated, every house leveled, and the stones of its buildings had been used as missiles for the Dragonkind trebuchets. The blood of the dead, men, women, and children, stained the walls of the fortress, and bodies littered every yard of ground, some in heaps where they died, or piled aside to make way for looting. Within the fortress itself, it was apparent that a desperate, last-ditch fighting had taken place from room to room and hall to hall. And it was evident to all that the undamaged gates of the fortress had been opened from within, which immediately fueled rumors of a traitor within the fortress, rumors which would vary and change but persist for centuries. But no one (except Lyrium) knew the identity of the traitor, until 870 S.A., when Robby Ribbon, through dreamwalking, discovered Pellen in Shatuum and delved into his nightmarish dreams.

After regrouping at Tulith Attis, Serith Ellyn was given general command. She quickly reorganized all of the forces, and within a day, they were pursuing the Dragonkind along the banks of the River Saerdulin. Fighting was intense and vicious, with the Dragonkind deftly turning and wheeling in an effort to outmaneuver their pursuers, laying ambushes and traps, and splitting their forces to either side of the Saerdulin. But the armies of the realms split as well, and soon the east and west banks of the Saerdulin were vicious fighting as the rearguard of the Dragonkind were encountered. The rearguard succeeded in delaying their pursuers, which allowed the Dragonkind to recombine their forces on the western bank of the Saerdulin and cross southward, not without difficulty, over the River Lerse. There, using the Lerse to protect their north flank and the River Saerdulin on their east flank, the Dragonkind prepared to make a stand.

By now, Serith Ellyn's army was joined by various bands of Tracian Men and Elifaen, who reported that Tracia was awash with fighting, but the Dragonkind there had given up their siege of Forlandis and had suffered defeat after defeat, with Altorians and Masurthians entering the fray. They also reported that the Dragonkind were building defensive positions between the Lerse and Saerdulin.

Serith Ellyn quickly made her battle plan. The bulk of her army swung west and south to cross the Lerse, then turned east and then marched north, coming upon the Dragonkind defenses just before sunset. They did not tarry, but with the sun low behind her, Serith Ellyn immediately mounted a full frontal assault against the Dragonkind lines. Meanwhile, two Vanaran captains, Navis and his sister Esildre, each took a large party of Vanaran Fellfaere, one positioned directly across the Lerse from the Dragonkind and the other across the Saerdulin. When Serith Ellyn and her force clashed with the Dragonkind, Navis and Esildre waited patiently for nightfall, and then made their move. Stripped to their skin, and carrying nothing but their swords, Esildre and her force swam the freezing Lerse, while Navis and his company swam across the Saerdulin, each group came up the river banks behind the Dragonkind. Navis and his group engaged first, but had the misfortune of encountering an elite group of Dragonkind being held in reserve. In the intense fighting, all of the warriors with Navis were soon killed, and he alone fought on with cruel efficiency. At one point, surrounded by the enemy, Navis picked up a slain general with one arm and used his body as a shield against arrows as he continued to fight, advancing deeper and deeper into the rear of the Dragonkind ranks.

Meanwhile, only a few hundred yards away, Esildre and her company at last made it ashore through the swift waters of the Lerse and immediately charged uphill into the north flank of the Dragonkind, who were so intent on Navis that they entirely failed to detect her. Soon the front lines of the Dragonkind faltered, as Esildre's fighters picked up bows and shot arrows into them. Various accounts differ, but all agree that the battle lasted until just before dawn, when the last of the Dragonkind were slain. Legend has it the slaughter was so great that the River Saerdulin ran red and full of dead from there all the way to the sea.

Aftermath

During the next few weeks and months, Serith Ellyn's army continued to pursue Dragonkind stragglers throughout the Eastlands and Tracia. Although many boasted that all of the invaders had been hunted down, in fact at least a dozen Dragonkind, and perhaps many more, would eventually make it back to their own lands.

But soon divisions began to surface among the victorious armies, with the ranks dividing over blame for the fall of Tulith Attis. There were skirmishes, even, between Men and Elifaen, and bloodshed quickly threatened to undermine all semblance of unity. Duinnor's generals, not wishing to be drawn into a fight with their Elifaen allies, prudently withdrew their forces back to Duinnor. Meanwhile, within the Glareth ranks, many Men who had served with distinction were now being attacked by Vanaran Fellfaere. Bloodlust, it seemed, had filled the soldiers with anger and malice. At last, Prince Thalamir of Glareth and Serith Ellyn together announced that any violence amongst and between their forces would be treated as an act of high treason, and to convince their soldiers, they were forced to execute several dozen, with the two leaders personally carrying out those sentences upon their own fighters. Then, to emphasize their stern orders, they ordered the arrest and execution of several officers who refused to mete out discipline. It was a bitter and cruel policy, but order was quickly restored, even if resentment and suspicion were not allayed.

Every realm was touched in some way by the Great Invasion. Altoria, Masurthia, Tracia, and the Eastlands were the primary battlegrounds, with Duinnor and Glareth each losing many thousands of men (Duinnor lost thousands of men to Nasakeeria alone). Vanara suffered the fewest battlefield casualties, but its relationship with Duinnor was shaken. Tracia, the Eastlands, Altoria, and Masurthia would never fully recover. Vast tracts of land were utterly destroyed, with towns and villages entirely wiped out, forests obliterated, and fields burned. Forlandis, Tracia's capital city, survived but was heavily damaged. Solsorna, in Masurthia, was in ruins, and Draymoor would be held under siege for nearly the entire year. The region around Tulith Attis would never recover the wealth or power it previously held, and few could be enticed to live there. Attis, the town, would never be rebuilt. Obliterated by the besieging army, the site would become a forlorn plain, with two large barrows beneath the looming walls of the doomed fortress. The only evidence of the once-thriving community to survive would be two stone pillars that marked the location of the town's western gate. The fortress itself would be abandoned, left to the spirits of the dead and to the decay of time, while legends and tales about the place would soon be told.

By some estimates, over a million died, including almost all of the estimated 450,000 Dragonkind. At least 30,000 inhabitants in and around Tulith Attis were killed. Another 50,000 were killed in Draymoor and 60,000 in and around Forlandis. Virtually every village and town in Tracia and the Eastlands simply disappeared, along with entire populations, with higher estimates putting this at around 500,000 people. In Altoria, particularly along the Iridelin, thirty towns were completely destroyed, with 80,000 dead. Added to these were deaths suffered in Vanara (during the feint attack), at Nasakeeria, and at Fisenwold, estimated to have been around 125,000. At least 80,000 slaves and prisoners taken by the Dragonkind died of violence, starvation, and disease. These estimates probably do not include lesser known places. And the numbers of injured and wounded because of the conflict are likely twice as high.

The Eastlands was devastated and would never recover. Its population was greatly diminished, for many were killed, while disease and starvation took its toll on those who remained. Many others fled, never to return. Recovery was hampered by inept and corrupt rulers. Tracia's sufferings were only marginally less than those of the Eastlands, mainly because of the forewarning they had. This gave many people the chance to flee, some to the coastal islands, and it gave others the time to fortify and prepare. But its post-war fate was similar, with disease and famine, aggravated by corrupt and ineffective leadership. Eventually, the Eastlands lost its status as a Realm and became a territorial dominion of Glareth Realm. This, in turn, gave rise to further disputes with Tracia concerning borders, which in turn contributed to the unrest and discontent that lead to open revolt in the late Second Age.

Altoria and Masurthia fared somewhat better, since the Dragonkind did not seem inclined to venture far from their chosen routes of conquest. This allowed many people to escape the carnage, some into the Plains of Bletharn, some into the southern Thunder Mountains, while others escaped by sea to faraway places aboard ships and vessels of every description.

But the populations of all of the invaded lands struggled to cope. They suffered from hunger, sickness, and terrible dread for years to come. But the greatest lasting effect of the Great Invasion was the mistrust that plagued the realms of the world. Vanara never again trusted Duinnor. Tracia slowly recovered, only to tear itself apart with repeated civil upheavals. The Great Invasion was a turning point that presaged the decline of the Elifaen and the rise of Men. The center of power shifted firmly north to Duinnor and its Unknown Kings. And though Duinnor was never again trusted, it was the least affected by the invasion, and it quickly moved to assert its power over all other Realms, and in Vanara, particularly. Duinnor insisted on a permanent military presence within Vanara to defend against further Dragonkind incursions, and Serith Ellyn was forced to comply. Vanara continued to grow weaker and more dependent on Duinnor's support, which Duinnor's Kings used to further weaken and undermine Vanara's power.

Of course, the Dragonkind suffered, too, from this humiliating and costly campaign. Great upheavals among those remaining in power weakened the Dragonlands. Fortunately for the Dragonkind, the realms of the north were in no condition to push its victories into the deserts. So when the Dragonkind began to recover from the ill-conceived invasion, they did so relatively quickly. Within only a few centuries, they acquired unity, prosperity and power as never before.

To historians who have had the opportunity to carefully study the Invasion, certain aspects seem baffling. One is why the Dragonkind kept moving eastward rather than consolidate in Altoria. With the power devoted to the invasion, the Dragonkind might have conquered Altoria and held onto it, garnering vast resources and possibly establishing valuable agricultural colonies. But the manner of their movement was obviously carefully planned to thrust deep into the easternmost parts of the world. Many scholars propose that Tulith Attis was their ultimate goal, while others argue that had they not been confronted by the armies of the realms, they could have firmly taken and held Colleton. Until it was discovered otherwise, it was thought that the Bloodcoins of the House of Fairfir were taken by the Dragonkind at Tulith Attis, and that this was their primary goal. But there is no supporting evidence, from documents or from captured Dragonkind, that this happened. Thus the fate of those Bloodcoins remained a mystery until the end of the Second Age. Other scholars also argue that had the Dragonkind contented themselves with Vanara alone, the capture and conquest of that realm would have secured them immense wealth and resources, with strong defensive positions against any possible threat from Duinnor, Glareth, or other forces.

And so the debate continues. What is certain is that the Great Dragonkind Invasion forever changed the structures of power and set the stage for the dominance of Duinnor.

See Also:
Biographical Sketches (Esildre)
Tales of the High Houses (House of Fairfir)
****

Griferis

Griferis was an island that floated in the sky located over the Crack Between Worlds adjacent to Mount Algamori. Its upper surface was about a mile in area, roughly that of a circle, and was mostly covered by the grounds and buildings of a lavish estate, surrounded by high walls. The buildings including a palace of several wings, and the grounds enclosed a variety of gardens and wooded areas. The only access to Griferis was a bridge spanning the distance from a ledge on Algamori at a large arch located there to the front main gate of the walls of Griferis, facing east. The bridge was about a mile in length and would only appear when summoned to do so by the Judges of Griferis or, later, by King Philawain.

Griferis served as the legendary "Place of Judgment," where future kings and queens were supposedly evaluated for fitness to rule. There is anecdotal evidence that it was also something of a training place in some respects. It is said that those who survive the trials and tests of Griferis are fit to rule over others, whether they eventually do so or not. Only two people whose names are known went to and survived Griferis, Queen Serith Ellyn and Robby Ribbon (who became King Philawain). However, many unknown persons went to Griferis, and a few of them likely also survived and returned to the outside world.

According to Vanaran records, Griferis was first discovered by Elrasil the Hunter. He guided King Parthais of Vanara to see the place. Not many years later, Serith Ellyn went into Griferis and later emerged and succeeded in overthrowing Parthais. From that year, the last year of the First Age, until the year 870 of the Second Age, it was shrouded in mystery and lore, with many tales arising concerning it, most of which were wildly inaccurate. By the time that Robby Ribbon located Griferis, many people assumed that it was merely a fanciful legend and had never existed. Some of the legends and tales say that it is a place of fearful and strange visions, and where terrible monsters and ghouls feast upon those who venture there. Some people believed that it was the Land of Shadows, conflating Griferis with nearby Shatuum. Hence it came to be referred to as Griferis Vale, Grigferith Vale, or Bonewalker's Valley, a place (so it is said) from where nightmares spring, and to where all go to be punished for evil deeds before passing into the afterlife. When Robby Ribbon became King Philawain, Griferis was his first domain. During the last days of the Second Age, Philawain guided Griferis to various parts of the world, used it to overthrow the Sixth Unknown King (and thereby become the Seventh, and final King of Duinnor) and to transport his followers and allies to various places. Griferis has not been seen since the world was remade.

Until King Philawain took it as his domain, Griferis was a place of judgment. It was created by Aperion shortly after the Fall of the Faere and served as a place where potential kings and queens of the world could be tested and judged for worthiness; those who did not pass the tests did not survive; those who emerged do not necessarily become rulers, but they were said to have certain qualities of wisdom, intelligence, and fortitude in the face of adversity. Although she never spoke publicly about it, Queen Serith Ellyn went to Griferis when she was banished from Vanara by her father, Parthais. She later emerged and succeeded in wresting the throne from Parthais and became Vanara's Queen; the only other confirmed visitor and product of Griferis was King Philawain (Robby Ribbon), who became the ultimate ruler of all Realms.

As mentioned above, Griferis was a walled palace complex, its high walls at the very edge of the sky-floating island. The Palace consisted of several large wings and towers; in one wing was a library which magically obtained every book or scroll ever written (in any language). The library also obtained more ephemeral materials such as newspapers; but it did not contain personal letters or other writings (such as diaries, field orders, or business documents) unless they were reproduced or published for general sharing or for sale in book or scroll form.

Griferis had many observation towers, some higher than others. In one that overlooked the front gate toward Algamori was a room that contained an apparatus by which Griferis could be made to move. Another tower contained a large telescope observatory.

Covering over 600 acres, there were many gardens and trees, some of which were quite rare. There were also greenhouses filled with more delicate or exotic plants. Along one wall was a wooded grove, with a stream that gurgled up from the ground and ran into a small pond. Some wings contained elegant suites for guests, one of which King Philawain occupied for his personal use. There were also lesser rooms for other guests or servants. There was a throne room, a dining hall, many kitchens and workrooms, storage rooms, and lesser dining rooms, some of which were quite elegant. There were massive storage areas, including a huge coal bunker (a peculiar coal that did not smoke), places for liquid fuels (oils and alcohol), food (including cold storage areas), linens, and all of the material requirements needed to host and house its occupants.

It is also known that there was a special hidden place within Griferis where the mysterious Judges sat (on floating thrones). There was also a great "circle room" where once there were many doors (perhaps as many as 50) that led to other places and times. Candidates to Griferis were made to pass through these doors and be exposed to or involved with places and events, some of which were life-threatening. Upon returning to Griferis from such experiences, that particular door would disappear. It is thought that each candidate's experiences/doors were unique to that particular candidate. For example, King Philawain spoke about how he was taken to the time and place where Shevalia (Sheila) had collapsed when she was struggling to get to Boskland (after she was assaulted and raped) and the King managed to help her get to Boskland. Philawain revealed that time spent at Griferis during such trials was separate and apart from the outside world, and that, until he completed those trials, he had no idea that time passed very slowly on the outside. His many years of trials were only as a few hours outside Griferis. Indeed, his time in Griferis aged him by almost twenty years (since he was mortal at the time). But when Griferis became his own domain, and the Judges departed, time at Griferis became the same as for the outside world.

Many of the King's experiences and trials were depicted, under his direction, by the artist Borwain, of the House of Hemlock, whose paintings and drawings have an uncanny quality of animation. Working with Finn, he made an effort to record his experiences, but those documents have not yet been found and most likely disappeared when Griferis did at the end of the Second Age.

There were two other known occupants of Griferis during Philawain's time there. The first of these was a man called Finn, who was taken from the world by the Judges in order to serve and wait upon the candidates undergoing trials, that is, during those times when the candidate was back from a trial, back to Griferis, and needed recuperation. Finn revealed that he was not the first such servant, but had a predecessor who was killed by an irate, and unsuccessful, candidate. Finn was not sure how long he remained in Griferis, but speculated that it had been several hundred years at the least and had served and waited upon many candidates.

The other occupant was a girl called Celia. One of Robby's trials involved the task of freeing her from a large bell jar, in which she and her pet rabbit were kept in a state of suspended animation. Her age was unknown, but she appeared to be no more than twelve years old. Upon her release, Celia displayed certain peculiar qualities. She was woefully ignorant of many things, while at the same time had a certain sagacity about other matters. Finn and Philawain wondered if she might actually be Elifaen, but she did not have wings or scars as the Faerekind and Elifaen did. They would never discover the truth, that she was one of Aperion's daughters, placed in Griferis as a testament of innocence and to give the place, if conditions were met, a sense of home. She was not given wings, as the other Faerekind had, and although she would age but very slowly, she was not immortal. It is thought that she might still abide in Griferis, wherever it may be.

****

Battle of Grisland Strait

The Battle of Grisland Strait was a naval engagement that took place in the Grisland Strait between the Tracian Royal Navy (loyal to Prince Lantos) and that of the Triumvirate in the year 856 S.A.. It took place only a few days after the rescue of Loyalist forces fleeing from their defeat at the Battle of the Marshlands.

Prelude

After the Triumvirate of Tracia took power, a series of battles took place which eventually led to Loyalist forces being trapped in what has come to be called The Battle of the Marshlands. Under Prince Lantos, Royalist forces (accompanying and protecting several thousand civilians) fought a rearguard action in an attempt to escape encirclement. The Redvests forces failed to mount their offensive in time or effectively enough to encircle the Loyalists, which enabled the Loyalists to ensure a mass retreat through the Marshlands to the sea. Much aid was rendered by locals who used hundreds of small boats which navigated into the marshes along streams to take on board Loyalists who survived the battle. These boats, many making several trips back and forth, transported over three thousand soldiers and two thousand civilians, mostly women and children, to awaiting ships anchored along the coast. Each of these ships departed for Glareth as soon as they were full to capacity with passengers, and many escort vessels accompanied them.

Battle

Among the last Loyalist ships to pick up survivors were the Sea Horse and the Barge Royale, which lingered to take on Prince Lantos, his family, and many of his soldiers who had fought the rearguard action to prevent Redvest forces from overrunning the retreat. These two ships, along with four escorting warships, then departed. Their course was to take them east by north around Grisland Island before turning north toward Glareth. However, a squadron of Triumvirate ships had been dispatched to capture Lantos and were lying in wait off the eastern coast of Grisland Island. This forced the Loyalists to turn back south around the island where they made for the Grisland Strait to find a clear passage northward. This, however, was the Redvest intent, and several ships were sent to block the northern egress from the strait and trap the Loyalist ships within those confining waters. In the ensuing battle, six Loyalist ships faced thirteen Redvest ships.

Among the Triumvirate Redvest vessels were four biremes, eight triremes, and the heavy battle cruiser, the Scarlet Lance, a quadrireme (four rows of oarsman on each side) and the most powerful surviving ship in the Redvest Navy.

The Loyalists ships included the Trueblood, the Golden Swallow, and the Sea Horse, all swift Glareth-built biremes with the latest triangular sails and rigging, two older triremes, the Worthy and the Pyros, along with the Barge Royale, which was not a warship but a heavy transport quadrireme. Except for the Glareth-built ships, all were square-rigged and sluggish. Aboard the crowded Sea Horse were women and children, including the family of Prince Lantos, numbering some 225 or more. The Barge Royale was encumbered with nearly 400 surviving soldiers, including many wounded, as well as Prince Lantos. The Prince's intention was to see the faster Sea Horse safely out of Tracian waters with the Golden Swallow escorting, while the other four ships would safeguard the rear of the retreating ships. This, however, would not come to pass.

When the Loyalist fleet was almost halfway through Grisland Strait, the Golden Swallow and the Trueblood, acting as a forward screen, encountered the first of the Redvest vessels bearing down the channel from the north. Surviving accounts relate that the Golden Swallow and the Trueblood immediately engaged. Meanwhile at the far rear, some two miles behind, the remainder of the Redvest warships gained on the other Loyalist vessels. The Trueblood and the Golden Swallow coordinated their attacks, being highly maneuverable, and each was able to turn into an enemy vessel, ramming and sinking them. During this first encounter, the Trueblood was set afire, but her crew managed to contain the blaze while ramming yet another ship. At this point, the Trueblood was also rammed by another Tracian ship which was already ablaze from the Golden Swallow's catapults. As the three vessels burned and sank, the Golden Swallow rammed and sank the last of the Redvest ships that threatened to block the northern channel.

Meanwhile, at the rear of the Loyalist formation, the Worthy and the Pyros turned into their pursuers. They managed to damage one vessel and temporarily break up the pursuers before both were crippled and set afire. However, their action delayed the Redvests, giving the Sea Horse and the Royale Barge more of a lead and allowing the Golden Swallow time to come about and race southward.

What followed was one of the most daring, imaginative, and valiant naval engagements ever, pitting the small Golden Swallow, commanded by Martin Makeig, against six enemy ships, including the powerful Scarlet Lance.

Makeig first managed to force two of the Triumvirate ships aground, and when two other ships sought to pass, he successfully set them both ablaze, one of which collided with an as-yet-unscathed Tracian vessel, setting it ablaze as well. The Golden Swallow suffered only minor damage that was quickly repaired, and very few wounded.

However, the Scarlet Lance managed to make it through the melee, and was swiftly gaining on the Barge Royale. The Golden Swallow turned again, this time pursuing the pursuer. In spite of the narrow channel, all ships by now carried full sails in a race northward. It seemed hopeless, since the Scarlet Lance was much faster than the Barge Royale. Yet neither could match the speed of the Golden Swallow. Her innovative sail plan allowed for more sail area and better trimming, and her hull was both strong and stable. Expertly handled by her crew, she quickly gained on the Scarlet Lance. In a daring move, the Scarlet Lance then bent on even more sails. For nearly a half an hour, amid a channel strewn with sinking and burning ships and drowning men, the four ships raced northward, every oarsman at battle speed, every yard of canvas filled with air. The Sea Horse, outpacing all others, was far ahead of the Barge Royale. Then came the Scarlet Lance, and behind the Lance came the Golden Swallow. As the ships neared the northern stretch of the channel, and the open water beyond, the Golden Swallow sprang forward in a surprising burst of speed. After but a few more minutes, it was clear that the Swallow intended to ram the stern of the Scarlet Lance. However, with very little closing speed, the strike would likely not penetrate the hull of the Redvest ship, and its captain did not vary his course to thwart the strike. Soon they were within a few yards of each other, with the Swallow closing rapidly.

It was at this point that Makeig carried out an unusual maneuver, which he had prepared for during the pursuit. He ordered ramming speed, and when the Swallow came within range of the Lance, her crew dowsed the stern decks of the Lance with firepots, setting the stern ablaze. Then Makeig's catapults launched grappling irons over the stern. These were attached by ropes cleverly set into blocks and pulleys to the Swallow's two stern anchors. When the anchors were dropped, they pulled the two ships together so rapidly that the Swallow's ram completely penetrated the stern of the Lance. Makeig had guided the strike carefully so that, as soon as the ram was into the Lance, he had the anchors cut away and immediately ordered his sails pulled round. The Swallow, pushed by the wind, shifted its stern to port, coming around so that its ram pried out the rudder post of the Lance before it broke away. Thus freed, and the Lance now skidding rudderless under full sails. The Swallow continued to slip around until the port side of the Swallow crashed into the port of the Lance, facing the other way. Since the oarsmen of the Golden Swallow had pulled in their oars, and those of the Lance likewise, the two hulls met. The Golden Swallow's oarsmen then shoved narrow troughs through their oar ports and into those of the Scarlet Lance, and they poured flaming oil into the Redvest vessel. The Swallow's crew then set their own ship ablaze belowdecks.

By this time, both ships had firmly grappled together, portside to portside. Topdecks, a furious fight was taking place as the men of the Scarlet Lance poured over its side onto the Swallow. Makeig, however, had already ordered most of his own men into the water to make for shore while he and a few of his crew fought the boarders. By the time the Redvests realized that both ships were doomed and quickly sinking, most of Makeig's men were safely overboard.

Thus the Royale Barge and the Sea Horse were saved and eventually made it safely to Glareth by the Sea.

Assessment

The Battle of Grisland Strait is viewed as the last major action of the Tracian civil war, and is generally seen by outsiders as a net strategic victory for Loyalist forces, even though they were in retreat. Already weakened by previous battles and actions, at Grisland Strait the Triumvirate navy was effectively destroyed with little hope of replacing the thirteen lost ships and crews. Triumvirate docks and shipbuilding facilities had already been destroyed or heavily damaged, and most Royal Navy personnel remained loyal, escaping to other Realms. Thus hampered by the lack of able seamen, experienced commanders, and the means to build ships, the Triumvirate would be unable to rebuild its navy, forcing them to rely almost entirely on their land army for their planned invasions of the Eastlands and Masurthia.

See Also:
Biographical Sketches (Lantos, Martin Makeig)
Historical Sketches (Battle of the Marshlands)
****

Kajarahn

Also called the "Free City," located in the northwestern deserts of the Dragonlands, known in former times as Alaberbra.

As Alaberbra, it was originally a small agricultural community, growing meager crops of flax and wheat by using well water for irrigation founded sometime during the late Age of Strife or early First Age. Sometime in the First Age, perhaps during the time of Silmain, it began trading fabric both with Vanara and with the Green Citadel. Its relative isolation from the rest of the Dragonkind empire, and its proximity to Vanara soon made it an important stop for traders passing back and forth between Vanara and the Dragonlands, mainly those conducting illicit trade. Through Alaberbra, Vanarans and the Dragonkind could obtain commodities and resources that were scarce in their own lands. With its agricultural base supplying the needs of its citizens, usually with surplus, and its ample supply of water, it quickly grew. By the middle of the First Age, Alaberbra was a booming trade town, dealing in textiles, grain, steel, jewels, and spices, wood and lumber, and minerals. It became so important to both north and south that the Dragonkind and Vanara observed a tacit agreement restraining each from molesting traders coming and going to Alaberbra. This effectively made Alaberbra an independent city-state. Although both Vanara and the Dragonkind Kings would seek to wrest control of the city, mainly through intrigue, neither would succeed. Eventually, in the year 732 F.A., the Accord of Sianne was reached, a formal agreement between Vanara and the Dragonkind, with approval by Alaberbra's leaders, which sought to ensure safe trade routes to and from the town, mainly through Ladentree in Vanara.

Alaberbra quickly grew and prospered, and although the Accord would fail after only a few years, the city had by then become highly important as a conduit of precious goods between Vanarans and the Dragonkind. Yet the people of Alaberbra, mostly Dragonkind but a substantial number of Elifaen (and later, Men), successfully fended off efforts made by outside powers to control the city. This they did by continually negotiating pacts so favorable to each side that neither dared disrupt trade through conquest.

In 335 of the Second Age, a rebellious Dragonkind general named Ozradur set his sights upon Alaberbra, having failed to find refuge in the Green Citadel. He laid siege to the town and nearly captured it. During the siege, the Dragonkind Prince Nulamon and his family were killed. This nearly led to the capitulation of the city, but a Melnari named Collandoth quickly rallied the people. Under his leadership, Alaberbra's defenders not only repulsed several attacks that came against their walls, but also managed to conduct counterstrikes against Ozradur's encampment. Finally, in an audacious maneuver, Collandoth led several thousand defenders out of the city and around to come behind Ozradur. At the same time, those left to defend the city lit smoky fires which led Ozradur to think the city was burning. He ordered a renewed attack on the city, but Collandoth and his forces came behind him, destroying his encampment and catching Ozradur against the walls. Ozradur was killed in the fighting, and his forces were scattered.

So grateful were the inhabitants to Collandoth that they proclaimed him their new king, and they gave him a magnificent throne made of intricately carved oak. Collandoth accepted so that he would have the status to negotiate a treaty on behalf of the city with the Dragonkind King. The King was so grateful for the defeat of his rebellious general that he agreed to make Alaberbra a Free City forever ruled by its own people. Collandoth then organized a ruling council of town people and relinquished the throne. With trade re-established and Alaberbra's independence secured, Collandoth abdicated his throne to a council of city elders and leaders of commerce. Later, Vanara would ratify a similar understanding of the city's free status.

Four years later, the city once again faced annihilation, this time at the hands of demons, witches, and other foul creatures that infested the world in the year 343 S.A.. Alaberbra was not spared, large areas within the city became dens of dark enchantment and torture. Collandoth returned late in the year 347 S.A., this time as a member of the Nine Banes. They found a devastated city, filled with blood-sucking witches and terrible demons. Over half of the inhabitants were dead or maimed, and the rest were living behind locked doors, afraid to show themselves. The Nine Banes successfully eradicated the creatures, but only a few of Collandoth's old friends survived the scourge. The city would slowly be repopulated, and it would be renamed Kajarahn, known to most simply as the Free City.

By the late Second Age, Kajarahn was more prosperous than ever, and the city managed to maintain its independent status from the Dragonkind Empire by balancing delicate trade and diplomatic relations with both Vanara and with the Dragonkind. Although its walls formed the boundaries of its jurisdiction, it exerted control over certain key areas outside the city proper, mainly along nearby trade routes. Also, since it maintained its own system of laws, any person who reached the city would not face immediate arrest and imprisonment unless they had broken laws within the city. The city maintained a small standing army, which also served as law enforcement, and a considerable number of civil servants charged with enforcing regulations, inspections, and taxation. With well over 40,000 citizens, and thousands of visiting traders, it was a ever a hotbed of intrigue, with agents from the Dragonlands and the Seven Realms well ensconced and openly spying upon one another. It was also a haven for renegades, bandits, and unscrupulous traders as well as a playground for the most decadent and wealthy of the Dragonkind. Although ruled by a strict division of power amongst several city lords, it was a violent place where few went forth without armed guards. All manner of vice was commonplace and mostly tolerated, with very few things banned or made illegal as long as payment for such goods or services (including tribute) was properly made and trade agreements were not violated.

One of the interesting aspects of Kajarahn was that its people did not seem as vulnerable to the desert sickness as elsewhere in the Dragonlands. That is, they required less darakal to maintain their health. As this became better understood, various schemes came and went among traders to exaggerate Kajarahn's need for darakal to ensure greater supplies, the excess of which were smuggled back to various places to be sold on the black market.

****

Karkarando

A land to the far west and south within the Dragonlands. It bordered the western mountains and the Craggy Sea. In the early epochs of the Dragonkind history, it was the chief source of food crops, vegetables and fruit, all of which were almost entirely replaced with darakal cultivation by the beginning of the Second Age. The Dragonkind gradually became more and more cautious of sharing or publishing information about the region, as it gained more control over the area and over darakal production.

Along the Craggy Sea there were belts of sand and dunes extending north for about thirty miles. Beyond this boundary was a broad region of fertile ground that borders the western mountains and reaches some 200 miles eastward and almost 150 miles northward. In addition to its many wells, it was common for the entire region to experience long periods of dense fog and light rain, which fed many shallow streams. Dragonkind writings explain that many attempts to grow grain in the region failed due to various wilts and diseases that stunted wheat, barley, corn, and oats. However, several other crops, such as flax, were once common. Native grasses that grow along streams served as fodder for goats, horses, and other livestock. There were very few trees other than date palms, which grew near to the many oases north and south of Karkarando.

Before its medicinal value was known, darakal, a hardy plant native to the region, was treated as a nuisance and herders and farmers tried to eradicate it. Once its properties were understood, however, it would rapidly become the most important crop of the region, and its cultivation supplanted virtually all other market and food crops. By the mid-First Age, vast plantations had been established throughout Karkarando, with labor supplied by slaves consisting mainly of condemned prisoners and captives. Elifaen were particularly valuable workers since they were immune to the many diseases and deprivations of the harsh conditions. Darakal is cultivated and harvested year-round. To preserve the medicinal properties, the plant had to be properly harvested, with care taken not to harvest too many stalks, else the plant would become stunted. The pulpy stalks and heavy leaves then had to be slowly dried under shade to prevent the medicinal quality from being spoiled. Once dried, the leaves could be used to make a tea-like infusion, and the stalks could be processed to make a liquid elixir. This was labor-intensive work and from harvest to final product could take two months.

After darakal's use and cultivation became common, several regional tribes became extremely wealthy, and quite a few work towns and villages were established. The leaders of these tribes, while competing with one another, often cooperated with each other to seek better prices and terms for darakal, to secure labor, and for greater autonomy. From time to time, one tribe would try to forcibly take over the fields of another tribe, and there were times of intense feuds.

While darakal became the most important product of the region, other items, such as amber, rubies, salt, and goat products were also important. By the late Second Age, however, it was actually receiving more food from elsewhere than it produced, mainly grain produced in the eastern regions of the Dragonlands, along the western slopes of the Tulivana Mountains.

The rulers of the Dragonkind became increasingly wary of Karkarando's power, as well as the vulnerability of the supplies of darakal to unrest, embargos, and cartels, and sought to exert greater control over the production and distribution of darakal. Almost from the beginning of widespread darakal cultivation, efforts were made by the King Tajahnaman to take over and monopolize darakal, most often through bribery or intrigue. From time to time, he sent troops to enforce terms favorable to the throne. By the time his son, Churadu, took power, almost all of Karkarando was under the military rule of a royal governor with many garrisons provided by the king. Churadu formally established a quasi-religious order known as the Priesthood of the Dragon, which was charged by royal decree as the sole legal agent allowed to legally distribute darakal throughout the Dragonlands.

Soon the cultivation, harvesting, and processing of darakal was highly regulated, to the dismay of the native tribes of Karkarando who wished to grow and trade darakal freely. Ongoing corruption within the King's ranks, and among the priesthood, prevented the Dragonkind throne from having total control. Thus, over the centuries, power would wax and wane, with various kings having more control than others, and with many black markets springing up to trade illicit darakal. Draconian measures were put in place to punish those caught, but since its effectiveness against the desert sickness was so great, and thus darakal's value, there was little hope of eliminating the illegal markets. Even after it was made a capital offense to illegally harvest, trade, or sell darakal, there were always people willing to take the risk of doing so to profit from such lucrative activities.

In order to have the best troops and supporters possible, as free of the desert sickness as possible, the King, as head of the Priesthood, prioritized distribution. Darakal was preferentially channeled to his troops, his courtiers, and those in favor and good standing with the throne. Military service granted free darakal to soldiers, in some amount, anyway, which not only bolstered the health and fitness of the troops, but also the willingness among the very poor to join and serve. All civil servants and officials appointed by the King, along with their immediate families, were eligible for frequent and free supplies of darakal. It became a system of patronage that ensured loyalty. Those out of favor had no such allowances of darakal, and the poorest often could not afford even the minimum amount required to keep the sickness at bay.

Karkarando itself was not immune to the debilitating illness, and many people flocked to the region hoping to find both work and cheap darakal. Rumors were constantly circulating that plantation overseers gave their workers darakal to keep them healthy, but it is very likely that workers suffered from other forms of "normal" malnutrition, abuse, and terrible living conditions. Indeed, as mentioned before, many overseers paid for Elifaen slaves, either captives from battle or those who were kidnapped into bondage, because they required no darakal and very little sustenance, rest, or shelter. Yet the demands and pressures from the Kings for the region to produce more darakal more cheaply was a great cause of discontent even among the well-to-do tribes. There persisted guarded talk of resisting the yoke that Tyrsharat increasingly sought to force on the region.

At last, in the latter part of the Second Age, a major armed rebellion took place in Karkarando. A large army of rebels, united from many tribes, opposed interference from Tyrsharat and sought to establish autonomy by overpowering the King's agents and military in the region. They swept across Karkarando, and quickly eliminated the many small garrisons of the King's army, killing many and forcing the rest into slavery. Soon the rebels had nearly cut off the entire supply of darakal and were actively seeking to sell darakal to any and all throughout the Dragonlands via their own heavily armed traders. To counter this, a large Dragonkind army was sent against Karkarando, which was eventually led by Gurasa, and succeeded in defeating the rebel forces and reestablishing control over the region. Within a year, darakal production was back to pre-rebellion levels, with many thousands of the captured rebels, rebel supporters, and their families working the fields as slave laborers under a fierce and unforgiving military guard.

It might be noted that just south of Karkarando, and well within the belt of sand that borders the Craggy Sea, stands the mysterious Tower Zurlamont. Except that it is topped with a green dome, it is identical to the other six towers scattered around the world.

See also:
Biographical Sketches (Gurasa)
Glossary (Darakal, Seven Towers)
****

Kingsmen

The King's Army of Duinnor was the best trained and most professional force in the Duinnor military. Begun as a relatively small elite force charged primarily with palace duties, it grew in size and capabilities during the second half of the Second Age. All combined, it never numbered more than 70,000. Unlike the Duinnor Regular Army, the Kingsmen were financed entirely by public funds gathered through the Royal Treasury.

From the onset of its establishment, the King's Men were experts in the use of weapons and served as bodyguards and the palace guard during the reign of the First Unknown King. Under the Second Unknown King, the force was greatly expanded to enforce the King's Law within Duinnor, and was given the power to make arrests.

By the time that the Third Unknown King came to power, it consisted of approximately 5,000 men of all ranks assigned to various specialized divisions and units. It was under this king that a formal system was made in to law that required each eldest son of each Named House to serve in the King's Army, now referred to as Kingsmen. While some viewed this as a form of hostage-taking, to help enforce loyalty of the Named Houses, it also served to prevent some of the more powerful houses from serving in other armed forces. As control over other Realms expanded, the law was also expanded to include punishments, fines, and penalties for Houses that did not submit. Generally, these "conscripts" served with distinction rather than resentment. With this influx of relatively well-educated and wealthy recruits, the Kingsmen were able to enhance training and indoctrination of their soldiers, and several training facilities were created for that. Eventually, these would be combined under a single educational system, called the King's Academy, which became one of the foremost centers of higher education in the world. The emphasis was always on strict discipline, thorough training in law, and warfighting, but as the Kingsmen were given various additional duties and assignments, the curriculum also included courses in history, language, culture, mathematics, engineering, logistics, metallurgy, mapmaking, and medicine, to name a few. All Kingsmen were expected to graduate successfully from the Academy, unless they were given a special dispensation as a recruit from other armed forces and could pass certain tests and qualifications.

The organizational structures of the Kingsmen forces were unusual. All were responsible to a central command structure, independent from any specific army. Each "army" was a relatively small division of the overall Kingsman armed forces, and combat interoperability and coordination between every tier was essential. Consisting of around 5,000 men, each army varied in actual size during deployments and was divided into "battalions" that usually consisted of 800-1200 men, usually divided into companies. A single "first" general was in charge of each army, with second generals heading up each battalion. Companies were usually overseen by "captains," sometimes called "commanders." Within each company, there might be smaller units, sometimes called squads.

By the end of the Second Age, there were four fully provisioned and trained battlefield-capable Kingsman Armies that had established themselves as the core fighting forces of Duinnor. They served all over the world, and in the Dragonlands. There was also a separate "constabulary" which was organized to handle civil policing matters. Finally, there was a separate "King's Post," which was eventually formalized from the previous ad hoc systems of communications to serve civilian as well as military needs. There were also many auxiliary units made up of civilian contractors that supplied labor, goods, and services as needed, usually under the direct authority of the Kingsmen. These also included instructors at the Academy, servants and staff at various posts, stations, bureaus, and camps. Here is a summary of the main official units of the Kingsman Army:

1st Army -- Engineers -- 1st Battalion Assault -- charged with offensive building tasks such as road-making, mapping, bridging, siege weapons (including large engines), and logistical support. Various companies of this Battalion were often assigned to other armies to fulfill specific needs.

1st Army -- Engineers -- 2nd Battalion Fortifications -- charged with defensive construction tasks, including the building and maintenance of temporary or permanent forts, keeps, or watchtowers, with trenching and obstacles.

1st Army -- Engineers -- 3rd Battalion Logistics -- working with other units, this battalion was responsible for the supply and equipment needs, including the transportation of war materials, weapons, food, water, fodder, horses and supply depots. They worked closely to keep supplies flowing, to guard their supplies and routes, and to do light maintenance as needed on roads and bridges.

1st Army -- Engineers -- 4th Battalion Training -- As its name implied, this battalion was strictly for field training purposes, and supplied recruits under special officers to give members detailed training and experience within the other Battalions.

2nd Army -- Battle Group Foot -- 1st & 2nd Battalions -- These battalions were entirely devoted to battlefield operations, offensive or defensive, and often served long stints in the field, particularly in

Vanara. They were a "general purpose" fighting force used to supply fighters to any place where needed.

2nd Army -- Battle Group Horse -- This battalion was a swift mobile force, sometimes serving as shock-troops, and sometimes as a maneuvering force during battle. They were not calvary, although they were trained to fight from horseback and had several calvary units within the battalion, usually acting as lightly armed strike forces.

3rd Army -- Battle Group Foot -- identical in structure and purpose to 2nd Army

4th Army -- Heavy Assault -- Consisting of five battalions (one being a training battalion), this was the most renown and battle-hardened of all of the Kingsmen armies. It was the tip of the spear for many attacks, but also saw service as defensive forces. They often used heavier armor and weapons than other armies and, with their tactics, could withstand heavy blows from an enemy that was numerically superior. Their members were hand-picked, the best-of-the-best, from other units and armies. They endured training and deployments that were very demanding, and in battle they exhibited a cohesion that was matchless.

King's Constabulary -- Duinnor City -- This was a two-battalion force that was charged with law enforcement duties. Some of its members were former soldiers of other Kingsman armies but had been wounded or were recovering from wounds and were thus temporary members. About half, however, were enlisted men or officers on permanent assignment. Their duties ranged from patrolling Duinnor City, legal inspections, criminal investigations, keeping order, and supporting the judicial system of Duinnor. They operated from a central headquarters and maintained stations throughout the city.

King's Post -- This was an armed force that became chiefly responsible for mail and dispatches. In addition to their official duties of a military nature, they began serving as messengers and mail carriers for governing bodies and civilians. At its core were Kingsmen specifically assigned either as "route," "post," or "special couriers." By the end of the Second Age, this force included some local civilian riders and employees, and employed or engaged 12,000 men and women in various capacities. (see King's Post) Along with the expected duties of managing mail and post, Post Riders also regularly reported on general road conditions, bridges, route conditions, weather, and even local news. All were required to keep careful records of their activities and observations. Since this was a royal force, any interference with the King's Post was deemed a crime against the Unknown King himself, and any Post Rider that was abused, delayed, or attacked by bandits usually resulted in swift and decisive retaliation and punishment from the nearest Kingsmen army units.

All Kingsman uniforms were based on a dark green color trimmed with yellow or gold. Each Army had its own trim pattern, and all uniforms were required to display unit and rank insignias at all times. Most Kingsmen had three sets of seasonal uniforms, one for everyday duties which consisted of breeches, boots, blouse, tunic or jacket or coat, and a light helmet or cap. Another set was for dress occasions and were tunics of a lighter green color worn with white breeches, brass and gold buttons and gold embroidery, shoulder braids, and sashes. Finally, there was battle dress, or field uniforms, which varied according to each army and unit to suit their missions but generally consisted of dark green tunic and breeches with yellow piping and trim. Some units preferred kilts or shendyts during marches and adapted them to accommodate battle armor. Battle helmets also varied and changed over time, with most having a hinged visor. But all Kingsmen, regardless of rank, bore a standard-issue gladius, a pair of fighting daggers, and most were also assigned shields. Different units carried different bows, and most armies had dedicated companies of bowmen. Armor varied with time and among different units, but ranged from very light "arrow-resistant" protection to "heavy armor" that was virtually impervious to any blow. The King's Constabulary, as a departure from other Kingsmen, generally wore green with distinctive blue piping and trim. Post Riders were allowed a great deal of choice to wear what suited them while "out on the routes," and some preferred civilian clothing over formal uniforms, as long as they were readily able to identify themselves with official documents that they had to carry at all times. Most wore a blouse, usually green or blue blazoned with the Unknown King's emblem. Since they consisted of Kingsmen and civilians under Kingsman supervision, there was usually at least some consistency when it came to appearance and presentation.

Most Kingsmen were released after twenty-five years of service with a pension, but could remain enlisted if they chose to do so and were fit for duty.

Known for their discipline, loyalty, battlefield cunning, and strong traditions of law and order, the Kingsmen were frequently used to perform the most difficult or unpleasant assignments, often acting as shock troops at the vanguard of great battles.

In addition to the traditional duties of an army, the Kingsmen served other important functions. They were the palace guard, hence their name, serving the palace exclusively over all other armed units. And, within Duinnor City, they were the policing force, required to keep order, solve crimes, enforce laws, and see to the safety of Duinnor City and its citizens. The city was divided into several constabulary precincts, each with its own captain who often served as its chief investigator of crimes. However, any Kingsman serving any precinct could pursue investigations or criminals into any other portion of the city. Kingsmen were also sometimes used as temporary field occupation forces due to their familiarity and dedication to Duinnor Law.

It is worth noting that Duinnor's Regular Army was in no way affiliated with the Kingsmen. While a Kingsman can advance on merit and performance alone, regardless of title or background, the Regular Army is filled with soldiers that have received little or no real military training, led by "gentlemen" soldiers who are often men who wish to increase their wealth or power. Although considered a standing army, very few of its officers or men are permanent. As a result, although Duinnor maintains a permanent contingent of Kingsmen in Duinnor and along the southern border of Vanara, Duinnor Regulars come and go as various leaders vie for the spoils of war. It was the undisciplined Duinnor Regulars who made up the bulk of the armies that laid siege to the Green Citadel, with the expected disastrous results, but it was Kingsmen who fought to protect them when they hastily retreated, and Kingsmen who suffered the highest casualties when their flanks, held by Duinnor Regulars, collapsed. There was always tension and rivalry between Kingsmen and Regulars, and the Kingsmen openly despised the Regulars as uneducated, undisciplined, and uncouth opportunists, loyal only to themselves. Indeed, many saw the Regulars as merely a large mercenary organization. This attitude was only reinforced when, under Lord Banis, convicted criminals were permitted to serve their sentences within the Regular Army rather than in prison.

Although Lord Banis often contrived to have Kingsmen subordinate to officers of the Regular Army, the King never authorized this. Indeed, it is known that the Sixth Unknown King rebuked Banis for his attempts to control or manipulate the Kingsmen. When the debacle of the Green Citadel was repeated, and the King received reports as to its failures, he fined the generals of the Regular Army for their incompetence in planning and carrying out the expedition. Under pressure from the King, Banis discharged several high-ranking Regular Generals and, at least for a time, was forced to defer once again to Kingsman leadership for military matters.

Among Duinnor's allies, even those uncomfortable with Duinnor's power over their affairs, the Kingsmen retained a great deal of respect. Their fighting prowess and capabilities were well known, their organizational skills and planning almost universally respected. Even in Vanara, where there was much friction with Duinnor, the Kingsmen were treated with great respect and admiration. In other parts of the world, especially in the Eastlands, Tracia, and Altoria, Kingsmen were somewhat feared, even though there were seldom present in those parts in any great number. This stems greatly from the fact that the King often used special units of Kingsmen to carry out unpleasant tasks, including raids against criminals, tax enforcement, enforcement of Leases of Forfeiture. As well, some Kingsmen were used to hunt for those who might in some way usurp the King, particularly searching for people who did not have a rightful name (named in the old way, secretly, by a dying relative or friend, as Robby Ribbon was).

Among the Dragonkind, the Kingsmen were feared only slightly less than the Fellfaere of Vanara. The Kingsmen demonstrated their fortitude, skill, and discipline over and again to the Dragonkind at such places, among others, as Ladentree, Khanhar Pass, the two assaults against the Green Citadel, and Gory Gulch. Indeed, by the late Second Age, the Dragonkind viewed Duinnor with its Kingsmen as their greatest threat, even compared to Vanara.

See Also:
Biographical Sketches (Artais Teracue, Danig Tallin)
Historical Sketches (Battle of Soltani Pass)
****

Battle of the Marshlands

The Battle of the Marshlands, which took place in 856 S.A., was the last major land battle between Tracian Loyalist forces and Redvest forces of the Triumvirate. The battle itself was a victory for the Redvests, soundly defeating the Loyalists and putting them into retreat. However, taken as a whole, the battle is often considered a draw since the Loyalists were able to avoid annihilation and, for the most part, escape capture.

Prelude

In the years preceding the battle, almost all of the Loyalist forces within Tracia were defeated in a series of set-piece battles. By 856 S.A., only a few pockets of resistance remained, mostly in the region surrounding Waterstone and to the east near Sorghwall. However, in a series of sweeping flanking moves, the Redvests took Sorghwall and cut off the Loyalists. Under pressure from the more powerful Redvest forces, some 20,000 Loyalist soldiers under Prince Lantos, along with nearly 25,000 civilians, were pushed into a pocket to the southeast of Waterstone. With no hope of resupply, Lantos knew that his people would soon starve even if the Redvests did not mount a decisive attack on their positions. Rather than wait for the inevitable end, he decided to split his forces and his people in a bid to get as many of them away to Glareth as possible.

On the fourth day of Seventhmonth, Lantos sent 12,000 of his troops against the Redvest stronghold at Sorghwall. As he intended, the Redvests were surprised and retreated into their fortifications as the Loyalists made every appearance of laying siege. However, this was only so that the civilians could swing around Sorghwall unmolested and flee northward. The Loyalists very carefully coordinated their efforts. Each day, the Loyalists would assail Redvest defenses while, each night, a few thousand soldiers would march north behind the civilians to guard their flight. On the fourth day of the supposed siege, the Redvests awoke to a scene devoid of any Loyalist troops.

Prince Lantos, meanwhile, having been kept informed concerning these actions, led a series of feints against Redvests near to Forlandis. Most of his people escaped northward, but Lantos and his contingent were cut off from that direction. They numbered around 7,000 soldiers and at least 2,000 civilians, mostly women and children (including his own wife and two young sons). They marched back and forth, creating as much havoc as they could over the course of three weeks, but ever pushed southward by the growing strength of the Redvests. Very soon two large Redvest forces converged from Forlandis and from Waterstone, forcing Lantos to retreat into the northern swamplands called The Marshlands. With his back to the swamps and his other flanks surrounded by Redvests, Lantos again split his forces. A thousand he sent with the civilians into the swamps in a bid to find their way through and reach the coast. And he dispatched several messengers tasked with passing through the Redvests to carry word of his predicament and plans to Admiral Navostra, or any Loyalist Naval forces that could be found. Then he and his remaining men prepared to face the Redvests.

Battle

Redvest General Mar Henith, a former Kingsman and veteran of the Dragonlands, now led over 20,000 troops against Prince Lantos. Hard-pressed for time, Lantos nonetheless selected his battleground carefully, a large hammock some ten miles inside the swamplands, a low bit of ground less than fifty yards at the widest and one thousand yards at the longest, in somewhat of a triangular shape. However, it was surrounded on three sides by broad impassible bogs that prevented Mar Henith from bringing up his war engines or make use of his mounted forces. On the widest side of this hammock would be the only viable approach for the Redvests, and that was where Lantos intended to fight. The Loyalists felled many trees to make additional obstacles for the Redvests, prepared their positions, and waited. However, Mar Henith quickly realized the strength of the Loyalist position and ordered the quick construction of several raised platforms, some three stories high, from which his archers and small ballistae would have better range and coverage on the hammock. This construction lasted for two days and, once completed, the Loyalists fell under a constant barrage of missiles. Under the cover of his archers, Mar Henith then had dozens of footbridges and raised footpaths constructed using rocks and soil brought by wagon. While this was being done, he also had constructed many footbridges along which he could send his troops.

Seeing all this, Lantos and his men sought to destroy the construction by sending night-time raiding parties to set fire to them. However, this was anticipated by Mar Henith, and the bridges and platforms were constantly dowsed with water to prevent just such countermoves. At last, sooner than the Lantos expected, at dawn five days after the construction began, the Redvests attacked. Thousands of Redvests charged along the bridges and footpaths to within thirty yards, then waded the rest of the way to the Loyalist hammock. At first the Loyalists had an easy time picking off the few Redvests who made it to their lines. But as more Redvests poured against them and became better organized in their formations, the Loyalists felt the full brunt of the assault.

The Loyalists fought furiously, and the Redvests just as determinedly, and the swamp water surrounding was bright red with blood by midmorning. Back and forth they pushed each other. At times, it seemed the hammock would be entirely taken, then the Redvests would be routed and driven back the length of it before they could regroup and attack again. So littered was the ground with dead and dying that the fighting often took place with men standing or stumbling upon the piles of corpses. By some estimates, over five thousand Redvests were dead or wounded, and nearly as many Loyalists. And by noon, it was growing hopeless for the Loyalists.

Respite came shortly after noon when an extremely violent thunderstorm darkened the battleground and dumped heavy rain with high winds on the scene and all of the combatants, forcing each side to pause and regroup. During this lull, Lantos ordered a full retreat into the swamps, and by the time the storm had passed, they were away. Mar Henith gave chase, and over the next three days, many skirmishes were fought as the remnants of both armies moved deeper and deeper into the swamps and coastal marshes.

Rescue

Meanwhile, a minor miracle was taking place along the coasts. By the time Lantos and his men began their retreat, the first of the civilians reached the marshes on the other side of the swamplands. There they encountered local inhabitants, and word quickly spread concerning the Loyalists and their retreat. While some of these people who knew the marshes and swamps best moved northward to find

Lantos, a large number of ships began to gather and drop anchor just off the coast. With them had come hundreds of small boats, skiffs, prams, pirogues, and punts. These were poled and paddled up into the estuaries of the marshes and on into the swamps and emerged filled with passengers. Thus, over the course of two weeks, thousands were rescued from the swamps and from the Redvests. And as soon as each awaiting Loyalist ship was filled with refugees, it raised anchor and set sail for Glareth. By the time Prince Lantos and his remaining men were brought out, thirty ships had already departed northward. Prince Lantos refused to depart, however, until he was as certain as he could be that as many of his people as possible were brought away to the ships. At last, only six Loyalist ships remained, four warships and two others that carried the family of Prince Lantos, the Prince himself, and the last of the survivors that could be found. Four days after the Battle of the Marshlands, the small fleet set sail. However, this only set the stage for the Battle of Grisland Strait, as a fleet of Redvest warships was quickly closing in.

Assessment

If the intent of the Redvests was to put an end to armed Loyalist resistance within Tracia, then they certainly did so. However, General Henith's orders emphasized that he was to capture as many Loyalists as possible, mainly to subject them to public humiliation and for use as slave labor. In this regard, the battle was a failure for the Redvests. Less than 500 prisoners were taken, while at least ten times that number of soldiers and civilians escaped by sea from the Marshlands and would make it to Glareth. This is added to the estimated 50-75,000 Tracian Loyalists who escaped overland as a result of the maneuvers carried out by Lantos. Thus the Redvests aims were spoiled.

See also:
Biographical Sketches (Lantos, Mar Henith, Martin Makeig)
Historical Sketches (Battle of Grisland Strait)

****

The Melnari and Their Familiars

The Melnari were a small group of mysterious people, neither Man, nor Elifaen, nor Dragonkind. There were very few of them, perhaps less than a dozen, and they were capable of long lives, perhaps being somewhat immortal as the Elifaen are. Some regarded them as troublemakers, and others referred to them as mystics, although that term is somewhat inaccurate. However, in addition to their keen intellects, they possessed strange abilities and powers, similar to some of the older Elifaen.

There were six Melnari. In order of their appearance in the world, they were:

Barian the Counter
Micharam the Poet
Tolimay the Angry
Ishtorgus the Mariner
Raynor the Wise
Collandoth the Wanderer

Our information about the Melnari comes from widely scattered sources. More is known about Raynor and Collandoth because many aspects of their lives and experiences were recorded. The lives of the first four Melnari (Barian, Micharam, Tolimay, and Ishtorgus) are not as well-documented.

The mysterious nature and origin of the Melnari remained somewhat murky throughout the Second Age. However, facts revealed in 870 SA indicated that each Melnari came into the world (or into existence) when each Unknown King of Duinnor gained the throne. It would then seem that the Melnari were somehow tied to a particular Unknown King in some way, or at least to the mysteries surrounding the Unknown Kings. Indeed, it seems that upon the ascent to the throne, each

Unknown King was given a special advisor who was to remain with the king through his reign, replaced when that king was replaced. In *The Year of the Red Door*, it is told that the Sixth Unknown King had somehow discovered this fact, and that each Melnari that had come into the world was, in some way, a sibling (perhaps a twin) of the king's advisor. Whether these advisors were truly Melnari remains unclear. Oddly, it seems that the advisor assigned to each aged backwards, starting out very old, but becoming younger at different rates, according to the length of an Unknown King's reign, and gradually losing their sagacity. This was certainly not true of the other Melnari, who generally started out young and aged over time. Because we know very little about the nature of these "advisors" to the Unknown Kings, we confine this sketch to describe those Melnari as known to the world at large.

The Melnari performed a variety of feats and served various roles in the world. The word "Melnari" is derived from an ancient term that meant "helper" or "midwife," and was used in ancient texts in a general sense to describe someone whose duty or work was to be an assistant. Indeed, the Melnari sometimes served as advisors to kings and queens, and as warriors, ambassadors, explorers, tutors, mentors, and scholars. When a new Unknown King came along, these Melnari did not go away (as did the "advisor" Melnari did), but remained in the world. Some were acquainted with each other, at least superficially, but until the time of Raynor and Collandoth, it is not certain whether they ever coordinated any of their endeavors. Each seemed to act independently of the others to a great extent, focused on different interests, and had different temperaments.

Each Melnari acquired a companion, known as a Familiar, that was in the form of an animal, bird, or insect. These served the Melnari in various ways, often as messengers or spies, and the relationship between each Melnari and his particular Familiar seemed to vary.

There has been recent speculation that, in general, the "purpose" of each Melnari was to assist the world in such a manner as to allow the Elifaen to fulfill their task of using the Bloodcoins and of setting themselves free of the world. This, too, such writers say, was the original and ordained purpose of each King of Duinnor, to be helpmate to the Elifaen people, that is, to help the Elifaen do what they themselves could not or would not accomplish on their own. Yet the Unknown Kings seemed inclined to do the opposite, to thwart rather than aid. And, as it turned out, only two Melnari, Raynor and Collandoth, seemed inclined to such a role.

Barian the Counter (with Telliniece, a chipmunk Familiar)

Barian entered the world in the year 231 of the second age, when the First Unknown King came to power. He was renowned for his knowledge of the heavens and wrote many books on the subject of the stars. Sometimes called Barian the Counter, it is said that he possessed remarkable eyesight and made an attempt to put a number to the stars and to trace their movements. He had as his companion a Familiar in the form of a chipmunk, called Telliniece. It was Barian who first perfected a method of using a sextant to aid in navigation, which he shared with his friend and fellow Melnari, Ishtorgus. He was also able to accurately predict certain celestial events, and he was a proponent of improved calendars. While living in Altoria, he developed a reliable timekeeping device, one that operated by way of waterwheels and gears. Barian was among the chief scholars that gathered in 246 SA to work out a better calendar system. Not all of Barian's suggestions would be adopted into the New Calendar that was developed and put in use in 266 SA. Indeed, he warned that if certain regular adjustments were not made, the New Calendar could "drift" and become out of synchronization with the seasons and stars. This was, indeed, the case, but as of 870 SA, no scheme to make adjustments had been adopted.

In the year 417, while Barian was stargazing one night, a falling star struck where he stood, leaving no trace of him but a smoking hole in the ground. Three of his servants also died, but a fourth, temporarily blinded by the blast, escaped with only minor burns and bruises. This survivor wandered lost for weeks until reaching Karthia and eventually making his way to Glareth to tell

Ishtorgus. A year later, Ishtorgus and this survivor managed to locate the spot (in the Carthanes near Karthia), and saw that some great and fiery object had indeed struck, noting a crater some forty feet wide and ten feet deep, with charred rock and trees in abundance nearby.

Micharam the Poet (with Hanion, a praying mantis Familiar)

Micharam came into the world in the year 244 of the Second Age, when the Second Unknown King came to power. He was widely known as Micharam the Poet. Very little is known about him, but records indicate that he frequented Vanara and delighted Queen Serith Ellyn's court with his jests and witty poems and his sad ballads. He often boasted that he freely entered and walked within the Forest Islindia, but could offer no proof to skeptics. However, his fondness for woods and forests was well known, and it is said that he had a mysterious ability to understand insects. It was thought (and later confirmed) that the praying mantis that he called Hanion and that often perched on his shoulder was a Familiar.

Although Micharam sometimes traveled with Collandoth, he loved the solitude of the forest and was always venturing forth to explore the woods and forests of the realms. He was a fierce defender of wild lands, too, and some say that his zeal inspired some within the Pinewood Uprising, although he denounced all forms of violence for any cause. He was fond of jokes and pun-making, and could not restrain himself from extemporaneous verse, even when it was somewhat lewd or offensive. Perhaps it was his proclivity to provoke that led to his demise, for legend has it that one of Micharam's verses severely offended a butterfly, which then pursued him through a Vanaran forest and beat him to death with its wings. At any rate, he was last seen in the year 592 in Vanara.

Tolimay the Angry (with Fallendine, a vulture Familiar)

Tolimay came into the world in the year 292, when the Third Unknown King of Duinnor came to power. He is often called Tolimay the Angry, and stories abound concern his legendary bad temper. One tale says that he so offended King Inrick of Colleton that he was put in irons. He apparently escaped. Another story says that shortly after he escaped from Inrick, he was waylaid by a dozen highwaymen on the road to Glareth. When the bandits saw how impoverished that he was, they laughed and gave him coin from their purse. Apparently this offended Tolimay so much that he entered a brawl with them on the spot, and gave them such a beating that they fled. Another story goes that he attended a wedding, but was impatient for the feast that was to take place afterwards, and he so upset the bride that she threw a candlestick at him, which put out his right eye.

Some say the reason for Tolimay's behavior is linked to his Familiar. Tolimay's Familiar was a vulture called Fallendine, which Tolimay abhorred and with which he apparently never had any close relationship with. Although Fallendine faithfully followed Tolimay wherever he went, and was a willing messenger on occasion, by all accounts Tolimay treated Fallendine with disdain and with as much rudeness as he heaped upon others. Some, including Collandoth, said that Tolimay's temper was a mystery and did not manifest in any way until some while after Fallendine became his Familiar. It was speculated, then, that Tolimay's resentment over being associated with such a creature, often resulting in his being shunned, that he gave into the most selfish attitudes. Ishtorgus openly expressed his disappointment in Tolimay, observing that Tolimay had become an entirely different person than he once was. In fact, arguments between Ishtorgus and Tolimay were so heated that they had to be physically separated from one another on more than one occasion in order to prevent them from coming to blows. Eventually, Tolimay found himself a pariah among the surviving Melnari as much as among civil society in general. Tolimay never garnered (or perhaps deserved) respect or position of any kind, and was never involved in any events of importance.

The most famous tale of all has it that he was tricked into minding the spoiled son of an Eastlands farmer. The farmer told Tolimay that if he remained silent, no matter what happened, he would give Tolimay an entire keg of beer to drink, along with a fine roast to eat. He was to watch after the boy only for a day while the farmer went to market. Different versions of the story relate different ways in which the little boy, no more than five or six, played trick after trick upon Tolimay. Other versions of the tale had it that the boy was actually an imp sent by Secundur. But all have the same ending for, at last, so angry did Tolimay become, but so determined not to react, that his anger swelled up inside of him until he exploded into a thousand bits, apparently much to the delight of the lad. Of course, no one could confirm this story, and Tolimay was last seen in the world in the year 483 of the Second Age.

Ishtorgus the Mariner (with Wink, a firefly Familiar)

Ishtorgus came into the world in the year 308, when the Fourth Unknown King came to power. Later in his life, he was known as Ishtorgus the Mariner. He was an advisor of King Thalamir of Glareth, the last of the Sea Kings. His Familiar was a firefly called Wink. After they became companions, they were never seen apart from each other. It is thought that Wink served Ishtorgus in a variety of ways, as a messenger and scout. He once made mention of how it was Wink that helped him understand the seasonal changes in the tides and even which woods of the forest might serve best for various crafts.

During the Dragonkind Invasion of 322 S.A., Ishtorgus went to Tulith Attis with Thalamir (who was then a young Prince), and fought next to him at the Battle of Saerdulin. He was credited with much of Thalamir's education, and when Thalamir became king, Ishtorgus was a valued advisor to his court. It was in those years, 330-369 S.A., that Ishtorgus helped Thalamir rebuild and expand Glareth's maritime power. Ishtorgus advanced this cause by convincing master shipbuilders from other realms to come to Glareth to work. Using information and knowledge gained from Barian the Counter, Ishtorgus refined various navigation methods, mostly using the stars. He introduced a method of producing celestial almanacs and ephemerides for use with a sextant. He also experimented with clocks, and it is thought that he introduced a reliable type of compass to Glareth and conducted experiments on magnetism. Ishtorgus also helped in the development of a triangular sail system that was first used on small craft and that would slowly become a distinctive feature of larger Glarethian warships long before being adopted by other ships.

When Thalamir died, Ishtorgus remained in Glareth to continue developing his ship designs. He also served as a teacher at the Glareth Sea Academy and, later, as a trade representative. He was aboard one of four ships that sailed together from Glareth bound for Tracia when the Great Storm of 505 S.A. struck and the group was driven far out to sea. The ship bearing Ishtorgus and one other were lost in a maelstrom which pulled them under the waves.

Raynor the Wise (with Beauchamp, a woodland rabbit Familiar)

Raynor came into the world in the year 318, when the Fifth Unknown King came to power. He was a renowned tutor and educator with many notable students, including Navis and Esildre of the House of Elmwood. As a result of his learnedness, he was often called Raynor the Wise.

His name first appears in the annals of Duinnor in the year 326 F.A. when it is recorded that a Melnari possessed of peculiar skill was able to decipher some of the old manuscripts that were possessed by the Fifth Unknown King and which had been brought to Duinnor during the Vanaran Purge of Scholars of the First Age. He was apparently instrumental in organizing several lesser schools in the Duinnor area. He privately tutored many students as well, including Esildre and her brother Navis of the House of Elmwood, although their sessions would be interrupted many times.

Raynor's Familiar was in the form of a woodland rabbit, called Beauchamp. The two were very close to each other, but on several occasions Beauchamp was separated from Raynor due to various "missions and errands" that Raynor asked Beauchamp to perform for him. Some of these turned into epic adventures on the part of the rabbit, worthy of their own pages.

Under the Sixth Unknown King, Raynor was given a position within the King's Academy in charge of the instruction of Kingsmen in academic matters. The King's Academy was reorganized in

355 S.A. when the King ordered that all Kingsmen must have fundamental skills of reading, writing, mathematics, engineering, and geography, and be given knowledge of law and history. That same year, Raynor was made Head Scholar (in effect, the headmaster), and under his leadership that the Academy quickly expanded from its purely military training to become a center for learning and research. Independent of his work at the Academy, Raynor also worked with other schools, particularly those for women who were not permitted to be Kingsmen, as well as schools for the poor.

Raynor continued as a private tutor. After Esildre and Navis returned from the east, where they had gone to fight against the Dragonkind invaders, they resumed their lessons with Raynor. Navis was not particularly enthusiastic about learning to read and write, ever restless and argumentative. But Esildre was determined to learn, and she became one of Raynor's greatest successes. However, he noticed how despondent she was after her return from Tulith Attis, becoming ever more withdrawn and introverted, even as her brother became ever more boisterous. Raynor encouraged her to give up her soldierly profession and take up more formal studies. Although she agreed to put away her sword for a time, she could not bear the company of others and refused to enroll in any school, and she begged Raynor not to press her on the matter, and to remain her tutor. She may have confided to him her feelings of depression or her desire to escape the influences of Elifaen. At any rate, her reading and writing skills improved so that she spent much of her time reading and discussing books that Raynor loaned to her. Then, under pressure from her father, Lord Banis, Esildre abruptly decided to go to Shatuum, seeking the isolation she longed for. Raynor vehemently opposed this, seeking to explain to Esildre what kind of creature Secundur really was. When she departed, Raynor wept bitterly, and he mourned her loss as a kind of suicide.

Sixty-three years later, when Navis became determined to rescue his sister from Shatuum, Raynor strongly opposed his plan. Navis's expedition was doomed from the start, as it turned out, and he would fall victim to murder conspiracy. After his departure, he was never heard from again.

Meanwhile, Raynor made many enemies in Duinnor by refusing to advance cadets merely because of their family's position, wealth, or influence. Rather, he insisted, as did the purely military trainers within the Academy, on excellence in all subjects of the curriculum. His situation became more difficult when he began openly criticizing Duinnor for its policies toward other Realms which he said ultimately hurt Duinnor's authority.

Sometime in the mid-590s, Raynor learned that Esildre had escaped from Shatuum. He also learned that she had taken up residence at Castle Elmwood, where she lived a life of debauchery and wantonness. He soon learned, too, that she had been cursed by Secundur, a curse not only designed to make her a pariah but to also make others who might become close to her victims of madness. Without her knowledge, Raynor worked to supply Esildre with servants who, being blind, were immune to her curse. As a result, a change took place in Esildre's heart when she realized the evil that was being transmitted through her, and she began a long struggle to check it. Raynor kept himself abreast of Esildre's condition through one of the servants he had arranged for her.

Raynor traveled extensively to gather materials for the Academy, even into the Dragonlands on several occasions. On his return from one such trip, in 723 S.A., he learned that he had been replaced as the Head Scholar, and he was subsequently arrested on suspicion of spying for Vanara. However, his many friends in court helped him prove that the charges had no merit, and he was soon exonerated. He did not, however, seek to be reinstated at the Academy.

From then on, Raynor worked as a bookseller, copyist, and tutor. He seldom left Duinnor. In 870, Raynor discovered the fate of Navis, who had disappeared on a quest to release Esildre from Shatuum. Through Beauchamp, Raynor learned that Navis had been murdered. He also obtained evidence that Navis's own father, Lord Banis, was behind the murder plot. He then arranged for Esildre to come to Duinnor (to the Temple of Beras) so that he could reveal details of his findings and plan a course of action to bring Banis to justice. He somewhat failed in this, but his disclosures to Esildre provoked her on a quest to locate Bailorg, the accused murderer. What happened to her, and to Raynor, is well-covered within *The Year of the Red Door.*

It is not known what happened to Raynor when the world was remade. Ullin Saheed Tallin found clues that Raynor and Collandoth set out together from Duinnor and suspected that they were bound for the Familiar Wood, but he could not locate that place nor find any clues to the whereabouts of Raynor or Collandoth.

Collandoth the Wanderer (with Certina, a screech owl Familiar)

We know more about Collandoth than any other Melnari due to his long career, the many people who knew him, and the many references to him in various documents, records, and books. He also left behind a bit of his own writings, mostly in the form of reports or letters.

He was commonly known amongst Men as "Ashlord," and he was sometimes referred to as Collandoth the Wanderer, and sometimes as Collandoth the Watcher.

Collandoth came into the world in the year 332 of the Second Age, when the Sixth Unknown King came to power. By the end of the Second Age, he was 538 years old, so it is no surprise that he had a varied and complicated career (even more so than Raynor, his elder). He was a mystic, warrior, witch-hunter, teacher, academic, diplomat, and counselor to Queen Serith Ellyn and many other high lords and ladies. Some regarded Collandoth as a holy man, but he shunned organized religious groups and cults, and regarded himself as "merely a person with faith."

The earliest written records of him from are dated in 336 or 337 SA (by Duinnor's calendar) are in Dragonkind annals which recorded that he successfully defended the city of Alaberbra (later called Kajarahn) against a rogue Dragonkind general who laid siege to the place. When the prince of the city was killed, Collandoth led the city in its defense and defeated the general. So grateful were the people of the city that they made him their king. Collandoth accepted the title only long enough to take advantage of the Dragonkind King Xurnon IV's appreciation for defeating his rebellious general so that the city would be granted an independent, city-state status as a Free City, to enjoy trade with the north as well as the Dragonlands. This was granted. Collandoth then installed a council of leaders to rule the city, and he abdicated to them. These events took place roughly around the year 336 S.A.

Records in Duinnor, dated 347 SA, describe him as a great witch hunter, but is, in fact, he was only one member of an elite company of witch and demon hunters from the Duinnor region. This was during a great outbreak of witches, demons, and vile creatures across the world. Having successfully eliminated them from Duinnor, the Nine Banes worked their way south, assisting wherever they could. It is unclear how, but while in Vanara a brief accord was reached with the Dragonkind, and the Nine Banes traveled to the city of Alaberbra which was severely stricken by the witches. There, Collandoth found the city devastated, all his old friends dead or missing, and the people living in miserable fear, constantly harassed and attacked by swarms of witches, imps, and lesser demons. With their cunning and, it seems, with their special weapons, they quickly destroyed the invaders, but not without loss, as four of their members were slain by demons. Again, Collandoth briefly took charge of the city, cleansing its water supply, treating its many wounded, and reorganizing the city's governance. After six months, he and the remaining of his company returned to the northern lands.

Sometime between 350 and 400 S.A., Collandoth acquired a Familiar, in the form of a little owl. Her name was Certina, and they became very close. Collandoth often seemed to actually converse with her, although no one ever heard the owl say anything. But it became apparent that the two became very close over the years, and she was a valuable helpmate for Collandoth, even rendering assistance to others. More about her is told within *The Year of the Red Door.*

Some texts in Duinnor and Glareth refer to Collandoth as one of the Twenty-Four Watchers (although no list has been found that names the other twenty-three). In manuscripts he was sometimes referred to as one of the Forge Ores, because legend had it that some Melnari undergo severe trials during their stay on earth to prepare for their eventual transformation into another plane of existence.

Between the years of 585 and 760 S.A., he spent a great deal of time in Duinnor where he taught at the King's Academy. He departed and disappeared for a long while, reappearing in Glareth in 780 S.A., and then in Vanara in 796 S.A., where he taught various subjects at the Queen's Academy.

He traveled widely, but was often seen in the court of Serith Ellyn, and it is thought that he advised her on a variety of matters, particularly concerning Shatuum and the Dragonlands and on issues concerning Vanara's relationship with Duinnor. He was known to be outspoken in his criticism of some of the Queen's policies. Likewise, in Glareth, he admonished Ruling Prince Carbane not to support Tracia's Ruling Prince Lewtrah, but to invest instead in backing his brother Prince Lantos, who sought to reform Tracia's corruption.

By the late Second Age, Collandoth was out of favor in most realms, probably because of his stern advice to Ruling Princes about the need to reform their ways. In Vanara, he was tolerated by Queen Serith Ellyn, and was able to play an important role in seeking to forge some truce with the Dragonlands, even acting as a trade representative on her behalf. It is thought that during those years (roughly 800-840 SA), he was instrumental in the smuggling of darakal plants out of the deserts so that they might be studied in an attempt to cultivate them in the north (Such cultivation failed.).

While in the Dragonlands, he befriended a young Dragonkind named Gurasa who convinced Collandoth to bring him north on his return to Vanara. Collandoth and Gurasa traveled throughout Vanara and on to Duinnor, where Gurasa met and was befriended by Lord Tallin and his son Dalvenpar. Although Gurasa always traveled in disguise, and his identity was carefully guarded by his new friends, the fact that he was Dragonkind was eventually learned by others not friendly with Collandoth or the Tallins. As a result, and especially after Gurasa rose to become a powerful general of the Dragonkind, Collandoth and the Tallins came under some suspicion for their friendliness to Gurasa.

Years later, and well after the peace was broken, Collandoth at first refused to take up arms against the Dragonkind. When the retreat from the First Siege of the Green Citadel took place, he was far away in Glareth where he had gone to study manuscripts located there. It was said that when news reached Glareth of the debacle, Collandoth ranted and paced for four days and nights without rest. Yet he remained in Glareth, and traveled from there throughout the Eastlands, visiting Colleton and Tallinvale before going to Tracia for a time.

In 842, Collandoth arrived back in Vanara only to learn that a second attempt to lay siege to the Green Citadel was taking place. The Queen's scribe, Orinus, recorded that Collandoth severely scolded Queen Serith Ellyn for permitting her forces to go with Duinnor's on such a foolhardy mission. A heated argument ensued between Collandoth and the Queen, which was interrupted only when news came that a botched retreat was once again taking place (just as with the first assault on the Green Citadel) . Together, Collandoth and Serith Ellyn led a hastily assembled army to relieve a group of over two thousand of their comrades who were isolated and surrounded by Dragonkind in a steep ravine called Peldown, located in the Blue Mountains. They arrived, along with a contingent of Kingsmen, in time to turn the tide of battle and to rescue their surviving allies and kinsmen. The battle was so costly and bloody that the place came to be called Gory Gulch.

After this, Vanara (and the Queen, particularly) seemed more disposed to listen to Collandoth's advice. It is said by some that he worked to assemble a group of secretive peace-minded conspirators, to make overtures to dissident Dragonkind, and to thwart the rise of Duinnor's power in Vanara, and to weaken those who directed Duinnor Regular Army units who ever agitated for and even provoked battle and unrest with the Dragonkind.

Collandoth eventually enlisted several high-ranking Kingsmen to his cause who took on some of the more clandestine work in the desert lands. Then, mysteriously, Collandoth departed the west, traveling first to Duinnor, then east. In 859 S.A., he appeared in the Eastlands bearing a writ from

Duinnor that made him warden of Tulith Attis. A few years later, in 864 S.A., he would take up residence there. How he managed to obtain the writ is subject to speculation, but likely it was provided "on behalf of the King" by a high-ranking Kingsman.

Those familiar with the events of the Year of the Red Door certainly know of Collandoth's involvement and important actions. It was he who saved the life of the future king, Robby Ribbon (King Philawain), and thereafter sought to advise and guide him.

In 870 S.A., Collandoth was amongst the first to detect the invading Tracian Redvests, and he took warning of their arrival at Tulith Attis to Boskland, with the Redvests close behind him. While Garend Bosk, Laird of Boskland, put up a hastily prepared defense, Collandoth took many women and children with him and fled to Passdale. At Passdale, he and many others of the region fought a rearguard action to allow the people there time to escape to Janhaven, and he only barely managed to escape capture during the fighting. Shortly afterwards, he joined with a party intent on traveling west to spread word of the invasion to Duinnor. Although they intended to do that, it served as a cover for their more important mission, which was to deliver Robby Ribbon to Griferis, protecting him along the arduous way.

During this trek, while traveling along the western edges of the Carthanes, the group was attacked by a witch that Collandoth dispatched. However, while he sent the others on, he remained behind to seek out the dead witch's lair and to destroy it. As a result, he wound up doing battle with Valkose, a great demon from the earliest days of the world. As a result of wounds sustained in this fight, Collandoth's appearance, and somewhat his demeanor, changed, as is described in The Year of the Red Door. He would catch up with and rejoin the group some while later and guide them safely through Forest Islindia.

The group that Collandoth led eventually split. Robby Ribbon and Ullin Saheed Tallin would indeed make it to Griferis via Vanara. Meanwhile, Collandoth, Sheila Pradkin, Billy Bosk, and Ibin Brinnin went to Duinnor and immediately became embroiled in the conspiracies and corruption that Lord Banis was behind. As a result of Banis, Collandoth narrowly escaped assassination, and he (along with his comrades) also narrowly escaped a second attempt, due to the timely intervention of Eldwin of the Nowhereans.

King Philawain succeeded in taking the throne of Duinnor, but he immediately abdicated to his new wife, Sheila Pradkin (Lady Shevalia). Collandoth continued to serve her as her chief advisor, guiding her through various decisions until the world was remade.

It is not known what happened to Collandoth when the world was remade. Ullin Saheed Tallin found clues that Raynor and Collandoth set out together from Duinnor and suspected that they were bound for the Familiar Wood, but he could not locate that place nor find any clues to the whereabouts of Raynor or Collandoth.

See Also:
Biographical Sketches (Gurasa)
Glossary (Valkose the Demon)

The Melnari and the Familiar Wood

At some point in each Melnari's life, he acquires a peculiar companion, called a Familiar, in the form of some creature. The nature of the relationship between the Melnari and his Familiar remains mysterious but, once together, they are hardly ever seen apart from one another. Among papers discovered after the death of Lord Rolland Seafar (a friend of Collandoth) was an unpublished treatise upon the subject. He had the following to say:

> Over the ages, the Melnari have learned, somewhat, about themselves, but they keep that knowledge close. They know that whenever a new King comes to Duinnor, a new Melnari will come into the world somewhere, though it may be many years before he is known. They know, too, that they are not natives of the

world they were sent into, yet they are intimately connected to it. Although their memory is keen, and rarely do they become forgetful, they remember nothing prior to the morning that they first took breath and opened their eyes. But if they have no memory of the time before, they have something else of it, some sense of it, a sense of vastness filled with beauty and sublime harmony. And this was not a sense of loss, like the Elifaen feel of the time before they lost their wings. Rather, the Melnari have an inclination that the prior state of being lay ahead of them, not behind, and they feel a state of privilege to have that sense. It is an optimism about existence that informs them through all trials and challenges.

The Melnari's life in this world is divided into three stages. First there is the Wandering, a time when they first come into the world. During this time, they learn about the world by traveling through it, learning of its peoples and places and histories. Then comes the Settling, a period when they abide in one place to work and to meditate upon things. During this time, they learn what it is to work and labor, to serve and to lead. They ponder and assimilate those things they have seen in the world during their Wandering. Afterwards comes the time of Urging. This is when they become restless and uncertain, and they leave their home to participate in the world. During this time, each Melnari's path takes him to the same place as all other Melnari have gone before, though he does not realize what is calling him. This place, to all other eyes, is a small woodland that lies in a band of gentle hills along the southeast borders of the Vanaran frontier. It is out of the way to most travelers, unremarkable, and not a place you can find if you look for it, and those who do stumble upon it do not see it for what it is. But, somehow, the Melnari is pulled there, driven by some power within his heart, a heart that has come to feel lonely and somewhat lost. However long it takes, and by whatever roundabout path that leads him there, he comes. And when he arrives, he realizes that it is the urging of this unremarkable place that has been calling to him all the while. As he enters the soft shadows of its trees, peace touches his heart, and gentle gladness, too, as if welcomed by the modest woodland and all of its humble creatures.

Sometimes known in legend as the Familiar Wood, all things there are truly familiar to the Melnari, and to anyone else who may accidentally come there. All creatures, all trees, every stone, hillside, and valley, and all of the streams there seem utterly mundane, with nothing out of place or unusual. Everything is exactly what it seems. Utterly so, in fact, so that nothing is merely what it seems, disguised by openness. And does each thing understand what it is? Does a rock understand that it is a rock? One should think not, for a rock has no means of understanding, surely. And so, most people would do just what they should, and think not. But if you heft up any rock of this Familiar Wood, it would protest to you. That is, if you had the ears to hear. And the Melnari who comes to this little wood does. He and his kind have something of what the Elifaen have slowly lost. So the Melnari understands what the rock says. And why it is said. It is in the nature of the rock to be hard, to resist you as you pick it up, and that is what is said.

In this wood, are gathered those creatures of the Time Before Time, when the world was still being made manifest into the forms of the Faerekind. Indeed, all things here are creatures, gathered from all over the world, and in every form. But these are creatures who had not yet fully been born of the spirit of the earth into the form of the Faere, but were locked in their intermediate forms when the Faerekind lost their wings and all such growth in the world came to an abrupt end. The Urging, felt by the Melnari visitor, is not his own but that of those creatures and beings of the Familiar Wood, stunted in growth and forced to retain the form from which they would otherwise have sprung into the world.

When a Melnari comes, one has already been chosen to speak openly to him, and to thereafter go with him into the wide world outside the Wood to be his helpmate and companion. But the visitor must find that creature and give it a name that pleases it before this may take place. This quest within the Familiar Wood may take weeks, even years, but the patient and sympathetic Melnari will not leave until it is accomplished.

First, he listens to all, and thereby comes to detect the one that will not speak until named. It is a game the Wood plays with the Melnari, chattering its chatter as a distraction to him so that he must hear them. The trees creak their slow verse, inflected with the breezy shush of their leaves. The birds titter and whistle their songs, and the deer bray forth their panting exuberance. The snake hisses its admonishments while the chipmunks dance and squeak with laughter while their cousins, the squirrels, argue and complain. Careless and full of frivolous delight, the stream sings and laughs and repeats its verses with endless variation. And through this cacophony, the Melnari seeks the Hidden One, who remains silent all the while. When the Melnari finds this silent one, he will spend much time in consideration of the creature, observing with his eyes to see all of the ways of the creature, and listening with his ears to hear every noise it makes until at last he finds the Name. And when the Name is found, the Melnari calls to the creature, and it comes to him as all the other beings of the Familiar Wood become silent and watchful, satisfied that the Melnari has fairly won the game. It is now that the creature the Melnari has called forth reveals what sort of person it almost is and would have become. As if seeing for the first time, great secrets are thereby revealed to the Melnari.

Then, understanding his mission in the world as never before, the Melnari departs the wood, along with his Familiar.

Of the various Familiars, Certina and Beauchamp seemed to have developed the closest relationships with their companions. Indeed, Collandoth was not reticent to express his love and admiration for Certina, saying that he did not know how he could do without her companionship. He said that Certina was petulant, proud, prone to pouts, and was inclined to rapscallion stunts. But this only seemed to endear her to him all the more, for he also saw how attentive she was to all things, how she was ever reluctant to leave his company, and how she cooed so tenderly when the two were alone with each other. Many people who knew Collandoth and Certina noted the "bird's" uncanny expressiveness, even without speech or sound. And they noted their behavior toward one another was more akin to friends than master and servant, and that Collandoth seemed quite paternal towards her, as if she were a child, often to the extent of doting on her and lavishing her with compliments and praise before others. Even Raynor, who also had a close relationship with his Familiar, made comment that Collandoth was apt to spoil Certina, but then always added, "But why not?"

Yet equally mysterious were the other Familiars when their companion Melnari died. The activities of Wink and Telliniece and Hanion are obscure, yet they were apparently attentive to the happenings of the world. Fallendine, too, and perhaps more so. He actively engaged with Micerea and somehow developed a relationship with her akin to that which he ought to have had with Tolimay. He became her eyes, her messenger, and even on one occasion her courier to deliver items to Robby Ribbon. Yet these four familiars joined with Robby Ribbon's cause, along with Certina and Beauchamp, such that when he became King Philawain, they were able to perform for him various tasks. Indeed, they were essential to Philawain's effort to convince Queen Serith Ellyn to relinquish her Bloodcoins, as is described within the pages of *The Year of the Red Door*. That tale contains within it references to chipmunks and fireflies, but we do not know if these ever may have been Familiars in their common disguise.

For the Familiars, their form was their disguise, their nature, and their prison. None were intended to be as they were, it seems. All of their development from spirits in to living beings, into Faerekind, had ceased when Aperion called away the Faithful. Those not yet fully formed were stranded. Yet there remained within them a strong yearning to be freed of their intermediate form, to fulfill their initial Urge. Perhaps their motivation to aid King Philawain was entwined with such hopes and longings. Certainly they acted as such when they aided King Philawain.

****

Battle of Soltani Pass

On the 18th day of Twelfthmonth, in the Year 870, the Kingsman Fourth Army fought a decisive battle against Wickerman forces. With this Kingsman victory, a significant revolt against Duinnor was crushed.

It is estimated that the Wickermen numbered some 12-13,000 men, mostly on foot with a few riders, mainly captains. The Kingsman Fourth fielded its First through Fourth Battalions, leaving a garrison force behind them at Edgewold. The garrison force of about three hundred and fifty footmen consisted mainly of Kingsmen who had been wounded in previous engagements, as well as a small contingent of armored horsemen who were to fight their way through the enemy, if need be, to act as couriers (once clear of the enemy, these would shed their armor to ride faster and more nimbly). All told, the Edgewold force numbered around three hundred, leaving some 3,200 Kingsman to fight at Soltani Pass. General Teracue had also enlisted a small army of about 1,300 men and women from Edgewold to man flanking positions and act as a following force. The following force was to advance closely behind the Kingsmen line and dispatch or capture any Wickermen who made it through the front lines of the battle. Teracue knew that his force was terribly outnumbered, but he relied on the discipline and skill of his Kingsmen, with their better arms and armor, and the lack thereof on the part of the Wickermen.

Prelude to Battle: The Situation

In early spring of 870, a sinister cult sprang up in the town of Westlawn led by a man or Elifaen who was thought to have magical or supernatural powers. His name was Bunar, thought by some to be somehow associated with Secundur. He arrived in the town of Edgewold with about forty armed followers. They claimed to be followers and agents of Wotan, a godlike deity who lived in the vines that they planted in and around the town.

Within weeks, the vines, which they called "kudzu," quickly spread and became a nuisance. The vines grew up and over houses, spread into fields and pastures, and threatened to smother the entire region. The cult members cut and gathered much of the vines, and weaved them into a kind of wicker armor worn like a cuirass. Then Bunar announced that he could save the town and surrounding area from the kudzu if only they submit to his leadership. He demonstrated his power over the vines by walking about the town and invoking a god he called Wotan to make the vines retreat, which they did. This demonstration convinced many Edgewolders of his authority. The cult leader and his followers then attempted to convince the people of Edgewold and the surrounding area to join them. Bunar declared that Duinnor Law was no good and had no power over them. He stated that he intended to create a new realm, independent of Duinnor.

In spite of his power over the vines, the majority of Edgewold remained loyal to Duinnor and rebuffed the Wickermen (as they came to be called). Then the cult incited an insurrection. Using his followers as provocateurs, Bunar gained many disgruntled new followers and began rioting and looting. At the same time, he brought back the rapidly moving vines over the gates of the town and into the streets. He and his followers were then confronted by a very large crowd of Edgewolders bearing torches, scythes, and other tools. They attacked, cut, chopped and burned the vines away. At the same time, many of the town's people directly fought the Wickermen with what weapons they could muster. Thus, the uprising was quickly put down. But Bunar and his chief officers escaped capture, along with most of his followers and a few others that had been recruited (or coerced) from Edgewold.

Unbeknownst to anyone in Edgewold, the Wickermen had also started a similar campaign at Westlawn, some twenty miles south of Edgewold. They met with better success, having learned from their Edgewold mistakes, and soon had full control over the town. In Westlawn, the Wickermen quickly organized an army and began spreading their kudzu and taking over nearby farms and small villages. They also began raiding farms and small settlements outside of their territory, mainly east of Edgewold. By late summer of 870, they essentially controlled an area from about five miles north of Westlawn, extending some twenty miles west, south, and east. The Edgewolders were sufficiently alarmed to begin raising a defensive wall around their town, cutting vast tracts of trees to use as materials. At the same time, the Edgewolders sent word to Duinnor appealing for armed assistance. They made it clear that they needed a large army, and that they would also consider engaging the services of mercenaries in their cause.

The situation continued to escalate, and the Kingsman High Command consulted with the Realm Judges and with Lord Banis on the question of authority over those lands. It was promptly ruled that Edgewold and Westlawn were part of Duinnor Realm and were subject to the King's Law. A formal order was immediately issued to send an army south to Edgewold.

The Fourth Kingsman Army had just returned from duties in the desert, and since they were already on an active service status, they were given the order to turn around and march south to Edgewold. On the day of those orders, word reached Duinnor that its ambassador to Altoria and his entire party had been captured by the Wickermen. The ambassador was carrying sensitive documents and was traveling to Duinnor to deliver his routine annual report. The ambassador's capture prompted the Kingsmen High Command to issue new orders for General Teracue and his Fourth Army: they were to march immediately to the rescue of any Duinnor citizens held by the rebels. The orders gave Teracue broad independent authority. He was empowered to enforce Duinnor Law, to use whatever means or materials available, to defend Edgewold from further attacks, and to put down the Wickerman rebellion. Teracue was given license to go wherever he deemed necessary for the "defense of the King and His Law by confronting and defeating any rebellion" et cetera (Teracue would later use the orders as a pretext and justification for marching his army to the Eastlands.). The orders also specified that Teracue was to first attempt to negotiate with the Wickermen for the peaceful release of all prisoners and their effects. If that was not fruitful, Teracue was to use whatever force necessary to rescue and free all prisoners and to prevent further kidnappings. In essence, General Teracue had full discretionary control over the movements and actions of the Fourth Army.

The Arrival of the Kingsmen

The Kingsman Fourth Army arrived in Edgewold to find the town under siege. An army of some five thousand Wickermen was encamped outside of Edgewold. During the previous week, they had twice broken through the Edgewold defenses, setting fire to buildings, but were repelled both times. When Teracue arrived, the Fourth easily drove away the Wickermen. General Teracue then held a war council with the leaders of Edgewold. It was a diplomatic move on Teracue's part—a show of respect for the townspeople—but everyone understood that Teracue was really in command.

Within a day, Teracue's men began repairing and improving the town's defenses. Work on the defensive walls resumed with great vigor. Chevaux de fries and earthen walls were erected many yards out from the town wall, which would slow any enemy assault and create a killing field immediately below the walls. Hoardings with embrasures were built along the southern stretch of the town walls, and the most vulnerable areas were given drop boxes.

The work was difficult and demanding and involved nearly every able-bodied resident of Edgewold working day and night side-by-side with Kingsmen. Kingsmen also acted as guards for the workers, repelling frequent raids by the Wickermen. In spite of the scale of the construction work, it was nearly completed within three weeks, just in time to face the first real Wickerman assault.

The Wickermen's First Major Attack

The Wickermen failed to reconnoiter, so they did not know that the northern stretch of defenses were incomplete and vulnerable. Instead of attacking there, they concentrated their efforts on the south and eastern walls. The eastern wall, where the main gate to the town was located, was the scene of repeated assaults as the Wickermen tried to bring forward battering rams.

Teracue kept a strong contingent of Kingsmen well outside the town with orders to remain undiscovered by the Wickermen. They were to watch the attacks on the city and take advantage of any opportunity to stage a counterattack. This tactic worked repeatedly, with Kingsman horsemen acting as shock troops ahead of heavily armored footmen. On several occasions, Teracue himself led the counterattacks.

It became readily apparent that the Wickermen army had no effective leadership and lacked a clear strategy for taking Edgewold. They relied on frontal assaults, with battering rams and pots of flaming pitch against the wooden walls. But the attacks were not well coordinated, allowing the defenders to mass on the particular area of wall under assault. The Wickermen continually failed to scout the area and so remained ignorant of the Kingsmen forces positioned outside of the town within striking distance. The Wickermen did not construct siege engines such as trebuchets, nor did they attempt to mine the walls. Had they done either of those things, Teracue would have been hard-pressed to mount an effective defense. After two weeks, the Wickerman withdrew, leaving behind thousands of their dead comrades. By this time, Teracue had a clear understanding of the capabilities and tactics of the Wickermen.

During the following lull in the fighting, Teracue attempted to establish lines of communication with the Wickermen leadership, offering to negotiate for the release of prisoners. Each offer was rebuffed. Then Teracue received a message that his offer would be considered if he spoke in person with one of the Wickermen leaders. It was a trick. On his way to the meeting place, a large company of Wickermen ambushed his party. The Wickermen were heavily armed and succeeded in driving a wedge through the company of about thirty Kingsmen escort riders, and General Teracue became separated from his men. Unable to press through the Wickermen throng, Teracue fought furiously. His horse was soon killed from under him, but Teracue quickly got to his feet. With no shield, Teracue fought with gladius and dagger, making his way toward his comrades as they fought their way toward him. Fortunately for Teracue, the Wickermen were unskilled and undisciplined fighters. By the time Teracue and his escort rejoined, a score of Wickermen lay dead. The rest, disheartened, soon withdrew. Teracue and his entire escort, having suffered only minor wounds, quickly returned to Edgewold.

The Enemy Gathers

That same day, upon Teracue's return, a farmer who had been taken prisoner by the Wickermen escaped his captors and made his way to Edgewold with important news. The farmer told Teracue that all of the Duinnor ambassador's party, including the ambassador himself, were publicly executed in Westlawn. It was done as a sign, so said the farmer, that Duinnor had "no authority over Wokan and Wokan's people." He also said that the Wickermen's previous attacks against Edgewold were only feints. The purpose was to keep the Kingsmen busy at Edgewold so as not to discover the assembly of a much larger army at Westlawn.

This news was soon confirmed by Teracue's agents and scouts. It was apparent that a large army was gathering and preparing a massive attack against Edgewold. The scouts estimated that over eight thousand soldiers were already gathered and encamped about Westlawn, with hundreds more arriving every day. Many of the soldiers were mercenaries from Masurthia and Altoria, some were clansmen from the mountains south of Forest Islindia, and others were under the command of ambitious but weak warlords. They were all seduced by the Wickermen's dream of rebuffing Duinnor, by the promise of loot and riches gained from the expansion of Wotan's territory and by taking control of the Great South Road that ran from Duinnor City to Draymoor—an important and lucrative trade route.

Only Edgewold stood in their way.

Teracue surmised that the Wickerman army intended to do as they had before. That is, they would attempt a massive frontal assault against the walls of Edgewold. There was little chance that the town could withstand an attack by so many of the enemy. The only chance to defeat the Wickermen was to intercept them before they reached Edgewold. Such an army, ill-led and undisciplined, would have to come through Soltani Pass, a few miles south of Edgewold. That was the only place where Teracue's small force could make a stand. Preparations began immediately.

Battle

There are many accounts of the battle. One view of it was expressed in *The Year of the Red Door*. Other accounts, including reports later submitted by Teracue and other officers, were sent to Duinnor, and later found by Ullin Saheed Tallin (who was a participant in the battle). Ullin also found another account of the battle, that of Baroth Langdon, a councilman of Edgewold who witnessed the event. In his youth, Langdon had served with the Duinnor Regulars and had seen action in the desert. He was seventy-four years of age at the time of the battle. Although he had taken up arms to defend his people, he was not deemed fit enough to participate in the action at Soltani Pass. Nonetheless, he accompanied the army. Afterwards, he wrote an account of the battle in a letter to his nephew who was in Duinnor. The nephew passed the letter on to the Duinnor Star, and it was promptly published. After assuring his nephew that all his kin were safe and unharmed, Langdon summarized the general situation before proceeding with his account of the battle, which we share here:

> As you know, Soltani Pass is really a small vale that runs north and south. The vale is about a half-mile wide at the southern opening, bounded by gentle slopes. It narrows gradually northward for about two miles, as the sides of the vale grow steeper. At its northern end, the ground is nearly level and is only about two hundred yards wide, embraced on either side by hills that rise steeply to about fifty or so feet above the floor of the pass. It is as if a gigantic shovel had scooped up the earth in order to make a gentle opening to the north, some five miles from Edgewold. It was there, at the northern extremity of Soltani Pass, where it was naturally constricted, that General Teracue intended to meet the enemy.

> Two days before, word came to us that the Wickermen would march against Edgewold. Already Teracue's preparations had begun. He enlisted several thousand men (and a few strong women) to enhance his forces. He had a kind of palisade built along each side of the pass at the base of the hills, and these palisades angled inward with the hills toward the narrow north opening. The palisades were made of saplings and poles, something like a high fence with narrow openings between each post. They were lined with sharp stakes pointing outward to discourage and slow any assault. Brush and limbs that were cut from the saplings were scattered in piles on the ground some few yards away from the palisades to further obstruct an enemy charge against them. Behind the palisades were men and boys armed with swords and spears. Their purpose was to deny the Wickerman the high ground and to act as a sort of funnel to crowd and channel the enemy onward to the north and the awaiting line of Kingsmen.

> These palisades were about a hundred yards in length, and ended at the north ends of the pass where it is only about two hundred yards from side to side. It was there that General Teracue arranged his Kingsmen. Three battalions were deployed in a dense line, shoulder-to-shoulder, from east to west, fully blocking the way. In the very front was the Fourth Heavy Assault Battalion, armored from head to foot, in a

line three men deep. I was told that a fully armored Kingsman gained some sixty pounds in weight, not including shield or weapons. They were a wonder to see, otherworldly, like something from legend.   All of the Kingsmen carried tall rectangular shields, curved somewhat on the sides, and they all carried a rather short sword called a gladius. Its blade is about three inches at the widest, and tapered to a very sharp point. It is about three feet long and weighs about four pounds. Such a weapon is mainly for jabbing and stabbing, but both edges of it are sharpened all the way to the tang.

The second and third lines of Kingsmen—so close that their breath fell upon their comrades in front of them—were the First Battalion and part of the Second Battalion, armed with shield and sword like all Kingsmen, but with lighter armor than the Fourth.   Similarly, behind these were two more lines composed of the Third Battalion along with the rest of the Second Battalion. Altogether, from front to back, the lines were nine or ten men deep.

Behind the Kingsmen, and with a gap of about twenty or thirty yards, was an array of our countrymen and townspeople. They were armed as well as they could be, some with swords, some with lances, some with scythes or large knives, and some carrying only sharpened poles. None had any armor. Their hope was that the Kingsmen could withstand the brunt of the enemy attack, and that was Teracue's plan. It was understood that any Wickerman who made it through the Kingsmen line would be dealt with by our people.

By dawn, all were in position. I watched from the top of a hill on the east flank, my old sword in hand. From where I stood, the palisades on my side of the pass were about forty feet below me at the bottom of the steep hillside. I was with a group of elderly men such as myself. We were not supposed to be there at all, but each of us had managed to procure a pass that allowed us to come. I, myself, had to pay a tidy bribe for my own pass. We were all of us armed, although I doubt we could have posed much of a threat to anyone. But there we were, thinking that our presence might discourage any Wickermen from climbing the hill and coming around the Kingsmen.

Nearby to where we stood, and somewhat behind us, were about a hundred archers, made up of our people but commanded by Kingsmen. Also nearby were four trebuchets situated far enough behind the top of the hill so as not to be seen from below. I could see across the vale to the other side, and it appeared to be a mirror image to us with its own archers and trebuchets. I'm sure on that far side there must have been others who, like myself, by rights probably should not have been there, but who were determined to watch the engagement and, if need be, to fight.

I must say that my stomach fluttered and churned, just as it did in the days of my service to the King. I never was a confident soldier—every fight and skirmish filled me with fear. I did my duty well, I hope, and I intended to do thus again on this day. But I confess to having a sense of overwhelming dread and sadness and fear. Sadness that things should come to such a state where only terrible violence against one another could resolve matters. Dread that so many of my friends and quite a few of my kinsmen might have only a little while longer to live. And fear that, should we not prevail, my town would be defenseless against the wicked and the vile. I feared especially for my wife and three daughters. They are all as sturdy as they come, by virtue of their strength of heart, which more than compensated for any frailty of their sweet and lovely frames. I could not prevail upon them to flee northward, and when I last kissed them goodbye, they were busy sharpening daggers and tearing sheets into bandages.

I should say that General Teracue, though confident, touched every contingency with his plans. Horsemen in saddle were behind all of the front lines, and should we be defeated upon the field, the horsemen would swiftly carry word back to Edgewold so that they could brace for the inevitable attack. I did not know at the time (none of us did) that Teracue had long before sent secret orders that the Fifth Training Battalion should march to us and position itself a few miles north of Edgewold. The presence of the Fifth Battalion was a carefully guarded secret, and some of our riders would fetch them to the town's defense if need be. I also did not know that Teracue had reduced his force at Soltani Pass and sent nearly four hundred men and engineers southward with siege engines and other war machines, and that they were to meet us at Westlawn once the Pass was cleared of the enemy. It was perhaps audacious of Teracue, but his reckoning was that, should we be victorious at Soltani Pass, he would press the fight to the walls of Westlawn. And if we were not victorious, it would not much matter; the men near Westlawn, alerted by fast riders, were to harass and harm the enemy as best as they could.

The previous days had been full of intermittent rain that came down suddenly and departed just as quickly. General Teracue hoped that Soltani Pass would be boggy with wet ground and would thus hinder the enemy's advance. However, it seemed that Sir Wind or some other capricious entity kept the rain away from the pass. But for the morning dew, it was as dry as ever could be. So dry, in fact, that we could see clouds of dust rising from the south long before we could see the Wickermen army that stirred it up. I am afraid that for a long while I was entranced by that cloud of dust, and I fancied that I could hear the tromp of their approach. I was jarred from my trance by the sudden beat of a nearby drum. It beat slowly but steadily—bump, bump, bump, bump—and on the fourth beat three thousand Kingsmen swords were drawn and leveled, the wall of shields spiny with steel blades. Bump, bump, bump, bump, went the drum, and on the fourth beat the front three lines of Kingsmen stepped forward and gave a mighty call—RAH! Again on the fourth beat, they stepped forward with a shout, and the next three lines followed. Again, and the third tier of Kingsmen also stepped forward. Between each of the Kingsman lines was now a small gap, and I did not understand why they were positioning themselves as such. It would soon become grisly apparent.

By now the roar of the approaching Wickermen was almost as loud as the drum and shout of the Kingsmen, and when I looked southward I saw what can only be described as a terrible flood of men, obscured by a cloud of dust, as far as my eyes could see. And they were coming fast. It was as if a great storm rushed toward us. My throat went dry. Our lines were nine men deep, but our enemy was ninety men deep and more. Looking back upon it now, I do not understand why I did not take flight, for I trembled most violently with fear. Yet I seemed planted, as if in a terrible dream from which I could not rouse myself.

In front of the Wickerman horde rode a few of their leaders, captains or priests or thugs or whatever they were, dressed in white robes and pointed white hats. They rode back and forth in front of their shield-beating mob, whipping them into such a state of furor that the very scent of hatred was upon the air. Then one of those riders suddenly convulsed, jerking the reins so violently that his horse reared and turned in a bizarre spasm. Someone from the other side of the vale had made true the long flight of an arrow, burying its head and shaft right through that Wickerman's heart. As he fell dead from this horse, a shout of approval lifted up from our comrades opposite us and quite a few on our own side of the vale. But the death of one of their leaders only sparked in the Wickermen mass a greater roar of madness.

All the while, the gap between the enemy and the Kingsmen narrowed and narrowed. And whilst the Wickermen broke into a running charge, the unperturbed Kingsmen still slowly stepped and shouted "Rah!" Stepped and shouted, stepped and shouted. But now I saw what they did. They shifted their ranks so that every score of men or so one was out ahead with two just behind on either side of him, and each of those with several Kingsmen behind and beside them. The entire line of Kingsmen was transforming itself into an evenly spaced row of dense triangles, with the points to the Wickermen. The base of each triangle met that of the triangles on either side, and my people pressed close in behind all of these.

I had only just perceived this maneuver when the Wickermen and Kingsmen collided. I can hardly describe the sound. It was like a terrible crunch and clang of thunder, full of the grunts of men crashing into one another. Then the dust enveloped all, and I could make out nothing of what was happening below. But I could hear it. The Kingsmen still shouted Rah! with every fourth beat, but their voices were quite nearly drowned out by the yells and shouts and screams of the Wickermen. The dust seemed to thin somewhat, and I saw before me, from just below my vantage, all the way across the vale to the other side, nothing but Wickermen. Wickermen pressing into the Kingsmen, and more Wickermen pressing in behind those.

And that was precisely what Teracue had counted on.

With each shout of "Rah!" and in defiance of the legions that had collided with them, the Kingsmen still advanced. And their line, I now saw, was like a terrible jagged blade that cut into the Wickermen, that forced them between the wedges of Kingsmen swords and shields, that pressed the Wickermen into the very jaws of death. So densely packed was the horde that they could not swing their broadswords, they could not jab their spears or even thrust their long knives. And so the Wickermen fell. They fell, and they fell. And the Kingsmen stepped over the dead and dying in neat precision, seemingly without the least upset in their lines.

Then there was a great rush of air above my head as hundreds of arrows flew over me and down into the great press of men. A trebuchet behind me groaned and swung a bushel of flaming jars to rain down upon the horde. For a moment, I was overjoyed, for I now saw the inevitable outcome as the utter destruction of my enemy unfolded. Then I choked as the line of Kingsmen met up with where I was and continued on past me. My own people came behind them, and behind them trailed a field of blood and death.

The defenders of the palisades now poured into the Wickermen from both sides. Down from the opposing hills charged the archers who now wielded shields and swords. There was no stopping the Kingsmen from their duty, and no stopping my own people from their wrath. So gruesome the sight! So vicious! But a few moments later, the carnage was nearly complete.

I then witnessed, after the battle was clearly won, a sight that will forever haunt me. Many of the enemy plead for mercy, but very few received it. Many stood their ground, but none held it. And what was just a few moments before a vast army of Wickermen was now a red sea of dead and wounded. I saw men trying to crawl away, but were hacked to death by my townsmen. I saw boys begging for mercy who were run through with the swords and knives of my people or were beaten to death with clubs and mallets. I saw Kingsmen break from their ranks to try to stop the massacre of the wounded and the helpless. I saw Teracue himself, sword in hand, ride down a band of my people to drive them away from a group of huddled Wickermen who were upon their knees with their empty hands in the air. It was not long before the Kingsmen restored order. But, alas, it was not soon enough for many.

At some moment that I do not recall, I had dropped my sword and fallen to my knees. I had put my hands over my mouth to stifle my sobs, but I could not take my eyes from what I saw, blurry though they were. In horror and in disbelief, I, an old man, wept and moaned like a child.

Let no one say that battle is glorious. Let no one say that men are not made into the basest of animals when roused to fury. We of Edgewold were made the victims of the Wickermen, and we at last prevailed over them that day at Soltani Pass. Victims we had been, yet now we could no longer pretend to innocence. We were very glad that our own families were safe, yet many the family was broken that day, and lay in blood and death and ruin.

I cannot speak for those of our enemy, who were not long before our neighbors and friends. Nor can I fathom what may have driven them to act as they did, what malevolent force blackened their hearts against us and led them to take up arms. Yet now, looking over the field before me, I had much to wonder about concerning my own people. I think I will never look at them the same way as before.

I shall conclude, my dear nephew, with this:

The Kingsmen, I am told, have a tradition of meditating on their work when battle is done. They meditate, and they wash and bathe as they do so, cleansing themselves of battle's gore and, so it is said, of any guilt or shame. But I was made to wonder, watching from atop that hill, whether there was enough water in the all the rivers and seas to wash away the stain that the Wickermen left upon us and upon our lands. No longer have we any doubt as to what we ourselves are capable of.

The Monstrous Conclusion

The fighting at Soltani Pass was over just before noon. Teracue was prepared for victory, having sent by careful routes several small companies of engineers with war machines onward toward the Wickerman stronghold town of Westlawn. These were to remain hidden until notified of the battle's outcome, then, when reinforcements arrived, to move into position before the town's north walls. When the fighting at Soltani Pass was over, therefore, he quickly reformed his men and they began their march on Westlawn in all haste. Although weary from the fight, the Kingsmen paced themselves carefully, using wagons and carts to bring their heavy shields, armor, and supplies. By mid-afternoon, having marched about five miles, they approached a town in chaos.

The cult leader, whose name was thought to be Bunar, had conjured a great monster made of living human flesh and vines of kudzu. Bunar was devoured by it almost immediately when it became animated with the most malevolent spirit. This creature was some six stories high, and as Teracue rode before the walls of Westlawn to call for the surrender of the town, this monster began moving through the town toward the north gate, outside of which the Kingsmen were massing. As it through the town, it devoured all within reach of its spreading tendrils, spreading terror among the inhabitants. The Kingsmen watched in horror as it approached, while hundreds of people leapt from the walls to try to escape. The gates of the city burst open and thousands of people poured forth in terror as the monster strode through their midst. As told within *The Year of the Red Door*, as soon as the creature came within range of arrow and trebuchet shot, the Kingsmen engaged it, using fiery missiles, to ignite it and wielding axes and swords against its spreading tentacles.

All seemed hopeless until, just as the creature advanced into the Kingsmen, a vast flock of geese appeared on the scene and began tearing into the monster, pulling out bits of leafy vine and swarming the hideously roaring beast. This work sent the monster into a frenzy of distraction as it waved its arms around to fend off the birds. This allowed the Kingsmen to shoot pots of flaming oil against the beast, and soon it was burning in agony. As more missiles struck it, the beast toppled and fell and was consumed with an awful fire.

Somewhat in shock, the Kingsmen entered and took full control of Westlawn, finding the town much devastated by the monster.

Thus ended the Wickerman rebellion. Unfortunately, none of the hostages taken by the Wickermen were ever found, although some of their belongings were located. By most estimates, the Wickermen lost over 10,000 killed, with some 4,000 wounded. The Kingsman forces (including the Edgewold fighters) lost around 100 dead altogether, with some 1,000 seriously wounded.

With the cessation of fighting, and having received word of the Tracian invasion of the Eastlands, Teracue and most of the Kingsmen soon departed. Teracue led them on an epic fast march across the Bletharn Plains. Sweeping into the Thunder Mountains, they swept aside all Damar defenses, and they attacked and destroyed the Damar stronghold. Then, with little rest, they marched to the relief of besieged Tallinvale and were instrumental in the defeat of the Redvest Army surrounding that city.

****

The Thrones of the Dragonkind

Before the time of Kalzar the Great, the Dragonkind had developed writing, advanced geometry, engineering, and mathematics. Their culture was highly developed, replete with lore and literature long before the Faerekind were concerned with such things. This was during the Time Before Time, so it is not known how long it took the Dragonkind to reach the heights achieved by the time of Kalzar's reign, though some scholars surmise that it was some 12-15,000 years. The Great Destruction, that event that resulted in the Scathing of the Faerekind and the marooning of the Elifaen upon the earth, is recorded as being during the thirty-ninth year of Kalzar's reign. By some Dragonkind calendars, that would have been around the year 3,540 as counted from the time when the Beras destroyed the dragons. Other records give or take a few thousand years. But it is known that after Kalzar died (some say at the hands of Cupeldain), his son Diamases ascended the Dragonkind throne. However, records are scattered, reflecting the general collapse of Dragonkind culture and society that took place.

Of the sparse records and lore, it is said that there were brief periods of rapid development of cities, courts, and agriculture, only to as quickly collapse into ruin and chaos. This roughly corresponds to the period called the Time of Strife. But the Dragonkind slowly recovered, and their population increased, on average, in spite of many plagues, famines, and conflicts.

By the time Tajahnaman became King around 475 of the First Age, little more than lore remained concerning the past. Each tribe had its own customs and tales, its own way of life, and each its own way of marking the passage of years. But it was Tajahnaman who sought to unite all tribes under one rule. After Tajahnaman, there are additional gaps and discrepancies in the historical record. Below is an imperfect list of the known rulers of the Dragonkind, along with a few notes pertaining to some of them.

Kalzar the Great. Time Before Time	First known king of the Dragonkind
Diamases, Time Before Time	
???, ???	*(Great gap in the historical record)*
Tajahnaman, 475-494 F.A.	Wrests control of the darakal plantations of Karkarando in order to control the production of the heavily sought after darakal elixir.
Churadu, 494-??? F.A.	According to lore, Churadu establishes the priesthood of the Dragon, with himself as the head, in order to control the production and distribution of darakal elixir. Within a few generations, a new class of Dragonkind, free of the desert sickness, will emerge as the ruling class. They are called Alziekfria. The ordinary, working class Dragonkind, who continue to suffer from the desert sickness, are called the Drago.
???, ???	(Gap in historical record. Many tribal leaders fought for the throne.)
Aldiantur, ???-685 F.A	Amid ongoing feuds, Aldiantur gained ascendancy and establishes his throne in the city of Tyrsharat and began the reconstruction of the old palace of Kalzar.
Ralaram, 688-701 F.A.	Seizes the throne three years after the death of Aldiantur. He continued the work of expanding and commissioned many buildings and works.
Age of the Warlord Kings, 701-960 F.A.	With the exception of Salkasin, this age was characterized by a series of unremarkable kings, warlords, and general turmoil.
Salkasin, 960-971 F.A.	After coming to power, Salkasin quickly quelled all Dragonkind opposition, and raised an army of conquest, bent on invading Vanara. He was killed by Parthais at the Battle of Tamkal Plain.

Xurnon I, 205-235 S.A.

After a long period of various short-lived kings, Xurnon takes power. He establishes codes of revised laws, institutes various schemes of taxation and tribute, and establishes a standing army.

Xurnon II, 235-244 S.A.

Son of Xurnon I, he finances great smelters that use of newly discovered coal to increase metal smelting. As a result, steel, iron, copper, and tin production greatly increases.

Vaza I, 244-262 S.A.

Puts down a major revolt in the western lands where most of the mines are located. Vastly expands the system of roads, wells.

Nebalasa (Queen), 262-281 S.A.

The only queen of the Dragonkind. She expands agricultural production on the eastern slopes of the Tulivana Mountains; she reforms the Priesthood, ensuring greater supplies of darakal those favored by the crown; she establishes schools and libraries throughout the Dragonlands. She reforms the armies, establishing a system based on advancement due to merit rather than family or wealth. Her court is known for its lavish festivals and under her patronage, the arts flourish. She standardizes writing systems, weights and measures, and establishes crown control over coinage, lending, and taxation.

Vaza II, 281-308 S.A.

Expands the empire by establishing limited trade with the north, mainly between the cities of Alaberbra and Ladentree. In spite of his efforts to limit trade to that controlled by his court, a vibrant black market springs up with centers located in Alaberbra and all along the northwestern border of Vanara. Continues Nebalasa's policies for the most part, and reforms the courts of law.

Xurnon III, 308-330 S.A.

After putting down several minor revolts, and with his throne secure, he vastly increases the ranks of his armies. He plans, organizes, and launches the Great Invasion, but he himself remains in the Dragonlands, allowing his generals to carry out the invasion.

Xurnon IV, 330-355 S.A.

Overthrows his father after the failed and disastrous invasion. There is widespread discontent, and at last he is assassinated.

Vazamases I, 355-390 S.A.

Takes the place of Xurnon IV but is also beset with division, rebellion, and discontent.

Ozymandias, 390-430 S.A.

Last King of the Xurnon Dynasty. His reign is long, but his power is wholly dependent on the support of various tribal lords. He wastes much on ill-conceived building projects, many in isolated places.

Asadur, 430-436 S.A.
Denasalar, 436-459 S.A.
Bysalamases I, 459-461 S.A.
Bysalamases II, 461-510 S.A.
Durdalamon, 510-532 S.A.
Nasadur, 532-549 S.A.
Albenasadur, 549-577 S.A.
Seralaza, 577-604 S.A.
Albexurnon, 604-638 S.A.
Pelazarda, 638-653 S.A.
Nelabasadur, 653-660 S.A.
Shazabasadur, 660-681 S.A.
Zotanis I, 681-696 S.A.
Zotanis II, 696-729 S.A.
Gulaman, 729-755 S.A.
Oslanasadur, 755-771 S.A.
Utanis, 771-798 S.A.
Basadurmandis, 798-819 S.A.

This period of time is marked by a variety of mostly ineffectual rulers, and by much strife and disorganization. Many were rulers in name only, with the lion's share of power in the hands of various factions and tribes that waxed and waned throughout this period.

Salzadur, 819-845 S.A.

The Kalzar Dynasty is resurrected by Salzadur. Salzadur firmly establishes control over all of the Dragonlands. Although he is ruthless with his opponents, he is beloved by the people, who receive from his reign greater freedoms, wealth, and greater portions of darakal than ever before. He was keenly interested in maintaining diplomatic relations with Vanara, particularly with regard to trade agreements.

Belsalza, 845–870 S.A.

Crowned king when he was but 12 years of age. Ruled under his regents until he was 18. Then, one by one, he had all of the regents murdered or executed. By the time he was 25, he had sole control over all of the Dragonlands. He reversed many of the liberal policies of his father, increased taxation, instituted new, more restrictive controls on darakal, and cut diplomatic ties with Vanara. At the end of the Second Age, he was building a vast army, greater than any before assembled, with the obvious intention of invading other lands. However, much of this army was based in Tyrsharat and was destroyed or driven south when the floods reached the city. Amid the ruin, chaos, and efforts to evacuate, Belsalza lost all control. It is rumored that he drowned.

****

The Triumvirate

Also known as the Redvest Triumvirate for the reddish uniforms, surcoats, tunics, and banners of its soldiers. The Redvest Triumvirate was a trio of rulers that took power in Tracia in 853 S.A. during the civil war that drove out the Tracian Ruling Prince Lewtrah and his brother Prince Lantos after years of unrest. They were the noblemen Dargos Sagrin and Garg Bonovanti, and former general of the army Usler Vasos, who were all violently opposed to Ruling Prince Lewtrah for different reasons. Well before these three took power, Tracia suffered calamity and unrest. Years of drought, storms, and corruption turned much of the population against Prince Lewtrah. During this time, Dargos Sagrin, a Lord of the Realm, slowly began taking advantage of Lewtrah's inept rule to increase his own influence. He successfully led the House of Tracia (a kind of ruling body) to enact laws of sedition to fine or arrest any not directly loyal to Tracia. Soon afterwards, and without the authority of the Prince, General Usler Vasos joined with Sagrin, ordering the recall of all Tracian soldiers serving in other Realms as Kingsmen or in other capacities back to Tracia. Those that refused had their lands or the lands of their family confiscated. Vasos also began assembling an independent army, answerable to him, to enforce his orders. Many who joined his army were units previously serving the Ruling Prince, but many had not been paid for their services for many years.

Meanwhile, Garg Bonovanti, a charismatic agitator, went about the Realm advising that none give their taxes or tributes to the Ruling Prince, working an agreement with Sagrin and Bonovanti to divert half of what was owed to the Crown to them. Bonovanti used this as leverage to wrest control of the treasury (including coinage) and to undermine banks and lenders not under his direct control. Soon

Bonovanti was financing the activities of Sagrin and Vasos. Within months, civil war broke out between Loyalists and Redvests, and atrocities were widespread. However, the Redvests gained the upper hand, taking vast territories with great support of the people. In the wake of the Redvest armies, however, lands were ransacked, populations were compelled into forced labor, and a powerful elite of soldiers and noblemen quickly emerged in support of the Triumvirate.

Still Lewtrah fought on, sending his brother Lantos, who was still very popular, out from Forlandis. When Lantos and his Loyalists marched into battle at the Marshlands, they had been misinformed as to the size of the Redvest forces, and soon the city they left behind, Forlandis, was under siege. While Lantos fought a hopeless battle at the Marshlands, outnumbered nearly three to one and hampered by a shortage of food and supplies, Lewtrah escaped from Forlandis, rescued by a small band of Elifaen sailors from Glareth. A few weeks later, as the Royal Navy fought on, Lantos, too, would narrowly escape to Glareth.

By the end of 856 S.A., all of Tracia was under the control of the Redvest Triumvirate. They quickly consolidated power, purging from their ranks those they deemed untrustworthy, and began systematically taking control of the population. By this time, many who originally supported the Redvests were disillusioned with their lies, but any who spoke out were quickly arrested. The Triumvirate was inept at managing resources, but put down discontent with vicious zeal. In the years following their rise to power, prisons swelled beyond their capacities, the block or noose or forced labor were the most common sentences for anyone arrested, and in practically every village, gallows sagged with the dead. Hundreds of thousands of Tracians attempted to flee, going to faraway places to escape the assassins sent after them. Many men who could not leave and whose livelihoods had been ruined, had only the army to turn to, joining the Redvest ranks before they were conscripted. The women and children and old people fared no better, and many of them were forced into servitude as slaves.

During all this, the Redvest Triumvirate filled the streets with talk of how Duinnor, Glareth, and the other Realms opposed them and actively brought all this hardship upon them and threatened Tracia with invasion at any moment. With complete control of printers, they published and spread talk of how all other Realms were out to destroy Tracia. They began to take lands along the borders of the old Eastlands Realm and made incursions into Masurthia. Although hampered by the loss of their naval power (decimated by Loyalist raiders and by Redvest incompetence), the Triumvirate continued to build their armies, using up their resources to do so. It was evident to all that some grand plan was in the works, but it was not until 870 S.A., that the plan came to light with the invasion of the Eastlands. Evidence was mounting that the Triumvirate had somehow reached an accord with the Dragonlands to coordinate a vast offensive against Duinnor and the other Realms, which they planned to launch within the year. To this end, by the winter of 870, Tracia began marshaling its forces across the River Saerdulin southeast of Kalbrith.

As is described in *The Year of the Red Door*, several things happened that thwarted their plans. Firstly, Tallinvale remained independent of Tracian control and was supported by partisan fighters in the Eastlands. Tallinvale, with its strong defenses and small but determined army, posed a considerable threat to Tracia's northern flank. To eliminate this threat, they dispatched two expeditions against Tallinvale, the first of which was an utter failure almost from the onset due to its poor leadership and planning. Well before this force reached Tallinvale City, it was attacked and virtually annihilated by Lord Tallin's forces. This prompted a second attempt to subdue Tallinvale, this time with a much larger force, better organized and supported, and led by the very competent General Mar Henith. Against this, the people of Tallinvale gathered in Tallin City and made their preparations. Pressed for time, the Redvests laid siege to Tallinvale and immediately organized direct assaults against the city, but again the Redvests were utterly defeated.

Meanwhile, Glareth had been informed about the Redvest invasion in the Eastlands. It was not entirely unexpected, and Prince Carbane had already accelerated the building of warships, the gathering of supplies and equipment, as well as building, training, and equipping his large land armies. As well, Prince Lantos, located by now in Glareth, had organized his own army of exiled Tracians who were determined to strike back at the Redvests, remove the Triumvirate from power, and take back their homeland. These forces coordinated carefully, and in late winter of 870 they were on the move, by land and by sea. The Tracians were caught completely flat-footed. A large penetrating diversionary force of Loyalists and Glarethians moved southward, taking County Barley, Calletshire, and Colleton. Meanwhile, the main forces had embarked onto a huge fleet of warships and transports. About a third of these landed at Sorghwall, and after a quick siege, they overwhelmed the Redvests defenders. They began moving southwest as the main force, including many warships, fought their way across Spargers Bay and assaulted a completely unprepared Forlandis. Here the fighting was intense, but the Redvests, lacking the bulk of their forces (which were far away at their marshaling location), capitulated quickly. Bonovanti was captured, and Sagrin was killed. Vasos, who was at the time on his way to lead the forces at Kalbrith, was located and captured by special Glarethian marines who raided Kalbrith and were guided to Vasos by spies. A week later, when news reached the Redvests of the invasion, the capture and death of their leaders, and the devastation of Mar Henith's army at Tallinvale, all of the military forces west of the Saerdulin surrendered without a fight. However, many officers and men, fearing retribution for their acts, fled into the mountains.

During all of these incursions, over three million prisoners were released. These were mostly those rounded up as slave labor supporting the Redvest armies. Many, however, were held in prisons and camps, and most of them were starving, diseased, and injured. No official numbers were tallied, but it is estimated that almost two million Tracian civilians died in such camps and prisons during the Redvest reign.

Then, in Duinnor, King Philawain came to power and soon the world was remade. King Philawain summoned the Loyalist and Glarethian leaders and admonished them to subdue all vigilantes, to avoid illegal retributions, to resist yielding to the desires for revenge, to follow the law, to mete out justice and punishments that were due but without malice. When the world was remade, Bonovanti and Vasos had yet to be tried.

See Also:
Biographical Sketches (Prince Lantos, Prince Carbane)
Historical Sketches (Battle of Marshlands, Battle of Grisland Strait)

****

True Ink and the Scribblers

True Ink

True Ink was a magical ink that fades and becomes invisible if what is written with it is false. True Ink was discovered by Vanarans sometime in the middle to late Second Age, and its making was a closely held state secret. In fact, two types of True Ink were eventually developed, one from a special rare plant, which was deemed much more powerful and effective, and another formulation using various chemicals to dilute the original without too much loss of functionality.

True Ink was very sensitive to vibration, and it was reactive to most substances except amber and glass of a certain formula. Only silver nibbed pens could be used, else the inkwell's contents would be quickly contaminated. Various other conditions were discovered which limited its use or effectiveness.

Its discovery is still shrouded in mystery, but we know that it took many years to learn how to refine it consistently. Its existence and use was made public in 860, but no details were given on how it was made or how it worked. By the year 863, it was in use at Vanara's Hall of Ministers to verify the identity of those who came and went from that place. Its production and use were strictly guarded, and the most severe penalties were imposed for anyone caught and convicted of trying to transport

True Ink without permission. By decree, in some cases the death penalty was required. Because of its sensitivity, and how amber helped prevent its deterioration, Queen Serith Ellyn sought to obtain all supplies of amber stones large enough to be made into vials or containers, and she consistently but secretly financed buying agents to ensure that Vanaran traders would offer the highest prices to amber-hunters and suppliers from outside of Vanara.

The Scribblers

In late 868 (or early 869), a special intelligence-gathering service was established by Lord Brandis Seafar in Vanara, a unit of the Grey Guards called the Scribblers located in secret chambers within the White Palace of Linlally. Their task was to constantly write statements which, by fading or persisting, could be determined as truth and fact. They eventually learned to exploit its potential, and how to interpret its sometimes baffling results. But progress was steady and by late 869 the Scribblers had learned how to conjecture and garner information about virtually every topic of interest to Vanara.

At first, they had much to learn. Not only was True Ink somewhat finicky and easily ruined, but the information derived from its use was sometimes enigmatic or inconsistent with beliefs, sometimes contrary to other observations. In spite of this, by the middle of 869 they had worked out a system that was quite reliable. They operated in shifts at every hour of the day and night, and produced a prodigious amount of intelligence and information. To handle this, Seafar organized the Scribblers into "bureaus" that gathered particular kinds of information. For example, there was a Weather Bureau, a Dragonkind Bureau, a bureau for each Realm (including Vanara), and a Shatuum Bureau. Among other things, the Vanaran Bureau (or Home Bureau) was ever on the watch for any threats to Vanara, military or otherwise, or to the Queen. As an emergency system, the chambers that they used were equipped with a mechanical system by which they could rapidly ring alarm bells and gongs throughout the Palace.

They normally worked in teams of at least two people, sometimes calling upon others to assist. One person would write, using True Ink, a series of statements of a hypothetical nature, while their partner would copy all that was written in regular ink. Thus, if the True Ink faded, a record was still maintained. Eventually, most bureaus developed a standard set of statements to be regularly posed according to an established schedule (hourly, daily, weekly, etc.). However, Seafar and other commanders of the Scribblers often directed them to seek answers to particular questions of immediate interest.

By the end of 869, the amount of information produced was prodigious, and it was becoming more difficult to organize, sort, share, and analyze the results. At first Seafar sought to handle this by providing the information to others who did not know the source, but he eventually expanded the Scribblers so that they always had officers on-site to immediately assist and, if necessary, make immediate decisions about sharing information. A separate archive of past "scribblings" was established. This was readily available to the Scribblers and was organized and indexed for ease of reference.

Therefore, Seafar and others had the means to monitor the movement and activities of far-flung and varied groups or individuals. It was the Scribblers who discovered and warned of the intrusion of Faradan's men who were intent on killing Robby Ribbon within the White Palace, enabling him to be rescued and safeguarded from the assassins. Later, Seafar was able to somewhat track the movement of Robby Ribbon as he made his way to Griferis. He was also able to stay informed as to Queen Serith Ellyn's safety and her movements. Indeed, during the last days of the Second Age, Seafar used True Ink extensively to keep abreast of the many happenings outside of Vanara.

See Also:

Eighteen Objects of Power (True Ink)

****

Essays and Explanations

This section concerns itself with certain aspects of The Year of the Red Door that are not fully explained or detailed within that work or elsewhere within this Companion.

****

Being Elifaen

The Elifaen were the descendants of the first people to live in the world. Some of them, according to legend, were physically transformed from their previous bodies during the Time Before Time into the ones they would have after the Fall of the Faere. They lost their wings and much of their ability to communicate (and commune) with nature. But they retained many characteristics of their previous state of being.

By outward appearance, Elifaen are indistinguishable from typical mortal men and women, except for the two scars running from their shoulders down their backs to their hips. They did not have pointed ears, or horns, or animal-like parts. They had skin and hair of various colors and combinations. Their skin ranged from white to tan to dark black, and their hair likewise in hue, although some did have streaks of greenish or bluish strands.

The process by which the inherited scars form was called Scathing. Children conceived of parents who were both Elifaen were Scathed in the womb. Conception rates for such couples were very low, and many pregnancies did not lead to the live birth of a child, likely because of the Scathing process. "Sylphaen" were children born of an Elifaen mother and Mortal father. They were not born Scathed but underwent that process (which was an ordeal) later in life, usually in childhood, but sometimes much later in life. Some did not survive Scathing, as it was fraught with pain and severe mental distress while the scars formed on their backs. Elifaen children were only born of Elifaen mothers; that is, children of Mortal mothers remained mortal. While Elifaen born of two Elifaen parents did not mature beyond peak physical maturity (and therefore remained young in appearance), Sylphaen aged as all mortals do until they were Scathed. Afterwards, they matured until they reached their peak physical maturity. If Scathing came later in life, aging ceased, but the body remained in appearance at the level of maturity at the time Scathing. Thus, some Elifaen appeared older than others.

Elifaen were not entirely immortal, but could and did die. Although they had prodigious healing capabilities, they did succumb to serious wounds. For example, a cut to the heart or a severe blow to the head would kill them. Likewise, any wound that bled too much or too quickly (such as with the loss of a limb or a deep and long gash) would usually lead to death, especially if not stanched quickly. They could also be crushed to death, and they could drown. Small wounds and scratches healed very quickly. A serious cut might take a day to completely heal, such that no scar remained. A light scratch only a few moments. They never suffered, as far as is known, from any type of disease or malady. However, a wound suffered by any Sylphaen before they were Scathed could leave lasting scars or disabilities. Examples include Hazel, a servant of Esildre, who lost her sight because of a wound and did not regain it after being Scathed. King Philawain, too, carried with him the scars and lasting effects of injuries for the rest of his life, even after becoming Elifaen.

The Elifaen did not require as much food and water to survive as did Men. They would gradually waste away until they were mere skin and bones, but no Elifaen ever died of starvation. And they remained stronger for much longer during such deprivations than Men. This is why they were valued by the Dragonkind as slaves for hard labor.

Interestingly, the food and nourishment they consumed did not affect them in the same way as with mortals. Very few ever grew fat or obese from overeating. And, during a time when strength was needed, it was perceived that the Elifaen body would, almost suddenly, become quite fit and muscular. They varied in height; some were tall, some were short, but most were of average height compared to Men. There were no "giants" or "dwarves" among them.

The only known poison that could harm them was Foxdire (Sigh Mortabilis). Most poisons or toxins had little or no effect on them whatsoever. When it came to alcohol, the Elifaen had to drink a prodigious amount before becoming slightly tipsy, by which time, with the same quantity of drink, a mortal drinking companion would long be staggeringly drunk or unconscious.

As mentioned, their endurance was phenomenal. One example of this took place when Queen Serith Ellyn led a hastily assembled army to the relief of forces trapped at Gory Gulch. She, with over 2,000 soldiers, ran (or jogged), without pause or rest and with full battle gear, all the way from Linlally to the site of the battle. And then, also without having taken a rest, they immediately threw themselves into battle against the Dragonkind.

Normally, however, they rarely acted with such haste, due to their different perception of time, which seemed to often make them somewhat slower to act in the first place and less inclined to hurry once they set about a course of action. This trait would almost be their downfall, particularly during the Time of Strife and the early years of the First Age. Gradually, they learned the value of quicker decision-making and action.

****

A Kingsman Briefing Paper

Year 868 of the Second Age

The following summary was written in Duinnor around 868 of the Second Age, and it was used as part of the training curriculum at the Kingsman Academy. It is primarily aimed at cadets of the Academy from mortal families, particularly those who had little or no firsthand knowledge of the Elifaen (mainly those of the Eastlands, Duinnor, and Tracia).

Part I
Elifaen Inheritance, Scathing, and Immortality

1. Elifaen House Names are passed down along maternal lines, from eldest daughter to eldest daughter. The eldest female, usually the mother, is generally referred to as the "matron." Younger daughters may not become the matron of a Named House unless their elder sisters die without female issue. Sons may inherit an Elifaen House Name, but except in the case of the Firstborn, they may not pass it on unless they have a daughter whose mother is not the eldest daughter of another Named House. Many Elifaen Houses have special ceremonies for such marriages, such that the daughter-in-law is "adopted" and given full rights as a daughter by blood. However, should a daughter be subsequently born to the parents of the married couple, that daughter will be considered the matron of the House. Houses that have only sons that do not marry or bear children of eligible Elifaen (see above) will be dissolved after the death of the sons, or, if they predecease the mother, after her death.

In the case where there are two daughters, only one will become the matron should her mother die, and she will inherit and retain all such titles until death. To thwart or prevent violent power struggles, second daughters are often given substantial wealth and benefits to renounce their own House, usually in the form of a dowry upon marriage into another house. This practice was complicated by the rise of "joined" houses, which were becoming more common in the Second Age, wherein the Named House of the husband and the Named House of the wife were considered "joined" rather than one superseding the other. This, in effect, increased the power and wealth of such houses.

2.   The Elifaen do not have surnames. Surnames of Mortals are inherited from fathers to all children regardless of the mother's status as an Elifaen. For example, Aram Tallin, son of Danig Saheed Tallin (a Mortal) and Kahryna (an Elifaen of the House of Fairoak) inherited the Tallin surname, though Aram and his mother were both Elifaen, hence the "joined house" of Tallin and Fairoak. Grandchildren of an Elifaen Named House are permitted to cite the name, but not pass it on unless they are or will become Scathed. For example, Ullin Saheed Tallin, Aram's son by a Mortal mother, is permitted to lay claim to both Tallin and Fairoak Houses, but it would be improper for his children to do so. When no further eligible inheritors of the Elifaen House are available, the House Name passes out of existence and is considered dissolved.

3.   The rules of inheritance of Elifaen House Names were complicated by the arrival of Men in the world. Generally, prior to the Second Age, the Elifaen were more relaxed about maternal lines of inheritance. However, perhaps as a reaction to the encroachment of Men, the rules were codified by Vanarans in the House Edicts of Queen Serith Ellyn in the year 262 S.A.. Although never strictly or consistently enforced, the Edict served as a model for the other realms to follow, most notably in Duinnor and in Glareth for entirely different political reasons.

4.   Traditionally, female Elifaen control the House Name, including the actual ownership of land and property, while the male is responsible for maintaining, protecting, managing, or using the property. In the case of mixed marriages or "joined houses" (where an Elifaen marries a Mortal), all property rights are traditionally retained by the male regardless of whether he is Elifaen or Mortal.

5.   In order to become Elifaen, one either must be Firstborn (born during the Time Before Time) or else be the child of a female Elifaen. That is, Mortal females will conceive Mortal offspring; Elifaen females will conceive Elifaen offspring.

6.   Scathing, during which the formation of hereditary scars takes place, occurs within the womb of those born of both Elifaen mother and Elifaen father. Elifaen born of mixed parentage (Elifaen mother, Mortal father) undergo the Scathing later in life. If the Scathing takes place before adulthood, the child will continue to grow and age until physical maturity. However, Scathing may take place at any time in life. Although rare, there have been cases where Scathing did not take place until very late in life, at which point the person stops growing physically older. The rarest circumstance of Scathing was reported by a physician in Masurthia who attended an elderly man of some eighty years of age who had sustained mortal injuries from a boating accident. In that case, it was reported, the man's suffering was compounded by a strange, inexplicable fever, the appearance of scars on the back of the kind that the Elifaen have. Unable to endure, the elderly gentleman died before his injuries could heal and, presumably, before he became fully Elifaen.

7.   After being scaled, all Elifaen bear two scars that are the relics of a time when all Faerekind had wings and could fly. Each scar begins on the top of the shoulder and goes downward along one side of the back to terminate below the hip. The pattern of scars for each lineage is somewhat different, varying in the way they curve, the thickness or width of each scar line, and the pattern of radial scars (smaller scars that emanate outward from each of the two main scars). There is some variation of coloration of the scars, too, the most common being white, copper, red (or pink), or tan. The scars are painful throughout the remainder of the Elifaen's life. The level or intensity of pain was not constant, but waxed and waned according to individual differences and circumstances, with increased pain

during times of high mental or emotional stress. Elifaen reported the pain as variously burning or aching, and no salve or ointment seems to alleviate the Elifaen's suffering. In some cases, the pain was accompanied by renewed inflammation and even bleeding along the scars of Elifaen.

8. Elifaen are generally thought of as immortal, but they can and often do die. They do not succumb to sickness, and they do not age beyond the day of their Scathing (or beyond the maturity of their bodies), but they can die of wounds if the wounds are serious. Elifaen bodies have prodigious healing powers, but they cannot suffer loss of much blood, nor can they survive severe blows to the head, or serious wounds to the vital organs. They can be maimed, since they cannot grow new limbs if severed, and they can be poisoned with Sigh Mortabilis (aka, foxdire, or Grave's Breath) which results in sleep in mild cases or death, depending on the purity and amount of the poison. Also, with one notable exception, they can suffer blindness due to the loss of the eyes. The one exception occurred with Esildre of the House of Elmwood who put out her own eyes on at least one occasion only to have them grow back almost immediately (as recorded by a member of her household when Esildre lived near Averstone.). There are many known cases where an Elifaen has died of what can only be called melancholia or sadness; generally, all of these resulted in the person simply ceasing to live. Elifaen do require sustenance. Although there has been no definitive case of an Elifaen dying of starvation, it seems that the wasting away of the will to live often manifested in part in a refusal to eat, leading to a physical wasting away. In addition, depression and melancholia are so prevalent among the Elifaen that suicide is quite common. Efforts were made by Parthais to outlaw suicide, including provisions that any person who committed suicide would have all property forfeited to the crown rather than passed to heirs. Under these laws, Parthais distributed such property to those in his favor. This made it profitable to make murder look like suicide, and there was so much abuse that it was the first law that Serith Ellyn revoked when she became Queen of Vanara.

Part II
Houses, Names, and Race Relations

9. By tradition, Men have surnames, but Elifaen do not. In the ancient days, groups or clans of the Elifaen gave names to their people, according to the wish of their leader. These clans and groups came to be referred to as "Houses." At first, only the most powerful or influential Elifaen had House names. Later, groups of lesser standing also gave names to their Houses, perhaps in an effort to lend some legitimacy to their lineage. Elifaen not affiliated with any House often associated themselves with one. Others, particularly the woodland Elifaen, were reluctant to use any conventions that made them seem associated with Vanara.

10. At any rate, by the early years of the First Age, and particularly after Silmain became King of Vanara, House Names became so confusing that some system was needed to define and recognize these groups, particularly when they began to demand various rights such as land or property ownership and the right to petition the King. Within Vanara, Silmain made the first effort to codify some system, insisting that all Houses be recognized by his throne before being granted any rights. Silmain's method of recognizing a House was simply to have a petition brought before him by the leader of another House, and, if he then gave the new House his formal recognition, the House name was recorded into his annals, thus becoming a Named House. This tradition in Vanara remained in place throughout the First Age, but as more realms of the world were established, and more groups claimed to be a Named House, it was apparent that some better method was needed. Also, since many Houses fell into dissolution as their people died or as they recombined with other Houses, some method of recognizing these situations was also needed.

11. Matters were further complicated when, near the end of the First Age, Men came into the world. Their system of using surnames was at first confusing to the Elifaen, but when interracial unions began to occur, and the maternal nature of becoming Elifaen was discovered, the situation became more complicated than before. There were fears among many Elifaen that Men would eventually destroy their ancient lineages by "diluting" their bloodlines and dooming their descendants into mortaldom. This fear, along with the continued encroachment of Men into lands claimed by Elifaen, was the basis of some strife between the two races, including the Pinewood Uprising that took place in the early Second Age. As certain families of Men became powerful, they, too, began giving names to their lineage, names which sometimes were not their actual surnames.

12. At last, Queen Serith Ellyn, under pressure to resolve these situations and fears, issued the House Edicts of Vanara, which outlined the rules of inheritance of Elifaen House Names, and the rights, privileges, and responsibilities of the Named Houses. Many conservative Elifaen wanted intermarriage with mortals to be outlawed, but Serith Ellyn refused to go that far, saying that it was unnecessary and unkind, and that it would needlessly antagonize many people, particularly the powerful Men of Duinnor and Tracia of that time (262 S.A.). She also refused to permit the House Edicts to be highly specific, and she made conflicts and issues arising from the House Edicts subject to judicial rulings on a case-by-case basis.

13. Within a few short years, the House Edicts of Vanara would be adopted in some form or other in all other realms. In Duinnor, the process gave emphasis to the Houses of Men, dividing them into Named Houses and Honored Houses, the latter not having the standing of Named Houses, nor their responsibilities. In later years, the Duinnor system would become a method of exerting political control upon other Realms, and of building its Kingsmen army. When great Named Houses of Men began to join with Named Houses of the Elifaen, Joined Houses were formed, which never had any official recognition as such, as being a Joined House was usually only temporary (depending on which lineage, Elifaen or Mortal, that carried on). Among all the variation of rules throughout the different Realms, one rule was universal: A Named House of Elifaen must be dissolved when the children of the last Elifaen of its lineage die. Thus, mortal children (of Elifaen fathers, but mortal mothers), would be recognized as of a Named House, but the House Name must be dissolved upon their death.

14. By the late Second Age, the result of all these conditions were that more and more Men were of Named Houses, as the number of Elifaen Named Houses declined into dissolution. And Duinnor, through its power, enforced its rules over other Realms. Lesser Elifaen Houses persist, but they are small and relatively unimportant and very often in service to other, greater Houses (of either Men or Elifaen). And, in some cases, some of the women of these lesser Elifaen houses have had female offspring by the laird or master of a House of Men, and thus unofficially convert the House of Men into an Elifaen House. As the Second Age progressed, whether one was of a Named House or affiliated with one was growing less important. The population of Men outnumbered that of Elifaen by more than ten to one (some sources say it was only six to one). Duinnor, Tracia, the Eastlands, and Masurthia were ruled by Men almost exclusively, with Men also being the majority race in Glareth, Vanara, and Altoria, although they were still ruled by Elifaen Houses. It is interesting to note also that while the early part of the Second Age was characterized by the persecution and discrimination of Men by Elifaen, by the latter part of the Second Age the tables had turned, and Elifaen were facing increasing prejudice and persecution from Men. Only in Vanara and Glareth, where Men were accorded great liberties and high standing, equality between the races was normal and enshrined in law. And though Duinnor was the first to officially accord equal rights to all races, in practice it was not as welcoming to Elifaen as it had been during its early years, with many legal loopholes that permitted widespread discrimination. For that and many other reasons, tensions between Duinnor and the Realms of Glareth and Vanara were strained.

15. When the current Redvest Triumvirate took power, it at first actively sought to drive all Elifaen out of Tracia. Then, in a quick change of policy, it began capturing Elifaen within its territories to be their slaves, since Elifaen are less vulnerable to the deprivations of such a condition. That is, the Redvests did not need to feed the Elifaen as much as their mortal thralls, and obtained more work from the Elifaen slaves since they healed quickly of injuries and were immune to the diseases that abuse and deprivation brought upon their mortal slaves. These policies and actions are clearly contrary to Duinnor's law and the King's rule, but Duinnor has not yet sought to confront Tracia concerning these offenses, nor has Duinnor made any effort, through economic pressures, to force reform. (Note: Any actions against other Realms must be approved by the King. And although he has been presented with several appeals and indictments against Tracia for breaking the law, along with several plans concerning what actions to take, he has not given his approval to any.) Only Glareth Realm has taken any meaningful measures to support Tracia's exiled populations and Tracian refugees (which include Elifaen) who have fled persecution and injustice. Glareth has also severely restricted its trade with Triumvirate-controlled Tracia.

****

Elifaen Perceptions of Time

Elifaen individuals, as a rule, seem to have a different perception of the passage of time. Or at least their thought processes appear to be different. As was often mentioned within *The Year of the Red Door*, it seems that time could pass much more slowly than for mortals. As well, their thought processes did not necessarily slow. For example, an Elifaen might respond immediately to a situation, but when asked why they did what they did, they may reply by describing all of the different possible choices that they "contemplated," sifting through each, weighing each, before arriving at a decision and acting. During all of this, the world around them would appear to slow down, or even freeze.

The obvious benefit to this was offset by a considerable amount of confusion, often stirred up by highly emotional memories that would come into play in their thoughts. Sometimes one emotion, or one set of memories, would conflict with all others, or even hold sway. It is thought that their memory is nearly perfect, and that they can recall the slightest detail of something that they saw only once many centuries ago. But again, the complex of memories, and their power, only serves to confuse the Elifaen, to make them somewhat introspective, and to subdue their behavior toward others. Compared to mortals, their facial expressions were very often completely blank, and rarely did they smile or frown.

To Men, the behavior of Elifaen must have seemed erratic and unpredictable, often waiting months for a reply to a simple request, or reacting with keen intent and instant haste to solve some problem or issue. In fact, it was impossible for any Elifaen to predict or foresee how deeply their thoughts and feelings might run at any given moment. However, there are numerous examples of Elifaen in battle fighting in hand-to-hand combat with utmost precision and deliberation, and it was often said among the Dragonkind that one Fellfaere was more dangerous than ten Men. In at least one case, this intensity on the part of an Elifaen in battle became somewhat of a legend. Although they did not know her name, Mirabella Tallin was known variously as "green-eyed death," "red-maned witch of the North" (due to her red hair). In *The Year of the Red Door*, we find that some Dragonkind have said to Gurasa, "…if ever you see a Faere warrioress with long red hair, you must run away, for if you are ever close enough to see her green eyes, you will die."

It has been suggested that over the long course of time, this perception of time was not experienced by all Elifaen, and was noticeably absent from many born after the beginning of the Second Age. Others have suggested that all Elifaen continue to have such perceptions of time, but it only manifests in behavior during moments of great stress, be it emotional or physical.

****

Notes Pertaining to the Dragonkind

As of the Second Age, no union between Dragonkind and other races was known outside of Kajarahn, the Free City of the northwestern deserts. There, standing was strictly on an economic basis, with the wealthy wielding power. Few women of the Northlands, either of Elifaen or Mortal stock, ever ventured to the city, although many males did so. These Northmen, as they were called by the Dragonkind, came for various reasons; they were traders, merchantmen, craftsmen, renegades and deserters, fortune-seekers, or were engaged in other, more nefarious activities. Although Dragonkind women were discouraged from having any interaction with Northmen, there were instances of marriage, usually when a Northman came to have some wealth and power in Kajarahn and wished to take a wife. And only Dragonkind women were permitted to work within the brothels and other vice-oriented establishments within the Free City, and most of them were quite happy to engage with anyone, regardless of race, who had gold or silver to spend.

It might be worth noting that during the long history of the Dragonkind, they also sought to take Elifaen slaves, often captives from battle or those taken during raids into Vanara. The Elifaen, they discovered, were as vulnerable as they to the desert sickness, but they would not succumb to it and needed no darakal herb to sustain them. As well, since Elifaen slaves were immortal and would be able to labor for generations in bondage, their value was enhanced. However, Elifaen captives were often stubborn and willful, perhaps due to their ability to withstand punishment that would kill a mortal. There were cases of Elifaen slaves who were quite docile and eager to please their masters. Some even rose through the enslaved ranks to hold important positions within Dragonkind households. This might be due to the Elifaen's patience and longsuffering, confident that they would outlive their masters and eventually become free.

****

Calendars and Timekeeping

I.
Why Do Years Have Names?

The following was taken from a schoolbook published in Altoria in mid-870 of the Second Age. It serves as a basic primer on calendar systems used during that eponymous year.

As many children of the Second Age ask, "Why do we sometimes call the year by a number, saying 'It is the Year 870?' But other times we call the year by a name, and we say 'It's the Year of the Red Door?'"

The simple answer is that there are two kinds of year, and each has its own calendar. The first is the regular calendar that is well-known, starting from the Firstmonth of each year and ending on the last day of Twelthmonth. That year is numbered. Since the Second Age began the year that Queen Serith Ellyn of Vanara formally accepted the throne of that Realm, the years are counted from then forward. And so, this is the 870th year of the Second Age.

The other calendar marks the Royal Year of the Unknown King of Duinnor. That year ends on the day of the Spring Equinox and the new year begins the following day. On the day of the Equinox, the King is required by tradition (and some say by the law of the gods) to go forth from his palace in the city to the great Temple of Beras on a nearby mountaintop. There, with the monks and Oracle of that place presiding, the King renews his kingship for another year.

As most know, the King has a special servant that does his bidding, called the Avatar. This servant takes the shape of something of the world and floats along beside the King a foot or so from the ground or glides through the streets of the city when it is dispatched on the King's business. It does not speak, and it makes no noise. But whoever sees it is usually filled with fear and awe, since if it comes to your door, you must go away with it. And you may not be seen ever again. So when the people see it floating along through the streets of their city, they fervently hope that it will merely pass them by. Some people have such dread of the Avatar that they refuse to live within Duinnor City, since the Avatar may only go beyond the walls of the city in company with the King. And the King rarely leaves his palace, much less his city.

But each year, the Avatar must accompany the King to the Temple. When the King emerges from the Temple to go back to his palace, the Avatar comes out of the Temple with him in a new shape for the new Royal Year.

Thus, one year it was in the shape of a perfume bottle. Another year it was like fog. Still another year it was in the form of a terrible warlike battering ram. After a while, people began calling the Royal Year after the shape of the Avatar, and the practice continues to this day. That is why this Royal Year is called the Year of the Red Door, as it has been since springtime began and will be until winter ends. Then the Avatar will have a new shape. And the Royal Year will have a new name.

Editor's Notes:

With the above in mind, it is interesting to note that as time passed, the people of Duinnor began to view the Avatar, and the name of the year, as a sign of what might cause the downfall of the current Unknown King. During the Year of the Frying Pan, people wondered if the King might be induced to eat something ill-prepared or even poisoned, while during one minor public demonstration of that year, frying pans were carried by rioters who called for reform. Likewise, during the Year of the Red Door, people went about painting their doors red, saying that the time of the current King was at an end. The king responded by making it a crime to paint a door red, or to refuse to paint over any existing red door. This led many to believe that the shape of the Avatar was, indeed, a sign of something that threatened the King's rule or even lead to his death. And indeed, as was indicated within The Year of the Red Door, there were several doors of significance. One, located within the chambers of the High Tower, led to the room where the King secreted his Bloodcoins (discovered by Beauchamp the Familiar, even though it had been painted over). In addition, a red door was presented to Lord Banis during a nightmare through which he was told to escape only to fall to his death, thus ridding the King of his most powerful ally.

II.
Calendars and Clocks

A Brief Historical Overview

There are five commonly designated "ages" of the world:

The Time Before Time – from the creation and the beginning of the world until the Fall of the Faere, an unknown number of years, but speculated to be around 25,000 or more.

The Time of Strife – from the Fall of the Faere until the beginning of the reign of King Silmain of Vanara, an unknown number of years, but speculated to be around 7, 000.

The First Age – from the reign of Silmain until the overthrow of Parthais, when Serith Ellyn ascended the throne of Vanara

The Second Age
– from the reign of Queen Serith Ellyn until the Remaking of the World

The Third Age
– our present epoch.

This essay primarily pertains to the development and use of calendars and timekeeping during the Second Age of the world.

As of the year 870 of the Second Age, there were two commonly known calendar systems, the Royal Calendar and the "standard" Calendar of Duinnor, the former being for ceremonial purposes. It is the Royal Calendar, not the standard calendar, from which the names of years are derived (see below).

Until the middle of the Second Age, there were a variety of calendars in use in the world. The Dragonkind, Vanarans, Duinnor, and Glareth all used different calendar systems. It was common practice in the Eastlands Realm to use the Glareth Calendar, while Tracia and Masurthia used the Duinnor Calendar. Altoria used its own calendar before adopting that used by Vanara. All of these systems changed over time in various ways and used a variety of schemes when it came to the months of the year and the days of the week. Most were based on the lunar cycles, with Duinnor being a notable exception, using a solar calendar instead (as the Dragonkind consistently did throughout their history).

Realizing that trade depended upon some agreement on a consistent calendar system, in Year 246 S.A., the Council of Time was formed of scholars from all Realms. Their purpose was to discuss, debate, and decide on a new system. Vanara was chosen as a meeting place due to its many observatories.

For twenty years, scholars pored over documents, consulted with astrologers and time-keepers, and debated over proposed schemes. Eventually, three systems were considered, and the Duinnor Calendar was accepted with a few minor changes to it. Politically, this was an easy choice since Duinnor exerted little power and the choice of its system was deemed a compromise between vying representatives allied to Glareth, Vanara, and Masurthia (the most powerful Realms of that time).

The Duinnor Calendar (not to be confused with the Royal Calendar, see below) itself is something of an amalgamation of previous conventions. It consisted of twelve months of thirty days. Certain days of the year were not to be counted as part of a month. These were: (1) the first day of each year, called New Year's Day, (2 & 3,) the days of Winter and Summer Solstice, and (4 & 5) the days of Spring and Autumn Equinox. These made a year consisting of 365 days.

The names of the months were to be called Firstmonth, Secondmonth, Thirdmonth, et cetera.

This system had the advantage of retaining the general references to the lunar calendars of the other Realms, but was, in fact, based on a solar year. Unlike the old calendars prevalently used, New Year's Day would begin a week and two days after Midwinter's Day, rather than on the following day.

There are twenty-three standard hours in each calendar day, each consisting of sixty minutes.

Each day of the calendar begins at sunrise. The twenty-fourth hour of each day, called the Endhour, was the last hour before dawn, consisting of the remaining minutes until sunrise. Thus, the Endhour was sometimes the longest, and sometimes the shortest hour of the day. Dissatisfaction with this continued to mount, but those who viewed sunrise as the start of each day held sway over others who wanted the day to begin at midnight, which would allow a consistent length of minutes in every hour.

A standard hour was based on the time between sunrise on the day of and after the vernal equinox, divided by twenty-four. Although hours were not commonly used until the invention of accurate and cheaply produced clocks in the late Second Age, scholars understood them to be based on a standard of sixty minutes (each of sixty seconds). When clocks came into use, the daily adjustment of them by their owners became a sunrise ritual. Because of this and other irregularities, new calendar systems were being discussed by scholars in the late Second Age, systems that would do away with the inconvenient Endhour and compensate for seasonal drift that was taking place in spite of the intentions of the current system. It was noted, for example, that the length of each day was actually a tiny bit longer than 24 hours, which gradually added up so that the alignment of the stars and the date of the Vernal Equinox drifted. By 865, a new calendar had been devised, but languished without approval by the King or adoption by Duinnor or other realms.

The Royal Duinnor Calendar, which pertained only to the King's Year, started on the day after the Spring Equinox, sometimes called Spring Day, and was a ceremonial calendar for the regnal year of the Unknown Kings. On the morning of the Spring Equinox, the Unknown King of Duinnor went forth to the Temple of Beras and returned from there with a new Avatar. From thenceforth, the year was named after the shape of the King's Avatar. Hence, the Year of the Snowflake, the Year of the Red Door, et cetera. Why the Avatar took a different shape each year, and the meaning of the shape, remains a mystery. This calendar was begun by the First Unknown King and persisted until the end of the Second Age, although its value was primarily ceremonial.

Since the Vernal Equinox was the most important day for this calendar, and due to the problems of drift mentioned earlier, there was some discussion among scholars that it was perhaps best to do away with the Royal Duinnor Calendar altogether, except for ceremonial references, and to use a corrected standard calendar (as mentioned above) to determine the correct date of the King's renewal ceremonies.

When it came to timekeeping, it was traditionally left up to a town or village to designate a timekeeper, normally the mayor or other head person. Many regions used no system whatsoever for daily timekeeping, except that provided by the sun, moon, and stars. But as industry developed, including the need to regulate daily events, timekeeping grew in importance. Various instruments were developed over the ages to do this, including sandglasses, water clocks, and pendulum systems. By the 850s of the Second Age, clocks that used springs were being produced, and larger towns and cities erected a central clock, tended to by a timekeeper, that other clocks would be set to. By the year 870, clocks were being manufactured in every realm. In Glareth special attention and a great deal of resources were given to making seaworthy clocks to aid in the problems of navigation, but by the end of the Second Age no clock had yet been devised that could survive sea conditions and remain even relatively accurate.

****

Leases of Forfeiture

Leases of Forfeiture is the general name given to the Duinnor practice of acquiring lands and properties in other realms, usually in the guise of economic assistance, but just as often as punishment against a Named House for refusing the Kingsmen Summons. Using Duinnor's wealth, the Lord of the Exchequer, Lord Banis, first instituted leases in order to pressure Vanaran landowners to relinquish lands to Duinnor, primarily lands in the southern region nearest to the Dragonlands. When Lord

Banis became First Lord of the High Chamber, the practice of acquiring these leases steadily increased.

These leases required that the landowner sign over all rights to land or property to Duinnor to be held in trust. In the short-term, the rightful owner gained certain financial considerations, including substantial payments by Duinnor for a period of time, freedom from general tribute, and the right of the owners to continue to occupy and oversee the property. It was common that a stipulation would be that products, crops, or minerals produced on such estates must be sold exclusively to Duinnor at rates set within the lease. Other conditions or requirements were sometimes also included, such as provisions for the estate to provide land and support for military garrisons on the property. Duinnor was very strict in enforcing these conditions, and if not met, Duinnor had the right to foreclose on the property and expel anyone living there. Generally, it was akin to an equity mortgage and was seen by many as a means to retain their lands in times of economic hardship. Duinnor leases were, on the face, quite generous, but over time such properties were targeted with exorbitant fees and additional conditions, very often the condition that all products of the land be sold exclusively to Duinnor (at prices established by Duinnor). Sometimes, these leases stipulated that estate owners would only be paid a single one-time lump sum for all products of the estate for the term of the lease, usually 100 years.

Fees and property acquired in this manner amounted to a kind of tribute, since Duinnor's expenditures were always less than the fees for such support or the value received by the products of the land. Those who wished to terminate their lease agreement with Duinnor were required to repay Duinnor both the principal amount of the loan plus interest in addition to the worth of the products of the land over the remaining period of the loan. Most often, this period was for one hundred years. After many years, sometimes after generations, the fees demanded by Duinnor and the loss of income from the crops or products of the property exceeded the property owner's ability to pay, and Acts of Forfeiture were performed which gave the King full title to the lands and properties under lease. Such properties were usually disposed of at auctions held in Duinnor, auctions that increasingly became shams designed to benefit only a few select individuals.

Over time, as more lands were deeded away to Duinnor and people came to understand how dangerous these leases were, the term "lease" became a euphemism for corruption. As might be expected, these policies served to increase tension between Duinnor and the other Realms. Queen Serith Ellyn, along with many Ruling Princes, sought to prevent such agreements by instituting laws proclaiming that all lands were first sovereign to the realm, and that the realm within which the property resided had the first right to lease or purchase the properties. But this contradicted certain other Vanaran laws, already enacted, providing to property owners the right to lease, rent, sell, or dispose of their properties. A similar situation existed in most Realms. Many Rulers, including Queen Serith Ellyn, attempted to pay Duinnor the fees demanded, but Duinnor countered by simply increasing the fees to make this unsustainable. From time to time, a great furor against Leases rose up that in Vanara, Glareth, Altoria, and Tracia there was open discussion of militarily confiscating such leased properties.

Such leases were by law imposed on Named Houses that refused to send their eldest son to serve in the Kingsmen ranks or those Named Houses that had no son to send. However, these leases had a much shorter term (usually 15 years), and the Named House received no payment from Duinnor. As well, the Acts of Forfeiture were almost always performed well before any term of lease was up, in effect foreclosing on the properties. Additionally, any failure of a Named House to provide a Kingsman resulted in that House being officially dissolved. Until such acts were carried out, the House in question would be liable to steep fines imposed by Duinnor.

Leases became so common that they were objects of trade in Duinnor, with various accounting firms purchasing the rights to oversee the lease agreements. Holding such a lease often allowed the firm to specify the price paid for products acquired from the landowner and to modify other terms of the agreement. Properties that were foreclosed upon were at first often sold or given to those favorable to Duinnor, but by the late Second Age, Duinnor held so much property that most were allowed to fall into disuse and ruin.

Agents working for other realms often tried to use the trading system to take over such leases as they could, but under Lord Banis only certain parties were legally authorized to do so, being Royal Lease Agents. Non-Duinnor actors were excluded from this group, and of course the Royal Lease Agents were required to provide a large percentage of their earnings to the First Lord (Banis).

These leases were a contributing factor to the abdication of the Kings of Tracia, Masurthia, Glareth, and Altoria, reducing those Royal Houses to Ruling Principalities (with Ruling Princes, etc.). Each sought, as a condition of this change, for exemptions and various other conditions favorable to their own people. But, of course, overall, these abdications made those realms more or less subservient to Duinnor's will (The old Eastlands Realm became a protectorate of Glareth with no Ruling Prince of its own). By the late Second Age, only Vanara retained its Sovereign Ruler, Queen Serith Ellyn, partly because of Vanara's wealth and military power and partly because Duinnor needed Vanara as a buffer against the Dragonkind and was more dependent on good relations with Vanara than with other Realms.

****

Literacy and Education

The Beginnings of Writing

Phonetic alphabets began supplanting pictographic writing during the Time of Strife. The Dragonkind had developed several scripts and were transitioning from tablets of stone to linen and other fabrics. And with the necessity of maintaining official records, mostly because of rather mundane and administrative tasks and requirements, the drive for more efficient, reliable, and cheap writing methods developed fairly quickly. The same pressures came about in the northern Elifaen lands once they began to establish larger towns, cities, and especially when they began to organize under national governments.

However, the Elifaen were not as quick to take up writing. This was due to their long lives and excellent memories, so there was little perceived need to record information for future use, or even for transmission across distances. A courier could easily and accurately recite messages to and from leaders, and there was plenty of time, given their immortality, to hear orally given reports, stories, and accounts.

But as the First Tongue receded during the late Time of Strife, and especially after the urgent pressures of survival were better understood, the Elifaen began using various methods of writing, some modeled on the Dragonkind and some entirely unique. The speech of the Elifaen changed with the loss of the First Tongue, and eventually developed into what is referred to as the Ancient Speech, which itself changed over time.

When Silmain became king, and began to grapple with the affairs of state, the necessity of written records became urgent. Specially trained and trustworthy scribes were employed and soon assisted in every branch of governing. At the same time, in the early First Age, the Elifaen began exchanging letters and documents. When taxation and tribute were instituted, and especially when coinage came into use, record-keeping became even more important.

A variety of writing styles and methods competed. Pictographic writing, which held sway prior to Silmain, was slowly replaced by phonetic symbols to represent words and ideas, most often runic in character. Although certain symbols remained in use for numbers, these, too, were often written using phonetic characters. By the time Cupeldain came to power, there were at least seven commonly used alphabets. It was not uncommon for one government ministry to use one alphabet and another to use a different one, depending on the scribes employed. Likewise, those systems that were common in one region were often quite unintelligible to Elifaen living and working elsewhere. Some alphabets were syllabary in nature, while others expressed specific sounds within the syllables of words. Others were combinations of the two.

The New Writing & the Purge of Scholars

In Glareth Realm, there was a coordinated effort to adopt a single unified system of writing. Likewise in Vanara, there were various movements to make writing and the written language more uniform and less arbitrary. Eventually, and with cooperation between scribes in Vanara, Glareth, and Altoria, a system of writing was developed that reduced the number of characters (letters) required and standardized their shapes and glyphs, yet allowed for both simplistic rendering both simplistic rendering and embellishments that without confusing the reader. This system also included a standardized orthography to indicate pauses, ends of sentences, special stresses on words or syllables, and emphasis such as questions or exclamations. In writing, these became represented by symbols or, in some cases, by using different characters for the words. Names or proper nouns were at first designated by surrounding symbols, but this was soon replaced by simply making the first letter of the word different or by heavier or bolder rendering. Eventually each letter had two versions, at least, depending on whether it was to be used for a proper noun or not.

The use of the "New Writing" varied greatly, and was often not used according to the rules. There was much resistance to its adoption by various groups, mainly because they were accustomed to their own long-established alphabets. In Glareth, some of the first schools were established in order to teach the New Writing to government workers and to trade workers. At the same time, experts fluent in several of the older writing methods were employed to act as "interpreters." All of these projects were supported by generous monetary grants and by flexible legal requirements.

Meanwhile, in Vanara, the transition was quite rocky, with large groups of scribes and scholars resisting change and continuing the use of their preferred writing methods well into the rule of Parthais. Several events and circumstances took place that brought the issue to a crisis. Parthais, paranoid about his power, insisted that all written criticism of him be discovered and rebutted, with the authors of such criticisms publicly shamed or even fined. At the same time, there was much confusion about record-keeping when it came to collecting taxes and tributes, including the necessary inventories and reports required. At the same time, laws that were adopted or changed had to be written in every system in use throughout Vanara. This required the employment of a vast number of scribes and writing experts. Then, in 1154, a major fire broke out in Ladentree which destroyed many of the town's buildings. Blame fell on certain royal magistrates, assigned by Parthais, and an official document describing the event and seeking compensation for the damage was sent by the town leaders to Parthais. However, because the document was not written in the New Writing, it had to be translated (as did all such missives) before submitting it to Parthais. And since it was deemed a matter for the Royal Treasury authorities, it was given to them to do so. As a result, those responsible for the fires were able to modify the document to express their own innocence and to contain insults to Parthais. However, all such written submissions had to be reviewed and read to Parthais (who could not read) by his royal scribe, Nimwill, who saw immediately that it had been falsified by the Treasury scribes. Nimwill managed to obtain the original document sent by Ladentree (which had not been destroyed), and he properly translated it. Then Nimwill notified Lord Banis, a judge of Vanara, who launched an investigation. During the brief but intense scandal that followed, blame was put on all sides by all other sides. Many Treasury ministers fled, while others were arrested. And when it came to light that many of the warehouses destroyed in Ladentree were filled with tribute destined for Parthais, his fury was further stoked.

Although Parthais was partially responsible for the incident, by appointing officials he knew to be corrupt, he instantly issued an edict stating that the New Writing was the only writing that was to be used anywhere in Vanara and for all purposes, and that all old writings were to be translated or destroyed. This essentially began was came to be called the Purge of Scholars. Suddenly, many of the corrupt officials (who had been cheating both Parthais and everyone else) realized that their activities would become known. Others, innocent of any wrong, opposed the edict on the grounds that older works of history and literature ought to be preserved as valuable artifacts, even if they had been translated into the New Writing. Thus, from every side, there was opposition. After a year of resistance, Parthais grew even more tyrannical, ordering raids on homes, businesses, and schools to discover and burn anything that was not in the New Writing. He further ordered the execution of any scribes that continued the use of other writings. No one knows how many people were punished, but at least 2,000 were imprisoned and over were 300 executed. These not only included scholars, writers, and teachers, but also many journeyman scribes, traders who smuggled books or fleeing scholars, and even soldiers who refused to carry out arrests.

A mass exodus of scholars and written materials began immediately, along with many high-ranking officials, including Lord Banis. These refugees flooded into welcoming Duinnor and Glareth, both places where such Vanarans would be employed for their services and rewarded for the books and documents that they brought with them. Seeing how all this would benefit their growing realm, Duinnor's the ruling lords united behind a policy of openness and encouragement to any scholars who wished to come there, even so far as sending money and teams of servants to help with the move. In Glareth, King Gardin likewise granted special status to Vanaran immigrants, offering to purchase outright under generous terms any books that they brought with them.

Parthais responded by conducting more raids, which netted very little. Unknown to him, his chief scribe, Nimwill, was secretly working against him, warning people about impending moves against them, assisting in the smuggling and transport of scholars and materials, and, by creating false documents, redirecting funds from the Treasury to those in need of help. That he was never discovered was something of a miracle.

Eventually, Parthais began issuing threats against Duinnor and Glareth, saying that if all people and books were not returned promptly to Vanara, he would send his army against them. His armies were in disarray, though, and everyone knew it. So while rebuffing the threats of Parthais, Duinnor began building defensive works around the city and organizing its own army, albeit at a studied pace. Glareth entirely ignored the threats but issued warnings of its own to Parthais to refrain from molesting any citizens of Glareth in Vanara or hampering any trade or travellers to and from Glareth. Then Parthais backed (some say instigated) an attempt to assassinate King Gardin. The attempt was thwarted and evidence was discovered that strongly implicated Parthais, which of course made Glareth very angry.

The political and social repercussions of the Purge of Scholars were long lasting. And in some ways, it led to the downfall of Parthais and the rise to power of his daughter, Serith Ellyn. But the New Writing did take hold, and it became the dominant form of writing in all regions except the Dragonlands.

The coming of Men complicated things. Their native tongue was not all that different from the speech used by the Elifaen, but with many variations and even additional sounds that had to be accommodated. For example, all vowel sounds spoken by the Elifaen up to this point were long. And every letter of every word was pronounced. In the Ancient Speech, it was rare to give any syllable any greater stress or accent than the others of a word. Here are some examples using Common Speech equivalents or approximations:

Word	Approximate Pronunciation	
	Ancient Speech	Common Speech*
Vanara	VAY NAY RAY	Vuh NAR ah

Cupeldain	CU PEEL DAY INE	COO pell dane
Silmain	SILE MAY INE	SILL main
Linlally	LINE LAY LEE	len LAY lee
Serith Ellen	SEER I TH EEL LEEN	SAIR ith EH lin

* With, of course, wide variations between the localities and dialects of Men

As might be expected, spelling varied wildly, especially when striving to render the Ancient Speech. By the middle of the Second Age, however, with the power and population of Men, the letters of the New Writing had been adapted, rather inconsistently, to reflect their own ways of speech and words, even though they were based on the adopted Elifaen language. This was called the Common Speech, as opposed to what was generally referred to as the Ancient Speech. At first, the Common Speech, in all its forms, was considered uncouth or even barbaric by most Elifaen. But it was quickly adopted, and adapted, and by the middle of the Second Age, Common Speech was the dominant language in use both in writing and in speech, with many regional variations and dialects. As a result, from around 500 S.A. onward, spelling, lettering, and pronunciation became more uniform, if not fully standardized.

Yet, regional differences in the pronunciation, and sometimes the meaning, of words produced a variety of dialects, idioms, and accents, especially among those with little or no formal education. This was often reflected in their local writings.

Printing

Reproducing written works that were legible, durable, and somewhat portable was for centuries a time-consuming and tedious affair performed by scribes and copyists by hand. Various mechanical tools were developed quite early. Blocks of wood or stone carved with symbols and words were in common use throughout the First Age. Metal tokens cast or etched with specific messages or denoting specific authority to the bearer were common. Well before the end of the First Age, written works intended for wide dissemination, such as proclamations and decrees or important announcements that required distribution, large plates or blocks were made of wood, metal, or stone that were inked (sometimes in multiple colors) and pressed against sheets of linen or paper materials.

As materials such as linen and paper became cheaper and easier to produce, new systems of mass printing were developed, including roller printing and moveable type. Sewing sheets together into books quickly replaced scrolls. In the early Second Age, a method of making paper from wood fibers was discovered in Glareth, and such paper would become one of Glareth's most important exports. Around this time, methods of consistently casting movable type were developed in Duinnor, and more efficient methods of printing soon followed.

A variety of printers, therefore, existed by the middle Second Age. Most specialized in certain types of material or literature. At first, the various governments of realms made the most use of these. But by the late Second Age, private printing establishments had proliferated across the world. In Glareth alone, there were nearly 200 different privately operated printing businesses. In Duinnor, there were over 300. It is estimated that, by the end of the Second Age, there were over 1,500 printers in the world (excluding the Dragonlands).

Thus, a multitude of types of printed material were produced, according to the myriad of needs, subject matters, and profitability. Books, pamphlets, broadsheets (or newspapers) were all readily available in virtually every major city. Pre-printed forms, such as ledgers or applications or forms for submitting reports, were widely made and used.

Schools, Libraries, and Literacy

Almost as soon as writing became fairly common, and especially after there were sufficient means of copying and printing, libraries and archives sprang up. At first, these were centered on the needs of governments. But as time passed, people began recording information about other topics. Everything from common "how to" writings, to those concerning weather observations, the night sky, plants, and animals. Many were instructive in nature, while others were simply records of observations. At the same time, people began recording their stories and histories, their legends, and myths. Works of poetry and song were produced. Many types of ephemeral materials were produced, including announcements, newspapers (broadsheets), invitations, and even town directories. And all manner of works were gathered into myriad collections, large and small. Although expensive, books were highly sought after, and, for the wealthy, a well-stocked library was an essential symbol of status. The book trade therefore flourished in the Second Age.

Libraries were natural centers of learning, sometimes quite by happenstance and other times of a purpose. As these centers grew and became more formalized, their programs included not only instruction but also supported exploration and mapping expeditions, research, testing, and development of new tools and materials, as well as investigations into various aspects of nature.

In Glareth, a special academy was established for the training of sailors and officers of the Royal Glarethian Navy. It quickly expanded to include all manner of disciplines, and it merged with other schools over time to become the Glareth Academy. By the mid-Second Age, this was a place of higher learning for all who could qualify and pay the required fees (citizens of Glareth could attend without cost should they qualify). Applicants were required to show that they possessed good reading and writing skills, a general knowledge of history. Certain certificates and recommendations from their prior schools were required by applicants, often supplied by regional or local teachers or scholars. It was this school (Glareth Academy) that Robby Ribbon and Billy Bosk planned to attend, but were thwarted from doing so by events.

The other two great centers of learning, at least outside of the Dragonlands, were the King's Academy in Duinnor and Vanara's Queen's Academy. Like Glareth Academy, these were large institutions that delivered instruction on many subjects and supported research into many topics. Graduation from the King's Academy (Kingsman Academy) was required of all Kingsmen. It operated independently of other schools in Duinnor, some of which served the wealthy and others that were specifically designed for (and affordable to) the less affluent or the poor. As in other Realms, many schools in Duinnor were trade-oriented, or were specialized in some way (such as music schools). Likewise in Vanara. In Linlally were several important schools (and libraries).

Basic education in the fundamentals of reading, writing, and mathematics was slow to spread into smaller towns and rural areas. But by the late Second Age, there was a school for children in or nearby to virtually all but the most remote villages in Glareth. As the importance of an educated citizenry became better understood, local schools sprang up in the Eastlands and Tracia. In Vanara and Duinnor, by various edicts and laws, many publicly funded schools were established and operated.

By the year 870 of the second age, literacy, at least at the basic level of reading and writing skills, was as common in most regions as illiteracy. In some regions, virtually everyone knew how to read and write. Still, in other areas, due to their remoteness or conflict or repeated misfortunes, literacy was very low or almost non-existent. For example, in some regions in the Eastlands, depopulated by war, plague, drought, and famine, had not the means to support schools. In other regions, such as the high Carthanes or the relatively isolated fishing villages of Altoria, where poverty added to isolation, there were not the resources nor the pressures to obtain much formal learning. In many villages, a special person would be designated to serve as the scribe and often as a tutor. In other places, schools and teaching sprang up and faded away as the population grew and contracted, or as their purses did. Overall, though, by the end of the Second Age, the world was fairly literate. Almost everyone had at least an elementary ability to read and write.

So it is somewhat ironic that literacy was lowest among the Elifaen for a very long time. Due to their long memories and lives, many simply did not see the need, or benefit, of learning to read or write. This attitude was certainly changing during the latter part of the First Age, and by the middle of the Second Age the Elifaen not only were usually highly literate, but a great proportion of teachers and scholars were Elifaen.

In the Dragonlands

Less is known about the development of writing and literacy among the Dragon Peoples. However, by the beginning of the First Age, they were well ahead of the Elifaen. By virtue of their short lives, they depended much more on the written word than on oral traditions, and great importance was given to all manner of writings. In later years, many books written by Dragonkind would find their way to northern lands, and would spread much learning in the fields of mathematics, engineering, and metallurgy.

Such was the importance of learning in the Dragonlands that every person, even the lowest of society, was expected to learn to read and write. Of course, the better-off and wealthy sent their children to school, one of which existed in virtually every village. In Tyrsharat, schools and libraries were hardly distinguishable on the outside from the most lavish palaces. And by the Second Age, Sarapolis was the greatest city of learning anywhere, with over forty libraries and sixty schools and academies, some of which were supported by the Dragonkind Throne and others by private individuals.

Although not widely known for its erudition, the Free City of Kajarahn was also an important center of learning and the arts. Not only was this a crossroads for books and information passing between Vanara and the Dragonlands, but it was also a place where many writings (and writers) that were banned by various Dragonkind Kings found refuge. And here, too, the importance of an educated citizenry was recognized as all depended on the accurate and well-operated trading concerns and marketplaces that sustained the city.

The Library of Griferis

One library deserves special mention. It was the ever-growing library of Griferis. As related by Robby Ribbon (King Philawain), it contained every book ever published, and was continually growing as new works were published, copies of which magically appeared on its shelves. In addition to books, the library also obtained newspapers. The only works not included were those that were never copied and published (made public). How Griferis, or the powers that sustained Griferis, was able to physically expand to accommodate these works, and how its catalog was continually updated remains a mystery. But its existence, verified by many witnesses, was essential to how the world came to be remade. Whether it, along with the rest of Griferis, still exists is unknown.

****

Prerogatives of the Realms

The Prerogatives of the Realms was the name for a set of agreements between the King of Duinnor and the rulers of the other realms. It evolved over time, and gave certain rights and responsibilities to each of the Ruling Princes, the rulers of the other realms. The specifics of each agreement or condition of the Prerogatives varied somewhat from Realm to Realm. In essence, they were treaties between Duinnor and the Realms that consigned certain rights to Duinnor and others to the Realm.

Generally, these included provisions allowing the Ruling Princes to make laws that did not contradict agreements with Duinnor. It also required each Realm to keep and maintain armed forces sufficient to defend its own territories or to come to the aid of other Realms when required. Other notable provisions included the exemption of a certain number of persons serving the Ruling Prince from service as a Kingsman, the right to petition the King of Duinnor directly, the right to institute its own courts, and the right to levy and collect taxes of its own citizens within its own territorial bounds. In return, all Realms would be required to submit to Duinnor Law, Duinnor courts and arbitration for any disputes involving trade or territory, to collect taxes levied by Duinnor and transport those taxes to Duinnor, and to use Duinnor weights and measures for trade outside of their own Realm. Any Realm had the right to pursue and arrest any fugitive from their own Realm into any other Realm, as long as such fugitives were given the opportunity to appeal to Duinnor for redress of injustice. All roadways and waterways were required to be maintained and no Realm could levy tolls or road taxes without express consent of Duinnor. Duinnor alone had the power to impose any conditions on travel, including tolls or taxes to be paid by travelers. Duinnor, in writing at least, agreed to come to the defense of any Realm that was threatened by another or by the Dragonkind, to assist with road construction and maintenance, and to fairly arbitrate any disputes of trade or territory, and would give the representative of each Named or Honored House the right of hearing before Duinnor courts. Duinnor also agreed not to impose any religion or any ritualistic practices, and would confer on each Realm the power to control or limit commerce within its borders.

To facilitate all this, each Realm was required to conduct a yearly census of all its inhabitants, and each head of household was to attest to their property and livelihood. Likewise, every subject of every Realm was required to swear allegiance to the King of Duinnor, and to submit to the King one-tenth the annual value of profits from commerce or trade, to be collected by the King's representatives. So that Duinnor would support the Ruling Prince of each realm, every Realm was to pay to Duinnor a Surety of profound value, agreeable to the King, to be held in perpetuity. The amount and nature of each Surety paid by each Realm was negotiated, but was never made public. In exchange for these agreements, all kings and queens of the other Realms, except Vanara, eventually abdicated, becoming Ruling Princes or Princesses. Since the agreement did little to restrain or limit their power within their Realm, the Ruling Princes had nearly the same power as kings, but they were not allowed to use that title.

Some Ruling Houses, most notably within Glareth and Vanara, did much to circumvent the taxes that Duinnor sought to impose, offsetting the amount by trade. Other Realms, such as Masurthia and Tracia, struggled to maintain tributes.

These Prerogatives would go far in fostering resentment against Duinnor and, in some cases, against the Ruling Princes. In Tracia, the Prerogatives would be cited by many as one of the reasons for the revolt that eventually overtook that Realm.

In Vanara, the Prerogatives were never formally ratified or agreed to. Instead, much the same conditions were agreed to in an agreement called the Realm Accords Between Duinnor and Vanara, a treaty which stipulated, on paper, that Duinnor would support Vanara as a fully independent Realm with its own Sovereign Queen. However, in order to ensure Duinnor's continued military support against the Dragonkind, most of the conditions of the Prerogatives were also stipulated and agreed to in the Realm Accords.

****

Biographical Sketches and Tales

We obviously cannot include a detailed biography of every person mentioned within *The Year of the Red Door*. Generally, items in this section have been deemed too lengthy to include in the Glossary Section of this Companion. And the selection of persons in this section is merely a sampling. However, we have included sketches of less prominent figures, including those who played some important historical role or because aspects of their lives touch upon or shed light on other people, circumstances, or events.

Some of the individuals in this section are mentioned in *The Year of the Red Door*, while a few are not mentioned at all. As we continue our work, we may at some future date include more people in this section, and we may make revisions according to new discoveries.

We have not included biographies of certain individuals who played prominent roles within *The Year of the Red Door* (such as Mirabella, Robby Ribbon, or Sheila Pradkin, etc.) because much of their stories is revealed within *The Year of the Red Door* itself.

Some of what follows is in story form, as they are taken almost verbatim from other documents and notes, or from interviews. Other sketches are a blend of our own narrative with information or descriptions from others. As indicated in the introduction to this Companion, not all sources are cited here.

****

Alonair

Alonair was a Firstborn of the Faerekind, a maker of fabulous statues and carvings of stone. It was Alonair who set before the Dragonkind the challenge of the Great Stone and by doing so precipitated the disastrous conflict between Faerekind and Dragonkind that led to The Fall of the Faere. For this, he came to be ostracized and eventually became reclusive.

During the Time Before Time, Alonair was one of the first of the Faerekind to manipulate things of the world, shaping and making new things of old materials. He used the First Tongue to do this, as well as his hands, and was able to coax and convince stones into sculptures. As his skill grew, he decorated the new city of Linlally with some of his works, as well as placing some in gardens and parks in other parts of Vanara. Faerekind would come from far and wide just to see them.

Alonair's finest sculptures had uncanny, lifelike characteristics. In daylight, the people and animals that he carved seemed to follow viewers with their eyes. Many people reported that the carvings actually turned their heads or slightly shifted their posture. He himself always seemed dissatisfied with his work, and he implied that he always worked to make his statues more lifelike, even animated with movement and with other characteristics of beings. Yet his reputation grew, and eventually his renown spread to the Dragonlands. This resulted in Kalzar, King of the Dragonkind, to commission a work by Alonair, one of massive proportions. Alonair agreed, but only on the condition that the block upon which he was to work was to be of a certain type of stone, of a massive size, and successfully quarried and transported to the place where the statue was to be made. In return, Alonair promised that he would carve a statue that exceeded all others in grandeur, size, and quality.

Kalzar accepted the terms, and even succeeded in quarrying the stone (see Great Stone). But the effort drained his resources, and he was unable to transport the massive block across the desert to its intended place. Meanwhile, much resentment was aroused among the Dragonkind due to the vast resources of labor (often slaves) and treasure that Kalzar expended. Eventually, Kalzar became convinced that the whole affair was a ploy to weaken and discredit him and his people. His ire and the sentiments of the people grew to such a furor that he launched a massive invasion into Vanara. This sparked a terrible but brief war, to which Aperion put an end, and which resulted in a split among the Faerekind, with most following Aperion out from the world, while the ones who refused to depart the earth lost their wings.

Like Cupeldain, Alonair lost his wings when he refused to leave the world and go with Aperion to a new home in the heavens. Alonair's fame eventually turned against him as the suffering of the Elifaen increased and his role in their condition became more widely known. He never enjoyed the popularity that seemed to protect other Elifaen such as Cupeldain and Silmain who had just as much to do with the Fall of the Faere. Once Alonair and the Elifaen recovered from the loss of their wings and began to reestablish their culture, Alonair resumed working as a sculptor under the protection of Silmain and Cupeldain. But his ambitions were soon outstripping his skill as the First Tongue weakened within him.

During the Time of Strife, and well into the First Age, Alonair assisted Silmain and Cupeldain with the remodeling of the White Palace to make it better suited to people who walk rather than fly. He carefully avoided becoming embroiled in the politics and intrigues of the Vanaran Court.

Opinions about Alonair varied greatly, but as stories concerning the Fall of the Faere spread, he was held in blame for the Elifaen's fallen state. He was physically attacked several times, and some of his statues were defaced or destroyed. He steadfastly refused to take up arms against the Dragonkind, or be directly involved in the factions vying for power in Vanara. This served to further erode his reputation in the eyes of many. He therefore became increasingly more reclusive.

According to written accounts later discovered in Vanara, during the First Age, Alonair lived on the outskirts of Linlally at a small estate. And he continued to work, producing around three statues and stone carvings each year for almost fifty years. His behavior became increasingly erratic and prone to outbursts of anger. He often drank heavily, worked frantically, and was never satisfied with his work. He destroyed many of his statues, some not long after completion, until his admirers began removing them from his estate before he could do so. The disappearance of this work outraged Alonair, and when he discovered that it was carried out by his friends, he flew into such a violent rage against them that he was put in chains. After several months, his anger subsided and he became morose. His caretakers reported that he rarely spoke and that he seemed distracted, constantly pacing and muttering to himself. The decision was made to release Alonair from confinement and, perhaps somewhat shamed by his behavior, he peacefully returned to his estate. But he only remained there for a season before he departed in a wagon full of his tools.

Later, somewhere in the Blue Mountains, Alonair somehow managed to evade the squad of Fellfaere that were assigned to guard him. It was later reported that he was seen in the region of Ladentree in the company of a sorcerer who he had hired as an assistant. He had also hired many other servants and laborers, one of which kept a journal. All this was about the time that Silmain became King of Vanara. Alonair made a huge repository of stone blocks that he had quarried from lands far away to the west. Most of the blocks were of granite, taken from the great western cleft in the earth that other Faerekind had made. Using the First Tongue, Alonair easily floated them to his repository. It is said that he boasted that he would use the stones to fashion what would be his greatest achievement. He set about his work by making thousands of blocks of various sizes. Then he began stacking blocks in a manner that was roughly in the shape of a person, with two legs, two arms, and a head. Taking up his chisel, he began to carve, speaking the First Tongue to his tools and to the material that he carved.

Once he had roughed out one figure, he would go to the next figure. Then he started over with additional touches to the carve hands, fingers, ears and mouths of each statue. As he worked, day after day, night after night, he grew increasingly frustrated and annoyed that his creations were not as fine as he wished. In fact, they were nothing like his previous work at all, and barely better than what an inexperienced child might make. The First Tongue was leaving Alonair, and along with it, his skill. Finally, as he labored on a single carving, one that was much bigger than the rest, he realized what was happening to him. He abruptly halted his work and spent the next several weeks muttering and pacing around rank upon rank of crude man-like carvings, coming again and again to the last one that he worked on. For an entire week, Alonair stared at the single statue. At the end of that week, a terrible storm struck the region. Torrents of rain fell, bolt after bolt of lightning shot across the sky, and the hills surrounded shook with ceaseless rolling thunder. Alonair remained where he was. His servants implored him to take shelter, but he angrily refused. According to notes taken by one of his servants, Alonair raised his fists skyward.

"What am I to do?" he shouted heavenward. "What if I am required to fulfill the promise made to Kalzar? And what of these creatures before me? If I complete them, the last of my skill, the last of my First Tongue, will be gone! And the Great Stone will forever remain a stone! Is that what you would desire? But if I do not finish my work here, what will I have accomplished but another curse and bane upon the world? Is that what you wish?"

In a sudden frenzy, Alonair sprang forward to the nearest statue and put his hand upon it, speaking to it so softly that no one could hear what was said. Alonair then backed away a few steps just as a bolt of lightning shot downward and struck the head of the statue. All who peered out of their tents and huts were blinded and could not see or comprehend what was happening. But a strange fire glowed within the chest of the statue that was struck. Then the next statue was struck in the same manner by the first, and as the crash of it pounded the air and the great bolt faded, another likewise struck yet a third statue. Over and over lighting struck, and chests glowed. Alonair laughed in the rain, but his laughter could not be heard over the terrible, constant boom of thunder. Some of the servants fled. Others hid themselves behind rocks, pulling their coat over their eyes and covering their ears with their hands. This went on for over an hour. Then it was suddenly over. A heavy and silent darkness covered the area.

But Alonair was mortified that the rough unfinished figures—squarish and inelegant—would be seen as examples of his skill. All but one lacked any real intellect, any motivating will. All were crude in form, squarish, with none of the natural elegance of truly living creatures, no curved limbs or shapes, no flowing movement, and no subtlety of expression in their faces.

So, according to accounts, he forced all of his assistants to make vows of secrecy concerning them, and then he instructed them to go away. Once they had departed, Alonair transported all of the figures and his materials thousands of miles eastward, and he deposited them in the southern region of the Carthane Mountains. Before he abandoned them, he charged each with the command that they would all be obliged to obey his will. He left one of them, the single most refined, to be their king, who came to be called Thunderfoot. Alonair instructed all of the others to do the bidding of Thunderfoot in the absence of himself, their creator. Then he abandoned them to fend for themselves. There they would come to be known as trolls.

While in those mountains, however, Alonair discovered a seam of fine granite. From it he carved many columns that he intended to carry back to Vanara for further use. But the unruly trolls constantly interrupted him, and he abandoned his work, leaving all of the columns behind. In later years, these would be located by a sorcerer who merged them with soldiers of Heneil's guard at Tulith Attis, to be always ready to repeal intruders should the Great Bell ring out.

And so, Alonair's work on the trolls ended in the year 130 of the Second Age. The trolls terrorized the mountains where they lived. They were crude, ignorant, and had very low intellectual capacity, the only exception being their king, known as Thunderfoot. The mountains would eventually be named after their noise (the Thunder Mountains). There the trolls abided, eking out their lives by eating both rocks and animals, and often simply mulling about in an aimless manner. They were the bane of settlers, raiding farms for cattle, stamping and crushing crops, and waylaying travelers. King

Thunderfoot did little to restrain them. As a result, the Thunder Mountains became a land occupied by the most desperate outlaws, warlords, and fugitives from other regions.

All of this work upon the trolls depleted much of Alonair's skill and knowledge of the First Tongue, which he had possessed in greater abundance and was more persistent than with other Elifaen. And he suddenly realized that, for him, the First Tongue was not something that could be maintained by practice and use, but was rather of a limited supply, the use of which grew more difficult with the passage of time. He thus withdrew from the society of others, assumed a different name, and began a long period of travel. He went back and forth from place to place, from east to west, and from north to south. It is thought that he visited every realm and even the Dragonlands. He never lingered for very long, because his identity was easily discovered and when that happened, he was frequently expelled from the places that he visited. Eventually, he was given safe refuge at the Temple of Beras, and the Oracle and monks took pity on him and kept his presence a secret in order to protect him.

In the year 798 SA, Alonair decided to travel alone to Glareth. He took with him two large sacks of jewels. These were part of the vast collection of gemstones that he had discovered in his various quarries and mines. Much of his treasure he gave to the Temple. The rest he delivered to a trusted agent in Glareth to be used to support his family. Although his children lived in Vanara, by charging an agent in Glareth with the task, Alonair hoped to mislead anyone who might discover the source of his family's wealth.

On his way back to Duinnor, Alonair was traveling through the Carthane Mountains when he was set upon by bandits and made a captive. The group of bandits sought to make Alonair tell them who he was so that they could hold him for ransom, but Alonair refused. Seeing the scars on his back, the bandits knew that he was Elifaen and from the weighty purse of coins that they took from him, they surmised that he was someone of importance who would bring a large ransom. They were preparing to force him to drink a homemade concoction of foxdire when he was rescued by Lord Danig Tallin, who single-handedly killed all of the bandits and liberated Alonair. Tallin, who had somehow discovered Alonair's identity, managed to extract a promise from Alonair that, in exchange for this life, Alonair would assist in the construction of defensive works around Tallin's planned city in Tallinvale. This Alonair did, making use of his ability to communicate with the trolls. Alonair and the army of trolls (who did all of the work) were able to complete their task within a year, leaving Lord Tallin with a well-fortified city and the promise to further help defend Tallin City should the need ever arise. Lord Tallin merely needed to send word to Alonair (at the Temple of Beras), and a secret password would be sent to Lord Tallin. This password would rouse the trolls from their deep slumber and carry out the last command given to them by Alonair.

The key part of Tallin's design, constructed by the trolls, was a vast underground lake outside of the north side of the walled city. A thick roof was held up by the trolls, acting as supporting columns, and over this roof was spread soil such that crops could be planted on the surface, itself crisscrossed by irrigation canals. The underground lake was constantly fed by springs and streams, and the runoff helped feed boggy weirs to the east and west of Tallin City, further enhancing its defenses. Huge oil tanks were devised which could dump thousands of gallons of flammable oil into the canals and underground lake. Upon command, the trolls would lower their arms, collapsing the fields above into the lake, which would be set afire from the safety of the city walls. And this, indeed, eventually happened when Tallin City was besieged by Redvests in the year 870, resulting in the utter defeat of the attackers.

Alonair conceded to Tallin's wishes with great reservation, overseeing the work of the trolls for nearly a year. They were impervious to fire and heat, and made vast kilns to form glassy rock into the city walls. They cast brick and blocks to line the underground lake, above and below. Doing so, they moved countless tons of rock and earth, reshaping the land inside and outside of the city. When all was done and approved by Tallin, Alonair took his leave and returned to the Temple of

Beras. Over the years, Lord Tallin made several visits to the Temple to implore Alonair for the password needed to invoke the trolls. But it was not until Tallinvale came under attack by the Redvests that he relented, sending the word to Lord Tallin via the Familiar called Fallendine. After the battle was over, King Thunderfoot took charge of the trolls and led them away westward, where they would serve Robby Ribbon (King Philawain) for a time. Their final endeavor was to push mountains of stone and rock into the place where they had been originally quarried, in the Crack Between Worlds, creating an immense dam. This forced the waters that flowed within the chasm to rise and overspill, coursing through the Megrinor Mountains and spreading over the Dragonlands. In this way the Dragonlands were cleansed of the poisons that plagued the Dragonkind, ancient lakes and rivers were restored, and thus began a transformation of the desert lands that would continue during the Third Age.

Alonair remained at the Temple of Beras, his presence and identity closely guarded by the monks. In the autumn of 870 SA, a man appeared at the Temple, demanding to see Alonair. He was very peculiar in appearance. Dressed in a simple short toga, he was tall, broad-shouldered, athletic of frame, with flesh as hard as rock. The monks were fearful of him, though he showed no inclination toward violence. At last, the Oracle intervened to quell fears, and the newcomer was taken to Alonair. He became Alonair's servant and companion. Alonair called him Lythos. He was the only "stony guard" of Tulith Attis that survived after the ringing of the Great Bell.

Meanwhile, over the years, Danig Tallin made several visits to the Temple, to try to convince Alonair to share the secret words that would give the trolls the order to release their burdens and collapse the ground above, which they supported. Alonair consistently refused to do so until Tallinvale was besieged in early 871, and then, almost too late, he sent the phrase via a Familiar (Fallendine) to Tallin, who then used it to decimate his attackers. It is thought that Collandoth, who had recently visited Alonair, convinced him to do this, but it is also speculated that Robby Ribbon perhaps visited Alonair in his dreams and urged him to do so.

After the battles at Tallinvale were over, King Thunderfoot took charge of the trolls and led them away westward, where they would serve Robby Ribbon (King Philawain) for a time. Their final endeavor was to push mountains of stone and rock into the place where they had been originally quarried, in the Crack Between Worlds, creating an immense dam. This forced the waters that flowed within the chasm to rise and overspill, coursing through the Megrinor Mountains to spread across the Dragonlands. Sir Sun made the waters into clouds, and Sir Wind blew them across the deserts, provoking them to pour down rain. In this way, the Dragonlands were cleansed of the poisons that plagued the Dragonkind, ancient lakes and rivers were restored, and thus began a transformation of the desert lands that would continue during the Third Age.

It is known, because Alonair said so himself, that Robby Ribbon revealed to Alonair that he would, indeed, have an opportunity at last to work the Great Stone. Ribbon arranged for trolls to move the Great Stone to the abandoned ancient city of Darini. The trolls placed the stone on an island at the center of the artificial lake in the center of the city, then the trolls departed. At last Alonair, too, was taken to Darini to fulfill the promise that he had given to the Dragonkind and make a fabulous carving from the Great Stone in the city that would soon be reoccupied by the Nasakeerians and others.

When Alonair came, he examined the Great Stone and was pleased by its condition. Witnesses say that was heard to cry out loudly the following:

"Let me do this as penitence for the ills wrought by my hands. Let my hands now fulfill the promise that I gave. Let the language of the Beginning return to my lips so that I might whisper to my hands and to this stone, in praise of Creation and its Founder, in my plea for mercy, in my expressions of gratitude. Let nothing be spared of me, of any humble skill given to me, of any remnant of my being. Bestow upon this work some sign of your Great Mystery, some inexplicable spirit of wonder and awe, so that all who behold it shall have such like spirit in their hearts. Let my work be thy work, done at last as it should have been done in the first."

Alonair then set to work, and he carved a splendid statue of a vast spreading tree, with bold limbs dividing into delicate branches and leaves. Alonair worked day and night for two weeks, as the waters of the lake were restored and began to rise. At last the work was done, just as the lake reached its ancient and proper level. Miraculously, the tree siphoned water from the surrounding lake to be gently released from the carved leaves and branches as a fine, ever-falling rain.

Thus, Alonair completed his greatest work. He then was transformed, and witnesses say that he assumed the form of an airy and multicolored flower with long, waving petals, rising into the heavens and out of sight.

See also:
Glossary (Great Stone; Darini; Nasakeeria)
Tales of the High Houses (The Fall of the Faere)
Biographical Sketches (Danig Tallin)

****

Artais Teracue

Born in 817 S.A. in Duinnor Realm, the son of a farmer, Artais Teracue was educated at home until he passed the King's Academy entrance exams. Teracue scored higher than any of his co-applicants and, as was customary, was granted a full scholarship to begin studies in 832. Two years later, it was discovered that he had lied about his age on the entrance exam, but by then he was two years in school and one of the top students academically. He was a quiet, retiring student, somewhat small of stature. He was ridiculed for his humble upbringing by some cadets and came to fisticuffs on at least three known occasions. In all of these altercations, he soundly trounced his opponents, once even though outnumbered three to one by much bigger opponents. Although his altercations won him the grudging respect of his fellow cadets, he continued to be singled out for ridicule. He added to his fighting reputation by consistently scoring in the top five during the annual Last Man Standing* contest held by the Academy. Meanwhile, he performed at the top of his class academically, and also received commendation for outstanding performance during field training maneuvers. During his last years at the Academy, Teracue was much desired as a member of every training squad.

Upon graduation, he applied immediately to the Fourth Army but was instead assigned to the First Army with the rank of Lieutenant. He saw minor action in the Dragonlands on various patrols near Ladentree (Vanara). With the First Army, he took part in the Second Siege of the Green Citadel, and was slightly wounded during the retreat. He was among those Kingsmen and Fellfaere who were trapped within a small ravine by Dragonkind soldiers at Gory Gulch. During the first eight days of their entrapment, the higher-ranking officers were killed, leaving Teracue in command of the remaining units of the decimated First Army along with stragglers from various other Kingsmen units and a good number of Elifaen fighters from Vanara and other Realms. Although they were completely surrounded, with no hope of a massive breakout from the rough valley, Teracue organized a cohesive effort which held back the Dragonkind, managing to lead several sorties to punch through the lines so that some of the wounded could escape and so that word could be sent north to Linlally. The Dragonkind forces continued to build, and after two weeks, no more such sorties were possible. Using hastily erected defenses of brush, saplings and stones, Teracue organized a strong defense, made difficult by the constant rain of arrows and missiles from the heights surrounding.

By the sixteenth day, they were completely without food and very low on water. Teracue later said that he was inclined to surrender, but he had little doubt that they would all be massacred had they done so. At last, with fewer than two-thousand men remaining, Teracue saw the end coming as the Dragonkind massed for a crushing attack. Among those who remained were several stalwart Elifaen, including Mirabella Tallin, although it is unclear whether she and Teracue ever met. Her brother, Aram, had been killed six days earlier during a failed sortie to find food for their comrades.

Dramatically, shortly after the Dragonkind initiated their assault, relief forces began to arrive, including Queen Serith Ellyn herself, her brother Thurdun, and Collandoth the Melnari, along with two-thousand Fellfaere, as well as over six thousand soldiers of the Duinnor Fourth Army. In the battle that ensued, the region acquired its name, for the bloodletting continued day and night for three days. Very quickly, the Dragonkind found that they were now surrounded and cut off from retreat. Communicating via signals, Teracue coordinated his forces with those of his rescuers, and together the Northmen systematically boxed in and annihilated the Dragonkind, giving no quarter whatsoever. When it was over, nearly seven thousand Dragonkind were dead. Among the Northmen, four thousand were killed.

After the battle, and upon hearing Teracue's report of the siege of Green Citadel, of the botched retreat, and upon receiving the testimony from many survivors concerning the young officer's bravery and skill, the commanding general of the Fourth Army insisted that Teracue be transferred to the Fourth and given his own corps with the rank of Commander. He showed himself to be a master logistician and a masterful field tactician. Within five years, Teracue was given command of the Third Battalion, which saw action in and around the Mirse region. He served in this capacity until 857, when he was made commanding general of the Fourth Army.

Although Teracue's prowess as a fighter and leader was unquestioned, his criticism of corruption and nepotism within Duinnor's courts and especially within the Duinnor's Regular Army made him socially unpopular. Teracue was twice censured by the King for making statements of a disparaging nature concerning Lord Banis, and he was only narrowly spared from being removed as Commanding General of the Fourth. When one of his staff officers was killed in a duel, Teracue learned that the duel had come about as the result of insulting remarks that had been made concerning Teracue's loyalty. Teracue's investigation revealed that six other such duels had taken place in as many years. Somewhat humbled by the loyalty of his Kingsmen, he was nonetheless quick to put a stop to the duels. He publicly issued a formal apology to the King and the people of Duinnor (in a printed statement), and he forbade any Kingsman under his command from dueling lest they be summarily drummed out of the ranks. He also restrained himself thenceforth from overt criticism of Duinnor while in doubtful company.

In 870, the Four of the Fourth were sent to Edgewold to see to its defense against the Wickerman rebels. He adroitly lured the bulk of the Wickerman army into a decisive battle at Soltani Pass, between Edgewold and the Wickerman stronghold of Westlawn. The battle was brief and bloody, but the Fourth under Teracue sustained relatively few casualties while virtually annihilating the Wickermen who foolishly charged into his well-laid trap. Unknown to many, he had called up the Fifth of the Fourth, normally a training battalion, to be secretly encamped some miles north of Edgewold with orders to stand ready for action should he be defeated at Soltani Pass. After the victorious battle and the occupation of Westlawn (the former stronghold of the Wickermen), Teracue called upon the Fifth Battalion to assist with occupation and law-keeping duties. He then took the majority of his other battalions eastward on an epic march across the Plains of Bletharn. Living almost entirely on jawrock until they reached the Thunder Mountains, they quickly sacked and burned Damar City, then marched swiftly to the relief of Tallinvale during the Redvest invasion and siege of Tallin City.

****

Belmira and Elmira

During the first years of the Second Age, not many years after Lyrium and Heneil returned to Vanara, an incident took place that was told to Faslor of the House of Elmwood. Hundreds of years later, Faslor, who was in the party that came upon the wounded and nearly dead Ullin Saheed Tallin, managed to transport the sick man to safety, tending to him all along the way. To keep Ullin distracted somewhat from his pain, Faslor engaged Ullin with many stories and anecdotes. This was one of them, which Ullin would later write down.

There was an old friend of Heneil's, a Man named Ross, a Newcomer to the world, who lived and worked in Vanara as a stonemason, and whose little girls played often with Elmira and Belmira whilst the parents visited one another. But it came to pass that the man was injured one day when his horse slipped on ice and fell. As soon as they heard of it, Lyrium and Heneil went to see their friends, taking Elmira and Belmira along. They found the family gathered around the father's sickbed. His eyes were closed and his breathing was labored. His wife sat on the bed next to him, holding his hand tightly, and his two little girls stood at the foot of the bed, all with tears running down their faces. Lyrium immediately went to her friend, while Heneil knelt on the other side of the bed and put his hand on his friend's brow. Belmira and Elmira put their arms around their little friends and cried as they did.

"Is there nothing to be done for him?" asked Heneil. "Are his injuries so terrible?"'

"He was awake when he was brought here," said the man's wife. "He could barely speak, but said he could not feel anything at all, but for a slight ache in his neck, nor could he move his arms or legs. He said that he loved us, each one, and then he groaned and fell into this sleep and he has not opened his eyes since. Nor does he seem to hear my voice. Oh, my love, my dearest love!"

His two girls then broke away from their friends and flung themselves upon their mother, hugging and weeping, and Lyrium moved away to give them room. She saw, meanwhile, that Belmira and Elmira, at the foot of the bed, were holding hands, their eyes closed, and seemed to be mumbling softly to themselves, while tears ran down their faces. She thought they were praying, which puzzled her because she had taught them very little about prayer. Then, after a few moments, Belmira and Elmira opened their eyes, looked at each other, and nodded. They then hugged each other and wept so bitterly that Lyrium went to them and, kneeling with them, hugged them both and wept, too. When ample tears had been shed, the two girls took Lyrium's hand and led her to the door, where they spoke in soft tones to Lyrium.

"Soon this man will pass away," said Belmira.
"No power will make him stay," said Elmira.
"We prayed just to know, my sister and I..."
"...which way he might go, to live or to die."
"We wish we were not so sad that he must go..."
"...we wish we had not this power to know."
"We are so sad for his wife and his daughters..."
"...and for the despair of his friend, our father."
"How will they bear this awful turn?"
"And what can we do? Oh please, let us learn!"

Confused but deeply touched, Lyrium hugged them again and wept even more as she looked toward the bed.

"There is nothing for you to do but love," she said. "Love, and be kind and be gentle."

A few minutes later, Ross was truly gone, his breathing forever stilled. Other friends arrived, and relatives, too, and the house was one of terrible grief, for Ross was a good and kindly man, respected and big-hearted to all, well and earnestly loved.

This was the first time that Belmira and Elmira, not yet even six years of age, encountered death so near. And it was how Elmira and Belmira first discovered their peculiar ability to judge whether a person might live or die. Lyrium and Heneil were filled with wonder. Over the years, they demonstrated their propensities over and again, and they were never wrong. Yet, the girl's parents tried to guard their abilities from common knowledge, lest they were beset with pleas and requests from all sides. It was difficult, for the girls had no desire, it seemed, to refrain from performing such a task whenever asked to do so, as if it were their duty or obligation, sad though it often was. And Lyrium sometimes thought that perhaps Belmira and Elmira did not foretell life or death as much as negotiate, somehow, with the powers of the cosmos concerning such matters.

As for Ross's family, Heneil and Lyrium, along with many others, saw to it that they were supported with goodwill, and assisted the mother and daughters with keeping their home, with financial support, and by being good friends. Eventually, though, Ross's family moved away from Vanara and went away to Glareth to live with relatives there. And so they lost touch with one another.

Thus was what Faslor told Ullin. For his part, Ullin knew, or at least suspected, that they were the two "gentlewomen" who came to visit, and some say bless, his cousin Robby Ribbon when Robby was a sick child, near upon death. In his notes, which he never completed, Ullin implied that he was told about the incident by Robby's father, but was warned never to speak of it, nor to ask Robby's mother about it because she was very sensitive concerning the subject.

We relate this first, before all else about Elmira and Belmira, because so much concerning them remains a deep mystery. It is known that the twins were born in the year 217 of the Second Age in Vanara. In appearance, they were identical except for their hair. Elmira had blonde hair, while Belmira's hair was dark red, but both had eyes of deep green. They learned to speak quite early, and the two girls immediately began conversing constantly with each other, each matching in rhyme what the other said. It was a source of great amusement to their parents, and all else who knew them, and of quite a lot of wonderment. And, like many twins, they remained inseparable.

While Heneil took up his work in Linlally, being a prominent builder and advisor to the Queen, Lyrium took up the raising and educating of her children. They quickly learned to read and to write, to comprehend complex ideas, and to grasp things of great importance. And they also had an uncanny knack of observation, expressed, as ever, in rhyme. As they grew, it seemed that their minds were often as one, each knowing the thoughts of the other, or at least deeply entwined around the same thoughts. Sometimes when in conversation with each other, they would speak only single words which, of course, rhymed.

But they developed a special relationship with those near death, the old people of the race of Men, those who were sick or injured. As they seemed to be able to discern whether or not a person would recover into health or proceed into death, people came to think that they had the power to make it so, one way or the other. Of course, they did not possess this power, and they were mortified that people would think such a thing. But some people did believe this, leading to awkward misunderstandings, and Lyrium became ever more cautious about permitting the girls to attend to the suffering. Over the years, as they became young women, and as rumor and word of them spread, they received many such requests from near and far. At first, in spite of their parent's concern, Elmira and Belmira were quite obliging to such requests, and even willing to travel to far parts to carry out what they saw as their duty to their gift.

Meanwhile, Heneil and Lyrium became ever more uncomfortable not only with the increasing fame of their daughters, but with that of their own situation in Vanara. Heneil was increasingly in demand, for his organizational skills were quite profound, and he was ever more involved in matters of military concern, particularly when it came to designs and construction of fortifications and strongholds in far parts of Vanara, places that remained in watchful fear of the Dragonkind. These duties required Heneil to travel much. His designs were robust and when he supervised construction, his works were well-made, strong, and innovative. But they were expensive to build, and they had to be placed in locations that would be key to their purpose, and to their success if ever attacked. Many Vanarans were against spending the Royal Treasury on such schemes, saying that the local people of each region ought to do so of their own means. Other Vanarans objected to the placement of such projects on their lands, fearing that such installations would be used against them, as they did not yet trust Serith Ellyn to act differently than Parthais. Heneil was caught in the middle of these debates, which frustrated his efforts.

In additon, Lyrium, as keeper of Seven Bloodcoins, was ever under pressure to show them. Dignitaries, powerful lords and ladies of the realm, and many others hounded her to display the mysterious items as the Queen was in the habit of doing for those Bloodcoins in her keeping. Some people went so far as to suggest that Lyrium ought to have an equal right of rule over Vanara as the Queen, if possession of Bloodcoins was a legitimate basis for such a claim. Lyrium dismissed any such talk. Likewise, she refused to show her Bloodcoins except on very rare occasions and to private visitors such as the Queen herself, and only to assure the Queen that the Bloodcoins of the House of Fairfir were safe and secure.

Lyrium had secrets, too. With her gift of Sight, she saw through many mysteries. One secret was that her Sight had led her to locate and secure the sword Ethliad, which had been lost by Silmain upon his death in battle. She had told no one about possessing this sword, fearing even to tell Heneil. Indeed, while Heneil and Lyrium were courting, she discovered that Heneil had such strength of character, love, and trust toward her that he would not insist or pry into matters too close to her heart, or inquire into secrets she did not wish to tell, or concerning mysteries of her gift of Sight. So Heneil did not know about the sword, which she kept hidden from all in the same place where she kept safe her Bloodcoins. The sword, she thought, was too powerful, perhaps too seductive, and she often pondered how to dispose of it, using her Sight to strive, albeit unsuccessfully, for such an answer. Since it was well known that she was a keeper of Bloodcoins, she feared that if she ever had to relinquish them, or if she could no longer safeguard them, the sword, too, might be in similar danger.

So, too, was another object of power that she possessed, the Ring of Hearing. Wearing this ring, a person could know the thoughts of others nearby. This power led to its being used for ill purposes, but when it was lost, Lyrium found and took possession of it. Since the Ring of Hearing only worked if worn by mortals, and not by the Elifaen, she was never tempted to use it. But she kept it secret, like Ethliad, awaiting a time when she could resolve how to properly dispose of it, or to whom it ought to be given. And, like Ethliad, she feared that this object might someday be discovered.

Lyrium did not speak of these objects or her worries about them. She and Heneil did discuss the Bloodcoins, in light of how they brought Lyrium unwanted fame or celebrity. Just as they discussed Heneil's aggravations and pressures and problems concerning his work in Vanara. But Elmira and Belmira were too astute not to comprehend a great portion of these worries and concerns. So it came as no surprise when Heneil and Lyrium announced to the girls that they would be departing Vanara for the Eastlands Realm. There, Heneil would take up new work and Lyrium would help however she could. Elmira and Belmira were encouraged to come along so that they could all remain together, at least until they knew whether their new home was more peaceful or not for them.

And so, in the year 256 of the Second Age, the family moved eastward, to the newly established town of Attis in the Eastlands Realm. This was a trading town, quickly growing, and Heneil had been previously asked by an envoy from the town to consider becoming their advisor on construction, roads, bridges, and on military and security matters. When they arrived, the family settled into a small home in the center of the town, and Heneil saw immediately how the old fortress atop the nearby heights could be remodeled, strengthened, and used as a base of defense should the need ever arise. There was already a major stone bridge across the River Saerdulin under construction to replace the old wooden one. So Heneil took over both these projects and became very busy, indeed. His congenial nature and his knowledge and experience paid dividends for the community, and Heneil was eventually put in charge of all security matters. The town leaders, with their coffers overflowing, granted Heneil vast sums to hire builders to complete the bridge and to greatly improve and expand the fortress that would be called Tulith Attis.

Meanwhile, during these years, Lyrium and her daughters made themselves useful, too, by assisting with or even organizing schools, health and sanitation works, and community centers. They, too, were quickly recognized as important leaders and, like Heneil, were greatly respected and admired. As for Belmira and Elmira, they came and went. They traveled to Glareth many times, to Colleton, and back and forth to Vanara and Duinnor. Sometimes Lyrium or Heneil went with them, but often Elmira and Belmira traveled together without their parents, and often even without any guides or servants. As refined as they were, they seemed not to mind the hardships of travel, and acquitted themselves well on the few occasions when they encountered bandits or other unsavory people. They even had a few encounters with trolls, but these did not result in any conflict or harm.

While enjoying a lengthy stay in Glareth, the sisters received word of the Pinewood Uprising which had finally boiled over into active fighting. They first received letters from Heneil, one addressed to them and others for them to deliver to Prince Thalamir, describing the situation and how Attis was gathering a force of fighting men to protect their region and to oppose the rebels. The situation was confusing, with various clans and groups shifting allegiances and sides, with the lackluster response from King Inrick of the Eastlands, and the wavering of King Kapol of Tracia. They also received a letter from Lyrium, describing some previous letter that she had written to them in which she confided certain things. But that letter was never received, and since Lyrium had received no response, she wrote again to ask after them, and whether all was well in Glareth. The sisters decided to return to Attis, and King Thalamir sent a company of soldiers to be their escorts, to deliver word of the King's support to Attis, and to serve Heneil until they received further orders from Glareth.

Upon their return, they found Attis in a state of war. Several trade caravans had been attacked by Pinewood rebels, and the town had repulsed three minor forays against them. Heneil was in the final stages of putting together his "army of defense," with over four hundred men in various stages of training and equipping, plus several regional militias that sided with Attis. Notably, most of these were Men, but quite a few Elifaen were also in the ranks. Although work had not yet been completed on the fortress, a plan to evacuate the residents of the town into the fortress was developed. As well, several small scouting units were constantly moving in and out, reporting directly to Heneil. In fact, while Heneil was in charge of all military forces of the region, he was also now the de facto leader of government, too, since the town leaders consulted with him on all matters and deferred to his decisions and judgment.

The twins were also surprised at the growth of Attis in their absence. The town now spread from the base of Tulith Attis all the way across the plain to the west to the ridge nearly a mile off. New warehouses, stables, smithies, shops, and inns had been established to support trade, and many new houses, some quite fine, had been built. Wagon and cart traffic flowed in and out, coming and going night and day to and from points all over the world. And, in spite of King Inrick's efforts to impose tolls on the roads connecting Attis, and to tax trade entering Colleton from Attis, such measures were repeatedly overturned. It was a sign of the growing power and influence of Attis that Inrick wished to garner for himself.

When the sisters met with their parents, they were told about all of the incidents of violence that were spreading across the Eastlands and Tracia, about the preparations, and about many other things, too. But Heneil's duties soon called him away, and Lyrium took this opportunity to ask about the letters that the girls had never received, written in the cypher that the three had agreed upon. Now in person, Lyrium recounted the contents of the coded letter, and she told them that she felt it best that they know about Ethliad. This was the first time she had ever revealed to anyone that she possessed it.

She explained how she came by the sword, led to it by her gift of Sight, and why she did not wish to reveal its whereabouts to any, not even to her husband.

"Since times are now not as secure as before, I thought it best that you know that I have in my care yet another item of great power. Besides, of course, Ethliad and the seven Bloodcoins. I also possess a ring of great and terrible power, which I will tell you about only if needed. For now, know only that, should matters arise that threaten their safety, or their secrecy, I will see that they are taken away. But they are not as valuable to me as you are. For this reason, be prepared to depart soon, making this only a short visit. Since you come and go often, your departure will not be deemed much noteworthy. Many families here in town have sent away some of their kin to safer parts, mostly to Glareth or Vanara. But I will not have it thought that I fear for our safety just yet. So when, or if, you depart, we shall let it be known that it is to attend to other matters not having to do with this strife."

"We understand what you say..."

"...and we will do things your way."

"As for us, we trust our Father's skill..."

"...so we do not worry, come what will."

And so it was that Belmira and Elmira remained in Attis for only a few weeks, then departed to take word and letters to the Queen in Vanara and then to Duinnor, where their aunt and uncle, Myrium and Pellen, lived.

It is not precisely known where the sisters traveled, other than to those realms mentioned. But it is thought that they also traveled to Masurthia and Altoria. After the end of the Pinewood Rebellion, when all was at peace, the sisters returned by ship from Altoria to Colleton, and then to Attis, which was now a prosperous place, indeed.

Many years passed, and the two sisters abided at Attis, sometimes traveling as they were wont to do, but always returning to be with their parents. But then came the dark days of the Great Dragonkind Invasion. Those events, and what became of things, are told elsewhere. But when Lyrium's dreams and Sight became ever more frightening, and as the Dragonkind quickly approached, she sent her daughters away, making them promise not to return, no matter what, until the Dragonkind had been completely vanquished.

"I will see to the safety of those things in my possession, the Bloodcoins and those other things of power. And I will strive to see to my own safety as well. I do not plan to depart from here as long as we manage to hold against the invaders. But know this: I fear not only the Dragonkind, but other powers, too. It is my fear that the Bloodcoins in my possession are coveted by others, and that this conflict may bring with it some effort by those powers to take the Bloodcoins. For this reason, I must do things secretly. And when you leave here, once you are away from all who know you, enter into disguise. Let no one know who you are. Go to Blueshoals, on the Osterflo, and take up your abode there using the names of Brynya and Elyna. There, await word from me. If I must escape from here, I shall do so with as much secrecy, too. You may have to wait a very long time before it is safe for me to send for you or to write to you."

They traveled this time northward, then turned west to pass through the high Carthanes, near unto the Osterflo, before working their way across Middlemount. The journey was slow and arduous, and everywhere along the way people had heard about and were in fear of the great invasion and the great battles that were taking place. But at last they arrived at the little river town of Blueshoals. There they found a small cottage, and set themselves up as seamstresses to make and repair clothing for the townsfolk and the bargemen of the river. It was a good place, for though it was far from conflict, it was busy with travelers and traders who brought word with them of the happenings of the world. Thus they were able to learn the terrible news of the fall of Tulith Attis, and of the great slaughter that had taken place. For the first time, the girls had a serious and heated argument. In fact, they had two. First, Elmira urged Belmira that they should break their promise and go as quickly as possible to Tulith Attis in order to see for themselves and to search for their parents, if necessary, among the dead. But

Belmira prevailed, arguing that they should let the wisdom and instructions of their mother hold sway over their actions, that they should, meanwhile, abide as they were told to do, keeping care of their true identities, and listening to every scrap of news or rumor that came their way.

The next day, with second thoughts, another argument ensued. Belmira had had second thoughts, and she now urged that they do as Elmira had first suggested. But now Elmira had changed her mind, and she took up the argument against doing such, citing all of the reasons that her sister had given, and adding more. Elmira prevailed, and with new resolve to be patient and watchful, the sisters remained where they were.

Thus they abided at Blueshoals year after year, waiting. Waiting, yes, but not idle. They took on more and more business, not only repairing the work-clothes of the river men and townsfolk, but also making various and sundry decorative but sturdy house linens for the families of the small town and region. Their work was so fine, their stitches sturdy and firm, and their choice of materials so well suited to the needs of their customers that soon they had to hire seamstresses to work under their supervision. Then, a few years later, a weaver built a great water loom not far from the River Whitefall, and began to supply them with cotton and wool cloth that was much less expensive than that which had to be brought from Altoria or Glareth. So again they expanded the business, now having one shop for repairs and alterations and another larger shop for making towels, tablecloths, curtains, and even large heavy tarpaulins for the river barges.

The sisters obviously became well known in the region, and well respected, too. They lived simply, needing but very little, and so they paid their workers very well and at the same time charged very little for their products and services. In times of need, they gave amply of their own income to help their neighbors. Once, after an unusual winter flood had destroyed and damaged many homes and businesses along the river shore, Belmira and Elmira not only paid for many of the repairs and reconstruction, but they also rolled up their sleeves and joined in with the carpenters and stonemasons to assist them in the work of rebuilding. Their spirit of helpfulness and willingness inspired many others to join in, as well. Afterwards, once all had been resettled back into their homes, the entire community of Blueshoals held a fine town festival, with the sisters being the guests of honor.

It was the very next morning, well before sunrise, that a knock came on their door. The sisters stirred and opened the door to see Tyrillick, the same Tyrillick who had been the captain of their mother's guard at Tulith Attis.

"Your mother is alive," he said immediately. As the two sisters wept for joy, hugged each other, and dragged Tyrillick into their home all at the same time, Tyrillick continued.

"She bids you come with me to be with her once again," he told them. "Your father, I am sorry to tell, did not survive the battle of Tulith Attis."

Now they wept both for joy and in grief. Tyrillick, who had prepared himself as well as he could, but he was deeply moved by the agony of their emotions. But, sooner than he thought might be the case, they dried their tears.

"We had almost given up hope…"

"…and had almost learned to cope…"

"…for all and everyone, far and wide…"

"…insisted that Lyrium and Heneil died."

"That they were half right, we now grieve…"

"…but that they were half wrong, is our grief relieved."

"For our father, we will ever weep…"

"…but great joy for our mother we keep!"

"An infinite treasure, broken in twain…"

"…is still yet infinite, and so will remain!"

So it was that the sisters made the necessary arrangements to depart Blueshoals, which had been their home for nearly sixty years. Generations of townsfolk and riverfolk had come and gone, and much had changed. The little village was now a full-fledged town, busy with all the various activities that occur in every town, and becoming busier with each passing year as the traffic along the Osterflo increased. Although the river at Blueshoals was not deep enough for the large freight and passenger barges, it was ample enough for the numerous smaller craft that brought labor, travellers, and goods east and west. The main road from Blueshoals, recently improved, connected the town to Duinnor City, passing through many towns and villages along the way. So now Blueshoals had two inns, several coopers, wheelwrights, and blacksmiths, and many boat repairmen, besides all of the other shops and services needed for the bustling river and road trade. Elmira and Belmira, with their humble start as seamstresses, had more to do with the prosperity of Blueshoals than might be imagined, for not only did they make it a good place for boatmen and traders to find repairs, but it inspired others to do likewise for items other than clothing that needed repair or provisioning. And the sisters employed many women and youngsters, too, providing a balance of income for many families of very modest means.

So it was not without some sadness and a great deal of regret that the town learned that the sisters would be leaving them. A buyer for their business was easily found, and it was stipulated that all workers and all business would continue on as before for at least two years, overseen by a board of governors made up of employees and townsfolk.

It was not until they were well away from Blueshoals that Tyrillick informed the sisters where they were going. To Forest Islindia, it was. This gave Belmira and Elmira much consternation, but also a nervous excitement. The tales and legends of Islindia, its foreboding landscape that few had ever penetrated, and the prospect of seeing their mother once again all combined to maintain their excitement and anticipation. Along the way, Tyrillick recounted what he knew of the last days of Tulith Attis, his own failed mission to see the Bloodcoins safely away, and the loss of them along with Faeanna. He recounted his own ordeal and capture, and his subsequent rescue by Lyrium. And he spoke of their failed efforts to discover the fate of Faeanna and the precious Bloodcoins. He told them how Islindia had granted Lyrium and the people of her House safe refuge in the forest, and how they began gathering members of the House of Fairfir together in Islindia.

They arrived at last and entered Forest Islindia on its northernmost reach, passing safely through the ring of thorns and into a region that the Queen of the Wood had set aside for the House of Fairfir. The reunion of mother and daughters was a bittersweet one, indeed, and the sisters heard from Lyrium herself all that Tyrillick had told and much more. By then, through the means of carefully guarded letters and trustworthy couriers and messengers, Lyrium had gathered into Islindia over five hundred of her House, mostly those who had remained in safety in Vanara and Glareth during the Great Invasion, and many others who had been scattered across the world. They made for themselves, with the permission of the rulers of that forest, a little village that was adequate for their needs, and they settled in to a life of waiting, of recounting their woes, and of watchfulness.

More is told elsewhere of the centuries that passed. And in other stories it can be learned how Belmira and Elmira first came to meet the future King Philawain, long before any hint of his destiny was known or apparent. And elsewhere, in the chronicles of *The Year of the Red Door*, it is told how Lyrium herself met the king-to-be, how he saw to the destruction of the Ring of Hearing, and how he refused the temptation of Ethliad. In that saga, it is also told what became of Lyrium's Bloodcoins, which were ultimately delivered to King Philawain and used to remake the world.

But two things remain for us to describe.

First, that Lyrium finally discovered what to do with Ethliad. She privately discussed her thoughts and feelings about the great power of the sword, and how she could find no way of destroying it. She and her daughters discussed how best to rid themselves of it, where it might be hidden forever, or what might become of the world should it ever be discovered. With her Sight, Lyrium delved and delved, but her visions gave her little that she could comprehend, much less act upon. That is, until at last, and without struggle, her Sight revealed clearly what it was that she should do with Ethliad. The time of this revelation was during the same week when the great storms of King Philawain's coming were striking Duinnor City, just before he ascended the throne.

On the night of that last fearsome storm, a dreamwalker came unto all three women, Lyrium, Belmira, and Elmira. This person was called Finn, and he told Lyrium that the new King of Duinnor required her attendance unto him the following day. Finn told them that Islindia had agreed to provide them with transportation by way of her flying horses. Finn also said, without mentioning Ethliad, that should Lyrium desire to perform another duty or some other task along their way to Duinnor, that it should be good for it to be done, and that their flying mounts would oblige to take them wherever they should go.

So it was in gladness that Lyrium knew, from her Sight and from the dreamwalker, that not only did Robby Ribbon succeed in his quest to become King, but also that she could relieve herself of the terrible burden of Ethliad. And before dawn on the very morning they were to fly to Duinnor, Lyrium and her daughters mounted the magical flying horses provided by Islindia and first made their way south by southwest, across the wonders of the forest, now alive with Islindia's dream brought forth into temporary reality. They flew on until they reached the lake just outside the town of Lochton.

This was the very lake where Cupeldain, Loura, Shevalia, Bychanter, and so many others had been murdered by drowning. It was in this lake, held by the curses of Parthais that their spirits remained, in a half-life of spirit and flesh, gnawed and eaten and tortured by the serpent that Parthais had let loose into those waters. The very chains that had held their sinking bodies had likewise held back their spirits from leaving that place, and their existence was one of sadness, grief, longing, and frustration. Lyrium knew that this was where Ethliad was needed. And she knew that there was only one person there, in that lake, that was wise enough to take Ethliad for its proper use, wise enough to know what to do with it afterwards.

With the eastern rim of the world growing purple with the coming day, they flew over the still-darkened lands and as the sky grew brighter, they came to the mist-shrouded lake. There, not far from the old ferryman's place, the ladies landed on the lakeshore. As Belmira and Elmira watched, Lyrium took from her bundle the sword, Ethliad, and strode with it to the very edge of the still waters. There, she fell to her knees, with the sword in hand, and strove to find her Sight and to use it as she had never before done. In her mind, a swirl of murky blackness immediately surrounded her, and she stood on the muddy bottom of the dark pool. Then, just as the sun above came over the treetops, rays of light shot down into the murk. A face came into view, floating toward her through the water until she was within reach. It was Loura, wife of Cupeldain, kind and generous one, strong in her compassion and love. Without words, she said to Lyrium, "I am ready."

Lyrium immediately awoke from the vision and stood. With a powerful overarm swing, she threw Ethliad with all her might, and it flashed violently through the airy sunlight toward the middle of the lake. Then, just as it was about to strike the surface, Ethliad halted in air just over the still water, pointing skyward. Then a ghostly hand, lovely in form, reached up and took Ethliad by the hilt. With barely a ripple upon the surface, arm and sword together descended out of sight.

Lyrium smiled, for she knew. For the first time in her eons of existence, Loura held a sword. And with it she would slay the terrible serpent below, and she would free all those spirits that had been imprisoned in those waters. Then, when came the time, all would rejoin Aperion in the heavens, and Loura would deliver Ethliad to the King of the Faere, who would do what was then required.

This act is not related within *The Year of the Red Door*, or elsewhere. But it was told by the sisters to Finn on the same day that it happened. Finn later wrote down what they had told him, and he left his notes in Duinnor for Ullin Saheed Tallin to find and read many years later.

Another thing that was not told concerns what happened to Belmira and Elmira when the world was remade. It is not told because no one knows. They have not been seen since. Perhaps they departed from the world as most did. Perhaps they remain, having other things that they wish to do for the good of our world.

****

Danig Tallin

Kingsman, Lord of Tallinvale

Introduction

To understand Danig Saheed Tallin, it is good to know something of his lineage, for it is an ancient one steeped in history and surrounded by legend.

The Tallin name was associated with one of the first Men to come across the sea in the great City Ships that began landing on the eastern coasts of the world around 1,126 of the First Age. Little is known or recorded about the early years when Men made settlements and learned to live on land. It can be presumed that some of the skills they learned during their generations-long voyage served them well on land. Other skills or habits might have been deadly in the forests and fields of the eastern world. So they suffered many hardships, and centuries would pass before they became fully accustomed to life in the new world. And for a while, the Elifaen of the eastern world remained aloof of Men because they did not understand their ways, their short mortal lives, and their weakness. At first, the immortal descendants of the Faerekind associated Men with the Dragonkind, who were also mortal, and this caused further reason among the Elifaen to be cautious of the Newcomers, as Men were sometimes called.

Parris Tallin was the first recorded ancestor in the Tallin lineage, born in the Eastlands Realm around 260 of the Second Age. By then the Tallin family was well established in and around the western banks of the Saerdulin and north of the River Lerse in the shadows of the Thunder Mountains. Parris established a home in a valley in that region where he operated a mill, a successful farm, and other small trades. The name of his wife is not recorded, but his son, Leander, was born in 297 S.A.

Family lore has it that sometime around 315, Parris and Leander brought timbers away from the coast that previous generations of Tallins had carefully preserved and hidden. The timbers were parts of the City Ship that had brought the Tallins across the sea. Fearing that the timbers would be plundered by other Men, previous generations of Tallins had carefully removed the timbers from the grounded vessel. Then they were hauled inland and stored within a cave located somewhere near the present-day town of Mimblewan. It is not known what prompted Parris to move the timbers, but it took several wagons and two years to move them all to their home across the Saerdulin. It is also said that, during all this, Leander Tallin learned to fight as there were still many marauders and highwaymen in those days.

In 318, Leander volunteered as a soldier under Heneil to serve at Tulith Attis. Those were peaceful times, with few threats to speak of. Leander took to his training well, became accomplished with the sword and bow, and owing to his natural leadership qualities he would soon be a member of Heneil's personal guard. During this time, Leander married and had a son, called Ullinessin.

In 322, the Dragonkind came. It was the year of the Great Invasion, and soon the armies of King Xurnon swept across the whole of the Eastlands. Parris fled into the mountains with his grandson, Ullinessin, and successfully eluded the Dragonkind. Leander, however, was at Tulith Attis where the Dragonkind converged.

Little is known about the battle at Tulith Attis, or what role Leander played. Afterwards, his body was found within the fortress, and it is surmised that he died in an attempt to defend the Treasure Room when the fortress was betrayed and overrun by the enemy.

After the invasion, the Eastlands Realm was in ruins, rife with political chaos, and nearly without the rule of law. The Dragonkind were defeated, but they had destroyed fields and farms. Entire towns and villages had been obliterated. Starvation and disease soon followed, and many Men migrated away, some to Glareth and some to Vanara. But the Tallins remained and rebuilt their farms and trades.

In 357 of the Second Age, at age 38, Ullinessin Tallin was summoned by the Sixth Unknown King of Duinnor to receive a boon in honor of his father. In Duinnor, at a grand ceremony, Ullinessin was made a Lord of the Realm, one of the first Men to be so named. The new Lord Tallin was also granted a formal deed of all lands within Tallin Valley not already in true deed or charter, from *"Tallin Town to the Saerdulin, to the first ridgeline of the Thunder Mountains, to the River Lerse, and to 50 miles northward of the town."* Thus was established the Named House of Tallin. Similar grants of land were given to many other Men, in greater or lesser amounts, along with titles of prestige. In this manner, Boskland and the Honored House of Bosk, was established in County Barley, in honor of Bilaylin the Hammer, a Boskman who served and died with Leander Tallin at Tulith Attis. Ullinessin Tallin died in 398, and his son, Seamus, became the second Lord Tallin.

Over the next many decades, the Tallins lived modestly in their valley. Life was difficult, but their valley was fertile. There were trolls in the surrounding mountains, and it was difficult for them to entice other settlers into the region. Many tracks of land were sold or given away to others who came to the valley, now called Tallinvale. Meanwhile, political strife continued to plague the Eastlands. King Inrick, who ostensibly ruled the Eastlands, died and his son came to power. Inrick II was as incompetent and inept as his father. All during this time, Tallinvale began to prosper, far away from the intrigues of Colleton's court.

In 420 S.A., King Inrick II died, leaving no heir, sending the region in to turmoil. Lord Barsus, who was nephew to the late king, seized power and declared himself the new king. He then announced that the Eastlands would be entirely independent of Duinnor. Riots fueled by hunger and years of discontent almost immediately sprang up, and Colleton was almost entirely burned to the ground during the ensuing chaos.

Realizing beforehand that the Eastlands was headed for greater ruin unless something was done, Lord Aramoor Tallin arranged an alliance with Glareth and with the Bosks of the Attis region. When Lord Barsus seized the throne, Tallinvalers joined with Glarethians and Boskmen and converged on Colleton. Nearly all of the people of Colleton quickly joined with the alliance, and in the fighting to take the city, Lord Barsus was killed. A new provisional government was established until the question of rule could be resolved, with Lord Tallin as an advisor to its organization and work.

Late in the year, an envoy of the Unknown King arrived in Colleton, along with representatives from Altoria, Masurthia, and Vanara. Having already laid the groundwork for their proposal with Glareth, they told Lord Tallin that the Sixth Unknown King of Duinnor wished to make Lord Tallin the Ruling Prince of the Eastlands, and that, as king, Tallin would be fully accepted by the rulers of the other Realms. Tallin was deeply honored, but he refused the offer. As a fallback, Tallin was urged to take charge of the Eastlands as Regent Governor. Again, Tallin refused, saying that he wished only to return to his own people in Tallinvale. The representatives meeting with Tallin tried their best to persuade him, but he was steadfast.

Aramoor Tallin's refusals set off a new round of crises, and it led to resentment against the House of Tallin which would not be soon forgotten. Eventually, Glareth was given stewardship over the Eastlands. Disputes immediately sprang up with Tracia over borders, tribute, trade rights, and other matters. Tallin, meanwhile, had other concerns. Fever was spreading throughout the lands, drought caused crops to fail, and people continued to depart from the Eastlands, all of which served to deplete the realm of its people and resources. Aramoor and subsequent lords of Tallinvale would struggle for generations to recover from these setbacks.

Ten generations passed, the Tallin name and title going from son to son, until Lord Arlam Tallin died. He had no son, but his only daughter, Finteri, was made Lady Tallin. She met and married Dalcadian, an Elifaen son of Pellen, and the grandson of the first king of Vanara, Silmain. Finteri bore a son, named Metlar, who would remain a Man because Finteri was not Elifaen. Thus, Metlar inherited the Tallin name and titles from his mother. During his time, the House of Tallin and the House of Silmain were a Joined House. Finteri and Dalcadian had no other children. When Metlar was born, Dalcadian and Finteri went with him to live in Vanara, Dalcadian's homeland, while the Tallin lands in the Eastlands were left in the hands of overseers.

Metlar grew up in Vanara and eventually married Carylla Spritsul, a lady of Glareth Realm. They named their son Danig Saheed, after Metlar's great-grandfather and Carylla's father.

Part I: At the Kingsman Academy

Danig Saheed Tallin was born in Vanara in the 750th year of the Second Age. He was schooled at the Queen's Academy in Vanara and when he was of age he enlisted in the ranks of the Kingsmen, as required by law. Some who lived in Duinnor remembered how Danig's ancestor had rebuffed the King. They shunned Danig, spoke ill of him behind his back, and spread rumors that implied he would be disloyal. Some of those people sought to make his time at the Kingsman Academy difficult by influencing the Kingsman instructors to be especially hard on Danig.

If Danig was aware of the prejudice against him, none of it seemed to matter. He was undeniably an excellent student, somewhat bookish, and he developed a special interest in defensive fortifications. During free time, he was often to be found in the libraries and map rooms of the Academy, reading or studying charts and maps, and copying engineering designs of various fortresses. In the classroom, he was unassuming, but asked many questions, sometimes about topics only tangential to the day's lesson. His inquisitiveness was always respectful, and his observations keen. He was diligent, performed well beyond what was expected, and completed his assignments on time. And he was honest. When opportunities were made for him to cheat on particularly difficult assignments, he did not take the bait, even when offered bribes to do so. Upper classmen assigned to Danig treated him with disdain at first, but with growing respect as time passed. Although he was somewhat aloof, he was never snobbish or haughty.

Tallin also displayed remarkable leadership qualities. Although never overbearing, he seemed to know how to get the subordinate cadets under him and the upper classmen over him to work together so that all would complete their assignments. He even tutored some of his fellow students, including upper classmen. During field training, instructors soon learned to give Tallin's squad the toughest assignments that severely tested Tallin's leadership and the endurance of his teams. Many students sought to avoid any training or assignment that put them with Tallin, fearing that they would fail, while other students actively sought to join with Tallin's squads and teams, knowing they would perform well. Indeed, by the time he was a sophomore, it was recognized that no team or squad that Tallin was put in ever lost a single combat exercise, or failed any field exercise. During the traditional Nasakeeria Exercise* that all cadets were given, not only did Tallin's squad reach the final marker first, with all of the correct information recorded along the way, they continued on around Nasakeeria, continuing their survey of the markers until they met up with the opposing squad. This was done, so said Tallin, because of the particularly bad winter weather, with a foot of snow on the ground. His reasoning was that any effort to shorten the exercise would be best for all of the cadets and officers, allowing all to make shelter as soon as possible. His supervising officer did not oppose, and the opposing squad was grateful. It may have saved their lives, since the snow storm developed into an unusual blizzard, putting two feet of snow on the ground the next day. But by then, all were bivouacked safely together.

Tallin's training at arms was just as intense, and he quickly developed an unusual fighting skill. Indeed, Danig Tallin was the only cadet in the history of the Academy to receive top honors in both swordsmanship and archery for two consecutive years.

Part II: Last Man Standing, Years 768-772

Probably the most famous competition held annually at the Kingsman Academy was the Last Man Standing contest, a grueling sparring match. The rules of the game were simple. The entire school was randomly divided into two teams and two single file lines, opposite each other on either side of the field of combat.   Each cadet was then randomly assigned a spot in their team's line. Each cadet at the head of each line fought, and the winner of each bout was declared by judges. Immediately, the next cadet from the loser's team would step forth to challenge the winner of the bout. If the loser's team was depleted, the winner's team was required to immediately face him, one by one, and the bouts would continue until the final winner had no challenger, the Last Man Standing. Points were awarded to each team according to the number of opponents defeated, to the team with the Last Man Standing, and to each individual according to the number of bouts he won during the match. The winning team enjoyed a day of rest, the Last Man Standing was awarded a medal, and the winning individual, overall by score, was awarded a trophy.

The game was intentionally unfair, since it did not always pit cadets against each other that were equally matched in size or fighting ability. But it mimicked the often random nature of real combat and the unknowable skill of the enemy soldier one might be pitted against during battle.

The cadets were allowed only bucklers and stout wooden practice swords, and they could wear no armor other than a helmet. There were no rules of fair combat, and almost any tactic or move was allowed, unless it was one that could never be seen in actual battle. No cadet was permitted to resign, withdraw, or surrender during a bout until he was "killed or wounded" by his opponent, according to the judges. Any cadet that deliberately allowed his opponent to win was severely reprimanded, put in his opponent's line to fight again, and would later be given additional punishment by the academy instructors. And any semblance of mercy was likewise punished by the judges.

Every cadet, regardless of skill, was required to participate. None were exempted for any reason, and any cadet who failed to participate was summarily expelled from the Academy.

During his first year at the Academy, Danig Tallin proved a formidable opponent, and he scored in the top five of individuals with eleven "kills," even though he was on the losing team. In his second year, however, he happened to be placed last in line. His team did well, and led the match until about halfway through when the opposing team slowly crept up and then moved ahead in the scoring. When his turn came, thirty cadets remained on the opposing team, and Tallin's team was down by seven points. In less than an hour, Tallin had defeated every one of his opponents, winning the game for his team and exceeding any individual score ever before recorded. The following year, Tallin was the seventh in line and fought for a full three hours, defeating seventy-seven opponents until he was bested. He had broken his own record. His team also won by exactly seventy-seven points, making Tallin something of a hero.

In his final year at the Academy, all of Duinnor turned out to see the match, which was held outside of Duinnor City for the first time due to the crowds. The King, it is said, watched from his tower window. And, it was rumored, those who harbored resentment against the House of Tallin had their chance to satisfy their ancient grudge.

For the first time, the rules were changed. The two opposing lines were ranked according to their academic average, rather than at random, with the weakest fighters first and the strongest last in line. And, due to his record-breaking skill, Danig Tallin was placed last in line of his team once more, and so would face the strongest challengers. And anyone could see that Tallin's team was deliberately made up of the weakest fighters at the Academy.

The Last Man Standing competition began at dawn. As expected, Tallin's team did poorly. The match lasted all day and throughout the night. The spectators came and went, but the bleachers remained full to capacity, and even more watchers stood at the ropes around the arena, many standing on crates or chairs to see over the heads of others. When Tallin's turn finally approached, dawn was breaking, and his team had already lost. Word spread throughout the city that Tallin's turn had come, and people flocked out of the city to the field for a chance to see him fight. The score was 2,399 to 2,260. The winning team still had 140 swordsmen.

When Tallin stepped up to the combat line, the spectators and cadets erupted in cheers and calls. They watched, half-amazed and half-horrified, as Tallin bested cadet after cadet. Two hours later, when he defeated the seventy-eighth opponent, and for a third year in a row had scored a new all-time high, the noise of the crowds was deafening. By then, the tops of the city walls were jammed with people, many with spyglasses, and the south window of the royal High Tower glowed with bright golden light. The Sixth Unknown King was also watching. And everyone wondered how long Tallin could last.

Yet Danig Tallin only seemed to be warming up. He defeated the next and the next in short order. Ten more went down. His score rose to eighty, then ninety, then one hundred. The day wore on, and the crowds cheered all the more.

Noon came and went. Tallin's score reached 130, and he was by now showing every sign of weariness. He was not as quick as before, his blows were not as powerful, it seemed, he groaned at every stroke he gave, and he grunted painfully at every one he received. His only rest came in the few moments after each bout, as the next challenger girded himself and approached. During these moments, a cadet would sometimes break onto the field with a cup of water, only to be shooed away by the judges (who were, in turn, subjected to the boos and jeers of the spectators). And each time Danig staggered or tripped, the crowds caught their collective breath.

The 131st challenger fought hard, pressing Danig with powerful strokes, fast lunges, and hard hits with his buckler. But Danig persisted and returned the treatment he received, using keen judgment with his counterstrokes and careful dodges.

Then his sword suddenly shattered. A cry of dismay went up from the crowds. Replacement swords came flying onto the field from both teams. Tallin's opponent, however, did not let up for a single instant, coming on all the more furiously, swinging both sword and buckler against the disarmed fellow cadet. Scrambling for a sword that had been tossed his way, Tallin used his buckler as his only defense against the blows of his opponent who sought to block Tallin from getting to a sword. At last, Tallin's dented and bent buckler broke apart. He ducked a slash and charged, slamming into his opponent as new bucklers flew in from the spectators. The two fighters went sprawling and rolling across the ground, but it was clearly a calculated tackle, for it took Tallin's hand closer to the replacement sword. The two continued to kick and jab with knees and elbows as they wrestled, sending up clouds of dust. Then Tallin's hand found a sword, and he immediately delivered the "fatal" blow to his opponent. Picking up a buckler, he proceeded to defeat all of his remaining opponents amid raucous applause and cheers.

When it was done, he had fought for over seven hours without rest, food, or water, and he was truly the Last Man Standing. Within moments, he was no longer on his feet. The crowds charged onto the field, and he was swept up by his fellow cadets, even those he had defeated. They carried him up and down the city streets on their shoulders for another hour before they allowed him to descend to the ground. Danig Tallin had begun the match as a cadet with a good bit of renown. He ended a legend. He was twenty-two years old.

Part III: A Visit to Tallinvale

It was the year 772 of the Second Age. Danig Tallin graduated as a Kingsman with the advanced rank of lieutenant and was assigned to the Fourth Battalion of the Fourth Army. After graduation, he was given a six-month leave before he was to report to duty. By the time he reached home in Vanara to see his parents, news had preceded him concerning his accomplishments at the Academy, and many of his parents' friends and associates desired to meet the Kingsman. After a month in Vanara, however, Tallin grew weary of Vanara's social life, and with his father he traveled to the Eastlands to visit their ancestral homeland in Tallinvale.

In the Eastlands, they found that their family lands were being mismanaged, and the old Tallin manor house was ill-kept and in need of repairs. Although lacking in funds, Lord Tallin and Danig quickly began reorganizing things. They hired workers to repair the manor and to keep the grounds. It was only his third time visiting, but Danig was captivated by the valley's beauty and impressed with its potential. He decided that, should his fate allow, he would like to live out his days in peaceful Tallinvale.

While in the Eastlands, Danig Tallin visited the ruins of Tulith Attis. He wandered the crumbling battlements alone and walked among the barrows nearby. He was mindful of the terrible battle that took place there. He remembered his ancestor who died there and to whom he owed his present status and title. And he began to worry that another Dragonkind invasion could take place. If that happened, and if it was as devastating as the last one, Tallinvale could hardly hope to defend itself.

Mulling on all this, and in a somber mood, Danig returned to Duinnor and reported for duty. Almost immediately, the Fourth Army was sent on an extended assignment in Vanara, to help patrol the Blue Mountains against Dragonkind incursions.

Part IV: Ladentree

In the year 776, after four years of routine patrols and minor skirmishes with Dragonkind infiltrators, Tallin at last saw real action. A renegade Dragonkind general led a small army through the Blue Mountains into southwestern Vanara and established a fortified encampment near the town of Ladentree. From there, the Dragonkind conducted raids on caravans and wagon trains, disrupting trade between Linlally and Ladentree, and between Ladentree and the Free City of Kajarahn. A small army of Fellfaere under the command of Prince Thurdun was dispatched to the region by the Queen, and with them went Tallin's Fourth of the Fourth. They laid siege to the heavily defended Dragonkind encampment, and after a week were able to break through its lines.

The Dragonkind defenders were more numerous than had been reported, and when the breakthrough happened, a fierce and disorganized battle erupted. The attacking Kingsmen were cut off from the Fellfaere in short order, then a counteroffensive was launched from within the encampment. There were no clear battle lines, and pockets of renegade Dragonkind appeared out of nowhere from concealed positions, shearing off entire companies of Kingsmen at the flanks. It quickly turned into a melee, with no coordination, no communication between units, and no way of telling which side might be winning. After only a few hours, Danig Tallin and about sixty of his comrades found themselves near the center of the enemy encampment. They had pushed well beyond any support, and into a kind of city of pavilions and huts. Amid fleeing servants and women, freed prisoners and slaves, Tallin's company fought incredibly determined Dragonkind. Tallin was astounded at the skill and cunning of the seemingly frail warriors that he faced. It was as if some zeal motivated them beyond normal bravery.

Suddenly a tall figure appeared, dressed in burnished copper-colored armor cloaked in green. His head was covered by an imposing helmet of steel, and he wielded a sword in one hand and a hammer in the other. Tallin was momentarily agog at the sight, but he had no time to ponder, for the figure struck away four Kingsmen in a mere moment and was now swinging his hammer at Danig Tallin. Throwing up his shield against the blow, Tallin twisted away from the sword thrust and spun around. But the Dragonkind was too quick and parried Tallin's counterblow with his hammer and gave Tallin's helmet a glancing blow with his sword. Eyewitnesses later reported that Tallin then pushed into the tall Dragonkind with his shield, then quickly butted his head hard upward on the chin of the Dragonkind. The Dragonkind staggered and Tallin shot his sword upward through his exposed neck. The fight had lasted only a moment, but when the Dragonkind fell, the others around lost heart and began to flee from the Kingsman rather than face him. Killing the renegade general did not win the battle, but it shortened it. In less than an hour, the Fellfaere and Kingsmen were giving chase to the enemy. In the following days, the pursuers saw to it that the few Dragonkind who managed to escape fled far into the deserts and away from Vanara.

Danig Tallin had seen his first real action, and he had survived unscathed. He mourned his lost comrades, but he came away with an abiding respect for Dragonkind fighters, even though they were rejects and renegades from the real Dragonkind armies. He took the lesson to heart and would never underestimate the skill of his opponents, nor their determination.

As a result of the Ladentree action, Danig Tallin was promoted to captain and awarded the Distinguished Combat Medallion.

During the next few years, Tallin saw action in a variety of small desert skirmishes. They were insignificant when weighed against the grand scale of things, but many of the fights were vicious and bloody. Every few weeks, it seemed, he lost another comrade, either a fellow Kingsman or one of their Fellfaere allies. And it was during this period that he developed the habit of repeating aloud the name of each fallen comrade, even in the heat of battle, as his personal way of acknowledging and honoring the death.

Tallin also had ample opportunities to visit his parents in Linlally. And it was not unusual during those visits to find his parents entertaining various ambassadors and other important people.

But the desert people were preparing his next challenge. A large Dragonkind army marched from the desert city of Calamandor, also called the Green Citadel. With them came thousands of slaves and a long train of wagons bearing supplies. They went northward into the Blue Mountains to a place called Khanhar Pass. It was a pathway between Vanara and the Dragonlands, broad and easily traversed, and it had been used by armies from both north and south for eons. Once within the pass, the Dragonkind set to work erecting a series of fortifications throughout the pass. They meant to secure Khanhar Pass once and for all, and to create a doorway into Vanara itself, one which they could open and close at will.

Part V: **Khanhar Pass**, Tallin's First Major Engagements

Vanaran soon scouts reported the activities of the Dragonkind. Serith Ellyn quickly summoned a council of war that included the generals of the Fellfaere and those of the Kingsmen Fourth and newly arrived Duinnor Regulars that were stationed near Linlally. It was quickly decided that the Kingsman Fourth Army, along with Duinnor Regulars and Vanaran Fellfaere, would assault and capture Khanhar Pass. They were to prevent the Dragonkind from completing their fortifications by driving them out, then they were to occupy the pass and hold it until relieved.

The Dragonkind received word well ahead of their enemy's arrival, and they were well-prepared. Some six miles north of Khanhar Pass, the Dragonkind unleashed a furious attack head-on upon the Kingsmen who marched ahead of their allies. Meanwhile, the Fellfaere and Duinnor Regulars who guarded the flank of the column were also attacked. Thus began a three-week battle.

Although outnumbered, the Northmen drove the Dragonkind forces into their incomplete fortifications within Khanhar Pass itself. After a brief lull of a day or two, a second battle then began. The Kingsmen meticulously surrounded and overwhelmed each of the thirty or so smaller fortifications one by one, using trebuchets and rams to knock down the incomplete walls protecting the Dragonkind. After two weeks, only the largest and strongest forts remained, and those took another four weeks to capture. Casualties were high, especially among the ill-trained Duinnor Regulars. After the last fortress in the center of Khanhar Pass was stormed, pockets of Dragonkind in the surrounding hills continued to harry the Kingsmen for days.

Tallin had by now gained a new appreciation of the Dragonkind soldiers. They were well-trained, well-led, and well-organized. As individuals, the Dragonkind were agile, cunning, disciplined, and possessed of incredible stamina. Dragonkind units coordinated their actions with each other efficiently, and using flags and mirror signals by day and lamps by night, they communicated across great distances. By all accounts, their field officers were just as fearless as the foot soldiers, and their generals showed every sign of being deliberate and careful in their planning and leadership. And it was Tallin's opinion that, had the Dragonkind gone unopposed for another two weeks, they would have completed their fortifications work and secured Khanhar Pass for all time. As he and his Fourth Army prepared to withdraw, Tallin wondered what the Dragonkind might have done had they gained full control over the pass.

The forces of Duinnor withdrew, leaving Vanara's Fellfaere to occupy the pass. They immediately began the work of rebuilding the captured fortifications, adding improvements, making walls higher and thicker, and erecting additional towers and other features. But like the Dragonkind before them, the Vanarans were soon hampered by a shortage of water and supplies, and the work was slow, laborious, and taxing. The pass was windy and cold at night, and brutally hot by day. Many wells were dug, but none produced water, so all food and water had to be brought to the occupation force, often by long trains of wagons guarded by Kingsmen. Over the next months, Danig Tallin was among those sent on resupply missions, and each time he became more alarmed at the difficulties faced by the occupying force.

Within the year, the Dragonkind attacked with fresh troops, and after only two weeks of fighting, they forced the Vanarans to abandon the pass. So once again Kingsmen were sent to retake the pass, which they managed to do in spite of heavy losses. It would be a story repeated time and again over the next four years. As soon as one army had settled into Khanhar Pass, the enemy would arrive to force them out.

Part VI: Kahryna of Fairoak

Although the House of Fairoak was once a proud and powerful people, over the centuries their homelands in southern Vanara were repeatedly devastated and destroyed by the wars with the Dragonkind. At last, almost destitute, the Fairoaks abandoned their lands and settled into a small estate just outside the city of Linlally where they lived modestly, though comfortably. One by one, the scions of Fairoak were killed or passed away until, by 785, Lady Kahryna was the last remaining heir to her father and mother's legacy.

In the late summer of that same year, a grand ball was held in honor of Lord Seafar's birthday, and it took place at the White Palace of Queen Serith Ellyn. Lady Kahryna was in attendance, and it was there she met Danig Tallin, dashing and handsome in his dress uniform. He asked her to dance, and by the time the ball had ended, the two were in love.

Over the course of the next few weeks, they made it a point to see each other as often as possible until at last Danig asked for Lady Kahryna's hand in marriage, though he was Mortal and she Elifaen. It did not matter to her any more than to him. Rather than wait, they had an autumn wedding at the Fairoak estate. It was a lavish banquet the Tallins and Fairoaks put on, with hundreds of guests in attendance. There were not only many Kingsmen present but also Lord Seafar, Prince Thurdun, and many dignitaries of Vanara. It was a happy occasion, with Captain Tallin and Lady Kahryna amongst the most beautiful and handsome couples that one could hope to see. The banquet and festivities were well under way, and the newlyweds had just completed their first waltz, alone upon the dance floor, when, as the applause died away, a messenger appeared at the door bearing a note for Captain Tallin. It was a summons to report to the Kingsmen Headquarters without delay. Tallin tried to make the best of it, saying that all should continue their feast and that he would return as quickly as he could. So, amid the guests' expressions of dismay and astonishment that a Kingsman should be called away on his wedding day, Danig Tallin took leave of his new wife and all his family and guests.

When Tallin reached his army's headquarters, he was seething with anger. He knew full-well that his commanding general was aware what day it was, the same general who was invited but did not see fit to attend the wedding. Tallin had no chance to protest when he was escorted into the Kingsmen headquarters in Linlally. The top generals of the Kingsmen in Vanara apologized to Tallin for interrupting his wedding, then they set to business. The Fellfaere that had recently retaken Khanhar Pass from the Dragonkind had suffered many casualties, and fewer than 2,000 lightly armed Vanarans remained. They were too few to hold the pass and in desperate need of reinforcement. Tallin was then informed that he was promoted to general and was now in overall command of the Third and Fourth Battalions of the Fourth Army, along with 1st Army's 2nd and 3rd Battalions for supply and engineering support, and two battalions from the Third Army. The force was assembling as they spoke. He was to march immediately to Khanhar Pass and hold it until relieved. They must assume that at some point in the future, but not likely any time soon, the Dragonkind would try to retake the pass. Tallin's force was to give the leaders in Vanara and Duinnor time to plan a permanent and robust occupation of Khanhar Pass, and then assemble the troops and materials required for such a task. Meanwhile, Tallin's force would be more than enough to rebuff any enemy harassment.

General Tallin mentally did the numbers. He would have around 7,200 men, at most, plus the Fellfaere already at Khanhar. From experience, he knew the difficulties posed by the pass and its terrain. When he asked, he was told that no other troops could be sent for some time, perhaps many months. The First and Second Battalions of the Fourth were still deployed around Ladentree, the available Fellfaere could not assemble in time, and standing orders from High Command in Duinnor prevented Vanaran Command from depleting its own forces any further without authorization.

Part VII: Khanhar Pass, Years 785-786

General Danig Tallin dispatched a courier with a note to his wife, then hastened to order his troops. Many of the Kingsmen who had been at Tallin's wedding had also been recalled, as well as all those others of the Fourth Army's Third and Fourth Battalions. By the first hour after dawn, they were marching southward from Linlally to Khanhar Pass, and behind them came a supply train, with wagons full of water, food, and equipment. Along the way, Tallin constantly sent riders ahead to carry news and to report back to and from the Fellfaere at Khanhar. He also dispatched strong parties of scouts all along his flanks and well forward. Their destination was almost 500 miles south of Linlally, so Tallin also arranged for the purchase of additional supplies, wagons, and mounts from towns and villages along the route. After ten days, the mountainous land became treeless and barren, and being autumn, the days were chilly and the nights cold. On the day they reached Khanhar Pass, some fifteen days after setting out, there was a scattering of snow in the air.

Fortunately, the Fellfaere had kept scouts reconnoitering the Dragonkind, and they reported to Tallin that although there were small parties in the region, the nearest large force of Dragonkind was over a hundred miles away. There were no signs of an imminent attack. Tallin set to work right away, first surveying all of the fortifications up and down the pass, which was some twenty miles long and five miles at its widest, and ran from the southeast to northwest. At its southernmost end, it broadened into the deserts of the Biradur Waste. To the northwest, the pass narrowed to only a few hundred feet before the road leading north climbed around and through the Blue Mountains. Tallin already knew the pass well, and he knew that there were almost seventy keeps of various sizes along the flanks of the pass, with three fortresses at the northwest end. Seven more fortresses lined the broad southeast entrance, and a single large fortress sat right in the middle of Khanhar Pass. But he soon learned that several hundred of the Fellfaere at Khanhar had been recalled to Linlally, leaving just over a thousand with him. That meant that he would have roughly eight thousand men to defend the pass. And he remembered that the Dragonkind, even they with their fighting prowess, failed to hold it with over eighty-thousand troops. Now he better understood why.

Because there was no source of water anywhere in the pass, it had to be collected in the mountains and carried to each and every keep and stronghold, along with food and equipment. That alone was a massive undertaking, requiring the transport and distribution of hundreds of barrels of water every day. Tallin calculated that the task would take hundreds of men, constantly working in the open, vulnerable to attack, and therefore in need of hundreds more to guard them. He also noted that the ground throughout the pass was soft with deep sand, making the use of wagons and war engines difficult. One had to dig many feet down to reach more solid ground. And that meant that the fortifications, built in haste by the Dragonkind without deep foundations, were inherently weak. Many were severely damaged from previous battles. And every stone of their construction and repair had to be quarried and moved from the surrounding mountains.

After two days of surveying the pass and surrounding hills, Tallin set to work. He ordered all outlying fortifications and keeps abandoned except for those to the south that had tall watchtowers. Troops were massed at the large central fortress. Signal posts were established along the ridges on both sides of the pass. Relays of guarded wagon teams were established to fetch water.   He set his men to work on the fortress itself, which was really only a broad campground surrounded by fairly low walls, in some places barely the height of a man's knees. It enclosed an area of about a quarter-mile from one side to the other. Stones from the abandoned keeps were brought, and the fortress walls were made four times thicker and three times taller. All gates but two were blocked up. Outside the fortress, the sand was scoured and hauled well away, clearing the ground for a thousand yards in every direction. In that area, broad deep pits were dug and filled with powdery sand from which no man or horse could escape. Other pits were even deeper, and their bottoms were filled with jagged rocks. It was during the digging of these pits that tunnels were discovered leading away from the fortress toward the keeps on both sides of the pass. They had been started by the Dragonkind, but had never been finished. They were broad and tall enough for men to pass through easily, but they were not very deep beneath the ground. But what impressed Tallin the most was the fact that since there were no trees to be had, the Dragonkind had stacked blocks as columns to support stone crosspieces to hold up the ceilings. But in spite of this clever engineering feat, all of the tunnels were dangerously weak. He realized that if he had ropes attached to the stone columns supporting the tunnels, they could be collapsed underneath the enemy.

Work continued at a steady pace. After two months, the progress was evident. Wagon trains constantly came and went, bringing additional stocks of water and food. Tallin thought that if he could supply his men for another three weeks, he could make the fortress impregnable. Only food and water would limit their ability to withstand an attack. In fact, he had only three days.

On Midwinter's Day, 785, scouts reported that a Dragonkind army was approaching from the Biradur Waste.   They numbered roughly forty-seven thousand footmen, with two thousand horsemen, and a thousand men with rolling stock. Tallin recalled all of his men to the fortress and dispatched a fast rider with a change of mounts to inform Linlally. It stated only the following: "Fifty-thousand Dragonkind approach. We are as prepared as we can be and will stand firm. Send reinforcements quickly."

The Dragonkind sent several thousand troops around the fortress to the northern approaches of the pass and sealed it off. Then they surrounded the fortress and encamped beyond arrow range to assemble their engines, three heavy trebuchets, seventeen large ballistae, and two battering rams on carriages. Three days later, the Dragonkind made their first assault on the fortress. As they closed in on all sides, the attackers fell victim to the many deadly traps and pits that General Tallin had prepared. These included the collapse of many of the tunnels, into which fell many Dragonkind and many of their engines. Fighting continued nonstop for three days and nights, and casualties were extremely heavy on both sides. On the fourth day, the Dragonkind fell back and regrouped. Then they attacked again. This would be repeated for weeks. Meanwhile, the Kingsmen and Fellfaere defenders received no relief or reinforcements, and had no word from Vanara.

Six-weeks later, the defenders of Khanhar Pass had been without any water at all two days, and without any food but jawrock for five days. They had one day of jawrock remaining. This in spite of strict rationing and fewer mouths to feed. Indeed, only three thousand of the original eight-thousand defenders remained. They were weak, many were wounded, and some were feverish. All they were weary. The days were warm and the nights very cold. Sometimes at night, flecks of snow fell, and the men stuck out their tongues in hope of catching one.

The interior of their fortress was littered with thousands of corpses. There was no fuel to burn the dead, nor the time or strength to bury them, nor even to shoo away the vultures that picked away at the bodies. Moving them out of the way of the living was as much as could be managed. Beyond their cracked and broken walls was an even more horrendous scene of carnage. The killing ground that Tallin had meticulously prepared had been put to its use, and it was now a hellish jumble of corpses, shattered equipment, and the burning wrecks of war engines. At Khanhar Pass, the dead outnumbered the living, and it seemed the vultures outnumbered all. Hyenas and jackals prowled without caution, and clouds of flies swarmed.

On the walls of the fortress, the men did not stand. They kneeled or squatted, saving their strength while they waited for the next wave of night attacks. Swords were in hand, daggers at the ready, and arrows notched to string. It had been almost two hours since they had repelled the last assault. It was past time for the next. In some places, ladders leaned against the outer side of the walls, rising up from a jumble of bodies at their bases. Soon, said one soldier to another, the piles would be so high that the Dragonkind would no longer need ladders. So the defenders watched and waited. All had rags wrapped about their faces, a pitiful barrier to the dust and the stench. From time to time, eyelids would droop and heads would momentarily dip only to snap back up from the relentless call of sleep, often with sudden fear in their eyes. But there was nothing new to see, no sounds of an approaching threat.

General Danig Tallin was one of those who, on his knees and leaning against the battlement, watched the southern field beyond his wall. Now and then he put his eye to his spyglass resting on the block of stone he leaned upon. In the deceiving predawn light, he could discern no coming attack. They were running late. It had been well over two hours since the last attack. His mind wandered, and he thought of his wife and his parents. Turning his head, he gazed across the interior of the fortress. There were only a few buildings here and there, and he could easily see across to the opposite wall and the men there were as still as statues, most sitting or kneeling as he did, watching the northern fields as he did the southern ones.

He knew he should begin his rounds, that he should see to his men. But he dreaded it. There was nothing new he could say. No new words of hope he could give. His eyes passed slowly across the interior. Nearly all of the men under his command were dead. He did not realize what he was doing, but he began reciting their names, such as he knew them. His eyes were too dry, else they would have released a flood.

He turned away and looked again through his spyglass. By now, there was more light. The sun was nearly up and would soon clear the mountains. There. There they were. The Dragonkind that were so determined to take this horrid place. They were only a few hundred yards away. Close enough to see without the spyglass. They were getting to their feet and ordering their ranks. He could see their fine lances and their colorful banners lifted high. With the spyglass, he could even discern the dust on their shields and, he thought, a weary expression here and there amongst them. And there he was, too. Their general in his beautiful and terrible armor, astride his handsome mount, emerging through his ranks to the front. Some fifteen yards ahead of his soldiers, the Dragonkind general came to a halt, facing the fortress, and he waited. Tallin watched as the thousands of soldiers formed their orderly ranks behind the patient general. Tallin did not warn his men. They would see them soon enough. Soon enough, the Dragonkind general would lift his hand. And when the hand was lowered, they would come again, slowly at first, tightening their ranks. Then more quickly, gaining momentum like an avalanche of death.

It was a sight to see. Each time they came, it was with such deliberate purpose, their shields and lances before them, the ranks behind with drawn swords, and the archers behind them with their powerful bows and long, green-fletched arrows. It was like watching a splendid show, awesome and terrifying.

Tallin could not take his eye away from the glass. He wanted to see it all. He decided to wait until the last moment before standing and drawing his sword. He was certain that this would be the last time he would see such a sight, the last time he would stand and draw his sword.

The Dragonkind general raised his hand.

Tallin tried to lick his dried lips as he watched. But he had no spit, his mouth and tongue were dry. The Dragonkind general kept his hand raised longer than usual. Tallin watched as the ranks gripped their lances and raised their shields. They were ready. The hand remained in the air. This was something new, something ominous. Tallin tried to swallow, but could not. He wished he could have but one sip of water before he died. That hand. It was still raised. Tallin was almost impatient. What were they waiting for? Why prolong this agony one moment longer?

Suddenly Tallin knew what it meant, why the Dragonkind waited, and his empty stomach twisted and fluttered. He took his eye from the spyglass and looked at the Dragonkind general in the distance, his hand still raised. Tallin slowly stood. Then, with his men looking on and too astonished to speak, Tallin stepped up onto the stone he had been leaning upon, exposing himself fully to the enemy. He gazed across the slaughtered at the Dragonkind general, then he raised his own hand. For a long moment, and for the first time since the battle had begun six-weeks ago, the two generals acknowledged each other. Then the Dragonkind general, his hand still raised, turned his horse around and rode slowly through his troops, lowering his hand as he went. The Dragonkind ranks turned and followed their general southward and away. Tallin slowly lowered his hand, then he sat down and watched them all go.

A week later, Prince Thurdun was riding at the head of an army of Fellfaere and was within a day's ride of Khanhar Pass when he spied a strange sight on the road ahead. It was a slow-moving train of wagons, all being pulled at an agonizingly slow pace by teams of bone-thin men. Thurdun rode quickly to them but pulled up when he neared. They were Kingsmen. They halted and fell to their knees to rest, all with unkempt beards, ragged tunics and cloaks that hung loose on starved frames. In the wagons were scores of wounded. Looking farther down the road, Thurdun counted sixty-two such wagons and carts.

"Who commands you?" cried Thurdun.

"General Tallin is still our general, good sir!" came the sharp reply from one wounded man.

"And the pass? Who holds Khanhar Pass?"

"Who else but General Tallin?" said another Kingsman.

Meanwhile, without being told to do so, those who came with Thurdun had dismounted and were sharing their water and ministering to the needs of the Kingsmen. Thurdun hurried on, his lieutenants barely able to keep pace with him. When they came to the opening and rode down into Khanhar Pass, they rode more carefully. They slowed even more when they came within sight of the central fortress. Thurdun eased his buckmarl to a walk, his expression one of horror and grief. At last, Thurdun halted. Staring all around at the carnage, he dismounted, his face wet with tears as he carefully proceeded.

"The children of Duinnor," he was heard to say, "pay the price for Duinnor's neglect. Oh, but what shall I say to General Tallin? How can I face him?"

Since receiving Tallin's message that the Dragonkind were coming to Khanhar Pass, there had been nothing but delay and indecision amongst the Kingsmen in Vanara. Although Thurdun had raised a Vanaran army within days to go to the relief of Khanhar Pass, Duinnor's representatives in Linlally proved either too disorganized or too inept to issue orders to send any Kingsmen to the region. Even the commanding general of the Fourth Army, who still had two full battalions at his disposal, was prohibited from marching to the aid of his own men until given clearance to do so. At last, exasperated, Prince Thurdun and his Fellfaere set out without any Duinnor men. But snow and ice on the mountain road blocked and hampered their progress.

Prince Thurdun was still wondering how to explain the shame of his late arrival to General Tallin when he came into the fortress. And Tallin, informed of the approach of the Prince, was there to meet him. Tallin immediately knelt before the baffled Prince.

"Prince Thurdun, I alone am to blame for this disaster," Tallin said, his eyes to the ground. "Those of your people who remained with me fought valiantly. And the Dragonkind marked them especially. That so many died was because I did not prepare quickly enough, nor thoroughly enough."

"How many are left of you? How many altogether, of all that you commanded? Look at me and answer," Thurdun demanded. There was no tone of anger in his voice, and Tallin looked up.

"Less than two thousand, my lord."

Thurdun knelt before Tallin and put his hands on Tallin's shoulders.

"Yet you denied this place to seven times your number," Thurdun said. "You did not fail in your duty. But we who should have come sooner failed in ours."

When the full story was revealed to Thurdun by Tallin and by many of the survivors, he was even more moved and astounded that the defenders had held for even a week. For the first three days, the fighting was non-stop, furious, unrelenting, and savage. Those first three days of fighting claimed the lives of fully half the men on both sides. After that, the siege became one of attrition, regular assaults, regrouping, and renewed assaults, all to wear down the defenders, to slowly choke them of resolve. But, in the end, it was the Dragonkind who lost the will to continue.

Before he withdrew with what was left of his men, Tallin took the time to write out a complete report and send it ahead to Linlally. He included everything he could about the fighting and the names of all of those under his command that died or who remained missing and unaccounted for. Prince Thurdun also submitted his own reports to his sister the Queen of Vanara, and to various ministers of Vanara as well as representatives of Duinnor.

In part due to these reports, but also because of the tales spread by his men, Danig Tallin and his Kingsmen were welcomed as heroes when they marched into Vanara. When they entered Linlally, the Queen herself was there to greet them. And beside her stood Lady Kahryna. Queen Serith Ellyn presented Tallin with the Order of the Flying Shield, one of the highest Vanaran decorations to be bestowed. And she further declared that every man who served with General Tallin would be given a ring made of silver and sapphire as well as seven Vanaran gold sovereigns as tokens of gratitude for their defense of Vanara. Then, turning back to General Tallin and gesturing at Lady Kahryna, she grinned and quipped, "And you may kiss the bride, with all my blessings."

Tallin did just that, and everyone applauded and cheered as he and Kahryna kissed and embraced.

Danig Tallin, the legendary Last Man Standing, had become a hero. He was thirty-six years old.

Part VIII: The Ring of Valor

Kahryna was just as glad to have her husband home as he was to be with her at last, though it was not as either of them could have predicted. While the two did have some chance at last to get to know each other as husband and wife, they also had to contend with newfound fame. Over the following year, there was hardly a week that went by in which they did not receive an invitation to some event. Many were held in honor of General Tallin, but others merely wanted some guest who would lend esteem to the gathering. Kahryna was proud of her husband's status, and she thought it only bolstered the honor of their Joined Houses. She was as responsible as any for promoting Danig's fame, and she used every occasion to make the most of her husband's prestige. Danig Tallin, on the other hand, found it irksome. While he appreciated and enjoyed his time off from military duty, he felt he was missing opportunities to influence Duinnor and Vanara's military preparedness. He was assured, though, by his commanders and by all else that although Khanhar Pass had seen much conflict, there was little to be found elsewhere. Indeed, on all fronts the Dragonkind were quiet, and other than a few skirmishes with renegades, there were no signs of any hostilities on the horizon. There were even rumors that behind-the-scenes overtures were being made by the King of the Dragonlands for a formal treaty of peace. Tallin was skeptical. So, for the remainder of the year, he satisfied himself with visiting those Kingsmen who had fought with him at Khanhar Pass and were still in Vanara. He also visited many of the families of the fallen, or, if they were far away, he wrote letters expressing his condolences and saying how proud he was to have had such brave comrades during such a trying time.

Then, on Midwinter's Day, a year after he had dispatched his last message to Linlally before the battle at Khanhar Pass began, he himself received two messages from Duinnor, delivered in person by both his commanding general and the Duinnor ambassador to Vanara. One message consisted of new orders for him to report to Duinnor as soon as winter eased up enough for travel. The other note was from the First Lord of the High Chambers, Lord Banis, who expressly requested that General Tallin and his wife come to Duinnor for an audience with the King.

It was a mild winter, so General Danig Tallin and his wife Lady Kahryna made arrangements by post to rent a small villa just outside of Duinnor City. Then they began their journey, and arrived at their temporary home at the beginning of Secondmonth, 787. The next day, just when Danig was bidding his wife goodbye and mounting his horse to ride into the city to report for duty and then on to the Palace for his audience with the King, a contingent of Kingsmen rode up. As it turned out, word of the couple's arrival had preceded them, and arrangements for a reception had immediately been made. This was communicated to General Tallin as he dismounted and was given a note from Lord Banis. Concerned, his wife came down the steps into the yard.

"It seems that we, the both of us, are to be conveyed to the city at noon," he told Kahryna. "And we are to prepare ourselves for a formal reception."

"Oh?"

"Yes. So this will be your chance to show off that new gown of yours. And I suppose we should unpack my dress uniform."

Three frantic hours later—after a frenzy of unpacking, rushed hair styling, a number of tears, and a few sharp remarks—the two were climbing into an elaborate open carriage drawn by a team of four black stallions. Lady Kahryna was positively stunning in her winter frock, her diamond bracelet over her white elbow-length gloves, and her black fur-lined cap. And her husband was no less handsome in his black breeches and polished boots, his dark green Kingsman tunic trimmed in gold, his cloak thrown back to show his medals and decorations, and his battle sword across his knee. He wore an open-faced brass helmet with a white horsehair plume, but he frowned just as intensely and appeared as every bit as uncomfortable as Lady Kahryna appeared proud and happy, grinning and enjoying every moment. Across from the nervous couple sat Lord Banis himself, smiling and appearing rather sanguine, if not smug. As the carriage started out, preceded by a full company of Kingsman horsemen in ceremonial uniforms and shining ceremonial helmets, Banis explained that they would take a rather circuitous route to the Palace, for it was the King's wish for as many people as possible see the hero they had all been waiting to welcome. At Tallin's question, Banis further explained that the broadsheets had reported the general's exploits and his victory over the Dragonkind at Khanhar Pass, and that over the past few weeks, new versions of the tale had been circulated throughout the Realm.

"It is only right," Banis went on as they approached the eastern gate of the city, "that the people have a look at the mighty general who almost single-handedly held off the hordes of Dragonkind."

"But I did no such thing, my lord!" declared Danig. "The only reason we held the pass at all was because the Dragonkind gave in and gave up before we did. Had they known how weak we were, they would have surely mounted one last attack. And it would have been the end of us!"

"Then it is a doubly good thing they did not know," replied Banis. "For not only would we have lost Khanhar Pass, but also a splendid occasion such as this day shall prove to be!"

"My lord, I shall tell you what I have told countless others..."

"Danig, don't—" said Kahryna, seeking to rein in the topic.

"...and that is that the death of thousands of men is not a thing to celebrate, but to mourn. And if any honor is to be had in the remembrance of those who died and were wounded, it is that the remembrance should be somber and dignified."

"My dear General Tallin," Banis replied, "we do not make little of those who were lost. We celebrate their accomplishment, the accomplishment of those who fought for our Realm, and especially the accomplishment of the man who led them! This is a day for us to honor you, in particular, since it was due to your leadership that there is anything to celebrate at all. And it is good for our people to know what kind of men serve the Realm. Men like you. In you, we all take example."

"Ah. Men like me. I see. But is it not so that you are Elifaen? And this is not your Realm?"

"Lady Kahryna, did you know when you married this Kingsman that he was so prickly?"

"I am afraid I suspected, my lord," she replied. "But I suppose that is one of the qualities that I rather like in him."

"I see. Well, I have sought to express my opinion to your husband," Banis nodded with a smirk. "Let us now hear that of the people!"

In fact, he was almost shouting, for they had come into the city and the streets were lined with cheering onlookers. The carriage kept on, albeit more slowly, as they passed back and forth from street to avenue. At every turn there were new throngs, it seemed, and the Duinnor Regulars, Kingsmen, and Kingsmen Constabulary that lined the way had a difficult time keeping the tumultuous crowds away from the carriage. Winter blooms were thrown at the carriage, sometimes from the taller buildings they passed, and from time to time a few landed in the carriage itself. Sometimes a lady or girl would break free of the cordon and race forward to the carriage with a basket of flowers, only to be hauled safely out of the way by a uniformed man as she struggled to toss her posies. On toward the palace they went, and though the avenues became wider, they were all the more congested with well-wishers, some standing in their carts or carriages in order to see the passing celebrities. At one juncture, yet another woman broke free of the sidelines and rushed to the carriage, rummaging through her apron as she came. Just as she hurled an overripe tomato at Lord Banis, her arm was gripped by a Kingsman Constable, her aim spoiled, and the tomato only splattered on the seat beside the First Lord.

"Oh, my!" gasped Kahryna. "That was close!"

"Indeed," frowned Banis. "Why some people do such things is beyond me."

"Clearly the lady did not think things through," said Danig. "Something a bit harder than a juicy winter tomato would have made a better missile."

Banis was about to speak, but he was prevented by a deafening blare of trumpets, and he had to settle for scowling at his fellow passengers. The trumpets were announcing their arrival at Duinstone, the palace of the Unknown Kings, and the carriage stopped at a red carpet leading into the palace doors. Banis got out first. Danig stood to climb out, and he could be seen from a long distance. A great cheer and applause erupted from all around, nearly drowning out the trumpets. He bowed to the crowds, stepped down, and gave Kahryna his hand to help her out. Then, arm in arm, Danig and Kahryna followed Lord Banis who led the way between two long lines of saluting Kingsmen and then into the palace. Inside was hardly less noisy, for the great foyer, and every hall and staircase was lined with the lords and ladies of Duinnor in their finery, with Kingsmen in their uniforms, and with many foreign dignitaries and special guests. And all were clapping or shouting, "Huzzah!" All but the Kingsmen, that is, who stood rigidly with swords drawn and held upright in front of their faces as a sign of honor.

Up and up they went. Up and around and around the spiral stair, higher and higher. They went at an easy pace, just as all must do if they do not wish to be exhausted at the top, just when they needed all the coolness that could be mustered. For at the top, which the trio came to at last, was the High Chamber of the Unknown Kings, presently occupied by the Sixth Unknown King. As they entered, Danig saw the Avatar, in the form of a lady's fan, floating at one side of the room. There was a green curtain drawn across the width of the room, and in front of the curtain awaited the King in his Golden Mantle, which burned with a cold, blinding light. All knelt and averted their eyes.

"My King," said Lord Banis, "I have with me General Danig Tallin, of the Kingsman Fourth Army. And with him is his wife, Lady Kahryna of the House of Fairoak."

Danig and Kahryna both felt an odd sensation inside their heads just above their brow. It was not pleasant.

"No, Lady Kahryna," said the King aloud for all to hear, "it is not a pleasant sensation for most. But I shall forego my usual way of conversing with those who have audience with me and speak aloud."

"You are most gracious and kind, sire," said Lady Kahryna, dipping her head but not looking up.

"Please rise, everyone."

When they had all stood, their heads still bowed, Danig noticed for the first time several high-ranking Kingsmen were present, including his own superior officer as well as the Commandant General of all Kingsmen.

"General Tallin," said the King, "I wish to offer my congratulations to your accomplishment at Khanhar Pass."

"Thank you, Sire."

"I know that the engagement was costly," the King went on, "and that you feel responsible for the loss of so many fine soldiers. However, I have reviewed the action reports, the reports that you and your surviving officers have submitted, as well as a few of those that have been shared by Vanaran sources. I have also conferred with the Commandant, here, concerning Khanhar Pass, and I have asked many questions concerning the battle itself as well as about your reports. Not only do I wish to exonerate you of any guilt you may feel concerning your casualties, but I also wish to say that all who have knowledge of the details of the actions at Khanhar Pass are unanimous in their admiration and respect for your leadership there. I, too, am full of admiration and respect for you."

"That is most kind, my King."

"Indeed, all of Duinnor is proud of you and your men, as your reception no doubt indicates. It has been more than a year since the battle. It is normal for officers of the throne to prepare recommendations and observations beyond the usual after-action reports. I have been informed that you have done so, and that you have brought your detailed reports and recommendations with you."

"I have, sire."

"Would you be so kind as to briefly summarize the most important of your recommendations?"

"It would be my honor to do so," replied Danig, glancing at his Commandant, who nodded. "In my full report, I have listed twenty recommendations, of which almost half pertain to Khanhar Pass, specifically, and the rest concerning training, equipment, and organizational matters. But, pertaining to Khanhar Pass, the most important issue is one of food and water, particularly water. Many who died did so simply because they were too weak to defend themselves in combat. My proposal is to construct a system of aqueducts and canals to bring water from the mountain streams to Khanhar Pass. The water would be channeled into deep cisterns for storage so that the flow could be cut off should any enemy attack the pass. The attackers would be denied water, whilst the defenders would be well-supplied. Secondly, stores of dry foodstuffs should be built up so that, like water, it would be in ample supply for the defenders of Khanhar Pass. Third, rather than trying to man and defend so many forts and keeps, or even a central one, as we did, I suggest that a long-term effort be made to construct a high and defensible wall across the northern end of the pass, where the ground is naturally higher. Those are the chief recommendations, sire."

"I see. Would not such projects fall to the Vanarans, since Khanhar Pass resides within their realm?"

"Yes, King," answered Danig. "My proposals are not new. I only repeat and reiterate those that have been made by previous Kingsmen and by Vanarans alike. However, since the defense of Vanara is a joint effort, perhaps the strengthening of Khanhar Pass ought to be so as well. Particularly if it means fewer casualties."

"Hm. I shall instruct your superiors to study and consider your proposals seriously," said the King. "Meanwhile, as a sign of Duinnor's esteem and of the Throne's appreciation of your service, Lord Banis shall present you with a token of our favor."

A Kingsman stepped forward and gave a small box to Lord Banis. Banis opened the box and held it in front of him for all present to see. It held an ornate ring of gold, inlaid with onyx.

"Let it be known," said Banis, "that in recognition for heroism in battle, for leadership, and courage in the face of a determined and ruthless enemy, for honorably performing his duties with skill and determination, and for securing victory in spite of many hardships, the King of Duinnor has bestowed upon Danig Saheed Tallin the right to receive and wear upon his finger this Ring of Valor. Lady Kahryna, would you do the honors?"

Danig knelt once again, as Kahryna took the ring from the box that Banis held out. She took her husband's right hand, and she smiled broadly as she spoke.

"On behalf of the King of Duinnor and the people of this realm," she said, "and by the King's own decree, please accept this for all to see, a sign of your loyalty, your gallantry, and your honor."

She slipped the ring onto his finger, then took both his hands and leaned to kiss him on both cheeks.

"Please rise," said Lord Banis.

As Danig did so, all but the King clapped their hands.

"Sire, I am deeply honored by this gift," Danig said, bowing. "I shall proudly wear this ring in humble remembrance of those who fought, suffered, and died at Khanhar Pass, and as a sign of my esteem for the King they all so valiantly served. Thank you, my King."

Danig bowed again.

The audience with the king was over, and Lord Banis led General Tallin and Lady Kahryna were ushered out of the chamber, with the other dignitaries following. A little while later, they were taken to the wall overlooking the palace gate, a place where the royal proclamation could be loudly repeated and where all could see and cheer their hero. The trumpets were blown again, and the herald loudly read the proclamation, repeating what had already been said by Banis, but now for the benefit of all the people. And again, the crowds cheered and cheered. Danig was prevailed upon by his wife to wave at the people below. He gave in and did so, and he could not help but break into an amused grin, and Lady Kahryna smiled broadly as she clutched his other hand tightly. She laughed and elbowed him when he was about to lower his arm, and it shot back up higher than before.

At last, it was time to descend from the wall and go to their carriage and on to a series of banquets that would culminate in a grand ball that very night. On the way to the carriage, several men who represented the broadsheets of the city shouted questions past the Kingsmen escorts at the proud couple.

"What is it like to be wife to such a distinguished Kingsman?"

"Where will your next assignment be, General?"

"How many lizards would you say were killed at Khanhar Pass?"

Danig spun around and faced the man who had shouted that last question. Such was the suddenness of his movement and the ferocity of his expression that all hushed to hear his answer. He composed himself somewhat.

"Not a single one," he stated, glaring at the questioner. "But a good many men died there. Men with fathers and mothers. Men with brothers and sisters. Men with wives and children. Men with cunning and courage. Men of honor."

He threw a contemptuous gaze across the entire group of onlookers and turned sharply away, taking his wife's arm and proceeding to the awaiting carriage. Behind them, more questions flew, some of which were impolite.

For nearly a month, the dashing Kingsman and his exotic Elifaen wife were celebrated all over Duinnor City. As had previously happened in Vanara, Danig and Kahryna were invited to one celebration after another, and their door was crowded with visitors and well-wishers almost constantly. But Danig Tallin was not idle when it came to his official duties. He was called upon to deliver his reports and recommendations in person to many high-ranking Kingsmen officers. The

Kingsman Academy also requested that he deliver a series of lectures concerning the Khanhar Pass engagements for the benefit of the cadets. These lectures were open to the public, and were so well attended that they had to be moved to a larger venue than was originally planned.

Eventually General Tallin received new orders. He was to take command of the Fifth Battalion of the Fourth Army, which was a training battalion of new recruits who would serve as replacements for the nearly decimated Third and Fourth Battalions. It was not an assignment that he would have wished for, but he threw himself into the work with his usual zeal and effectiveness.

It was toward the middle of summer that he learned of the decision made by both Duinnor and Vanaran leaders pertaining to his recommendation to redirect water to Khanhar Pass via aqueducts. They were deemed too costly. Not only that, but it was decided to abandon Khanhar Pass altogether. This infuriated Tallin and many others in Duinnor and Vanara. After lodging an official protest over the decision, Tallin began a campaign of letter-writing. In his letters, he laid out the greater costs of retaking the pass should it be reoccupied by the Dragonkind. In some letters. he even enclosed estimates of the construction costs for the aqueducts and the new fortifications that he proposed, and he compared those estimates against the costs of supplying and supporting an army that would be required to oust the Dragonkind from Khanhar Pass. His letters caused a great stir, and quite a bit of controversy. Generally, the common people and the rank and file of the armies were convinced by Tallin's arguments. Vanara even reversed itself and proposed that his recommendations be acted upon. But the leaders in Duinnor were steadfast in their opposition. They even hinted that Tallin's efforts were somewhat disloyal, since the King was also opposed to his recommendations. For an entire year, during which he trained thousands of Kingsmen, he kept up his efforts to convince his superiors to take his advice concerning Khanhar Pass.

Eventually, Tallin found himself quite unpopular with the command staff. And Kahryna, who supported her husband's efforts wholeheartedly, was quietly shunned. Expected invitations to social events did not arrive, and she found that many ladies of the realm did not wish to receive her when she called upon them at their homes.

Part IX: The Hero Fades Away

In 789, after nearly a year and a half in Duinnor, Danig Tallin was reassigned. His new duty was to oversee the security of the town of Ladentree, in southwestern Vanara. It was an important assignment, but he knew it was to get him out of the way, so to speak. So it was with mixed feelings that he and Kahryna departed Duinnor.

Over the next years, Danig Tallin's fame receded. He found the work at Ladentree somewhat boring. The town was an important waypoint on the route to the Free City of Kajarahn and was a prime target for bandits and renegades. Still, Tallin found that the town's defenses and security were more than adequate, and that it had been bolstered considerably since his last visit some years earlier. He did assist with outlying defenses, and he instituted a system of road patrols to keep the ways free of bandits and highwaymen. But the work was not to his liking. And he traveled back to Linlally whenever he could to see his wife and his parents and his newborn son, Dalvenpar. Soon he would have another son, called Aram.

In 793, he traveled to Duinnor in order to personally deliver a report on the state of Ladentree's defenses. He traveled alone, since it was to be but a very short stay of only three weeks. While in Duinnor, he was disheartened by the decline in general discipline at the Academy and by the increasing decadence in the streets of Duinnor. Graft and corruption were at every turn, and the newly established Kingsmen Constabulary was hard-pressed to enforce law within the city. Tallin was glad, therefore, when it came time for his return to Vanara, and he traveled home as swiftly as he could.

Upon his arrival in Vanara he learned of the terrible fever that had swept through the land, striking down Men throughout the realm. The Elifaen, of course, were unaffected. Although his two boys were spared, both of his parents were dead. The new Lord Tallin grieved terribly, and he was hardly consoled by the birth of his third child, a daughter named Mirabella. And although there was no evidence of Dragonkind activity in the region of Khanhar Pass, he constantly worried over it. And more bad news came when he received letters from his estate managers in the Eastlands saying that rampaging trolls had driven out many of the farmers in Tallinvale.

In spite of his many worries, Danig Tallin continued to serve as Kingsman advisor and liaison at Ladentree. Through his friends and contacts in Vanara, he closely followed the treaty negotiations between the Dragonlands and the northern realms. He did not hold much hope for them, and he continued his campaign of trying to garner support for fortifying Khanhar Pass. The Vanarans, though generally supportive of his ideas, made it clear that without Duinnor's help, the project could not be financed. And Duinnor was intractable.

At last, in the year 799, Danig Tallin applied for retirement from active service, having served for over the normal term of twenty-five years. His retirement was granted, effective with the first month of the following year. As soon as he received his discharge, he sold all of his Vanaran properties and traveled with his family first to Duinnor, then down the Osterflo to Glareth by the Sea. There he established his family in a temporary dwelling while he traveled to Tallinvale to see to the restoration and remodeling of Tallin Hall and see to the management of his vast land holdings in that valley.

Part X: Tallinvale

During those days, trolls continued to abide in the Thunder Mountains, and they sometimes ventured into Tallinvale to carry off livestock and to make mischief by knocking over houses or stomping down orchards and crops. Since they were made of stone, no weapons could deter them, and very few people could be enticed to farm or take up trades in the valley. At last, in the winter of 801, Lord Tallin raised the alarm that trolls were moving into the valley, and he told everyone to evacuate the region. If they went to Glareth by the Sea, he told them, he would pay for their travel expenses and see to it that they found employment. He also told them that he planned to make Tallinvale safe from the trolls and that, should he succeed in doing so, the people would be invited to return.

When Tallinvalers began showing up in Glareth, Lady Kahryna was greatly troubled. But one of the new arrivals brought a letter for her from her husband that explained that he was very hopeful that the region would soon be made safe, and that he intended that Tallin Hall be made a suitable home for his family. He also assured Lady Kahryna that although the trolls were greatly feared, he was in no danger.

"Indeed," he wrote, "I will not only see to it that our valley will be safe from the trolls, but I also aim to construct walls and defenses large enough to enclose and protect not only Tallin Hall but also a small city within those walls. The defenses will be such that no invading army could succeed in taking the area enclosed. So do not fret. My days and nights are busy ones, and you shall soon see for yourself the fruit of this labor."

It seemed that Lord Tallin foresaw some uncanny and mysterious event, for it was shortly after this time that people in the region nearby to the Thunder Mountains began to notice the absence of the trolls that once numbered in the many thousands. At first, people were wary. No longer did the mountains rumble with the noise of the trolls as they tromped along or as they delved rock and stone. Travelers who braved the region no longer reported sighting any trolls. And a few adventurous explorers climbed into the mountains to look upon the troll towns, only to find them abandoned.

By the middle of 802, not a single troll had been reported by anyone. And, at the end of that year, messengers went about the villages and towns of the Eastlands. They tacked notices on trees and posts announcing that the Thunder Mountains were no longer the abode of trolls and that all were invited back to Tallinvale and would be welcomed by Lord Tallin with fair and generous leases and loans to establish themselves. The notices were also carried to Glareth, and news reached Lady Kahryna concerning these announcements only days before her husband arrived. He had come, he said, to take any of his people back to Tallinvale who were willing to return, and to make it worthwhile for them to come with generous grants of land and property. He told his wife that he would return after a few months to see her and their children to their remodeled mansion located in the new town that now surrounded his estate.

When the people returned to Tallinvale, and arrived at the northern end of the valley, they were flabbergasted by what they saw. Whereas before the valley floor was rocky and deep, and the promontory whereupon Tallin Hall sat jutted up some sixty feet above all else, now the northernmost valley floor was level and smooth, crisscrossed with irrigation canals. And Tallin Hall, in the distance, was now surrounded by a vast enclosure of smooth high walls, an area large enough for a good-sized town.

From a variety of sources, we now know that Lord Tallin secured from Alonair a promise to harness the trolls and to make all of these changes come about. As described elsewhere, once they had built up the city's defensive walls, they constructed a large underground lake on the north side of Tallin City. Over this, they constructed a roof which was itself covered with soil. The trolls acted as the columns to support this roof and were, in effect, put to sleep by Alonair. A password was arranged so that when the trolls heard it, they would wake up, lower their arms, and collapse everything above into the lake in which they stood. Any besieging force located above would be destroyed. In addition to these structures, Lord Tallin also designed a system to pour huge quantities of highly flammable oil into the lake to be set ablaze and cause further destruction. And, as events would prove during the Year of the Red Door, when Redvests attacked Tallinvale, this system worked just as planned.

After the construction work was completed, and with the trolls no longer a threat, Lord Tallin worked feverishly to entice workers of all kinds to Tallinvale. Woodworkers, metalworkers and blacksmiths, farmers and cattlemen, weavers and potters and glassmakers, coopers, farriers, and craftsmen of all kinds were invited to come, and many were first hired by Lord Tallin to work on his own mansion and estate. Others were given grants or loans to begin their shops and businesses. By the time he departed to fetch his own family to Tallinvale, the valley population already exceeded three thousand, with new arrivals every day.

Soon a bustling town surrounded Tallin Hall. However, when he arrived with his family, Lord Tallin was vexed to hear that Duinnor tax collectors were exacting a heavy amount from his people. Upon investigation, he discovered that many of the collectors were not reporting their collections to Prince Carbane in Glareth, as was required since Glareth held regency over the old Eastlands Realm. Tallin was further infuriated when he discovered, through a series of letters with the King's Exchequer in Duinnor that the sums collected in Tallinvale, and throughout the Eastlands, were not being properly reported. A system of embezzlement, it seemed, was in place.

After several years of letter-writing, during which Lord Tallin personally saw to it that the correct taxes were levied and collected, he decided to travel to Duinnor himself to get to the bottom of the trouble. This he did, taking his oldest son, Dalvenpar, along.

Part XI: Gurasa

In the year 809 of the Second Age, Lord Tallin and his son Dalvenpar traveled first to Glareth to acquire letters and statements from Prince Carbane's tax men, documents that confirmed Tallin's own version of things. Then he and Dalvenpar traveled westward along the Osterflo until at last they reached Duinnor City in early summer. Although they had much to do in the way of business, Lord Tallin made sure that Dalvenpar met as many of the former general's colleagues as possible, including a number of Kingsmen, retired or otherwise. They also had time to tour the city itself, and spent a number of days seeing the sights, visiting the Kingsman Academy, looking at the various works of art in Hanton Hall, and looking at a number of fine mansions within the city. They also traveled outside of Duinnor City, including to the Temple of Beras overlooking Duinnor City.

Lord Tallin had private business with the monks of the Temple, so private that Dalvenpar was not permitted to attend. However, he was free to roam the Temple grounds, and it was while walking about the gardens of the Temple that he met with an old acquaintance of his father from Vanara, Collandoth the Melnari. Collandoth was recently arrived from Vanara and he was showing the Temple sights to his travel companion, a sickly youngster named Gurasa. The two young men hit it off right away, and when Lord Tallin rejoined his son, he was happy to renew his acquaintance with Collandoth. Although they were not close friends, they had a lot to chat about. It was a time of peace between the north and the Dragonlands, and Collandoth had recently spent a good deal of time in the Dragonlands as a kind of trade representative. And Lord Tallin was keenly interested in all that Collandoth could share concerning the royal city of Tyrsharat, the court of the Sun King, and all else pertaining to the desert lands.

While Lord Tallin and Collandoth talked, Dalvenpar and Gurasa also talked. Gurasa was curious about the Eastlands, and when he learned that Dalvenpar lived there, he naturally asked if he had ever been to the old fortress at Tulith Attis. Dalvenpar told Gurasa all about it, and he answered many of Gurasa's questions about the forests and fields of the Eastlands, about crops and wildlife, and about the trolls of the Thunder Mountains and their mysterious disappearance. Dalvenpar answered as well as he could, while his own curiosity was piqued by the thin and frail-looking youngster. But Gurasa would not say where he was from, nor what accounted for his odd accent and manner of speech.

Over the next few weeks, Gurasa and Dalvenpar saw each other many times, and while Lord Tallin conducted his business with the King's Exchequer, Collandoth continued showing the two boys around Duinnor City. The news that Lord Tallin brought concerning the corrupt tax collections in the east was something of a minor scandal. Many clerks and bureaucrats were sacked as a result of his reports, and many others lost lucrative shares in the wealth that had been embezzled from the Eastlands. The scandal reached all the way up into the highest ranks of the King's court, and Lord Banis himself vowed to launch an investigation into the affair, although he himself was implicated in covering up many facts concerning the collection practices.

Working alongside the Glareth Ambassador, Lord Tallin at last secured a declaration that no tax collections would be performed by Duinnor in the Eastlands unless the collectors were accompanied by Eastlander representatives and overseen by those appointed by Prince Carbane. With this settlement in hand, Lord Tallin and Dalvenpar departed Duinnor to travel back to Glareth by the Sea by boat via the River Osterflo. With them also went Collandoth and Gurasa.

The journey was easy and full of cheer among the foursome. They were all amazed by the Locks of Karthia, and awed by the river vistas as they floated downstream. But, not long after they cleared the locks, Lord Tallin accidentally discovered that Gurasa was a Dragonkind, and he was terribly dismayed and alarmed by the dangers faced a Dragonkind outside his own lands. Unknown to all, including Gurasa, Dalvenpar knew this fact well before departing Duinnor, but had kept Gurasa's secret. By this time, Lord Tallin was himself quite taken by Gurasa, and he was only upset because he alone, of the four travelers, was kept in the dark about Gurasa's race. But, as far as Lord Tallin was concerned, Gurasa's race did not really matter beyond the care needed to safeguard him. Indeed, with his true identity revealed, new lines of conversation and sharing opened up, which Lord Tallin, fully of curiosity, certainly enjoyed. Gurasa was moved to hear the Kingsman general express his admiration for the stalwart Dragonkind that he had faced at Khanhar Pass. He promised Gurasa that he should have no fear of betrayal. Indeed, Lord Tallin told him, although they were far from Tallinvale, Gurasa should consider himself a guest of the Tallins, with all of the protections and courtesies that a guest should expect of any host. Collandoth, who was present during all of this, seemed immensely pleased.

With two new protectors and friends, Gurasa arrived in Glareth by the Sea. He was, by all accounts, utterly charmed by the realm, and amazed. He had never seen a body of water as large as Salfin Bay, and at first he mistook it for the Great Sea, much to the amusement of his travel companions. When at last he was taken to the bluffs overlooking the sea, Gurasa stood in awe of the sight for many moments, then sat down to gaze at the expanse of water. When Dalvenpar raced down the hill and fetched a cup of seawater for Gurasa to taste, he was even more amazed. While at Glareth, he met Dalvenpar's younger brother, Aram, who was attending school there, and the Tallins and Gurasa enjoyed dinner with Aram's sailing instructor and his family, the daughter of whom Aram would eventually marry.

Eventually, Gurasa, Dalvenpar, and Lord Tallin departed for Tallinvale, leaving Collandoth behind in Glareth. The three traveled first to Formouth, and there they were given passage on a small sloop and sailed down Lake Halgaeth, much to Gurasa's delight.

Gurasa remained in Tallinvale for nearly a year, and he traveled out on various excursions with Dalvenpar and Lord Tallin. By now, Tallin City, as the town around Tallin Hall was being called, was a bustling and growing place. Lord Tallin was often pressed by business, so Gurasa spent a good deal of time with Dalvenpar, and even the little Mirabella. He especially enjoyed playing Hide and Seek with Mirabella, but he always saw to it that she found him no matter where in the great mansion he hid himself.

After many months, Collandoth arrived in Tallinvale to guide Gurasa back home to the Dragonlands. By then, Gurasa and Dalvenpar had become very close friends, confiding in each other their concerns for their lands, their families, and for peace between their peoples. Gurasa and Collandoth departed, taking a circuitous route back via Masurthia and Altoria, and eventually back to Vanara. When Collandoth escorted Gurasa back home to his town of Almedian in the Dragonlands, the first thing that Gurasa did was to commission a special ring to be made. He then arranged for the ring to be carried by traders to the Free City of Kajarahn and then through Vanara all the way back to Tallinvale, where it was delivered to his friend. Dalvenpar proudly wore it for the rest of his life.

Meanwhile, after the departure of Gurasa, something of a conflict arose between Dalvenpar and his father. Dalvenpar wished to go to Duinnor and enlist as a Kingsman, but Lord Tallin opposed it. They both knew that by Royal Edict, all eldest sons of Named Houses must serve as Kingsmen. Failure to do so would result in heavy fines and levies against the Named House. Lord Tallin, who was by now very wealthy, had enough treasure to pay the fines, and he wanted Dalvenpar to remain in Tallinvale. He explained to Dalvenpar that he did not trust Duinnor, nor those alongside which Dalvenpar would serve, and had no confidence that the peace between the Dragonlands and the northern realms would last. Lord Tallin did not want his son to face the kind of Dragonkind fighters that he himself saw at Khanhar Pass. But Dalvenpar was adamant, and he enlisted the support of his mother, Lady Kahryna. She was able to convince Danig to give his blessing to Dalvenpar by allowing him to do as he wished. So, within two weeks of receiving the ring from Gurasa, Dalvenpar set out for Duinnor where he enlisted and enrolled in the Kingsman Academy.

Part XII: Renewed Hostilities

In Tallinvale, Lord Tallin continued to work with the people to increase prosperity. He invested in glassmaking trades, and formed partnerships with vineyards throughout the Eastlands that wanted to use glass bottles that were produced in Tallinvale. Tallinvale was granted county status by Glareth, and Lord Tallin consulted with town and country leaders to formulate commonsense laws and regulations pertaining to deeds, trade concerns, taxes, and the establishment of free schools. He also embarked on extensive roadway improvements that included the construction of many sturdy bridges capable of supporting heavy trade wagons.

Meanwhile, Lord Tallin invited many young Men and Elifaen to visit Tallinvale, and he made no secret that he was looking for a worthy suitor for his daughter, Mirabella, who was now a beautiful young lady. She, however, was uninterested in any of the would-be suitors.

In 821, both Aram and Dalvenpar came home to visit. Dalvenpar had been serving with the Kingsman Fourth Army in Vanara, and Aram was near to graduation from the Glareth Academy. It was a great homecoming. Lord Tallin sponsored an elaborate banquet, and a grand Midsummer's Ball at Tallin Hall. A few days later, the Tallin children were convinced by Lady Kahryna to sit for a painting. When the painting was finished, it was given a prominent place in the Hall. In the portrait, Mirabella sits before her two brothers, each with a hand on her shoulder. Clearly visible, and captured in detail, was the ring that Dalvenpar always wore, the one given to him by Gurasa.

Little could they guess that, in faraway Vanara, peace had been shattered when a caravan of Dragonkind traders were set upon by Vanaran highwaymen. In retaliation, several Vanaran travelers were kidnapped by the Dragonkind and sold into bondage. Soon raids were taking place back and forth across the border between Vanara and the Dragonlands. Queen Serith Ellyn tried to quell the violence, but her efforts were fruitless, and her appeals to the Sun King were not answered. Then, just a few days after Dalvenpar departed Tallinvale for Vanara, a small Dragonkind army cut northward into Vanara, burning and looting small villages in the Blue Mountains. War had returned. And within a few years, it would cost the lives of both Dalvenpar and Aram. Lady Kahryna would die of grief. Mirabella would be estranged from her father. And, far away, their Dragonkind friend Gurasa would be disgraced.

So the last years of the Second Age were very hard, very sad, and very lonely for Lord Tallin. Yet he had an important role during the final year of the Second Age. As described in *The Year of the Red Door*, he successfully delayed, then annihilated a large portion of the Redvest military. By doing so, he effectively prevented the Redvests from conducting their planned invasion of the West, and enabled forces led by Prince Lantos and Ruling Prince Carbane to carry out their own successful invasion of Tracia.

See Also:
Biographical Sketches (Gurasa)

****

Esildre

Introduction

Esildre was perhaps one of the most enigmatic Elifaen, with a life that stretched from the Time Before Time until near the end of the Second Age. It seems hardly credible that someone like her, with vast age and experience, should never assert herself into lofty positions of power or prestige. But she never sought rank or status. And, battle-hardened though she was—even somewhat vicious in a fight—she was, on occasion, equally soft and forgiving. As an Elifaen, and not very prone to physical injury, she had all of the characteristics of her kind, moody, melancholic, and even a certain shiftlessness, or at least a singular lack of ambition. Hers was a tragic life, filled with setbacks, losses, and anguish. Yet she, like many of her kind, found it within her to "carry on," if not as before, then at least in some different way, some different direction, for good or for ill. In this she was not so much different from other Elifaen. But her decisions were sometimes reckless to the point of outrage, and her conduct for many years was scandalous, and she often seemed rudderless, lost, or even apathetic. But, as with many of the actors that shaped events of the Year of the Red Door (before and during that year), Esildre certainly grappled with uncertainty and self-doubt. She quite literally had internal demons, which caused her and many others great grief. But one of the remarkable things about her is how she made efforts, eventually at least, to rectify her behavior and her life. As detailed in *The Year of the Red Door*, she played a critical role in the lives of the Nowhereans, thus affecting the outcome of Robby Ribbon's quest.

She was not what one would call wise. At least, she was not a font of advice or insight to be shared with others. It seems odd that an Elifaen, a Firstborn, would not accumulate vast stores of knowledge and wisdom, or could not find suitable ways of coping with existence. One might think that, after a long time, an Elifaen's path would become more defined, more purposeful, or at least more predictable. Not so Esildre. Perhaps, as some have said, she never really grew up, never really matured, or was never gifted nor acquired the intellect to become sagacious. Or, as Raynor observed, perhaps her innate introspection was, for her, terribly stormy. But one thing seems certain: She was resigned to a life on earth. She never expressed hope that the Bloodcoins could be used as they were intended, or that she would be redeemed or even forgiven for her mistakes. As time passed, her thoughts became darker and darker, her despair harder to deny, and her view of the future held little hope of improvement. Until, that is, two remarkable things occurred which she did not expect nor could have foreseen: Her introduction to Tyrin Spritsul. And her death. It was, after all, these two events that changed her, and changed the course of history.

The information and stories about Esildre come from a variety of sources. Raynor the Wise, her somewhile tutor, made much comment about her to Collandoth and to others in his letters. As well, when she was his student, she recounted many of her memories and experiences to Raynor, which he noted and used as lessons for her to copy as she learned to read and write. Esildre apparently talked to Raynor much more than she did with others, more comfortably sharing her past and her thoughts with him than with anyone else. These notes, some very detailed, and some in Esildre's own hand, were found by Ullin Saheed Tallin during one of his "literary" quests. Eldwin of Nowhere spoke much about her, and these stories were written down by his kinfolk, with copies later given to Ullin Saheed Tallin. But earlier records, documents, and letters also mention Esildre. Nimwill's court records of Vanara mention her. Shortly after the debacle with the House of Walnut, Lucinda's son, Jarvis, wrote about Esildre to a friend in Vanara, describing Esildre's role in saving the King's life and clearing his family of wrongdoing. Court documents pertaining to that affair were later copied and made available to the Royal Archives of Vanara. Ullin Saheed Tallin, whose own experience of Esildre was not pleasant, later interviewed surviving members of her staff and household, who had escaped Castle Elmwood. Some of those did not immediately transform and depart the Earth, and when Ullin's dreamwalkers came across them, they shared much about Esildre. Indeed, sources of information, although sometimes seemingly contradictory, ranged widely in nature, from court archives to letters to official documents. And yet, when put together, these reveal long gaps in her life for which nothing was ever recorded, as if she did not even exist. Ullin himself noted that he found her long life's story, though full of gaps, to be one that connected her to so many important events, that he felt it was worthwhile to make such information pertaining to her available.

Besides those insights given within the pages of The Year of the Red Door, most of what we have to go on are external accounts made by others, not her own observations. She never kept a diary, and hardly ever wrote letters. Indeed, it was only rather late in her long life that she learned to read and write. Unlike her boisterous brother, Navis, she was reticent to talk about herself and when she did, her words (at least what we know of them) seemed quite guarded. So we may never really know why she did the things that she did. Why she made certain decisions. Or what she hoped to achieve by her actions.

The following, therefore, is a somewhat disjointed portrait. The manner of relating her life varies below from a distant or dry perspective to some personal narratives derived from her own words, with certain license taken by the narrator. But we have done our best to provide the most salient facts, at least, with a few descriptions, where possible, about her life, her thoughts and her feelings.

The Time Before Time and the Age of Strife
Lady Esildre was one of the Firstborn of the Elifaen, daughter of Banis and Tiryna of the House of Elmwood, sister to Atlana and Navis. For a time, she was infatuated with Parthais, son of Cupeldain,

and in order to be with him, she refused to depart with Aperion and was Scathed of her wings. When she fell to the earth, it was many leagues from where Parthais fell, and the two would remain separated for many years. As did the rest of the Elifaen, Esildre struggled to overcome the hardships of her new existence.

The First Age

When at last Esildre and Parthais were reunited, Esildre quickly became disenchanted with his desire to make his House of Fairlinden supreme over all other Elifaen Houses. Parthais sought every opportunity to increase the power and authority of his father, Cupeldain. However, many Elifaen held a deep grudge against Cupeldain for his role in their downfall. Esildre was one of these, and she was suspicious and wary of Parthais. But her father, Banis, courted Cupeldain's favor, and he was dismayed when he learned that Esildre no longer sought favor with Parthais.

"Do you not know that, if you joined in union with Parthais, our own House would benefit?" he argued. "Do you blame his father for our condition?"

"Yes, father. That I know," she said. "But I do not love Parthais, and he does not love me. Parthais has become an irksome shadow of his father, always recruiting others in support of the House of Fairlinden, always nudging his father to wrest power, territory, and authority from others."

"I think you blame Parthais for the loss of our wings," said Banis.

"He is not entirely to blame. Nor is his father," she answered. "They but ignited a passion of hatred, the fuel of which was already prepared in our hearts. I am to blame for the loss of my wings, and you for yours, and every Elifaen likewise. I love you, my father, and I know of your loneliness without Mother. But she is with Aperion and we are not. She enjoys his guidance and compassion, but who may guide us? Who would have compassion for us? Who is to blame? Perhaps that is the wrong question. Perhaps the right questions have been lost to us, and so the answers, just as our wings are lost. Perhaps the words we now use cannot suffice for such. This language we now speak, an echo of how we once communed with the earth, is weak and faltering. All has become a great mystery. As if there is something we ought to know, but do not. Something we ought to remember, but cannot. Why do so few of us realize this? Feel this way? Parthais does not. And his heart no longer shines with the light that once drew me to him."

"My daughter," said Banis. "These are true words, surely, that you speak. But because others of our kind do not say them does not mean we do not think them. And who knows what may now come to pass? Surely our lot is a great struggle and not everyone will survive. Can you not see that I only want our own House, our family and our few followers and servants, to be safe? To have allies in a time of strife? We cannot and ought not hope and yearn for the return of our wings, for the return of life as it once was when the days were not counted and the seasons were all one and the same. That is gone. We must look to the present and to the future. That is now our lot and our fate and our challenge."

"Yes, I do understand that," Esildre agreed. "But how we do those things is what matters now. I will not seek the affection of Parthais. But I will not interfere with your efforts to curry his favor or that of his father Cupeldain. It was my mistake to remain here and to lose my wings. It was my mistake to be blinded by infatuation. I will strive not to make that mistake again, but if I do, the consequences surely cannot be as great as what I have already suffered. Aperion gave our people the way to redemption, but I do not see any desire among us to act upon his gift, to use the Bloodcoins as they were intended. So, as we all must, I must make my own way, my own life, for however long I live."

The subject was closed, and Lord Banis never again mentioned the matter to Esildre. Nor did he encourage his other daughter, Atlana, in such a manner.

Eventually, a ruler did emerge. It was Silmain who consolidated enough power to make himself king. "First King of the Faere" is what he called himself, a title that angered and insulted many Elifaen. But Silmain situated himself in the city of Linlally, and he made the great White Palace his home. Cupeldain threw his support behind Silmain, and he worked to rebuild Linlally and to make the palace a suitable place for people who had to move by using their feet instead of with wings. Many other Elifaen Houses allied themselves with Silmain, including the House of Elmwood. For her part, Esildre was relieved that Silmain was king instead of Cupeldain, for she feared what Parthais might do should he gain even more power. Meanwhile, there were enemies that had to be dealt with and defended against. So Esildre took up a new sword.

During the time of Silmain, Esildre and her brother Navis participated in many campaigns against the Dragonkind, and they earned reputations as fierce and merciless warriors. Navis was the more hot-headed of the two, and Esildre often had to sway him from risky adventures. When Navis desired to realign the House of Hemlock with that of Ormace's House of Fairbirch, both Esildre and her father opposed the idea, saying that Ormace was unwise and foolhardy in his ambitions, and that Fairbirch and Cupeldain's House of Fairlinden were at odds. To throw their support to Ormace could not but be interpreted as an insult, if not treason, by Silmain and Cupeldain. And Ormace had not the power nor the influence to prevent any retaliation that such a move might prompt. Navis was eventually made to understand this, and with Esildre's constant coaxing, he abandoned his desire to by an ally of Ormace.

Years later, during the battle against the Dragonkind in which Silmain was killed, Navis and Esildre saw for themselves how incompetent Ormace was, and they blamed him for failure to protect Silmain's flank. Things instantly escalated, and words flew hot and piercing. Cupeldain himself had to intervene to prevent a what would have been a violent feud between the House of Fairbirch and that of Elmwood. A feud that he feared would draw in many other Houses, including his own. It also threatened to turn Cupeldain against his own son, for Parthais was fanning the passions between Navis and Ormace, and was encouraging them to resolve things by taking up arms. Cupeldain angrily commanded Parthais to hold his tongue and to have nothing to do with either feuding House, even though he felt that Ormace was, indeed, to blame for Silmain's death.

Cupeldain arranged for all parties to meet under his protection to resolve things once and for all. Navis, Esildre, and Banis attended. Ormace came, too, attended by many of his warriors. But Cupeldain's soldiers outnumbered all and made certain that no violence took place. Many others came, too, and Cupeldain addressed them all.

"Silmain was not only my King, he was my friend," he declared. "Under his authority, we were united against the Dragonkind. And under his rule, our lands have prospered, our towns and villages have prospered, too. And let me say that no one present here, save his two sons, Heneil and Pellen, regret and mourn Silmain's death more than I do. It makes me sad and angry and I struggle for words. Yet he died in battle. It was the Dragonkind that killed him. The Dragonkind, I say, and no one else. If anyone failed in their duty to Silmain, all of us failed likewise. If Ormace was unable to protect Silmain's flank, I, too, was unable to come quickly enough to his aid. So if anyone here blames Ormace or threatens Ormace with violence or retaliation for Silmain's death, then I, too, must be blamed and threatened, as many of you must be likewise."

Cupeldain then ordered that all parties present put their names and to a written vow, and to say the vow aloud, that they, each and every one, have some blame for the turn of events and that, forthwith, each and every one will refrain from insulting any other concerning Silmain. Afterwards, Cupeldain spoke again.

"I will enforce this pact," he said. "The House of Fairlinden will take up the sword against any who break it. Any Elifaen House named in this pact that turns against another will suffer utter destruction! So let us go hence from here untied against our common enemy, the Dragonkind. Against those who slew our king."

"Who will be king now?" cried Navis. "Will you not take the throne, Lord Cupeldain? Will you not be our leader against the Dragonkind?"

"No. I will not be King. My eye is upon the south, upon our enemies. Decide amongst you who will be King. But consider not the House of Fairlinden!"

"Father," said Parthais to Cupeldain so that others could not hear, "you are needed! Only our House has the power to rule and reside over others! Without us, there will be discord among our people. What other House can unite us? If we are not united, our enemies will be encouraged by our discord. And surely it is your right and your destiny as keeper of the Seven from Aperion!"

"Say no more, Parthais," replied Cupeldain. "I will not hear of it from you."

Esildre, who was close by and who heard this exchange, clearly saw that Parthais was angry and impatient with Cupeldain. Looking about, she could also see that many others present had expressions of discontent, in spite of the pact they had just made.

"My lord," she said, somewhat reluctantly, "hear, then, from me. Will ink and parchment suffice to quell passion? Will words said aloud be enough to stifle resentment, and to forestay confrontation? You may enforce our pact, but who may guide and advise us in the obedience of our agreements? Who is there, but you, to take Silmain's place, and to give us order under law?"

"I think it is not for me," said Cupeldain. Then, loudly, he proclaimed, "I go to the Dragonlands! I go with my sword to confront the Dragonkind that now come through the mountains and strike our towns and our people. I go to smite the enemy, to cast him out from our lands, and to push him far back into his own lands. And if sufficient of you come with me, together we will destroy the Dragonkind!

"I shall go with you!" cried Navis, stepping forward.

"I, too, shall come," cried Lord Marhew of the House of Fairoak.

"And I!"

"We, too, shall come!"

In spite of his reluctance, this was, in fact, the beginning of Cupeldain's path to the throne of Vanara. He led a massive army of Elifaen southward, splitting his forces east and west, pushing the Dragonkind out of the Blue Mountains and back into the deserts. But the Dragonkind were stubborn and courageous. They gave ground slowly, often bogging down Cupeldain's forces in slow sieges of well-fortified positions. But months turned to years, and the Dragonkind slowly yielded. Esildre and Navis fought side by side, each taking advantage of the other's fighting skill. Navis was strong and heavy, and whenever he could he used his weight to simply crash through Dragonkind shields. Directly behind him came Esildre, lithe, lovely, and lethal. Rarely carrying a shield, she instead spun and whirled with fighting dagger and sword, moving so that arrows bounced from her armor, so that Dragonkind fell away from her slices and lunges like wheat from the scythe. She found that she was good at killing, and that when the fight was on, killing was easy, easier than thinking, easier than breathing. After each victorious battle, she would wonder at her abilities, at her cold-hearted lack of mercy. And when things were quiet, when she was alone with her thoughts, she worried about her ruthlessness. And she worried about those around her, her comrades in arms. But she said nothing. Not even to her brother. And for his part, Navis reveled in the fight, and he seemed to experience a kind of ecstasy that beamed from his face, that glinted from his eyes, that terrified Esildre.

While all this fighting was going on in the south, things were sinking into chaos back home in Linlally. In spite of the pact, factions of Elifaen feuded with each other over land, over who had authority, over just about everything. Chance encounters turned into deadly fights. Murder and kidnapping were rampant. And Silmain's law was ignored. Many an entreaty was sent to Cupeldain, begging him to return with his army, to quell the fighting by dint of his power, and to take the throne of Vanara. Whenever word spread in Vanara that Cupeldain might return, the violence died somewhat, since many rightly feared Cupeldain's might. But Cupeldain was skeptical of the news that came to him. He ignored many reports, thinking that they were politically motivated. Instead, he turned his attention back to the Dragonkind. Eventually, violence would again beset Vanara, and more appeals would be made to Cupeldain. At last, Cupeldain sent for

Esildre to come to him secretly, late one night when all in his encampment were a-slumber. When she came into Cupeldain's tent, she saw a weary and agitated leader sitting before a large table covered with letters, maps, and scrolls.

"My lord, I have come," she said.

Cupeldain stood and nodded. Then he dismissed her escorts.

"Will you take a cup of wine with me?"

"Certainly, my lord."

As he poured, he asked, "Does anyone know that you have come to me?"

"Only the escorts who brought me here. Navis was away when they came to fetch me, and my servants, save one, were fast asleep. But she only wakened me and does not know where it was that I was summoned to go."

"Good."

She took a goblet and drank as Cupeldain did. Then he motioned her to sit, and he took a chair nearby.

"I trust you," he said. "I trust you because you are fair-minded. Because I have heard that you care not for my power, and that you do not contrive with my son Parthais to increase the authority of my House."

"That is so, my lord."

"I asked you here so that I might ask for your help."

"I will do what I can, my lord."

"I grow concerned over conditions in our homeland. No doubt you are aware of the spreading chaos in Linlally, the feuds and rivalries."

"Yes. I, too, am worried."

"These past many years, we have been fairly successful in ousting the Dragonkind from our lands. But it has not brought peace at home."

"That seems to be so."

"I have rebuffed many entreaties, entreaties brought to me by emissaries of one House or another, begging me to march on Linlally and take Vanara by force. But some of those entreaties are motivated by the hope that I will favor some House or faction over another. Indeed, I have had very much the same requests brought to me by Houses on opposite sides of the latest feuds. So I do not trust the news they bring to me. My own agents, sent to gather news for me, have returned with much the same tidings. But my servants are biased and would have me be King."

Esildre sipped, listening.

"I want you to be my eyes upon Vanara. I want you to go and see for yourself how things are. I want you to be my ears, too, in as much as you can. Listen to the complaints of our people. Hear the contentions of the Elifaen Houses that are in conflict. See how things are, and how Vanarans fare with one another. Then, when you are satisfied that you have seen and heard enough to know, bring your tidings to me. That is all I ask. But it is much."

"It seems easy enough, Lord Cupeldain."

"I do not wish for it to be known that I send you," he stated. "I beg you not to reveal why you go, why you watch and listen, or to whom you bring word of such things. I fear that if it becomes known that you come on my behalf, then people will skew what they say one way or another in order to influence you and, through you, influence me. Do you understand, Esildre?"

"I do," she said. "But it seems to me that there are many here among us that could serve you better. I am not well known, nor is my House of Elmwood very influential."

"That is why I think many different sides can trust you," Cupeldain countered. "Because the House of Elmwood is small and almost entirely devoid of power, few will feel threatened by you and may speak and act more frankly than otherwise. And I wish you to be my agent because this may be a dangerous mission. You might be required to enter the very dens of murderers and assassins. And if one side learns that you have visited with their foes, you may have to defend your life. So, if you agree to do this, I beg you sleep where you cannot be disturbed, and even then with your dagger in your hand."

"My father and my sister are in Vanara," Esildre said, standing and putting her goblet on the table. "So I shall go on the pretense that I miss their company and wish to visit them. Which, for what it is worth, is not false, for I do long to see them, and to see my nieces and nephews as well."

"Then go as soon as you can," said Cupeldain, putting his goblet aside and bowing to Esildre. "Stay as long as is required, but return with all speed. I shall be patient, but I shall not rest easy in the meanwhile."

Esildre did as Cupeldain requested. She traveled to Vanara, stopping first at her sister's estate near Ladentree. While there, she learned of the dangerous and unpredictable conditions surrounding Linlally. Her sister, Atlana, who had learned to read and to write, corresponded by letter with many friends, and so she had gathered a great deal of news. Their father, Esildre learned, sought to avoid confrontation and was far away from the unrest and intrigues of Linlally. In his most recent letter to Atlana, only a month old, he said that he had located a very small island surrounded by a mountain lake that he was surveying, perhaps to build a castle upon it. Being quite wealthy, he had also engaged a small army of mercenaries to safeguard the region.

With that news, Esildre then traveled onward to Linlally. What Esildre soon learned, added to that which Atlana had told her, made her fear for all the Elifaen of Vanara. Violence was everywhere. Bands of highwaymen waylaid travelers. Street fights in Linlally escalated in small-scale battles, sometimes involving hundreds of fighters. Linlally was constantly in the throes of some riot or other. Shopkeepers could not safeguard their shops. Tradesmen could not work without fear for their families left at home. Farmers dared not come to market without guards to protect them. Poverty as a result of violence only fed more violence. Several times, as she went from place to place, Esildre had to defend herself against attackers who sprang from alleys or stalked her. Most of them only wanted her purse, but a few, embolden by their numbers, sought to rape her. She had no trouble dispatching them, and their bodies joined the many others that were unburied, littering the streets and byways. Everywhere there were damaged or abandoned buildings and homes, some having been burned, others with their doors knocked off their hinges. Riderless horses and buckmarls, many still saddled, wandered the streets seeking food and water. And she even saw wolves.

Her progress, therefore, was slow. She visited every ale room and tavern that she could. She drank with men who were certain to be dead by morning. She invited herself into the homes of acquaintances, and she listened to wives and widows and orphans. Back and forth she went over the course of nearly a month, slowly making her way through the city of Linlally. And so, she at last came before the great Falls of Tiandari. Surrounding the lake side were many homeless, sheltering as well as they could in makeshift tents or under tattered and dirty blankets. But at least there was clean water, she thought, making her way carefully through the encampment. The grand park nearby to the lake was likewise full of the homeless and the abandoned. Their faces were blank, more akin to stone than the wondrous statues of Alonair that dotted the grounds, statues so lifelike and alluring, but more alive, it seemed, than the people huddled amongst them.

It was strange to see so many strong Elifaen so devoid of vigor, so grief-stricken and fearful that their youthful bodies seemed somehow withered, somehow ill, like horses or cattle might become. But what illness could affect an immortal? Esildre knew: Hopelessness. Despair. Grief. Fear.

She wandered through the destitute crowds around the lake and grand monuments, all alike coated with the mists of the great falls, she stopped at a makeshift tent, outside of which sat a woman, pale and thin, in tattered clothes, holding a babe.

"Why is it that you remain here, at this place?"

"Why here?" the lady responded. "Because we have water. Because it is here, beneath the high White Palace, that we may be the first to receive help and succor for our condition. That we may receive redress for the wrongs we have suffered."

"Help from who?" Esildre asked. "Redress from who?"

"Anyone. We once hoped Cupeldain would come. But now we do not care. Let Ormace have the throne, if he wants it. And let him have power over us and all others of Vanara! We care not as long as we can return to our homes and shops, to our families."

"Then who occupies the White Palace above?"

"Ormace is there. Or so we have heard. But so are other lords. I cannot say. But none have made any move to help any but members of their own Houses, or their own followers."

Esildre returned to Cupeldain, and he received her in the presence of his war council, and before them all she related all that she saw and heard. They listened, asked a few questions, and then Cupeldain spoke.

"I have made the mistake," he said, "of thinking better of Ormace and the others. Of thinking that, if I protected Vanara from the Dragonkind, such security would allow for right actions elsewhere. But I see that it is not enough. I tell you first, Esildre, the laws established by Silmain are not enough, by themselves, to make us united, nor to give peace or justice. I will go to Linlally. I will take Silmain's throne. I will serve Vanara and our people, and I shall seek to bring order, peace, and law to all our lands, to all our people."

This made many present very glad, not the least Parthais, and immediately they began making their plans, ordering their troops, and preparing for the return to Linlally. In two days, they were on the move. Messengers were sent ahead to tell of their approach, to implore any who were willing to join with Cupeldain, and to warn all that Cupeldain's intention was to impose law, punish wrongdoers, and reform all bodies of governing. Esildre, who rode ahead as one of Cupeldain's scouts, saw for herself the effect of all this. Thousands of Elifaen flocked to join Cupeldain, and village after village along the way celebrated their arrival. By the time they reached the outskirts of Linlally, Cupeldain's host numbered some two hundred thousand men and women, most of whom were armed in some way, and the van of this procession was even larger. Even more thronged from the city to meet them. Among those who came were many lords, including Ormace, who knew they were over matched, to give their oaths of loyalty. And, of course, many thousands fled away, fearing the justice and the retribution that was their due.

And so Cupeldain became King of Vanara, and Esildre was present when the crown of Silmain was placed on his head and when he first took his seat upon the throne.

Cupeldain

After Cupeldain became King of Vanara, Esildre continued to fight as part of his Fellfaere armies, and when she was not deployed, she was often seen in Cupeldain's court. Her cousin, Shevalia, was a close friend of Cupeldain's wife, Queen Loura, and the three ladies spent a great deal of time together. And indeed, much changed in Vanara under Cupeldain. It was not always easy, nor always swift, but as the years passed, Vanara became safer, more peaceful, more prosperous, and more just. Esildre had few duties of the soldierly nature during these times and, according to Raynor, she considered these to be the happiest years of her life. She grew close to Loura and Shevalia, and became friends with Serith Ellen, daughter of Parthais. Esildre, though not as sophisticated as the other ladies, was made to feel so at home and comfortable with them that she was seldom far from their company. Serith Ellyn would comment many years later that Esildre actually brought much humor and laughter into the group, and she even taught Serith Ellyn the art of playing the lyre, along with some of the rather lewd songs that the soldiers sang in barracks and taverns.

But all was not perfectly peaceful in the lands, for a great feud, brewing for decades, finally erupted in the lands across the Iridelin. Each of the warring clans sought to draw Cupeldain into the conflict on their side, but the King steadfastly remained neutral. But he also worked diligently to resolve the conflict, receiving representatives from the conflicting sides to hear their complaints and to listen to their grievances and allegations and to seek solutions that would bring peace. At last, he succeeded in brokering a cessation to hostilities, agreeing with all parties to act as a fair enforcer of peace and just arbitration of any disputes. When all was ready, Cupeldain departed Linlally on a mission of goodwill to seal the agreements and encourage cooperation. Esildre was at first assigned to accompany Cupeldain's small party, but at the last moment she was reassigned to train new recruits to the Fellfaere, which required her to remain in Linlally. She happened to be present when Parthais received the terrible news that his parents and all in their party had been murdered, and Esildre accompanied Parthais as part of a large army he led to the scene of the crimes. There, she was shocked and dismayed at the cruelty with which Parthais exacted punishment, executing the innocent along with the guilty, but she did not dare contradict Parthais.

Glareth

Unlike his father, Parthais did not have widespread support of the Elifaen at first, and his ascent to the throne was delayed by wrangling, with various Houses vying to secure their positions or to make gains. During these years, war broke out between Masurthia and Altoria over lands bordering the River Wachee. This eventually disrupted Vanaran trade so severely that Parthais marched into those lands to quell the fighting and to force the warring sides to a settlement. Esildre did not go with him, as she was on station in Ladentree to guard the trade routes between Ladentree and the Free City. But all the while, Esildre remained troubled over Cupeldain's death, and the death of her dear friends. At last, Parthais returned to Vanara and was duly crowned king. But Esildre found herself much distracted by her grief from performing her duties. When on leave to Linlally, she begged to be released from duty, saying she wished for some time to ponder her grief, perhaps while roaming eastward to Glareth. Parthais granted her request.

"Let us part in good will, then," said Parthais. "And do me a small service, if you would be so kind. Go to Glareth, and carry for me a few missives that I send to the House of Walnut. I give them, too, a note of introduction for you so that they might afford you welcome. Walnut and Fairlinden are fast friends, although far apart, and I'm sure that you receive from them all hospitality as their guest. And, to offset any discomforts along the way, I give you a small purse to use as you wish, needing return none to me."

"That is most generous, Sire," said Esildre. "I shall do as you ask and deliver your missives directly upon my arrival in Glareth, be it day or night."

And so Esildre departed Linlally alone upon her buckmarl. She traveled at a leisurely pace along the forest road that wound northward through the mountains, tracing its way through canyons and beside streams until at last she arrived at Averstone. From there, she took the westerly path to her father's castle that was nigh upon completion. The location used for the castle was a small rocky island that jutted up in the center of a cold mountain lake. There was no bridge and the only way to approach was by a ferry linked to the castle landing by a long thick cable, pulled by able ferrymen. It would be a difficult place to assail, she saw, with high sheer cliffs that transitioned upward to form the foundation and of the castle.

When the barge landed, she was shown through a fortified portal carved into the rock and into a carved gallery for stores. Then she was shown the way up many flights of stairs, ascending higher and higher until at last she was brought into an anteroom. She could hear voices from the room adjacent. She recognized that of her father, but not the other voices, one of which was ordinary. But the other voice was strange, almost a loud whisper. She knocked, and from within she immediately heard a sound not unlike that of rushing air.

"Come!"

When she entered, Banis was pulling open some heavy curtains on the far window while another man was lighting lamps and candles. She wondered why they had been in a darkened room, but before she could express her surprise, she was greeted.

"Esildre! My pet!" cried Banis with a wide smile as he came to give her a hug. "Such a pleasant surprise! I was not expecting you."

Pleasant or not, Esildre had the distinct impression that she had interrupted some business. Looking around, she did not see the source of that odd third voice.

"Allow me to introduce you to an associate. Delcorman, this is my daughter Esildre. Esildre, this is Delcorman, on business here from Duinnor town."

"My very great pleasure," said Delcorman, bowing as he took Esildre's hand. "Much have I been told concerning your prowess at arms. But if it is but half as great as your beauty, then it is surely prodigious."

Esildre smiled politely, saying, "You flatter me. And people exaggerate, one way or the other, when telling tales."

"Surely. But I now doubt little that which has been told to me."

"So, are you the only visitor at Castle Elmwood today?" she asked, glancing around. "I thought I heard more people as I came to the door."

"Oh, yes. I have come alone."

"Perhaps a trick of an airy draft," said Banis with a slight gesture at the window.

"As our business is concluded," said Delcorman, "I will bid you adieu and be on my way."

"Very well, then," said Banis. "I thank you for attending to matters so expeditiously."

"My pleasure."

The two men shook hands. Then Delcorman bowed to Esildre and departed.

"So, my dear! What do you think of our castle?" asked Banis, motioning Esildre to a couch.

"A very strong position, in terms of its defensive placement. It would be quite difficult to assail, certainly. But just as difficult to supply, being not only on this island, but also in a remote region, far from provisions. Will not the roads and paths be inaccessible to snow for much of the year?"

"Yes, that is so. But as you may have seen upon entering, there is ample storage for a prodigious stock of provisions. Fresh, clean water all around, too. Late summer and early autumn will be busy times for resupplying, but Averstone, though small, is adequately situated nearby for use as a waypoint, and the north-south road passing through it is well attended and maintained."

"And as for the occupants? Will you be acquiring men-at-arms?"

"Not unless necessary," said Banis. "Except for a few household staff, I merely intend this to be a home. My agents in Vanara and elsewhere will give ample warning of any threats, in time to do what may be necessary for our defense."

"Are you still wary of Parthais?"

"I am wary. But not alarmed. Let us say that I am only being prudent and watchful."

"He is the reason I am here," continued Esildre. "As you know, I was severely shaken by the deaths of my friends, Shevalia and the others. And distracted enough to ask for a leave of absence from the Fellfaere. Parthais granted it to me and commissioned me to travel at my leisure to Glareth by the Sea, to deliver missives from him to the House of Walnut. Before departing, I wanted to visit you and see the progress of Castle Elmwood."

"Ah, well. Parthais apparently trusts you more than he does me! I am glad to know that our relationship has not tainted yours. To Glareth, then? The House of Walnut. Yes, Walnut is closely aligned with Fairlinden, or was in times past. Many say that it is through Walnut that Parthais keeps a watchful eye on Glareth and its rulers. And that Walnut has aspirations for greater power in that realm than it presently enjoys."

"So I should tread carefully."

"Indeed."

"I hope also to see Lucinda. It has been many years since I last saw her, before she departed for Glareth, and we hear so little about her. But she was very kind to me after Shevalia's death."

"Well, it might do the both of you good, then, to share good company for a while. Will Navis accompany you?"

"No, he remains in the Blue Mountains. I shall travel alone."

Banis seemed a bit distracted all throughout Esildre's stay, so much so that the sense that she had somehow intruded upon some secret business grew in her heart and mind. She wondered what it might be, and about the third person that she was convinced lingered somewhere nearby, and about the darkness of the room in which the interrupted meeting took place. But she did not press for answers. As the minutes passed by, she felt more and more uncomfortable in her father's presence, until at last she resolved to depart right away.

"What? Won't you at least stay a few days?" Banis politely asked.

"No, Father. The sooner that I am on my way, the sooner I hope my anxieties will fall away."

And so it was. She departed Castle Elmwood, passed through Averstone, and took the north road. It was mid-spring, and the snow had all melted, the trees were leafing out, and all of the birds and animals were busy with song and chores. She almost immediately felt some weight drop from her heart, and she often had a sense of very pleasant déjà vu, even though she had never traveled this way before. She went along without hurry, stopping only when she felt the desire to ponder things or when her buckmarl needed rest.

"Something good may happen along this way," she said to her buckmarl one day. "To someone, if not to me."

She turned eastward at Minion Gap and left the forests behind and continued on across the Great Bletharn Plains until she was within sight of the Carthanes, then she turned northeast to reach around Middlemount to the Osterflo. Thence she went by river road to Karthia and, once beyond the rapids, she and her buckmarl boarded a felucca to travel the rest of the way to Glareth.

She did not know what to expect. She had never been so far east, never seen any part of the Carthanes, the Osterflo, or Glareth Realm. But the great and dramatic beauty of the landscape awed her and filled her with wonder, perhaps even calm. The troubles of Vanara and the Dragonlands, of the court of Parthais, of the tragedies of violence and corruption and intrigue, piled century upon century, were all far away. No, she did not know what to expect, and there was a part of her that remained wary, alert, and considerate of what she might find in Glareth. But as she sailed across Salfin Bay and neared Glareth by the Sea, she was surprised by her own lack of great concern. She would see what there was to see, and take things as they came, she resolved.

To say that she was impressed by Glareth long before she landed at the city would be an understatement. The waters were busy with all manner of craft and commerce, from fishing vessels to trade ships to ferries, constantly moving hither and yon. Everywhere along the shore were docks and quays and wharves and warehouses. As she approached Glareth by the Sea, its graceful towers and palaces loomed above and behind the shoreline homes and places of commerce. Her boat, though not equipped for sea travel, rounded the tip of the long peninsula for which the city is named, and for the first time she saw the vastness of the Great Sea stretching out eastward to the horizon. Taking care to give much leeway, the boat passed almost a mile from the tip of Glareth by the Sea, and Esildre looked with wonder at the high sea-dashed cliffs upon which was the city itself, from edge to edge. Then they turned west again, entering a long bay to reach the home docks of the felucca where she and her buckmarl came ashore. It was by now mid-afternoon, and she engaged a guide to show her the way to the estate of the House of Walnut, some ten miles away in what was being called the "new" city.

Her reception at the House of Walnut was cordial and correct, but was not overly warm. Lord and Lady Tasliod smiled, and were generous enough to give Esildre the use of a guest suite situation on the guest wing of the estate house, as well as the service of attendants. And they gave no hint of any expectations of Esildre to keep company with them, nor any for her to attend them, even when dining. But they seemed distracted, not very social, and not at all interested in Esildre's travels, life, or impressions of things. In effect, Esildre was left to her own designs and plans during her stay, which suited her very well. So began her exploration of Glareth, sometimes wandering alone, following only her curiosity, sometimes accompanied by an attendant to show her the way. She was, for the most part, comfortable staying with at the House of Walnut, and only after the debacle described below did she find lodgings elsewhere. And so she saw the sights, visited the great palaces, looked upon the docks and ships, wandered the parks and gardens, and browsed the many wares, fine clothes, and goods made and sold in Glareth and those brought from far-off places.

For the first time, she saw a Man. In fact, she saw many Men. She was somewhat shocked, for many had beards that covered their faces. The various styles of beard trimming made them seem to Esildre bear-like, or goat-like, or sometimes like Dragonkind. They were pale, for the most part, and many had scars on their faces or arms from their hard work, or their fighting. When they laughed, they did so through a mouth often lacking in some teeth. When she first saw an old Man, she was deeply moved. He was so frail that he had to use a stick and be led by others due to his poor eyesight. His thin hair was white as snow, his beard, too, and his face was covered with wrinkles. Her thought was that life had injured him terribly, but as she learned more, and saw more Men, she came to understand how short their lives were, how frail they were, and yet, by all accounts, how determined they were to live as well as they could. From what she gathered, the settlements of the Newcomers were expanding rapidly all along the coasts and forests to the south. And although there was friction, even the occasional feud, between Men and Elifaen, the Men seemed eager to live in peace with the immortals they encountered.

She even had occasion to speak to a few of them. The Newcomers that she spoke with did so in the language of Glareth, but with their own way of pronouncing many words that was oddly and sometimes sing-song. She thought it odd that such unbecoming people in general spoke so beautifully. One day, while passing through a market, she came upon a group of Newcomers who were minstrels, singing and playing their instruments for whatever coin the passers-by might toss into a bucket. She lingered for a long time to hear them. They played stringed instruments they called "guitars," and some they called "violins," and also pipes and whistles, among others. Some of their songs were very lively and full of spirit and joy, but a few were haunting and sad, ballads of love, hardship, and mourning. Before leaving them, she took several gold coins from her purse and dropped them into their bucket. The refrains echoed in her mind for days afterwards, and she came to the conclusion that Men were just as capable of sadness and joy as anyone. And maybe more expressive of such things, at least in music, than were the Elifaen.

Among those in Glareth who were acquainted with Esildre was Lucinda of the House of Faircedar, who had fled Vanara to avoid persecution after the death of Cupeldain, which she constantly mourned, claiming that her House had nothing to do with his death. Esildre sought her out, and found Lucinda to be cordial, almost happy to receive the visitor, but was notably melancholy. Lucinda told Esildre that it was a terrible mistake that the Seven High Houses failed to use the Bloodcoins as they were intended, and that the strive that continued was a tragic and unnecessary result. Lucinda's estate in Glareth, located just inside the old city, was comfortable and grand, in its own way, although quite small. The House of Faircedar maintained its own full retinue of household staff, security guards, and the people of Walnut who lived throughout Glareth were productively engaged in business, commerce, and trade. By all accounts, her people enjoyed their lives in Glareth. With her two sons managing the affairs of Faircedar, the House and its people indeed prospered. King Gardin was glad to have them in Glareth, since they brought with them many skills, both in trades and in professions (such as alchemy, architecture, etc.), which they shared with Glarethians. The House of Faircedar also enjoyed a 50-year release from Gardin that allowed them to avoid many of the taxes and tributes normally expected of great estates, although this fact did cause some minor friction between Faircedar and many of the old Glarethian estates.

As for the Bloodcoins of the House of Faircedar, Esildre learned that one condition of the continuance of their special status in Glareth was for Lucinda to show her Bloodcoins to the King and his court once every two years. This was so that Glareth could rightly claim to be the home to such important objects of power. According to Lucinda, King Gardin never once even hinted at a desire to remove the Bloodcoins from her keeping, but he did promise the full support of Glareth for their security and continued safekeeping. It was on that account that the House of Walnut was granted the estate in the old city, due to its strong defenses.

Esildre visited often and attended many social events sponsored by Lucinda's House, so she became a familiar face to Faircedar's people.

And so it was that Esildre could not help but notice the often comings and goings of Faircedar's captain of the guard to and from the Walnut estate. From the first, she felt it odd, but said nothing for several weeks.

"Is that Captain Sequis, of Faircedar, that I saw just now entering the courtyard, and whom I have before seen at a distance at odd hours?" she at last asked her maid.

"Maybe it was, madam."

"I think that it was. And this time, as on all previous occasions, I have seen him cross through the garden path in a stealthy manner to the side door just across from my window, at the far side. And twice I have seen him depart from that door, with adieus to Lady Tasliod."

"Well," said the maid, coming close and speaking in a whisper, "as it happens, I shall tell you. But you mustn't say to anyone what it is that I have to impart to you. It is this: Lady Tasliod and Captain Sequis are having an affair."

"I hardly think so!"

"Aye, madam! That's what I said, too, when first I was told."

"Though he is strong in appearance," Esildre stated, "tall and broad of shoulder, I would not call him handsome at all. And as I myself have spoken with him, I would not say that he is either charming, or witty, or even very friendly of manner. I simply cannot conceive of any attraction Lady Tasliod might have for him."

"T'is more the wonder, too," said the maid. "For the Lady is so very pretty and vivacious and charming in every way."

"And," Esildre went on, "I have never seen them greet or part company in the way that lovers might do. No kiss. No embrace. No hand-holding. Lady Tasliod never seems glad upon his arrival nor sorry at his departure."

"That's just it," replied the maid. "They hide it marvelously well! As unlikely a pair as ever would be imagined. In appearance, in wit, and in charm they are as distant as sunrise and sunset!"

"Indeed."

"But it is so! It could hardly escape the notice of the gardener, who is my uncle, or the night butler, who is my cousin, nor the footman who takes the captain's reins and gives them back, who is my nephew. In fact, the whole of the household knows of it and keeps the Lady's secret, even though we cannot understand how it is kept from Lord Carras. For the captain and the Lady take no pains to conceal their company once he comes within the house itself. But out and about, they act as if they hardly know each other."

"Oh? Is that so?"

"They would not, and do not, even seem to recognize each other, so I hear, when they happen upon one another in town."

"I see. It is all very odd."

The following day, Esildre made a point to call on Lucinda, and on the way there, she considered how she might bring up the matter of Sequis and Lady Tasliod. Or whether she even ought to do so.

When she arrived and was shown through, Esildre found Lucinda in a state of absolute fury. Ryan, Lucinda's eldest, was just leaving his mother's chambers when Esildre arrived.

"Oh, Lady Esildre!" he said, rushing to her. "I am so relieved by your visit. Perhaps you might calm Mother. She is in such a state!"

"What has happened?"

"We have just learned that there is a rumor that she, or rather our House of Faircedar is the target of the many malicious tabloids that have been posted around and about the city."

"What tabloids?"

Just then, Captain Sequis emerged from Lucinda's chambers, somewhat red-faced, clutching a wad of parchment.

"Ah, Captain. Show Lady Esildre the tabloid you have there."

"Yes, my lord. My lady. Here it is."

Esildre glanced through the doorway as she took the large document and saw Lucinda being embraced by her daughter while her other son stared into the crackling hearth. Then a servant closed the door.

"Captain, please tell Lady Esildre what you just related to us."

"Very well. This tabloid I found late last night, nailed to a tree outside the Royal Palace. Copies have been turning up all day, all over the city. As fast as we pull them down, more appear elsewhere."

Esildre nodded as she opened the sheet and looked at it.

"I am sorry, but could you please read it to me? I cannot make out this script."

In truth, Esildre could not read, which was not unusual among the Elifaen, and Ryan was familiar with the courtesy that required Esildre to make an excuse and dictated Ryan's own response.

"Yes, of course," Ryan said. "The spelling is atrocious, and the script is hurriedly crude. Allow me."

Take Notice All ye Guyd Loyall Sitzens of Glareth!!
A Witch and a Snak hath come amongst us
To Maketh Diskord and to bringe fowell harm to Owere Fayer King
And to Owere Prinz.
Beewayr, the tree what sheds not its green in Wyntur!!

"It is a thinly veiled hint," concluded Ryan, "that this House of Faircedar—a tree that sheds not its green in winter—threatens the King and his family."

"So it seems. And who is the author of these lies?"

"We cannot even guess!" said Ryan. "We have made no enemies here. We threaten no one! And we have received good welcome from the King and all his family."

"If we were in Vanara, we would have no shortage of suspects," said Sequis.

"But we are not. And surely we are beyond the care, if not the reach, of Fairlinden," stated Ryan.

"Please excuse me, my lord, my lady," said Sequis. "But I must see to my men, who are scurrying about hither and yon in search of these articles of trash."

"Surely if the people of Glareth saw men in the livery of Faircedar going about tearing these down, it would raise greater suspicion."

"Indeed, Lady Esildre," said Sequis. "That is why they have been ordered to wear their common plain clothing today. Please excuse me a moment."

Ryan and Esildre watched Sequis as he departed, and Esildre was suddenly more hesitant than ever to ask about Captain Sequis.

"This is perhaps not a good time for me to visit, after all," she said.

"Oh," said Ryan. "But I was hoping a calm word of reassurance from you might help settle her emotions."

"Sequis said that he found this tabloid last night, did he not?   At the palace?"

"That is so."

"And he had business at the palace?"

"Indeed, he did. There are many Vanarans lately come to Glareth, and the First Lord invited all head captains and chief watchmen of Vanaran families and Houses to dine at the palace. To be addressed by Prince Thalamir."

"Oh?"

"Yes, it is a rather routine event. The prince wishes all to be familiar with the laws and practices of Glareth as they differ in many respects from those of Vanara and elsewhere."

"I see. And Sequis reported what he found upon leaving the palace? Reported it right away? Last night?"

"No. He said that he did not wish to alarm us until he had investigated further. He reported this morning after finding several more examples of this posting, and after ordering some of our guard out to search for others. They found them in places where many people pass, along streets, in markets, and such."

Esildre thought for a moment, then nodded.

"I should go."

"Will you not speak to Mother?   It is awful to see her in such distress!"

"I do not think that I have the words to calm her. And she is right to be distressed. Do not belittle her concern or her alarm. Do not be too trusting, either, of those around you. This is obviously a planned and intentional work of some enemy of Faircedar. Cast your scrutiny near and far."

"What do you mean? Why do you say that? Of whom do you speak?"

"I will not say more until I have more to say. But be cautious   Stay close to you mother. For my part, I shall look, too, and see what is to observe. And I shall endeavor to return tomorrow with more to say."

"You make me more apprehensive."

"Good. Turn your apprehension into caution."

Esildre departed and walked briskly back the way she came. She did not take a carriage, but preferred to watch for any of the same tabloids as the one she was shown. She saw none, though. At last, as she approached the side gate which she normally used to come and go from the estate of Walnut, she saw four men making their exit. They did not see her, and she instinctively stepped aside into the cover of some tall shrubs. She stood still and silent as they approached and passed by. They were jovial, carrying on, and joking about. Esildre thought they had the look of mercenaries, dressed in leather and bearing swords and daggers at their belts. But what struck her as very odd was that each of them carried a bundle of what appeared to be laundry or clothing of some sort. Just as they neared Esildre's hiding place, they paused and broke into laughter, one of the men giving another a good-natured shove. The recipient laughed, too, but nearly tripped as he attempted to shove back, but he only managed to fumble his bundle. He quickly gathered it back together, but not before Esildre saw a portion of a purple frock-coat with a gold tree embroidered upon it. A cedar tree.

The men went on along their way, and when they were out of sight, Esildre emerged and continued her own way toward her guest entrance. She hesitated, her hand on the door pull, realizing the meaning of the things she had heard and seen. Captain Sequis was conspiring with the House of Walnut. He was likely responsible for the posters denouncing Faircedar, in spite of his sworn fealty. And since he had ordered his men to go about without uniforms, it was an easy matter to steal a few and to deliver them to Lady Tasliod. Esildre then wondered about the letters that she herself had delivered from Parthais. Could it be that Walnut was doing the bidding of a spiteful monarch?   That

Parthais was kind to Esildre only so that a secure means of delivery could be secured?   Her mind quickly went over what she knew of Parthais and his late actions, his temperament, and his aims. It all fit. He wanted Lucinda to return to Vanara. He wanted her Bloodcoins most of all.

Esildre turned about abruptly and looked toward the path.

"I let them pass," she muttered. "And those men will do some mischief in sight of others to cast more disdain and suspicion upon Faircedar. I should have challenged them!   I should have thought faster!   I should have stopped them!"

She walked swiftly, almost at a jog, the way she had come. Once along the streets, she hailed a carriage and went straight back to Lucinda's home. She found the place abuzz, with a great many people coming and going, with additional guards posted all around the grounds that bordered Lucinda's estate. But she was allowed to pass without question, and she quickly made her way to the manor. There, on the front steps, she found Ryan and his brother Jarvis, who were chatting. When they saw her, they hurried down to meet her.

"You are back so soon! You must have news, then?"

"You appear quite agitated," said Jarvis.

"I have no real news, only strong suspicions," she said. "I beg to speak with you and with Lady Lucinda in private."

Seeing the urgency in her expression, they immediately led her inside and to Lucinda's chambers. They entered and Jarvis closed the door behind them. Lucinda immediately started up from her seat and approached.

"Lady Esildre!   You have chosen an ill day to visit, as we are quite distracted by a most disturbing turn of events. How shall I explain?   Where shall I begin?"

"Mother," said Ryan, "this is Lady Esildre's second visit to us this day. You were in such distress upon her first visit that she begged pardon to leave you undistracted by her. Nonetheless, Captain Sequis and I both spoke with Lady Esildre and conveyed to her the reasons for our disquiet, our distress and confusion. She saw for herself an example of the slander against us."

"Upon further thought and consideration," Esildre immediately picked up, "I have come to beg you to withdraw all of your guard and men and servants who have gone forth from your estate. Those who search for tabloids, and all members of your House who might be beyond the bounds of your estate. Send word immediately to recall everyone most urgently, putting aside all their activities. Muster all and make an account of them all to know if any are absent from you. Further, I beg you, have all of your House attired in their proper livery and uniforms so that you may know all who stand with you during this dark time."

Jarvis was already pulling the bell rope, and in but a moment there was a tap on the door. Jarvis went and spoke first with Lucinda's lady's maid, then he stepped into the hall to speak to others. He returned quickly.

"It is being done," he said.

"Why?' Lucinda asked. "You fear for our safety?"

"Only insofar as some rabble might be stirred to rash actions," Esildre answered. "My greater fear is that Parthais reaches from afar to work against you, perhaps in an effort to make you inclined to return to Vanara."

"Parthais!" Ryan uttered. "Many missives from him have we received from him on just such a topic. He has made entreaties, offers of wealth and station, and even a few veiled threats to us."

"Never did a fruit fall so far from the tree!" declared Jarvis. "But what reason do you have for suspecting that he is behind these rumors and accusations against us?"

"I have no evidence," said Esildre. "But that may be forthcoming as things develop further.

"But you think our people are at risk of harm?"

"Yes, harm. Or the risk of blame for something not of their doing. The tabloids are, I think, a way of preparing the kindling, so to speak, for a fire about to be lit."

"Well," said Jarvis, "our people have been summoned, and Captain Sequis, too, of course. But many of our House are out and about on business or errands, besides those who look for the tabloids. It may be some time before all are located and arrive back here. Our trusty footmen go forth to find them."

"The city is especially busy today," Ryan added, "so it may take some doing just to find everyone."

"Why?" Esildre asked. "What is happening today?"

"King Gardin passes the mantle of First Admiral to his son, Samis."

"A great procession of high lords and ladies goes forth with the King to the Admiralty, where the official ceremony is to take place."

"When?"

"The ceremony is to take place at mid-afternoon. So I imagine the procession has already started out from the palace. Wait! Where are you going?"

But Esildre was already through the door and was running swiftly along the street, dodging people and carts and carriages as she went across the city. She did not know what she would do, only at least try to warn the King. And as she ran, she became increasingly convinced that Gardin was in danger.

She at last caught up with the procession as it neared the Admiralty, and as she pushed through the throngs, she cast her eyes in every direction, looking for threats. Just as she burst through the cordon that kept back the cheering crowds, she saw movement along the roof of a building ahead and caught a glimpse men in the colors of Faircedar engaged in some work among scaffolding that ran up the building's side. Then, over the noise, she heard the sound of cranking mechanisms and cracking stone.

She shoved aside a Royal Guard, ran past the King's carriage toward the building with the scaffolding, and, shoving aside Guards that sought to remove her, she waved for the carriage to halt. But they came on, oblivious to her cries and warning. Several more guards came at her, grabbing her to drag her away as she backed up before the horses of the carriage. Then a loud bang resounded, followed by thundering cracks as the entire side of the building, just ahead, tottered and collapsed into the street, completely obliterating the way, killing and maiming dozens of spectators, and sending shards of rock, stone, and glass flying, bouncing, and rolling in every direction. Esildre was struck from behind by a beam of wood, sending her sprawling along with those she struggled with. The leading pair of horses pulling the carriage were knocked off their legs, and a cloud of dust choked the air. But the King was unscathed.

In the confusion that then took hold of the scene, many things happened. Esildre was dragged away under arrest. People, and the King himself, sprang into action to help the injured and to dig victims out of the rubble, while many others, thinking an earthquake must be taking place, fled.

Esildre yielded to her guards without struggle, biding her time until she could explain herself. She was taken this way and that by the confused guards until at last an officer took charge of the squad and ordered her taken to a nearby prison. There, she her wrists and ankles were quickly shackled to chains. She was shoved into a small cell, the door slammed shut, and the crossbar fell into place with a bang. And so she waited. Night fell, and it was nearly dawn before the door to her cell was thrown open. A jailer entered and lit the brazier within the cell and departed. Then King Gardin himself immediately entered, along with two guards, a scribe, the Captain of the Palace Guard, and three other officials. The king's robes were soiled and stained, there was blood on his sleeves, and his hands were cut and dirty.

"Remove the shackles," he ordered, and it was done. Esildre stood, then bowed.

"I am satisfied that you saved my life today," he said. "But my Captain, here, and my advisors wish to have your story before I release you."

"Yes, sire. I will tell all that I know, all that I saw, all that I heard."

And so Esildre began at the beginning, relating all pertaining to Parthais, the dispatches, the House of Walnut, Lucinda, and the Men that she saw. She told of the missing uniforms of the House of Faircedar, of the posters decrying Faircedar, and of her observations of Captain Sequis coming and going from the House of Walnut. All the while, Gardin and the others listened without interrupting her, and the scribes recorded what she said.

Gardin then turned to his captain.

"Does this satisfy you? Does not what she said align with your findings?"

"Yes, Your Highness. Our search revealed discarded uniforms nearby to the catastrophe. Our interview with Lucinda and her people confirm what Esildre has said. Captain Sequis cannot be located. Her story also bears out our investigations, already well advanced, into certain activities on the part of the House of Walnut. And we have tonight prevented Walnut from burning several documents, including the missive from Parthais. These are in a cypher that we seek to unravel, but will likely provide further evidence against Walnut."

"Then I order the immediate release of Esildre," the king said. Then, turning to her, he reached out for her hand and held it firmly. "I hope you will accept my apologies for your arrest and for any rough handling that you endured. I also hope that you will accept my deepest debt of gratitude to you for your actions today. I beg you to attend to me at the Palace on the day after tomorrow, when we convene to review and to begin our work to bring justice to those who died and who were injured this day, and reckoning to those responsible. What say you?"

"I would be honored to help Your Majesty in any way that I can. I am confident that justice will be done, that any blame or suspicion upon the House of Faircedar will be lifted. Sire, I also fear that the long hand of Parthais may do other things to disturb your peace and security."

Gardin nodded, but said nothing for a moment.

"I understand that your belongings remain at the House of Walnut. I would prefer that you relocate to the Palace as my guest for a time."

"Sire, I would be most happy and honored to be your guest."

Gardin turned to go, but hesitated before turning back once more.

"I feel I must ask you this openly: What are your ties with Parthais? What is your relationship with him?"

"Sire, Parthais is my king, king of my homeland, king of my people. In our traditions, we swear allegiance to the Throne of Vanara, not to he who may sit upon it. Many see them as one and the same. Many, such as I, do not. I knew Silmain. I knew Cupeldain. And, of course, I have known Parthais nearly all my life. Silmain and Cupeldain were kings, were leaders, of an entirely different order than is Parthais. Parthais may be my king, but I do not trust him. I do not agree with much that he does. And I do not trust those that surround him. I love my Vanara. I love my people. But I, and people like me, must tread carefully."

Gardin nodded again, "I see."

Then the king and his escorts departed, and Esildre was taken by carriage to gather her things from the House of Walnut, thence to the Palace where she was given a lavish suite overlooking the sea. Here, Esildre remained for several months while the courts conducted their inquiries. Walnut blatantly denied all allegations against them. But their work to cast blame on Lucinda continued unabated, and they spread lies and suspicions to divert the people's attention away from their own guilt. This did not influence those in power, but many Glarethians fell victim to the lies. There were continued protests against the House of Faircedar, and a few instances of vandalism. Soon, Lucinda did not feel safe in Glareth. The King of Masurthia, who wanted Lucinda's Bloodcoins for himself, sent emissaries to Lucinda offering safe passage by ship to Masurthia, a grand palace for a home, and lasting protection of the Masurthian crown. He never mentioned his lust for the Bloodcoins, of course. Eventually, his entreaties took effect, and against all advice from Esildre and from King

Gardin, she and almost all her household departed by ship for the long voyage to Masurthia. Indeed, this was their doom. Lucinda, her husband and children, and almost all that went with her would be lost, and her Bloodcoins, too.

For her part, Esildre grew restless, too. Rumors were reaching Glareth concerning Parthais's growing tyrannical ways. Vanarans, mostly scholars, were arriving each day seeking escape from his latest oppressions, which would become what was called the Purge of Scholars. At last, she made her desire to go home known to King Gardin, and he agreed to her departure, and by way of appreciation for her deeds and conduct, he awarded her a large sum of gold and jewels.

So Esildre, full of misgivings, returned to Vanara. She arrived in Vanara just as Parthais was gathering a great army to march into the deserts. Resuming her duties, she went with the Fellfaere to fight with her king. In the battle that developed at Tamkal Plain, Esildre and Navis fought together once more, seeing for themselves the duel between King Parthais and the Dragonkind King Salkasin. Although the Elifaen were victorious, and Salkasin was killed by Parthais, the price was high. More than two thousand Elifaen were killed, including Desira, who was Esildre's aunt (and Shevalia's mother). It was during this battle, though, that Esildre and Serith Ellyn, daughter of Parthais, became friends, each finding the other quite unlike their fathers.

The Downfall of Parthais

Not much is known about Esildre during the centuries that followed the battle at Tamkal Plain. However, she was in attendance at court when King Parthais received Elrasil the Hunter and heard his tale of Griferis. Esildre did not accompany the king and his party on their expedition to that place, although it is not known why. Upon their return, she was surprised at the change that had taken place in Parthais who had become moody and reclusive. Esildre was further alarmed when Parthais banished Serith Ellyn and her brother Thurdun. During the subsequent years, as Parthais became more tyrannical, Lord Banis, who had become a High Judge of Vanara, found it increasingly difficult to deal with Parthais, having many disputes with the king over various legal matters. Eventually, fearing for his life, Banis fled Linlally, taking Esildre and her brother Navis with him to their northern estate at Elmwood Castle. Atlana moved her family for a time to Airemoor. Banis often traveled from Elmwood Castle to Duinnor, and it was during one of these absences that Navis and Esildre received a mysterious guest who would not reveal his identity until they could meet in secret. It turned out to be Prince Thurdun who had come to ask Esildre and Navis to join with him in an attempt to overthrow Parthais and free their people from his tyranny. It was his intention, Thurdun said, to depose Parthais and put Serith Ellyn on the throne of Vanara. Thurdun explained that he had raised a sizable army, but that King Gardin of Glareth was reluctant to send aid since he was not sure he could trust anyone from the House of Fairlinden. Esildre agreed to go to Glareth and persuade Gardin to join in the conspiracy, while Navis accompanied Thurdun to Altoria to put their plan before King Felthain. Eventually, both Esildre and Navis would take part in the invasion of Vanara led by Thurdun and Serith Ellyn, and Esildre was present when Serith Ellyn slew Parthais.

The Second Age

During the early years of Queen Serith Ellyn's rule, Lord Banis, Esildre, and Navis all returned to live in Vanara, where Lord Banis was reinstated as a High Judge. However, Banis became disenchanted with the reforms that the Queen put into place and eventually resigned and moved to Duinnor. Esildre and Navis both remained in Vanara for a long time, until well after the First Unknown King came to power in Duinnor. Shortly after the Fifth Unknown King came to power, both Navis and Esildre journeyed to Duinnor at the request of their father. As it happened, neither sibling knew how to read or write (having long ago lost the use of the First Tongue), and Lord Banis wanted them to learn how to do so and also to increase their knowledge in other areas. Reluctantly, Navis agreed, but only on the condition that he not be made to attend school. Esildre also agreed, but only on the condition that she and Navis be allowed to receive their instruction together. Banis soon found a tutor for them both, a Melnari scholar called Raynor, who agreed to take the two on as students.

Esildre proved to be a quick and eager learner, while Navis tended to be argumentative and impatient. Raynor soon realized that Esildre would surpass Navis in her abilities and was trying to determine the best way to give them separate lessons when news reached Duinnor about a Dragonkind incursion into Vanara. Esildre and Navis both immediately rode southward, probably passing along the way Serith Ellyn's envoys riding northward to Duinnor with the latest news. It was no mere foray into Vanara, as it turned out, but a full-fledged invasion of the Northlands, and Queen Serith Ellyn sent word to Duinnor that she would be leading an army eastward behind a large Dragonkind army that was marching swiftly across the plains toward the Eastlands. Navis and Esildre encountered Serith Ellyn's army as it rounded the northern boundaries of Forest Islindia at Minion Gap, and they accompanied her eastward.

Accounts of the Great Invasion are replete with stories and tales of the battles that took place. Suffice it to say that when Serith Ellyn's army came to Fisenwold on the eastern side of Bletharn Plain, they found the city decimated by the Dragonkind, and evidence of the fierce fighting in the form of thousands of dead. But the Dragonkind had swept through quickly, and had already entered the Thunder Mountains. As she had promised Duinnor's Unknown King, Serith Ellyn's army waited at Fisenwold for the Duinnor army that was to join them there. However, due to the incompetence of a few Duinnor generals, the first army sent out was destroyed at Nasakeeria. A second army, comprised almost entirely of horsemen, was immediately dispatched eastward, and they at last caught up with the Vanaran armies three days after Serith Ellyn had given up on Duinnor and had departed Fisenwold. Delayed by two or three weeks, the Duinnor and Vanaran forces were hampered by winter ice and snow, but marched steadily on, not knowing that the Dragonkind had already overthrown Tulith Attis. There, the Dragonkind tarried, making the most of the spoils of food and treasure they found, but when they received word that armies were approaching, they quickly made their way southward. Esildre, along with the rest of those who were supposed to relieve Prince Heneil at Tulith Attis, were shocked and outraged by what they found. Not a living soul remained at Tulith Attis. Such was the carnage and the mutilation of the Dragonkind's victims, that few of the slain could be recognized. Esildre searched for an entire day and most of another for her niece, Faeanna, who was one of Lady Lyrium's household guards. But it was to no avail.

Meanwhile, forces from Glareth led by Prince Thalamir arrived to join with those already gathered around Tulith Attis. The combined armies quickly reorganized and set off in pursuit of the Dragonkind, filled with anger and the desire for vengeance.

Some days later, at the Battle of Saerdulin (described elsewhere), Esildre and Navis were instrumental in bringing about the Dragonkind's utter defeat. Such was the slaughter at that battle, that the river waters ran red as far south as Kalbrith, nearly two hundred miles away. But the violence did not end with the defeat of the Dragonkind. Accusations flew concerning the fall of Tulith Attis, and Men were blamed by some for betraying the defenders, while certain Elifaen were blamed by others. Arguments led to violence, and soon the countryside was awash in new blood as parties of vigilantes scoured the lands for traitors. The violence threatened to pit the Glarethian army against that of Vanara, and Duinnor against both, and had it not been for Prince Thalamir and Queen Serith Ellyn working together to enforce peace between the armies, all would have been much worse. As it was, the Queen ordered that all those who were not part of her Fellfaere contingent to depart immediately to their homes, on pain of arrest. Esildre and Navis obeyed, making their way briefly back to Tulith Attis to search again for the body of their niece, Faeanna, before turning westward once more through the Thunder Mountains.

As they traveled, Esildre became more despondent, and Navis angrier. Then there was an incident that took place in the mountains, when they came upon loot taken from Tulith Attis by Bailorg and his

Dragonkind guards. Bailorg and Dragonkind had already fled when Navis discovered the wagons of loot and the slaves that had been forced to pull them. What happened then is told within the pages of The Year of the Red Door.   Suffice to say here that Navis was filled with rage. He was about to slaughter the cowering slaves when Esildre caught up to him. Seeing their pitiful condition, she stopped her brother from doing any harm to them, and then she heard their story. This did not fully abate the ire of Navis, who leveled a curse at them which made them physically shrink. That was in addition to a curse that Bailorg has already laid on them, binding them to that area of the mountains. Filled with anger herself, but also with a touch of compassion, Esildre put her own curse upon the now little people, which gave them long life, to "suffer the fullness of their punishment." But she also blessed them with the ability to quickly move from place to place in order to survive. In later years, she would say that these curses and blessings were given in the throes of a deep and profound emotion, and could not be lifted by those that gave them.

Of what became of the former slaves, their curses, and the loot is part of the tale told in *The Year of the Red Door*. For her part, Esildre was deeply shaken by all her recent experiences, the war, the aftermath, and the encounter with the slaves of Bailorg. On their return to Duinnor, Navis said little that was not boastful, but Esildre said little at all. They attempted to resume their studies with Raynor, but Navis was even less patient than before, having taken to drinking more than he should have, and Esildre was increasingly brooding and silent, her heart heavy, and her mind far from any studies.

When their tutor, Raynor, became the head of the King's Academy, he no longer had time for private students. Very little is known about Esildre during these years, but Navis is said to have pursued various endeavors, including several ill-fated business adventures.

Seeing the condition of his daughter, and unconcerned for her wellbeing, Lord Banis secretly sought to use her as a bargaining tool with Secundur, in order to gain the use of Secundur's black eagles. Over the course of a year, he privately convinced her to seek refuge from the world and its woes by going to Shatuum and becoming a companion of Secundur. To do this, Banis only encouraged her despair at the happenings of the world, gave her reasons to withdraw, and sought to increase her sense of hopelessness. At last, in 420 of the Second Age, Esildre conceded, and she traveled to Shatuum. Rumors soon spread that she had become concubine to Secundur. It would later be discovered by Raynor and others that her father, Lord Banis, had persuaded her to go to Secundur. And it seemed apparent to Raynor, too, that Secundur rewarded Banis by giving him the use of his black eagles as spies, since they were creatures capable of sharing what they saw and heard.

Navis, not knowing that his father had made the arrangements between Esildre and Secundur, determined to rescue his sister. He eventually led a small expedition to Shatuum in order to do so, but he was never seen again.

Esildre would remain in Shatuum for nearly two centuries, emerging suddenly from that place in 590 S.A. She would later claim that she spent much of her time there asleep, but it is not known if she meant that in jest. What is apparent is that she slowly realized how evil Secundur was, and how much he plotted vile deeds against all his perceived enemies. Although Secundur sought to keep her isolated from his doings, she must have discovered much about his plans and his growing might. At any rate, her decision to leave resulted in a terrible argument with Secundur, who had become infatuated with her. He did not wish her to leave, but had no real power to stop her. Esildre would later imply that during a portion of her flight from Shatuum, she had to fight her way through a variety of creatures, wraiths, and goblins. She did escape, but not before Secundur (or one of his minions) laid a dark and terrible curse on her.

It soon became apparent to Esildre that any who looked into her eyes would be filled with an insatiable desire for her, and she likewise for them. And for several centuries, Esildre did not know how to resist the curse. Instead, it seems she did not really try to do so. She learned that she was reviled in Vanara for having been in Shatuum.   It is known that she made at least one journey to Vanara and met with her niece and nephew, Coreth and Faslor, since her sister Atlana would not receive her.   It was then she learned the fate of Navis, or at least that he had disappeared during a quest to release her from Secundur.   The meeting with her niece was unpleasant, and the two argued terribly, with Esildre, in shock at the news of her brother, claiming that she knew nothing of Navis and that surely if he had come into Shatuum she would have learned of it. She departed after only a little while, in grief and shame.

She then took up her abode in Elmwood Castle where she hosted the most extravagant and depraved orgies. However, as a result of Esildre's curse, anyone who had relations with her, whether man or woman, soon succumbed to madness and usually committed suicide shortly afterwards. Yet that did not deter new guests from coming, and she continued to attract the dregs and outcasts of society to her remote and forbidding castle.

The only people who were not vulnerable to Esildre's curse were those without sight. So, in order to have a staff of servants who could interact with her and remain unharmed, she solicited blind people into her employ.

As related in *The Year of the Red Door*, in 682 S.A., Esildre suddenly expelled all her guests, and she made it known that visitors would no longer be welcome at Elmwood Castle. The few visitors who dared go there were either turned away, or, if they were cunning enough to enter the castle, they were never seen again. Otherwise, Esildre remained a recluse for nearly two hundred years, rarely leaving her place of self-imposed exile.

According to *The Year of the Red Door*, that was how things remained until the year 870 S.A. when she was summoned to the Temple of Beras by Raynor. Without realizing it, she fell in love with Tyrin, the mercenary sent to fetch her, and he likewise with her. This would profoundly affect her decisions and actions, and her fate during the remaining months of her life and thereafter, as told within *The Year of the Red Door*. Indeed, her deep love for Tyrin would lead to Esildre becoming a ghost (or apparition), and in that state of being, she played an essential role in Philawain's effort to subdue Secundur. After this accomplishment, she regained her wings, rejoined Tyrin, and together they passed from this world into the next.

It is worth noting that Esildre and Sheila Pradkin were almost identical in appearance. This is a deep irony, because Sheila's actual name was Shevalia, and she was the grandchild of the same Shevalia that had been Esildre's close friend. And, unknown to Esildre, Shevalia was likely her half-sister, a love-child of Lord Banis. So, Sheila was the grandniece of Esildre which might have explained their resemblance. This close resemblance to one another certainly caused some confusion, as related within *The Year of the Red Door*.

See Also:
Biographical Sketches (Parthais, Tyrin Spritsul)
Glossary (Banis, Navis, Saerdulin, Battle of)
Historical Sketches (The Great Dragonkind Invasion)
Tales of the High Houses (The House of Faircedar)
****

Felthain

Felthain was a Firstborn of the House of Mulberry, husband to Rose, eventual king of Altoria. Felthain and Rose established the House of Mulberry in the northwest territories of Altoria along the River Iridelin sometime in the early First Age, during the time of Silmain's reign.

Neither Felthain nor Rose much desired any role of leadership, and they toiled in their own fields and carried their own harvests down river to trade. Felthain became interested in boat-building and sometime around 400 F.A., he had established several barge companies. Rose convinced Felthain to join a council of head men from various nearby clans and tribes who wished to discuss cooperating on several matters of trade and civic affairs. Soon after, the House of Mulberry was more or less in charge of the region, and began gaining more influence and power as other Elifaen houses joined into Mulberry.

In 610 F.A., Queen Therona demanded all within her domain to pay tribute to her court, but Felthain and his people resisted. Therona then threatened to send an army against Mulberry, but Felthain knew that drought had severely damaged the farms in Therona's domain, and he threatened to blockade the river, and to arrange for Vanara to send its goods overland to Masurthia rather than to Therona's city of Draymoor. Gambling that Therona was bluffing, he further stipulated that the Mulberry domain was to be made a principality, and that only he, as prince, could exact tribute from his people. In exchange, he promised to send a portion of that tax tribute to Therona. Therona was hard pressed for resources and treasure, and could not at that time supply any military force capable of subduing Mulberry, especially considering the food and fodder requirements. She soon conceded to his terms without bloodshed, and Felthain was made Prince of the Realm. Therona proclaimed to her people that this was her plan all along and that the relief provided by new shipments of food and a new source of revenue was only brought about by her own skill and power. Most Altorians knew better, and within the region of Mulberry there was much celebration of their new status.

During the following years, Felthain would become a staunch supporter of Therona's efforts to expand trade with Vanara and with the east. He emphasized the building and maintenance of roads and bridges, of docks and foundries, and the establishment of schools and vocational training centers. When war broke out between Altoria and Masurthia, Felthain sent a small army to secure his easternmost villages against Masurthian attacks, and he personally led several raids against King Barindon's forces when they crossed the River Wachee.

Meanwhile, Felthain appealed to Vanara for assistance against Masurthia, but his case was undermined when Queen Therona confiscated shipments of trade goods arriving in Draymoor from Vanara, along with shipments from Mulberry destined for Tracia and the Eastlands. It was Felthain who informed King Parthais of this, and when Parthais marched into Altoria, Felthain and Rose together rode out to meet him in an effort to negotiate their alliance. But Parthais was in no mood for such, counter to his advisor's council. Instead, he took the Felthain and Rose as prisoners and ransacked several Mulberry towns on his southward march. However, Heneil persuaded Parthais to be lenient with the House of Mulberry since Vanara relied upon them to assist with their river trade.

After the peace between Altoria and Masurthia was enforced by Parthais, Felthain and Rose were released from his service, and they traveled to Draymoor to view the Bloodcoins. This was done by the Queen during a ceremony that took place every twenty-four years but had been interrupted and postponed due to the war. However, the Queen refused to carry out the ceremony, saying that peace was still too tenuous and that Masurthian agents were still plotting against her. Felthain tried to convince Therona to show the Bloodcoins, saying that they were an important part of the heritage of all Altorians, and it would help restore the bonds among Altorians who had suffered during the war. But he was rebuffed by the Queen.

In the years that followed, the House of Mulberry would continue to increase its wealth and power. Felthain joined a group of Altorian lords who sought to codify Altorian law. He spent a great deal of time traveling throughout the realm, often with Rose coming along, and they collected information from villagers and chief men concerning local customs and laws. During this time, Felthain was called upon to resolve and arbitrate several disputes, some of which threatened to sink into bloodshed. His reputation for fairness and his ability to find solutions and agreeable compromises to difficult problems gained him the respect and admiration of his fellow Altorians.

When, twenty-four years later, Queen Therona still refused to show her Bloodcoins, Prince Felthain was traveling through northeastern Altoria, along the borders of the Bletharn. Several of Therona's ministers sent word to Felthain and asked him to come to Draymoor to speak with the

Queen in an effort to convince her to show the Bloodcoins. Felthain traveled swiftly back to his estate, and then, in a stroke of foresight, he mustered several hundred of his most trusted soldiers to travel with him to Draymoor. Rose, ill at ease with all this, tried to convince her husband not to go, for she deeply mistrusted Therona and was worried for his safety. Felthain assured her that he would be safe, and he and his men boarded boats and traveled down river to Draymoor. Before Felthain arrived, however, it was learned that the Bloodcoins were missing, and he entered Draymoor amid riots and unrest. Felthain first went throughout the city speaking to the people to instill calm and promising that he would do his utmost to locate the Bloodcoins. When he arrived at the Palace, he went straight to the throne room where Therona sat in anger, for she had been kept from leaving by her own Palace Guard, who now ushered in Felthain and many of his captains and several high ministers of Altoria. When she saw them, she commanded them to leave her throne room. But Felthain knew the laws and customs of the land as well as any.

"Show us the Bloodcoins given to you by Aperion," Felthain said to her in a calm but firm voice. "By your own law, and by your own mouth, the Bloodcoins are symbols of Altorian sovereignty, making the Bloodcoins objects of Altoria and not belonging to any individual. As Queen, you are the caretaker and guardian of those objects. As such, theft of the objects is to be considered a High Crime. Unless you produce them, or inform us as to their whereabouts, you will be placed under arrest and face justice in the courts of this land."

"I will not show them, and I will not speak of them," Therona said firmly.

"You know the punishment for High Treason as well as any," Felthain stated.

"I do," Therona replied haughtily. "But my House of Fairwillow is ancient and has many loyal subjects. Do you think they will tolerate their Queen to be treated so?"

Before Felthain could respond, one of the ministers stepped up and spoke to him so that all could hear.

"My lord," he said. "The queen does indeed have many supporters, and if she is convicted of her crimes and punished according to our law, there may be an uprising of vengeful violence among her people."

"Let there be violence, then," said Felthain. "The House of Mulberry will stand with the people, so if there is not to be a trial, then open the gates and open the doors. Let them in and let us see what they will do with Therona! My captains! Go throw open the gates to the people and invite them in to see their Queen. Let them have their will upon Therona and upon the House of Fairwillow!"

Therona was aghast, well aware of the mob outside her palace.

"I beg you!" cried Therona, who now stood from her throne in fear of her life.

"Then tell us where the Bloodcoins are."

Therona looked at Felthain helplessly, then, saying nothing, slowly sat back down.

"Then you will not say."

Therona said nothing as tears fell from her eyes.

"My lord?" said one of the captains. "Shall we open the gates?"

"No," said one of the ministers. "If she dies, she will never speak or answer. There is another path for us. Summon the Royal Scribe."

It was done, and a proclamation was prepared, which Queen Therona then signed, abdicating her throne. Another document was prepared and presented to Prince Felthain, who then agreed to Therona's abdication. This document also declared Felthain to be King of Altoria. When all of the ministers also signed and put their seals upon the documents, Therona was taken aside and Felthain was ushered onto the throne. The Royal Seal was brought to him, as well as the scepter, but there was no crown for his head, since Therona alone had ever been sovereign up to this moment, and her jewels were not deemed suitable for Felthain. King Felthain then spoke to those gathered.

"By my order and decree, Therona is to be placed under arrest. She is to be striped of any vestige of royalty, any symbols of her former status. She is to have no attendants, courtiers, company, or visitors except those admitted by the throne or its authorized ministers. She is to be taken to a place of exile far from this city where she is to remain for all the remaining days of her life. Her only hope of pardon and forgiveness is in the restoration by her own acts of the Bloodcoins. But she is on no count to be made a spectacle of the public, nor is she to be tried for her negligence, her actions, or her crimes, and neither is she to be subjected to any abuse, poverty, or torment. I, King Felthain, act as sole judge and declare that her sentence of exile is by my own order to be carried out by those who are loyal to Altoria and its throne. So let it be written. So let it be done."

When that was written, Felthain put his seal upon it and then spoke again.

"By my order and decree, the House of Fairwillow is hereby dissolved of name, of standing and status, and of all boon, reward, or privilege that may have formerly been awarded that House. Be it so forever. So let it be written. So let it be done."

When that was written, Felthain put his seal upon it and stood.

"Let all these things be proclaimed to the people!"

To say the least, Rose was surprised when she received word by fast-riding messenger that she was summoned to Draymoor by the new King of Altoria himself, and that she was not to delay but come immediately. The messenger was ordered to say no more, not even to tell her who this king was who commanded her so. The messenger could only assure her that Felthain was safe, but quite busy. After three days of hard riding, the two travelers entered Draymoor in the middle of the night and were ushered straight to the throne room. It is said that when she entered the room and saw her husband sitting on the throne, she laughed out loud, then, embarrassed, put her hand over her mouth, trying to stifle any further giggles. It took some convincing for her to believe that Felthain was now the King of Altoria, and she was his Queen.

By all accounts, King Felthain was a fair and just king for all of the days of his rule. Under him, Altoria remained at peace and grew prosperous. He reformed the legal system under a single code of laws to apply to all Altorians, and he established good relations with Vanara and Masurthia. Under his direction, working closely with his trade ministers and emissaries, Altoria's ports, especially at Draymoor, saw increased trade, and the port facilities greatly expanded. Roads were improved, new bridges were built to connect the trade routes will the more isolated towns and villages. Systems of governance were reformed, including the judicial system. Legislation was overseen by an elected body of representatives from each region. And the Crown subsidized loans and made grants for improving river navigation, for new waypoints, and for regional safety patrols.

Each year until her death, Felthain traveled to the villa where Therona was exiled to try to convince her to talk about the Bloodcoins. She never did, and he saw that she sank deeper into depression and madness with each passing year. When word came of her death, he was deeply troubled, though it was apparent that she took her own life. And, throughout his reign, he launched investigation after investigation into the whereabouts of the Bloodcoins. He even offered a tremendous reward of silver and gold to anyone who could find them and bring them to him. But the Bloodcoins were never found, and Felthain never received any credible word on their whereabouts.

Felthain continuously negotiated with Parthais for better trade terms, and traveled to Linlally himself on several occasions. However, he found Parthais difficult and prone to revoke agreements on a whim. When Felthain at last understood how untrustworthy and violent Parthais was, he began diverting resources in order to strengthen Altoria's northern defenses. He well knew the power and might of Vanara, and he knew that should Vanara invade, Altoria could offer little resistance. When word arrived that Parthais had exiled his son and daughter, Felthain redoubled his efforts to strengthen Altorian defenses. He also initiated the first systematic defense of the Hinterlands by constructing the first interconnected system of causeways, bridges, and keeps. But during his rule, neither the Dragonkind nor Parthais invaded.

In 206 S.A., to encourage visitors from other realms, he started the Mulberry Race, a long distance horse race from Draymoor to Duinnor, via Vanara and sponsored a generous prize to finalists, it was held every ten years until 800 from which it was held annually. The Mulberry Race eventually became one of the biggest sporting events, attracting participants and spectators from every realm. The villages and towns along the course of the race garnered much trade as inns and taverns filled with visitors. Farriers, blacksmiths, shops and trading posts did brisk business during the races. By the end of the Second Age, the race took place every two years, with over three hundred horses and riders entering the contest (although no more than fifty riders ever completed the race).

Felthain's wife, Rose, who was with him constantly from their union in the Time Before Time, died in a boating accident in the year 217 S.A., and Felthain was deeply affected by her loss. At last, still sad from his wife's death and weary of rule, King Felthain abdicated to his son, Prince Gerald, in the year 224 S.A. He then returned to his estate and lived a life of solitude, fishing and painting, until he died in his sleep in the year 237 S.A. No evidence of foul play was found, and it is believed that he died of melancholia.

See Also:
Biographical Sketches (Parthais)
Glossary (Mulberry Race)
Historical Sketches (Altoria)
Tales of the High Houses (House of Fairwillow)

****

Gaiyelneth Labret

Serving Mistress to Queen Serith Ellyn

Gaiyelneth was the chief handmaiden of Queen Serith Ellyn during the late Second Age. She was known to be precocious, spirited, outspoken, and fiercely loyal to the Queen.

Born 849 of the Second Age in Vanara, Gaiyelneth was the youngest child of Cyril Labret, who served for a time as the Vanaran ambassador to Glareth, and Lady Gina of the Mortal House of Coral. Gaiyelneth was from her earliest years headstrong, precocious, and outspoken, with boundless energy and possessed of great intelligence. She first came to the attention of the Queen when, at the age of six, she sneaked into the Palace and wandered around for hours, making herself at home wherever she went. She was discovered by the Queen herself when, going to her barge, she found Gaiyelneth sitting on the Queen's pillows, throwing crumbs of bread to the swans. With Serith Ellyn were several lords and ladies and Collandoth, the Melnari, who recognized the girl since he was a friend of Gaiyelneth's father. Collandoth eventually coaxed Gaiyelneth to allow him to take her home to her parents who, it turned out, were anxiously searching for her.

Gaiyelneth had a brother, Chanter, who was older than her by a decade, and who was little inclined to play with his sister. But he taught her how to use the rapier until she exceeded his skill. At the age of ten, and in disguise, she lied about her age and entered a competition consisting of much older swordsmen. Although she was small and did not have the reach of her opponents, she proved quick and aggressive in the bouts with remarkable reflexes and skill. As a result, she advanced to the finals in the rapier division of the contest. When she faced her final opponent, a boy from Duinnor, she was soundly and quickly defeated in the best of five bouts, her opponent disarming her each time with only a few strokes. Enraged, Gaiyelneth would not concede, and she argued with the judges to permit a rematch. They refused, but she vehemently insisted, coming very close to insulting the judges by asserting that she was more than a match for any of them. She challenged any one of the judges to face her, and if she won the bout, she would have a rematch with the boy. If she lost, she said, she would concede peacefully.

The boy who won against Gaiyelneth stood by patiently, and he calmly awaited the outcome of the argument, saying only that he would leave it to the judges. Amused by her spirit, the Queen signaled for one of the judges to face Gaiyelneth, and it fell to Brandis Seafar, son of the Lord Chancellor of

Vanara, to meet her. He gave Gaiyelneth every opportunity to win the bout, obviously leaving himself open to her thrusts and cuts, but at last he tapped her with a winning blow on the side of her helmet. Embarrassed, she conceded the match and the entire contest to the boy from Duinnor. However, just as the judges were about to award the medal to the boy from Duinnor, the boy's father, who had just arrived, interrupted the proceeding. He revealed that his son had run away from home, and that he was not old enough to compete, being only fourteen. Since the boy had lied about his age, the judges disqualified his win, and the boy's father led him away.

Then the judges, in order to award her the medal, called the name that Gaiyelneth had used to enter the contest. Since she, too, had not only lied about her age, but had given a false name as well, she was very nervous when she accepted the medal. Then the judges called for her parents to come forward so that they could share the crowd's acclaim with Gaiyelneth and accept the Queen's personal congratulations. Gaiyelneth panicked, stammering that at first that she was an orphan. Then she suddenly insisted that the medal should be given to the boy from Duinnor, since, she said, any boy of fourteen as skilled as he was must surely deserve to win. She thrust the medal into the hands of Seafar, ran from the rostrum, and stole away into the crowd. This left the judges in something of a muddle since the boy who had defeated Gaiyelneth had already departed with his father. So judges awarded the medal to the boy who had before been in third place.

While all this was being sorted out and done, Gaiyelneth discarded her disguise to watch as a spectator, but not before being recognized by a keen onlooker who was, once again, none other than Collandoth.

Whether it was by Collandoth's doing or not, Gaiyelneth's parents received a letter on the following day requesting that they enroll their daughter at the Queen's Academy, at the express invitation of the Queen, herself. The Queen's Academy was the highest center of learning in Vanara. Students were drilled not only in the usual academic arts, but were also trained in martial arts as part of physical fitness training. It was at the Academy that Gaiyelneth received her education and somewhat her discipline. The ranks of the Fellfaere as well as the Queen's Gray Guard recruited from the school, with men and women being treated as equals in the armed forces, and by the time she was fifteen, she was already being closely watched by military recruiters. Indeed, Gaiyelneth proved as capable as her male schoolmates. However, rather than join the armed forces when she graduated at the age of sixteen, she instead applied to the court as a serving mistress, and soon after that, she became the Queen's own preferred handmaiden. Under Serith Ellyn's influence and guidance, Gaiyelneth further matured, although her spirit remained undiminished and unrepressed.

Serith Ellyn traveled quite often throughout Vanara to see firsthand how her people were doing and to hear their concerns. On many occasions she traveled on a buckmarl or by horseback with only a small contingent of her guard, rather than by royal coach with full retinue. Either way, Gaiyelneth often accompanied the queen, proving as hardy on the road as anyone and good company to have along. During one such trip to Ladentree in the summer of 867, Serith Ellyn learned of the deteriorating condition of several bridges along the main road from there to Kajarahn, and she insisted on inspecting them firsthand. With Gaiyelneth and a force of twenty Gray Guard as well as three-dozen Fellfaere out of Ladentree, the Queen set off for a two-week tour of the roadway. The party traveled light and rode quickly, with scouts carefully deployed all around and ahead of them, knowing that bandits had been harassing travelers along that route. Traveling swiftly, they stopped only to camp, to query the traders that they encountered, and to carefully inspect the many bridges along the way.

Nearly every bridge was in need of repair, and one of them was so unstable that many of the traders did not trust it with their heavy wagons (although it remained safe enough for horsemen). Instead, the traders were in the habit of taking a rugged and dangerous detour of thirty miles to go around it. The detour passed down a steep canyon and back up the other side, and it was a favorite place for bandits to lie in wait for their victims. Hence, most of the traders only traveled with a large body of guards in their employ.

The Queen ended her inspection of the road almost within sight of The Badlands, there being no other bridges to inspect. On the way back to Ladentree, she ordered half of her escort to travel the detour around the untrustworthy bridge and to engage with any bandits along the way. When her party, including Gaiyelneth, reached the bridge, they found the approach had been blocked by a small avalanche. And when they dismounted to clear the way, they were attacked by a considerable number of bandits, mostly renegades, who attacked in concert. While some of the bandits sniped from above with arrows, others charged into the Queen's party. The attack was so swift that there was no time to find cover or to form a defensive line. Although the bandits were out-matched by the skill of their intended victims, several attackers broke through to the Queen and had it not been for Gaiyelneth, she may have fallen to harm. The two women fought back to back and were responsible between the two of them for as many dead bandits as the rest of their party combined. The bandits were driven off, and several were captured. When it was over, the road was littered with dead and dying bandits. Three Fellfaere were also wounded by arrows, and two Gray Guard by swords, but none seriously.

Though only eighteen years of age, Gaiyelneth's value was thus proven to the Gray Guard, who said that only the Queen herself had exceeded the ferocity of Gaiyelneth's steel, and that her only care was to defend the Queen. When Lord Seafar received the incident report upon their return to Linlally, he issued standing orders for Gaiyelneth to accompany the Queen on any future outings whenever possible. Queen Serith Ellyn did not object, and Gaiyelneth was pleased.

Many said that Gaiyelneth was the Queen's only true female friend, so close they became, and that the Queen was never as morose or as dark-humored as she was before Gaiyelneth came along. And certainly her skill at arms was a comfort to those whose duty it was to watch after Serith Ellyn's safety.

See Also:
Biographical Sketches (Grantham Farby)

****

Gardin

Gardin was a Firstborn Elifaen of the House of Beech. He established a small domain on the northeastern coasts of the world that would later grow to become Glareth by the Sea. Gardin was made Sea King of Glareth in 550 F.A., and he quickly expanded his domain south and westward as well as along the coast. He was uninterested in the intrigues of the west and sought to keep his people uninvolved. However, he did have kin in the west, including an aunt who was related by marriage to Cupeldain, as well as other relatives who lived in the western forests nearby to the Hemlock lands. When Cupeldain was slain, and Parthais exacted punishment of the feuding parties that led to Cupeldain's murder, Gardin was sorely troubled. None of Gardin's relatives were killed, but they wrote to Gardin telling how the violence had taken many of their friends. In spite of pressure from his courtiers and kin, he refused to retaliate against Parthais or against those various parties accused of the initial feuds.

Hearing that Lucinda wished to leave the west, he invited her to Glareth and asked her to bring with her any of his kin who also wished to come. Lucinda only stayed a few years until the intrigues of Parthais forced her to depart Glareth (against the wishes of Gardin).

After the departure of Lucinda, Gardin continued the expansion of his domain, and may have been the first to refer to it as a "realm." By 1100 F.A., he had established a province on the northern shores of Lake Halgaeth called Connassa and several communities along the Osterflo. He also invited some of the Newcomers to the world to his court to share their stories, lore, skills, and knowledge.

Gardin remained wary of Parthais, and he sent spies into Vanara to report on the happenings there. When he heard of the growing tension between Parthais and the scholars of the region, he made it known that Glareth sought scholars and scholarly works of every kind and made an open invitation for any to come to Glareth. He also let it be known that he was purchasing manuscripts brought to Glareth to bolster his growing library (which would later become part of the Glareth Academy). Later historians speculated that Nimwill of Vanara secretly contacted Gardin to arrange this. Soon, scholars were migrating rapidly away from Vanara, and Glareth received a great many of them along with nearly a thousand manuscripts and tablets.

Parthais, learning of this, was infuriated, and threatened Glareth with war, but King Gardin only redoubled his efforts, making it known that any Vanaran who could read and write in any script or language would receive a stipend to help with the expenses of their relocation to Glareth. Soon Glareth was awash with Vanaran refugees, receiving more than any other place outside of Duinnor. The manuscripts they brought were quickly acquired by Gardin, and many scholars who came were put to work in his new academy or in other schools in the region, making Glareth a center of learning for the eastern realms of the world.

Copies of certain manuscripts released to the public some five centuries after Gardin's death revealed that he and his son, Samis, met secretly with Thurdun, Parthais's son, and with Heneil. Gardin agreed to supply arms and financing to Thurdun, and made arrangements for weapons to be sent upriver (the Osterflo) and thence to The Middlemount, where Thurdun was assembling his army in exile. It is thought that a few of the Newcomers (Men) who later went with Thurdun to Vanara came from Glareth.

Gardin died suddenly in 1269 F.A. and it was rumored that he was poisoned by the agents of Parthais. As a result, Gardin's son, Samis, immediately sent word to Thurdun and dispatched several thousand men to join Thurdun's forces with a promise of additional support to defeat Parthais. Whether or not Parthais was actually responsible for Gardin's death remains a mystery, but the forces that Samis sent to Thurdun doubtless made the defeat of Parthais much easier than it otherwise would have been. As a result, Glareth and Vanara, under Queen Serith Ellyn, enjoyed close ties and the support of each other throughout the Second Age.

See Also:
Biographical Sketches (Esildre, Parthais)

****

Grantham Farby

Grantham was the son of the Farby's of Duinnor, Blain Farby and his wife, Lady Elyna, born in the year 845 S.A. He would prove to be intelligent but somewhat peculiar, with a penchant for adventure. When he was very young, perhaps only six or seven, he ran away from his governess and found his way onto the grounds of the King's Academy. There he climbed a tree and spent the afternoon watching Kingsmen practicing their swordplay before he was discovered and escorted home. His second adventure came two years later on a trip with his father to the mines of Mount Vendril. He stole away, managed to climb the mountain to the base of Tower Vendril at its summit, even though it was forbidden by local law to go there. When he was discovered by local men, and his outraged father, Grantham was shooting rocks with his slingshot at the skeletal remains that still hung high up against the tower from a failed climbing attempt many years earlier. Grantham was apparently, and with some success, trying to knock down some of the bones that still dangled there. His father had to pay a substantial fine to the local authorities for the incident.

Upon his return to Duinnor City, Grantham was immediately enrolled in the Gentilly School, a boarding school known for its high academic standards and for keeping unruly boys in check. At the school, Grantham quickly mastered all of the studies and gave over his attention to perfecting his fencing skills. His classmates remembered him as being extremely bright and very bored.

At the age of fourteen, Grantham ran away once more. This time he made it all the way to Vanara where he promptly entered in a fencing contest. Hot on his heels was his father, who appeared just when his son was about to be awarded the highest medal in the rapier competition. He failed to receive the award when the judges learned from his father that he was only fourteen, and not the required minimum age of sixteen.

Soon after returning to Duinnor, Grantham's father secured a commission for his son to attend the King's Academy and to become a Kingsman. Since he was only fourteen, he had to wait a year and a half before he could be enrolled, but at last he seemed happy and contented, much to his parent's relief.

At the Academy, Grantham excelled in all subjects, particularly at language arts, engineering, and swordsmanship, and he advanced quickly through the curriculum. It was noted by his training officers that, in field maneuvers, he was a master of maps and tactics. On one of the standard training missions, which was to map and survey the warning markers surrounding Nasakeeria, Farby's squad was pitted against another squad of cadets to reach the easternmost marker first, one squad going around the north side, and the other, Farby's, making their way eastward along the southern border of Nasakeeria. Not only did Farby's squad win the match by two days, but along the way Farby drew detailed sketches of the wooden towers that could be seen under construction within the forbidden land. On the way back, drums were heard sounding from within Nasakeeria, and Farby, using his knowledge of musical notation, was able to record the cadence and patterns of the drumming. It had long been theorized that the drums heard from within Nasakeeria were methods of communication, but no real effort to understand them had ever been made. Upon his return, Farby's extensive notes on the subject were given over to the academics of Duinnor for study and would become the basis for a new course of study at the Academy, which from then on sent parties expressly to listen for Nasakeerian drumming.

Grantham's career as a Kingsman cadet came to an abrupt end when he engaged in a street duel. Farby was leaving a pub when he came upon a man engaged in mistreating a young lady who turned out to be a prostitute. Grantham intervened as the man struck the girl. It became a vicious fight when the man turned on Grantham, who was at first reluctant to draw on the intoxicated man. Grantham was wounded several times, and only drew when the man lunged with his rapier at the young lady. Still, Grantham was reluctant in the fight, suffering still more wounds. Realizing that the man would not desist, and in pain and weak from his wounds, Grantham at last fought back in earnest. The man died of his wounds, and Grantham was arrested and tried for murder. Although exonerated by the many witnesses, the man turned out to be the secretary of the powerful Lord Banis, and Grantham was forced to resign his Kingsman commission and give up his place at the Academy. However, since Grantham was one of the Academy's top students, and was well liked and respected by the Kingsmen, he was granted a certificate that listed his academic achievements and a letter that acknowledged his sense of honor and duty.

Lord Banis, who was known to be vindictive, protested the verdict. He also quickly obtained from the King an edict which made any interference with those in the employ of Lord Banis a crime. Fearing for their son, Farby's parents sent him away to attend school in Vanara. However, a month after arriving in Vanara, Farby abruptly set out for Glareth. He traveled overland to Solsorna, where he embarked on a merchant vessel bound for Glareth, paying for his passage by working as a deckhand. His ship called on the ports of Forlandis and Colleton along the way. By the time Grantham arrived in Glareth by the Sea, he was enthralled with the sea and all things having to do with ships. He managed to find work as a part-time draftsman in one of Prince Carbane's shipyards, supplementing his income by working on local fishing vessels. He spent as much time as he could studying every aspect of shipbuilding and boat handling, often paying men to allow him to watch them work and to ask questions. Knowing that his father's men were earnestly seeking him, Farby sent several letters home begging his parents to let him be, but promising that he would try his best to remain in Glareth in spite of their wishes to come home. He learned that his father was sending envoys to Glareth to try to force Grantham's return, but through various intrigues, he was able to avoid returning to Duinnor for three years.

During his time in Glareth, Farby's interest and excellent work soon won him the respect of the boatyard workers and foremen. He spent several months at sea, going from Glareth to Colleton on the Eastlands coast and back again, usually as a crew member. At last, upon his return to Glareth by the Sea from one such sea voyage, men from Duinnor awaited him, having successfully tracked him down. These men had letters from his father insisting that he return immediately to Duinnor. However, Grantham resisted the entreaties. It would be two more years and many more envoys and letters before he at last returned with a passion for shipbuilding, and ideas concerning new ship designs that he was convinced would revolutionize seafaring. His parents did not share his enthusiasm, and they convinced Grantham that his duty was to take his place in the family mining business. Seeing that his father was not as healthy as he once was, Grantham reluctantly agreed, on the condition that he at least be allowed to visit the coast every few years. Thus he became a clerk in his father's concern, working mainly in the Duinnor City.

Grantham's work was not enthusiastic, to say the least, and he had a tendency to ignore his duties. When he did work, it was with diligence and care, but he was always restless and distracted. After a few months, he had become something as an odd gadabout. He spent a considerable amount of time reading, visiting Hanton Hall, and socializing with booksellers, merchants, and travelers. He gained a reputation for being a good-natured ne'er-do-well, highly engaging in conversation, witty, and prone to joking. He abhorred the "high" social circles that his parents moved in, and he was never comfortable at the soirées of the rich and "influential." Although he had dalliances with several girls, no lasting relationship developed, even though his parents pressured him to find a wife and "settle down."

In the year 870 SA, he happened to meet Sheila Pradkin, who was in the guise of Lady Shevalia. He was immediately infatuated by her, and tried to insinuate himself into her company. He eventually succeeded and was with Sheila during her Scathing. His amorous hopes were dashed when he learned of her love for Robby Ribbon. And yet he remained devoted to Sheila. He also gained the confidence of Sheila's other friends (Collandoth, Billy, and Ibin) and supported their efforts to pave the way for Robby to become the new ruler of Duinnor.

It is not known what became of Grantham after the world was remade. He always expressed a desire to return to Glareth, but he may have transformed and left the world as most people did.

****

Gurasa

(unless otherwise noted, all years are of the Second Age)

Introduction

Much has been said and written about Gurasa, both within his homeland and elsewhere. He is variously referred to as the White Dragon, the Desert Ghost, and Saltani Gurasa ("Great Leader" Gurasa). Stories are told about his legendary rise to fame, about his battlefield cunning, and about his political acumen. When news about Gurasa reached the Free City of Kajarahn, rumors quickly spread and it was even feared that the Dragonkind King might send the White Dragon to capture the city. When reports about Gurasa reached Vanara, Queen Serith Ellyn put her Fellfaere troops on a heightened state of readiness. This action served to trigger a series of events that resulted in Vanara and Duinnor joining forces to invade the Dragonlands and lay siege to the city of Calamandor. The campaign, aimed at destroying Calamandor's power to wage war, would succeed in that aim, but its aftermath would be disastrous for both the invaders and, as it turned out, for Gurasa.

As for Gurasa himself, thousands of soldiers met or knew him personally. Tens of thousands served under him, and even more fought against him. Each soldier has his own story to tell about

Gurasa. But there have been few descriptions of Gurasa that shed light on his character, much less attempt to explain the rather perplexing actions (or lack of action) that led to his downfall. What follows is an attempt to compile notes, scribbles, and sundry documents concerning Gurasa. It is presented as is, in a rather raw and unedited form. Perhaps there may be found within this a few clues to his true character.

In many ways, Gurasa was a tragic figure. In hindsight, it seems obvious that his career was doomed from the outset because of his relationship with the North—in particular, because of his friendship with Dalvenpar Tallin. Although his loyalty to the Dragon King was never really in doubt, his dedication and his will to fight for his king was suddenly and unexpectedly destroyed in one fell blow. The incident that triggered his downfall (described below) was the first of a succession of setbacks, reversals, and personal tragedies. It might be argued that, afterwards, he was never the man that he was before.

However, it could also be argued that Gurasa never was the man that most thought him to be. Those who knew him well and who served closely with him did not regard Gurasa as the fierce and unyielding warrior that was his popular reputation. He was never the unfeeling agent of his King. Nor was he a fighter by desire, by heart, or by choosing. And when at last things came to a tragic head, he made a choice that would baffle his friends and supporters. In effect, he resigned from service. At the tribunals held to determine his fate, Gurasa remained silent, refusing to defend himself while his enemies and defenders loudly carried on their tug-of-war over him. In short, he found at last a kind of dignity that was his own, simple, quiet, and honorable. He was a man who preferred to keep his own counsel.

He treated each person with equal respect, whether a common foot soldier or a prince. He never expected anyone to do that which he himself would not do, and he was more apt to lavish praise upon a courageous soldier than upon his superiors or sovereign courtiers. His soldiers were devoted to him, some perhaps even fanatical. They viewed him as shrewd and cunning, but knew him to be concerned for the welfare of his troops, fair in promoting worthy individuals and weeding out ineffective officers, and just in the discipline that he demanded. As Tareef al Binsalud noted in the foreword to his biography of Gurasa, "He did not demand, he inquired. He did not order, he directed. He did not punish, he disciplined. He tried to take care of us. He guided our skills, cultivated our prowess, and rewarded us with praise and encouragement. He fought beside us, and he mourned our losses. He asked for nothing that was not due any soldier. But we would have given him anything. Because we loved him."

Brief Summary

Gurasa was a Dragonkind general said to possess the greatest military mind since Kalzar the Great. His active military career was short, spanning only fifteen years, and his meteoric rise to fame kindled many legends and tales surrounding him. Some of these legends are the stuff of pure invention, but many have their basis in actual events. We are fortunate to have many first-hand accounts of Gurasa, including his own memoirs and those of other important figures. It is from such accounts and documents that we present this biographical sketch and, where feasible, we have cited our sources. We also gleaned much of our information concerning Gurasa's life from the journals of Tareef al Binsalud, who was from Gurasa's home region and served with Gurasa as a captain of the Al Sairs, Gurasa's elite household guard. Tareef, some six years younger than Gurasa, was with Gurasa throughout his leader's career and remained in service to Gurasa's household long after Gurasa retired.

According to Tareef, Gurasa was of a slight and unimposing stature and bearing, soft-spoken and humble in demeanor. Always neat in appearance, he dressed rather plainly and eschewed the ornate and lavish armor and robes that were his right. In public and when with his troops, he preferred practical clothing, light but sturdy weapons and battle dress. At home, he was even more casual, often wearing a simple gandoura and chechia and going about his town in bare feet. Both as the leader of Almedian and as a general, Gurasa was a meticulous planner, cunning tactician, and insightful leader who inspired his followers to great feats of courage and endurance. He was fearless in battle, and there are many stories of him riding at the spearhead of his armies when he could have easily and honorably guided things from the rear. He received many wounds as a result, yet even after losing his hand in combat, he continued to lead from the front. A brilliant tactician, he was famous for his traps, surprising battlefield maneuvers, and imaginative use of terrain to gain the upper hand against generally stronger and more numerous opponents. He never lost any battle or campaign. And his strong preference was for capturing rather than annihilating his opponents. His spies and agents were almost fanatical in their loyalty and zeal, and his troops were renown as the most disciplined soldiers who ever saw battle. In defense, his troops withstood withering blows from more powerful forces without giving ground. On the offensive, no other army, even those superior in numbers to his, accomplished nearly so much, inflicted nearly as casualties to the enemy, nor suffered fewer casualties while on the attack. His army was famous for appearing unexpectedly out of nowhere, like the ghostly White Dragon that was Gurasa's battle standard.

Gurasa was learned, was tutored from a very young age, and he traveled extensively in the Northlands and all throughout the Dragonlands as a youngster. He was fluent in the dialects of the Northmen, and was as knowledgeable about the histories of the North as he was about his own Dragonlands. Only once did Gurasa face Northmen in battle, during the final campaign of this career, one which resulted in his fall from grace.

Early Years

Gurasa was born in 795 S.A. into a wealthy merchant family in the remote desert village of Almedian located in the northeast region of the Dragonlands near Tamkal Plain. His father, Talbas, was an active trader with trading partners throughout the Dragonlands. Gurasa was the eldest of ten siblings, but the only one who survived into adulthood. He had a keen interest in botany and insects, often wandering out into the desert to collect specimens, and spending long hours making paintings and sketches of them. He was very interested in history and lore, and he especially loved to hear stories of far-off lands, particularly tales and fables about the forests of the north. By the time he was twelve, all of his younger brothers and sisters had died.

A Tour of Foreign Lands

At the age of fifteen, and during those years of peace between the Dragonlands and Vanara (805-835 S.A.), Gurasa's father sent him to Tyrsharat to further his education. There Gurasa met Collandoth, a Melnari who was serving Vanara as a minor ambassador to the Dragonlands, sent to negotiate preliminary trade agreements. Collandoth was impressed with the boy, and Gurasa somehow convinced the Melnari to allow him to travel north with him. Perhaps at Collandoth's suggestion, Gurasa disguised himself as a sickly old vagabond in order to avoid persecution. Together they traveled to Linlally where Gurasa busied himself with learning all he could about Vanara and other realms, spending a great deal of his time in libraries. After traveling with Collandoth throughout the region, the two went to Duinnor.

Collandoth was very careful about keeping Gurasa's disguise intact. Whenever possible, he spoke for Gurasa in order to hide Gurasa's accent. And he rarely allowed Gurasa to accept invitations to dinner or to other gatherings, sometimes by using Gurasa's fragile health as an excuse to be absent. When it was not possible to avoid interactions with others, Gurasa kept his head and much of his face covered, saying that his illness had left his face pock-marked with scars. The disguise worked only too well, and on several occasions Collandoth had to reassure mortal people that Gurasa was not contagious and posed no danger at all.

Meanwhile, with Collandoth's help, Gurasa's command of Common Speech quickly improved, and he was better able to hide his accent. When needed, he took up the surname Bintalbas, which meant, in his own language, "son of Talbas."

Gurasa and Dalvenpar

While in Duinnor City, Collandoth took Gurasa all about the city, visiting its shops, schools, palaces, parks, and galleries. Collandoth also took Gurasa to the Temple of Beras, just outside of the city, and they enjoyed wandering the gardens and viewing the monks at their work and prayers. It was in the library of the temple that Collandoth was greeted by the son of Lord Tallin. Tallin was an acquaintance of Collandoth's and his son, Dalvenpar, explained that his father was at the temple on some private business. Collandoth introduced Gurasa to Lord Tallin and Dalvenpar as a fellow traveler from "the south." Of course, Lord Tallin's name was well-known in the Dragonlands. So Gurasa was somewhat nervous at meeting the Tallins and on being left alone with the famed general's son. But the two were about the same age, and it was the first time either of them had visited Duinnor City. And since they had friendly dispositions, they hit it off splendidly, even if Gurasa was somewhat reticent about revealing much about his past. Since he kept his head low and covered by the hood of his cloak, he was not too worried about his race being discovered. Gurasa later wrote:

> We conversed for about two hours, I think, while we wandered the various gardens of the temple. Collandoth left us to find one of the monks that he knew, and Dalvenpar's father was also meeting with someone at the temple. It was my good fortune that it was a lengthy meeting.
>
> Dalvenpar was jovial and talkative, and I think he enjoyed our conversation quite a lot. He was as relaxed as I was nervous, but his manner and his respect soon put me at ease. He never seemed the least impatient for his father's return, and he was as delighted with answering my many questions as he was with the wonders and serenity of the temple gardens. He answered my questions with enthusiasm. He told me all about Tallinvale, about his journey from the old Eastlands Realm through the Thunder Mountains and across the wide Bletharn Plain. In only a short while, I had learned quite a lot about his family, too. Dalvenpar took pride in the fact that I knew of his father, the famed hero of Khanhar Pass. My obvious ignorance of matters pertaining to the Seven Realms was so great that at one point he blurted out that I must be the most sheltered person in the world not to know more about its history and lands. But I could see that he immediately regretted the outburst, judging perhaps from my posture or my expression (if he could see it) that I was embarrassed. I stammered something to the effect that he was probably right.
>
> "Oh, never mind that!" he said. "I'm not exactly an expert on history myself. I imagine that our education, yours and mine, emphasized different matters. For instance, you seem to know a lot about plants and insects and such, which I know very little about. And as for importance, I daresay that plants and insects and such will be around a lot longer than either of us or even any history!"
>
> That was, as I was to learn, typical of Dalvenpar. He always seemed able to put matters right whenever there was an uncomfortable or embarrassing moment. He had a genuine desire, I think, for everyone to get along with each other without strife or hard feelings. And he was always aware or even sensitive to the feelings and opinions of others, even when he did not share them. He was as generous with his handshakes and embraces as he was with his infectious smile. In all the years since, I do not think I have ever met a more good-natured or gentle person. I regret that he was destined to be a soldier, for he would have made a splendid diplomat.

It was late in the afternoon before Collandoth and Lord Tallin returned. They agreed to dine together that night and to spend the following day seeing the sights of Duinnor City. They met at a modest inn just outside of the city, and enjoyed a good meal and conversation, although Gurasa noted that Lord Tallin seemed somewhat distracted. Starting early in the morning, they entered the city and began their tour, visiting shops and schools, museums and parks, viewing the grand buildings, and sampling the many foods and treats offered by street vendors, stalls, and tearooms. Gurasa's disguise worked well. Seeing his manner of dress, indicating a sickly person, the people they met with kept their distance and rarely addressed him.

Lord Tallin seemed somewhat distracted and spoke very little, although he was amiable enough throughout the day. Gurasa overheard Collandoth ask Lord Tallin what was troubling him, but Lord Tallin declined to answer. As for the two new friends, Gurasa and Dalvenpar were jocular and even boisterous as they went about the city. Lord Tallin later recounted that he had never heard his son talk so much, laugh so much, or be as jovial as he was with Gurasa, and that the two seemed like old comrades rather than new acquaintances.

While Gurasa and Dalvenpar gaped and gazed at the city, the two older gentlemen talked. Lord Tallin was keenly interested in Collandoth's sojourn in the Dragonlands. He asked about the routes that Collandoth took, the condition of the people, and the state of the cities. They talked about Dragonkind food and customs, about music and poetry, about Tyrsharat and court politics, trade agreements, and even about the Dragonkind armed forces.

All this talk of the Dragonlands made Gurasa very nervous, although he knew that Collandoth would let nothing slip that might give away the secret of his identity. Fortunately, Dalvenpar had not the least bit of curiosity about the Dragonlands, and indeed seemed completely bored by the topic. And so it would not be long before Dalvenpar managed to change the subject, often by injecting some joke or by asking about a passing object or building of interest as they toured the great city.

By late afternoon, Dalvenpar had decided that Gurasa and Collandoth ought to join the Tallins as they made their way home. Lord Tallin did not seem to mind the notion, but Gurasa was reluctant. He was keen to know more by way of the Tallins' company, but he worried that traveling in close company with others might be too risky. Collandoth was also was concerned by the very same thing, and he took Gurasa aside to privately discuss the matter. Dalvenpar would not hear otherwise, though, and gave Gurasa and Collandoth every assurance that he would keep his sickly new friend safe and well and as comfortable as could be on the long voyage. As for Lord Tallin, he knew better than to argue with his son, and he appeared somewhat amused by Dalvenpar's enthusiasm. Eventually, Gurasa and Collandoth agreed to do as Dalvenpar desired. But Collandoth insisted on certain conditions. Without giving much of an explanation, Collandoth insisted that not only should Dalvenpar and Lord Tallin refrain from asking about Gurasa's family and home, but that they should protect Gurasa from the inquisitiveness of others. Although this made Gurasa feel somewhat awkward, Dalvenpar was quick to agree, and Lord Tallin also gave his oath to Collandoth. Lord Tallin later said that he knew Collandoth would not ask such a thing without good reason, and that he was only too happy to oblige. So, Gurasa and Collandoth joined the Tallins early the next morning, and the foursome departed Duinnor City.

It was the beginning not only of a great friendship, but of a thrilling and exciting adventure for Gurasa. Their route took them first to the River Osterflo. There they boarded boats and began the journey downriver, through the Locks of Karthia and onward by river toward Glareth by the Sea. It was a scenic and easy route, taking them through the dramatic Carthanes that pitched high on either side of the river for nearly a hundred miles. There was time for fishing, conversation, good food, and gazing at the stars as they floated eastward.

Whenever I dined in the company of others, I was careful to keep my face as covered as I could and in shadows. I implied that I was ashamed or embarrassed by my condition and by the appearance of my face, and that I could not bear the stares of shock or disgust that my appearance might provoke. My accent was explained by an impediment of my speech due to my disfigurement. The Tallins were sympathetic and even sought to make my meals as private as possible, or in such places where I would not be uncomfortable. Thus we traveled in good company, and in good spirits.

It was just after passing through the Locks of Karthia that my true identity—my race, that is—was discovered due entirely to my own mistakes. Some weeks before, shortly after we first met, Dalvenpar had asked my age, and I thought nothing of giving it. Then, while having dinner at a private table in the courtyard of a riverside inn, the topic of age came up again, this time in regard to Lord Tallin's age. That night, Collandoth was not dining with us. He was out wandering the hillsides in search of herbs and would not rejoin us until dawn when we were to cast off and continue our barge journey eastward.

For some reason, the subject of growing older came up. I confessed that I was a terrible judge of a person's age, but that I thought that Lord Tallin looked quite hale for a man of his years.

"Indeed," he said. "I have been touched by the Faerekind, though I am a Mortal Man."

"I do not understand what you mean," I said. "Have you had an encounter with those who kept their wings? And have been somehow blessed by the experience?"

"No." Lord Tallin chuckled. "I have not. I use a figure of speech when I say 'touched by the Faerekind.' I have married an Elifaen lady of an ancient House. Being so joined, my years do not wear upon me as they do to others of my race. I assure you that I am some forty years Dalvenpar's senior."

"If you can believe it, my father and I are often mistaken for brothers," Dalvenpar said. "Of course, he would be my much older brother!"

"And my goodly wife," Lord Tallin picked up, "has every appearance of being Dalvenpar's sister, almost as youthful as his actual little sister, Mirabella!"

"That is most incredible!" I blurted out.

"You'll see for yourself when you meet them!" said Dalvenpar.

"I take it that you have not met many Elifaen," ventured Lord Tallin.

"No, I admit I have not. I met a few when Collandoth and I visited Vanara. But I was introduced to very few people during my stay there. And I certainly did not come to know any well enough to have such a conversation as this."

"I'm tempted to break my promise to Collandoth and start pestering you for wherever it is that you are from!" declared Dalvenpar. "I might think you are from Tracia or Masurthia, since there are so few Elifaen left in those parts."

Lord Tallin sent a warning gaze at his son, which I noticed.

"Oh, Father! I jest! Gurasa, I have no intention of doing any such thing. I would never break my word!"

"I am relieved to hear it," commented Lord Tallin.

"I mean," Dalvenpar went on, "if I did and Collandoth found out, he might turn me into a newt or some such!"

Lord Tallin closed his eyes and shook his head.

"I don't understand," I said.

"The Melnari, such as Collandoth, are not sorcerers or enchanters," Lord Tallin said, "in spite of the tales concerning them. And my son takes his jest too far. He forgets that witty words should never put in doubt one's honor."

"Father! It was only a jest! Gurasa, I assure you, with my deepest sincerity, that I have not contemplated breaking my word to you or to Collandoth."

It was the first time I had seen Dalvenpar the least bit upset about anything.

"Friend," I said to him, "we have not been acquainted for very long, but I have known you long enough to know that would never be the case."

Lord Tallin smiled at this.

"Then you do, indeed, know my son well. And what he says is true, in spite of his inclination to make sport of things. And by coming to know him so well in such a short time, you have shown your keen perception of things." Turning to Dalvenpar, he said, "In spite of being, at times, sorely tested!"

"My father once said that true friendship can stand any test," I recounted, "and that only those who are casual and insincere will fail the test. And so, he went on to tell me, many avoid the tests, knowing the friendship they seek to preserve is not true."

"A wise man, your father," said Lord Tallin.

We soon recovered our jocularity and jovial mood, and we enjoyed the rest of our dinner in good fellowship. Afterwards, we repaired to our barge, where we each had a cabin, and prepared to turn in for the night.

I was unfamiliar with the spiritual rituals of Northmen, but I felt that I should exercise the practices of my own people. Perhaps it was that I was always aware of how far I was from my own lands and people. I cannot say, but shortly after I began my sojourn with Collandoth, I began saying my evening prayers, as I was taught to do when I was a little child. Comforted and reassured by the private ritual, I would then take to my bed or bedroll and sleep.

This night was no different. Except, this night, I failed to latch my cabin door properly. Well-oiled, it easily swung open at the least wave or eddy that washed past our barge. I took off my clothes, all but my loincloth, as is the practice of my people, and I knelt on the cabin floor and said my prayers. As you might know, it is our custom at the end of our nightly prayer to remain in meditation for a while longer, to ponder upon things or, as my father taught me, to let peace come into our hearts. So when I at last opened my eyes and rose up to blow out the candle, I saw my cabin door wide open. And, standing there in the passageway, was Lord Tallin.

There was nothing that I could say or do. I do not know how long he had been standing there, but he plainly saw and heard enough. His face was expressionless as he looked at me, and I'm sure that my own face was covered with horror, embarrassment, and fear. Whatever happened next, I knew that I had to submit to it, that there was no use in words or resistance. So, I knelt again, and I bowed my head but could not bring myself to close my eyes. I saw Lord Tallin step into my cabin and stand before me. He turned and closed the cabin door and securely latched it before turning back to me.

"Get up, please," he said. "Please, get up."

I did so as he took a seat in my cabin chair. He gestured to my cot, and I sat facing him. Still there was no expression that I could read, which made me tremble all the more.

"I think you should tell my son," he stated. "I think he deserves to know. And although I cannot blame Collandoth for keeping your secret, nor for exacting our promises to look after you. But I wish he, and you, had been more forthcoming. I do not blame you, but I do not think that Collandoth knows me as well as I should like for him to."

"It is true," he went on, "that your people and my own have been sworn enemies for thousands of years, and will probably come to blows again when this precarious peace falls apart, as I am sure it will one day. But I have not raised my sons with hatred or animosity toward any people. I have not regaled them with hollow tales of valor, nor have I given them a shallow sense of honor. And I hope that regardless of what may transpire in the future, no act will ever put hatred or animosity in their hearts. But you must know that as the son of a Named House, Dalvenpar is required to become a Kingsman. I will attempt to prevent that from happening, but he is already keen to serve as I have done. So my efforts may be useless. And you know Dalvenpar well enough already to know that as a Kingsman he will do his duty, obey his orders, and will go where he is sent. All of that is on his heart and will be upon his plate. And it may be a bitter meal when comes the time for him to eat. So if you are to be a true friend, I hope that you would tell him fully who—and what—you are. I will not command or force you to do so. I can only say to you, as your own father might, that such a test will only strengthen the friendship between you."

By this time, I admit that I was so overwhelmed with relief that tears ran down my face. Somehow, I had felt ashamed all along for keeping the secret of my identity from Dalvenpar, and Lord Tallin's words only served to bring that feeling of shame up into my throat.

"I shall go to him at once," I said.

"No. Allow me to bring him to you," he said, rising. "I think you should dress, since we must be careful with all of this opening and closing of your door."

"Yes, sir."

Not long afterwards, I answered the knock on the door. Dalvenpar entered, obviously in some confusion. Lord Tallin did not come in.

"I shall let you two have a chat," he said. "And perhaps once that is done, we shall consult with one another on what we should do thenceforth."

He closed the door, and I latched it securely.

"What is the matter?" Dalvenpar asked immediately. "Father said that there was something serious and private that you might want to tell me. Has your health taken a turn? Are you in need of a physician?"

"No. My health is fine, thank you. Better than it has ever been. But there is another matter that I should put before you."

I had, as Lord Tallin suggested, gotten fully dressed, with my usual coverings over my head and face. I always wore a sort of veil over my face, one that covered my eyes for the most part and that was commonly seen being worn by people of the North who were very sick, who had leprosy or some other terrible ailment. And that was how I was attired.

"When we first met, you asked why I have no surname," I said.

"Yes."

"And I told you that it was not the custom of my people to use surnames, and that the one I used was invented in an effort to conform to the customs of others."

"I remember. And I asked you if you were Elifaen, and you said that you were not."

"And when I told you my age, you said that I looked a bit smallish."

"I'm sorry. I did not mean to give you offense."

"No, that is not it. I was not offended. It is true. I am, by your standards, very slight of build. But, even for my size, I am one of the most healthy and hearty of all of my own people. You see, most of my people are destined to die young because of a sickness that we are cursed with. Some of us—the wealthy, the powerful—can afford a special and rare medicine which makes us able to withstand the terrible effects of the sickness, but which does not cure us of it or make us invulnerable to it. I think you should see me. And then you may decide if we are to remain friends."

"Whatever can you mean by that?"

I unfastened my head coverings and dropped them to the floor so that he could fully see my face, my eyes, and my hair. He simply looked at me, as expressionless as his father had been earlier. Then he nodded.

"So I assume that you have a supply of darakal that you have brought with you," he said at last. "Has it run out? You said that your health was fine, though."

"What? So you already know that I am a Dragonkind?"

"Of course I know. I've known practically since the moment we first met, whilst rummaging around the gardens at the Temple of Beras."

"What? How?"

I was so flummoxed that I had to take a seat.

"My dear fellow," he laughed, "I thought it was all an act to keep my father from finding out, so I just went along with it."

"But, but..."

"It was when we were in the south garden of the Temple," Dalvenpar went on. "There were some flowers there that you recognized and rushed over to see. I don't think you realized it, but you said rather loudly that you had no idea that they could be cultivated so far north. Remember? And remember the monk who overheard you? He said that you were right, that the flowers had arrived only a month earlier, as a gift from a patron who was just back from the Dragonlands. The monk said that the flowers were doing poorly and that most had already died, that the rest were not expected to last another fortnight. Remember? Remember how you and he laughed at that?"

"Yes. Yes, of course I remember that. But how could that have let on anything about me?"

"Well, I might not know much about flowers and such, but I do know about the legend of Ormace and his love, the beautiful Eyrice."

"I have no idea what or to whom you refer."

Indeed, I was as confused as ever.

"It's a legend about how those flowers came to be," he explained. "Cronosis, you called them, which I know from my lessons is what they are called by the Dragonkind. We call them Semiluna, the Fortnight Flowers. And there is only one place where they grow, in the deserts of the Dragonlands, and only in those rare spots where there is ample water. But that day at the Temple, you recognized them immediately, and you were genuinely surprised, I could tell. I certainly did not know what they were until you blurted it out. And the monk was surprised by your knowledge, too, although he did not press you on it. The only possible way you could have recognized them is if you had seen them before. And the only place you could have seen them before is in the Dragonlands."

"Oh. So you knew ever since that day."

"Pretty much. By the time of the flower incident, I had already asked about your surname. I had my suspicions then. The Fortnight Flowers cinched it for me."

"Why did you not say anything? Why did you go along with the promise to Collandoth?"

"My dear fellow! It was not my place to say anything," he explained. "I might be a bit of a jester, but I'm no fool. I was struck by the terrible risk you were taking by traveling outside of your own lands. And I think I judged rightly when I came to the conclusion that you have uncommon courage and pluck!"

"I can hardly believe it!"

"It's true! I grappled with myself over whether I should let on that I knew. But when Collandoth made us promise, it just brought home to me how much protection you need. So I thought I'd be better able to look out for you if I just went along with the promise. That way, if you made a slip, perhaps I could interfere and cover for you with no one the wiser."

"I am completely—what is the word Collandoth taught me? Gobsmacked. I am completely gobsmacked."

Having held it back for nearly the entire conversation, Dalvenpar began laughing. He could not stop laughing. That made me laugh. Lord Tallin told me later that when he heard us laughing, he knew that all was well. When he came in, he had a difficult time getting us to settle down. He wanted the three of us to have a serious talk about how we should handle my disguise so that there could be no possibility of anyone else learning my secret, which was now our secret, together.

It was the best thing that could have happened. Then Dalvenpar's pent-up curiosity poured out, and from then on he asked incessantly about my home and people. He was as curious about me and my people as I was about him and his. We learned to guard our conversations so that they were never overheard, but whenever we had the chance, we talked ourselves hoarse. Lord Tallin was no less enthusiastic than his son, with many questions to ask, and with stories of his own to tell. That is truly when my education began. Never could I have found better friends than Dalvenpar and his father, the Lord Tallin.

Many years later, Collandoth recorded in his journals what happened later that same night. Long after Gurasa and Dalvenpar had gone to bed and were fast asleep, Lord Tallin waited ashore near the gangplank for Collandoth's return. When Collandoth approached and saw Lord Tallin, he at first thought something had happened during his absence.

"Lord Tallin, I am surprised to see that you are not asleep. You wait for me? Has something happened?"

"Yes, Collandoth," Tallin answered. "Something has happened. Perhaps we could step away from the barge, just a short distance on down the path."

It was apparent that Tallin did not wish to be overheard, so we followed the path along the riverbank for a short distance until we were well out of earshot of the boatmen, but still within sight of our barge.

"As a soldier," Tallin began, "it has been my unfortunate duty to place in harm's way many a good man. My duty has also made me responsible for the loss of many lives. Those who served under me, and those who opposed me in battle. Never have I taken that duty lightly. Never have I disregarded common sense and prudent measures to safeguard the lives of others whenever I could."

"I am certain that is so, Lord Tallin. You have a well-deserved reputation for both cunning and prudence."

"Then you will forgive me if I do not understand how it is that a Melnari of your experience, to say nothing of years, could be so careless of another man's life!"

"I beg your pardon. What do you mean by that, sir?"

"When we agreed to travel together, and you asked me and Dalvenpar to respect Gurasa's privacy by not questioning him, I was of course curious, if not suspicious. After all, your reputation for intrigue and diplomacy is fairly well known. So I assumed the best. That you and Gurasa had good reason to maintain his disguise as a sickly person. But his manner of walk, to say nothing at all of his stamina, belies that ruse. Still, I kept my word, thinking perhaps that Gurasa was someone important, perhaps even the son of a lord or prince, though his costume would certainly not be necessary if that were the case. As I said, it never occurred to me that Gurasa might be in any real danger, regardless of who he might be."

Lord Tallin spoke very fast, which was quite out of character as he was normally very deliberate in his manner of speech. He paused for a long moment, obviously weighing what he was about to say.

"That young man," Tallin pointing at the barge, "is a Dragonkind!   His very presence outside of his own lands is tantamount to a death sentence for him. How could you permit him to come out of the Dragonlands with you?   What's more, why did you not inform me of his race so that I could safeguard him?   No, no!   Gurasa is safe and sound. But anyone could have discovered his identity as easily and as accidentally as I did. And I daresay it would have gone badly for Gurasa if someone else had happened along his open door whilst he was at his evening prayers."

Then Lord Tallin explained to me all that had happened while I was away. He was genuinely upset, and I let him fume away at me for many moments.

"Good sir," I said, "it was not for me to tell you. Gurasa is fully aware of the dangers posed to him. You are right to be upset at the close call. Perhaps it was my mistake not to take Gurasa along with me this evening. But if he is not to be trusted with his own safety, then, soon or later, anything I might do to safeguard him would be in vain. We are the only passengers on this barge, so the likelihood was quite low of anything going amiss. And Dalvenpar?"

It took a while longer before Tallin would accept my apology. I am sure that he felt that I was careless. Little did Lord Tallin realize that my good Certina was keeping watch all the while at Gurasa's cabin window, and she would have fetched me right away if any threat to Gurasa had materialized. I did not point this out to Lord Tallin because I knew that it would eventually occur to him that I did not leave Gurasa unguarded. Besides, I could not help feeling a little insulted by his insinuations, and so I reserved for myself some modicum of smugness.

An Uncomfortable Incident in Glareth by the Sea

With two new protectors and friends, Gurasa arrived in Glareth by the Sea. He was, by all accounts, utterly charmed by the realm, and amazed. He had never seen a body of water as large as Salfin Bay, and at first he mistook it for the Great Sea, much to the amusement of his companions. Having arrived late in the day with little daylight left, they continued on into the city on to the easternmost and oldest part of Glareth by the Sea, built high up upon the rocky cliffs and bluffs. In their carriage, they passed through the ancient and fabled Gate of the Sea Kings and into the Old City. The carriage halted near the palace of the Ruling Prince, and the foursome continued on foot, going along the old fortress ramparts until, coming around a keep, the full sweep of the eastern sea came into view. Far below them, greenish-gray waves crashed and boomed into white spray, and as far as the eye could see eastward was the heaving Great Sea in all its might and mystery.

Gurasa stood in speechless wonder of the sight for many moments. Then, overcome with awe, he suddenly sat on the cobblestones. Collandoth and Lord Tallin nodded, for Gurasa's reaction to the sight reminded them of the first time they had seen the majesty and power of the Great Sea. Dalvenpar, borrowing a cup from a street vendor, raced down a steep stairway and disappeared. A little while later, he returned, carefully bearing a sip of seawater which he offered to Gurasa to taste. The look on Gurasa's face was one of astonishment. Collandoth later recounted:

"It is salty!" he said. "Like some of the bad wells in the desert. Tell me, is it safe to drink?"

"Perfectly safe," Dalvenpar replied, "if you are a fish of the sea! For the rest of us, though, it does not quench the thirst, nor can it be given to cattle or used to water crops."

"In some places along the coast," Lord Tallin added, "the seawater is collected and poured out into great troughs. After it dries away, the salt is collected and sold."

"Yes," Gurasa nodded, "I have tasted sea-salt, gathered in a like manner by my people on the shores of the Craggy Sea. Then are all seas salty?"

"The Craggy Sea is a part of the Great Sea, Gurasa," I told him. "Its waters and that of the Great Sea mingle and mix freely."

"And your people, Lord Tallin, came across and from beyond this Great Sea?" Gurasa asked.

"Yes. We did."

"And your ancestors carried enough water to drink during their long voyage?"

"No. They learned to cleanse the salt water by some means, perhaps by distilling it. No one is sure how it was done, for most of the stories and the knowledge of day-to-day life aboard the mighty city ships have been lost and forgotten."

"Oh."

They tarried in Glareth by the Sea only a few days. During that time, Gurasa met Dalvenpar's younger brother, Aram, who was attending school there. Gurasa says little about Aram in his journals, only that he was not as boisterous as his older brother, somewhat more thoughtful and reserved, but every bit as kind and gentlemanly. Dalvenpar and Gurasa tagged along with Lord Tallin, who seemed to have had friends and business associates everywhere they went. Lord Tallin, somewhat anxious to get home, hurried hither and yon throughout the city. One of the places where he had business at the Admiralty of the Royal Glarethian Navy. According to Gurasa's biographer, Tareef al Binsalud, a telling incident took place at the Admiralty which was only mentioned in passing in Gurasa's own travel journals, but one that Gurasa elaborated upon during a conversation with Tareef many years later. Tareef reconstructed the account thuswise:

Lord Tallin had a friend who was soon to retire from the Glarethian Navy and planned to buy a trade ship and be its captain.

"I hope to convince him to let me invest in his company," Lord Tallin told the boys upon their arrival at the Admiralty, "and to influence him to place Tallinvale's trade before all others. For a generous commission, of course. If so, we can base our operations out of Colleton and shave nearly three hundred miles off the overland route from Tallinvale to Glareth."

"Is not the city and port of Forlandis nearer?" asked Gurasa.

"It is, indeed," answered Lord Tallin. "You have a shrewd eye for maps. Yes, Forlandis is some fifty to a hundred miles closer to Tallinvale than is Colleton. But I would not trust the safety of any cargo to Tracian ports."

"They are dishonest, then."

"Dishonest? Not exactly. They are open and up front about fees, taxes, and tolls on their roads, on all shipping, and on foreign visitors. Especially those with Elifaen connections. Dishonest? That is not the word. Rapacious would be a better one."

"Rapacious?"

"There are other words. Greedy. Predatory. Ravenous."

"Oh."

"They will strangle themselves out of existence, or worse, if they are not careful,"

Tallin said as they walked up the steps of a very large building with ornate columns and high glass windows.

They entered the great foyer of the Admiralty, a broad room with several staircases leading upward, walls covered with portraits and seascapes, and a high ceiling from which hung bright lamps.

"Why don't you two look around while I find my friend," Tallin said. "His bureau is upstairs. I don't think I'll be very long. Avoid speaking with others you may meet. Be careful. And for goodness sakes, don't get in the way! Meet me here at four bells. You'll hear the chime wherever you are."

At that, Lord Tallin was away, tromping upstairs and out of sight, leaving the lads free to explore the surroundings. Everything was of a maritime theme. The stairs had polished brasswork, there were thick ropes draped over doorways, and gimbaled lamps hung from the walls, as if the entire building might heel at any moment. Here and there, the two explorers came to foyers where several hallways met, and a few of the larger intersections had staircases leading upward and downward. In one such place, a large ship's anchor leaned against a rock in the middle of the room, and in front of it was a life-size statue. It depicted a bearded man holding a sextant in one hand whilst with the other he pointed at the door through which the boys had entered. Even here, Gurasa retained his sense of direction, and he knew that the figure was pointing due north.

"Ishtorgus the Mariner," Dalvenpar stated. He gestured to the placard nearby. "He was a good friend to King Thalamir. A great inventor and shipbuilder. Glareth owes its maritime power to him, for he taught Glareth much about seamanship, navigation, and ship-handling."

"A great man, indeed," said Gurasa. "And I am still astounded not only at the tremendous expanse of water that is the sea, but that men traverse it hither and yon as a routine matter of course."

"Well," said Dalvenpar, "I would not call it a routine matter at all! Sailing is dangerous, and I personally tremble every time I step into a ship or sea-boat. And the motion of a boat, up and down, tilting this way and that, heaving back and forth, makes me so ill that I cannot hold down any meal!"

"Really? Is the movement all that bad?"

"Worse! And, worse still, ships break apart at the slightest bump, or for no reason at all! They spring leaks and sink right out from under you. They turn over, dumping you into the sea to drown. That is, if you haven't already been crushed to death by falling masts or shifting cargo. And then there are pirates."

"Pirates? What are pirates?"

"They are like the renegades of the Badlands. In boats and ships they go out to sea and attack the hapless, stealing cargo, enslaving some passengers and casting all others into the sea. Sometimes, when ships are battling sea-storms, the pirates lure them onto rocky shores by putting up false lights and lamps in the safe channels and taking away warning lights up on the rocks."

"That is terrible!"

"Yes," nodded Dalvenpar. "But not so terrible as the creatures that lurk below the waves, ones that make the sea their home. At least with pirates, you have a chance to survive."

"Fish, you mean? Such as those creatures that we took from River Osterflo and cooked for supper?"

"Aye, fish!" joined in an elderly man who had paused to look upon the statue and had heard Dalvenpar's explanation of maritime dangers.

"Fish, indeed!" he proclaimed. "Some are so big that ye could barely fit the tail of one into this room. And if ye did, the thrash of it would surely destroy this entire building with but a few sweeps."

Gurasa, wide-eyed, gaped.

"I do not mean to make ye suffer fear or apprehension unnecessarily," said the old man, gesturing slightly at Gurasa's coverings. "To add to yer condition, that is."

"No, no," said Gurasa. "I am fit in that regard. But surely you exaggerate. How can a fish be so big?"

"They just are," said Dalvenpar, giving Gurasa a little nudge away from the old man. "Perhaps we should move along." But Gurasa desired to hear more.

"And then there're sharks!" declared the man, putting his face close to Gurasa's. "The very demons of the sea, they are. They come swift and sure, smellin' trouble from miles away, and comin' to add terror to distress. Look yonder, boy! What d'ye see?"

Gurasa turned and looked up at a large white hoop hanging on the wall. So large it was that Gurasa would have had no trouble stepping through it, if only he could avoid cutting himself on the short, wide blades protruding inside the rim.

"Some sort of ship-making tool?" Gurasa guessed. "Perhaps for cutting peculiar patterns?"

"A tool? Aye, it is! A tool it is!" cried the old man, his voice echoing. "A tool for killin' and maimin'. The jaws and teeth of a great shark!"

Gurasa stepped closer to the display. Some of the teeth were as big as his hand.

"Oh, the sea is a fearful place!" Gurasa said a bit too loudly. Overhearing this exclamation, a group of sailors passing by nodded and grinned.

"Yes," said Dalvenpar. "There you are in your puny little boat, surrounded by all manner of terror. And just when you think you are safe from sharks and whales and eels and great lobsters, other creatures will come and lure you from the rickety safety of your boat and into the water and right down beneath the waves."

"Other creatures?"

"People-creatures," said Dalvenpar, now forgetting his father's warning and joining fully into the conversation. "Selkies, Finfolk, kelpies, mermaids, and sirens. All sorts of sea-folk! And very few of them the kind of folk you'd care to meet, I'm sure."

"Sea people? People who can breathe water?"

"Aye! When they want to," said the old man. "They say that when the Faerekind fell from the skies, some of them landed in the sea and in lakes and rivers and such. And so their wings were not completely torn off of 'em. And them remnants is that's what gives 'em their magic. They got gossamer fins, some do. And they fly through the depths of the sea like birds do in the sky, sometimes even dancin' atop the sea-waves. Some of 'em got so used to the sea that they turned half into fish, part scales, part skin, with powerful fish-like tails instead o' legs."

Gurasa was, by now, fairly overwhelmed, and he was unable to come to grips with this news about dangerous sea-creatures. But all boys have a kind of morbid curiosity about such things, and Gurasa was no different, so he hung on every word.

"Some of them are beautiful to behold, they say," added Dalvenpar.

"Aye, that's true!" And if their beauty don't attract ye to 'em, then the music they make and the songs they sing will do the trick. Many's the seaman what stepped off a good sturdy ship to join the sea-folk, sinkin' down with 'em, probably to be eaten once they drowned. And many's the sailor what heard them songs or seen them folk and came home safe and sound only to pine and long to go back out yonder, to the sea and to them sea-folk!"

"No!"

"Aye! T'is true! Come, come!" said the old man, tugging on Gurasa's sleeve and gesturing down the hall. "Come see this paintin' just yon."

Dalvenpar and Gurasa followed the old man a few yards along a hallway, then he stopped and pointed.

"Look!" he cried, pointing to a very large painting. Gurasa and Dalvenpar stepped closer.

It depicted a rocky coastline, white with churning surf. Out to sea was a foundering ship, breaking up on the rocks. Men were fighting for their lives, some clinging to drifting spars or planks, others splashing helplessly, and others, already dead, rolling against the rocks with the waves. And sitting on the rocks, as if oblivious to the peril, was a creature. She was half-woman. Down to her waist, she was beautiful and alluring. From her waist down were green scales, and instead of legs she had the tail of a great fish. She sat, her tail languishing in the water, her back to the sea, with a silver mirror in one hand and a silver comb in the other. She blithely combed her luxurious red hair as men cried out and died in the waves all around her. Beneath his coverings, Gurasa could feel himself blush at the sight of the creature and feeling guilty for doing so whilst those men suffered and died.

"What d'ye think of that?" whispered the old man.

"She's...she's beautiful!"

"That she is. A mermaid, she is. Aye, beautiful. Beautiful and unconcerned with the likes of poor sailors and seamen."

For a long moment, none of the trio could take their eyes from the painting. Then Dalvenpar started at something he noticed. He pointed to one of the sailors, clinging to a rock not five yards away from the mermaid. The man had a distinctive tattoo on his forearm, two round figures that represented Sir Sun and Lady Moon. Gurasa nodded, then he, too, did a double-take. The two boys looked at the old man's forearm, adorned with the same tattoo.

"I've had this tattoo ever since me first homecoming when I was just a snivelin' midshipman," said the man. "When I was a second lieutenant and thirty years of age, we fought a typhoon for four days, doin' our best to stay out to sea. On the fourth day, we hit the rocks and our ship broke up. It did."

He pointed at the painting.

"That's me. I was there. And that's a fair depiction of what I saw, 'cept not half so beautiful as the actual creature. And I ain't the only one what seen her sittin' there. Twenty of me shipmates came ashore where I did, and they seen her, too. When finally I got up on the rocks, she spotted me, and it was like I startled her for a moment. Then she looked out at the wreckage comin' in, the bodies roilin', the men cryin' for help. And d'ye know what she did?   She heaved a great sigh, as if we were an inconvenient interruption. Then she slipped into the water and was gone. No offer to help, though bein' half fish and so a powerful swimmer, she could've saved many a life that day. But, no!" The old man shook his head. "Cold creature! Cold-hearted."

"Aw, that ain't cold!"

The three turned around and saw another old man standing behind them. He was well-dressed, lanky, with a stark, weather-beaten face.

"I say it was," said the first old man. "I was there, warn't I?"

"Aye, sure. Maybe ye were," answered the second. "But ye don't know cold 'til ye get to the Dragonlands, an' come face to face with a lizard wearin' plate."

"Plate?"

"Armor, mister. Armor!   Them slinky lizards ain't got no betters when it comes to uncarin', callous, an' cruel ways!"

Dalvenpar tugged Gurasa's sleeve.

"Come, Gurasa! I think we ought to get on back," Dalvenpar said.

"Why, sir," answered the first old man, "I daresay ye have never been at sea."

"What lizards?" asked Gurasa.

"An' I'd wager ye ain't never been to the deserts!"

"Gurasa!   Let us go!"

Gurasa was staring back and forth at the two arguing men.

"What liz—?"

"An' if ye ever were in the deserts," went on the second old man, oblivious to Gurasa, "an' if ye seen what I seen, ye'd wonder if them devils even got hearts. But they do!   I know they do, 'cause me and me mates cut one open just to find out."

Dalvenpar clutched Gurasa's arm and pulled hard.

"That's disgusting!" he said to the old man as he pushed Gurasa ahead of him and away. "And I don't think we care for your company one little bit!   Let's go, Gurasa!"

On down the hallway, while the argument behind them grew heated, Gurasa glanced over his shoulder at the two men.

"Dalvenpar, I think that man told tales," he said. "There are no lizards that wear armor."

"I know."

"There are no lizards big enough to wear armor," stated Gurasa.

"I know, Gurasa."

"Well!"

They continued to hurry along back the way they had come, and soon they could see the main entrance foyer ahead. Dalvenpar slowed and then drew to a halt.

"What is it, Dalvenpar?"

Dalvenpar sigh and shook his head. He put his hand on Gurasa's shoulder.

"Listen," he said. "I'm really sorry about that. But there's no use in denying that there are a lot of people who think the same way as that man back there."

"What do you mean?"

"I mean that people throw hate around because it's so light and easy to toss. And when it comes to people, my people, who have fought in the deserts against your people, there's no lacking in hateful feelings."

"Yes. I can understand that. Especially if some of your friends died in fighting. Did I misunderstand something back there?"

"Yes, you did."

Dalvenpar's expression was one of embarrassment mixed with anger, but he did not look away. Gurasa thought for a moment that his friend was on the verge of tears. Then he understood.

"Oh."

Dalvenpar nodded.

"Lizards," said Gurasa, gesturing to himself.

Dalvenpar nodded again. "I'm sorry."

"No. Don't be," said Gurasa, now visibly shaken at the hateful man's words. "Oh, my! Do you think he told the truth? About what he and his friends did?"

"I'm sorry to say that I don't doubt it," answered Dalvenpar.

Just then, the bells rang four times, their signal to return to the main foyer. Looking that way, they saw Lord Tallin appear down the stairs, craning his head to look for them.

In Tallinvale and the Old Eastlands Realm

The following day, Gurasa, Dalvenpar, and Lord Tallin departed for Tallinvale, leaving Collandoth behind in Glareth. The three traveled first to Formouth, and there they were given passage on a small sloop and sailed down Lake Halgaeth. This delighted Gurasa immensely. Dalvenpar was sick for the entire journey. They put in at Northwick, then took the road along the lake's western shore. They passed through the small town of Passdale, and then by way of Janhaven they entered the forests of the Thunder Mountains. Gurasa had already witnessed forest-country on his journey from Vanara to Duinnor, but he was no less enchanted as the trio neared Tallinvale. Wildlife was in abundance—rabbits, deer, hawks, and turtles—and Dalvenpar took great delight in pointing them out.

Gurasa's time in Tallinvale was not very well recorded, or at least many of his notes pertaining to that part of his journey did not survive. An entire trunk that held many of his Tallinvale journals was lost. And Dalvenpar himself did not keep many notes. What is certain is that by the time of Gurasa's visit, Tallin City, the newly established town surrounding Tallin Hall, was a bustling and growing place. Dalvenpar probably explained to Gurasa that many people feared that Dragonkind armies might come again as they had centuries before, hence why Lord Tallin had the walls and defenses built. Gurasa would later mention to Tareef that Tallinvale's defenses were formidable, and though her fighting strength was small, it was highly trained and disciplined.

What survived of Gurasa's notes were mostly sketches and notes pertaining to the many insects and plants that he collected. He made watercolor renditions of wildlife and domestic animals, as well as colored sketches of flowers and trees. Most of the plants and creatures were unknown or legendary to his people in the Dragonlands. He also collected quite a few specimens, mostly of insects, filling boxes and bottles with them.

Having left the Dragonlands with only a single small pack, by the time he reached Tallinvale, he had two large trunks filled with journals and specimens, and he was soon to have a third full trunk. Lord Tallin generously arranged for Gurasa's trunks to be transported to Kajarahn, the Free City of the northern Dragonlands. From there, they would be taken to Gurasa's home town of Almedian to await the traveler's return. As it happened, so productive was Gurasa's stay in Tallinvale that by the time he departed, five full trunks had been dispatched ahead of him, including one that would become lost.

It was through one of his specimens that, years later, it came to light that one of the excursions that Dalvenpar and Gurasa went on had been kept a secret from Lord Tallin, no doubt to avoid his displeasure. Mention of it appears nowhere among Gurasa's journals. As it happened, very many years later, a visitor to Gurasa's home in Almedian recorded in his diary how Gurasa had on display within his home a small collection of insects. They had all been gathered, Gurasa told the visitor, while he was on his travels in the northern lands. There was a particularly beautiful butterfly in the collection. When the visitor made a comment about it, Gurasa said that the butterfly was taken after it alit atop the western wall of Tulith Attis, right beside where Gurasa's hand was resting as he gazed out from the parapets. The butterfly landed, said Gurasa, moved its wings a few times, and died. The visitor, a fellow Dragonkind, was surprised by the revelation, and he pressed Gurasa to say more about his visit to the legendary fortress. But Gurasa said very little about his impression of the place, and he guided the topic of conversation to other matters.

During Gurasa's stay in Tallinvale, Lord Tallin was often pressed by business, so Gurasa spent a good deal of time with Dalvenpar, and even Mirabella. She was vivacious and merry, and he especially enjoyed playing Hide and Seek with her, but he always saw to it that she found him no matter where in the great mansion he hid himself. Years later, legends sprang up among the Dragonkind about a fierce green-eyed, red-haired warrioress and how she slaughtered any who came within reach of her sword. When Gurasa eventually learned her identity, he was shocked that it was the self-same mirthful girl that had played games with him in Tallin Hall.

Gurasa Returns Home

After many months, Collandoth arrived in Tallinvale to guide Gurasa back home to the Dragonlands. By then (812 SA), Gurasa and Dalvenpar had become good friends, indeed, and they confided in each other their concerns for their lands, their families, and for peace between their peoples. It was not without regret that the two took leave of each other at last. Gurasa and Collandoth departed, taking a circuitous route westward through Masurthia and Altoria, and eventually back to Vanara. Collandoth then escorted Gurasa back to Almedian and remained as a guest for several days. The first thing that Gurasa did after Collandoth's departure was to commission a special ring. He arranged for the ring to be carried by traders to the Free City of Kajarahn and through Vanara and all the way back to Tallinvale, where it was delivered to his friend. Dalvenpar proudly wore it for the rest of his life.

Gurasa continued to travel for several months, going to every corner of the Dragonlands until, at the age of nineteen. This was when he married an Almedian girl named Sefina, the daughter of a local weaver. Gurasa took up the work of his father, who was seriously ill, and began raising a family, his first child being born the same year. However, by the end of his nineteenth year, he was forced to enlist in the military because his father had not the wealth to bribe authorities, nor the influence to exempt his only remaining child. Over the years, throughout his military service, Gurasa would return home to his family at every opportunity, even if his visits were very short. Each time he came, he brought with him any earnings, boons, or bounties to share with his people. And, over time, he and Sefina would have four children. All but one would die before adulthood, victims of epidemics and the desert sickness. Only his youngest child, and only daughter, would survive into adulthood.

Although small and unimposing, Gurasa's intelligence enabled him to survive his military training. He demonstrated a talent for leading other recruits and conscripts, and he quickly advanced through the ranks. When his training was complete, he was given several unimportant field assignments, mostly leading patrols to safeguard trading routes. His superiors took notice of him after he rescued a caravan of traders and noblemen that was attacked by a large contingent of renegades. Among those that Gurasa's patrol rescued were several relatives of the Dragonkind King. As a reward, Gurasa was given the command of a battalion under the illustrious General Saris. The following week, Saris marched with his army to put down a rebellion in the southern region of the Dragonlands known as Karkarando.

The Rebellion in Karkarando

Since the discovery of the healing properties of darakal, a plant that could only be grown in the Karkarando region in the southwest, the Dragonkind rulers sought to systematically took over all crop production. By royal decree, all darakal production and products belonged to the throne. And the kings of the Dragonlands constantly forced its cultivation instead of precious food crops needed by the Karkarando's people. It was difficult to control the growing black market in darakal, and as the fortunes of the various kings waxed and waned, the tendency was for the Dragonkind throne to exert harsher conditions on Karkarando and its people.

After years of oppression, there was a general uprising in 816 SA. Darakal fields were burned, royal overseers were put to death, and many supporters of the crown were killed or driven out. The Dragon King reacted by sending troops to the region to quell the violence and punish the rebels. However, the inept and weak force that arrived in Karkarando only made matters worse. Within days of their arrival, they had been completely routed by organized resistance, and many of the troops had deserted to join the ranks of the rebels. At last, a unified rebel army was formed, armed with captured weapons. The rebel leaders aimed for complete control of darakal cultivation, and to use control of the vital elixir in a bid for regional autonomy. Their methods were violent and extreme. They gave the people of the region a stark choice: join the rebellion or die. Many of the villages that were part of the early revolt now faced an enemy far worse than the Dragonkind King. The only thing that prevented the rebels from gaining complete control of Karkarando was the fact that it was an enormous area to conquer and administer. Yet, the rebels made steady progress, led by the seasoned fighters under the overall command of a self-made warlord, called Jahawalez. Within two years, they consolidated their forces in the westernmost areas, and pushed steadily eastward, defeating in detail the royal garrisons of each village or stronghold before moving to the next. With each victory, their ranks increased in numbers, and with greater experience and better leadership and logistics, the rebels were as formidable as any that might be fielded against them. And in 819 S.A., they faced their greatest threat, as the King sent a newly formed army to the region.

The rebels' opponent was the brilliant, if elderly, General Saris. A veteran of northern battles (he had even seen action against Lord Tallin at Khanhar Pass), Saris led a force of some two-hundred thousand southward in early 819 S.A.. However, Jahawalez had warning and prepared carefully. In a daring and massive raid, the Jahawalez surprised Saris's forces. The rebels, numbering perhaps 125,000, drove straight into the forces led by General Saris, driving a deep wedge then turning left and right, subdividing the confused Dragonkind army. Saris was killed along with all of his officers. The only officer that was spared was Gurasa, during this attack, was many miles away with his battalion guarding the supply trains. He quickly rode to the scene and saw that the army was in disarray and on the verge of collapse, and, as the most senior surviving officer, Gurasa assumed command just in time to prevent a complete rout. He quickly reorganized, promoting capable junior officers as needed, and he redeployed against renewed rebel attacks. To confuse the enemy, Gurasa hastily changed all of the battle standards of his army to a new one depicting a white dragon, which in the legends of the desert represents "ghost" or "apparition."

By now, it was apparent to Gurasa that his surviving forces were severely outnumbered. He began a series of tactical retreats and managed to avoid direct confrontation with the rebel forces. Gurasa's forces numbered around 70,000, including thousands of men of the supply trains who were not trained to fight. By some estimates, Jahawalez had some 180,000 fighters under his command. But they had been bruised and bloodied, too, with many killed on their side. There was a high rate of desertion and defection, and so there may have been many fewer rebels. Regardless, Jahawalez knew that his forces were far superior in numbers. Moreover, the manner of Gurasa's retreats led Jahawalez to believe that Gurasa's entire force was in disorderly retreat. Confident of his strengths, Jahawalez halted further pursuit for two days in order to reform and resupply his troops before delivering a devastating blow. It was the break that Gurasa was looking for.

When Jahawalez was ready to resume, his scouts reported that they could find no trace of their opponent, only a rag-tag band that was still in hasty retreat north and east away from the region. This led Jahawalez to believe that complete victory had already been attained, and he began moving his forces back into Karkarando. That night, the far north flank of the rebel army was attacked by a small band of fast-riding horsemen. The attack was easily thwarted, and when the horsemen turned tail, a host of rebel horsemen rode after them into the night. Only one managed to return, severely wounded, saying that his comrades were all killed by ghost soldiers fighting under the banner of a white dragon.

The next morning, nearly a hundred miles away to the south, another attack occurred, this time by about two-thousand footmen against the unprepared rebel flank. They drove about two miles into the rebel-held territory, then, just when the rebels were in full retreat, the attackers melted away into the hills. They, too, had flown the white dragon.

When news of these attacks reached Jahawalez that night, he did not believe the reports. How could the two attacks, hundreds of miles apart, have come under the same banner only hours apart? While he was busy deriding his officers for such rumors, the alarm was raised in his own encampment. No sooner had he donned his battle gear than his camp was overrun with enemy horsemen who set tents afire, cut down those they galloped past, and continued on. Almost as suddenly as they had come, the raiders departed, driving straight through the encampment and out the other side and fading into the night. They left behind hundreds of dead and dying rebels, tents afire, and wagons scattered.

And Jahawalez himself saw, by the light of the fires, the banner they carried: the White Dragon.

The attacks were all insignificant militarily, but had a devastating blow to rebel morale. Within but a few hours, word of a ghost army come to mete out the King's anger shot through the rebel forces like lightning. It was exactly what Gurasa intended.

Over the following days, the stings and pricks and uncanny appearance and disappearance of Gurasa's forces upon those of the rebels took its toll. The rebels did not know which way to turn, from which direction the next attack would come. If only the ghost army would stand and fight! But Gurasa was not ready. Instead, he kept up the relentless harassment campaign, keeping the rebels off balance, not permitting them the time to react. Under his leadership, his small forces lured rebel details into well-laid ambushes, then melted away into the surrounding desert only to turn up somewhere else on a different flank. He even sent spies into the rebel camps to gauge what effect the skirmishes were having, and thus Gurasa learned that Jahawalez itched for a pitted battle where he could mass his entire army against the vexing White Dragon. Gurasa intended to give Jahawalez his chance to do just that.

After a week and a half, Gurasa judged that his enemy was sufficiently weakened by these hit-and-run tactics, and sufficiently goaded, too. He finalized his plans with his officers, deployed his troops, and then he allowed the rebels to pursue his army into a carefully planned defensive position to the west of the main rebel force. The rebels halted for the night to bring up additional forces and to prepare for the morning's assault. Jahawalez was thrilled by the prospect of a set-piece battle, and he meant to completely crush his enemy. That night, Gurasa erected a series of fake encampments with bright campfires. Leaving a few hundred men behind to make noise and commotion throughout the night, Gurasa quietly marched the bulk of his army fifteen miles around and behind the rebel camps. Outnumbered almost three to one, he attacked at dawn with the rising sun in the eyes of his enemies. It was a complete and utter surprise, and within two hours of vicious and intense fighting (during which Gurasa was wounded), the rebels were completely defeated. The rebel general Jahawalez took his own life rather than be captured. After winning the battle, even though seriously wounded (he would lose his left hand as a result), Gurasa marched into the rebellious territories, putting down several more minor uprisings before triumphantly returning to Tyrsharat.

News of his feats had preceded him, and the city welcomed Gurasa, the White Dragon, as a great hero. He was feted by the high and mighty, praised by King Salzadur in person and in proclamation. And because the darakal supplies had been restored, all the people were relieved and thankful to Saltani Gurasa.

Peace With the North Comes to an End

There was little rest for the Dragonkind's new hero. Within a month, Tyrsharat was attacked by yet another rebel army commanded by King Salzadur's own nephew who sought to gain the throne by force. Before the city could be cut off and besieged, Gurasa rode out with a small company of his Al Sairs (Gurasa's personal army, numbering around 500). In a bold, quick strike, they captured the rebellious nephew, and Gurasa personally brought him before the King, who promptly beheaded the unrepentant relative.

Gurasa's fame was at its pinnacle, and it was whispered that the King privately feared the young general. Hearing that Gurasa had spent time in the Northlands, King Salzadur's agents began spreading rumors that Gurasa was not as loyal as he ought to be. Although this caused the upper class and many within the military to distance themselves from Gurasa, it did nothing to cool the ardor of the common people, and particularly those soldiers who had served with him. Militarily, all now seemed secure within the Dragonlands, as no one else dared to oppose the King.

Thus, for several years, Gurasa was more or less inactive militarily. He spent much of the time at home in Almedian with his family. In Almedian, he worked to increase the wealth of his village by using his influence to garner trade deals. He had numerous new wells dug, irrigation systems built, and improvements made to the surrounding roads. He also spent a good deal of time rebuilding his small palace in Almedian, employing many craftsmen and workers. For the first time since his return from the north, he had time to look through the notes and journals and specimens that he had brought back with him. He even managed to paint a few depictions of the places he had visited in the north and in his own Dragonlands.

Yet Gurasa remained aware of the tensions between the Dragonkind and the realms of the north. Through various contacts, he learned of the growing might of Vanara and Duinnor and grew concerned. As more trade goods flowed through the Free City, people of the Dragonlands began to fully realize how rich and prosperous Vanara was, with abundant natural resources such as timber, water, farmlands, and livestock. And Gurasa was aware that whispers of envy within the court of the King were turning into open suggestions for conquest. Some feared that the Free City would become a Vanaran ally and suggested that the city be captured and annexed and placed under the rule of a governor appointed by the King. A great sense of foreboding settled over Gurasa.

Unbeknownst to most, including Gurasa, King Salzadur had authorized new forays into Vanara with the aim of probing Vanara's military strength. These actions resulted in many attacks into Vanara and the destruction of several villages and small towns. Very quickly, general hostilities broke out and the peace that had been in place for nearly twenty years was falling to bits. Reluctantly, Gurasa traveled to the Green Citadel in order to offer his services and that of his Al Sairs. It was there that Gurasa learned that the city was the base from which the attacks on the north were being launched by the King's brother-in-law, the governor of the city. Gurasa warned the city leaders that such actions could have terrible consequences, and pointed out that the Green Citadel was ill-prepared for hostilities. He offered his services and those of his Al Sairs to help bolster the city's defenses. But instead of accepting Gurasa's offer of assistance, he was rebuffed, and the prince ordered Gurasa to cease his interference and gave him orders to report to the King in Tyrsharat.

While Gurasa was traveling to Tyrsharat, a powerful force was marching south into the Dragonlands. The combined armies of Duinnor, Vanara and other Realms converged on the Green Citadel and laid siege, determined to end the city's aggression. Word reached Tyrsharat the day after Gurasa arrived, and though he was anxious to return north, he was delayed by court rivalries that prevented him from seeing the King or receiving any marching orders. Meanwhile, learning that Gurasa was in the city, the people clamored to have him lead an army north to break the siege and rescue the Green Citadel. Within a week, rumors spread within Tyrsharat that the Green Citadel had fallen and the Elifaen were marching to Tyrsharat with a vast army of Kingsmen and other barbarians. Panic spread, the most fearful fled southward, and a few riots even broke out. At last the King commanded Gurasa to deploy immediately, with all of the forces that could be mustered, to head off the approaching invaders and to vanquish them from the Dragonlands. But again, court rivalries prevented Gurasa from quickly taking command of the forces or of securing the necessary supplies for the campaign. Thus it was that the army intended to relieve Calamandor only managed to depart after yet another week, and Gurasa drove the great force northward swiftly.

The threats to Tyrsharat were only rumors, and no southward-bound enemy force was encountered. But as they approached the region of Calamandor, the long column of smoke rising on the northern horizon grew denser with every passing mile. Gurasa was unable to reach the Green Citadel in time to prevent it from being sacked, plundered, and burned. He entered the charred and devastated city a day after the Northmen had withdrawn, and he was profoundly shaken by what he saw. Fires still burned across the city, and slaughter was in evidence everywhere, bodies strewn wherever he went. Some survivors told how the Northmen cried, "Remember Tulith Attis!" as they killed both women and children. The city had been stripped of its riches, with much of its fabled Glowing Stone broken and hauled away, and even the sacred tomb of Queen Nebalasa ransacked of its treasures. Gurasa saw evidence, too, that many citizens of the city had turned on each other, with as much looting and murder by its inhabitants against each other as by the invaders.

Leaving a strong army to secure the city and enforce order, Gurasa immediately took the rest of his army in pursuit of the retreating Northmen. Within two days, the slow-moving invaders were encountered. Instead of keeping their forces together, the Northmen had taken various different routes, with no communication or support between them. The slowest-moving consisted of long trains of loot-laden wagons that traced their way north, guarded by thousands of Vanarans and Kingsmen soldiers. It was this force that Gurasa's army first encountered. The surprised Vanarans and Kingsmen quickly reorganized and turned to face the horde of Dragonkind.

Ordering the main body of his army to perform a standard attack, Gurasa led his Al Sairs and several battalions of Dragonkind regulars around the Northmen, outflanking them near Khanhar Pass and blocking them from further retreat. The Northmen dug in and formed defensive lines. After three days of fighting, the invaders were cut off, without food or water, and were entirely surrounded, yet they fought on.

Gurasa knew that he would be unable to control his outraged army, and he could easily foresee the outcome. Although he ordered that prisoners were to be taken as slaves to rebuild the city, his orders were largely ignored, and those Northmen who were forced to surrender were more often killed on the spot. See this, the Northmen fought all the harder and the fighting soon devolved into hundreds of vicious skirmishes, with little coordination or control. Casualties on both sides mounted, with the frenzied Dragonkind falling in droves. Only the Al Sairs remained loyal and obedient to his orders. Gurasa rode frantically from hotspot to hotspot, sternly imposing order and exerting his authority over his troops. He finally was able to maneuver them into a complete encirclement of the Northmen. With the Blue Mountains at his back, Gurasa called for a halt to all attacks upon the surrounded invaders. In a bid to prevent useless bloodshed, he secretly sent a message through the lines using a captured Kingsmen as courier. He offered a way out for the Northmen. Gurasa promised that if the Northmen surrendered their arms and gave their oath never to enter the Dragonlands again, he would open the way north through the mountains and permit them to safely pass.

Just as he sent his offer, a new Dragonkind general arrived from Tyrsharat, and he learned of Gurasa's plan. He ordered Gurasa to relinquish command and go immediately to the Green Citadel to answer for his actions and to await judgment. Gurasa's Al Sairs nearly revolted at hearing this, but Gurasa reminded them of the consequences to their families if they were disobedient. However, Gurasa insisted that the change of command be made according to strict protocol that dictated that command changes should be performed in the presence of the troops. The new Dragonkind general conceded to this, and Gurasa's last order to the army was to call a halt to any further actions so that he could meet with all commanders and address as many soldiers as possible. Meanwhile, he sent a second message through the lines to the Northmen explaining that the truce would soon end and, hence, they should use the pause in fighting as an opportunity to flee. He then recalled the Al Sairs, who held the pass that blocked the retreat, and, as soon as he learned from his scouts that the retreat had resumed, he led his men away.

Gurasa's sense of honor was apparently greater than that of the Northmen, for they regrouped once more, and in a flanking action they staged a massive but ultimately futile counterattack against the Dragonkind. The fighting was brutal and thousands were slaughtered. Then the Northmen's momentum ran out and their lines began to disintegrate. The Dragonkind successfully regrouped and came back at the Northmen from every side. Soon there were once again hundreds of small pockets of desperate fighting.

Within a few hours, Gurasa learned of the new battle and was deeply insulted that his gesture had been so outrageously wasted. He returned to the scene with the knowledge that the Northmen now had little chance for quarter. It was, indeed, a horrible slaughter, with fresh Dragonkind troops pouring in from every side by the thousands. It was during this slaughter that Gurasa saw and recognized Dalvenpar, who was Elifaen and had changed but little in appearance during the years since they had last seen each other. But, just as Gurasa rode closer, Dalvenpar threw himself in front of a comrade to save him from a hail of arrows. Dalvenpar was struck many times and was mortally wounded. His comrade took Dalvenpar's sword and turned to face Gurasa as he rode up, but then turned and fled. Gurasa ordered his men not to pursue. Instead, he dismounted and, to the astonishment of the Al Sairs, he cradled the dying Dalvenpar in his arms. It was later rumored that Gurasa screamed and wailed when his friend died, rocking the dead man in his arms as a mother might do her child. He then took a ring from the dead Northman's finger, and ordered that Dalvenpar be buried rather than left for the gathering carrion. While the fighting continued for miles around, he stood for a long time over the grave of his friend, silent and heedless of the surrounding violence. As the Al Sairs looked on, he remained until well after dark. Then he rejoined his men to proceed back to Tyrsharat. Tareef relates that during the journey, Gurasa spoke almost not at all, and gave no orders, leaving it to his captains to decide how fast to ride, when to break for the night's camp, and when to resume. Unlike his usual custom, Gurasa invited no one into his tent for evening tea and Tareef relates that he doubted if Gurasa ate anything at all.

Tribunals

When they arrived at the gates of Tyrsharat, he was given a summons to appear immediately before the King's Tribunal at the Royal Palace. According to the customs of the day, representatives, lords, and high-ranking officers of the armies stood before the king to pronounce their opinions. These were all gathered in the court of King Salzadur, and Gurasa immediately saw that it was a gathering of cronies and others who held grudges against him. With only three of his chief captains, Gurasa knelt before the king.

An official court scribe and his two apprentices recorded the event into the Chronicles of King Salzadur. As one of Gurasa's captains, Tareef was present, and he recorded what happened along with his own observations. What follows is a sort of narrative assembled from both of those sources. It begins with Gurasa's arrival:

> "I have come, my King," Gurasa said.
>
> "You have come," replied the King. "Stand just there, and face my court."
>
> Gurasa did so, with his captains behind him, and turned to see his enemies.
>
> "It is my wish," said Salzadur, "that any may now speak of Gurasa."
>
> A member of the Great Council immediately stepped forward.
>
> "Sire," he said, "I wish to express my concern for our people and especially those of our great city, Calamandor, who have been insulted and grievously harmed by Saltani Gurasa's failure to rescue them from our enemies. And, sire, I call upon any who may bear witness to speak."
>
> "Very well," said the King. "Is there anyone here who may wish to speak a complaint against Saltani Gurasa?"
>
> "Yes, my King," said a general of the army. "My honor as a servant of this throne has been insulted by Saltani Gurasa. That a servant of the king such as he, famed for his skill as a warrior and commander, should choose not to act according to the wishes of this Throne."
>
> "I, too," said another man, a captain of the Calamandor forces. "With my own eyes, I witnessed treachery, authored and carried out by this traitor, Gurasa!"
>
> "I, too," said a Calamandor councilman. "witnessed how my city was overtaken and sacked, its people slaughtered, its riches plundered, and its homes, shops, and courts burned and destroyed. All of these acts were done by our enemy, who took our gates and overcame our defenders. And all the while, this Saltani, leading a powerful army, delayed coming to our rescue."
>
> "I, too," said another, "beheld how this Great Saltani, honored by the throne with acclaim and favor, gave comfort and relief to our enemies."
>
> The king nodded as each person spoke. Then he turned to Gurasa and gestured for

him to speak. But Gurasa remained silent and looked upon his accusers with no expression on his face. After a long moment, Captain Tareef, of Gurasa's Al Sairs, stepped forward, clearly angry.

"My king, these lies and slanders insult not only Saltani Gurasa, and all those who have served him," he said loudly. "But that they should be uttered in your presence is an even greater insult upon your honor and dignity and the honor and greatness of our people. I beg that you permit me to punish those who bring such lies and offense into this court and before your exalted throne!"

Tareef's hand went to his hilt, and he stepped closer to those who had spoken against Gurasa.

The opposing general, who had spoken earlier, stepped forward.

"As a faithful servant of our King and his people," he cried,"I clearly see that it is Gurasa's lackeys who bring insult. I beg leave, Your Highness, to indulge my sword with their blood!"

"Nay and cease!" cried King Salzadur, standing from his throne. "This is a time for words only!"

Tareef looked at Salzadur sternly.

"My King," he said at last. "I am obedient."

Tareef then bowed and took his place beside Gurasa once again. Reluctantly, the general bowed and returned to stand with his faction.

"Then, sire, I, too, must speak!" said another of Gurasa's men. "I bore witness and can bring before you a thousand men who saw likewise that my Saltani Gurasa did all that was possible to reach Calamandor, to bring relief to the people of that city, and to drive out the invaders. I beg the King to invite my further words on this matter, but also to invite all else who may say what they saw. And I can bring you ten thousand citizens of this city who know and saw how my Saltani labored against delay and disorder created by unfaithful servants of your throne. Unfaithful servants who saw only an opportunity to bring down Saltani Gurasa. Unfaithful servants, I say, who blocked your orders from reaching my Saltani. Who conspired to hoard away and hide supplies and fodder necessary for our quick movement. Unfaithful servants who did those things and many other things to hobble Saltani Gurasa and to prevent our timely arrival at Calamandor! Sire, permit me to bring these witnesses before you, to name names and to recount what has been done against your declarations and edicts."

The King stirred in his seat, suddenly uncomfortable. For many moments, Salzadur considered things, his gaze seeking to penetrate Gurasa, his Al Sairs, and those who stood against Gurasa. The great room was silent as all waited to hear the King's words. Then, from the open windows behind the Royal Dais, a distant sound came, somewhat muffled at first, a repetitive noise that swelled. Those closest to the windows, including the King himself, made out a chorus from thousands of voices.

"Gurasa! Gurasa! Gurasa!" they chanted.

Salzadur rose from his throne and, with his hands together as if in contemplation, he went to the far window behind his throne. With royal nonchalance, Salzadur looked upward upon the sky for a long moment. Then, slowly, he lowered his eyes to look down from the lofty window. From his vantage, Salzadur could see over the gates of his palace and beyond, where a great crowd gathered. In their colorful robes and turbans, the people filled the streets and yards, and were arrayed on rooftops. Men, women, and children alike chanted and clapped. And he saw, here and there among the press, the glint of helmets and armor. Many flags of the White Dragon were waving in the air.

Salzadur returned to his throne and sat once again.

"I shall consider your request," Salzadur said to Gurasa's supporters. "Who else here may bring words upon this matter? And who else here may have knowledge of Saltani Gurasa's acts? Who else do you know that can do so?"

There was a chorus of "I, my King!" from every man present, for and against Gurasa. But Gurasa himself remained silent.

"What say you, Gurasa?" asked the king. "What say you to these charges and these accusations?"

Gurasa now at last stirred, but slightly. He bowed to Salzadur, and spoke softly.

"My great and mighty King," Gurasa said, "I serve you as I always have. I have acted upon your wishes, and I have carried out your commands. I beg the King to judge whether I have failed or succeeded. Whether I am a traitor or a worthy servant. But I shall not address lies, and I do not feel any sting of guilt from the words of my accusers. Any words I might say in return would vaunt and tout my actions and the valor of my soldiers, for we have always done our duty faithfully. And though the responsibility is my burden, I shall not boast, nor shall I be a braggart before you. Therefore, my King and Judge, let me not speak at all."

Salzadur gazed upon Gurasa. He realized that should he command Gurasa to speak, it would seem as if he himself backed and encouraged Gurasa. And should Gurasa answer the King, his accusers would be reluctant to speak against him because it would seem as if they spoke against the Throne. It was a trap. Gurasa had judged rightly the weakness of his opponents, how they craved the favor of the throne, how they fawned upon every nod and word of King Salzadur, and would never dare challenge their king. Thus Salzadur saw that Gurasa was not only a keen military planner, but was also possessed of an accurate understanding of the machinations of the Throne and its courtiers. All this, King Salzadur now understood, and his countenance settled into an expression of grim appreciation.

"Very well, Saltani Gurasa, you may speak when you wish, if your wish, or not at all," said Salzadur. "Yet heed all to my wishes and my command! Let there be a tribunal formed. Let all throughout our domain come to bear witness. Let all be written, so that all may be done that must be done. Saltani Gurasa, you shall remain in Tyrsharat until such a time comes when the tribunal has heard all and until I shall be made aware of all matters pertaining to your conduct.

Salzadur stood and cried, "So let it be written into the Book of My Law. So let it be done!" He quickly departed as all bowed at his passing.

Thus began the great tribunals that sought to ruin Gurasa and bring punishment upon him. In essence, these were trials. And many who served in these proceedings sought not only to bring about Gurasa's ruin, but also his execution, for they feared Gurasa's popularity and power.

Gurasa was repeatedly accused of giving aid to the enemy and of being disloyal to the King. As soon as he was cleared of one charge, and one tribunal ended, another charge was leveled against Gurasa and a new tribunal begun. It was clear that his enemies were out for blood, and they sought to strip Gurasa of his station and rank. His accusers spoke of Gurasa's sojourn in the Northlands. They said that he was infected with a devotion to the enemy. They argued that his fame and greatness hid his true nature, his treasonous affiliation to Men and Elifaen.

During all of this, there were several attempts on Gurasa's life, all thwarted by his vigilant and cunning Al Sairs. When that effort proved ineffectual, Gurasa's enemies began to target his supporters. Witnesses that testified in favor of Gurasa were retaliated against, three were killed outright within hours of their testimony, and two others were severely beaten. This was when Tareef, as captain of the Al Sairs, ordered that all witnesses should enjoy the same protection as Gurasa. At the same time, perhaps to show that Gurasa's enemies were not immune, three of Gurasa's accusers were poisoned to death, and two more were found hanging from the city gates. Although Tareef denied involvement with these incidents, Gurasa reprimanded him in private, telling Tareef that never before had he, Gurasa, deigned to play by his enemies' rules, and he would not begin now. He had never seen Gurasa so angry. According to Tareef, Gurasa gave him such a ferocious dressing down that he feared he might be expelled from service. But Gurasa had no such intention. Tareef, for his part, made certain that Gurasa's message was quickly relayed throughout the Al Sairs and to others who supported Gurasa. Although attempts were still made upon Gurasa and his supporters, no further attacks were carried out against his accusers.

Still Gurasa refused to speak or to answer any of his accusers' questions, but many testified on Gurasa's behalf, in spite of the threats made against them. They presented lists of people, merchants and traders, who were lackeys of those who accused Gurasa. And they presented witnesses who described how these minions conspired to withhold supplies so that Gurasa and his army were delayed from carrying out the King's will. How precious days were wasted while the Northmen sacked Calamandor.

Meanwhile, the tribunals fueled a growing discontent among many of the common people who were staunch supporters of Gurasa. Fearing unrest, the King ordered a curfew. However, in defiance of that order, angry crowds gathered and riots threatened to break out in Tyrsharat, for there were thousands who idolized Gurasa, and there were many more than that who resented the King's courtiers and their power and saw their opportunity to defy them. It was suspected that soldiers who had served under Gurasa fomented and fueled the discontent. Efforts to break up the crowds grew increasingly violent, and within the palace there was fear of insurrection.

Meanwhile, with the exception of the Al Sairs, Gurasa's army was dismantled. Its officers and soldiers were reassigned en mass to serve under other generals who promptly took their armies far away from Tyrsharat for training exercises. Desertion was rampant, and many soldiers took their families and fled into the Badlands toward the Free City of Kajarahn.

While all this was going on, and still mourning for his good friend, Gurasa secretly had his personal battle standard sent to the Free City of Kajarahn. From there it was taken by traders to the north and then on to Tallinvale. He sent a note with it, unsigned, saying simply, "In exchange for one ring."

After two years, the King, fearing further unrest, intervened to end the tribunals by royal decree. The King's proclamation retired Gurasa with honor and with the Throne's gratitude for his service and his deeds. He awarded to Gurasa a generous bounty in gold and silver as well. But all knew that Gurasa was effectively banished, and many believe that Gurasa had been warned to never return to Tyrsharat. As for Gurasa, he was weary, a broken man suddenly old beyond his years. In the dark of night, he and his Al Sairs quietly departed Tyrsharat.

Home Again

It was 829 S.A. when Gurasa returned to his home in Almedian, to his family and to his loyal friends and neighbors. He was greeted as a great hero, and a festival was given in his honor. Afterwards, Gurasa secluded himself within his small palace. Later that same year, a fever swept through Almedian. Three of Gurasa's four remaining children died of the fever. Only his youngest child, his daughter Micerea, was spared. Gurasa's wife was also stricken and would never fully recover her strength. Sadness and depression settled upon Gurasa's home.

A few years later, in 842 S.A., the Green Citadel was once again besieged and sacked. Gurasa never stirred from his home, and by his order none of his household guard, the Al Sairs, were to leave Almedian for any reason. When news came to him concerning the great slaughter, Gurasa sank deeper into grief and despair. He isolated himself from most of his people and relatives, but he doted on his daughter, Micerea. She, alone, prevented Gurasa from wasting away, and the two spent a great deal of joy-filled time together. He rarely ventured from his palace, and traveled only when absolutely necessary. Other than a few business journeys to the Free City of Kajarahn, he remained in Almedian. And, when traveling to Kajarahn, he always took the long way either south or north, to go around Calamandor. This was so that he would not see the city or pass any of the battlegrounds. One of Gurasa's Al Sairs, wrote:

> We traveled slowly and carefully. Our Saltani had no desire to visit Calamandor, nor did he wish to look upon the old battlefields that were north of that city. We did not stop at any village except to replenish our water. At night, we pitched our tents far away from any other caravans. Our Saltani spoke very little, as was his manner, but was never stern or unfriendly towards us.
>
> I can only guess that our Saltani did not wish to make his business known to any, lest news of his approach traveled ahead of us. He was recognized, of course, by many fellow travelers or village headmen, and those who did not know his face certainly knew the household standard under which we rode.

Gurasa's wife died in 850 S.A., leaving only his daughter, Micerea, the last surviving member of his family. Gurasa became her teacher, and he devoted himself to his daughter's education and upbringing. When she was eleven years of age, and Gurasa began to teach her to ride, and to use dagger and sword. He lavished her with tutors, teaching her not only the language and literature of the Dragonlands, but also he taught her the Common Speech that he learned during his travels as a youth. When he was not with Micerea, Gurasa occupied his days and nights with painting and writing poetry. From time to time, old comrades would come to Almedian to visit Gurasa. But they would not stay for very long.

During this time, Gurasa recorded in his journals that he was concerned for Micerea's health. She often had difficulty sleeping, and this made her suffer terrible bouts of fatigue. When she did sleep, it was fitful and full of odd dreams and anxious nightmares. Therefore, it was not uncommon that she would awake in the middle of the night, and, unable to settle back into slumber, she would roam the palace. It was not unusual for her to find her father busy with his collection of specimens and notes gathered from the travels of his youth. He often stopped whatever he was doing and, hand in hand, they would go to the balcony. Sometimes he would point to the stars and tell her stories about them. Gurasa often read to her from his notes or from old books. Or he might read from books that he brought out of Vanara or Duinnor or some other place he had visited. These he read aloud as they were written, in the dialect of the Northmen.

Nothing he did seemed to help Micerea to sleep more soundly. And her waking behavior was often melancholy and distracted. And, strangely, she seemed to know things about which no one could have told her. Once she said she dreamed of a terrible sandstorm in which dunes marched up and down streets and avenues. A month later, news came that, indeed, there had been an awful sandstorm that drove high dunes into the streets over some roofs of faraway Tollipi. It was reported that the dunes went first this way, then turned suddenly and went that way, as if they were lost.

Unbeknownst to Micerea, Gurasa invited many wise men and apothecaries from far and wide so that he could consult with them concerning his daughter's peculiar sleep disorder. He allowed them to observe Micerea, but not to speak to her about her "condition" so as not to alarm or disquiet her. He wrote that his greatest fear was that she was succumbing to some new malady that would take her life, something that Gurasa said he would not be able to bear. But each wise man in turn assured him that Micerea appeared quite healthy. So they came and went, and his diaries note that he learned much, but he never wrote what it was that he learned.

He also noted in his journals that Micerea became evermore curious about the peculiar ring that he always wore, the one that had once been worn by his friend, Dalvenpar Tallin. It was Micerea's habit to ask about it, but he always put her off. By piecing together various accounts, all of which have gaps, we can imagine that it went something like this:

"Father, will you now tell me about your ring?"
"Not yet, my princess," he would always say.
Micerea continued to ask, and Gurasa continued to gently refuse.
Until one night, they went to the balcony and watched the bright stars slowly wheel. Together they stood at the banister, and neither of them spoke for a very long time, until Micerea asked once again.
"Father, will you now tell me about your ring?"
Gurasa turned to her and nodded.
"Yes, my princess. The time has come for you to learn about it, and about much else. I will tell you that which I suspect is the cause of your bad dreams. And I will also speak to you about a great hope that may come to our people from the north. I will tell you about the coming of a great king who will unite all people and who will bring about lasting peace between our kind and his. And when I have told you all about those things and all about the ring, it will be yours to wear on my behalf."

And thus it was that Micerea became Gurasa's helpmate and messenger and confidant. And because he eventually confirmed that Micerea was a dreamwalker, he groomed her carefully to use her gift so that she might help the coming of the New King.
See Also:
Historical Sketches (Karkarando)
Glossary (Darakal)
****

Gustan Broadweed

Born in 825 in western Glareth, Gustan Broadweed was orphaned at the age of six and became the foster child of his aunt and uncle. They treated the boy as a servant and habitually abused and mistreated him. At age eleven, after careful preparation, he stole away one night and fled to Glareth by the Sea. There, he apprenticed to a cooper and learned to read and write. By the time he was fourteen years old, he was an avid reader, frequenting the many libraries and bookshops of the city during his spare time. At work, Broadweed was often found reading or teaching other apprentices to read rather than attending to his duties. The cooper in charge was at first annoyed by this, but he noticed that the productivity of his workers was increasing. He realized that Broadweed was teaching the other workers how to keep records and share written instructions with each other about how to make certain parts and items. The cooper himself, a person who could barely read, arranged for a regular time when all his workers, including himself, could attend Broadweed's lessons.

When his apprenticeship was up, Broadweed applied to the Royal Glareth Academy (a school for sailors who intended to be officers). He had one of the highest scores on the written and oral exams, showing a command of language, history, mathematics, maritime history, and law, but he was denied entrance due to his poor eyesight. In 844, after a few years struggling to make a living in the shipbuilding trade, he found employment as a clerk with Ned Arbuckle, a merchant who sold marine supplies. Broadweed soon convinced Arbuckle to change certain aspects of the business, which resulted more customers and a rapid expansion of the business. As his reward, Arbuckle gave Broadweed a generous salary and put him in charge of all of the accounts and other clerks.

During his time with Arbuckle, Broadweed married Lydia Rose, the daughter of a frequent customer who was the owner of a small fishing fleet. The couple, though happy, would never have children.

In 849, Arbuckle's business was destroyed by a fire. Arbuckle was ruined, and Broadweed was once again unemployed. However, in 851, he happened to meet Alfred Greardon, the son of a miller from Passdale in Barley County of the Eastlands. Greardon was so impressed by Broadweed that he asked him to come to Passdale and serve as their as schoolmaster, which Broadweed readily agreed to do. When he arrived in County Barley, he saw the bridge-building project that was underway in Passdale. Learning that there were a few difficulties with the project, he wrote to Ned Arbuckle begging his old employer to come. Arbuckle did so. Not only was Arbuckle helpful during the final stages of construction, he became the bridge tender once the bridge was completed. Broadweed, meanwhile, had become schoolmaster for County Barley. With the support of Harrald Bosk, Robigor Ribbon, Greardon, and many others, Broadweed's school was soon producing literate graduates, able to read, write, and solve arithmetic problems.

As Schoolmaster, Broadweed not only taught the youth of the county, but he was also a strong advocate for the protection of children from abuse and maltreatment (working closely with Harrald Bosk). In addition, Broadweed was called upon from time to time to advise those who governed Passdale and Barley on certain points of Realm Law, particularly when it came to tolls and taxes. But his greatest influence was as a teacher. He crafted his curriculum according to the nature and abilities of his individual students, often tutoring them after school hours and on non-school days. He worked closely with parents and with the various places of employment around the county to assess the needs and conditions of his current and former students. By doing so, he was able to shape his curriculum to include lessons that would help his students become good workers, sometimes taking them on field trips to see how things were done on farms or in the workshops in the county. Broadweed also conducted weekly classes at the various work places to help older workers learn to read and write.

Broadweed also managed established a relationship with various schools in Glareth that enabled him to write letters of reference for any of his students who successfully passed his curriculum. With a letter from Broadweed, his graduates could apply to take the entrance exams for a number of schools of higher learning, including the prestigious Glareth Academy. After twenty years, there was hardly an adult under the age of thirty within County Barley who could not read and write and "do numbers."

Broadweed was among those driven out of Barley during the Redvest Invasion of 870. On the night of the invasion, Collandoth (who was leading a large group fleeing away from Boskland) passed by the schoolhouse and the cottage nearby where Broadweed lived. Fortunately, Broadweed had just returned from the Fall Festival in Passdale, with a borrowed wagon that he planned to use the following day to bring children to the festival. Warned by Collandoth about the coming Redvests, Broadweed quickly loaded a number of books and teaching materials into the wagon before fleeing to Passdale with his wife. When the invaders reached the schoolhouse, they burned it to the ground.

The following morning, Broadweed helped organize the evacuation of Passdale. He sent his wife ahead to Janhaven with the wagon, but he remained behind to protect a group of straggling children, and he thus took part in the melee in Passdale when the Redvests attacked the town. Broadweed was slightly wounded, but he got the children safely away to Janhaven. Within days, had a classroom set up within Furaman's stockade. There, he took care of those children who had no parents and those whose parents were missing. By conducting lessons, he was able to reduce the natural anxiety that the children felt during the turmoil and hardships of being refugees.

See Also:
Biographical Sketches (Ned Arbuckle)
Essays and Explanations (Literacy and Education)
****

How the Blacksmith Got His Iron

(Pertaining to the Clingdons of Passdale)

The source of this story is unknown.   However, we include it here due to its relevance to The Year of the Red Door. In the opening volume, many bells are mentioned besides the Great Bell. One bell of significance was the warning bell, fashioned by Passdale's blacksmith, used by the Passdale Militia. Its ringing led to a case of mistaken identity and the kidnapping of Billy Bosk, with Robby Ribbon in pursuit. This meant that the two friends would not be present at the deadly fight that took place in Passdale the following day, their absence perhaps saving their lives. The reason that the local blacksmith could fashion such a large bell in the first place is related in the following tale.

A large covered wagon slowly creaked and rattled southward along the old road that traced its way around the western shores of Lake Halgaeth. The two oxen that pulled it were in no hurry, and the driver of the lumbering wagon had no inclination to encourage them. They knew that his faithful old beasts would keep to the path before them, and would stop all by themselves if they had any doubt as to the way, or if any obstacle presented itself.

Slumped comfortably on the bench with the reins across his lap, the driver puffed his pipe and gazed across the wide expanse of water off to his left. It was a clear day, fairly warm for so early in the spring, and hardly a breeze disturbed the lake's sun-speckled surface. The trees passed slowly by, some that were just beginning to show the very first signs of green. The driver shifted himself slightly, and he absently adjusted the blanket across his knees, never taking his eyes from the lake. There was a sailboat out there, far off, going in the opposite direction, its white sails full. He noted to himself that no air stirred along the path he took, and yet the boat had found plenty of it far out yonder. But that was the way of water and wind and land, he knew from experience. The boat made him think on his past, for he was formerly a blacksmith of Glareth Realm. He had made all manner of tools and braces, pins and pintles, and even some weapons for the Glarethian Navy and for the trade and fishing fleets. Indeed, he had enjoyed a prosperous business for ten good years, ever since he had set himself up with his own forge after completing his apprenticeship. But it was his ill-fortune to enter into business just when loads of iron and steel began flowing to Glareth down the Osterflo from Duinnor. Before long, awash in good metal, everyone seemed to be opening their own smithies. Unable to compete well enough to keep his forge running, he instead began transporting iron goods made by others to far-flung villages and towns. And he always brought along his own small anvil, his bellows and tools, a big sack of charcoal, and a small stock of metal to do repair work for those he met with. But other blacksmiths had the same idea as he, taking up their own wagons, and he was forced to travel farther and farther to find work. At last, he sold his shop in Glareth, packed all of his belongings into a single great wagon, and had lived ever since on the road. Now, the year 726 of the Second Age, he ventured farther south than he had ever gone. As he rolled along the shoreline road, he watched the lone sailboat which reminded him of the easier days of his vocation in Glareth by the Sea.

He sighed and tapped out his pipe, tucked it away into his coat pocket, and shifted the reins on his lap just as his oxen pulled him and his wagon around a wooded bend and along a broad cove of sorts where the path descended mildly almost to the water's edge. He sat up suddenly, squinting. About a hundred yards out, jutting up from the water, were two gigantic arms. A slight shiver coursed its way down his spine. The two arms, the elbows of which were underneath the water, reached upward, and in each hand was held aloft a broad flat bowl.

"Whoa, there," he said softly, pulling the reins to stop the oxen. The creaking of wheels halted, and the sudden silence that descended seemed odd, almost eerie.

"What place is this? And what are those?" he asked himself.

"They are beacons."

The driver jumped, jerking around to see who had spoken. To the right side of the road, and up the hill about five or six yards, was a young man sitting with his back against a tree. He had on a thick coat of an unusual fashion, somewhat like the dress coats of the Glarethian Navy. But this man's coat was white, somewhat travel-stained here and there, and was bulky—obviously a winter coat—with a fur-lined hood that was tossed back. The man also wore a white cap with flaps on the sides and back that were folded upward around the hat, and it had a bill that jutted out from the front.

"Ye nearly startled the daylights out of me!" the driver declared.

"You were so intent on watching the lake that I thought I ought not interrupt your thoughts," answered the young man. "But when you asked your question, I thought I should answer you."

"I see."

"They are beacons," repeated the young man.

The driver glanced back at the strange arms.

"Seems an odd place to put beacons," he said, "seeing how ye'd need a boat to haul wood an' oil an' whatnot to 'em."

"So it might seem. But there is an ancient quay out there, completely underwater but for those two arms at the very end of it. This used to be a place where boats came to and went from, carrying trade goods, soldiers, and passengers to and fro across the lake up to Formouth. It is called, or was called, Surthquay."

"Oh. I see."

The driver looked back and forth from the lake to the young man at the side of the way.

"So I reckon that when the lake rose up, after Lord Heneil built his dam, a lot got covered over," said the driver.

"That is so," said the young man.

"Hm."

"You are from Glareth, I take it. Judging by your manner of speech."

"That's right. An' yerself?"

"I was born not too far from here. But I'm only passing through. It has been a good while since I've passed this way, and I thought I'd stop here to rest and to think on my memories before continuing on."

The driver nodded, looking around the place where the young man sat.

"Travelin', then?"

"In a manner of speaking."

"I don't see no horse, nor any pack or such."

"I travel lightly, and on foot."

"I see."

"And where might you be going with your great wagon? Are you a tradesman, or do you transport goods for sale?"

"I do a bit of both," answered the driver of the wagon. "I'm a blacksmith by trade, an' a travelin' ironmonger by necessity, there bein' little need of me back home in Glareth."

"A bit far afield, aren't you?"

"Aye, that I am. I have to go farther an' farther, it seems, roamin' wider an' wider, as it were, every season. Me goods don't wear out soon enough to need much replenishment. An' me handiwork at the anvil, likewise."

"Do you own your wagon yourself, and your load? Or do you travel in the hire of another to sell and trade on their behalf?"

"Oh, it's all me own! I buy an' resell, rather than take on consignments, because I don't care to be obliged to others for such, nor to be told where to go or what to do by them what don't know the trade, but only have coin to invest, so to speak. So this is all mine, bein' me store, me shop, an' me home, all on these four wheels!"

"And you've been doing this for a long time?"

"Four years, come this summer."

"Do you ever grow weary of travel? Don't you miss being away from your wife and children, or your friends?"

"Well, as for that, I ain't got no wife, nor any children. And me friends are wherever I meet or make 'em. Truth be told, I'd fancy settlin' down an' make a family somewhere. But blacksmithin's the only trade I know, an' what good woman would have such as me as a husband, a blacksmith with no work but what can be found by wanderin' all 'round, far an' away?"

"I see."

The young man stood, brushed a few stray twigs from his coat, and stepped closer to the wagon.

"Well, if you keep going on southward, the way you are going, you'll come to a very small village on the Bentwide River. This path runs alongside the river, so just keep to it until you find the village. It is a small village, once called Dalefath, but I don't think anyone remembers that. Some are starting to call the place Passdale."

"That's what I heard, back up a ways at Northwick. They say folks are startin' to settle into the parts south of the lake once again. I thought I'd take a chance on things, even though I hear tell folks ain't been too well off since them Dragonkind came through. And that folks're a might skittish about more Dragonkind comin' along someday."

"That might be so," said the young man. "But the Dragonkind won't be back, regardless of what people might be afraid of. And the folks down the way in Passdale need a blacksmith, I happen to know. That's because they have to send their horses, what few they have, all the way to Tallinvale to get shoed decently, and are just as apt to throw a shoe on the way back. And they have no one to make or mend their tools. There's Boskland, nearby, but the blacksmith there has all the work he can handle, and anyway it is across the river from Passdale, with no bridge across it. There are ferries on down river, but they take too much coin from those who have little enough to spare."

"So yer sayin' that I might find good work that'll last for a good while?"

"I think so."

"Hm."

"And I know a place where you can get plenty of good iron, not too far off. Some steel, too."

"Do ye?"

"Free for the taking."

"Oh?" The blacksmith squinted. "An' why ain't nobody already took it?"

"Well, for one, who would need it but a blacksmith? For another, it is in a place where people don't much like to go to. And, finally, I don't think they know what is there."

The two looked at each other for a few moments, the young man waiting, apparently for the blacksmith to consider things, and the blacksmith running through all of the reasons why he should be suspicious and wary.

"You are wondering what else there is to it," said the young man.

"I am. Seems too simple, the way ye put it. Iron just for the takin' is like coin just for the takin'. Don't seem right, somehow. Must be some reason nobody's already took it."

"It isn't cursed, or hexed, or in a haunted place, or any such as that," the young man grinned. "It is simply out of sight, in a place where no one has cared to look. I know all about it, how it came to be there, and for how long. I, myself, have no need of the metal."

"How much do ye reckon? Enough to keep me in business for a season or two?"

The young man eyed the wagon.

"This looks to be a sturdy wagon," he said. "So I imagine you could fill your wagon with iron bars, flat iron plates, and steel to the tune of maybe a thousand pounds, if your wagon can carry that weight. And if that ran out, you could get just as much again, over and over. I'd say there's probably twenty wagon-loads, or thereabouts. You'd be the better judge. And you'd be a better judge of the worth and quality of the metal than I am. Some of it is apt to be rusty by now. But I was made to understand that much was packed and covered with some kind of grease or wool wax."

The blacksmith's eyes alternately squinted, then grew wide, and squinted again as he took in what the young man was telling him.

"I'm sure you don't know whether to believe me or not," continued the young man, seeing the blacksmith's confusion. "But since you go southward anyway, perhaps you might get a chance to go look for yourself. I will tell you all that I know about it, if you'd care to hear."

The blacksmith nodded.

"Well, you know all about Tulith Attis, I suppose," said the young man.

"Aye."

"It fell to the Dragonkind nearly three-hundred years ago. When their armies came, they brought with them vast supplies of weapons, great bars of steel and iron, and large plates of iron, with which they made their engines of war to lay siege to Tulith Attis. The Dragonkind have always been masters and artisans of iron and steel, owing perhaps to how precious those metals are to them. So when they came, they not only brought a great deal with them, but they also looted the cities and towns they conquered along the way, taking the best iron and steel that they came upon as they burned and plundered. But when they at last overthrew Tulith Attis, they received word that armies were approaching to do battle with them—the armies of Glareth, Duinnor, and Vanara all converging upon them. So the Dragonkind, after having massacred those within the fortress and looted the place of valuables, attempted to pack up and march away. Besides their loot, they also took away much of their metal stock, it being highly valuable to them, as I said. But all of the wagons slowed them down as they fled south along the Saerdulin. At last, pressed by pursuing armies, the Dragonkind had to find a place to make a stand, and they had to get there in time to prepare for battle. I suppose you have also heard of the Battle of Saerdulin, too?"

"Aye," answered the blacksmith. "That's where the Dragonkind were cornered an' entirely vanquished."

"Cornered, yes," said the young man. "But not entirely vanquished. A few—only a very few—survived and made it all the way back to their own lands and homes. And they told how, three days before their defeat at the battle of Saerdulin, they abandoned all of their iron and steel, except what they would need for battle. They put thousands of laborers to work, and they erected great barrows some twenty miles north of the River Lerse, and three miles west of the River Saerdulin. They also put a large stone marker right along the old road, and the barrows are three miles due west of that marker. The marker is made of large blocks of square stone, about twelve feet high. It has no markings on it, and people around here think it is older than it really is and they don't know its purpose. It signifies the place where one must go west to find the barrows. Yet the Dragonkind did not put their dead into those barrows. They bundled great bales of iron together, wrapped in grease-soaked cloth. And they covered over their great hoard of metal with earth in such a way so that no moisture could get at the metal. That was what they put beneath their earthen barrows. And now those barrows have been worn away, by rain and storm and wind, and only thinly cover their precious abandoned iron and steel."

By now, the young man was leaning against the wagon comfortably, and he smiled at the blacksmith.

"Well!" said the blacksmith. "That's quite a tale, if it is to be believed."

"You can judge for yourself, if you go with shovel and pick and have a look."

"And how might ye know about all this, eh?"

"I ventured into the Dragonlands, some years ago when I was younger, and I heard the tale myself from a descendant of one of those Dragonkind who buried the metal. He even had an old map, drawn by his grandfather's grandfather, and he showed it to me."

"Hm."

The blacksmith scratched his chin, still not sure what to make of all this, and glanced back at the strange arms reaching out from the lake.

"North of the Lerse, you said. An' west of the Saerdulin?"

"That's right. It is mostly forest, now. But the marker I spoke of cannot be missed. As for the barrows, for some reason trees won't grow on them, although weeds and grass do grow there. I will tell you an easy way to get to the place, though it is almost a hundred leagues from here. You follow this road. After it passes by this lake, it follows along the River Bentwide and, farther away, along the Saerdulin…."

And so the young man carefully explained the way to the hoard of metal.

It is often the case that what people at first think is an odd thing, they later grow accustomed to and remark about it no more. So it was with the blacksmith who arrived one spring day, determined, as he said, to buy a small bit of ground within the village where he could build his shop, construct his forge, and ply his craft and trade. This was soon done, and he set to work immediately. From time to time, the blacksmith went off with his wagon for a week or so, always going southward along the old river road, and always returning along the same way. He never said where he went off to, but he always departed with an empty wagon and returned with it heavily loaded and covered over with tarpaulins. It was an odd thing, but the villagers were grateful to have such a valuable addition to their community, especially since his iron and steel products were always strong and worthy of their purpose. And his skill was as good as his metal, too, for he was able to make all the things needed by the small but growing village, everything from hinges to hammers, from cowbells to chisels, and from barrel hoops to bridle bits—all done with skill and economy. He traded his goods and his work with the villagers for their goods, for food, and for their own work, and he never demanded coin if anything else was agreeable.

At first, they also thought it odd that no ironmongers ever came to their village to sell plate or bars to the blacksmith, and yet the blacksmith was never without the material that he needed for his trade. After a few years, so amiable was his nature and so joyfully he conducted his business, that few ever wondered about his supply of metal. The villagers simply assumed that if a thing of metal was needed, their blacksmith would be able to make it. His shop, heated by his forge, was always warm and welcoming, too, even on the coldest of winter days, and it was there that many of the menfolk often gathered to trade tales or to swap tunes on their fiddles and guitars. Before too long, the blacksmith met and married a girl of the village, and soon their children played and laughed as happily and as readily as the parents.

The blacksmith was blessed with a son, and from the earliest age the boy was shown all the mysteries and dangers of the forge, of hot iron, of ringing anvils and hammers, and of flying sparks. The boy learned to stoke the forge, to pump the bellows, and to hold steady the tongs. From small hammers to larger ones, he learned to strike red iron, and to twist and shape things. The boy grew strong, like his parents, and he came in his own time to run the shop whilst his old father watched from a nearby stool, often with a grandson or granddaughter on his knee.

That was how a wandering blacksmith found a home. How he settled in Passdale, and how he obtained all of the iron he could ever need. His descendants, each in turn, were told the secret of where to find good metal for the forge, and how their supply came to be found in the first place. It was a special time when this secret was passed along, and a solemn occasion each and every time, for it was incumbent upon each generation to tell the next of the grim source of their livelihood, and how it was up to each of them to turn their supply of metal to a good purpose.

So the years passed, as did the generations, and never was there a hardier family, or a happier family, than the Clingdons of Passdale. Then came a day that one of them was called upon to make something that none of his forebears had ever been asked to make. It was to be a signal bell, made to summon the local militia and to spread warning to the people should any peril come. By the time he received his commission to make the bell for Passdale, blacksmith Clingdon had all the skills required for such a task, learned and passed down from father to son for generations. Unlike most bells that are made of liquid iron cast into molds, this one was made of plates of iron skillfully welded and riveted together. It did not take very long to make, either. When it was done, and the bell was hoisted up into the tower from which it would hang, never was there a prouder blacksmith. And, in the dark days that afterwards came, the blacksmith who made it was given pause to wonder. For the bell that he had made rang out one fateful night, and because of its warning his own family and many other families were saved from capture by an invading army.

But what blacksmith Clingdon pondered the most was how things might have been so different had not his ancestor met with a perfect stranger one spring day at a place called Surthquay on the shore of Lake Halgaeth.

****

If Not for Galafronks

(About Billy Bosk and Ibin Brinnin)

The following was found at the Library of Darini among a packet of notes left by Ullin Saheed Tallin. However, the handwriting was not Ullin's, so we do not know the true source. We do not know how the author of this story came by his information, or whether this story is accurate. We have included it in this Companion because it may shed some light on people who played vital roles during the fateful final year of the Second Age.

Mr. Broadweed, the county schoolmaster, had a problem. He sat at his desk late one autumn afternoon and thought things through.   The students were all gone for the day, and the schoolroom—the only room in the place besides the cloakroom—was once again neat and tidy. Broken bits of chalk had been swept up along with all of the detritus that school children produce. One of his students, Ibin Brinnin, had stayed late to help with all of that and to chop and stack firewood for the morrow. Ibin was not a good student, at least as far as learning went. At seventeen, Ibin was the eldest of all students, but he had not learned a thing in at least six years. At least, not anything significant. He was, as everyone knew, dim. But Ibin did have a gift for remembering rhymes, and he could hear a song once and sing it well. Indeed, during such recitations and singing, his stumbling stutter, full of hesitation and restarts, completely went away. And he had a very good voice. Never any trouble, always willing to be helpful with chores, nearly always smiling, and not very talkative. He was something of a rock for Mr. Broadweed. A student that, while not very bright, was reliable, always on time, always obedient. And he was huge. Back when he was but ten years old, he was already a head taller than any other student. He was never lanky. His years of chores and labor, along with his prodigious appetite, gave him a somewhat stocky appearance, in spite of his height, with a broad chest, and powerful arms and legs. Thus he was somewhat in demand, not only taking care of his elderly parents and their cottage and little farm plot, but he was often called upon by local farmers to help with baling or clearing or other odd jobs requiring strength and endurance.

Broadweed sighed. If only Ibin's mind was as well-developed as his physique. It was a shame. But as Broadweed saw it, Ibin made up for a lot by his genuinely friendly demeanor. Indeed, during recess he was always found in the center of the youngest students, playing tag, or being smothered by the children's playful wrestling. Ibin was their favorite swing, able to hoist and twirl four little ones at a time, around and around, while others clamored on his back, all screaming with delight. Yes, if only. And if only other students could be half so well mannered, and half so nice.

Which brought the teacher back to the problem at hand. Billy Bosk, rapscallion, teaser, jokester, expert exasperater, and almost always at the center, if not the cause, of disruptions. Billy was not a bully, strictly speaking. His antics were always carried out with the greatest glee, with an almost maniacal joy which was often the source of laughter or amusement among the children. He never intended cruelty or harm, but Billy was not averse to picking on older and bigger boys, as scrawny as he was, and the evidence of the resulting scraps were almost always present, from black eyes, to bruises and cuts, or torn clothing. Broadweed mentally reviewed some of Billy's activities, which included tadpoles (more than once) in the water pitcher, honey smeared on doorknobs (and other places), putting walnuts into the woodstove (which then continually popped so loud that lessons were interrupted), lizards in desks, peashooters, red pepper in some students' water cups, excessive talking, and (although Broadweed didn't know quite how or why) continually provoking the most ill-tempered boys into scuffles. His zest for a good joke was matched only by his laziness when it came to books and lessons.

Broadweed found himself staring at his water glass. It was too ornate, really, for a simple teacher in a one-room schoolhouse, etched with decorative motifs all around. But he used it at his desk, as it was a gift from the people of County Barley for his service. Costly, unique, and specially made for him in Tallinvale. Writing on it simply stated, "With Great Appreciation." Chief among the citizens of the county, and probably one of the biggest contributors to its expense, was Billy's father. Indeed, it was Billy's grandfather who brought Mr. Broadweed to the county to establish this school, years ago. For a while, Billy's own father had been one of his first students. The grandfather had long ago passed away, and now Billy's father was master of Boskland, a vast estate and Honored House of the King's registry. Powerful. Wealthy. Mr. Bosk was thick-set, muscular and strong, somewhat serious and brusk, prone to scowling, and a bit short-tempered, but successful, hard-working, and, overall, a fair-minded man. Billy was not a chip off the old block. Scrawny, red-haired, freckled, and usually grinning—the very image of mischief. Never serious about anything. The incorrigible jokester and minor terror of the county. Or, certainly, of the schoolyard.

Broadweed reached for the pitcher and carefully poured water into his glass. He was relieved to see no tadpoles or minnows, only clean, clear water. He sipped, still baffled as to how Billy had managed to sneak them into the pitcher last week, as it never left his desk, and he always filled it himself at the well. But just last week, as he was about to take a sip, he spotted the wriggling creatures just inches from his lips, just at the moment when Gina, a girl sitting nearby, saw them. Gina screamed, Mr. Broadweed flinched in violent disgust, and, far to the back of the room, Billy burst in to a fit of hysterical laughter, pounding his desk and stomping his foot in delight.

That was the thing about Billy. He did not seem to care a wit if he got caught, and often gave himself away or simply confessed. He never put the blame on anyone else. Billy acted as if any amount of reprimand was worth it, a fair price for a good jest. And none of Broadweed's punishments prevented the next onslaught of pranks. None of the notes sent to Billy's parents made any difference in the long run. After a short period of good behavior, Billy was sure to be back at it. And so it went. Year after year.

Though a very patient man, he was capable of sternness when required, and Broadweed had twice expelled Billy from school, which was within his authority to do. Each time, Mr. and Mrs. Bosk came to see him to beg Billy's reinstatement. Both times Broadweed relented. Then the tadpole incident happened, and Broadweed almost expelled Billy on the spot. Thing of it was—blast it—it was funny. And when Broadweed went home that evening and told his wife, she laughed just as hard as Billy had, which made Broadweed laugh, too.

But today Billy had crossed a line. He put down his glass and reached for a note on his desk. It was a love letter addressed to Broadweed from "SG," the initials of one of the older school girls. In the note, she declared her everlasting ardor and promised never to marry or even court unless it should come about that Broadweed might take a second wife. This she promised to say in person should Broadweed but ask her to speak of it.

He shook his head. It was a forgery, of course. And to Broadweed, who knew every student's abilities, it was obvious who penned the note, for none of his students' spelling and penmanship were as atrocious as Billy's. It was annoying and on the surface would have been easy to dismiss. Broadweed said nothing about it at all, biding his time until he could think about it.

The problem was this: Billy had broken one of the most important rules of conduct, had broken part of the primary pact shared between each citizen of Barley, and their oath to the King. He had broken a rule, one that would be a scandal if any adult was caught breaking it.

Billy had lied. He falsified SG's signature, and by forging such a letter, he essentially cast false shame on SG. That could not be ignored. Each year, everyone took an oath to the King and to each other—a public oath—not to lie. And every student took the oath, too, no matter how young. It was something Broadweed could not ignore. Billy had gone too far. A third and final expulsion was warranted. He really had little choice, and Broadweed determined to begin the process tomorrow when Billy arrived at school. He would send Billy back home immediately upon his arrival with a note to carry to his parents stating that Broadweed would come to Bosk Manor to speak to them personally at the end of the school day.

Broadweed tossed Billy's note aside. It was a shame, really. Billy was, if not bright, at least capable of being a decent student. If only he had a smidgen of his older sister's intelligence, only a fraction of her discipline, only a tad of her calm. If he had but a modicum of his father's work ethic, or his mother's grounded wisdom. He might never be a brilliant student, but if only he was less disruptive. As it stood, for the sake of the school, Billy had to go.

Of course, Mr. Broadweed had no idea that Billy would not come to school the next day. As Mr. Broadweed contemplated Billy, Billy himself was contemplating a large oak tree, looking from branch to branch, occasionally scratching his head or his chin in thought. This he did while also continually glancing up the path that ran under the great tree. He knew that Ibin would be coming along the little-used path, as he normally did each day, cutting through the woods as a shortcut on his way home from school. Today, Ibin was staying late at school to do chores for Mr. Broadweed, but Billy knew he did not have much time to set things up. Having selected the branches he would use, two very large ones quite high up, he set to work.

He tied one end of a long sturdy rope around his waist, and the trailing end to a sack of hanging moss he had collected over the past days. Then he began climbing. The first few feet were easy enough, but the higher he went, trailing the rope below him, it became a bit more difficult to reach the first big limb that he aimed for, carefully hugging the trunk and using smaller branches as footholds. At last he made it, and began crawling out onto the large limb, slowly working his way outward until he was almost directly over the path some twenty-five feet below. He carefully positioned the rope over the limb so that it would dangle several feet over the path, and then hoisted up the sack of moss. He almost fell when he grabbed the sack, but managed to save himself as he straddled the limb. Now he pulled all of the free rope upward, intending to tie the two ends together in one great loop. That way, when all was done, he could untie the one knot and pull the rope back down to the ground and carry it off back home. He secured the knot, then used the slack to tie the sack of moss to himself. He retreated back to the trunk and began moving to the next limb. This would be the one that he would launch himself from, covered in moss like some wild tree creature, and swing right at the approaching Ibin. Billy chuckled to himself in anticipation of Ibin's terror, and kept on navigating to the next limb, passing the rope and sack over and around intervening branches as he went.

The whole process was tedious, and as Billy reached the limb from which he would launch himself, he discovered that the rope was snagged across a limb that he somehow forgot to bypass. As was bound to happen, this was when things began to go wrong. Try as he might, he could not figure out how to free the rope without going all the way back, and somewhat upward, to that interfering branch. But as the rope was now many feet out from the trunk, with many lesser branches between the trunk and the rope, he had no choice. So he pulled in all of the slack and began backtracking. The sack he carried was catching on small branches as he went, and one little branch caught it in such a way as to jerk it right out of his grasp. The sack filled with his mossy costume tumbled to the ground, spilling open as it went.

"Well, dang!" he said. "This ain't goin' to plan, is it? I guess I'll have to start all over."

So it went. Or didn't, as the case may be. He managed to get to the offending snag, but had to gather all of the rope to himself, somewhat wrapping himself with it, so that he could get at and free the snagged bit. Then, glancing from his perch, he spotted through the trees Ibin's head bobbing along the approaching slope. That was exactly when the branch cracked and sagged and, in a tangle of rope, Billy slipped from it and fell head first. The rope caught around one leg, and the other shoulder, twisting him sideways and flipping him around. Several loops passed around his neck, then the rope freed itself from his leg, only to drop him right over the path. Various branches caught different parts of the rope, snapping and bending as he fell, and their springiness somewhat cushioned him as he bounced to a stop with his flailing legs some five feet above the ground, bobbing like a cork on a fishing line, the rope firmly snaked around his neck, choking him as his weight tightened the loops. He squirmed and kicked, but that only made matters worse. Clutching for the portion over his head, he tried to get a grip on the two lines that now held him, but as he pulled one rope, the other only tightened around his neck.

In no condition to pay attention to other things, Billy did not notice the sound of Ibin's pounding feet approaching at a charge. Suddenly he felt Ibin's stout arms around his legs, pushing him upward.

"I'vegotyou! I've...I've...I'vegotyou, Billy!" Ibin cried.

With Ibin lifting, the rope slackened just a bit, enough for Billy to breathe and catch hold to both lines above him. He gasped for air, coughed, panted, and groaned, and could not stop himself from trying to kick and flail, in spite of Ibin's hold.

"Billy! I'vegotyou! Iwon'tlet...Iwon'tletgo!"

Billy was still trying to free the rope from his neck, to no avail, but at last he got a good enough grip to lift himself slightly. But his hands soon began to slip.

"Oh! Oh! Oh! Now I've done it! This is the end of me, for sure!"

Anyone else might have had immediate questions. Like "How did this happen?" or "What were you doing up there?" Or, "What were you thinking?" Or they might have been sharp enough to see what was going on, concluding that Billy was at last getting his just reward for attempting such a stunt. Someone else might have laughed at Billy's predicament, too amused (or satisfied) to see the danger.

Not Ibin. Though labeled as "slow," he immediately understood the essentials of the situation at hand, running to Billy's aid. But all of the whys and hows mattered very little at the moment.

"I'vegotyou! I'vegotyou!" Ibin shouted again.

"Oh, Ibin!" Billy muttered, more to himself than to Ibin. Hot tears were rolling down his face by now and dripping onto Ibin's thin hair.

"Putyourfeet...Billyputyourfeetonmy...onmy...onmyshoulders!"

Billy understood, and after a moment he managed the attempt. Ibin put his hands under Billy's feet and lifted a few inches, and directed Billy's feet onto his shoulders. This lifted Billy somewhat higher, especially when Ibin stood fully erect, but the overhead branches, like springs trying to bend back upward, kept the rope taut.

Now a little more comfortable, with better breath, and somewhat calmer, Billy tried to gaze down at Ibin, but only managed a slight glimpse of the top of Ibin's head and of Ibin's hands firmly gripping his ankles. Billy then looked up and down the path, up into the tree above. No one used this path much. Only Ibin's regular tread kept it clear of the encroaching brush and grass.

"Now ain't this a situation!"

"Iguessso,Billy."

"A real fix."

"Uhhuh."

"Ye wouldn't happen to have a knife on ye, eh?"

"No,I...no,Isuredon't. I left... Ileft... no,Ileftmypenknife-atschoolonmy... onmydesk."

"Ah. I ain't got one, neither, though me old man always says I oughtta always have a knife on me, even if it's only a little 'un. Always tellin' me ye never know when ye might have need of one. Gave me a bunch, too. All in me bedroom back home, though."

"Oh?"

"Yeah. And I reckon this here is one of them times me old man said might come about for needin' one."

"Ireckon."

"Gonna try again to see if I can climb up, so get ready."

"I'mready."

Billy managed to grip both of the downward lines of rope pretty well, knowing now that if one slipped, the other would only tighten around his neck. He pulled, but the branches overhead only bent downward, and his feet never left Ibin's shoulders.

"Argh! Blast!" Billy screamed. "These ropes! They got me good! Whoa!"

Ibin was doing a little dance to keep under Billy, to match his squirming. But Billy quickly saw the futility of the effort and the danger of mishandling the rope. Trying to resume his balance on Ibin, desperation swelled in his heart.

"That ain't gonna work!" he said, trying to steady himself.

A long while passed. No one came along. And the overcast day was now darkening. The breeze picked up and hissed through the woods, the birds began leaving off with their evening singing and tittering, and all was settling into the coming night.

"It's... it'sgetting... It'sgettingdark,Billy."

"Yep. It is."

"Whatareyougoingtodo,now?"

"I dunno, Ibin. I ain't too sure what to do," Billy's voice cracked. "It's about as bad as it can be, I reckon."

Then, with a few random and dispersed ticks of sound to lead things off, it began to rain. Several gusts swept through, with big drops flying, then came a downpour, filling the land with the noise of the soaking gush, and drenching the two hapless young men. The water ran down the ropes and over Billy's hands and down his arms. Suddenly the ropes were very slippery, and they felt thinner in Billy's grip. From time to time, the branches swayed in the gusts, pulling Billy this way or that way.

"Oh, oh!"

Billy fought to hang on, constantly reclamping his hands. He couldn't really tell if the rope was stretching or shrinking as the limbs danced overhead. There was nothing to do but hold on, but by now the ropes were truly too slippery to climb. Ibin's grip on Billy's ankles never lessened. Billy, in pain, his arms aching, in this ludicrous position as a result of his own ludicrous actions, had nothing to do but think his thoughts. Neither of them said anything at all for a long while, as the rain eventually eased to a drizzle, and at last halted altogether. The dark was complete, not even relieved by lightning. Only the sound of dripping woods, the occasional groan of a tree limb, and his own breathing met Billy's ears. The drizzle diluted his tears, and the blackness only mirrored the bleakness of his heart.

After a while, Billy found himself listening more carefully to the tick and drip of the woods, and there was only the slightest movement of air at all. He listened for the padding of footsteps, the clop of a horse, or the creak of rolling cartwheels down the track. But he did not hope. He knew this stretch was lonely and seldom-used.

For his part, Ibin listened, too. But his mind was of a kind to hear patterns, or at least what he took for patterns, in the random watery noise. It seemed to him that one drip answered another, or that one creak of a limb was a comment to what another branch had said. And he wished he knew what the wet woods was saying to itself.

Billy suddenly burst into sobs.

"I'm sorry, Ibin!" he moaned. "I'm sorry for bein' so mean to ye! I'm sorry for being a good-fer-nuthin, just like my folks say I am. I'm lazy an' I ain't careful for others. I don't even stop an' wonder what a fella might feel inside. How a fella might not feel good inside, might be hurtin' all the while I joke an' play an make wisecracks. I never pay any mind to that, or how mean an' low-down I am, an' how my fun ain't any fun at all for other folk. I'm sorry I'm such a mean good-for-nuthin rascal!"

"Billy,don't...don't...Billy,don'tcry! Iain'thurt. Iain'thurton... on... Iain'thurtontheinside. Yeragoodfor...agoodforsomethinrascal."

"No, yer wrong 'bout that. An' I want ye to do something. I want ye to ease me off yer shoulders an' then run on home. Ye can bring yore papa in when morning comes, get me down, an' take me home."

"Idon'tthinkI'lldothat, Billy. Idon't... Idon'twant... Idon'twanttogo. Iain'tgonnaleaveyou, Billy. Andit's... andit'sdarksoImightgetlost."

"Ye ain't gonna get lost, Ibin. Go on, now. Get on home."

"No. Iain'tgonnaleave."

Ibin tightened his grip on Billy's ankles as he spoke, and he seemed to stand straighter under Billy's weight.

Billy tried to argue, but all that came out of his mouth was a choked gulp as he tried to suppress his mixed feelings of gratitude and regret.

The night wore on, with long stretches of nothing said between the two. From time to time, Ibin shifted his stance and Billy his grip on the ropes. He at last managed to use only one hand at a time, allowing the other to dangle so that some feeling could return, painful though it was. Ibin did the same with his grip on Billy's ankles. Neither spoke. The breeze picked up and shook most of the raindrops from the woods. The two boys shivered in unison. A few night birds cooed in the distance. Above, narrow cracks formed in the thinning sky, and a few misty stars winked. Off to the east, a lopsided crescent moon glowed as it ascended. Billy noticed it through half-shut eyes, and he wondered if it meant that the morning was any closer at hand. Somewhere in his blurry mind, he thought so, but this hour of the night was not one that he was often awake to notice things. And although he knew many people who could tell time using the moon from one night to the next—sometimes holding up their hand to measure its height—Billy had never bothered to learn the art of doing so. A few times his parents had made him rise for early morning chores, and he had sometimes seen Lady Moon, and he recalled that she never seemed the same, sometimes shy, sometimes quite bold. Broadweed even talked about how it all worked, but at the time Billy had not been paying attention. So now it was impossible for Billy to make any calculation. And it was pointless, anyway, he concluded. This wood was far from any road or common track, and it might be days, rather than hours, before anyone happened along this path.

He thought of his parents. And he thought of Ibin's parents, too. How worried they must be. How they might have fretted for hours before setting out to find their boys. This gave Billy hope, but it also filled him with more regret. While his own parents were hardy and hale, he vaguely remembered, from someone, perhaps his mother, that Ibin's parents were elderly and frail. He realized how little he knew about them. About Ibin. Only, from what he had heard, that Ibin did almost all of the labor around the cottage, when he was not at the school. That Ibin fetched water, chopped wood, fed the chickens, tended to the garden, and all manner of things. He recalled someone saying that Ibin's mother was often in bed, and that his father used a crutch or a walking stick. Billy wasn't sure if that was so, or if any of it was really so, since he had never bothered to ask, and he could now recall only once passing by Ibin's home, some two or three miles away. How little he knew! And as he considered things, the more and more his regrets piled up. Although he tried to stifle them, every once in a while a quiet little whimper pushed out.

In fact, around that same time, Billy's mother was fretting about in the kitchen of Bosk Manor, her headquarters, one might say. Billy's father had ridden out hours ago. He first rode to the school, carefully tracing the road by which Billy usually went. He went slowly, having a storm lantern up on a pole, seated in a lance cup on his saddle, carefully moving it right and left along the way, searching the sides of the roads and paths. By the time he reached the school, the rain was coming down in torrents, and he dismounted to look carefully into the yards and outbuildings. Calling out, he received no reply. He stepped up onto the covered porch and opened the door to look within, but the place was empty. Then he quickly and carefully refilled the oil for his lamp, using a school candle to see by, trimmed the lamp's wick, and cleaned the glass. Later, back in the saddle, he continued on to Broadweed's cottage not far away, almost within sight of the school, and pounded on the door.

Meanwhile, Ibin's father clumped back and forth in his cottage, peering through the small windows into the night, puffing furiously on his pipe. He had laid aside one crutch so that he could carry a candle, and he lit several lanterns outside. The wind and rain had extinguished one, but he saw that the others still glowed. His wife called to him from the next room, and he went to her.

"No sign, dearie," he told her. "As I said, I reckon he worked late helpin' Gustan at the schoolhouse. Getting' caught in the rain and the dark, I imagine he's found shelter somewhar an' awaits the morning. I know, I know! But our worry won't help matters. When light comes, I'll stoke up the stove for ye, put the kettle on, an' set off towards the school."

"I am as alarmed and puzzled as you," Mr. Broadweed said to Mr. Bosk. Mrs. Broadweed stood across the room heating some tea for Mr. Bosk. Bosk was still standing and dripping at the doorway. "I dismissed school today around mid-afternoon, hours before sunset. And, as usual, Billy was immediately to the door and well on his way before most students had risen from their desks."

"Well, as I said, we've seen not hide nor hair of 'im, so I'll move on."

"Maybe he went to Passdale," suggested Broadweed.

"That's whar I go from here," said Bosk. "But he had no errands to do thar, nothin' to get from the store or such. Still, Robby might know somethin'. I thank ye once more for openin' yer door to me. No, Mrs. Broadweed, I'll not take any drink, thank ye just the same, but will be on me way."

"I'll go the other way, then," said Broadweed, reaching for his coat. "I can at least alert the neighbors along the way towards Weepingbrook."

"That is good of you," nodded Bosk. "It's the long way 'round for Billy to go home by, so I doubt he's yonder way."

"Nevertheless, I will go."

"Very well. Much appreciated. Be careful 'round Steggan's place, as ye know how ornery he is. At least the rain seems tapering off."

"Good luck to you!"

In the wood, and all around, the inconsistent breeze fell to a steady whisper. Thin mist began to form over the ground, and it slowly ascended. Above, the sky began to clear, but was just as quickly obscured by the restless and thickening fog. The moon, now somewhat higher, became a mere spot of gray glow. All the while, Billy continued his thoughts, his mind often circling around and back in a tiresome repetition. Although he sensed that his people were alerted to his own disappearance, and were probably out looking for him, he thought that in all likelihood there was no one out looking for Ibin. This made him gulp again with shame and sorrow at the thought of their crushing weight of worry, two old people with nobody nearby to help them. No one aware of their plight.

"Well," he thought to himself, "one way or other, it won't be much longer." His arms were rapidly losing strength, his hands almost without sensation, and his legs aching with shots of fire that made him twitch on Ibin's shoulders. "Even if I don't give out, surely Ibin can't stand much more of this, bull ox though he is." He pulled in his breath and held it for a moment, then spoke to Ibin.

"Ibin. Let go of me. Just ease me off yer shoulders an' go on home. Ye can fetch a knife for me an' come back. I'll just hang on. I think that's the best thing to do."

"I'mnot… I'mnotsosure, Billy. Andit'sstill… Andit'sstill… It'sstill-toodark."

Billy would have nodded if he could have. So they waited. Ibin stood fast, and Billy dangled. Time crawled by. Billy's mind, as numb as his arms, wandered aimlessly.

"What'sthat?"

Ibin's voice jarred Billy back to attention.

"What?"

"Billy,there's… There'salight."

"It's just the moon, Ibin."

"No,not… No,not… Notthemoon… It'snotthe… It'smoving, Billy! It'smovingthisway!"

"Naw, it's just yer eyes playing… Oh! What's that!?"

A light it was, but in the mist it was an eerie bluish glow, none too big, and it was slowly moving. But moving it was, and it was coming nearer. What with the brush and the fog intervening, it went from dim to bright, sometimes small and sharp, sometimes a mere diffused glow.

"That ain't no torchlight," said Billy. "An' no kind of lamp nor lantern that I've ever seen. See how blue it is?"

"Help!" cried Ibin.

"Help!" called Billy.

Both began yelling so desperately that they almost shook themselves apart from one another. The light stopped moving, but then proceeded faster toward them.

"I'm a comin'!" a voice called. "Where are ye?"

"Here! Over here!"

Now the two could hear clunking and stomping and soon enough a man appeared carrying a blue-glowing lantern on a short pole. It was difficult to see his features, but it was plain that he was burdened with a very large pack, with many items dangling from it, making various clunking and thudding sounds as he approached. Coming along the path, he got to within ten feet before he saw them. Abruptly stopping, he held up his lamp for a better view. It was an odd lamp, in the shape of a large bottle, tied and dangling with twine from the pole, but when the man agitated it, it glowed even brighter.

"Lord Beras Almighty!" the man cried out. "What on earth are ye two fellas up to?"

"A knife!" cried Ibin.

"I need a knife to cut meself free!" cried Billy. "Quick! Afore we give out!"

"But I ain't got no knife."

"A dirk, then."

"No dirk."

"Sword?"

"Nope."

"Lance?"

"Nope."

"Yer jokin'!"

"Scissors?" Ibin asked.

"Nope. I don't carry no metal."

"The lamp!" Billy cried. "Ye could pass it up an' mebbe I could burn through this rope!"

"There's no fire in this lamp. It's a flask of sea-stars."

"What! No fire?"

"Just sea-stars. As cool as the water they're swimming in."

"Sea stars? Never heard of that."

"Well, thar little teeny-tiny bugs what live out in the Great Sea. A feller over in Glareth catches 'em an' raises them for folk like me. When ye add a bit of dried sea stars to water, even fresh water, they come back alive an' start glowin'. Add a tad of sugar an' a pinch of salt with a bit of rotten leaves, an' they get real bright, like right now."

"It's glass, ain't it? Ye can bust it an' we can use it to cut with!"

"Never gonna do that! I need it too much!"

"But ain't ye got some kinda firesticks or some kind of flint an' steel or the like?"

"No metal. No firesticks. I don't use any fire at all."

"What kind of fella are ye, then!?" Billy cried in exasperation. "Ye just eat raw stuff? Ye don't make hot tea on the trail? Ye don't cut things?"

"Nope. I'm a hunter."

"A hunter! Some hunter! Ye ain't even got a knife. An' I don't see no bows or arrows or even sharp sticks on ye."

"I hunt galafronks."

Ibin stiffened. Billy's mouth fell open.

"Galafronks!" Ibin whispered. "Ihategalafronks!"

"Galafronks're just stuff, just tales, Ibin! Thar ain't no such thing."

"Ah," said the hunter. "That's what a lot of folk say. But look at this."

In the growing light of faraway morning, the hunter put down his pack and opened a flap, then drew out a small pouch. From this he pulled out a long and broad sheet of thin, black cloth. It floated in the air like the lightest gauze ever, black as coal, and after a moment, the breeze seemed to be trying to tug it away from the hunter's hands as he held it up.

"Do ye notice something odd here? Do ye notice which way the breeze is blowin'?"

Indeed, while the sheet of black waved off toward the west, the breeze itself was very distinctly coming from the south. Yet the material was not at all inclined to move in any direction but west.

"This is the skin of a galafronk. I took it not six nights ago, down not far from Bessinton. An' if I let go of it, it'd float away off westward. They all do that, no matter the breeze or wind. I sell bits to sailors an' other folk to put on lines an' rigging to always know, out at sea, which way is west."

"Well, I admit that's some trick," said Billy. "But it don't prove nuthin' an' it don't help us none."

"I might be inclined to try to give ye some help," said the hunter. "But first I'd want to know what got ye into this, well, this situation. I don't want to be helpin' no rogues or murderers or the like what's getting thar justice an' such."

"We'rejustboys. Weain'trogues. Weain'tbad!" Ibin said.

"Then tell me all about it, then."

"Well, I'm Billy Bosk, an' this here's Ibin, Ibin Brinnin," Billy said.

"I don't think I'll give ye me own name just yet," said the hunter. "But do go on with yer tale."

Billy told all. He described his harebrained plan to have a bit of fun. He described all of the work he did up in the tree, how he got tangled, how he fell, and how Ibin came along in the nick of time. Of course, this took a good while, due to Billy's way of roaming about in his tales. And as he did a bit of that roaming, he let onto the hunter more about his own rapscallious nature than he might have thought. At last, though, as the light of day had grown enough for him to see the hunter better, he wound up his story.

All while the hunter listened, he fiddled with his pack. First he put away his galafronk skin, which took some doing as it seemed to fight his efforts to get stuffed back into the pouch. After this, glancing at Billy from time to time and nodding to indicate he was still listening, he rummaged until he found another roll of cloth, long and thickly padded, which he put onto the ground and then unfastened the tethers binding its flap. Opening it up and letting it roll out, several long curved white items rattled. Each was flat, as wide as two fingers, as long as an arm. Each was oddly curved, with one end flat and coarse, as if it had broken from something, while the other end tapered to a point.

"An' that's about it," Billy concluded. "Now, do ye think ye can go off an' find somebody better to help us out?"

"Nope. Don't think I will do that. But I'll give ye some help."

He bent and began examining the white objects as he spoke.

"You see, galafronks don't like fire, don't like the sight of it, nor the smell of it, and won't come near anyone smelling of smoke or oil or charred stuff. Won't come near a candle or fire of any kind. That's why I don't have no use for any fire. And metal is worse than useless on 'em, as not even the sharpest knife makes any difference to 'em. Knives, arrows, and all the like just pass right through 'em. When they're alive, you see, they are like smoke itself. Don't ye know the old rhyme about 'em?"

"Yes… Yes, I do… I know it," said Ibin. Then he recited:

> *Galafronks, galafronks!*
> *Big as a house, small as a mouse,*
> *Brown and black and gray.*
> *Squeezing between the door-cracks*
> *Up between the floor-cracks*
> *As thin and flat as smoke are they!*
>
> *With iron-strong arms,*
> *And saucer-plate eyes*
> *They mumble their charms*
> *Through teeth like scythes*
> *To get you they come, rum duma-dums!*
> *Stomping their trollfeet,*
> *Like thunder, like drums.*
>
> *Galafronks, galafronks, shadows and dust!*
> *Galafronks, galafronks, gristle and rust!*
> *Rude little girls they love to boil*
> *With beetles and spiders and bugs.*
> *And bad little boys they like to broil*
> *With maggots and leeches and slugs!*

"Yep," said the hunter, "that's it. Yer mighty lucky ain't none about, is what I say. An', just so ye know, the only way to kill a galafronk is with the teeth of a galafronk."

He held up one of the long white objects which now almost appeared in his hand like a curved blade.

Billy was by now nearly beside himself with impatience.

"Now that's just mean!" he cried. "A fella like Ibin, doin' his best to help out another fella, an' thar ye are, just makin' him all the more scared! That's just mean."

"Hm," said the hunter, "Well, that's a purty speech comin' from a fella who ought to know 'bout such things as being mean. What I oughtta do is let things be as they are an' get on me way. Mr. Ibin, here, won't be none the worse for wear after a bit of rest, an' the world'll be rid of another imp."

Ibin gulped, and Billy was duly rebuked to tearful silence.

"But I figure this big feller here has been through enough."

The hunter suddenly threw the long galafronk tooth, sending it right over Billy's hands and slicing through the ropes as neatly as scissors through thin thread. Billy tumbled backwards, landing on his back, knocking the breath out of him. Ibin stumbled forward and fell to his hands and knees. Billy twisted around on the ground, clawing to free the rope from his neck when he felt a boot on his chest, pressing him down. Towering over him was the hunter, galafronk tooth in hand.

"Yer old life ended on that rope," said the hunter, bending over to put his face close to Billy's. Wide-eyed and filled with renewed terror, Billy froze.

"An' now the new life ye have ain't entirely yer own. Part of ye, perhaps the most part, now belongs to this man." The hunter gestured toward Ibin. "This man, who showed compassion for yer plight. Who knew not of yer trickery an' carelessness. This man, who ran to ye, who truly supported ye in yer time of need, who remained with ye long past his natural endurance. What past crimes, tricks, an' cheats ye've done ain't of no account. This man gave ye all he had to give. He did not abandon ye when came darkness an' storm an' fear. He cared naught for his own safety an' tied his own fate to yers."

"Now," continued the hunter. "Now. He owns ye, after a manner of speakin', though he would not be yer master. He, not I, freed ye from yer doom. But now. Now! Can ye match the strength of his heart? Can ye ever safeguard him, if ever need be, as he safeguarded? What is the quality of yer heart, I wonder? Is there kindness within it? Might ye have the courage, I wonder. Might ye have a grain of this man's concern an' common goodness? Might ye look after his well-bein', should it come to that, as he has done this night for yers?"

The hunter drew back his face and stood upright, leaving his foot on Billy's chest.

"Ye've been given the gift of the rest of yer life," he said. "Do not forget! Never forget!"

Billy, his face streaming, managed to nod as the hunter lifted his foot and stood aside. After a stern gaze at Billy, as if sizing up things, the hunter went to Ibin and offered his hand. Ibin took it and the hunter helped him onto his feet. Ibin stood, a bit unsteadily, a bit fearful. The hunter held Ibin's hand firmly and gave it a shake.

"It has been me honor, an' me instruction, to meet ye," said the hunter to Ibin. "Me name is Tarl, Johannes Tarl. Mister Ibin, ye have the natural makin' of a great friend, should anyone decide to be a friend to ye. An' may ye ever be just as ye are! The world'd be a fine place, indeed it would be, if others whar as steadfast an' as kind. Adieu! Adieu to ye both!"

The hunter released Ibin's hand, quickly put away his things and hoisted his pack, picked up his eerie lantern, and—without another word—ambled off into the morning mists and disappeared from sight.

When the hunter was gone, Billy got to his feet. The two looked at each other.

"Ithink… Ithink… IthinkIneedtositforaspell. IthinkIneed-tositdown," Ibin said.

"Yeah. Me, too."

Billy followed Ibin to the trunk of the tree and the two sat down and leaned back upon it, their legs sprawled out.

"Oophf!"

They rested. The mist dissipated, the light of day increased, birds began their morning tittering and their singing practice, and the countryside woke up. Across the way and just above the trees, the Morning Star still beamed, though the sky all around was blue, and not far from it remained the shy crescent face of Lady Moon. Then the treetops received a wide touch of yellow from the rising sun which gradually spread downward like golden butter melting. A chipmunk hopped onto a nearby clump and chirped at the two, and a rabbit hopped out from under a nearby bush a few yards away.

Ibin closed his eyes and maybe he napped a little. Billy tried, but could not. Every sound and movement attracted his attention, his eyes going from thing to thing, from sky to tree, from bird to bird, and his ears pricked at every sound, the creaking woods, the birdsongs, and the hush of the breeze through the weeds along the path.

Billy rubbed his neck with his sore hands, then paused, turning to gaze at Ibin. He began to shake, but it was not with shivers or cold, and his mouth quivered. He closed his eyes. But, though tightly shut, they could not stop the newest stream of tears that poured forth for a long while.

"I ain't got the words," Ibin heard Billy say. He looked at Billy, who was now staring blankly at the scene of their misadventure.

"Mebbe I can figure them out someday. I dunno, Ibin. If I said a thank-ye, that don't seem enough. If I said that I was sorry, that don't seem enough. If I said I was wrong an' pretty much a heel an' a bully, that wouldn't get to the truth of it. An' if I said that I shoulda known better, that I shoulda done different, that'd be just words an' air, too."

Ibin listened, but said nothing.

"But I think, right now, I ought to be gettin' ye home," Billy concluded. He rolled over onto his hands and knees and pushed himself first into a crouch, and then stood.

"Come on, big fella," Billy said, offering his hand to Ibin. "Let's get ye home."

It was not the end of things.

Billy first went with Ibin to his cottage and saw how Ibin was tearfully and joyously received by his parents. The two were given cups of cool water to drink and ushered to the hearth to warm themselves. Of course, Mr. and Mrs. Brinnin wanted to know what had happened, and so Billy tried to explain how Ibin had saved his life. Uncharacteristically brief, Billy only said that he had fallen and gotten tangled in the rope when Ibin came along. He was about to say why it all came about, but got so choked up with shame that he could not bring himself to utter a thing for a while. Mrs. Brinnin, who had for hours been up and about from her sickbed, gave Billy a hug, which made him cry all the harder, and Mr. Brinnin patted Billy on the shoulder.

At last, wiping his face, Billy nodded.

"I am terribly sorry," he said. "I'm awful ashamed of bein' the cause of all yer worry."

"Put that out of yer mind," said Mrs. Brinnin, taking up Ibin's hand. "I'm just so happy that the two of you are safe."

Billy could sense that they refrained from saying many other things, things he deserved to hear. Certainly they were far more restrained than his own parents would be, and for the first time he got a glimpse, a real glimpse, of Ibin's little family.

"Ibin is a good man," Billy said. "A son to be proud of."

"We are proud," said Mr. Brinnin. "We've always been proud of Ibin. Most don't understand why. But now you do, at least somewhat."

"I do. An' I'm proud, too, of Ibin. Not just fer what he's done for me. But fer who he is, fer what's inside of 'im."

Presently, they heard the clopping of approaching hooves, and soon there was a rap on the door. It was Billy's father. Mr. Bosk was not a man of great patience, especially when it came to Billy. But when his son rushed to him and flung his arms around him, all his angry and scolding words stopped-up his heart. Hugging his son, he looked at the others and sensed that all was well. Unexpectedly moved by the scene, the smiles, and by Billy's clinging, he said nothing at all. Indeed, his own eyes glistened with inexplicable feelings. Feelings of relief, surely. Of weariness, too. And, too, of love.

After handshakes and expressions of gratitude, Mr. Bosk helped Billy settle onto the horse to sit behind him. Billy put his arms around his father's waist, and Mr. Bosk took the reins in one hand and put his other on those of his son to hold him tight. And that is how they went all the way home, miles and miles. At many a steep or rough stretch, Mr. Bosk put the reins in his teeth and gripped Billy's arms with both of his own to be sure his son would not slide away. Perhaps Billy slept. They did not speak at all. Later, Mr. Bosk carried Billy upstairs to his room, with Billy's mother trailing alongside, wiping her son's hair back from his brow. A shake of Mr. Bosk's head forestalled conversation and query. With his wife looking on, Mr. Bosk silently helped Billy take off his clothes, washed some of the mud and grime from his son's little body, and tucked him into bed. Then the mother and father pulled two chairs together close to one another and sat.

Early the following morning, Mr. Bosk dispatched a rider to go to Broadweed and to all around, informing everyone that Billy had been located and was back at home after spending the night in the rainy out-of-doors. Not knowing the details himself, Mr. Bosk instructed the rider to say that Billy was safe and well enough.

As for what Billy told his parents, he left out much. He did say that he got tangled up in some ropes, although he did not mention why. And he described how Ibin came along and helped him out. He said it took all night, and Ibin stayed with him until he managed to get free, with the additional help of a passing hunter. When pressed as to what Billy was trying to do up in that tree, he only said that he thought it would be fun to make a swing. At this moment, Billy burst into tears, and his parents only thought it was because of the close call, not knowing the weight of shame on Billy's heart. His hand kept going up to rub his neck, now banded with red chaff marks and blue bruises. And of course he was scolded for everything he had put everyone through, all of the worry, the effort of searching, and the unnecessary alarm. Billy repeated his tearful apologies over and over.

Late the next afternoon, Broadweed came. Mr. and Mrs. Bosk were both at home, and Billy was still in bed, now suffering from a minor fever and chills. But he was well enough to sit up, and the three adults gathered around his bed.

"While I am certainly relieved and happy that you are safe," he said to Billy, "my business here has nothing to do with your unfortunate escapade. Did you write this note?"

Billy looked at the note that Broadweed held up, which had already been shown to his parents, and he nodded.

"Yes, sir."

"This is a lie," Broadweed said bluntly.

"Yes, sir. I made it all up."

"Yet you have taken an oath not to lie. To always say the truth."

"Yes, sir. I'm sorry. I reckon I got took by how much fun it might be to see yer face when ye read it."

"Did you?"

Now the weight on Billy's heart played in, and he realized the meanness of it.

"I guess it kinda got away from me," Billy said. "I'm very sorry. I guess I warn't thinkin' right."

"I cannot have liars in my school," said Broadweed.

"Yes, sir."

"It isn't fair to the other students, and it sets a bad example for others to go by."

"Yes, sir."

"When I ask a question, I must know that my students speak truthfully."

"Yes, sir."

"Lying is like cheating on your lessons to steal good grades that do not belong to you."

"Yes, sir."

"And it goes against the promises that the people of Barley have made to each other, and to the King."

"Yes, sir. I'm sorry that I did that."

Broadweed looked at Billy. He did not expect Billy to argue or to deny anything, as it was always Billy's way to own up to his antics. But he saw Billy trying to control his emotions, visibly shaking, eyes watering, voice cracking. This was uncharacteristic, but perhaps it was due to Billy's physical ailments and his fatigue.

"So," Broadweed continued, "I cannot allow you to continue coming to school."

Billy nodded, but at first could not speak.

"I will not further your shame by telling anyone about this," said Broadweed, "not even the young lady against whom this is also an offense."

Billy's parents did not speak, but were obviously upset, angry, and disappointed with Billy. Mr. Bosk almost spoke, but Mrs. Bosk put her hand on his knee to forestall him. Everyone stared at Billy, somewhat expectantly, while Billy, sitting up in bed, stared down at his hands that were clutching the quilt that covered him.

"I… I know that I have no worth," he said. "I know I've dun bad things. I can't undo 'em. I've been showed, over the past short while, how careless I've been when it comes to things, when it comes to other folk. I guess I got a hard heart, if I got one at all. An' thar ain't no one to blame but meself. I've got away with a lot, I reckon. So now I reckon all this is just my comeuppance, what's owed, what's right. I'm sorry, Mr. Broadweed. I'm just as sorry to ye as I am to me family. I'm just as sorry for what I put Ibin through, too, and his folks."

"This is not about that," said Broadweed.

"But I reckon it is, indeed," Billy said. "An' I figure that I gotta try to pay back some of what I took. Even if I'll never be able to. I don't know that I'm man enough. I don't know if I'm smart enough. An' I don't know if it'll ever make any difference to anybody. An' out of all the folk out thar that I joked an' teased an' made fun of, thar's one, more than anyone else, that I owe the most to, an' that's Ibin Brinnin. He looked after me, you see. And he needs lookin' after too, is what I see. My Pop came out lookin' to find me the other night. But nobody came lookin' for Ibin. I came home to folks to take care of me. But Ibin went home to take care of others. So, now I've been thinkin', been tryin' to figure out what I oughtta do. An' the least I can try to do is to be his friend. He ain't got none, I don't think. A lot of folks pick on Ibin, an' I've done me share of it. He don't seem to mind it, he don't seem to feel the sting of it like the rest of us would. But that don't matter, don't make it alright."

"Ibin is, in his own way, a fine young man," said Broadweed. "Whatever happened to you two, which I understand was because of your thoughtlessness, is outside my own duties. My duty is to the school, the children, and all their parents."

"But ain't it up to ye to help out a fella? Can ye help a fella change, if a fella really wants to, really needs to? Ain't that what school is for? Ain't it about learnin' things? Ain't it about tryin' to learn? So as to be better than before? Won't ye help me be better? Please let me come back to school. Mebbe not right away, as I'm pretty busted up. Mebbe after a while. An' mebbe give me one last chance? I know ye don't trust any promise I might make to ye, but I'll do me best to be better than before. I'll do me best to learn an' not be so much a burden to ye."

Broadweed sighed and stood, shaking his head.

"I don't know, Billy. You are right. I don't trust you. And I can't use up all of my time at school watching over you."

Billy was now struggling to get out of bed. His mother and father stood, uncertain whether to force him back. But Billy pushed them aside and wobbled across the room to his clothes chest. He lifted the lid and rummaged through it until he produced an ornate leather pouch and brought it to Broadweed. Mr. and Mrs. Bosk, recognizing it and knowing what it contained, were confused. Billy opened the pouch and produced a cloak clasp. It was as big as Billy's palm, in the ornate shape of a round knot, cast in silver, heavily tarnished, with a long steel pin hinged to the back of it. He handed it to Mr. Broadweed.

"This is all that was found of me forebear, Bilaylin the Hammer, the man I was named after. He died at Tulith Attis tryin' to protect others. This is all that was found of him, his mark is on the back of it. My Grandpa gave it to me on the day I was born. When I was very little, Grandpa told me all about it, an' all about the man it belonged to. My own Pop has told me, too. Well, I can't be the man what wore this. An' I don't deserve it. Take it. Keep it. An', someday, if I ever do come to deserve it, then give it back to me."

"Billy…" Broadweed glanced at the parents, who appeared as confused as he was. He turned the clasp over in his hand and saw the ancient marks of its onetime owner. "Billy, I cannot do this. It's your heirloom from your namesake."

"I reckon I gotta give up a lot of things if I want to shift me ways," said Billy. "Please let me come back to school."

Broadweed carefully put the clasp back into its pouch, searching Billy's eyes as he did so.

"What say you?" he asked Mr. Bosk. "For this object is as much yours as anyone's."

"It is up to Billy," stated Mr. Bosk. "What do you say, Frizella?"

Mrs. Bosk shook her head, saying, "It is something like a ransom, ain't it? An' yes. It is up to Billy to pay it, to own up to its worth."

"Very well," said Mr. Broadweed. "Let this be a pact between us. To be known only to the four of us. And my wife, too, from whom I keep no secrets. Although, I know not how I am to be the judge of things, the judge of what you may deserve in the future. I shall keep it safe. I give you this one last chance. When you are well enough, come back to school. We shall have a talk about your studies and what you must do, and must not do."

Very few know the whole story of what happened the night that Billy dangled and Ibin supported him. Ibin never mentioned it. Billy told little enough of it to his parents, never mentioned the galafronk hunter or what that man had said. Indeed, Billy rarely mentioned it at all for the rest of his life.

But in the days and weeks that followed, Billy did seem different. The sparks of change sometimes smolder long and only slowly come to light and life. Billy soon enough resumed much of his carefree and jovial ways, and even rose to new heights of laziness. But only when it came to certain things. He tried to become a better student, and although he would never be brilliant, Broadweed had to admit that he became a passable reader, could do numbers well enough, and actually took to lessons about customs, lore, and history better than some of the other students. And, at least on the school grounds, Billy refrained from playing jokes, and almost always his antics were harmless. Sometimes, though, he directed his efforts to insult or to humiliate some of the bullies, especially among the Passdale boys. It did seem that he got into just as many scrapes, but not during school hours, taking home just as many shiners as before. But what most did not see was that these fights were often in the defense of someone else, and not entirely of Billy's provocation.

Along those lines, woe be unto anyone who slighted Ibin in Billy's presence. If it happened at school, retribution would surely be had later on and elsewhere.

Eventually, Mr. Broadweed paired Billy with Robby Ribbon, son of a local merchant and one of the better students, and this helped Billy keep his mind from wandering too much. The three, Ibin, Billy, and Robby, sat together at the back of the schoolroom and eventually became very good friends.

But Billy and Ibin became almost inseparable. In Billy, Ibin found a friend and companion who seemed to care about him. In Ibin, Billy found someone tolerant of his chatter, amiable to his laziness, and, most importantly, someone who was an example of stolid kindness. Billy almost always took the long way home, first accompanying Ibin to his cottage. Mr. and Mrs. Bosk suspected this was only a ploy so that Billy would often be too late to do certain chores. But Ibin's parents seemed to appreciate it, often inviting Billy in for tea before he walked the rest of the way home.

After much effort, Billy talked the blacksmith at Boskland into taking Ibin on as a helper, since he was big and strong and could sling fuel and metal with ease. This was agreed to, with Mr. Bosk's permission, and so the two boys were able to see more of each other. Mr. Bosk was skeptical, thinking Billy would seek to spend too much time lingering about the forge rather than doing his own chores.

But Mrs. Bosk thought it a good idea, since help was needed and Ibin could take home a few coins each week to help out his parents.

So for almost a year, the two boys changed their homeward route from school to go to Boskland first, where Ibin would work until sunset. Sometimes Billy would see Ibin home, chattering the entire way about this or that, with Ibin's patient attention to all that Billy said. Sometimes, Ibin went home by himself after a long day, almost always with a basket prepared by Mrs. Bosk, one filled with food or candles or sewing things, or even hand-me-down clothes. On many occasions, when there was much for Ibin to do, he remained overnight at Bosk Manor. And whenever there was little for Ibin to do at the forge, he spent his time mostly in Mrs. Bosk's kitchen. That is, except for those times when Billy managed to entice him away to ride around the estate, to go fishing, to idle away errands to Passdale, or to simply watch the sunset. All the while, of course, Billy had his chance to hold forth on some subject or other, for hours at a time, with the agreeable Ibin nodding often and rarely interrupting. Billy's parents, Mr. Broadweed, and many others made comment on the pair, and some observed how Ibin's friendship seemed to have steadied Billy, at least a little.

Then, almost two years later, an awful fever swept through the county, and Ibin lost both of his parents within two weeks of one another. Billy was there both times, along with his mother. Afterwards, and every day, Billy returned to Ibin's place to help his friend, or at least just be with him. Mrs Bosk was none too surprised, in the days to come, that Billy took up the argument that Ibin should come to Boskland to live. Otherwise, as Billy said, he would need to move to Ibin's cottage. Strong and capable of many things, Billy argued, he simply did not have what it took to run a small farm, to make sensible decisions about keeping house, or about trade or money. He needed looking after, Billy argued. And if he had to do it alone, he told his parents, then so be it. His parents laughed at the prospect of disaster if Billy was to be in charge of such things.

It was never to come to that, as his parents had decided long before Billy brought it up, that Ibin should live somewhere on their estate, under their caring eye. To live in Bosk Manor, taking one of the many spare bedrooms, was not something they had really considered until Billy suggested it. But it was the right and sensible thing to do, they all had to admit. With Ibin's permission, of course.

Indeed, just as Billy had reported, Ibin had been struggling to understand all that was now upon him. The loss of his parents was very sad, and he often went about the homestead, aimless and often tearful. He was sad and muddled, not knowing what to do around the farm, or in what order to do things. There was no one to tell him what to do. Billy was not much help in that regard, either, though Ibin was always happy at Billy's company. So, on the day after the Bosks made their decision, Billy went to Ibin to talk to him about it. He laid out all the points, including his own inability to be of much help with Ibin's place, and together they weighed the options and Billy gently suggested to Ibin the notion of living at Bosk Manor. Ibin immediately said that he would like to do that. And he went on to say that he could cut and carry wood, he could scrub walls, spend more time with the blacksmith, he could feed chickens, fetch water, and do all the things he had been doing all along.

"Andmebbe…mebbewecould…wecouldhavesupper…suppereverysingle-night,too."

So it was, and Ibin became part of the Bosk family. Over the years, the two would continue in their friendship, and it would deepen as time went by. Sometimes they privately discussed the fateful night that Ibin saved Billy. Sometimes they talked about galafronks, and while Ibin had developed a great fear of them, Billy always insisted they were just the stuff of tales meant to frighten small children. They spent hours and hours together, walking, fishing, gazing at the clouds, with hardly a word passing between them. And Mr. Broadweed, who had come to see Billy's good heart, did indeed return the cloak clasp to Billy.

See Also:
Biographical Sketches (Gustan Broadweed)
Glossary (Galafronk)
****

Laeleth and Sir Wind

Many versions of this story abound, each with varying details, both in oral traditions as well as in many books and manuscripts, some dating from the earliest years of the First Age and recorded in some of the earliest known runic alphabets of those years. It serves as a glimpse at what the early Elifaen might have thought of those who had departed with Aperion, the place they went to, and how the seasons came to be. This particular version, written in the Common Speech, appeared in a book of stories for children that was published in Glareth during the middle years of the Second Age.

Of those who departed the earth and went with Aperion into his heavenly abode was one called Laeleth. There are many stories told about her, and how she so loved one of the Fallen Ones that she contrived to return to the earth, forsaking her own kind so that she could seek out her love, whose name was Celefar. It happened like this:

It was Aperion, King and Lord of all the Faerekind and Laeleth's father, who had laid the curse upon Elifaen hosts, causing those who wished for violence to be stripped of their wings and to tread the earth like the lowly animals. It was he, Aperion King, who led the Obedient Ones away to a heavenly abode prepared for them by Beras.

Aperion was sorely displeased at Laeleth for wanting to return and forbade her to go, fearing that if she returned to the earth, the curse upon the Elifaen might be lifted before its time. So he set a watch about her and set a gate before his starry castle, guarded by Wind so that any Faere who passed through the gate would be blown by Wind's powerful breath back into the castle. Many times did Laeleth attempt to depart, spreading her wings to fly down to the earth, and yet each time was blown back into the castle by the breath of Wind. Until at last, distraught at her separation from Celefar and driven unto extremes, she prepared a draught of poison and drank it full. This poison could not kill her, for she was Faere and immortal, and untouched by the curse of the Elifaen, but it caused her wings to become brittle and they filled with decay and broke from her shoulders and fell from her back like broken glass. Then Laeleth threw herself from the gate and Wind had no power over her and, fearing his failure and the wrath of Aperion, he turned into a tempest and blew even harder, but still he could not force her back.

But because she had no longer the Faere wings of her kind, she fell through the forest of stars and plunged downward through the mountains of the sky and passed by the island of Lady Moon to the earth. This was a great calamity and filled all of the earth and heavens with fear. As she fell, Wind gave chase, following her downward until at last she struck the earth with such force that her body was broken and disfigured. At that moment, for the first time since the world came into being, all of the leaves of all of the trees withered and fell away at once. When Wind came soon after, and found her lying on the ground, so filled with grief and anger was he that he blew his cold breath all about Laeleth's body and covered her with the new fallen leaves and, to hide his failure, he blew his cold breath upon the clouds, making them fall as snow upon all of the lands, which had never happened before. And so she lay there, covered by a blanket of leaves and snow, while Wind raged all about the earth, tearing at himself in anguish and despair, uprooting trees and tossing them aside, spinning himself into great whirlwinds of dust, and kicking the waves of the sea against the shore, ever restless in his fretfulness and fear. And all the creatures of the earth hid themselves, thinking the End of Days had come, and took to burrows and caves and other deep places.

One day, Aperion was walking about his starry castle, going from room to room and from floor to floor and from chamber to chamber looking for his daughter, but he could not find her. Then he noticed that the gates were quiet and that Wind did not howl and blow, and he immediately grew angry at her and at Wind, realizing they had gone. So Aperion himself flew to the earth, seeking his daughter and there found wandering over the earth Wind, muttering and moaning and cringing in cold fear and Aperion asked Wind, "Wind, where is my daughter? Did I not charge you with thwarting her departure from my castle?"

But Wind could not answer and only flew desperately from north to south and from west to east, seeking to avoid Aperion's eyes.

"Wind," Aperion called to him, "what is this that you have done to the earth? What is this cold white stuff that blows from the sky on your breath? And why are the trees naked and without their green clothes?"

At last, Wind calmed himself, settled, and whispered to Aperion.

"Laeleth took poison to dry up her wings and to break them off from her body and thus she threw herself from your castle. I had no power to stop her, for without her wings my breath found no purchase against her. And so she plunged to the earth. Dreadful was her fall, and she now lay yonder. The trees, in grief for her, shed also their wings, their leaves, and she is covered over with them. Then, I, fearful of my failure to stop her, blew my cold breath into the clouds and made snow to cover the leaves. Here, o mighty King, is your daughter."

And so Wind blew a gentle warm breath upon the ground and the snows melted and the leaves blew away, revealing the broken Laeleth still lying there, upon a bed of new green grass and blossoms of purple Sorrowcups and red Heartflowers. Upon seeing his daughter's form, Aperion was filled with remorse and grief and regretted his attempt to keep Laeleth from leaving him. As he hovered over his daughter, once lovely and delicate, great tears welled up in his eyes and as he reached for her, these tears fell upon her face and she stirred into wakefulness.

"Oh, Laeleth! What have I done?" he cried out, lifting her gently. "Let me take you from here and unto our home to mend your body and heal your heart."

"No, my father! Let me lie. Let me remain where I have chosen to be. There is no healing of my heart, save by the hand of he that I came to find. And there is no mending of my body, except by the company of this earth upon which he treads. Leave me. Perchance one day my legs will carry me as his has surely learned to do for him, and my back will hold up my proud head and my silver-white hair will thicken again to the color of gold that it once was. But if that never shall be, this is the place of my undoing by my own desire and my own longing. Never shall I fly until he that I love flies also. So long as he walks this earth, so shall I remain. His sufferings shall be my sufferings and his trials shall be my trials. And even if yet we never meet again, perhaps at least his dream will mingle with my own and together we shall be."

By now, most of the Faerekind had gathered behind Aperion, floating about nearby, listening and looking on with sadness and concern. And while Aperion and Laeleth spoke, the wind blew warm and gentle, causing the snows of the earth to melt away and the Sun pushed his golden head through the clouds and stretched his golden arms across the sky and parted the heavens so that he could look upon the scene. The grass pushed itself up through the fallen leaves, carrying up the blooms of all manner of flowers, and the trees put forth new leaves, and animals came forth in peace with one another from the dens where they had hidden themselves. And that is how the first Spring came to be.

"How can I leave you here?" said Aperion. "How can I remain Lord of the Faere, to guard and protect our kind, when I have abandoned my own daughter?"

"Let it be known, my father, that this is both the desire and punishment of she who disobeyed you. That you do not abandon me, but leave me to the making of my own way."

"Very well, child my daughter," sighed Aperion. "But watchful I shall ever be, and my eyes will ever be upon you. And if you ever call upon me, I shall come to you and with all my host. Farewell, my daughter!"

And so Aperion and the whole host of the Faere took leave of the earth and flew back through the mountains of the sky to Aperion's castle. So sad and distraught were they that they shed tears all the way and their tears became a trail of stars in the heavens, known to some as the Milky Way, which even now leads to their heavenly abode. And so great was their mourning that even the clouds, lingering aside, wept and so the first rains came to the earth.

When the Faere host arrived back at their home, Aperion sat upon his throne and summoned Wind, who came mildly before his lord.

"Wind," said Aperion King, "you have failed me and I must mete some punishment upon you. But I cannot hold you entirely to blame in this matter, for the dark cunning of my daughter and her will was greater than even I could surmise."

"My shame is boundless, oh lord, and my grief at failure brought forth a madness in me I have never known," said the Wind, striking his chest with thunder and twisting around in the air. "And though I was given a task beyond my power, I do not plea for mercy."

"It is as well you do not waste your breath so, for my anger is not sated by my grief. This curse I lay upon you: Never shall you know rest. From this day hence, the earth will ever be your abode and in no part of it may you find peace. You will be cold and you will be warm and for a time every year you will relive your grief and fear and the discovery of your failure. Go now! And be forever banished from my realm!"

And so Wind departed from the heavens unto the earth and for a time blew warm and gentle, graceful in his acceptance of his doom. But after a time, he grew troubled and restless and blew colder and colder and caused again the trees to drop their leaves in fear. And his breath became even colder, so cold that snow was made to fall again for a while. But as madness passes to grief, and grief to meditation, and as resignation sprouts hope, so did the mood of Wind change. And that is how the seasons of the year were made.

Meanwhile, Laeleth slowly recovered from her fall and at last could stand with the aid of a branch cast down to her by a tree which took pity on her.

"Maiden of the Faere, take ye this branch of mine to give thee aid and support. Let it be a sign of my love of thee and of my friendship thereof. Wheresoever ye may go, green leaves shall sprout from the branch so long as it is grasped by thee, and if ever ye shall need it no longer, thrust it into the ground and thus it will grow into a mighty tree and, over time, a great forest shall spring from it to shield thee."

So she took up the branch, which sprouted leaves from its top, and bent and haggard as an old woman, with a crooked back and thin, white hair, she began her search for her only true love, Celefar, which is another tale worthy of the telling but one that must await another time.

****

Lantos

Prince Lantos, of the House of Bayberry, was the younger brother of Lewtrah, Ruling Prince of Tracia. Lantos was almost entirely opposite in character and demeanor than his brother. Nearly twenty years younger, Lantos was handsome, athletic, and dashing, although somewhat serious-minded. He was keenly intellectual, as comfortable with a book as he was with the reins of a spirited horse or at the tiller of a close-hauled boat. He was privately a fierce critic not only of his brother's ruling policies, which contributed greatly to the revolution, but also to his brother's womanizing, drinking, and gambling ways. Where Lewtrah was jovial, haughty, and loud, Lantos was quiet and intense. Where Lewtrah lavished favors on those who fawned after him, Lantos financed public works such as wells and irrigation, free schools, libraries, and roads. Where Lewtrah was contemptuous of the working people, Lantos strove to understand and resolve the economic and trade difficulties of Tracia and to alleviate poverty.

During the years immediately prior to the Triumvirate, riots were common as people were swindled of their lands and livelihoods by Lewtrah's clique of courtiers, lords, and corrupt ministers. At last, after crop failures, devastating storms, and a series of outrageous acts of blatant judicial favoritism, open rebellion broke out, and soon the Triumvirate was leading armies against Royalists. Prince Lantos tried to negotiate a settlement, but it was too late. Although he privately expressed sympathy for the people, he publicly backed his brother, and led a campaign of defense against the Redvests that was doomed to failure.

When the capital city of Forlandis fell to the Redvests, Prince Lewtrah narrowly escaped, aided by a band of Glarethians sailors who staged a daring rescue. Lantos, meanwhile, continued to lead the fight against the Redvests. By 856 S.A., most of the Loyalist resistance had been defeated in a series of set-piece battles, with only the much reduced forces under Prince Lantos remaining, mostly in the region surrounding Waterstone and to the east near Sorghwall. However, in a series of sweeping flanking moves, the Redvests took Sorghwall and cut off the Loyalists. Under pressure from the more powerful Redvest forces, some 20,000 soldiers under Prince Lantos, along with nearly 25,000 civilians, were pushed into a pocket to the southeast of Waterstone. With no hope of resupply, Lantos knew that his people would soon starve even if the Redvests did not mount a decisive attack on their positions. Rather than wait for the inevitable end, he decided to split his forces and his people in a bid to get as many of them away to Glareth as possible.

On the fourth day of Seventhmonth, Lantos sent 12,000 of his troops against the Redvest stronghold at Sorghwall. As he intended, the Redvests were surprised and retreated into their fortifications as the Loyalists made every appearance of laying siege. However, this was only so that the civilians could swing around Sorghwall unmolested and flee northward through the Eastlands to Glareth. The Loyalists very carefully coordinated their efforts. Each day, the Loyalists would assail Redvest defenses while, each night, a few thousand would march north behind the civilians to guard their flight. On the fourth day of the supposed siege, the Redvests awoke to a scene devoid of any Loyalist troops.

Prince Lantos, meanwhile, having been kept informed concerning these actions, led a series of feints against Redvests near to Forlandis. So while most of his people escaped northward, he and 7,000 of his troops, along with many members of his own family (including his wife and two young sons who would not abandon the Prince) and around 2,000 other persecuted civilians who had flocked into his camp, marched back and forth creating as much havoc as they could over the course of three weeks. Very soon two large Redvest forces converged from Forlandis and from Waterstone, forcing Lantos to retreat into the northern swamps called The Marshlands. With his back to the swamps and his other flanks surrounded by Redvests, Lantos again split his forces. A thousand he sent with the civilians into the swamps in a bid to reach the coast while he and the rest turned and faced the Redvests.

Redvest Mar Henith, a former Kingsman and veteran of the Dragonlands, now led over 20,000 troops against Prince Lantos. Hard-pressed for time, Lantos nonetheless selected his battleground carefully, a large hammock some ten miles inside the swamplands, a small bit of relatively dry ground less than fifty yards at the widest and one thousand yards at the longest, in somewhat of a triangular shape. However, it was surrounded on three sides by broad impassible bogs that would prevent Mar Henith from bringing up his war engines. On the widest side of this hammock would be the only viable approach for the Redvests, and that was where Lantos intended to fight. The Loyalists felled many trees to make additional obstacles for the Redvests, prepared their positions, and waited. However, Mar Henith quickly realized the strength of the Loyalist position and ordered the quick construction of raised platforms from which his archers would have range of the hammock. This construction lasted for two days and, once completed, the Loyalists fell under a constant barrage of missiles. Under the cover of his archers, Mar Henith then had dozens of footbridges and raised footpaths constructed using rocks and soil brought by wagon. While this was being done, he also had constructed many footbridges along which he could send his troops.

Seeing all this, Lantos and his men sought to destroy the construction by sending raiding parties out at night to set fire to them. However, this was anticipated, and the bridges and platforms were constantly dowsed with water to prevent just such countermoves. At last, soon than the Lantos expected, at dawn five days after the construction began, the Redvests attacked. Over twenty thousand

Redvests charged along the bridges and footpaths to within thirty yards, then waded the rest of the way to the Loyalist hammock. At first the Loyalists had an easy time of it picking off the few who made it to their lines. But as more Redvests poured against them and became better organized in their formations, the Loyalists felt the full brunt of battle.

The Loyalists fought furiously, and the Redvests were just as determined, and the swamp water surrounding was bright red with blood by midmorning. Back and forth they pushed each other, and when it seemed the hammock would be entirely taken, the Redvests would be routed and driven back the length of it. So littered was the ground with dead and dying that the fighting often took place with men standing or stumbling upon the piles of corpses. By some estimates, over five thousand Redvests were dead or wounded, and nearly as many Loyalists. By noon, it was hopeless for the Loyalists, and Lantos knew it.

Salvation came shortly after noon when a violent thunderstorm darkened the battleground and dumped heavy rain on the scene and all of the combatants, forcing each side to pause and regroup. During this lull, Lantos ordered a full retreat into the swamps, and by the time the storm had passed, they were away. Mar Henith gave chase, and over the next three days, many skirmishes were fought as the remnants of both armies moved deeper and deeper into the swamps.

Meanwhile, another minor miracle was taking place along the coasts. By the time Lantos and his men began their retreat, the first of the civilians reached the marshes on the other side of the swamplands. Here they encountered local inhabitants and word quickly spread concerning the Loyalists and their retreat. While some of these people who knew the marshes and swamps best moved northward to find Lantos, a large number of ships began to gather and drop anchor just off the coast. With them had come hundreds of small boats, skiffs and prams and pirogues and punts. These were poled and paddled up into the estuaries of the marshes and on into the swamps and emerged filled with passengers. Thus, over the course of two weeks, thousands of were rescued from the swamps, and from the Redvests. And as each sailing ship was filled with refugees, it hoisted anchor and set sail for Glareth. By the time Prince Lantos and his remaining men were brought out, thirty ships had already departed northward. Prince Lantos refused to depart, however, until he was as certain as he could be that as many of his people as possible were brought away to the ships. At last, only six Loyalist ships remained, four warships and two others that carried the family of Prince Lantos, the Prince himself, and the last of the survivors that could be found. Four days after the Battle of the Marshlands, the small fleet set sail. However, this only set the stage for the Battle of Grisland Strait, as a fleet of Redvest warships was quickly closing in on the Prince. Only the ship bearing Prince Lantos and one other survived the battle, and both made it away to Glareth by the Sea.

In Glareth, the Tracian royalty quickly established a community in exile, with Lantos working hard to find his people gainful work and places to live. Meanwhile, Lewtrah hardly paused in his philandering, and squandered both the resources and the goodwill of his people. Lewtrah was an embarrassment not only to his brother but also to Ruling Prince Carbane who had risked so much to host the Tracians. When Lewtrah suddenly died in 865 S.A., he was officially mourned, but many were relieved. Tracians in exile were jubilant when Prince Carbane recognized Lantos as Tracia's Ruling Prince in Exile, a title Carbane never acknowledged for Lewtrah. As a result, Lantos gained prestige with his own people, but was also able to quickly rein in or even punish those former Lewtrah supporters who shared so much of the blame for Tracia's strife and who vexed Glareth and his own people with their corruption and intrigues.

During the troubles in Tracia, Glareth had not been idle. Aghast at the events in Tracia, and fearful of Tracia's territorial aspirations, Prince Carbane initiated a program to bolster Glareth's armed forces, including its naval power. When news came of the Redvest invasion of the Eastlands, Carbane put his plan in to action. A powerful army, led by Prince Danoss and Prince Lantos, made up of Glarethians and thousands of exiled Tracians, marched south. News of their approach was deliberately spread so that the Tracians would gather their strength to face the northern threat.

Meanwhile, the main invasion force boarded ships and sailed south in a vast fleet to strike in the southern regions of Tracia. Caught between two great armies, the Redvest military was smashed in a series of battles until the entire Realm was under the control of the liberating forces, and Prince Lantos was declared the new Ruling Prince.
See Also:
Historical Sketches (Battle of the Marshlands, Battle of Grisland Strait)
****

Loura

Loura was a Firstborn of the House of Fairlinden, and was the wife of Cupeldain. She was exceedingly shy, and would never say of what spirit she was born. She was brown-skinned, with silver hair, and her wings were like flakes of snow while her eyes were as the blue sky. She kept to herself, preferring the treeless mountaintops so that she could fly into the sky if anyone else approached. Legends say that Cupeldain flew over her mountaintop one day and when she saw him, so handsome and fair of form, she did not run away to hide among the rocks or fly off the mountain to avoid him. Seeing her staring at him, he alit and asked her why she gazed at him so. She did not speak, but her cheeks blushed and she turned away. When she lifted her wings to fly away, Cupeldain took her hand and begged her to wait, for he was smitten by her beauty. When he asked again why she gazed at him so, she turned back to him and stroked his long, brown hair, and touched his strong wings. She touched his face, running her fingers over his brow and nose and lips, and she put her hands upon his broad chest.

"Will you come with me?" he asked. "I have built a palace upon a high mountain lake. It is fair to look upon, but needs someone of your beauty to grace it. Will you come look upon it?"

She nodded and together they went to Linlally's high falls, called Tiandari, and he showed her the palace built at the top of the falls upon a blue lake.

Loura never spoke a word, and never would her entire life, and Cupeldain knew that she would not. But, somehow, he always knew what she wanted, and what her gestures meant, and could tell from the expression of her face and the light in her eyes what she had to say. And, mysteriously, without words, Loura was able to impart anything she wished to those around her without the use of words or sound, and with only a few graceful gestures of her hands or expressions of her beautiful face.

Loura stayed with Cupeldain, and hated to be apart from him from that moment on. Such was their love that they vowed themselves to each other, and from their union was born Parthais, their son. With Parthais flying along, the threesome enjoyed life. Cupeldain worked to improve his city, and Loura helped him shape it, often indicating to Cupeldain where Alonair the Sculpture might place one of his works, or where gardens might be. It was Loura who befriended a flock of swans and they came to live in Linlally to be near her, gliding across the lake while Loura and Parthais played with them. When Parthais fell in love with Mena, a Faerekind of the forest, Loura encouraged their union, and from it Parthais had a daughter and a son, called Ellyn and Thurdun.

But Cupeldain was ever harassed by Secundur and perplexed with thought and consideration, so that he often flew away to be alone to think his thoughts. This made Loura sad and worried, but he was never away for very long, and she rejoiced at his every return.

When Kalzar attacked the Faerekind, she clung to Cupeldain to try to prevent him from going away with his bright sword. Later, when Aperion called all of the Faerekind to gather before him, Loura went, too, and as Aperion spoke, she sought out Cupeldain and found him, breathing hard with his hatred for the Dragonkind. When Aperion departed, and Cupeldain flew away southward to continue his attack upon Kalzar's people, Loura followed after him, with Parthais, Ellyn, and Thurdun, too. And when Cupeldain's wings withered, and he fell to earth, hers melted away into the air, and she fell, too, many miles away. Legends say that it was many years before they found each other once more, and even longer before they were reunited with their children and grandchildren. But during these years Cupeldain gathered to him others of the Elifaen who had fallen, and strove with them to remake their lives upon the hard earth, Loura was always with him. It was she who pointed out the linden tree to Cupeldain, and after which he named his House.

They were separated only once more, when Aperion called the leaders of the High Houses and gave to them the Forty-Nine. When he returned, and explained the purpose of his seven sapphire objects, Loura most excitedly nodded her head, but he shook his, saying that he could not leave the earth for the Dragonkind alone to have. This deeply disappointed Loura, but she nodded in understanding.

Loura and Cupeldain remained together. She was with him when he went with King Silmain to war with the Dragonkind. She took up arms and fought at Cupeldain's side, more to protect him than to fight the Dragonkind. They were together when Silmain called for the Forty-Nine to be used to make the Nimbus Illuminas come so that they all could join Aperion. And she saw how adamantly Cupeldain and others refused.

In later years, Loura was with Cupeldain when he became King of Vanara, and she became his queen. Loura was there when Cupeldain decided to call again upon the High Houses to use the Forty-Nine. She was present when Ormace defied him, and she saw how Cupeldain checked Heneil's wrath against the lord of Fairbirch. And she saw the sadness in Cupeldain's heart that never went away from that moment on.

The centuries passed, and under the rule of Cupeldain and Loura, Vanara prospered and grew. But all was not well in Vanara's eastern regions, across the River Iridelin nearby to Forest Islindia. There, disputes amongst the forest Elifaen led to violence, and Cupeldain worked hard to resolve the disagreements and end the bloodshed. In the year 920 of the First Age, Cupeldain at last negotiated a truce between the feuding parties, threatening to bring his own army to quash the violence should a settlement not be reached. His terms were quite generous, promising aid to all parties once peace was established. But Cupeldain was led to believe that the truce he had negotiated held only until he could personally oversee a permanent treaty between the feuding factions. He and Loura, with a small party of peace-minded Vanarans, gladly traveled into those lands, and they expected to be received as honored guests. However, his company was attacked by a large party of masked Elifaen, and all were captured and taken to a forest lake. Loura and Cupeldain were forced to watch as their friends, including Shevalia and Bychanter, were drowned. Then Cupeldain was forced to watch as Loura was drowned. His spirit soon joined hers at the bottom of the cursed lake wherein they were cast. It is said that a sole member of Cupeldain's party survived and escaped back to Linlally, saying that the blame was upon the House of Hemlock, one of the feuding houses, for it was within the lands of that house that the murders took place. When Parthais heard the news, he immediately brought his army into those lands and, after a brief campaign, put down the fighting there. Then, it is told, he executed many members of each clan of Elifaen by having them drowned in the same lake as Cupeldain and Loura. Afterwards, Parthais released a demon-serpent into the lake. Some say it was to guard them and keep them, and some say it was to feed upon the spirits of those Parthais killed. Others say it was to show that he, Parthais, was now the sole ruler of Vanara. Serith Ellyn and Thurdun were not with their father when all this happened, as they were far away in Glareth. When they returned and heard the news, they were devastated, and went to the lake to mourn and weep for their grandparents and for their good friends.

It is said that sometimes the lake almost gives up its dead, Loura, Cupeldain, and all the others who were murdered there. Sometimes, on moonlit nights, they are seen rising up from the dark waters of the lake. Witnesses say the forms of these spirits are likened unto those the forms they had in the Time Before Time, yearning to be free of the lake and the world, but unable to lift their drooping wings. But, somehow, the creature that Parthais released into the waters holds them to the lake. It is whispered that Parthais uttered an oath when he put the serpent into the lake, that those spirits would never be released, until the world itself is remade, when all oaths are made meaningless, when all bonds are broken, when those who wish to be free may become free, when those who long for reunion will be reunited, and when there will be a new earth and new stars in the heavens.

Editor's Note: We have reason to think that the curse mentioned above was broken, and that it was Loura who broke it. The weapon she used to do so was Ethliad, delivered to her by Lyrium.

See Also:
Biographical Sketches (Belmira and Elmira)

****

Martin Makeig

Some of the following was related in bits and pieces by Makeig himself. Other parts were pieced together from accounts told by his friends and associates, by his god-daughter, Sally Bodwin, and others.

Part 1: Early Years

Martin Makeig was born to Gargeoff and Alice Makeig in Sorghwall, Tracia Realm, in the year 825 of the Second Age. Gargeoff was an able seaman in the Tracian Royal Navy. Three years after Martin's birth, the transport ship that Gargeoff Makeig served upon was driven by storms into the Craggy Sea and wrecked. Over two hundred sailors and troops bound for Draymoor went into the sea, but only sixty made it ashore onto a small uninhabited island. Amongst the survivors was Gargeoff Makeig. The only officer, a young second lieutenant, was severely injured and unable to take command of the survivors. Gargeoff, though only twenty years old, took charge. He saw to it that rainwater was collected, fish were caught, and that the injured were cared for. He did this in spite of being less senior than other seamen, perhaps by dint of his size and assertive manner. By the time the second lieutenant was well enough to resume command of the group, Gargeoff had things managed as well as could be expected for the inhospitable conditions. The island had no fresh water, no plants, and no animals other than shorebirds and scorpions. The men managed to survive by collecting rainwater and eating raw fish. Wood from their wrecked ship occasionally washed ashore and was collected, along with bits of rigging and tattered canvas. After three weeks, they were discovered by an Altorian fishing vessel that was also caught in a storm and cast onto the rocky shore. It took only a day to mend the fishing boat, and its crew departed with as many survivors as their boat could carry away. Within a week. the boat made it safely to Altoria with word of the shipwrecked Tracians that had been left behind. It was another two weeks before the remainder of Gargeoff's crew were rescued, but by that time Gargeoff and several others had died of exposure. The Tracians were taken first to Draymoor where they were tended to and cared for, then as berths could be found for them, the crew returned to Tracia.

The second lieutenant that Gargeoff had saved was among the last to return to Tracia. He related the ordeal to the authorities and told how he and the others who were shipwrecked with him had been saved by Gargeoff Makeig's efforts. The lieutenant's father, an influential man in the Tracian court, was so grateful for his son's safe return, that he arranged through his connections for Gargeoff's son, Martin, to receive a letter of service into the navy as soon as he was old enough to go to sea. Should Martin serve well, a trust to pay his commission as a midshipman was also put aside for him. In the meantime, a pension was arranged for Martin and his mother to live on.

In 837, at the age of 12, Martin Makeig departed Sorghwall and traveled to Forlandis where he joined the navy as a seaman (which would later qualify him for his commission). His benefactor had arranged for him to serve aboard the bireme Hazard, a light escort warship under the command of Captain Egan Navostra. During the next four years, Makeig's life was typical of all cadet-candidates during that era. He served and received training at the oars, learned about rigging, sails, and all other aspects of life at sea aboard a warship. During this time, the Hazard was almost constantly at sea escorting Tracian trade ships through the pirate-infested waters off the coast of Masurthia or taking part in various fleet maneuvers.

At age fourteen, Martin saw his first sea battle not far from Solsorna when the Hazard and its escorted trade ships came under attack by several pirate ships. The Hazard put herself in harm's way to protect her escorts, engaging all three pirates. After sinking one of the marauders by ramming, the Hazard was boarded by another pirate ship. Makeig was slightly wounded in the fight that ensued, yet he helped to repel the attack and turn the tide. The enemy ship was itself then boarded and ultimately captured. The other pirate ship withdrew and retreated. The captured ship and its cargo were taken as a prize, and the prize money was considerable since it was carrying a quantity of gold. For his heroism, young Makeig was awarded the Battle Ribbon with Star to wear on his coat. He sent half of his share of the prize home to his mother.

Makeig was formally made a midshipman aboard the Hazard and began the second phase of his training. This involved learning navigation, ship maintenance, and command structure and protocol. He was also schooled aboard ship in reading, mathematics, geometry, and history.

At age 18, Martin passed the last of his lieutenant exams. Due to his exemplary performance aboard the Hazard, Captain Navostra submitted Makeig's name to the admiralty for confirmation. It was done, and Makeig was awarded the rank of junior lieutenant under Navostra's command.

Part 2: Advance to Captain

In 848, a loose-knit band of rebels and pirates flying a red flag carried out a series of raids against villages and shipping along the northeast coast of Tracia. Accordingly, a squadron of four warships, including the Hazard, was dispatched to locate the rebel strongholds with orders to sink or capture the rebels and to bring as many as possible back to Forlandis to face trial.

News reached the Tracian task force that a group of small pirate boats were harassing the fishing villages along the coast near Sorghwall. In an effort to box them in, two of the warships in Makeig's group were sent ahead and far off from the coast. They were to turn back and sail from the north into the Bay of Lasstra, while the other two ships would come up from the south. The plan worked, as far as it went, but instead of facing a few small raiding boats, the four Royal Tracian ships found themselves confronted by seven rebel warships with a score of smaller craft. Every captain tried to get the weather gage. In this, several of the smaller craft, especially those with no oars, were at a disadvantage, unable to quickly turn and maneuver or spread enough sail. After an hour of such maneuvering, a series of accidents occurred. Two small coastal vessels collided, and the entanglement sent all other nearby craft veering out of their way, setting off a chain reaction. Suddenly all of the ships and craft found themselves in close quarters, and within moments a violent melee broke out. Three Royal Tracian ships, five rebel ships and a score of smaller craft were rammed or set afire, all sinking within minutes of each other. Only the Hazard remained of the Royal ships, and it was engaged by four small vessels. The two remaining rebel warships took advantage of this and sought an escape to open sea. By the time the Hazard had cleared from its attackers and turned in pursuit, the two rebel ships were miles away, making northward.

Two days later, the Hazard overtook the slower of the two rebels, and forced it aground. During that engagement, the other rebel ship gained an additional lead, fleeing northeast between Portalrock and Lowland Islands. Captain Navostra of the Hazard decided to gamble on the more dangerous route through the channel between the coast and the islands of Lowland, Canis, and Little Canis, seeking to position his warship ahead of the rebel ship.

It worked. Just as the Hazard gained sight of Colleton, its lookouts spied the rebel ship broad on the starboard beam, making a run to port from further out to sea. It was a race. If the rebel ship made it to port, they might claim safe harbor rights from the Eastlanders, having committed no crimes in Eastland waters. But the wind and current were favorable to the Hazard, and it closed the gap quickly.

Barely a mile from port, and within view of Colleton's inhabitants, the Hazard engaged the rebel ship in a furious battle. Arrows and flaming pitch shot from one ship to the other as the two circled. But neither ship could close for boarding actions. After the first few passes at each other, Captain Navostra was seriously wounded, the First Officer was dead, and most of the other officers dead or seriously wounded, too, leaving Makeig as the only remaining officer fit to command.

In an audacious maneuver, Makeig ordered full sails and all spare hands to oars, swinging around and beyond bowshot of the rebel. Due to their relative positions, the rebel ship had only two choices: either bear aground or run straight into port at full speed. Since the port of Colleton was just upriver from the broad mouth of the River Northford, and it was now low tide, the rebel put every man at the oars and every stitch of sailcloth to the wind and pulled toward port, hoping that the Hazard would not risk the narrow channel. For a few moments, both ships ran dead abeam of each other, with the rebel ship only thirty yards on the Hazard's port side. Already they were within the mouth of the river, and the rebel ship was amid channel, knowing that the Hazard would have to turn off or soon run aground on the low side of the channel. This is just what Makeig had gambled on, hoping that the rebel would think the Hazard too careful for any risky maneuver. Instead, Makeig ordered ramming speed, and the Hazard pulled slightly ahead, then violently turned the Hazard into the rebel ship, ramming it athwart with such force that the more fragile rebel was nearly cut in half. Makeig then reversed oars and backed sails, and pulled away as the rebel ship broke apart and sank. Swinging around, the Hazard came to a stop and dropped anchor just yards from Colleton's docks.

Makeig ordered his marines and sailors into boats to capture as many survivors as possible, including any that might swim ashore. Meanwhile, the mayor of Colleton and the Glarethian governor, who had watched the entire engagement, took to boats themselves and rowed out to the Hazard. Once aboard, the two officials promptly and loudly gave Makeig their protests since the incident had endangered the town and disrupted shipping. However, Makeig knew that Glareth supported Tracia in its efforts against piracy and that the protests were a mere show of formality.

Almost seventy rebel sailors were captured, including the captain of the rebel ship and several officers. Among those who managed to escape the sinking rebel ship were seventeen Glarethian travelers who were thought to have been lost at sea. They related how their passenger ship had been attacked by pirates six weeks earlier and how they had been held for ransom. One of the passengers was none other than the niece of Prince Carbane, Ruling Prince of Glareth. Ignoring the local officials, Makeig personally arranged for the rescued party to be given housing in Colleton until they could be transported home. Meanwhile, Captain Navostra and the other injured of the Hazard were taken ashore and treated for their wounds.

As for the rebels and pirates that were captured, although it was within his right to summarily hang them all, Makeig saw to it that they were transported back to Forlandis to await trial along with those many others who had been captured at Lasstra. Most would face charges of piracy and treason.

Makeig and the crew of the Hazard remained in Colleton for three weeks. During this time, the Hazard was repaired, the crew refreshed, and the wounded recovered. Besides official reports to the Admiralty, Makeig also wrote home to his mother. He also made arrangements for the safe transport of the rescued Glarethians, lately prisoners of the pirates, to Glareth by the Sea, sending with them a letter detailing his actions. Their safe arrival caused a great sensation and no little celebration. Ruling Prince Carbane of Glareth Realm, in a gesture of gratitude to Tracia for freeing his niece and the others, announced that one of his new Swift-class warships that was being built would be made a gift to Tracia.

Captain Navostra recovered quickly and reassumed command. Soon after, the Hazard returned to Forlandis. Navostra testified before the admiralty of Tracia concerning the naval actions at Lasstra and Colleton. Already made somewhat famous by news that had preceded them, Navostra lavished praise upon young Martin Makeig for keeping his head and making victory come about. Makeig was afterwards asked to wait upon Ruling Prince Lewtrah and his brother, Prince Lantos. At court,

Makeig was received with great ceremony and awarded the Ram and Oar, a medal for conspicuous bravery. He was then informed of his promotion to the rank of Captain. His first orders were to travel to Glareth by the Sea, and there receive and assume command of the Golden Swallow, the new warship gifted to Tracia by Prince Carbane. After sea trials, overseen by Glarethians, Makeig was to bring the Golden Swallow back into Tracian waters and continue the campaign against pirates and rebel shipping. Captain Navostra, in turn, was promoted to admiral, and he thus relinquished command of the Hazard to take up duties of naval planning

Part 3: The Golden Swallow

Thus, at 26 years of age, Martin Makeig was the youngest captain in the Royal Tracian Navy. He traveled to Glareth by the Sea to take command of the Golden Swallow. Upon his arrival, Makeig was met and greeted as a hero, feted in the court of Ruling Prince Carbane. After a few days of shore leave, Makeig spent a month conducting sea trials aboard the Golden Swallow, learning his way about the ship, and training her crew.

He was, to say the least, astounded at the performance of the Swallow from the onset. Although it had two decks of oars, eighty all together, it hardly needed them. It had two masts, the main that supported a huge triangular sail, and a mizzen-mast almost as high as the main. It also had a removable bowsprit and could carry three foresails. Although only a bireme, the Swallow was heavily built, and the masts were reinforced to withstand the shocks of ramming. The sail plan was carefully laid out so that they could be used in battle (as opposed to most designs that required lowering of sails when being rowed). The hull was long and relatively narrow, curving downward sharply below the waterline to a relatively deep keel. When on a reach, the Swallow heeled, of course, but its oar ports were made to close tightly against the sea (with the oars drawn in). Indeed, Makeig was skeptical of the design at first, but he soon appreciated the Swallow's speed, even without men pumping the oars. And he well appreciated the fact the sails would take much of the work from the rowers. The rowers were well-enclosed and protected, with a strong relatively uncluttered deck above them for the placement of weapons (such as catapults and ballistae), archers, and fighting men. Bunks and hammocks for off-duty crew were ample, storage for provisions was generous, and there was even a small cabin for the captain.

There was much to learn about the ship, much to test and try. But at last, Makeig was satisfied, rightly proud of his first real command. At a public ceremony, he formally received the ship from Ruling Prince Carbane. Then, with her new captain and crew, the Golden Swallow made its departure.

On the way home, the Golden Swallow captured two small rebel vessels, arriving in Forlandis with two prize ships carrying several tons of cargo. Now Makeig was not only famous, but he was relatively wealthy. While new catapults and ballistae were being built for the Swallow, Makeig took an extended shore leave, the first in over five years. He traveled to Sorghwall to visit his aging mother. While there, he married his childhood sweetheart, with whom he had been corresponding for years.

While at Sorghwall, news came of the fate of the pirates and rebels he had captured the year before. In a horrendous display, they and three-hundred other prisoners were tried en masse and publicly hung from gibbets erected along the docks and streets of Forlandis. Makeig was deeply disturbed by this, knowing that some of the prisoners had been conscripted and forced to serve in those ships, some had even been chained to the oars. Many other people who supported Prince Lewtrah were outraged that the Prince would order such a thing. Makeig's own misgivings were soon fulfilled as unrest spread across Tracia. In Sorghwall, there were many who sympathized with the rebels, and the region was quickly beset with feuds as people took sides for or against Ruling Prince Lewtrah. Uneasy about leaving his new wife and his mother, Makeig remained in Sorghwall as long as he could, for almost four months, until he was informed that the Swallow was long ready for his return, and he was recalled to duty.

During 852 of the Second Age, unrest spread throughout Tracia, and many people openly revolted. Factions of the Royal Tracian Army deserted their posts to serve a group of disgruntled lords. These lords began seizing property and estates belonging to those who remained loyal to the ruling order, but their methods and cruelty were hardly more humane than Lewtrah. And it was, of course, ordinary people who suffered the most.

Makeig resumed command of the Golden Swallow, charged with intercepting shipments of arms intended for the Tracian rebels. Although he managed to sink three small rebel warships, Makeig thought his orders were a waste of resources, since most arms were being provided overland or from within Tracia itself. He strongly advised the use of naval forces to support the beleaguered Royal Army under Prince Lantos. His suggestions fell upon deaf ears amongst the old senior naval staff. Instead, they sent the Golden Swallow far afield, into Masurthian waters to patrol for coastal smugglers.

After nearly a year on patrol, the Golden Swallow arrived back in Forlandis only to find the city in flames and a great battle raging between the Redvests and Loyalists. Under cover of darkness, the Swallow eased northward up the Saerdulin a few miles past Forlandis and anchored in a safe place. Makeig ordered some of his crew to form heavily armed parties and to go ashore for supplies. He himself led a separate party carefully back to Forlandis to obtain news about the situation. He entered a city in chaos, with street fighting and looting widespread, and he learned that the Redvests had formed a new government under a so-called Triumvirate. While he and the men with him were in the city, the Redvests consolidated their forces around the city, quite nearly cutting it off. Trapped, Makeig's party had to fight their way out and away to rejoin the rest of their comrades aboard the Golden Swallow.

With dawn approaching, and fearing that the Redvests might blockade the river, Makeig ordered an immediate departure downstream. With the sails of the Swallow lowered and lamps shrouded, they quietly rowed past the lurid glow of flames that engulfed Forlandis. Suddenly, the Golden Swallow was hailed by a small boat frantically rowing toward them. In the ruddy light, Makeig saw a Loyalist admiral and a few other officers were aboard the boat. He then gave orders to slow oars to only the minimum speed necessary to control the ship in the river current. It therefore took some while for the small boat to catch up to them.

While Makeig anxiously awaited the boat, he witnessed the rescue of Prince Lewtrah and his family by Glarethian marines who had landed from their own ships, fought their way into the city, and soon returned with the Prince. The Glarethians cast off and were quickly away, while Makeig still waited for the inept crew of the small boat to bring it alongside. When at last they did, Makeig was glad that he had waited, for the admiral was none other than Navostra.

After thanking Makeig for saving him and the men with him, Admiral Navostra told him about a secret rendezvous where many Loyalist ships were to gather. Other ships, Navostra said, had orders to bear on, some to Altoria and some to Glareth. Makeig asked about Sorghwall, and Navostra reassured him that although the Bay of Lasstra was controlled by rebel naval forces, Sorghwall itself was under the protection of Prince Lantos (brother to Ruling Prince Lewtrah) and the Loyalist army that he commanded.

Part 4: The Secret Harbor

A week later, and full of misgivings, Makeig brought the Golden Swallow to the rendezvous on the southwestern coast of Tracia at the mouth of River Massaro. Almost forty other ships were there, mostly transports and trade ships, but also twenty warships. Many of the ships were in terrible shape and in need of major repairs. At least a dozen of the transports were in constant need of bailing, as well as three of the warships, not to mention the awful state of their sails and rigging. While repairs were attempted, an encampment was made on shore where provisions were gathered and plans were discussed and debated.

Most of the senior officers were of the opinion that their Realm was lost to the Redvests and that all should make for Altoria, or, for the most daring, to Glareth. Others, like Makeig, argued that the most seaworthy ships should set out to make contact with Prince Lantos in order to take their orders from him.

The weeks stretched out, and as winter approached, with the expected storms and lack of provisions, the arguments continued. Makeig felt that the opinions of the civilian captains carried too much weight, that they craved the continued protection of the navy over the welfare of their country. Thus, Makeig grew increasingly assertive and acerbic toward his fellow officers who, in turn, looked down on the rather uncouth young captain who had no family to speak of, had had no position in court, and was, by all accounts, brash and impetuous. However, there emerged a small group of senior officers under Admiral Navostra's leadership who agreed with Makeig, and together they privately made their own plans.

It was arranged, with the consent of all of the ship captains, that at least three warships should always be on patrol, scouting for Redvest ships that might come against the fleet. However, it was secretly agreed amongst Navostra's officers that each ship should conduct raids, whenever possible, to obtain food and provisions for the warship crews and fighting men. The most senior officers within this conspiracy carefully coordinated such activities with one another and guarded the surreptitious operations from the other admirals and officers of the fleet, and from the even more timid merchant captains.

Winter came, and it was harsh. The ships that were able moved farther out to sea, but three of those that did so were lost, including a warship. Several other ships, unable to risk deeper waters, were driven onto the beaches during storms. Food was scarce, and weakness and disease soon began taking a toll. Aboard the warships, things were marginally better due to discipline and the strict rationing of supplies. It was a relief to all when winter finally came to an end, and by late spring, things amongst the paralyzed fleet eased somewhat.

Everyone fretted about their families in Tracia. Throughout the previous autumn, small boats disguised as fishing vessels had been sent out on a regular basis to scout and to bring back news, but during the long winter, those missions had all but ceased. When they resumed in the spring, the scouting parties brought back word that Prince Lantos was fighting on. Tracia was effectively divided, they said, with several regions, particularly in the north and east, steadfastly holding out against the Redvests. But the Redvests had taken Kalbrith and all of Tracia west of the Saerdulin. There was no word concerning Sorghwall, nor which regions, if any, that the Loyalist forces firmly held.

Makeig feared the worst, knowing that unless the coast near Sorghwall was secured, the town would make easy pickings for even a moderate Redvest force if landed by sea.

Winter had passed, but fair weather brought new worries for the Loyalist fleet. It was only a matter of time before the secret harbor was discovered by the Redvests. Many of the scouting parties that were sent into Tracia had not returned. The few that had come back only reported bad news, if they had any at all to report. Makeig refitted the Golden Swallow as best as he could with dwindling resources, and he sailed monotonous screening missions to look for any wayward Redvest vessels that might venture too close to their harbor. Weeks passed, and spring passed into summer. Boredom and hunger were the ever-present companions to a growing anxiety. Just when Makeig and the other naval captains were beginning to grow alarmed at the restlessness and unease amongst their crews, they received new orders. They were to make preparations for a raid on Forlandis, to depart within the fortnight. The goals were simple: First, to raid the warehouses and stores for food and supplies. Second, to cripple the Redvest navy by destroying or damaging ships and port facilities.

Part 5: The Raid

On a calm summer night some three weeks later, long after Lady Moon, with her face half-covered by her fan, had disappeared into the west, twelve ships of the Royal Tracian Navy quietly slipped into Spargers Bay and approached Forlandis. Among them were the Golden Swallow and seven other warships, along with two transports full of Loyalist marines and two cutters to serve as messengers. In the lead and well ahead of all the others was Admiral Navostra, commanding the warship Pyros, escorting the two transports into Forlandis Harbor. They were to quickly raid the warehouses for needed supplies and provisions, burning the warehouses upon their retreat. Having deciphered the Redvest harbor signals, the Loyalist transports successfully docked along the supply wharves. Navostra took up his position in support of the marines while, one by one, the other warships quietly slid into the bay, with the Golden Swallow coming last of all. They took up their stations just outside the harbor and waited. When they saw the docks afire, they were to attack the Redvest warships at anchor within the harbor, trusting that all eyes would be turned toward the flames and the other way. It was a chance not only to obtain the supplies they needed, but to deliver a crippling blow to the Redvest navy.

Makeig began to sense something very wrong almost as soon as he arrived within Spargers Bay. There were no patrolling Redvest ships in sight. There were none of the smaller harbor boats that would normally be going back and forth servicing the ships, and he could see only a few anchor lamps. He counted those lights through his spyglass, unable to tell if they hung from warships or merchantmen. But it was clearly not the number of ships they had expected. He signaled one of the cutters to move ahead and scout, while he waited anxiously and scanned the faraway docks for any sign of fire. After an hour, the cutter returned, reporting that the only ships in port were several trading ships and two warships. None of the main Redvest ships that were to be their targets were in port, a battle fleet of over twenty-five warships. Especially disappointing was the fact that the Scarlet Lance was not in port, a powerful quadrireme that was to be attacked by the Trueblood and the Golden Swallow simultaneously. Makeig certainly wondered where all the ships could be, but speculation would have to wait; a new plan was needed.

Makeig obtained the positions of the two warships from the cutter, assuming that the other cutter had reported the same information to Admiral Navostra. He then quickly signaled each of the other warships in his group, giving each one new target assignments. And if Navostra knew that the main warships of the Redvest navy were absent was now irrelevant since by the time Makeig's orders were received, fires among the far off warehouses were blazing. It was the awaited signal. It was time to strike.

At first, no rowing drum sounded on any of the attack ships, the oarmaster calling a cadence by voice only loud enough for his men to hear. The oiled oars dipped rhythmically and splashed softly, and unseen water gurgled past shadowy hulls. The Golden Swallow and the Trueblood moved ahead swiftly through the darkness, making for the two Tracian warships, the farthest away of all the enemy vessels. The slower Loyalist warships followed, each coming to attack speed toward its own targets.

Soon the Trueblood and the Golden Swallow were far in front, weaving between and around the anchored merchantmen. On board one of these, an alert watch called out in dismay and began ringing his ship's bell frantically. Then loud cracks and crashes could be heard across the harbor as, one after another, Makeig's fellow captains found their targets and the merchantmen were rammed. Oaring drums now thudded loudly across the bay. Then loomed the two Redvest warships, both large triremes sitting motionless, oblivious to the peril that slid quickly across the dark waters. Makeig ordered ramming speed. There was a rush of water as the Swallow accelerated. Then she struck with such force that the enemy ship broke from its anchor as seawater poured into it amidships. Extricating herself from the listing wreck, the Golden Swallow then turned, came up to speed once more and swept between two merchantmen, dowsing both with so many flaming missiles that the very sky seemed afire.

The Trueblood, too, had sunk its quarry and had already turned into and rammed yet another merchantman astern. By now, the harbor was brightly lit with flames and awash with the crack and groan of sinking ships and the cries of drowning men. The other Loyalist warships each sank at least one ship apiece. Then trumpets were heard blaring in the distance, the signal that Admiral Navostra's Pyros was coming back out with the transports. The eastern horizon was growing pale before the coming dawn, and the Loyalist war fleet departed Spargers Bay. Behind them billowed smoke and flames from ashore and across the harbor. No Loyalist ships were lost or even very much damaged, and the marines had successfully set afire many warehouses after first carrying away food, canvas, rigging, and other vital naval stores. Altogether, twelve Redvest ships had been destroyed.

However successful the raid had been, the fact remained that it had not gone off as planned, since the main target, the Redvest war fleet, was not in port at the time of the attack. Makeig knew as well as his fellow captains that it could only mean that the Redvest navy was busy elsewhere. Where was open to speculation, and something for Loyalist spies to determine. For now, it meant that the most powerful ship of the Redvest navy, the Scarlet Lance, would have to be faced elsewhere, and probably under less favorable conditions. Certainly, it was very unlikely the Loyalists would have the element of surprise a second time. So it was with some trepidation that the Loyalist fleet sailed away, heading back toward their base at the Massaro.

Had Makeig known where the Scarlet Lance was at that very moment, he would have been filled with even greater worry. While Forlandis glowed with the reflected light of destruction, some five hundred miles to the northeast, a Redvest armada entered into the Bay of Lasstra. In a sweeping move, twenty transport ships put ashore over six thousand troops under the protection of a watchful fleet of warships. That the warships were there at all, and not at anchor in Forlandis, was an ironic result of the Loyalists' success in masking their own fleet's location. The commanders of the landing troops were terrified that the mysterious unaccounted-for Loyalist warships might intercept the hulking transports long before they made their disembarkation point. Hence, they had insisted on the strongest possible escort. The Triumvirate agreed and sent nearly the entirety of its navy along with the landing ships. Only two ancient and unseaworthy warships were kept in Forlandis, each now at the bottom of Spargers Bay.

By the time the fires along the docks of Forlandis were put out and the raiders were long gone from sight, Sorghwall was under attack by Redvests. It would fall in less than two days, and nearly every one of its inhabitants, staunch Loyalists, would be put to the sword or taken away as slaves. Amongst those taken aboard the transport ships bound for Forlandis, and ultimately for Kalbrith where they would toil for the Redvest army, was Makeig's three-year-old son that he had never seen and his wife whom he would never see again. Like so many thousands who fell victim to the Redvest tyranny, they were taken as slaves and would disappear forever.

When it was clear that they were safely away from Spargers Bay, Admiral Navostra ordered his fleet to gather near to shore and drop anchor. He signaled that all officers were to report to him aboard the Pyros. After hearing all their reports, Navostra issued orders for the two cutters. They would be provisioned and manned for a long voyage, and would be taking along four of Navostra's experienced spies to be put ashore in various places. Their mission was to learn the whereabouts of the Redvest fleet and report back as quickly as possible. The two cutters would travel together, sharing all reports with each other so that if one was lost, the other might return with all information. And if they did not make contact with the Redvest fleet by the time they reached the Eastlands coast, they were to return, picking up their spies along the way.

Navostra asked for a volunteer to command the expedition, and Makeig stepped forward, but Navostra turned him down, saying that Makeig was too valuable aboard the Golden Swallow. Niels Bodwin then offered himself as commander of the two cutters. He was Makeig's first officer and a good friend, and he well knew why Makeig was so keen to go. Navostra and Makeig agreed that Bodwin should go, and preparations immediately began. On the way back to the Golden Swallow, Bodwin privately assured Makeig that he would strive to learn the situation at Sorghwall and also, if at all possible, bring away Makeig's wife and child. While Bodwin gathered his things, Makeig wrote a hasty and carefully worded note to his wife, telling her that he was safe, giving her his love and his best wishes, telling her to trust Bodwin completely, and saying that he looked forward to seeing his family soon. An hour later, the ships resumed their way westward, and Makeig watched the sails of the two cutters disappear over the eastern horizon.

Part 6: The Chase

The Chase Begins

With contrary winds and currents, the fleet proceeded slowly westward. Three days later, as they approached Massaro, the lookouts aboard the Golden Swallow spotted a sail off their port quarter, far out to sea on the southern horizon. Climbing the mast, Makeig watched the distant square-rigged ship and saw how it was outpacing his own fleet. He signaled a report to Admiral Navostra who immediately ordered the Golden Swallow to pursue, overtake, and, if Redvest, to sink or take as a prize the ship and its crew. If it turned out to be friendly and cooperative, no harm, no foul. But, friendly or not, in the event the ship or its crew sought to resist or evade Makeig, he was to sink or take her without hesitation, and bring back any survivors if that was convenient. Makeig ordered all sails and extra relief to the oars, then put the Golden Swallow on an intercept course.

After four hours, the Golden Swallow was within five miles of the mystery ship, and it was apparent that it had no intention of being overtaken. Makeig recognized it as one of the large new Glarethian-built schooners, a fast ship with no oars, two masts, and many sails. As he watched in his spyglass, the ship put on even more sail, sending up a jib and flying jib. Glancing over his starboard quarter, he saw that he and his quarry were far ahead and nearly out of sight of the fleet.

He knew that the Golden Swallow, though swift under full sails and full oars, could not match the endurance of the schooner. His oarsmen would tire, but the schooner's sails would never grow weary. He ordered every inch of sail aloft, and every man not required at the helm or rigging to the oars, to take turns in rounds. Then he ordered battle speed, stripped to his waist, and went below to take his first turn at the oars.

Too Close

It did little good. They rowed throughout the night, altering course as the wind favored, and followed the mystery ship by moonlight. When the sun rose, the Golden Swallow had gained two more miles. But Makeig knew they could not sustain their effort for long. As noon came, the winds shifted and strengthened, the Golden Swallow heeled, and oars had to be drawn and portholes sealed. Their speed increased slightly with the new winds, but as Makeig went aloft after a night of rowing, and the men below rested, he saw that the mystery ship was again almost three miles ahead. The wind was helping the mystery ship with its great sail area more than it helped the Golden Swallow. Peering through his glass, he saw the ship actually reduce sail, yet with all the sails the Swallow could carry, it barely kept pace. And with the overcast skies, when darkness came there would be no moonlight. The mystery ship could easily turn and slip away. But one thing Makeig could not fail to notice. At the stern of the mystery ship flew a large red flag with a white triangle, the ensign of the Redvests Navy. Almost despairing, Makeig lowered his spyglass.

Suddenly, the wind eased. The Swallow briefly righted, then another puff sent her heeling once more. A minute later, the wind fell to a mere breeze. Throwing his glass to his eye, he saw his quarry's sails droop. This was his chance.

Before he could give the order or descend from the loft, sails were being lowered, the oars were put out, and the rowing master had the oarsmen pulling at battle speed. The gap between the Golden Swallow and its quarry began to narrow once more. Makeig watched as the day dimmed toward night, and as the light failed, the Swallow approached to within a mile. Then it was too dark to see.

A half an hour after the last sighting of the mystery ship, Makeig ordered all stop and complete silence. The Swallow coasted to a halt, and every man on deck and aloft strained his eyes and his ears. Makeig listened, too, judging from the whiskers of his beard which way the light air moved. Nothing was heard, and no light, near or far, could be seen, and Makeig felt nothing across his face. Taking off his hat, he stroked the long, puffy plume that decorated it. Then, unable to see it at all, he held it close to his face and closed his eyes. After a moment, he moved the plume so that it barely touched the side of his nose, then he slowly turned around. Yes, there was a very slight air, so slight that only a ship with a tremendous sail area could be moved by it. A ship such as the Glarethian schooner. Abruptly, he shoved the hat back on, ordered the oars to cruising speed, and gave the helmsman a change of course. The Swallow moved once more at the dip of oars, and Makeig sent for his captain of marines.

"Captain Garner, do we have any o' them Vanaran flares?" Makeig asked.

"Yes, sir," answered the captain. "About three or four, I think."

"Have yer strongest bowman fetch 'em along with his best bow. Tell him to meet me at the mainmast."

"Yes, sir."

A few minutes later, the marine captain presented a young man to Makeig.

"What's this? Yer strongest bowman?" Makeig asked. "A boy?"

"He's our best, Captain Makeig. Has a way with the bow, and he has beaten all of my men at contest with range. Not all that accurate, but if by strongest you mean the one who can throw an arrow the farthest, then Winterford's your man, sir."

"Well. I take yer word. Winterford, is it?"

"Aye, Captain Makeig."

"Ye understand how these flares work, do ye?"

"Aye, Captain. I've used 'em afore."

"An' are ye good in the riggin' at night? Answer true, an' don't be ashamed to say no, for thar's a number of us what don't like goin' up yonder in the pitch dark."

"Aye, sir. I got no qualms 'bout it, sir. I've got a sure hand an' steady feet. An' I ain't scared at all of great heights."

"Good, good! Now take a bit of line an' tie them flares to yer arrows. One per arrow. Tie them real good, like, so as to make the arrows good to fly. Then get ye up as high as ye can go, on up well above the loft. Make yerself fast with some rope so as to be able to get at yer bow an' arrows, see?"

"Aye, sir."

"I'll be right behind ye, but I'll stop off at the loft, since my hulk's a sight too heavy for the topmost to hold me. Now, when ye hear me call up at ye, get a flare lit an' send it up just as high as ye can make it go. We're gonna try an' spot that ship by yer light, see?"

"Aye, sir."

"Get yer flares ready on yer arrows, an' then go on up. I'll be up behind ye directly."

"Aye, sir."

Makeig ordered all lamps to the deck, unlit, to be affixed at the bow and stern and all along every rail and at the end of every spar. Every lamp was to have a man beside it, ready to strike firestick to wick, and every lamp was to be shielded so as only to shine out over the water.

"We want to see out but not be blinded by our own light," he explained. "Light the lamps only when I say so."

"Aye, sir."

"Helmsman, at the next turn of the glass, swing hard a port to due south by the northmetal."

"Aye, Captain. Hard to due south, at the next turn of the glass."

Knowing that the sandglass would soon run out, Makeig scrambled aloft to the lookout perch on the mainmast. Above him, the archer had climbed to the very top of the mast and had suspended himself with ropes so that his arms were free. Sooner than he expected, before he had regained his breath from the climb, Makeig felt the ship turning. When it straightened course, Makeig began counting to himself. He knew that it was unlikely they would spot the mystery ship, no matter how much light they threw out. But there was little else to do. He kept counting, mentally calculating until he reached five-hundred. He opened his eyes.

"Winterford, can ye hear me?"

"Aye, Captain Makeig."

"Then let's have some light, son."

"Aye, sir."

Makeig averted his eyes to look down and away. Suddenly he was looking at the eerie shadows of the mast and rigging cast onto the deck far below by a brilliant white light directly above him.

"Flare away!" Winterford called.

The burning arrow shot upward. Makeig's eyes quickly scanned the sea all around, just as everyone on decks did, too. But he was looking too far away. When he saw it, he hardly had time to react. A huge glowing form, greater in height than Makeig's perch, billowed and floated dead ahead, not even forty yards off the bow moving slowly from left to right.

"Ramming speed! Ramming speed! Brace yerselves!"

But the mystery ship reacted, too, turning into the oncoming Swallow.

"Light all lamps! Battle stations! Make ready the—"

At that moment, the Swallow's ram struck a glancing blow on the schooner's starboard side, nearly throwing Makeig out of his perch. The next few moments were full of noise and chaos. Oars cracked and shattered as the schooner and the Golden Swallow scraped past each other. The oarsmen below struggled to pull in their oars, arrows and missiles began raining down on the Swallow's decks, and a few torches were lit on the enemy vessel and tossed over, too. Meanwhile, the clank of catapults being cranked, the crack and splintering of oars, the yelling of men below decks, Makeig bellowing orders from above, and the seemingly endless grinding of hull against hull had transformed the peaceful night. Almost as quickly as they had collided, the two ships pulled apart in opposite directions. Makeig was scrambling down from his loft, when he saw a long arc of white light fly from overhead toward the enemy ship, just beginning to fade ghostlike into the darkness. Winterford had let go a long shot, and it struck the mainsail of the schooner, setting the cloth ablaze. Its crew quickly cut it free and pulled it down and away, but not before two other sails had also been set afire. The two ships receded, each wounded and limping away the from other. Fires were also being put out on the Swallow's decks, now littered with dead and wounded men. Lamps were lit, and Makeig threw his spyglass to his eye just in time to see the name across the fading schooner's stern.

"Scarlet Revenge!" he muttered, then bellowed, "Damage report! Helm, come about. Let's after him!"

"Aye, Captain!"

"Captain, should Winterford stay aloft?"

"No, bring him on down, if ye please."

All eyes that were not upon their tasks watched the Scarlet Revenge, now some four hundred yards off as the Swallow came around. The enemy was still battling small fires on deck, and by the glow Makeig could see that it was already hoisting new sails and was making a slow turn to port and northward.

"Captain, how did you know he'd turn back at us?" asked one of the deck officers.

"With these light airs, what else could he do?" Makeig shrugged. "That's what I'd have done, anyhow. Damn! He knows that he'll pick up a land breeze if he gets in close enough to shore. If he does, he'll swing west again."

Makeig glanced eastward. "Sun'll be up in a couple of hours. Have the oars at cruising speed. We'll let him have a lead, and then we'll turn west before he does."

"See if he catches up on us?"

"Aye," nodded Makeig as a midshipman hurried to him.

"Damage report, sir!"

"Where's Lieutenant Tavis?"

"Dead, sir. And Lieutenants Lestin and Charn, too, sir."

"What else?"

"Six others dead, as I've been able to count. About nine wounded, three very badly. Twenty oars broken, several more damaged, but the carpenter thinks they can be repaired. Not enough spares to go 'round 'til the repairs are made. Minor hull damage at the oar ports, nothing that can't wait until the oars are repaired. Fires are out."

"Very well, carry on."

"Yes, sir."

"Captain Garner! Yer report?"

"Sir!" the captain of the marines stepped forward. "I have four dead, two wounded."

Makeig shook his head.

"They really let us have it, sir," Garner said.

"Twelve dead in but a moment of time," Makeig muttered.

"They were ready for us, they were."

"Indeed, so it seems. So be it. I want twelve of your men at the oars. The rest are to make dang sure them catapults are ready at all times. Next time, no waitin' for orders, just let go at 'em if we come in range."

"Yes, sir!"

At this moment, Makeig spotted Winterford coming down from aloft.

"Mr. Winterford!"

"Aye, Captain!"

"Did ye hear me say to shoot at that ship?"

"No, sir, Captain, sir. I just—"

"Well, it was quick thinkin' is alls I got to say. Keepin' yer head an' all. I think ye did him fair damage, too, an' it might just make all the difference."

"Aye, Captain. Thank ye, sir."

"Captain Garner, I'm hereby takin' Mr. Winterford, here, an' makin' him midshipman. I need a good solid man on decks with a quick eye an' quicker action."

"But, Captain Makeig, that'd put us at only eleven marines, with the others at the oars."

"Winterford can have watch of the catapults an' ballistae, when not needed for other things."

"Yes, sir."

"How does that suit ye, Winterford?"

"Suits me just fine, sir. Does it mean I'll get a fancy blue coat?"

"As soon as one's to be had an' ye've paid for it proper. I reckon ye've been aboard long enough to know most of the routine on deck."

"Mr. Brancara!"

"Aye, sir!"

"Ye know Winterford, here, I expect. Take him in tow, as he's our newest midshipman."

"He's a bit old, ain't he, Captain?"

"Then he'll not be as whiny as the others, we'll hope. Ye'll have him as long as no enemy's in range, but then he's to look to the deck weapons as we've lost Lieutenant Charn."

"Aye, sir. Come along, then Wint'ferd."

All this while, Makeig continued to watch the Scarlet Revenge, still visible in the distance. Going to the helm, he glanced at the binnacle.

"He's gonna have to turn again if he's to make westward again," he said to the helmsman. "Let him have his course until the next bell, then let us turn about due west."

"Aye, sir. Due west. Is he makin' for Solsorna, maybe, sir?" asked the helmsman.

"Could be. But Masurthia ain't all that fond of Redvests. Draymoor would be my guess. Not that they care all that much for Redvests, neither. Hard to say. Hard to say."

"I don't understand, sir. They could've turned in and soundly thrashed us to bits."

Makeig took off his hat and gave the plume a wipe, then jammed it back on.

"It means they're more interested in running than fighting. Maybe they've got to be somewhere important by a certain time. And maybe some special cargo or something too important to risk in a fight."

Cat and Mouse

At the appointed time, and some little while after the Scarlet Revenge had faded from sight to the north, the Golden Swallow altered course due west. It, too, picked up a favorable breeze, and with sails and little heeling, the oarsmen had an easier time of it. Makeig ordered speed reduced to three-quarter cruise when the sun came up. And, in spite of the glare, they could easily see the enemy ship's white sails on the horizon behind them. It would be a delicate thing, Makeig knew. If the Swallow outpaced the Revenge too much, the enemy could slip out to sea and race around them. If they let the Revenge come up too fast, though, the Swallow would have only one chance to make an attack. The trick, Makeig knew, would be to keep the Revenge between himself and shore, to limit the enemy's maneuvering, while at the same time giving the Revenge every indication that the Swallow was in no shape for much of an attack. And if the Swallow could get the weather gage, all the better.

"Cat an' mouse," Makeig was heard to say several times as he gazed through his spyglass, sometimes at the Revenge, sometimes at the low line in the north that was Masurthia's coastline. "Cat an' mouse."

"Aye, Captain," agreed a nearby sailor. "But who's the cat, sir, and who's the mouse?"
"Aye, there's a riddle," answered Makeig.

Stalking Ahead

For three days and three nights, the ships paced westward. The Swallow led on slowly by day, and more swiftly at night. Makeig ordered full speed at night to assure his lead, unable to keep the Revenge in view. By day, at least as soon as the Revenge was spotted again, the Swallow's speed and course were constantly adjusted according to what Makeig thought would keep the Revenge on his starboard quarter. He knew that they would soon be off the coast near Solsorna, as he reminded his crew, and there was little chance a Redvest ship and crew would be welcome there.

All the while, he kept an eye on Winterford, learning and going about his new duties. And from Brancara, Makeig learned that Winterford knew much more than expected, including the use of compass and sextant, could read and write, and was familiar with all parts of the Swallow, having been aboard for over a year. The four other midshipmen, all still in their early teens, were somewhat in awe of Winterford and were glad of his experience and maturity. Apparently they knew him fairly well already, even though marines and ship's crew didn't usually mix.

All the while, the winds remained favorable to the Swallow, and the warship was aided by her oars during the few slight lulls so that they maintained their lead over the Scarlet Revenge by a few miles. For its part, the Revenge did not seem disposed to overtake the Golden Swallow. Makeig speculated that Winterford's flaming arrow might have done more damage than he could see through his spyglass. Perhaps the spars or rigging were damaged, or maybe the Revenge neglected to have enough spare line and cloth available to replace the destroyed sails. These were reasonable possibilities, but Makeig remained alert to any clue from the trailing ship of some hidden strategy.

Pressing his luck, and in order to aid his navigator, Makeig had the Swallow edge northward nearer the coastline. When the islands to the east of the River Wachee were spotted, they knew that Masurthia was behind them and that they were now in Altorian waters. But this did not allay Makeig's worries. He nor any of his crew could say where the Altorians stood when it came to the rebels who overthrew Tracia. But Altoria's capitol city, Draymoor, was steadily drawing nearer, and the closer they came, the more certain Makeig was that the Scarlet Revenge was headed there. That presented even more questions. Why would the Redvests be so intent on sending a ship to Draymoor? Could it be that there was a pact of some kind between the Redvests and Altoria?   As unlikely as it seemed, the possibility nagged Makeig's thoughts.

The Chase Ends

On the seventh day of the chase, and within 200 miles of Draymoor, Makeig prepared his crew. Soon the Revenge must turn northwest toward the Iridelin River and sail upriver to the port of Draymoor. The Golden Swallow would follow and, in the restricted waters of the river where the Revenge would be hampered, they would attack and ram the Redvest ship. The enemy ship would then be boarded and taken, with the aim of learning its mission and taking as many prisoners as possible. Makeig was sure that such action would elicit strong protests from Altoria, and it might even mean imprisonment for his crew. So, at mid-morning, with a fair wind that required no oarsmen to pull, Makeig called all men to decks and gave them his plan. It was simple. They would first slow to allow the Scarlet Revenge to draw closer, then the Swallow would pull ahead by a few hundred yards and lead the Revenge into the river, as if going to Draymoor themselves. But, picking the best moment, they would turn and attack downstream, taking as many prisoners as they could for questioning.

"Our comrades back home need to know if the Redvests have some partnership with Altoria," he said, "an' I mean for us to find out. As soon as we have our answers, we'll put the prisoners ashore somewhere along the coast to fend for themselves. An' we'll take aboard what provisions we can hold, then head home with all speed. That's the size of it. Now let us do our duty!"

The Golden Swallow altered course to the northwest then slowed so much that she barely made headway, all to permit the Revenge to catch up. But the Revenge made no move to change course. She kept on westward, so that the Swallow crossed her bow some half-mile ahead. When the Revenge was directly astern, showing no sign of making any course change, Makeig brought the Swallow to a dead stop. By this time, the mouth of the Iridelin was in sight almost due north. Several ships could be seen outbound on the tide. Also within sight, to the west, were the first rocky islands of the Craggy Sea, rising gaunt and sharp against the horizon. Makeig could not help but think of his father.

"What's she playin' at, Captain?" asked the helmsman. "If she don't turn soon, she'll head right into them rocks."

"I've got me own eyes, Warren," Makeig replied testily, his eye to his spyglass. "An' I've got the very same question."

Incredibly, as the Swallow's crew watched, the Revenge put on additional sails, now racing away westward. Then Makeig turned his spyglass to the southeast and saw a line of squalls running before a wall of black. His first mate saw it too, at nearly the same time, and barked out orders.

"Make ready the storm sails!" he called. "Secure for heavy seas!"

"Mr. Warren," Makeig said calmly, "put us on course to intercept. Mr. Boradattas, bring us to battle speed, if ye will."

"Aye, sir!"

"Let's get right in afore the storm, if ever we can," commented Makeig, swinging up his spyglass once more as Boradattas shouted orders to the oarmaster below. "Well, I'll be damned! She's turning southwest!"

Indeed, the Revenge seemed intent to make a run right into the treacherous Craggy Sea.

"She's got a fool of a captain," said Boradattas.

"Or else that's been her aim all along," Makeig replied, glancing at the men bringing down the regular sails and sending aloft heavier canvas. "Ship oars an' secure oar ports as soon as we get the first great puff of that storm."

"Aye, sir."

"Mister Arns, we'll not be reefing, so prepare the men for shifting as we heel. An' let us have the full storm jib, too."

"Aye, Captain!"

By now, the Swallow was already slicing through the choppy waters, coming around to bear behind the Revenge. It was only a few minutes later that the first gusty rain swept in. The Swallow heeled, the oars were shipped, and the ports closed. Makeig caught a glimpse of the Revenge putting even more sails aloft before his lens was obscured by rain.

"Have all spare crew on the windward rail," he ordered.

Once again, Sir Wind seemed to favor the Golden Swallow over the Revenge, although that ship was designed to take full advantage of every puff. However, the damage done to its sails and rigging by Winterford's flaming arrow could not be overcome by its crew. Splices made with worn line gave way in the gusts, sails not designed to take high winds parted, and rigging that was scorched by fire four days earlier stretched and parted. From the heaving deck of the Swallow, Makeig watched, as best as he could through the rain, while the crew of the Revenge fought to keep her running ahead. He saw through the watery lens of his spyglass the enemy crewmen pulling away tattered sails and hoisting new ones, scrambling into the swaying ship's rigging, and lining the windward rail. Meanwhile, the waves pounded the ships as the Swallow edged closer. At last, Makeig brought the Swallow around to follow dead astern of the Revenge, ranging ahead by a half-mile.

"Due west, Captain!" the helmsman shouted over the noise of the storm.

"Aye. Mr. Brancara! The lead, if you will. Keep the reports coming."

"Aye, sir!"

"Keep us on her stern, Mr. Warren."

"Aye, Captain."

Makeig made his way to the bow as the lead was tossed.

"Seven fathoms, sand!"

Mr. Brancara joined Makeig at the bow, the two of them ducking as the bow wave crashed over them. The rain suddenly ceased to a fine mist, while the wind and waves continued as heavy as before.

"Five an' a half fathoms, coarse sand!"

Makeig gazed through his spyglass beyond the Scarlet Revenge at what he at first took to be a gray bank of dense fog. He was about to order the men to their oars so as to gain on the Revenge before she entered the fog bank, but then he looked again. It was not fog at all, but a line of rocks looming high, obscured by the mist. And the Revenge was bearing right for the wave-battered crags.

"Hard a port!" he shouted back at the helmsman. Brancara ran astern, repeating the order at the top of his lungs. Makeig followed.

"Run out oars!" he cried as the Swallow lurched sharply and heeled away from the turn.

"Captain!" one of the deck hands shouted, pointing ahead. Turning, Makeig saw the long arc of a flaming arrow shoot up from the bow of the Revenge. As well, she had lit all of her running lamps. Almost as soon as the arrow disappeared, another arrow shot upwards.

"Four fathoms, coarse sand an' pebbles!"

Now the rocks ahead were plainly visible, some well over a hundred feet high over the white spray of a pounding sea. To the left, at the top of one of the higher rocks, a light glimmered through the mist, then grew brighter. On the top of another rock not very far from the first, another light appeared.

"Signal fires!" Makeig shouted over the wind. "Well, ain't this something!"

The Scarlet Revenge suddenly turned to starboard, making for an opening between the two lights.

"Mr. Warren, bring us back on her stern!"

"Boats, ahoy!" cried a lookout from above. "Two points on the starboard bow!"

Makeig turned that way, but could not see the boats.

"How many? What kind?"

Before the answer came, Makeig heard a loud crack and turned back in time to see the top of the Revenge's mast fall, its sails suddenly billowing and whipping about wildly. The Revenge slid out of control just as the ship came to the opening between the signals. Instead of entering the break between the rocks, it was tossed by contrary waves right against them.

"Three an' a half fathoms, clean lead, solid rock below!"

"Hard to starboard, Mr. Warren! Bear away thirty degrees, northeast. Lookout! Those boats?"

"Five or six, sir! Smallish, no sails, about eight oarsmen apiece."

Now within three hundred yards of the wrecked ship, Makeig could see for himself. While the Revenge was being pounded to bits, heaving up against the rocks and crashing back down, the intrepid boats fought the heavy seas to swarm to it. Makeig made his way slowly along the port rail, and he saw men leaping from the stricken ship, now careening onto its side, while ladders were being put over the side. Throwing up his spyglass, he saw several men scrambling over the side, moving down the heaving ladders to the awaiting boats. One of the men was crushed when the boat he aimed for suddenly lurched up and against the ship's hull. He could make out yelling and screams over the howling wind and hissing surf.

"It boggles the mind, Captain," Mr. Brancara said. "What kind of place is that for a rendezvous? Bound to be dicey, even in the calmest seas. It's deliberate suicide!"

"What shall we do, Captain?" Captain Garner asked. "Should we put out boats and give a hand? Maybe get a few answers in the way of prisoners?"

"No. No, I don't think so," Makeig replied, still watching through his glass as the enemy shipwreck receded off the stern. "I think we'll never know what they are up to. But it don't seem like the Altorians are in on it, whoever lit those signal fires up yonder. No, Captain Garner, I won't put the Swallow or crew at risk in that surf, with little hope of gain from it."

Makeig dropped his glass to his side, took off his hat and shook it out. Then, with a last glance at the Revenge, he jammed the hat back on his head and turned to the men around him.

"Make course for Draymoor, Mr. Brancara," he said. "We shall provision as quickly as we can an' be on our way. The deck is yours."

And, with that, Makeig stormed down to his cabin.

Part 7: The Loss of the Golden Swallow

Things did not go as planned. Redvest emissaries had already reached Draymoor weeks earlier. In something of a coup, the Loyalist Ambassador, it seemed, had been "arrested" by the Redvest contingent and sent back to Tracia. A new Redvest ambassador was installed, and he immediately set to work rounding up other Loyalist Tracians. In addition, the Redvest ambassador submitted a list of names to the Altorian authorities, a list of those they claimed were pirates and wanted men, including Makeig and his crew. Ignorant of this, the Golden Swallow entered the port of Draymoor where they were immediately confronted by a Redvest delegation waving papers and seeking to place Makeig and his crew under arrest. They were thrown overboard just as the Altorian authorities arrived on the scene. Although Altoria was skeptical of the Redvest claims, they also confronted Makeig. After a heated discussion with Makeig, they permitted Makeig and a limited number of his crew ashore to secure provisions. But they would not permit the Golden Swallow or any of its crew to depart Altorian waters until the question of piracy was resolved. Thus Makeig was caught in a legal and diplomatic tangle, with Altoria trying to determine whether or not to recognize the Triumvirate as legitimate.

Once he understood the situation, Makeig destroyed all documents, logs, and maps that might give away the location of the Loyalist base at Massaro. This still left Makeig with many documents to show the Altorians, including the Golden Swallow's Royal Commission Seal, his own commission and those of his officers, official maps and navigation charts bearing the Royal Seal, and so forth. Upon examining these, the Altorians conceded that they were indeed a legally commissioned ship and crew. They forbade any Tracians from boarding the Swallow without permission, provided the Swallow with limited shore passes for the purpose of acquiring provisions or obtaining supplies needed for repairs. But since Altoria neither recognized the Triumvirate nor had affirmed any support for the Ruling Prince, the situation remained in a legal limbo. What to do with forces hostile to one another within Altorian waters, even if they posed no threat to Altoria, was a quandary. But the Altorians made it absolutely clear that any act of violence, regardless of who might be to blame, would bring swift and severe consequences against both parties, Redvest and Loyalist alike, including imprisonment.

The situation remained unchanged for six months. Makeig, not wishing to allow his ship to rot, arranged for entirely new sets of sails to be made. He saw to improvements made to the rigging, as well as weapons and fighting stations. The damaged oars were replaced and new spares brought in. The damage sustained to the Golden Swallow's hull was repaired as well. Not wishing his men to become dull, he conducted daily drills, including rowing in place (with the stern firmly anchored), gave training to his midshipmen on various nautical subjects, and held nightly meetings with his officers. He continued to be impressed with Winterford, a quick and eager learner, and a nimble and good-natured junior officer. He quickly learned the proper etiquette and procedures, and he was already an example of discipline and insight, even if he was a bit too free with his observations at times. To be sure, Makeig confirmed his own impressions by consulting the men and officers concerning Winterford, too. Makeig was more than satisfied with Winterford, and he felt that the ship and crew were in better shape than they had been for years. But it was not enough to make Makeig content with things.

And so he wrote almost daily missives to the Altorians, arguing and sometimes pleading for the release of his ship and crew. At last, three months into the new year, a private note from the Altorian Admiralty reached Makeig which indicated that, should the Golden Swallow make an attempt to leave port, no Altorian vessel would interfere, but neither would any assistance be given if the Redvests tried to intervene. Late that very night, the Altorian ships that had anchored around the Swallow to box her in quietly moved away, and the Golden Swallow slipped back out to sea.

Upon his arrival back at the secret base at Masarro, Makeig found that most of the transports and merchantmen were gone, and none of the warships could be seen. However, one of the cutters that had been dispatched with Bodwin was at anchor, and soon Makeig was reunited with his First Officer. Bodwin grimly related what he had learned about the fall of Sorghwall and the fate of its inhabitants. He returned the letter that Makeig had written to his wife, and he expressed the hope that she and Makeig's son might make it to the Eastlands. Bodwin also reported that he had sent his own wife and infant daughter away toward the north, and that many other people were fleeing Tracia.

Once Makeig understood all this, Bodwin reported that Prince Lantos and his army continued to fight the Redvests, but they were desperately short of food and provisions. All the Loyalist warships that Makeig had expected to see had departed that very morning to serve as an escort to the merchantmen and transport ships that were carrying all of the supplies they could muster. They hoped to put ashore at the north mouth of Grisland Strait and make contact with the Loyalists. The Golden Swallow was ordered to join them there as soon as possible.

With his First Mate back with him, Makeig ordered the Swallow to sea as soon as fresh water had been taken aboard, along with replacements for the lost crew and oarsmen.

However, things developed more quickly than Makeig's admirals expected, and took a turn for the worse. While the Loyalist ships maneuvered around Grisland Island, with the Golden Swallow fast catching up, word reached the fleet that Lantos and his army had been pushed into the swamps of the northern Marshlands where Lantos hoped to make a stand, his back to the swamps and sea. The fleet turned and quickly devised a plan for rescuing as many of the Loyalist fighters as could be saved. In a cunning series of moves, some of the Loyalists sailors lured the Redvest warships away from the area while the main fleet dropped anchor in the shallows of the Marshlands coast, dangerously close to Spargers Bay. With the help of knowledgeable and loyal local folk, a great rescue operation began as hundreds of small boats went into the marshes and swamps to ferry out the Prince and his army, still fighting a rearguard action against the Redvests.

During the desperate sea battle which shortly followed, later to be known as the Battle of Grisland Strait, Makeig had to sacrifice the Golden Swallow in order to ensure the escape of Prince Lantos and the thousands of men aboard transports that were trying to escape capture. In an unusual maneuver, the Swallow drove its ram into the stern of the Scarlet Lance, a ship much more powerful than the Swallow, and managed to disable the Lance's rudder. Amid flying arrows and missiles, with both ships mortally damaged, Makeig swung the Swallow all the way around and grappled onto the Lance, pouring flaming oil into the Lance's lower oar ports. Both ships afire, they sank swiftly with much loss of life on each side. But the transports escaped.

Of the one hundred and eighty members of Makeig's crew, one hundred and five made it to shore. Among the dead and missing were all of the young midshipmen except Winterford, all of the marines and their officers. They were a hostile territory, albeit their homeland, and Makeig organized his crew accordingly, assigning Winterford the rank of lieutenant to serve alongside Bodwin to provide leadership. Ahead of them was a long and dangerous journey northward. Their aim was to eventually reach Glareth. However, they had few supplies and fewer weapons, and many did not even have shoes. They moved at an agonizingly slow pace, carefully scouting ahead for trouble as they went. Several crewmen who were seriously wounded and died within a couple of days. The rest of the men were in terrible shape, and they were all soon enough hungry, cold, and weak.

Part 8: The Arduous Journey

When Makeig's scouts reported a small encampment of about a hundred Redvest soldiers nearby, he made the decision to attack them in order to take horses and food. The raid was carefully planned for surprise, and carried out at dawn when there was just enough light to see. They divided in to three groups to come at the Redvests from different directions, and those without swords or knives armed themselves with rocks and stout branches. Essentially, Makeig's men overran the Redvest camp, which had only a few guards posted, and caught them completely unawares. The Redvests who did not run away were killed, but several of Makeig's crew were also killed. They gained a few horses, boots and blankets, some food, and a few more weapons.

But they had barely started their long journey.

Over the next week, Makeig led many raids to secure more horses and food. But word of Loyalist marauders quickly spread across the land, and there would be few easy victories. The cost was high. Every few days, during a raid or skirmish, another one or two of Makeig's men were killed. Barely a hundred miles from where they had started, Makeig's crew numbered only eighty. The farther north they went, the harder they were chased by Redvests, and the more difficult it was to find food. Time and again, they were cut off and pushed west of their intended course. Over and over, they were forced to fight their way out of traps laid for them. Makeig dared not try to enlist the help of local people, for fear of reprisals against them. Instead, he pressed his men on, sometimes backtracking many miles to find a clear way north.

One day, as they made their way through a dense wood, smoke hung thick in the motionless air. Suddenly they came upon the smoldering remains of a small village. Every cottage was burned to the ground, and every shop and workplace destroyed. Too weak for a fight, Makeig and his men nonetheless unsheathed their swords and slowly rode between the crackling ruins toward the center of the village where a tremendous oak stood with massive, sprawling limbs. Makeig drew his horse to a halt, sheathed his sword, and took off his hat as his men gathered around. A large sign was nailed to the truck of the tree.

Friends of Loyalists
Beware This Fate

Bodwin pulled up beside Makeig, staring aghast.

Hanging throughout the tree were many bodies, young and old, men, women, and children.

"Should we cut 'em down, Capt'n?" asked Winterford.

"No. Let others who come this way see what the Redvests do."

"Aye, sir."

"Well," said Makeig, giving his old plume a stroke and putting his hat back on, "I reckon we'll be not be stoppin' 'til we get into the Eastlands."

Two weeks later, and a good three months since the Battle of Grisland Strait, it was a weary and much-diminished group that entered the Eastlands. Makeig's men now numbered less than fifty. When they approached a village in County Bransondale, they were met by a large group of Eastlanders wielding pitchforks and scythes. The Eastlanders made it clear that no Tracians were welcome in that county, no matter how needy, for they had seen too many already and would not abide any more thievery. After a good bit of shouting back and forth at one another, Makeig gathered that a large group of Tracian people had passed through some weeks before. Starving and desperate, the Tracian refugees set about looting, stealing, and rustling from local farms and shops. There were many fights, and a few local people had been killed. Makeig tried to ask where he and his men could trade for a bit of food or a few blankets, and he showed them a spyglass, a gold coin, and even offered to give up their weapons in exchange for provisions. But the villagers were unmoved. In fact, they only shouted and cursed at Makeig even more vehemently.

Makeig turned his men away, going eastward and then north around Bransondale. It would be the same story over and again, at village after village, as the weary men moved farther north into the unwelcoming Eastlands. But they pressed on, almost too weak to stay in their saddles, bedraggled and hungry, and the horses were as bad off as any of the men.

When they camped, few had the strength to keep watch. Their flint was gone, and without the means to make a fire, or enough blankets to go around, they huddled together in an effort to keep warm. When it rained, the lot of them shivered as one.

They did manage to find a bit of food here and there. Once was from an abandoned farmstead where they found a few potatoes in the ground that were not rotten. Another time was when they came upon a camp of six Redvest scouts who were so confident of their safety that they set no watch. But the Redvests roused themselves to a good fight, and before they were overwhelmed, four more of Makeig's men lay dead. The little bread and meat that was found was hastily divided so that each of Makeig's men had at least a morsel or two. They savored every tiny bit, too weary to even speak.

They found no more food the next day, the day after that, nor the day following.

Somewhere between Bransondale and Bessinton, one of the horses stumbled and broke a leg. That night they had a feast, even though they had no fire to cook with. The next morning, sick with horsemeat, the men slept much longer than they should have. But at last Makeig stirred himself and went about trying to wake his men to another day of travel. They grudgingly complied, silent and wet with the morning dew. Four of the men would not wake up, though, amongst them Niels Bodwin. Makeig knelt beside his old comrade, begging him to stir. But Bodwin was dead.

They had no shovels, and the ground was too hard for their thin hands, so they moved their dead comrades as far away from the horse carcass as they had strength to pull, and they arranged the bodies together. Ashamed that he could not provide a proper burial, Makeig directed that the bodies be covered with pine straw. This was done in silence, and though the straw was light enough, it was still an exhausting task. Afterwards, Makeig stared at the straw barrow for a good while. Then, without a word, he walked some distance away from his men. While they waited by the horses, they watched him go to the top of a nearby hill. There, he took off his hat, sat heavily on the ground, and wept.

Some while later, after he had regained his composure, Makeig continued to sit. It was a high overlook, bare of trees at the top, and he could see forests and patches of farmland off to the north. An overgrown path lined its way down from where he sat, and he watched as a man emerged from the trees below and slowly ascended the hill toward him. At first, Makeig was inclined to get up and move away as quickly as he could, for he had no desire to speak with any strangers, nor to explain himself, the sorry condition he was in, or his plight. And he had not the heart to withstand yet another refusal of help. But Makeig remained where he was and watched the man approach. He was a young man, perhaps not much more than twenty or so. He was neatly dressed in jacket and breeches with sturdy walking boots of brown leather. And he had a shoulder bag as if he was a kind of messenger or perhaps a clerk of some kind.

"Good morning," the young man said when he was near enough to be heard. He had curly black hair, and looked remarkably like a younger version of an oarsman who had saved Makeig's life during the battle of Grisland Strait and who went missing when they abandoned the sinking Golden Swallow.

"Mornin'," Makeig replied.

The man continued toward him and came to a halt a few feet away.

"You look tired," the man commented.

"I am, I reckon."

The man gazed for a moment past Makeig, and he could see down the other side of the hill to where Makeig's men waited with the horses.

"Might you be the band of Tracian raiders that is said to be about?" the man asked casually.

"Well," Makeig glanced over his shoulder at his men, "if so, we're a right poor bunch of raiders."

"And far from a troubled home."

"Aye. A troubled home."

The man nodded. Makeig picked himself up and stood. He brushed out the plume on his hat, put it on his head, and turned away.

"I reckon we'll be off, then."

"Very well," said the man. "But if you might be looking for work, I know of a farm not two leagues from here that is in bad need of labor."

"We're Tracians, ye know."

"I don't think it matters to the farmer if you are Tracians or even Dragonkind, so desperate he is."

Makeig stopped and gazed back at the man.

"Mind, it's some trees that need moving. They blew over in a terrible storm last month, right into the farmer's barn. The trees need moving, and the barn needs repairing, and he's trying his best to get his fields ready for planting. It's only him, by himself, since his son died a year ago. And there doesn't seem to be anyone nearby he can call upon to help him out."

"Ye don't say. Well, there's a bunch of us, not just me."

"He can't pay you," the man went on. "But he's a good man, and a good farmer, and he has more than ample laid by. So perhaps you can agree to meals as trade for doing the work. He can feed you a meal or two every day. You might have to help cook and clean up, though. And, what with so many of you, the work might not last but a few days."

By now, Makeig was fairly staring at the man in disbelief.

"But it'd be long enough to get some rest," the man continued. "And shelter. Your horses can get some pasture, too."

"We're Tracians."

"Like I said, I don't think it matters. Just follow this path for about a league or two, and it'll take you right to the place. The farmer's name is Pearl. Walford Pearl. I just came from there, and saw for myself the mess those trees made and heard for myself all his woes about it. You'll see for yourself when you get there. Right along this path. And after your work is done, you might go northeast, crossing over the Saerdulin, then north until you get to Newstone Ferry. Then take the west road and on up into the Thunder Mountains. Some of your people are up there, I hear, and have made a settlement of sorts. I hear they've been getting arrivals from your homeland pretty regularly these past few months."

Makeig nodded. He turned and looked downhill at his men, still waiting for him. He nodded once more, took his hat back off, and scratched his head.

"I don't know," he said, still watching his men. "We were aimin' for Glareth. But I reckon we do need some help." Makeig turned, reaching out to offer a handshake. "I'm much obliged to ye for the—"

The man was gone. Craning his neck and turning this way and that, Makeig could not understand where he had gotten off to.

"Now I'm dreamin', wide awake," he said to himself. "I reckon I'm as sick an' bad off as any of us, imaginin' good things, good people, an' a kind word from a stranger. A make-believe stranger."

He walked down the hill toward his men, deep in thought.

"Winterford!" he called as he arrived among them.

"Yes, sir?"

"I reckon we're kinda tuckered out, lad," Makeig said. "But I wonder if ye have it in ye to do a bit of scoutin' around?"

"I think so, Capt'n."

"Well, on the other side of that hilltop is a path what runs down into woods and such. Why don't ye ride along it for a few leagues, being careful as ye always are, an' see what there is to see that way."

Winterford mounted up and was turning his horse around when Makeig put a hand on Winterford's leg.

"Sir?"

"If ye happen on a farm or such," Makeig said quietly, "an' if ye see the farmer about, why don't ye strike up a conversation with him an' find out what prospects there might be for tradin'."

"We ain't got much to trade, Capt'n."

"I know. But, here, take these." Makeig handed Winterford the last two coins he had, a small gold piece and an even smaller silver one. "Just ask. Maybe we can trade our labor for some food or some such."

"We ain't so much in the way of labor, neither, Capt'n," Winterford said.

"Don't get smart. Just ask. That is, if ye happen on a farm an' such, which ye might not at all. I think we'll wait here until noonish, unless we get pushed off by any what happen on us."

Makeig watched Winterford ride off, then announced to his men that they would wait for Winterford's report before riding on. Almost immediately, the men sat down. Within minutes, nearly all of them were asleep. But Makeig, as tired as he was, paced around and around his sleeping crew.

It took longer than Makeig wished. Noon came and went, and though his men continued to sleep, Makeig paced all the more. At last he began rousing the men, all but one who, like those found that morning, would never wake again. Makeig was examining this man to make sure of his condition when Winterford returned riding on a cart with his horse tethered at the rear. At the reins was an old man who wore the plain but sturdy clothes of a farmer. All the men stared as the cart came to a halt among them and as Winterford and the farmer climbed down from it. Before Makeig could say anything, the farmer spoke.

"There ain't much here," he said, going to the back of the cart and pulling out a couple of baskets. "But it might keep ye 'til mornin' when ye can come on to me place. It ain't far, but Wint'ford, here, told me 'bout yer condition, so I brung some food an' a few blankets. Thar's some firesticks in this basket." He handed the basket to the astonished Makeig. "An' thar's some cookin' things, a pot an' pan, some lard, in this'un. Got ye some eggs here. That one's got a slab of bacon. Here's some bread. Ain't much since I ain't had time to get down to Missus Fanner what does some bakin' an' such. Just down the road, but I ain't had time, like I said. I'll need to ask around for more blankets an' such, too, since I ain't got enough by a long shot."

He was pulling out baskets an' bundles from the cart, talking all the while so that no one else could get a word in.

"I done told Wint'ford 'bout the work, so he can tell ye when he gets a chance. We done made a deal, so I hope he spoke for the all of ye. Yep, a sorry lot of workers, indeed, just as Wint'ford said. But since thar's so many, it'll be light work, I reckon, an' won't take much more than a few days, or a week at most. Here's a couple of spades for yer fellers what died. I'm sorry for yer loss, too. But times ain't good are they? Purty rough all 'round, I'd say. Me name's Pearl, Walford Pearl."

"Martin Makeig." Makeig took the man's hand and shook. "I reckon we already owe ye a day's work for all these victuals."

"That's right," said Pearl, "an' I appreciate the right way of yer seein' it. Now, I've got to get on back an' see to makin' a place for all of ye. I think the barn'll hold most of ye, but I'll need to move the cows out."

The man got back onto his now empty cart and reined it around.

"Don't dawdle!" he cried out as he drove away. "Lest ye want to miss both work an' breakfast, too."

"Wait!" cried Makeig. "How'd ye know? I mean, how'd ye know ye can trust us?"

"Oh, well, a feller came by early this mornin' an' said he'd send some trustworthy men to help me out."

"Who? What feller?"

"Don't know. Just happened along. I gotta go. Got a lot to do! See ye in the mornin'!"

Over the next several days, whenever Makeig had a chance, he asked Pearl again and again about the stranger. But Pearl had no ideas about him, except that he "just seemed right, if ye know what I mean. Like someone ye can trust to do the right thing."

"Well, what about the settlement of me people he mentioned?"

"Oh, I was the one what told him 'bout that," Pearl said. "I got it from a reliable feller who knows a trader up in them parts. He come over the Saerdulin south o' the Bentwide a bit, an' was comin' through here to make deals for gettin' grain an' such. That was awhiles back. A month ago, I reckon."

"Do ye know them parts?"

"A little bit. When I was a lad, I did some loggin' over the river a ways."

"Do ye know the best way to get to our folks over there?"

"Well, the easiest way would be to go over the river an' up through Tallinvale lands, then north up the forest road. But I wouldn't do that if I whar ye an' ye whar me. The next best way'd be across the river an' up the old river road up to Passdale in County Barley. Then west through Janhaven afore headin' south an' west. But I wouldn't do that, neither. See, I hear tell that Barley is hard-strapped on account of havin' some witches come to them parts an' doin' mischief with the crops an' all. I hear tell it was the Lord Tallin hisself what paid the witches to do it, too, on account of him not likin' County Barley much."

"Sounds like a tale."

"Yep, but tales or not, Lord Tallin ain't one to fool around with. An' them Barley folk was havin' a time of it last year. Or mebbe it whar the year afore last. Now, wait. I reckon it whar three years ago that I heard the story of all that. Oh, goshalmighty! I don't recollect when I got the story!"

"Then maybe things've sorted out somewhat."

"Could be. Or mebbe not."

Meanwhile, there was indeed work to do. And it was hard work, especially for men in such a wretched state. A large old pine had uprooted and toppled onto Pearl's barn, smashing through a portion of the roof and wall. Had the barn not been so sturdy, the damage would have been far worse. So there was much chopping, sawing, and clearing away to be done, along with carpentry work. Day after day, Makeig and his men grew a little stronger than the day before, and a little less afraid of any sudden appearance by Redvests or angry villagers. So the men of the Golden Swallow applied themselves to the work with great skill, and they accomplished more each day than the day before. They slept in the stalls of the barn, in a shed nearby, and in a makeshift tent. They all had warm blankets, too. But it was not without sadness. Six of the men continued to grow weak, and, one after another, they died.

Farmer Pearl, with the help of a woman who lived down the way and several of Makeig's men, prepared breakfast every morning at dawn. They had a light lunch every day at noon, and were served a hearty supper after every sunset.

After a week, and as the workers settled into the stride of their labor, they began to worry that they might finish too soon, for none wished to give up the steady meals and warm berths. It was a somewhat misplaced worry, for as the second week began, Pearl started asking a few of the men to help out with this or that other chore, such as greasing the axles of his carts and wagons, or carving new handles for his tools, or mending a bridle or harness. The farmer had a labor force the likes of which he had never known, and for the first time in his life, he spent an entire day doing nothing but watching others work, sitting on his porch and smoking his pipe with a very pleased and satisfied expression.

One day, about two weeks after the sailors had arrived, Pearl called Makeig aside and asked, "Do ye reckon ye can manage the farm for a few days without me? I've in mind to go over to Bessinton so as to fetch a wagon-load of supplies an' such."

"Well, we ain't farmers, ye know," Makeig answered. "But we'll manage things the best way we know how."

"That's all I ask. Just keep at it, keep gathering the eggs, milkin' the cows and such. Take any spare eggs and milk down the road to Missus Fanner, an' she'll give ye some bread. Just keep up the good work, as ye've been doin'. I'll depart afore dawn, an' I think I'll be back in five or six days. An' don't mind if the neighbors on down the way come by an' look in on ye. It's just our way of things 'round here."

Farmer Pearl departed the following morning, and Makeig put himself in charge of directing the work. The barn was mended, the walls and roof repaired, the fallen trees were all cut up and split for firewood, the tools and harnesses all repaired, and the various carts all greased. The cupboard doors were mended, the cottage table stoned and oiled, and the chimney re-mortared. The tool shed was nicely organized, the farmer's cottage cleaned and swept, and all the fences repaired. Weeds had been pulled from the garden, and the spring had been unclogged and set free to run its cool water through the springhouse. Every lamp, lantern, and candlestick was repaired, cleaned, and polished. A new fence was put around the pasture, and a new gate put on the corral.

By suppertime, on the sixth day, Makeig had run flat out of ideas. The men sat around supper trying to come up with things for themselves to do on the morrow. But it was a paltry list, hardly consisting of enough to keep the all of the men busy for very long.

As luck would have it, Pearl returned the following morning, pulling his heavily laden wagon into the yard. Makeig was glad to see him, and the men set about unloading the wagon.

"Now be right careful of them bales thar," Pearl directed. "Some special things wrapped up inside of 'em. Why don't ye leave 'em out over by the porch until after the kegs an' sacks are put away into the barn? When all that's done, come all of ye an' gather round at the porch."

They finished unloading the wagon and unhitching the horses, and soon they were all gathered together before the cottage porch. Pearl lit his pipe and addressed them.

"Now, then. I reckon this farm's in better shape than it's ever been in, thanks to yer hard an' skillful work," he said. "An' I saw right off it'd be that way. Thing is, I do believe I got the better part of our bargain, an' all that's come yer way's been a few meals. An' I reckon ye noticed how I spent a whole day watchin' ye. I knew the work was comin' to a finish, an' that ye'd need to be on yer way purty soon. So I thought I'd better be quick about payin' ye the best I knew how. Well, open up them bales. Inside yer gonna find something for each an' ever' one of ye."

What they found were bundles of clothes. A neatly tied bundle for each one of the men. Breeches, belts, blouses, coats, stockings, and even hats. Every set was sized just right, with room for each man to fill out as they continued to get back their weight and frames. Within another bale were brand new boots.

"Now as to the colors of the cloth," Pearl explained. "Thar's so many of ye that the five tailors worked day an' night, using what they had on hand. But all are sturdy wool an' linen, mind ye! Only I had to take the colors they had already dyed up, ye see? So now, at least, when ye ride off away an' find yer countrymen in the hills, ye'll look a mite more respectable, like."

That's how the remaining men of the Golden Swallow at last changed out of their tattered sea-going threads and into the colorful outfits that they would be known for afterwards. Needless to say, it was a grateful captain and crew that parted company with Farmer Pearl two days later, after all had bathed and shaved and had trimmings all around. They put on what was to them their finest clothes, and saddled their restored horses. After handshakes and a few hugs, they waved a hearty goodbye to the man who had saved them all, who had restored some of their faith that there were still good people in the world, and who had even perhaps instilled the hope that they might find their own way in the world, too. Martin Makeig was the last to rein around, and the last to express his gratitude.

"It ain't me own doin'," said Pearl to Makeig. "It's all on account of that stranger what passed through just when I was at me lowest. The one an' the same what passed by ye, too, at yer own low-water mark, as ye might put it."

"An' ye still don't know who he was, do ye?" asked Makeig.

"No. But he told me that if ye persisted in askin' 'bout him, to tell ye only that he hopes ye'll be kindly disposed toward folks up around County Barley, should ye ever venture that way."

"Well, I don't reckon we'll be headed that way, unless it's on the way up into the hills."

"I see. Well, Capt'n, I hope ye find some good place to settle down in," said Pearl, offering his hand once more. "An' best of luck to ye all."

"Thank ye, sir. And fare thee well!"

Part 9: Conclusion

What remains of Martin Makeig's story is part of history and is better told in other tales. A few more words should suffice to summarize things.

Makeig and his men located the community of refugees from Tracia in a place called Hill Town, up in the Thunder Mountains north of Tallinvale. There he found Niels Bodwin's wife and his tiny daughter, named Sally. Mrs. Bodwin was very sick, having never recovered from her long trek out of Tracia and the hardships along the way. Makeig did not have the heart to tell her the fate of her husband, but she guessed it by his demeanor and hesitation. And she begged Martin Makeig to be godfather to Sally, and to take care of her to the best of his ability. He readily agreed, promising Mrs. Bodwin that he would do just as she wished. She died the next day.

Makeig did not know how to properly take care of the little girl, but he was sure that the trip on to Glareth would be too dangerous for her. So he determined to remain in Hill Town until such a time when things were somewhat more peaceful. Or until the Tracians in Hill Town, himself included, could return to their homes in their own land. And he enlisted several women of Hill Town to help him with Sally.

But Hill Town had its own problems. It was a somewhat squalid place, and set upon at every side by warlords, feuds, and disorganization. So Martin, along with his band of former sailors, soon took charge of the place, saw to its defense, and put able men and women in charge of overseeing how things were done. It was the least he could do for his fellow Tracians, he thought. And the least he could do to give his old friend's daughter a safe place to live. And so it was that Hill Town, in its own way, began to thrive as never before.

See Also:
Biographical Sketches (Sally Bodwin)
Historical Sketches (The Battle of the Marshlands, The Battle of Grisland Strait)

Notes:
Certain papers originating from the Dragonlands have come to our attention that shed light on the mission of the Scarlet Revenge. She was carrying a special envoy from the Triumvirate to the Dragonlands to finalize a secret pact between the Dragonkind and the Triumvirate. The envoy carried papers agreeing to a mutual alliance against Duinnor and laying out a plan for joint attack. The rendezvous on the outskirts of the Craggy Sea near Altoria was prearranged between the Redvests and the Dragonkind. However, the loss of the Scarlet Revenge was

obviously not part of the plan, as it was ordered to return at all speed to Forlandis as soon as it had seen the envoys delivered, if necessary without resupplying at Draymoor. Had the ship not been lost, the Scarlet Revenge may have tilted the scales against the Loyalists during the Battle of Grisland Strait.

****

Ned Arbuckle

Bridge Tender of Passdale

Ned Arbuckle was born in 785 of the Second Age in Altoria, the son of a shipbuilder. He worked as a shipbuilder's apprentice until 801 when he signed aboard an Altorian trade vessel captained by a young Glarethian named Miles Northstar. Arbuckle worked as a carpenter's mate and quickly adapted to shipboard life. After many voyages, his abilities were the equal to those of the Ship's Carpenter. Captain Northstar recognized Arbuckle's skill, and in 807, he recommended Arbuckle for the post of Ship's Carpenter on another vessel. Arbuckle, now as full Ship's Carpenter on the trade ship Westwind, traveled up and down the coast from Altoria and Glareth. After several years, and while in Glareth, Arbuckle visited Miles Northstar, who had become a sailing instructor at the Glareth Naval Academy. Northstar was overjoyed to see his young friend, and he offered to show Arbuckle around the Academy. During the little tour, Northstar introduced Arbuckle to several pupils, amongst whom was Aram Tallin. Northstar convinced Arbuckle to give up his post as Ship's Carpenter to serve instead aboard Northstar's training vessel, the Right Swift. Although enlisted men and officers rarely mixed, Arbuckle's skills were so well known, and Captain Northstar's respect so great, that Arbuckle was often invited to socialize with the cadets and officers. Arbuckle and Aram Tallin struck up an unlikely friendship, with the young Elifaen anxious to learn all that Arbuckle could teach regarding ships and ship's carpentry.

In 818, Arbuckle was asked to assist in the design and building of a new experimental type of cutter, a two-masted vessel powered solely by a new triangular sail plan that would be called the Osprey (it had no oars). The Glarethian ship designers in charge of the project were impressed with the valuable suggestions made by Arbuckle. In 821, the Osprey was launched and underwent sea trials. Many issues with the new sail plan arose that required modifications, including new and more robust blocks and tackle, and stronger masts and rigging. After refitting, and carrying a crew of 27, including Arbuckle as Ship's Carpenter, the Osprey set a new record by sailing from Glareth by the Sea to Colleton in only five days, a full two days faster than the fastest oared ships. Over the next year, that record was broken by the same ship on subsequent voyages.

A few years later, in 823, Arbuckle received word that his father in Altoria was very ill. Arbuckle resigned his commission and returned home. He arrived two weeks after his father died. Virtually penniless, and with an elderly mother to support, Arbuckle accepted whatever work he could find, going from job to job. He eventually found work as a carpenter repairing bridges in the region. This led to more work alongside hundreds of others who maintained the long wooden military causeways that crisscrossed the marshy Altorian Hinderlands. Although those years of work were strenuous and required Arbuckle to be away from home for years at a stretch, he rose through the working ranks rapidly and became a crew chief and then a foreman.

In 825, while working on the narrow wooden Hinderland causeways, Arbuckle drew from his knowledge of ships to suggest a way of building drawbridges and guard towers at regular intervals, thus making the causeway more secure against any Dragonkind intruders. Intrigued, Altorian generals put Arbuckle in charge of a company of workers in order to build such a strongpoint as a trial. Arbuckle completed the work, made entirely of timber, within four months. His ingenious design incorporated a system of pulleys and blocks so that only a few men were required to raise and lower a folding drawbridge that, when fully deployed, was supported by a system of suspension cables and counterweights and could withstand heavy traffic. Furthermore, should the system fail, the entire bridge span was made so that with only a few pegs knocked out, it would collapse into the marshy estuary below.

Enthused, Altoria began the work of refitting the Hinderland causeways, installing more than a hundred of the new bridges and towers with Arbuckle as a richly paid adviser to the engineers who took charge of the project.

As the Hinderland project neared completion (the year 827), Arbuckle was approached by a Glarethian captain of a merchant ship who was an acquaintance of Miles Northstar. The captain told Arbuckle that his own ship's carpenter was seriously injured in an accident, and he asked Arbuckle to join his crew. Arbuckle, who longed to return to Glareth, anyway, agreed to join only until the voyage is over. After making arrangements for the care of his mother, he joined the captain and his crew in Draymoor aboard a large cargo vessel called the Selkie, and they departed Altoria on Midwinter's Day.

The journey to Glareth was a rough one, with winter seas and storms battering the Selkie. Arbuckle's skill was sorely tested as he was continuously making repairs during the voyage. By the time the Selkie made Glareth by the Sea, and perhaps due to the crew's narrow escape from several violent winter storms, Arbuckle had decided that he no longer had any desire for seafaring life. Using his earnings from the Hinderland project, he started a trade business supplying tools and rigging supplies to fishermen and merchant sailors.

In 829, Arbuckle met and married a young widow, and together they had two sons. Over the next few years, Arbuckle's business grew in size. Among the various workers that came into his employment was a young clerk, Gustan Broadweed, whom he had met at a shipyard where Broadweed was seeking work. Gustan proved adroit at bookkeeping, and Arbuckle worked closely with him for several years to improve and expand the business. Then, in 848, a fire swept through the warehouse district where Arbuckle's business was located. Overnight, Arbuckle was financially ruined. With only a small sum put aside, he barely had enough to put food on the table. Fortunately, his two sons were already both enlisted in the Glareth Navy as ordinary seamen. Gustan Broadweed, Arbuckle's clerk, managed to find employment as a schoolmaster in the old Eastlands Realm.

For two years, Arbuckle struggled once more by taking odd jobs here and there. Tragedy struck again when the training vessel on which his sons were serving was reported missing at sea. A fleet of search ships turned up nothing, and it was rumored that the ship had run afoul of Redvest warships. Arbuckle and his wife were devastated by the news, and they were little consoled by the modest pension that Glareth awarded to the families of the lost sailors.

The following year, 851, Gustan Broadweed heard about his former employer's continued troubles, and he sent a letter to Arbuckle to invite him to come to County Barley in the Eastlands to live and to seek work. Broadweed related that the bridge at Passdale was being rebuilt. Knowing of Arbuckle's experience with such things, he suggested that Arbuckle might be useful to those in charge of the project. With no better prospects, Arbuckle and his wife decided to take Broadweed up on the invitation. They arrived in Passdale to find the new bridge across the Bentwide was nearly completed. Although impressed by the structure and the work required to build it, Arbuckle quickly saw several issues with the supporting cables. When he made these known to the bridge builders, he was employed to supervise a better system for stronger supports to the bridge spans. Soon enough, the bridge was completed, and was constantly congested with traffic. As a result of the easy access back and forth across the river, trade and marketplaces in Passdale began to flourish.

However, no one could decide how to manage traffic back and forth across the narrow bridge, and already there had been several close calls when crossing wagons met halfway. One incident nearly caused the drowning of two bridge workers who were forced to leap from the bridge into the river below. Arbuckle suggested a system of rope-controlled signs and crossbars to limit traffic to one direction only, switching to allow traffic to then flow in the other direction. The apparatus would be controlled by a bridge tender situated in a kind of box at mid-point on the bridge. He promised to design and build the system himself if he was supplied with materials and if he was given the position of bridge tender at a modest salary.

This proposal aroused some debate among the people of the region. Some thought that if people using the bridge did not have the common sense to avoid each other, they deserved to have accidents. Others feared such accidents would injure the innocent, hamper traffic, and might even damage the bridge itself.

But the method by which Arbuckle would be paid his salary was the most contentious issue. Some thought a toll should be charged of each person crossing the bridge. Most people, including Robigor Ribbon (a local merchant who had spearheaded the bridge building project) and the Bosklanders were strongly opposed to any roadway tolls. It was finally pointed out by Gustan Broadweed that, in a purely legal sense, all roads and bridges belonged to the King. Therefore, he argued, it might be appropriate to set aside a portion of the King's tithe that was collected each year to pay the bridge tender a modest sum. Also, Broadweed argued, another portion might be taken from the tithe to reimburse those who had contributed labor and materials to the project, and that a petition be sent to the King to explain and to allow for such. Since Mr. Ribbon and Alfred Greardon (a local miller) had kept careful records of the entire project, these expenses were easily calculated. A special referendum was held so that the county and town could decide by ballot after a series of public debates. The only groups opposed to the proposal were those related to the ferry operators downstream, but they were soundly trounced both in debate and at the ballot box. The proposal passed, the petition was sent to the King's Regent, Ruling Prince Carbane in Glareth by the Sea who promptly approved it.

And so it was done. Arbuckle officially became the bridge tender. He held the post until 870, when the Redvests invaded the land and he and his wife were forced to flee Passdale ahead of an invading army of Redvests. In the battle that followed, the bridge was set afire in order to deprive the invaders of its use.

See Also:
Biographical Sketches (Gustan Broadweed)

Notes:
•*Miles Northstar was the father of Sharyn Northstar who would become Aram Tallin's wife and Ullin Saheed's mother.*
•*The Osprey would eventually inspire a class of warships beginning with the construction of the Sea Swift, a bireme warship that incorporated much of the Osprey's sail design features. The Sea Swift would, in turn, inspire other ships like it (the Swift Class), including the Golden Swallow (under the command of Martin Makeig), the Trueblood, and the Sea Horse, all three of which would be transferred to the Tracian Royal Navy. All three were engaged against Triumvirate vessels during the Battle of Grisland Strait, with the loss of the Golden Swallow and the Trueblood.*
•*Unknown to Arbuckle and the rest of the crew of the Selkie, within its hold was a secret shipment consisting of a large crate from the Dragonlands. It was taken to Colleton from where the crate would be transported overland to Tallinvale. This is mentioned in The Nature of a Curse.*
•*Alfred Greardon, along with Harrald Bosk, was instrumental in bringing Mr. Broadweed to Barley to be schoolmaster. Like Robigor Ribbon, Greardon would later become one of Passdale's mayors. Greardon, Ribbon, and Garend Bosk (Harrald Bosk's son) were close friends from their youth and the three would be instrumental in bringing about many changes in Passdale and County Barley.*
****

Parthais

Parthais was born of Cupeldain and Loura in the Time Before Time. In that age, he wed Mena, and they had two children, Serith Ellyn and Thurdun. Parthais followed in his father's way, and when he refused to depart with Aperion, he was Scathed of his wings, as were his wife and children.

During the Time of Strife, he and his family reunited with Cupeldain and others of Vanara. Parthais became a fierce warrior of the House of Fairlinden, seeing many battles in the Dragonlands. He became increasingly volatile and hot-tempered, and when Cupeldain was King, Parthais often used undue influence to advance his own wealth and power, often by the use of unscrupulous associates. Throughout Cupeldain's reign, he pressed for greater action against the Dragonkind, for territorial expansion to the east and south, and he sometimes subverted his father's policies to influence matters, but always with mixed results.

When Cupeldain and Loura were murdered, along with the rest of their company, Parthais reacted with extreme violence. He drove a powerful army eastward into the feuding region and rounded up thousands of prisoners from each side of the feud, freely killing those who resisted, and hunting down those who sought to escape. Villages and towns were burned, and crops were destroyed until the population of the region was thoroughly subdued. He then convened a field court of sorts and put to death many leading families of those involved with the feuds, whether they were guilty of Cupeldain's murder or not. He had them executed in the same manner as was his father, by being weighed with stones and drowned in the same lake as was his parents. He then released into that lake a serpent that had been captured from the Iridelin, one of many monsters that for a time plagued the world. Some say that its purpose was to guard the spirits of the place and keep them there, while some said it was meant to feed upon the dead. Others maintained that it was Parthais's way of demonstrating his power and authority over all Elifaen the region and over Vanara.

Owing to strife within Vanara, and the need to bring an end to the war between Masurthia and Altoria, Parthais was not officially crowned until twenty years after Cupeldain's death. He quickly consolidated his power, ousting those he felt were too attached to his father's ways. Not long afterwards, he was fighting the Dragonkind once again, and Parthais aimed to secure the Blue Mountains through which many raiders passed into Vanara.

In 966 F.A., in an effort to flush out Dragonkind infiltrators, fires were set in the forests of the western Blue Mountains which quickly turned into an inferno that burned for five weeks, destroying huge swaths of forests, croplands, and many estates and small villages. Parthais was furious and ordered those responsible for the act arrested. When Lord Banis, the Vanaran High Judge, did not find any malicious intent on the part of those who set the fires, Parthais threatened to have him removed. Banis countered that he was only following Vanaran law. This led to a long series of court tribunals over which Parthais personally presided. It lasted for three years without bringing any verdicts and was interrupted by yet another threat from the deserts.

It was then that Parthais learned that King Salkasin of the Dragonkind aimed to establish a line of keeps and forts along the northern edge of the deserts, and it was feared that these would serve as forward positions where the Dragonkind could marshal before an invasion. Parthais set to disrupting the work, sending armies to destroy the keeps before they could be completed or fully manned. When it was learned that Salkasin was leading a large army to the east in an effort to outflank Vanaran forces, Parthais rushed with his own armies to intercept him. They met on Tamkal Plain, and during the battle, Parthais and Salkasin fought each other. How they came to face each other is something of a mystery, but it seems that a salient of Dragonkind wedged itself deep into Vanaran lines and overran the encampment of Parthais. Mounted his buckmarl, Parthais led the charge and drove into salient where he came upon Salkasin's guard who had charged in behind their own soldiers, led by their king. Thus Parthais and Salkasin came to face each other, and they immediately began a long dual whilst their men fought around them. When Parthais at last slew Salkasin, Vanarans rallied and the leaderless Dragonkind army soon collapsed into retreat. It was for a time called the Battle of Kings, but is more commonly called the Battle of Tamkal Plain. As a result of the victory, there would be relative peace for many years.

Meanwhile, another crisis was brewing in Vanara. In an effort to further his influence and power, Parthais had ordered that all previous methods of writing were to be abandoned in favor of the so-called "New Writing" that had been developed under Cupeldain. At first, Parthais was content only to have his court and his armies use the New Writing. But there was sharp resistance, particularly among scholars and scribes, that would reach a crisis in a few years.

In 1150, Parthais led an expedition to find the legendary place called Griferis, somewhere in the high mountains northwest of Vanara along the edge of the world. Upon his return, he was so disturbed by what he had found that he ordered the lands around Griferis to be laid with traps and snares to kill anyone who might attempt to go there. When confronted with this act by his children, Parthais banished Thurdun and Serith Ellyn from Vanara. He also made a secret pact with Secundur and ceded the lands nearby to Griferis to the shadowy Elifaen. Secundur thereafter made the lands into his own realm, which came to be called Shatuum.

Whether it was through the influence of Secundur or by his own character, Parthais thenceforth became more tyrannical. In 1156 S.A., he reacted to the continued resistance to the New Writing by ordering the execution of all scribes using any other script. He also ordered that all scrolls and books in the old scripts be burned and tablets broken. Called the Purge of Scholars, these acts led to the exodus of thousands of Vanarans who fled with their books and scrolls to far places, mainly Duinnor and Glareth. Many others who were not scribes also fled, alarmed by the erratic king. Parthais tried to force the return of the exiles, and he threatened war with Duinnor and Glareth should the Vanarans not be expelled from those lands. He also insisted that any Vanaran books and manuscripts be returned to Vanara. Glareth ignored Parthais and his threats, but Duinnor began to fortify its main city and began raising an army of defense.

Meanwhile, in Vanara, the court of Parthais grew more decadent and corrupt. Murder was often a way to advance, and the ministers of Vanara came and went rapidly while the governance of the lands fell to bribery and extortion. People began arming themselves for the protection of their homes and neighborhoods, mistrusting the king's army and his palace guard.

During these years, Thurdun and Serith Ellyn remained in hiding. But they were not idle. They maintained a reliable network of spies and informants throughout Vanara, even within the court and military. With the help of Glareth, Thurdun and Serith Ellyn secretly organized an army of exiled Vanarans and others, and, in 1273 F.A., using various tactics to hide their movements, they positioned their forces just outside of Linlally. They launched their assault in darkness, first sending an elite force to move quickly through Linlally and ascend to the White Palace where Parthais held court. Under Serith Ellyn's command, this force quickly overpowered the palace guards and issued the signal for the main army under Thurdun to attack Linlally. However, as soon as Thurdun's forces entered the city, all of the troops of Parthais laid down their arms and surrendered, and people flocked to join them. Serith Ellyn slew Parthais in his throne room, and Linlally fell in a single night with very little fighting. Serith Ellyn would become Vanara's new queen, and she would waste no time sweeping away the corruptions of her father and consolidating her own rule.

As a lasting symbol to her people of her own disdain for Parthais, and for the shame and ruin he wrought, Serith Ellyn had the body of Parthais burned so that nothing was left but his bones. These she ordered to be broken and crushed and then cast into large stepping stones and laid into the floor of the throne room. This was so that all who approached the throne would tread upon those who had disgraced and betrayed the trust of her people. And for this reason, she never permitted any carpets or rugs to be placed over the floor of the throne room, no matter how cold the floor became.

See Also:
Tales of the High Houses (The Last Book of Nimwill)
****

Pellen

Son of Silmain, and the twin brother of Heneil. Pellen wed Myrium, the twin sister of Lyrium. Unlike his brother, Pellen's interest in supporting Vanara waned after his father was killed. He continued fighting for Vanara for many years, but during the time of Parthais, he removed to Duinnor with Myrium. He took up arms to help Serith Ellyn overthrow Parthais, but soon after she began her reign, he left Vanara again to return to Duinnor.

Little is known about Pellen and Myrium's activities in Duinnor, but it seems they continued a cordial relationship with their families, mainly by correspondence. While in Duinnor, the couple had a son that they called Dalcadian. It is apparent, however, that Pellen came to the attention of the Unknown King, probably through Lord Banis, and on their behalf was recruited by Bailorg to obtain the Bloodcoins of Lyrium. It also seems likely that their plot was developed long before the Great Dragonkind Invasion took place. We do not know what kind of blackmail or coercion may have been used on Pellen in order to recruit him, but we doubt that he was, at first, a completely willing accomplice. Perhaps he held a grudging but hidden jealousy of his brother's fame and standing, too. Whatever his motives were, they certainly came from a darkened heart. In essence, Pellen was to use his good relationship with his brother to lay his hands on Lyrium's Bloodcoins, then deliver those objects to the Unknown King.

The real plot, of which Pellen was likely ignorant of, seems a bit more convoluted, with Bailorg perhaps promising the Bloodcoins to the Unknown King, to Secundur, to Banis, and also to the Dragonkind.   Being the opportunist, it isn't beyond belief that Bailorg may have wanted the Bloodcoins for himself. As it would eventually be revealed, both Secundur and Banis did not want for all of the Bloodcoins to be fall into the hands of the Unknown King for fear that he or one of his successors would open the Nimbus Illuminas. Banis apparently wanted eventual dominion over the Elifaen for himself, and Secundur wanted their destruction. On the other hand, in the hands of the Dragonkind, the Bloodcoins would represent a powerful insult against the Elifaen. As for Secundur, he stated that he did not fear the Bloodcoins, that many were lost and would never be found. His reasoning for entering into the plot was always as a method for obtaining a powerful warrior that he could co-opt and corrupt into his service, one to control Shatuum's growing and unruly hordes of creatures, a leader with the skill and power form them into an army.

So it is highly likely that Bailorg negotiated a separate agreement with the Dragonkind and influenced their planners to include a major assault on Tulith Attis. He probably arranged for much of their pre-invasion intelligence by providing maps, reports on the disposition of enemy forces, and by helping the Dragonkind plan their routes. At the same time, Bailorg apparently arranged things with Secundur, which is how he obtained the armor later given to Pellen. All of this took years to accomplish and unfold. How much Banis knew of these things is unknown, but it is reasonable to assume that he believed Bailorg and Pellen would deliver the stolen Bloodcoins to him, but report to the King that they could not be located. We do not know what the King's ultimate intended plan was, however, and he had no way of knowing about the impending invasion.

What we do know is that Pellen and Myrium traveled to Tulith Attis, ostensibly on an extended social visit to last several months. And we surmise that while there Pellen and Myrium grew renewed a closeness with Heneil and Lyrium. It is thought that a few weeks, at most, after their arrival, the Dragonkind invasion began. News that reached Tulith Attis was sketchy, with no one knowing that it was such a massive assault. But it seems likely that Pellen knew about it ahead of time and planned to use the Dragonkind's attack as a distraction that would allow him to steal the Bloodcoins and escape. And it seems likely that until the attack, his own plan was to deliver them to the Unknown King. But things moved rapidly. The Dragonkind outpaced the news of their breakout, and it was not until Fisenwold had fallen that word reached Tulith Attis of the approach of a great army. Thus the

Dragonkind posed a greater threat to his plans, and to Tulith Attis, than Pellen had been led to believe, so he was fully prepared to fight in earnest against the Dragonkind in defense of not only Tulith Attis, but to further his own scheme. Again, using the Dragonkind as a distraction. He probably had no idea the attack on Tulith Attis would be so massive.

As is told elsewhere, Pellen enlisted a sorcerer and deceived Heneil and his wife (with others) as to the purpose of guarding the Iron Door and the bell room of Tulith Attis. This he did, thus murdering those that the sorcerer turned into stone. But the Dragonkind assault was much more successful, much better commanded and carried out. Pellen clung to hope that, in the guise of Heneil, he would successfully lead the defenders to victory, or at least buy time for help to arrive, either of which would enable him to take the Bloodcoins and depart. And, it is likely that he was in communication with Bailorg, although ignorant that Bailorg himself had come with the Dragonkind. It may have been at Bailorg's suggestion that Pellen enlist the sorcerer, carry out the murders, and take Heneil's place at the head of Tulith Attis's defenders.

So Pellen, pretending to be Heneil, was captured during a foolhardy sally against the besieging forces. This was what Bailorg and the Dragonkind had planned all along. When Pellen saw Bailorg, he knew that he was trapped, and had been a pawn of their great game. He donned the enchanted armor, which multiplied his physical strength, and he took up his new role. Betrayal was easy, and the gates of Tulith Attis were thrown open to the invaders.

After the massacre, and when Pellen discovered that the Bloodcoins were gone, he knew that he had no place to hide, no place to go, that all of humanity would revile him should they discover his identity. This was, of course, known to Bailorg, Banis, Secundur, and, likely, the Unknown King. Of the Dragonkind who knew, they were soon afterwards killed at the Battle of Saerdulin. But Pellen suspected that Lyrium, who had escaped, knew as a certainty that he was the traitor. And he knew there was no hope of finding the Bloodcoins. He and Bailorg, with wagons of loot, began their journey back to Duinnor. But Pellen became increasingly morose as they progressed. Eventually, he and Bailorg parted company, with Pellen striking out on his own.

Pellen wandered, trapped in his armor, relentlessly attracted toward Shatuum by the enchantments within the armor he wore. He could not remove the armor, nor could he resist Secundur's dark and gnawing bidding. Though he may have tried to resist, his wandering tracks ever took him closer to Shatuum until at last he entered that place. Indeed, he only arrived shortly after Esildre had departed that place. And so Secundur took him in and began to groom him to his will. He was given a new name, Throgallus. And for the following few centuries, he served Secundur, rising to be his highest and most powerful general. And so it was, when the time came and Secundur was eliminated by Philawain, it was Throgallus who led the ravenous creatures of Shatuum out from that place and into the world on a frenzied invasion of nightmarish destruction.

****

Sally Bodwin

Sally Bodwin was born in 853 S.A. in Tracia Realm, the daughter of Niels Bodwin and his wife Tana. Niels was an officer of the Tracian Royal Navy and served as Martin Makeig's First Officer aboard the Golden Swallow. Like many Tracians, Bodwin sent his wife and young daughter away during the civil war between the Loyalists and the Redvests. However, Bodwin was unable to go with them, so mother and daughter set out for Glareth with a train of other refugees, following the Saerdulin north. They made it as far as Kalbrith, but there the refugees were detained by militias loyal to the Redvests and then informed they would have to return the way they came. Bodwin's wife and daughter, along with several others, escaped and continued northward, but were soon pursued into the Eastlands. Fearing capture, many set off westward and found their way to a settlement of Tracian refugees called Hill Town.

The Golden Swallow was sunk during the Battle of Grisland Strait, but Niels Bodwin and many of the crew made it ashore. However, he and many of his comrades would die during the dangerous trek out of Tracia. When Martin Makeig and the few remaining of his crew made it to Hill Town, he found Sally's mother too ill to relay the sad news of her husband's death. Tara Bodwin somehow learned the truth and, knowing that she did not have long to live, she asked Makeig to look after Sally, which he promised that he would do.

Perhaps it was because of that promise that Makeig remained in Hill Town rather than returning to fight in Tracia or pushing on to Glareth. At any rate, he was true to his word and immediately set about making Hill Town safe from raiders and warlords, and a fit place for little Sally to grow up in. As well, the women of Hill Town insisted that Makeig make a proper home for Sally, and that she be given every opportunity to learn all that could be afforded a young lady within the means of their little town. Her own personality also affected Martin, as he was never as brusque or stern with her as he may have been with others, and he sought to act as the father she never knew. As Makeig put it, "Not to act as I'd do naturally, but as I imagine good Niels Bodwin would do, as he was ever an upright, kind, and affectionate man, with a keen eye to his duty, be it to captain or kin."

Makeig made an effort to educate Sally himself, but as other Tracians came to live in Hill Town and a school was started, he saw to it that she attended regularly. She was a fair student, with a tendency to daydream, and she was soon an accomplished musician, playing both the dulcimer and the guitar (Makeig began teaching her the guitar as soon as she was old enough to hold the instrument.). And none could dispute that she had a strong and lovely voice. She often performed with other musicians of Hill Town at their many gatherings, and she was not at all averse to singing some of the bawdy sea songs that Makeig taught her. When she was not in school, she was a hard worker, keeping the cottage that she and Makeig occupied, gardening, and helping about town.

Some say that it was due to Sally's scolding influence that Makeig began steering away from the highwayman trade by which means he and his followers sometimes supplemented the town's treasury. And she was such a hardy girl that she often accompanied Makeig on forays against the Damar and to Janhaven on trading business.

Although Sally's personality was sometimes sharp, especially with Makeig, she was also prone to melancholia. Makeig, who always sought ways of cheering her up, accounted for it by acknowledging the loss of her family and by the lack of sleep that she suffered due to persistent night terrors and bad dreams. It was clear to him, too, that she was becoming a fine young woman, and he confided to some of the women of the town that perhaps an eligible beau might pay her some attentions and thereby cure some of her wistful sadness. He was assured by the women that although many young men of Hill Town pined for her, very few of them were brave enough to risk her displeasure or that of her intimidating adoptive father.

As it turned out, much of Sally's melancholia and fatigue (due to sleep loss) was because she was a dreamwalker. This fact was discovered by Robby Ribbon (King Philawain), and he placed her under the tutelage of Micerea. This was in 870 S.A., and during this time a great fleet was setting off from Glareth to take part in a massive invasion of Tracia. Robby recruited Sally to act as his liaison (and spy) aboard Prince Carbane's flagship, both to report on Carbane's fleet activities and to relay messages, through dreams, to Carbane.

****

Sir Sun and Lady Moon

(and how they were parted from one another)

The world's moon is often referred to as Lady Moon or Lady Luna, just as the sun is often referred to as Sir Sun. Indeed, Lady Moon often appears in the night sky as the face of a lovely and somewhat demur lady. But she is inconsistent, increasing and decreasing in brightness as portions of her face are covered and uncovered during the lunar month. Some say that it is her fan that she uses to cover her face and that the nearer she is to her husband, Sir Sun, the more shy she becomes for anyone but him to see her. When they are very close to each other, she almost fully covers her face, smiling upon her husband from behind her fan while he gazes back at her. When they are the farthest separated, she puts her fan away entirely and shows her face fully in order to look for him wherever he may be.

Legend has it that once Sir Sun and Lady Moon were never parted from each other's company and that they always walked the sky together. During that time, there was no day and no night upon the earth, and Sir Sun did not strive to outshine his beautiful wife. Hand in hand they stood on high, with all their children, the stars, with them. There are many stories that tell different accounts of how they came to be separated.

One story relates that when the Dragonkind first came to the Northlands bringing gifts to the Faerekind, and the Faerekind rebuffed them, Aperion was angry at his siblings for doing so. It is said that Aperion sent Sir Sun away, to bring darkness upon the world so that the Faerekind might be reminded that the Dragonkind live only for a short while and that the days of the Dragonkind are filled with toil and hardship. When Sir Sun obeyed Aperion, he went quickly away into the west. But Lady Moon, who loved to look upon the world, hesitated. Their hands became unclasped, and, after a time, she and her stars followed after Sir Sun. But, it is told, she could not find her husband, and when he came again to look upon the world, she was not there. Meanwhile, and perhaps this was Aperion's true purpose, the Dragonkind were given relief from the heat of their lands. Thereafter, Sir Sun continued his search for his wife, and she continued to look for him. Since then, they are seldom joined, and when they do come together, their union is brief, and darkness crosses the earth and the sky so that neither Lady Moon nor her husband can be seen for a few moments.

However, another tale says that it was Secundur, and not Aperion, who created the night, but he did not intend for Sir Sun and Lady Moon to be parted. Secundur wanted to send them both far away, along with all their children and heavenly kin, so that no light would fall upon the earth. Secundur was fond of dark caves and shadowy places, he suffered much pain by any source of light, and he strongly desired to freely roam the earth and to go wherever he wished without the risk of painful light.

So when the Dragonkind came to visit the Faerekind, Secundur whispered against them to his fellow Faerekind, inciting them to anger and making them rebuff the visitors' offerings of peace and friendship. Then, when the King of the Faere, Aperion, left the northern lands to personally escort the Dragonkind back to their abode, he took with him his comforting light. Sir Sun and Lady Moon continued to shine brightly, but Secundur wanted them to go away, too, for he was relieved at Aperion's absence. To accomplish this, Secundur sent a white eagle who could fly higher than any other to speak with Sir Sun and Lady Moon. The eagle told Sir Sun and Lady Moon that Secundur knew of a place far in the west where there was not yet any Faerekind nor any creatures at all. The eagle told Lady Moon and Sir Sun that they should go to that place so that their light could inspire the spirits of that portion of the earth to come forth into being, just as the Faerekind had done. Sir Sun did not wish to go, but Lady Moon, thinking it was only right for all the earth to share in the abundant joy of existence, wanted to find that place. Although Sir Sun and Lady Moon loved each other, the eagle, using Secundur's words, provoked them to argue. At last, in anger, Lady Moon departed into the west without her husband, taking all their children with her on the adventure.

Sir Sun remained for a long while. At first, he was angry at Lady Moon for her abrupt departure and at his children for going with her. But he began to miss them terribly, and he became sad. As his mood changed, he slowly moved in the direction his wife had gone, and as he went, his light faded somewhat from the earth. Then, determined to find his wife and to take her back into his arms, he resolutely marched over the far hills of the earth and out of sight.

The Faerekind were dismayed and filled with fear and foreboding, for they had never seen darkness. But Secundur rejoiced, going about from one to another saying, "It is but as it should be, for now I can be amongst you without pain or suffering."

But his brothers and sisters turned on Secundur, saying, "What have you done? We do not have eyes for darkness as you do. How are we to see the forests and the fields? How are we to enjoy the colors of the flowers, and the sparkle of laughing water? How may we see the love in the eyes of each other, or share our smiles? Go from us! It is a vile thing you have done!"

Secundur only laughed, traveling far and wide in but a short while, spreading himself all over the earth.

Meanwhile, Lady Moon and her children had crossed the great circle of the sky, but had not seen any land upon the earth without teeming life. But as she went, those Faerekind of the world underneath her flight praised her for her light, which came as a beautiful relief for them. But she marched on, with many of her children going before her and following behind, and she realized that she had been tricked and that Secundur's words were lies.

At last, Lady Moon returned to the lands where she had left Sir Sun, but he was not there. Below, the Faerekind were glad of her appearance, but implored her to bring back her husband.

"Where is he?" she asked. But they only pointed to the west and said, "He went over the hill."

All were happy when she moved toward the far western hills to find her husband and to bring him back. All but Secundur. He was writhing in pain from Lady Moon's bright light and was unable to speak to her at all. Even her children, the countless stars, gave him pain and continued to do so long after Lady Moon's face could no longer be seen in the west. Then, much to Secundur's increased suffering and dismay, the eastern sky began to glow. It became brighter and brighter, so that Secundur was forced to flee, darting from shadow to shadow to cover himself. At last, as Sir Sun completed his walk around the great circle of the sky and came again to the lands where he had last seen his wife, Secundur found a deep place within the crack of a mountain and hid himself there.

When Sir Sun saw that Lady Moon was nowhere in sight, he realized Secundur's trickery and gazed harshly upon the world to search for him, seeking to smite him with his burning glare. Secundur was nowhere to be found, but Sir Sun saw the white eagle who was Secundur's messenger circling over a deep mountain gorge. With all his fury, Sir Sun's fiery eyes landed upon the eagle, and so stunned and burned by the light was the creature that it dove downward to escape the heat, and he slipped into the very same cave where Secundur hid. Together they huddled, Secundur and the white eagle, both angry at the other for the failure of their plot. Their words to each other grew angrier and Secundur and the eagle fought, the eagle clawing at Secundur's wispy form, and Secundur clutching at the bird's feathers. At last, when Secundur with his hurtful words and terrible grip had subdued the eagle, he said to the bird, "You shall be my servant from henceforth, and all your offspring! You shall do my bidding and my will, going wherever I send you, and coming again unto me for my pleasure. Agree to this or die!"

So the eagle agreed. But he said to Secundur, "I dare not leave this cave, for Sir Sun's gaze is relentless, and I fear that he will kill me with his fire. And he is sure to see me, for I am the only white eagle to fly in these lands."

"Fear not, bird," said Secundur, "for I have stained you with my shadow, and now there is not a speck of white anywhere upon you. Only your eyes have I not stained, but I have put the blood of your heart into them, as a sign that you are my creature. Now go! Go and look upon the world, and return to tell me what it is that you see."

That is how Secundur came to have black eagles do his bidding. And that is how Sir Sun and Lady Moon were parted. And to this day they look for one another. Sometimes they come very close to finding each other, but rarely do they join hands. And even then, they are pulled apart once more by the paths that draw them on. It is said that Lady Moon ever looks for that place where life has not been, or from where life has departed, seeing for herself the spirits of those who have left their earthly form and those whose earthly forms have not yet come to pass. But always does she look to her husband, sometimes from far across the sky. Meanwhile, Sir Sun constantly searches for Secundur and his white eagle. His heart, it is said, is set upon revenge for the trick played upon him and his wife. Thus Sir Sun's heart is restless, and his feet ever move him onward, to search again in those places he has already been, to look for his wife, too, and his children. And neither Sir Sun nor Lady Moon nor any of their children will have anything to do with the happenings of the earth. Though they look upon the wide world and all of the things that happen there, they do not trust those who abide within it.

****

Tyrin Spritsul

Born in 835 S.A. in Glareth to a wealthy self-made merchant, Tyrin Spritsul was the youngest of five children. As all of the other children were girls, and Tyrin grew up in a rather domesticated setting. He was precocious, prone to teasing and playing jokes on his older sisters. By the time he was nine, he was sneaking out of his upstairs bedroom window to play with his friends throughout the night. This earned him a reputation for being lazy, for he often slept through his school lessons. When he was fourteen, he was enrolled in a boy's school but was forced to drop out when his father suddenly died. The business was sold, and the family moved into a modest house south of Glareth by the Sea. Young Tyrin became an apprentice clerk, but within a year he was summarily dismissed when he was caught inking his account books with unflattering sketches of his fellow workers. He moved from job to job, acquiring and losing employment with no great concern, until he rekindled his friendship with a group of former school chums who were training to be soldiers. They soon convinced Tyrin to join them, much to his mother's dismay. He proved quite skillful at arms, but had so little discipline when it came to duties that he was released from service.

Penniless, he fell in with a band of mercenaries bound for Tracia. This work was much more to his liking, since his fighting brethren were as keen to drink and carouse as they were to fight. In Tracia, they were employed to protect a small village against Redvest marauders, which they did with great skill. However, when the Redvest rulers began consolidating power in 854, they sent an overwhelming force against Tyrin and his small band. As the villagers ran away, Tyrin's group fought as their rearguard while they retreated. The mercenaries and many villagers fled to coast, fighting nearly the entire way. Tyrin managed to secure several boats so that his comrades could escape. But at the last moment, with the Redvests closing in, they gave their places to Tracian villagers, and they themselves were stranded. Having no choice but to fight their way overland, the mercenaries lost many men to the Redvests that were hot in pursuit. Tyrin and a few others managed to escape back to Glareth, but they soon learned that Tracia had put bounties on their heads, accusing them of being bandits and spies. Fearing for the safety of their families, Tyrin and several of his comrades left Glareth, going west along the Osterflo to Duinnor.

In Duinnor City, Tyrin and his band of eight fighters took various jobs, often acting as private guards for wealthy merchants who were unwilling to entrust the care of their goods to the corrupt Duinnor Regulars. Although the work was boring, the pay was good enough for Tyrin and his friends to take decent rooms in the same apartment house. It was there that Tyrin met a bookseller and academic named Raynor who also had rooms in the house. Tyrin probably did not know Raynor's reputation or history, but it likely would not have mattered. The two struck up a friendship. Often was the case when Tyrin's friends were out enjoying Duinnor nightlife that he himself was sharing wine and conversation with Raynor late into the night, sometimes at the kitchen table with the landlady joining in with them. Tyrin was also known to laze all day long in bed, reading one after another of the many books that he borrowed from Raynor.

One night, Raynor invited Tyrin along to hear a concert given by one of the chamber orchestras of Duinnor City. After the concert, the two had dinner at a café, discussing the music they had heard that evening. Still conversing as they walked home late that night, Tyrin was describing to Raynor a particularly talented cellist he had met in Tracia when they were suddenly set upon by a group of five armed men intent on relieving them of their purses. Tyrin burst in to laughter at their demands, then took the offensive. To Raynor's astonishment, all five assailants were soon unconscious, and Tyrin resumed his description of the Tracian cellist's masterful technique as if nothing at all had interrupted him.

Not long afterwards, Raynor offered Tyrin a job. Raynor instructed Tyrin to take a spare horse and travel several hundred miles south to the village of Averstone, in the vicinity of Elmwood Castle. Tyrin was to remain in Averstone until he was sent for, either by Raynor with a message to return to Duinnor, or by someone from the castle. Raynor explained that there was a blind pilgrim staying at Castle Elmwood who was intent on traveling to Temple Beras but would need an escort to do so. That was Tyrin's task, that is, to escort the pilgrim to the temple and, as soon as that was done, to immediately come to Raynor to let him know that all was well.

All this Tyrin agreed to do, and he departed Duinnor City the next morning. He arrived in Averstone some weeks later, and secured lodging at the inn using coin that Raynor had given him for that purpose. Raynor also gave Tyrin several books to read during his stay, since it might be several weeks before the pilgrim appeared. Tyrin settled in and waited. Weeks passed, Midsummer's Day arrived, and there was still no word from Raynor or anyone else about the pilgrim. Tyrin passed the time reading, walking about the village and countryside, and playing cards with the innkeeper and his family. The people of Averstone, at first somewhat suspicious of Tyrin, were soon won over by his jocularity and happy-go-lucky character. Tyrin often played hide and seek with the innkeeper's children, and even pitched in and helped the village blacksmith repair his furnace. More weeks passed, and as Tyrin re-read the books he was given, he began to grow ever more restless. At last, he wrote a letter to Raynor explaining that no pilgrim had come along, and he asked Raynor if he should remain longer since the fund to pay for his lodging was running low.

Tyrin sealed the letter, and he was sitting on the porch outside the inn waiting for the Post Rider to come along when he saw a man hurrying along the road toward him. It was the ferryman from Castle Elmwood, coming to find Tyrin. After relaying his message to Tyrin, the ferryman hurried away. Tyrin put his things together, saddled the horses, and strapped on provisions for the journey. Then he bade the innkeeper and his family farewell and made his way toward Castle Elmwood. Not long after arriving at the water's edge, Tyrin saw the ferryman pulling his barge across the lake from the gloomy castle with a single passenger upon it. And when the barge bumped against the landing, Tyrin was surprised that the pilgrim was not only blind, but was a young lady. It was, in fact, the notorious Lady Esildre, but Tyrin did not know that. Nor did he know that Raynor had arranged for Esildre to be temporarily blinded in order to safeguard Tyrin and others from her curse during the journey. In addition, Esildre told Tyrin that her name was Shevalia. Thus, Tyrin never knew the pilgrim's true identity.

Even though blind and in disguise, Esildre's charms were considerable, and Tyrin was soon completely besotted by the blind lass in his charge. Yet during the entire journey, just as Raynor knew would be the case, Tyrin remained honorable toward the "unfortunate" girl. For her part, Esildre also remained honorable, as her curse was held completely in check by the scales that covered her eyes. When Tyrin returned from the long journey, having safely escorted Esildre to the Temple of Beras as he had been instructed, he informed Raynor of the success of his mission. Then he proceeded to get very drunk. Hours later, and at the urging of his landlady, Tyrin tried to sober himself up so that he could ride back to the Temple to visit the girl he had left there. However, as he was on his way, a great cacophony of ringing resounded throughout the land, and the gates of the city were closed and barred before Tyrin could reach them. Indeed, that was the night that all the bells of Duinnor, and everywhere else for that matter, rang of their own accord, spreading great panic and alarm.

During the following two weeks, as Duinnor City was locked up, Tyrin briefly served as a conscript, drafted by a proclamation that all able-bodied men stand ready to repel any enemy that might assault the city. But the panic eased, the city gates were reopened, and Tyrin was released from duty. Returning to his boarding house, Tyrin looked for Raynor in order to ask about the young lady at the Temple, but Raynor was not at home. Not knowing that Raynor was himself on his way to the Temple to see Esildre, Tyrin made up his mind to do the same, that is, to go and see the girl he thought was called Shevalia.

However, before he could make his departure from the boarding house, Tyrin was beset by his comrades. They informed Tyrin that they had a very urgent offer of work from some farmers to the south, and that they were required to depart right away. Tyrin did not know that his landlady had spoken with his mates about his heartache over Shevalia, or that they, in turn, thought the best remedy was to get him well away as quickly as possible. As they reckoned, Tyrin was a good fighter and a talented leader, and they needed him. After hasty preparations, they hurried off with Tyrin and traveled a few hundred miles south to the town of Edgewold.

As it turned out, Tyrin and his comrades became embroiled in a little war against the Wickermen of the town of Westlawn who were attacking the people of Edgewold and raiding surrounding farms. The fighting intensified, as the Wickermen mounted larger and larger raids, sometimes sending a hundred men against a single farm. Tyrin would be the only one of his group to survive. He himself was taken prisoner by the Wickermen, but he managed to escape with the help of Robby Ribbon of Passdale, who was traveling through the region and was also taken prisoner by the Wickermen. Somehow the two escapees found themselves in the middle of Westlawn itself, surrounded by their enemies. The two became separated a few hours before a Kingsmen army and other forces from Edgewold began staging an attack upon the town. Just as the assault began, the mysterious leader of the Wickermen unleashed a monster against the Kingsmen attackers. The monster ran somewhat amuck, killing many Wickerman and Westlawn townspeople before setting upon the Kingsmen outside the gates of town. During the confusion, Tyrin managed to free over a hundred prisoners who had been captured and taken to Westlawn, and he successfully led them to safety while the Kingsmen engaged the monster. Soon it was all over, the monster was destroyed, the town surrendered, and Tyrin, along with those he had rescued, returned safely to Edgewold.

Tyrin, hearing of the plight of the Eastlands and the refugees at Janhaven, traveled alone from Edgewold and made his way eastward across the Bletharn Plains, with the apparent intention of joining those who were fighting against the Redvests in and around Janhaven. However, he never made it to Janhaven. Rather, it appears as if he lost his way in the Thunder Mountains and rode right into lands controlled by the Damar warlord. As it happened, the same Kingsmen forces that had fought the Wickermen arrived in the region. A small scouting patrol came across Tyrin as he was fighting several Damar mercenaries. Recognizing him from Edgewold, they observed Tyrin's rather unorthodox but effective fighting skill. Amused, the Kingsmen looked on, and when Tyrin dispatched the last of his opponents, they congratulated him on his victory and complimented him on his skill. In the conversation that followed, Tyrin convinced the patrol to permit him to act as their scout. Although somewhat dubious, they could hardly refuse the good-natured and capable rogue. In a written communiqué sent to their commanding general, the Kingsman patrol reported that Tyrin Spritsul, "who had recently distinguished himself against the Wickermen" was now acting as their scout, and that they would venture closer to Damar City in order to reconnoiter its defenses.

The Kingsmen conducted a blistering attack on Damar City, utterly defeating the few defenders within a few hours. Learning of the siege of Tallinvale, they immediately marched eastward, with Tyrin accompanying. Along the way, they picked up many other fighters, including some people of Nowhere and, unknown to Tyrin, Esildre was among them. They reached Tallinvale early in the morning, a day and a half later, just as the Redvests and Damar were beginning their assault on Tallin City's southern walls.

General Teracue organized his troops behind the besiegers and ordered an attack. The fighting was furious as the Kingsmen smashed into and through the rear of the Redvests. And, after but a short while, the Kingsmen and Tallinvale emerged victorious.

During the attack, Tyrin was among those in the lead. He was seen to fight his way up the ramp that the Redvests had built, killing his way through the rear of the pressing attackers. But he was marked by bowmen and several arrows brought him down. At this moment, Esildre, who was nearby, saw him and came to aid. After the battle, she tended to Tyrin, and never once left his side. Sitting beside the delirious and often unconscious man, she told stories to him as she stroked his brow. Once, he woke and smiled and spoke a few words. But the arrows had gone deep, and they were poisoned, and Tyrin faded, then died. Esildre, utterly heartbroken, gave up her will to live and quietly passed away, her head on his shoulder.

See Also:
Historical Sketches (The Melnari and Their Familiars)

****

Ullin Saheed Tallin

Ullin Saheed Tallin, born 836 S.A., was the son of Aram Tallin and Sharyn (nee Northstar), grandson of Lord Danig Tallin and Kahryna of the Joined House of Tallin and Fairoak. He served as Kingsman from 855 until the end of the Second Age. Trained as a combat engineer, he was assigned first to the First Army, First Engineering Battalion. In addition to active combat, he also worked in the Eastlands to conduct surveys and to make improvements to existing maps. His ability to navigate difficult terrain led him to be assigned as a courier for the Kingsman headquarters in Vanara. He was later assigned to the King's Post as a Special Rider under the direct supervision of Collandoth.

Ullin's role in the events of the final year of the Second Age is detailed within the pages of *The Year of the Red Door*, and due to his efforts Robby Ribbon successfully made it to Griferis. Later, Ullin and Micerea (who were lovers) went with the Nasakeerians when they returned to the Dragonlands and to their ancient city of Darini. Because many important events of his life are detailed elsewhere, we offer this brief outline of his life up through mid-870 of the Second Age.

Outline of Ullin Saheed Tallin's Life
(all dates are of the Second Age)

836: Ullin Saheed Tallin was born to Aram Tallin and Sharyn (nee Northstar) in Tallinvale.

843: Upon the death of Aram, Sharyn and Ullin depart Tallinvale to live with her family in Glareth.

844: An uncanny incident occurs while at a swimming hole with some of his friends. Ullin is overcome by a powerful sense of foreboding and fear, and he runs away to go home. His uncle finds him, almost insensible, but immediately takes a party of men to the swimming place. There they find only one of the boys, who is hiding in the brush and cannot describe what happened, except that "It came." The boy remained insane for the rest of his life. For his part, from that day on, Ullin had an uncanny sense of danger whenever any was about, indicated by the hairs on his neck and arms standing on end like goosebumps.

846: Ullin's mother reluctantly permits Ullin Saheed Tallin (age 10) to return to Tallinvale. Ullin has been miserable and unhappy in Glareth, and it is her hope that he will be happier with his father's relatives. In Tallinvale, he is received somewhat coolly by his grandfather, Lord Tallin. However, Mirabella dotes on Ullin, he being one of the few people with whom she is willing to keep company.

846-854: Ullin is educated in Tallinvale, and received good, if not sporadic, guidance from his grandfather. Mirabella also teaches him much from her own experiences. Ullin makes many friends and is well-liked and admired by all. In particular, he becomes good friends with Chrisafer Weylan, and the pair have many escapades together. Wishing to fulfill what he saw was his duty, in the spring of 851 Ullin secures certificates of education from his teachers and tutors, and he departs Tallinvale to enroll at the Kingsman Academy. This grandfather, Lord Tallin, provides him with a modest allowance and a letter of introduction, but is unenthusiastic and relatively unsupportive of Ullin's decision. Mirabella is distraught, but she does not seek to change Ullin's mind. Notably, she does not give Ullin his father's sword, one that was retrieved first from the dying body of Dalvenpar and later again by Mirabella from Aram when he was killed. Ullin arrives too late for enrollment, and since the Academy did not know he was coming, they did not reserve a place for him. Ullin had to wait a full year, but did not waste his time. He studied as much as he could, learned as much as he could from others, and prepared himself as well as he could for eventual enrollment. When, in 852, he took the entrance exams, he was exempted from and credited for many of the courses that freshmen were required to complete.

855: Ullin graduates with honors from the King's Academy, having completed his training earlier than most. He is given the rank of Junior Lieutenant and assigned to the First Engineering Battalion of the First Kingsman Army.

856: Ullin takes part in the Battle of Garmitor. His unit, tasked with bridging a gulch so that others could assault the Dragonkind, was attacked and cut off. After two days of continuous fighting, encircled, and having lost half of his company, including its captain, Ullin (who was himself wounded) took charge and stealthily led the survivors through enemy lines and out of the Dragonlands, using his skills to navigate the poorly mapped region. His gallantry resulted in being promoted to the rank of commander (captain while on active duty). After completing a two-year tour of duty in Vanara, seeing only minor action in the Dragonlands, Ullin is recalled to Duinnor for reassignment. While there, he receives as a gift the horse called Anerath, from the Thrubold family because their son Kurk was one of those saved by Ullin's actions at Garmitor. Ullin's new assignment was to gather information for the improvement of maps, and he was assigned to the Eastlands region of County Barley. By this time, his aunt Mirabella had wed and was living with her husband and young son in Passdale, so Ullin arranged to stay with them while he went about his duties. During this time, he briefly met Sheila Pradkin, a rambunctious "wild girl," and was kind to her. Ullin remains in Passdale for nine months before returning to Duinnor, where he supervised newly drawn maps based on his findings and surveys.

859: Impressed by his expertise and soldierly skills, High Command reassigned for special duties in Vanara that were of a secretive nature. It was then that he began carrying out lone forays into the desert, acting as a courier to deliver secret documents to and from Dragonkind contacts who were part of a clandestine effort to bring about peace. These assignments were difficult, dangerous, and lonely, and he was often away from Linlally, usually in the Badlands, for months at a time. His contacts were prearranged, but difficulties arose when avoiding detection by renegades and Dragonkind scout parties. On a few assignments, he waited for weeks for his contact to appear, and then only spoke a word or two before documents were exchanged and they parted. His contact was always disguised, and sometime traveling with a small party of armed guards, but they were clearly Dragonkind.

862: While on assignment in the Dragonlands, Ullin encounters Micerea, Gurasa's daughter, who is the courier he is to exchange documents with. But when her party was attacked by renegades, he managed to rescue her. Together, they made their eventual way to the Free City of Kajarahn.

863: Ullin left Micerea and departed Kajarahn to make his way back to Linlally with the important documents he was to deliver, but he was pursued by both renegades and Dragonkind scouts and driven well away from any easy route back. Eventually he was found by a party of Vanarans, but was suffering from wounds, dehydration, and exhaustion. It took nearly a month for his rescuers to transport him back to Linlally where Ullin was hospitalized for yet another month before he began regaining his health. During his stay, he was visited by Collandoth, the Melnari. Collandoth was part and privy to Ullin's missions (although Ullin did not know that) and was impressed by Ullin's service. Having already obtained agreement from high-ranking Kingsmen, Collandoth convinced Ullin to volunteer to work with him. Ullin agreed and all the arrangements with the Kingsman Command were made. Retaining his rank as commander, Ullin was commissioned into the Kings Post as a Special Rider, with exclusive orders to serve the needs of Collandoth who, in turn, reported only to a select few in Duinnor and Vanara.

866: Ullin assumes his assignments as Special Post Rider under the supervision of Collandoth. He begins routinely traveling by horseback from Vanara and Duinnor to Glareth and the Eastlands, and occasionally traveled to western Vanara (Ladentree) and to Altoria. Often, when traveling to and from Glareth, he would go through Passdale and then to Tulith Attis where Collandoth had taken up residence. These were brief stays, never more than a night, before carrying on his way. But in this way, through dispatches and letters, Collandoth was able to keep abreast of news and events reported to him from far-flung places. Ullin, for his part, did stop by and visit his Aunt on occasion, but never stayed overnight.

870: Queen Serith Ellyn departed Vanara on a long journey to Glareth. At first she planned her route to follow along that taken by most Vanarans who were migrating to Glareth by way of the Osterflo. She found, however, that many bureaucratic and legal obstacles were created by Duinnor to slow or discourage Vanarans from migrating. Among these were writs and orders that Vanarans must pay a duty or toll to each town or village through which they passed. Other hurdles involved special taxes and fees charged to Vanarans that booked passage eastward along the Osterflo. So instead of following that way, the Queen's party decided to travel across the Great Bletharn Plains, a lesser-used route, and then through the Carthanes and on to Glareth by way of Lake Halgaeth. Collandoth was privy to these plans and was kept abreast of the movements of the Queen's company, and he charged Ullin with going ahead to Glareth by the Sea to pass along this information to Ruling Prince Carbane, and to arrange with Prince Danoss of Formouth for the Queen's transport by boat across the lake and on to Glareth by the Sea. This meant that Ullin had to ride fast and hard, and had little time to visit when he passed through Passdale. Indeed, he was two days behind by the time he reached Passdale, and he enlisted Robby Ribbon to carry dispatches to Collandoth (known in the Eastlands as Ashlord). In this way, Ullin could continue eastward through the Mistwarren to Colleton, where he was to take ship passage to Glareth. Having Robby go to Collandoth (at Tulith Attis) meant that Ullin would gain at least a half day, or more. As it was, Ullin was late in arriving at Colleton and almost missed the awaiting ship. As for Robby Ribbon, the errand he ran for Ullin would be the beginning of his saga along the road to kingship.

Other Notes

Of course, Ullin would become one of the few who learned Robby's destiny and would become his guide, along with Collandoth, on the journey to Griferis. Along the way, Ullin's various skills and fighting prowess would prove essential to Robby's survival and to the success of Robby's quest. These events and activities are more fully told within *The Year of the Red Door*.

However, perhaps Ullin's most important work began after the events of 870-871; that is, after he took up residence in Darini. As an engineer, he greatly assisted with the restoration of the city. His greatest achievement, though, was the establishment of the Great Library of Darini. From there, Ullin led many expeditions into the world to retrieve books, manuscripts, and documents for preservation and for use. He created a system of "reading," whereby dreamwalkers could listen to various works being read by volunteers.

Ullin was a prolific writer, keeping copious notes and observations on his activities, his readings, and all the aspects of operating the Great Library. He also employed many helpers and assistants to copy, catalog, and preserve materials, not to mention those who accompanied him on his many arduous expeditions. Although the world was mostly depleted of its human populations, Ullin managed to locate many people who shared their memories and knowledge so that many first-hand accounts and impressions of the "last days" came to light.

As stated in the introduction, it is from this wealth of material that this Reader's Companion has been made possible. Even though Ullin has since departed the world, his work continues, and new insights and information will surely come to light as the Great Library continues to expand, and as more people delve into the collections of that institution.

Ullin always knew, better than anyone, that many mysteries and unanswered questions remained concerning the world and especially the events of the last years of the Second Age. In particular, although he tried, he was not able to obtain much in the way of information pertaining to Robby Ribbon's many experiences while on trial within Griferis, in the process of becoming King Philawain. For example, it is known that Robby was made to pass through many portals that took him to other places and times, but only a few of Robby's experiences were uncovered. In an effort to learn more, Ullin went back to Mount Algamori, to the gate of Griferis, but he was never able to gain access to that mysterious floating palace. He also sent dreamwalkers to explore Griferis, to look for any inhabitants and to learn whatever they might, but these explorers were also denied entrance.

As of this writing, one of the most perplexing of Ullin's activities involves a great mystery surrounding the old realm of Griferis, where a mysterious force blocked any and all dreamwalkers from visiting. The only thing dreamwalkers could perceive there was complete darkness. This region was discovered by Ullin's, Micerea, and many dreamwalkers attempted to penetrate it, but all failed. At last, with a mind to gather materials from the eastern world, Ullin's final expedition traveled into the region. We may never fully know what happened. Although he acquired some books from Glareth, he swore the members of his expedition to secrecy concerning their experiences there. He wrote about it, though, but he placed all of his writings and records pertaining to the "region of darkness" into the keeping of the Great Library, under a strict instruction that would not permit them to be seen until five hundred years had passed. His only comment about that was that he made a promise and that he hoped that, with the passage of time, the "situations pertaining to the Great Darkness would be resolved." As far as we know, all of those who accompanied Ullin on that expedition have kept their vow of secrecy.

Ullin worked almost constantly, even while traveling, on a history of the world preceding 870 of the Second Age, which he called The Prequalia. At his passing away it remained unfinished, but much of his work and his incomplete notes were made freely available to all visitors to the Great Library, including the editors of the Companion that you now hold in your hands.

****

Tales of the High Houses

The following is taken almost entirely from Ullin Saheed Tallin's notes related to his "Prequalia." He intended to include all of this as important background information about the various ways in which these Elifaen Houses and their peoples influenced the history that would play out during the Year of the Red Door. We see from his notes that some of these tales were translated by him from a variety of other manuscripts written in the Ancient Tongue using very old systems of writing. Other tales he composed from his own notes written in the Common Speech. We did not find explanatory notes but note that he must have been aware of some of the inconsistencies and repetitions. We offer his work, therefore, as we found it, and we made no changes to his work.

Introduction
The Seven High Houses

The Elifaen once had wings. In those days, they were called the Faere, or Faerekind. They came into being during a time before there was time, when the sun and moon and all the stars shone together in the sky with equal glory. They reveled in light and air, spoke with all things, heard all things, loved all things, and were loved by all things.

But strife and discord entered the world and was nurtured by one called Morgasir and his pupil, Secundur. This strife led to a terrible choice. The King of the Faere, called Aperion, gave all of the Faerekind of the earth an ultimatum: depart with him into a new heavenly abode, or remain upon the earth. Many departed, and they flew away into the sky with Aperion. But many elected to remain upon the earth. As a result, they were stripped of their wings, and became Elifaen, the Fallen Ones.

It was a catastrophe the Elifaen did not expect and were not prepared for. Many had never used their feet, had never even touched the ground before they lost their wings. Now crawling, they had to learn to walk, to eat, to stay warm. And, in the face of predators and enemies, they had to learn how to stay alive.

Yet, like the Faere they once were, the Elifaen remained immortal. They did not age beyond their body's maturity. All but the most severe wounds healed very quickly. They knew hunger, but could not starve. They knew cold, but could not freeze. Very few poisons would harm them. And no disease could touch them. But they knew pain, both of the body and within the heart. They were prone to melancholia and sadness, sometimes even dying from those maladies. And many, grieving too much for that which was lost, took their own lives or threw their lives away in foolish and hateful conflicts.

A few hoped for redemption.

Eventually, the Elifaen formed many clans and tribes throughout the world, and they learned to make the things needed for a better life. Civilized ways, law, art, music, culture, and great industries replaced the squalor and meanness of their previous days. Some of the clans formed into mighty Houses ruled by influential and gifted lords and ladies. Of those, these are tales of seven of the most powerful, the Seven High Houses.

The Seven High Houses were those that received the Forty-Nine Keys to the Nimbus Illuminas, otherwise called the Bloodcoins, or simply the Forty-Nine. Aperion returned to the earth at the end of the period referred to as the Time of Strife to deliver the Forty-Nine as a way for the Fallen Ones, the Elifaen, to break their earthly bonds and return to his fold, a way of leaving the world and regaining their status as Faerekind.

There are many legends concerning how this was done, but most suggest that Aperion took pity on the Elifaen and devised a method of testing them and of rewarding them should they pass the test. It is said that Aperion fashioned the Forty-Nine, then summoned the leaders of the Elifaen to the summit of Mount Cassos, giving them the means to come before him should they desire to hear his words. This summons, some legends report, was not in the form of a demand, but one of powerful urging. And some legends assert that he expected only one leader to come, Lyrium of the House of Fairfir, and that he was pleased that the leaders of six other Houses came, too. Other legends say that Secundur knew of Aperion's plan, and that it was he who urged the others to respond to Aperion's summons. Those legends have it that Secundur knew that he could not corrupt Lyrium, but if a group came before Aperion then the chance for discord was greater.

The Seven High Houses that responded to Aperion's call were Fairlinden, Fairwillow, Fairfir, Fairmaple, Faircedar, Fairmyrtle, and Fairbirch. These were established during the Time of Strife.

Each of the Forty-Nine Keys (or Bloodcoins) were fashioned of discs of heavy red gold approximately three inches in diameter and nearly a quarter of an inch thick, and each encircled a gemstone within its center. Seven different gems were used: amber, amethyst, diamond, emerald, ruby, sapphire, and topaz. To each High House Aperion gave seven of the Forty-Nine. During the First Age, they were redistributed, but the original manner of distribution by Aperion was as follows:

Cupeldain of the House of Fairlinden was entrusted with Sapphire Bloodcoins
Ormace of the House of Fairbirch was entrusted with Emerald Bloodcoins
Chantay of the House of Faircedar was entrusted with Amethyst Bloodcoins
Katrina of the House of Fairmaple was entrusted with Topaz Bloodcoins
Therona of the House of Fairwillow was entrusted with Diamond Bloodcoins
Pyros of the House of Fairmyrtle, was entrusted with Ruby Bloodcoins
Lyrium of the House of Fairfir was entrusted with Amber Bloodcoins

When Aperion gave the Forty-Nine to the High Houses, he also showed them in a vision how the Forty-Nine were to be used to open a way (which Aperion called the Nimbus Illuminas) for the Elifaen to depart the earth and come into Aperion's heavenly abode. However, Aperion warned them that it should be done quickly, as he foresaw misfortune and continued strife if they tarried too long. They accepted the Forty-Nine, but failed to act soon enough to avoid his prophecy.

During the First Age, there were two failed attempts to bring about an agreement among the Seven High Houses to use the Forty-Nine Bloodcoins and open the Nimbus Illuminas. After the second failure to do so, the Bloodcoins were redistributed so that each of the Seven High Houses would possess one Bloodcoin of each of the seven types of jewels (that is, all taking one Bloodcoin of each other High House, and retaining one of their own).

Eventually, most of the Forty-Nine Bloodcoins would be lost, and by the middle of the Second Age, all of the High Houses except that of Fairlinden would either have died out or disappeared from the world. And only the House of Fairlinden would still possess its seven Bloodcoins, passed from Cupeldain to his son Parthais, and from him to Serith Ellyn, daughter of Parthais, when she took the Vanaran throne as Queen.

The following tales variously describe each High House, its founder, and somewhat of its history. Some of these tales are apocryphal in nature since very little was recorded by the subjects of these stories. The many versions that exist were recorded long after the events took place, told by surviving descendants or by others who passed down their stories from generation to generation. Of these many stories, tales, and partial records collected by the author, very few are complete. The author has made an effort to discard blatantly false or confused renderings, and to sift through clues contained within seemingly unrelated documents and stories. Except where noted, he has made an effort to retell these stories in a coherent fashion while preserving for the reader those aspects that seem most reliable. Nonetheless, in spite of these efforts, contradictions, discrepancies, and curious gaps remain.

Taken together, these stories and legends describe the strife and tragedies that led to the events that took place during the Year of the Red Door. Some of the figures within these tales fought valiantly, but unsuccessfully, to avert the conflicts and violence that they foresaw. Some saw the error of their ways and sought to undo the sufferings they had inflicted upon their people. Others remained unrepentant and vengeful, and they insured the fate of all the others. By the late Second Age, almost all of the significant players in these tales would be dead, and many of them all but forgotten. But the power of their acts, stretching beyond the breadth of their lives, seeded the crisis that would take place during the year 870-871 of the Second Age, the Year of the Red Door.

Events mentioned within some of these stories are more thoroughly described in others. Therefore, the author suggests that the following tales be read in the order that they are presented, for some of the latter tales lack elucidating information that is contained within the previous ones.

The House of Fairlinden

The House of Fairlinden is arguably the most important of all of the High Houses. Its founder, Cupeldain, played an important role in bringing about the downfall of the Faerekind during the Time Before Time, but it was also due to his efforts that many survived that catastrophe. In later ages, Cupeldain would become King of Vanara, and his lineage would rule through and until the end of the Second Age.

The following passages describe how Cupeldain helped bring about the Fall of the Faere, how he was instrumental in establishing Vanara as a powerful realm, and how, ages later, his son Parthais almost destroyed everything that Cupeldain worked to achieve, but was ultimately thwarted by his son Thurdun, and daughter, Serith Ellyn, who would become Queen of Vanara.

The Fall of the Faere

How the Elifaen, who were once Faerekind, lost their wings.

There are many tales and versions of tales pertaining to the Time Before Time, the early days of the Faerekind, how they came into the world, their strife, and how their wings were taken. The Dragonkind have similar tales about how their own people came into being, with many versions and variations, and about their early encounters with the Faerekind. A comparison of those told in the Dragonlands with those told in the Northlands reveals that they are in agreement, at least in broad strokes. The following tale is a version of these events as related by Collandoth (aka, Ashlord) during the late Second Age to a party of his companions while they traveled westward. It was later set down by one of those traveling with him. Collandoth is brief, and he relates little pertaining to what happened after the Fall. However, Cupeldain and Secundur play important roles in the tale, so it is included here.

Aperion was appointed by Beras to be King of the Firstborn, the Faerekind. When the world was made, such was the power of Beras that each thing that came into being answered first to Beras and took form in the First Tongue. Through Beras, the Creator gave to these forms the power to witness and to have joy in the emerging creations of the world. So, as the forests grew, there came into the world the Firstborn of the Forest. As the mountains rose up, there also arose the Firstborn of Hill and of Dale. As rivers flowed, so came the singing of the Firstborn of the Rivers. Thus came into the world all the Firstborn of the Faere. Aperion came last, as the spirit of the Faere was strong, and out of their spirit he was created. It was he, Aperion King, whom Beras gave to the Faerekind as their leader, the one to give guidance to the others when need be.

No one knows how it came to be, but there sprang a jealousy of Aperion from the Faerekind of the mountains. Not all of the Faere were jealous, but some of those among the elders of the Firstborn. They, who had been upon the earth the longest, felt one of their own should be leader of all the Faere, and they chafed against the authority of Aperion, their younger sibling. Into the deep recesses of their mountain caverns they withdrew. They ceased to take fellowship with the others of Faere family, in sunlight or in moonlight, in forest or field or river, and so the Mountain Faerekind grew apart from the intent of Beras. They rejected Aperion's guidance and heard not his urgings to rejoin the others of their folk. It was one of those who came to power at last and who first brought sadness into the world by creating poison and death. This one, who was later called by the name of Morgasir, sought to have power over Aperion, and it was he who first spread death into the world and deceit and treachery. Some say that it was through trickery that he gained from Beras the power to beget other creatures, and that it was he who brought dragons into the world. But none of the Elifaen bards say so, and they take offense that Beras could be tricked. In any case, Morgasir's creatures were made in the most foul and unspeakable way. The shadow of that power, a corruption of Beras, reaches into every age. It was Beras, not Aperion, who destroyed Morgasir, and his domains and the places where Morgasir and his followers once dwelt sank into the sea by the hand of Beras. That place remains unto this day, in the far reaches of the world to the south and west, and it is called the Craggy Sea, a vast sea choked with great rocks, full of treacherous currents and shallows, beset with fog and storms so that no ship can pass through it.

Evil though Morgasir was, some of his followers and some of his creatures were permitted by Beras to escape his wrath, for no creature made by the hand of the Creator is purely evil. Eons passed.

Peace and tranquility returned to the world, and the passing of time upon the earth was not counted nor noticed. Then there appeared dragons in the lands of the far south, rising up from the depths of the sea, from that place of Morgasir that was destroyed, and they brought with them fire and destruction to the lush forests and fields. Like Morgasir, they, too, beget new creatures to toil and to labor for them and to be as slaves. Great alarm swept the Faerekind. They witnessed the death and disappearance of many trees and animals, and saw for the first time ever death come to some of their own Faere brethren. Thus the world was filled with fear. But it was at this time also that Beras made a way for offspring to come of all living creatures so that they might have some hope of continuing their own kind. And so, for the first time, the love of family came to the Faerekind, as children were born unto them.

Many of the Faere retreated from the devastated lands, but some grumbled against Aperion and against Beras, too.

"We do not know these dragon creatures, nor their slaves," Aperion argued, "and Beras is silent concerning them."

"Let us fashion the land over," said some. "Let us make the rivers run dry from those lands, and let us coax Sir Sun with his heat to parch these unwanted ones."

Those that spoke thus to Aperion then departed from him and they strove in the earth and sky and changed the path of the rivers and made the land of the Dragonkind harsh and barren. This angered Aperion who said only Beras may have such power. Such was Aperion's ire that he grew fearsome in aspect to his own kind. Indeed, even those that reshaped the lands regretted what they did, but they were powerless to undo their work. Yet, as a result of their labors, the dragons died away or receded back into the seas or burrowed into deep places into the earth where they yet grumble, sometimes sending forth their flames and their molten bile high into the sky and flowing across the lands, burning the plains with lava and covering vast areas with soot and ash. Even to this day, they sometimes do this.

The Dragonkind, who were the offspring of the monsters and had been made to be their slaves, dwindled in numbers when their former masters were destroyed, and once again peace came into the world.

But there was one among the Faerekind who sought to undo Aperion. He was called Secundur and had been a pupil of Morgasir. Secundur was fond of shadowy places and longed to take up the work of his former master. He nurtured resentment among the Faerekind who had lost their forests to the desert, and by his soft urges they were made to feel discontented. He gathered around him all those who, like himself, had escaped the destruction of Morgasir. Though they were few, they made much mischief among the other Faerekind by whispering against Aperion, and they even hissed against Beras when they dared. It is said that Secundur courted even the Dragonkind of the parched places, seeking to provoke them, but those people for the most part shunned and mistrusted him. The desert people eked out a miserable existence, but they considered themselves free of their former masters, the dragons who were now destroyed or in hiding.

In spite of all these things, the world was still favored by Beras and the Faere lived happily and without need but for sunlight and moonlight. Dew filled the ever-blooming flowers with nectar to delight the lips of the Faerekind, and the birds sang joyously to delight their ears. With their broad and airy wings, the Faere skipped along the waters and danced among the green forest treetops, and with the First Tongue, they took pleasure in conversation with every creature, every tree and blade of grass, and every stone. And their communion with each other brought forth for the first time children of their own kind, without pain or travail, and new joys were brought into the world.

One day, some of the Dragonkind appeared among the green hills of the north saying they were invited to feast with the Faerekind. As it turned out, it was Secundur who had invited them and welcomed them. Yet many of the Faere were mistrustful of these crude creatures who walked with their feet and were covered with the dust of their travels. Many of the Faere who had been driven out from their lands by the dragons remained aloof and resentful of the guests. But Aperion welcomed them, saying, "Are you not also the children of Beras, though your coming into the world was sad and harsh? Why should we not enjoy together the taste of these fruits and share with one another our songs and our laughter?"

Indeed, it was perceived by many that the Dragonkind and the Faerekind had much in common, and each found beauty where they lived. And it was shown by Secundur that, though the Dragonkind had no wings, they were little different from the Faere. The women of the Dragonkind were especially beautiful, and they aroused admiration for their poise and their grace. These women brought with them gifts made by their own hands of gold and ruby and lapis. Secundur was pleased, for it was he who showed them the art of making such things, and he well knew what the outcome would be.

"What is this?" one of the Faere cried out upon seeing the ruby-encrusted staff being presented to Aperion. "This staff is the arm of my old friend, a great and mighty cedar who once lived in the southlands!"

And another cried, seeing the emeralds that lined a headpiece being offered, "And these are the eyes of my dear friend the hare who danced and played in the meadows of the southlands!"

And so great discord came among them, prodded by the smiling whispers of Secundur.

"Aperion," Secundur breathed from the shadow of an elm tree, "it does not seem fitting that such gifts should be accepted. Our people grow angry, and their hearts turn against our guests. Give back these things and send the Dragonkind away."

This Aperion reluctantly did, apologizing for the temperament of his own kind and begging the guests to take with them what food they wished.

"I fear for you," he told them, "for I have never seen my people act in this manner. But I will see you safely home. Let us wish for a time when such things may be forgotten and when we may be friends."

And so Aperion accompanied them away, back into the desert lands, and he walked upon the ground as they did to keep their company and to converse with them all along the way for many many leagues. At last, when they reached their homes, he bade them farewell and took to the air with his wings and returned to his own kind in the north.

Some stories say that when Aperion returned, he spoke to his own people with anger in his face and in his voice, saying, "Who are we to deny communion with those others of this world who live and breathe? What fault of theirs is it that they may live in lands made barren by evil doers and misguided mischief-makers? What fault of theirs is it that they do not know how to speak with the things of the world? But are these not also children of Beras, who come from the same Font of Creation that brought forth us all? And look you at their plight, for they live but for a very short while, toiling against the ground without wings. Their lives are full of struggles, and then they quickly pass away. Yet we remain. I say unto you: Know now time, its measure and the weight of its passage! Let the day end, and let darkness come to the lands to cause you to think on the end of life for creatures such as these. And, after a while, let day come back anew to remind you that life has its beginnings out of darkness. Give thanks that you enjoy the creations of Beras as you do and are joined with him. Let your heart ponder what otherwise may be!"

And as he spoke, Sir Sun shrank away and sank low into the ground for the first time ever since the world was made, and the sky was filled with the red fire of his trailing robes. Lady Moon followed soon afterwards, alone and without her bright husband, hiding her face behind her hands in shame. All of the Faerekind shuddered at the coming dark of the First Night upon the earth. Yet, by this act, the Dragonkind were given relief from Sir Sun's pitiless gaze, and for the first time the cool of the night air was known in their lands, and they praised and thanked Beras for the respite.

Other stories say that the day and the night were made by Secundur's trickery, and was not Aperion's doing. Regardless, Secundur reveled in the hiding dark of night. He went about with ease and spoke to the others, whispering, "Why does Aperion put the creatures of the desert lands before us? Why does he give greater regard to those who live on lands that were taken from us?" And to others he said, "Aperion has turned away from Beras and has taken favor with those that Beras has punished." Thus he went, stirring dark thoughts among many.

He went also to the far-off Dragonkind and floated amongst them while they rested in the cool of the evenings. There he went about from one to another.

"Why should it be," he spoke, leaning over their shoulders with his lips near their ears, "that those of the northern lands may live easily and without struggle when you must scrape and toil?" And to others he declared, "Aperion sets himself up as a god, and he cares not if he offends you by refusing your gifts and your company. Yet you are the proud offspring of dragons!"

Thus for many passings of the days and nights without count, Secundur patiently aroused some of the Faerekind to doubt and to subtle anger. And he did not neglect the Dragonkind, either, going amongst them to spread worry, resentment, and discord.

There was one among the Firstborn who began to think as Secundur suggested, and yet he also sought to resist Secundur's words. These days, his name is remembered as Cupeldain, and he was one of those who had once favored the coastal forests far to the south and was driven out by the dragons who came from the sea. It was Cupeldain, too, some say, who had striven with rock and river to drive out the dragons and who, with some others lost to memory, angered Aperion by their works. Cupeldain had not forgotten Aperion's anger, nor the shame of his rebuke, but his spirit had arisen in those places now lost to the world, and Secundur's words filled him with melancholy longings for what was no more. Yet Cupeldain had not the power to restore the forests of the south, even though the dragons were gone. It was he who took to heart Aperion's admonishments, and he, more than the others, grieved not only at his loss but also at his failure to restore life to those lands as they once were. Never could he forget the shame of attempting what only Beras might do.

"Aperion's words were true," Cupeldain said to Secundur. "Look at our failure. It was we, not Aperion, who strove to be gods and to do what Beras has not seen fit to do. The dragons are gone, but our seeds grow not in the southlands. Sand and rock are parched, and the rivers we took away cannot be put back in their old courses. Surely it is as Aperion has spoken, that it is not our place to create but only to rejoice in that which is, and, if it must be so, to mourn and remember that which is no more."

This angered Secundur, for he knew Cupeldain to be powerful and that Cupeldain enjoyed the conversation of rock and river and would be a mighty ally if only he could be convinced.

"If Beras is in all things the intent of Creation," Secundur countered, "then how may it be that those things have come to pass and that the spawn of the dragons now roam the dry lands once lush with leaf, root, and twig? Is it not given to us by Beras to decide and to judge? Is that not why Aperion claims to speak for Beras?"

In this manner Secundur slowly urged Cupeldain, coming to him in the shadows of the forest or in the darkness of night. But Cupeldain listened not, it seemed, and Secundur grew impatient and went then to the Dragonkind.

"Why should you struggle so," he asked them, "when, just over yon mountains, is cool-flowing water, vines heavy with sweet grape and berry, trees laden with hearty nuts and with peaches gold and juicy?"

"We are not welcome there," was the reply from one.

"This is our place," said another, "given to us by our dragon-fathers."

So Secundur set about causing strife among the Dragonkind, and with his whisperings and shadowy words he created turmoil among them so that they fought among themselves and increased their struggles. This was difficult for Secundur to do, for there are few shadows in the Dragonlands, and Lady Moon watches brightly at night. And the Dragonkind people were mysterious to him. Although he knew that they were the products of dragons, and that dragons were made by his former tutor, Morgasir, Secundur did not understand the Dragonkind's resistance to him nor the mystery of their existence. For how could the rude dragon sire such a fair likeness, though crude, of the form of the Faere folk?

Still, for generation after generation of Dragonkind, Secundur patiently plied them with doubts and with longings until there rose up among them one who heeded Secundur's words. His name was Kalzar, a chief of one of the great tribes of the barren lands. To this tribe Secundur showed the secrets of smelting iron and forging weapons and tools. He suggested to Kalzar that he, among all his peoples, was the true descendant of the dragons, and that with the secret of fire and steel, he held the power of the sun itself.

As Kalzar came to have greater power over his kind, Secundur went also to Cupeldain and said, "Do you not see the stirrings of the south? Yet Aperion does nothing and claims to have kinship with them through Beras. Yet they do not rejoice in life as we do. They do not follow the intent of creation. See how they fight and slay one another? This they do without remorse. And now there is one, named Kalzar, who rises to great power in those lands. He builds cities and commands legions who worship him as a god. Yet Aperion cares not that they do these things."

"What is it to us?" Cupeldain replied. "We have our lands and they have theirs. If Beras is offended, let him make a change. Why do you whisper to me these thoughts and try to put fear in my heart?"

"Is it fear to be aware? Is it fear to be prepared to protect our lands? Or is it folly to be idle as Aperion is and to invite the followers of Kalzar into these untouched valleys."

"What may we do, anyway? Look at our last efforts! In our effort to destroy the dragon, we only made a place for these Dragonkind."

"You must learn what they have learned," said Secundur. "Make steel as they have. Forge and mill, cut stone and raise up walls."

To this Cupeldain eventually agreed, and so he and those also convinced by Secundur delved into rock and fire, forged weapons and built airy cities of glass and stone. They ceased in their conversations with oak and granite, refrained from singing with river and reed.

Aperion, when he saw this, went to Cupeldain and asked, "Why have you forsaken our ways and taken up the works of your own hands over that which Beras has provided?"

"We seek not to offend Beras," Cupeldain replied, "but only to learn and take joy in the abilities that Beras gave us. We wish to fashion with our own hands pleasing things for ourselves and, in doing so, to discover and rejoice in new things."

"For what purpose do you build these temples? Are not the halls of the forest and the columns of the mountains seemly enough places to rejoice?"

"We build them in fond imitation of the earth."

"Why do you then strike iron from the stones and make fire to forge metals?"

"The stone and the trees are willing to our hands, or else they would not give up their metal or their heat."

"For what use do you make, then, these sharp implements of bright steel? And what do you make when you stretch sinew across the cut and carved branch?"

"These swords we make because they are beautiful to hold, and they have within them mysterious powers of life and death. These instruments we make with wood and string to invent music like the brook does or the gurgling stream. Also, we may use these to send short branches far into the air as birds in swift flight."

And though the things they wrought were beautiful to behold, and the music of their lyres and bows comely and sweet, Aperion trusted not Cupeldain's words, for he had seen the use of such things in the hands of the Dragonkind. So he went away from Cupeldain full of misgivings. Secundur, watching and listening from the shadows, followed Aperion as a murky cloud and whispered to him.

"O, King of the Faere! Why trouble over the toys and pastimes of your fellows? Their hands were made by Beras, were they not? And so all works spring from him."

Then to Cupeldain Secundur went and suggested, "You answered wisely, Cupeldain, and yet perhaps you should assert yourself more than you do, for Aperion grows weak and you grow strong."

This troubled Cupeldain, and he flew to the sunlit plains where he knew Secundur seldom went. There he pondered all that had come to pass while he drank from the flower-cups of nectar and gave himself over to sing with the larks and to ride gaily on the backs of antelope as they danced across the plain.

Secundur did not follow, for on the plain the face of Sir Sun, ever the servant of Beras, shined unbearably. But he was satisfied with what he had said to Cupeldain. That night, Secundur went unto Kalzar, the new king over the Dragonlands.

"You have done well, Kalzar, and your sires, the dragon-gods, are proud and pleased with your rule. What say you to those Faere who north of here in the green mountains make sharp weapons and build great castles? It is not for each other they do these things, but to come and take back these places that have been given from them to the Dragonkind by Beras."

"Why do you come to me? Are you not one of them? Like them, your spirit is dark to me and arouses me from my peaceful sleep to pace the night in troubled thoughts. Go from me! You are not welcome, and your words do not bring comfort to me!"

Full of anger at the rebuff, Secundur left Kalzar, and he brooded in the deep caverns of the mountains. He prodded, for spite's sake, the ancient beasts of Morgasir that still survived in the deepest recesses. With skills taught to him by Morgasir, Secundur conjured the old dragons to breed demons, and these he set loose to bring pestilence and torture to the Dragonlands and to any place they might roam.

"It is not meet for me, who am Firstborn, to be shunned. It is Beras himself who strikes my heart, and I shall strike his! It will be my place to remake the world. To gain from all the Faere and all the Dragonkind their prideful spirit and their knowledge and turn it against the plan of Beras!"

And for a long time, Secundur was not seen or heard, but his followers, those Faere who bent to his will, gathered themselves unto him and did his bidding. And though seldom seen or heard, his hand has ever since been felt in all the world and no doubt it was he who somehow provoked the first war, and sundered the Faerekind one from another, and caused the Fallen Ones, the Elifaen, to be in the world as they now are.

In the grand White Palace that Cupeldain built, there stayed a Faerekind by the name of Alonair who was skilled in the making of stone likenesses of animals, trees, and even of his own kind. These he would place around the Faere city that Cupeldain had built, and Alonair made them upon the porches and in the gardens. These sculptures were a marvel to all who saw them, so lifelike that, especially in the moonlight, they seemed to move and breathe, sometimes even turning their heads. Alonair's fame spread throughout Faerum and even far away to the Dragonlands. Even Aperion was amazed at the skill of Alonair. Those of the Faerekind who never before went to the city now did so to see the works of Alonair. The visitors, from the plains and from the forests, were amazed at all the doings of Cupeldain and his people, at the grand structures and temples, the fantastic gardens and fountains, and the boisterousness of those who lived in the city. And especially were they filled with wonder when they laid their hands on the statues of Alonair and felt them to be warm to the touch. But the statues spoke no word, the stone of their making was silent, and the visiting Faere understood this not at all, for never had any material of nature been silent to them before.

When Kalzar heard of these statues, he marveled at the tales and sent emissaries to Aperion asking if Alonair might carve some statue for Kalzar in exchange for some similar boon.

"Alonair may decide for himself if he is to do this," Aperion said, "and the measure of his reward, too."

And Aperion summoned Alonair, but when he arrived, Alonair's heart was darkened against the Dragonkind, and he thought to himself, "I will agree to Kalzar's wish and ask a boon of great price of him, for his people walk the land where once I played with deer and where I once danced with the ram. Kalzar's land of sand once was full of green fields and forests that gave to me the juice of their berries. There, the chorus of leaves once spoke back to the beat of my wings as I passed through, and thus the trees sang as Sir Wind moved his fingers through their branches. Yes, it will be a great price."

So Alonair agreed to come to Tyrsharat, the city of Kalzar in the desert plains, and to make for him a statue like no other, and to ask in return a favor of his own choosing.

"Make ready the stone that I will carve. Cut it twenty times the height of Kalzar and the same in its width and breadth. Quarry this stone in a single block and make a place for it in the center of your city. When it is there and all is ready, send for me and I will begin the work of carving this thing for you."

"In what likeness may we tell Kalzar that you will carve this statue?" the chief emissary asked.

"You may say that it will be in the likeness of what once was but is no more, of what will be but has not yet come to pass."

When Kalzar received the emissaries back at Tyrsharat and they told of their meeting with Alonair, Kalzar asked, "Did he say no more? Did he not say what likeness he would carve?"

"No, Mighty One, only: 'It will be in the likeness of what once was but is no more, of what will be but has not yet come to pass."

"And did he not say what boon he would ask?"

"No, Son of Dragon, he never did."

Kalzar pondered this for a day and a night, then he ordered the preparations to begin. The Dragonkind labored long, and an entire generation was born into the task, for once the massive block was cut from a mountain, it had to be moved over a hundred leagues to the city Tyrsharat. Many of his people grumbled, saying it was impossible to move such a stone, as big as a hill, as heavy as a mountain. But Kalzar would have the thing done, and so he raised armies to conquer all of the Dragonkind and to make of them slaves. And he raised a great host of workers to pry away the stone, to forge tools for sliding it across the sands and gravel of the desert. When they faltered, Kalzar's taskmasters whipped the workers. When his counselors said the task was too great and cost the empire too much, Kalzar had them put to death. When at last the Dragonkind Empire grew weak from the task, Secundur emerged from his place of sulking and went to Kalzar and stood beside him on the high balcony of the palace. There, Kalzar cast his gray eyes over the city, beyond the place prepared for the stone, and outward across the moonlit desert toward where, far beyond sight, the stone still moved, inch by agonizing inch.

"Surely Alonair's gift has become a curse upon you, Kalzar," Secundur said in his ear. "The Faerekind delight in the sufferings of your people and rejoice in your vanity. You do not have the power, as do the Faerekind, to converse with stone and sand, and they resist your will stubbornly. Only the Faere may move this thing here, and this they know. While your empire falters into ruin, the cities of Cupeldain flourish and grow in beauty. Your numbers were once vast, but the ocean of your people recedes, while the Faere grow in number."

Kalzar thought about this and passed the night through with Secundur at his ear until morning when Kalzar walked out into the sun and Secundur departed.

"What power have I to do this thing?" Kalzar cried out at the blazing sun. "Have we indeed been tricked by the immortal ones who may wait with patient ease for our self-destruction? No! I shall not be treated so contemptuously!"

Then he gathered his generals and ordered them to make an army and to go north into the green lands, fearing not the Faere. There, this army was ordered to capture as many of those who lived there and could be brought back to be chained to the Great Stone and to pull against it. To take the fruit of the lands, too, and all the animals they could find, and to destroy what they could not sack, forest, field, and city alike.

Of course, the Faerekind saw these preparations. Many still flew the skies that once covered their homes of leaf and twig, looking down at the now-parched lands. They saw the many fearsome creatures below, scorpions and basilisks, which the devastated lands had spawned. And these Faere watched the building up of the Dragonkind and the rise of their cities. They saw how the desert dwellers made fields along the few rivers still flowing there, and how they slaved and toiled and fought and were beaten down by the sun and by the whips of their masters. They saw, often enough, Kalzar himself and his retinues, going forth in glory upon elaborate sedans to survey the movement of the Great Stone or to review the gathering of his armies with his many sons and wives and all the high members of his court. But those Faerekind that flew high overhead and watched did not speak to those creatures below, or those people or those rivers, or to the rows of wheat that they grew in some faint semblance of the grass that had once sprouted there. Rarely did they allow themselves to be seen, except in the distance, perhaps, safe from the bite of the high-flung arrow. To Cupeldain they returned to tell of what they had seen. As the marching armies came toward them, all of the Faerekind in Cupeldain's city watched in horror and disbelief. Some went to Aperion and cried, "What shall we do? For they are grim and vast in numbers, and they have murder upon their faces."

"They cannot fly into the air as we," said Aperion, "nor do they abide upon the earth but for a short while. They are weak creatures and are cursed with all manner of pain and longing, springing from their lowly bodies. What is there to fear of them? Let them be as they are and have what they wish, for all will return to Beras after a time, as is His intent, and we will see their passing away."

"What of our cities? What of our gardens that we made with our hands and that give us pleasure?"

"It is not from such made things that we sprang, but from that which made the stone of your cities, and from that which made the flowers that grow in your gardens, and we sprang also from the water that runs across your terraces, and from the air that blows the scent of your blossoms. The Dragonkind cannot unmake Beras, nor can they stay his Intent."

"But it is cruel, what they do. If we are but the hand of Beras, then surely it is an offense to him that the works of his children are cast down and trodden to dust."

Aperion then understood that many of his own kind had become attached to the things of the earth and to the objects made by their hands, and he saw that they no longer felt as strongly the Force behind those things.

"Beware that you do not act as those you fear," he said to them, "lest you take up their ways and become as they are."

But Cupeldain and the others with him understood little and heeded less of Aperion's words. From their high places in the cities, they watched the armies hack through the forests and swarm through the mountain passes between the Dragonlands and Faerum. Deer and elk, docile and tame, they slaughtered to eat, and birds for their feathers, and the bear for his skin. In horror, Cupeldain watched from the tower of his castle, his eyes stinging with tears. And when the armies came to his city, the Dragonkind were at first baffled, for there was no road into the city and no gate. But what use are these to Faere who are lifted up by their wings over the walls of their cities and who need not tread the ground or crush a leaf with their feet? Here, the Dragonkind camped and made engines of wood and stone and iron, the smoke of their fires and forges choking the air along with the sound of anvils, mallets, and drums. Strange and cumbersome devices they made, dark of purpose, and with them they came again unto the walls of the city. They pounded the walls with the great battering hammers they had made, slung by ropes from carriages and scaffolds. Day and night, they smote the walls, and day after day and night after night, until at last they made cracks in the statue-covered ramparts until they crumbled away into rubble and ruin.

It was then that many of the Faere, still innocent and without understanding, were taken by the intruders, and when Cupeldain saw them murdered, he cried out and fetched his sword and flew into the midst of the enemy and cut down all the Dragonkind that he reached. Others joined him, and in their fury they put to death all they found, soaking the ground with the blood of the Dragonkind, those that fought against them and those that tried to flee. But few Dragonkind escaped, and the fey defenders of the forest lands flew across the desert and, coming upon Tyrsharat, wreaked such blood that Kalzar himself was in fear and joined the battle.

Then, as the height of the battle was reached, and Cupeldain plied with Kalzar, sword against ringing sword, darkness fell upon the earth. Torch fires gave no light, nor did Lady Moon or any of her retinue of stars look down from the heavens. And a great fear came over all, Faere and Dragonkind alike, so that they paused in their killing.

Aperion's voice, full of the might and spirit of Beras, parted the black silence.

"Come!" he commanded, and the wings of all Faerekind moved and flew of their own accord, obeying some higher master than the bodies to which they were attached. Away they flew from Tyrsharat, and from all other parts of the earth, over the blackened desert and through the blinded sky and beyond the lightless forests and onto the wide plains where Aperion waited. All the Faere of all the lands of the earth were called, those in battle and those who knew nothing of it. Those of the forests, and those of the rivers, and those of the sea. All were gathered on the plain in a vast host, and they saw each other in the red light of Aperion's golden anger.

"A new place is prepared, and now we must depart this world to await the will of Beras!" he said to them sternly. "Follow now along the way I go."

But there was hesitation among many of the Faere, who muttered, "Why must we go? We have done no harm to any creature, and our conversation with the earth is not broken."

"We cannot depart and leave our work unfinished!" cried Cupeldain, still breathing with the heat of battle and soaked with the blood of Dragonkind. A rejoin of like sentiment went up from his people, still gripping their swords and anxious to complete their vengeance.

"You have parted yourselves from the intent of Beras and love too much that which Beras gives rather than He who gives it."

"We will not go!"

"We cannot go!"

"Look there!" Aperion pointed at Sir Sun, who was red with anger, and who was retreating with haste to that place beyond the western rim of the world. And very close at his side was his Lady Moon, who covered her face for shame.

"All those who stay beyond the passing of Sir Sun's purple hem shall bear the punishment of their desire. Verily, the weight of their hearts shall be their reward. All those who still rejoice are welcome into our new home."

And so Aperion departed quickly upward into the sky, followed by a host of the Faerekind. But many hesitated, not wishing to leave their lovers or their fathers or mothers or children. Some did not wish to leave their fields or forests, and many spoke to one another, muttering words of wonder that Aperion would leave so, and with him such a host of Faerekind. Those of the deep forest or gentle sea who knew nothing of Cupeldain made to depart back to their homes. And those who wished to resume their battle against the Dragonkind moved to return with Cupeldain to those lands. But as the sun disappeared, their wings grew weak, and they fell to the ground or into the treetops or upon the waves of the sea.

"Why does my body fail me!" cried Cupeldain as he alit on a high hill. "What sensation is this to be pulled to the earth? This pain that burns my back and this emptiness that grows in my belly? How is it that this sword grows heavy in my hand when it was but a feather moments ago?"

As he pondered these new and curious sensations, his dripping sword became too heavy to hold. The burning of his back grew more painful, the hunger of his stomach spoke loudly. He cried aloud, gathering his wings about him for warmth against the cold night air. But his wings did not obey him, and he pulled them with his hands, feeling the life go from them. And, as everywhere around him the sounds of agony and shock of all the Fallen Ones rose up from the lands, their wings crumbled and fell away as dust.

That was how it was that the Elifaen lost their wings. They bear the scars of what they lost even to this day, and all their offspring, too. From that day to this one, those of the Faere race who remained in the world have felt hunger and cold. The stone bruises their feet, and the thorn cuts their flesh. For all the days of their lives, they endure the memory of what they lost, yet they are unable to succumb to sickness, or to hunger, or to pain, or even to age. The peace of death comes to them only through violence or, sometimes, through deep inconsolable sadness.

The Throne of Vanara

During the long eons after the Fall of the Faere, Cupeldain established the House of Fairlinden. He arguably became the most powerful leader to emerge, and there is little doubt that the people of Fairlinden were the most numerous of any house, occupying much of Vanara. It was Cupeldain who established Linlally and built the White Palace at the top of the Falls of Tiandari. However, Cupeldain's obsession to overthrow the Dragonkind prevented Fairlinden from gaining ultimate ascendancy over the other Elifaen. As a result Silmain was able to consolidate power by bringing together a coalition of Elifaen houses and clans. Thus, it was Silmain who became the first king of the Vanaran Elifaen, even though many, if not most, would have preferred to see Cupeldain as their king.

Nonetheless, Cupeldain supported Silmain as long as Silmain pressed the Dragonkind. But when Silmain tired of war and strife, and sought to have the Seven High Houses use the Bloodcoins to open the Nimbus Illuminas, Cupeldain was outspoken in his opposition. Silmain's efforts failed, and the relationship between Cupeldain and Silmain was strained for many years. Still, Cupeldain's House of Fairlinden was the most powerful single Elifaen House, and Cupeldain continued to support Silmain in his wars against the Dragonkind. When Silmain was killed, it was Cupeldain who assured order in Vanara by quelling several uprisings. Many Elifaen pressured Cupeldain to take the Vanaran throne, but he was reluctant to do so. His son Parthais and his grandchildren, Serith Ellyn and Thurdun, also urged Cupeldain to assume the throne of Vanara because, like many others, they feared the incompetence of Ormace, who openly maneuvered to replace Silmain as king. Fearing Ormace, virtually all other Vanaran Houses banded together to urge Cupeldain to accept the throne, and he eventually did so.

Under Cupeldain, Vanara prospered, even though war with the Dragonkind persisted. New settlements along the Iridelin and north of Linlally became important trading towns, the city of Linlally grew and prospered and became a center for learning and the arts.

Yet, like Silmain before him, Cupeldain grew weary of war. And he foresaw that continued strife with the Dragonkind would only serve to weaken Vanara while other realms, such as Altoria and Glareth, grew in power. For those reasons and others, he called together the Seven High Houses once again to convince them to use the Bloodcoins. This time, most of the leaders of the High Houses were for the plan. But Therona and Ormace were adamantly opposed. As well, Secundur worked behind the scenes to bring about discord. Eventually, the discussions became so heated that violence was only narrowly averted. And, at the insistence of Ormace, the Bloodcoins were then redistributed so that each House would retain only one of their original Bloodcoins, exchanging the other six with each other so that all still retained seven, albeit of seven different gems.

Things went from bad to worse. One after another, the High Houses were destroyed or disappeared from the world. During this period, Cupeldain was murdered, and his son Parthais came to the Vanaran throne. At first, Parthais continued his father's legacy. He consolidated power in Vanara and sought to secure Vanara against the Dragonkind. However, his rule became increasingly despotic and tyrannical. Jealous of the growing power of other Elifaen realms, he authored numerous plots and intrigues against the rulers of other lands. With growing paranoia, he tolerated corruption and vice among his courtiers and supporters. During the Purge of Scholars, he almost single-handedly destroyed the cultural legacy of Vanara.

The following tale describes the discovery of Griferis (which would play a critical role during the Year of the Red Door), the establishment of Shatuum as Secundur's domain, and the downfall of Parthais.

About Nimwill

This tale was recorded by Nimwill, who was court chronicler under King Parthais of Vanara. As such, Nimwill attended and personally recorded many events taking place within the Vanaran Royal Court, and he also traveled with Parthais to record his various exploits and experiences. Nimwill was with Parthais when he executed those accused of murdering Cupeldain, and he was also with the king during his many campaigns in the Dragonlands as well as other parts of the world. He was with Parthais at the Battle of Tamkal Plain, and he was also with Parthais in Masurthia when he forced King Barindon and Queen Therona to make peace, and he traveled with Parthais to see the legendary Griferis (to which the following tale pertains).

After Parthais exiled his son and daughter and grew more tyrannical, Nimwill continued to serve him. However, during the Purge of Scholars, and without the knowledge of Parthais, Nimwill secretly assisted many scholars to escape Vanara along with many books and scrolls that were in danger of being destroyed. It was a delicate line that he walked, being at once the official chronicler of Vanara's Royal Court whilst at the same time seeking to subvert the will of his king. He worked tirelessly to transcribe materials written in the various old scripts into the so-called New Writing that Parthais sought to impose upon Vanara. It is thanks to his efforts that Vanara was able to retain as much as it did, although many of the original texts from which he worked were destroyed or smuggled away to other realms.

The following tale was most likely recorded by Nimwill after the fall of Parthais, since it spans a period of over 125 years, from when Parthais first learned about Griferis until his eventual overthrow. It says nothing of the Purge of Scholars, nor does it contain much information about Serith Ellyn or Thurdun during their exile, or the many plots and intrigues that Parthais authored against his contemporaries in other lands. However, it is a basis for understanding something of the events surrounding the demise of Parthais.

After the time of this tale, Nimwill remained for a while as Court Chronicler to Queen Serith Ellyn. He retired in the year 202 of the Second Age (S.A.), giving over his duties to Orinus. In the year 275 S.A., Nimwill traveled east, intending to go to Glareth to make copies of manuscripts sent there during the Purge of Scholars. He passed through Attis and visited with Lyrium and Heneil for a brief time before continuing on to Glareth, but he never arrived. No one knows what happened to him, and no trace was ever found of the party he was traveling with. Some speculate that they were killed or captured by Pinewood rebels, while others insist that King Inrick of Colleton imprisoned him. Still other legends have it that Nimwill's party became lost within Forest Mistwarren and never emerged. Since he was Elifaen, many suppose that he may still be alive somewhere in the world.

The Last Book of Nimwill

Part l.
The Tale of Elrasil

This, then, is the Tale of Elrasil the Hunter, as told by him to Parthais, King of Vanara, son of Cupeldain, in the year 1,149 from the First Day of Reckoning of the First Age, and set down by his scribe, Nimwill, in the New Writing, as heard in the company of the King's Court, including the Prince Thurdun and his sister the Princess Serith Ellyn, son and daughter of Parthais:

l am called Elrasil. l hunt the wild game for my people who live in a far valley, for our lands yield little from the rocky ground and so we eat flesh and make from the wild creatures warm clothes that we need to cover ourselves against the bitterness of wind and snow. l have come hither, sent by the elders of my people, to tell thee of what l have seen, and to ask what omen it may contain.

It was on the day after the first moon, two months ago, that l and several of my kinsmen departed into the mountains to hunt. Westward we went, up the slopes, and we took stag and many fowl for three days until there was ample to carry home. Then, on the morning of the fourth day, as we prepared for our return, there came upon a hill overlooking our camp a mighty ram. Its fleece was the color of bright steel and its great curled horns as polished copper, and we were amazed by its size and hue and at the majesty of its proud form.

"l will have that fleece," l vowed, taking up my bow and lance, "and of its horns l shall make a mighty trumpet!"

"But we are burdened enough," said my kinsmen, "and have no need of more."

"Go, then, and l will take it alone," l said, aiming my arrow. But as l drew my aim upon it, the ram kicked and leapt from view, and my arrow went far from it.

"Come, let us depart," urged my kinsmen. But l left them immediately and took up the chase of the ram, leaving my kinsmen to the bounty of our hunt and to return without me.

For ten days, l chased the ram, stalking it through the mountains and into places l had never been, westward and upward through passes filled with ice and along the terrible faces of sheer cliffs. Each day l neared close enough to him to let fly an arrow, but each time he stepped away unharmed, until on the tenth day l spent my last arrow. Yet l continued on, climbing after him, seeking to take him with my lance. But he was ever just out of reach of me. Deftly, and with great ease, the beast stepped from rock to rock and vaulted from ledge to ledge, while l climbed after him slowly and with great effort, hunger and weakness overtaking me as l went. Often he seemed to wait for me to catch up somewhat before climbing on, and sometimes he would let out a powerful bray that echoed loudly from wall to wall and from slope to slope, taunting me and encouraging renewed strength in my arms and legs.

Then, on the morning of the full moon, he stood over me as l awoke. But l was too weak to lift my lance. He brayed at me and tossed his head and stamped upon all four hooves. Turning away, he climbed a rock nearby and stepped out of sight. Mustering all my remaining strength, l climbed after him onto a broad shelf below the western peak of the mountain, and I was filled with wonder at what I saw.

How may I tell of it? For I overlooked the Crack of the World, that which few have ever seen except those who remember their wings. There it was, running north to south, straight and true, a deep, smooth-walled canyon filled with mist, and out of it from far below came a low rumbling. Beyond was nothing but air into faraway peaks, their tops bound with snow and towering over the place where I stood. Yet before me, at the very edge of the precipice, stood a gateway, fashioned of two columns of white marble, each standing eight cubits high, and the width of its opening between these was eight cubits. An untarnished silver arch spanned the two columns and at its apex was set a black disk three cubits in diameter. Upon the ring that held the black disk was inscribed figures likened unto those used by the Dragonkind for conveying messages. And as I gazed upon these figures, I understood their meaning, though I have no knowledge of writing, and they said to me the name of the thing I looked upon, "The Bridge of Rulers, Gateway of Worthy Sovereigns."

Then, lo, out of the sky came a stormy cloud, full of fire and drums. And the storm surrounded the gate and smote it with its blinding fire so that I was full of fear and cast myself down into the rocks and into a crevice to hide my eyes and to cover my ears against the terrible crack and rumble of skyward-drums. But soon there came a lull in the storm, and I looked up and beheld the black disk was afire with blue light, as a star in the heavens, and the silver arch in which it was set rang with a chime that did not fade from hearing. And then I perceived between the columns, stretching out into the air, a narrow causeway into the storm-cloud beyond. And in the cloud itself I saw a mighty castle floating. As I beheld the marvelous castle, the gates thereof opened, and from it came the sound of many trumpets, and onto the bridge from the castle came two figures. As the trumpets blared out and the clouds swirled around the causeway, the figures crossed over toward the gate and unto the mountain where I still hid myself. But I saw that it was a very young boy, still in swaddling clothes, walking beside and a little behind the magnificent ram that led me to the place. I watched as the boy guided the ram by tapping it lightly on its flank with a golden stalk of wheat.

When they stopped on the threshold of the gate, the trumpets ceased their blare and the boy held up his other hand in which was a sandglass. He held out the sandglass and turned it so that the sand ran from top to bottom, and all while the sand flowed, no sound but the ringing of the arch could be heard, though the clouds that blew around the castle and darkened the sky over the bridge were split by white fire all the while. From my hiding place, I looked on as they stood there. The sand of the glass fell, and so eerie was the sight that the hairs of my skin stood on end from the back of my neck to the back of my arms. I sensed a movement some small distance from me, and I shrank back as another figure emerged from nearby to where I hid. This figure was a person dressed in strange garb and fabric like those that the Newcomers weave and wear. Whether male or female, I could not discern, but the person approached the gate and strode resolutely through and stood before the ram and the child who waited there. Then the ram and the child turned, and together they led the person across the bridge and into the castle. When they had all disappeared within, there came a deafening clap of thunder as the gate shut behind them and once more the noise of the storm raged, and the castle faded from sight as did the causeway that led to it. Into nothing they faded, as the storm lifted and dissipated, and no sight of the castle or the bridge remained, but only the gate and the clear cold air and the distant snow-capped mountains beyond the Crack of the World.

All this I swear to thee, my King, that I did see with mine own eyes, and upon my life I assure that what I hath told is a true reckoning of what I saw and heard.

Part II:
Griferis

The King and his court were curious and asked many questions of Elrasil about his adventure.

"Tell us," asked Parthais, "couldst thou find the way back to the place thou hath told us of?"

"If the need was dire, my King, or the reward great, I believe so," answered Elrasil. "But it would be a mighty effort."

"I desire to look upon the place and to see with mine own eyes the Crack of the World and the gate thereupon it and to delve into this mystery."

Parthais declared to his treasurer to give precious jewels to Elrasil as a reward for his tale. The King then made preparations to go out from the city with many of his court to find the place Elrasil described. And so, on the very next day, Parthais departed with Elrasil and traveled into the mountains and unto the village of the hunter. This was in the springtime and the rivers and streams gushed with melting snow, and the way was difficult and slow. When they came upon the village of Elrasil, they were received with much honor and gladness, and they were made welcome by Elrasil's people. And Parthais lavished gifts upon the people there, and while they waited for the streams and rivers to subside, he built there a temple to honor Beras.

When the summer was full and Elrasil judged the conditions best, he led King Parthais and those who accompanied him into the mountains. And those that accompanied him, besides those of Elrasil's people who served as bearers and guides, were many of his court, the Prince and the Princess, his children, and I, his scribe, to faithfully witness and record these events.

It was a difficult task, full of deadly hazards. On the second day, some of the party were killed by an avalanche of rock, and others turned back, departing with the King's permission. For three weeks, we climbed. More were killed in falls and other mishaps, and many more were injured. On two occasions only the quick hand of Elrasil saved Parthais from plummeting to his death. But at last we made the summit and beheld the gate. I, Nimwill, his scribe, Elrasil, the hunter, the King's daughter and son, Serith Ellyn and Thurdun, my assistant, and several porters of Elrasil's village were all that remained of our party among all who had departed from below.

Parthais ordered a camp to be made upon the summit, and, as he had done many times before, he bade Elrasil to repeat his tale. Then Parthais, King, said, "I shall abide here and await a sign and see for myself if the mysterious bridge may appear. And, should Beras will it, I shall cross over and inspect the castle in the air."

"Sire," said Thurdun, "we have not the means to remain very long."

"Majesty," said Elrasil, "who knows if the bridge shall ever again appear?"

"The gate remains, does it not? Why should it remain for nothing? And, look ye all at the fashioning of it. The threshold and the columns are of one piece of marble. And, see, there is no grime or weather upon it, but rather it appears to be new-made. And behold the arch that spans it, what manner of writing is that so that we may all know its meaning? Like the First Tongue, it is. And look ye at the stone made into it, look at its sheen! Surely this is a work of Beras himself, or at least of some agent of Aperion!"

And so camp was made upon the windy place, and we spent our days in awe of the view around us. Often the clouds completely covered the scene so that we had to be careful of our steps. But it was more often clear, and we could look out from the gate and gaze downward a league or more into a straight cleft cut into the world. Wide, it was, and it was walled on the far side by straight, smooth cliffs, clean, as if cut with a knife. And farther away, blue in the distance was another mountain, higher even than the one we were upon, jutting up to a jagged point and covered on all its high flanks by snow and gleaming ice. On some days that far mountain was the only feature we could see, rising up from a blanket of clouds that spread out below us like an endless sea, stretching in all directions.

For many weeks we remained. When our food ran short, Elrasil and his kinsmen, the porters, made their way off the mountain, and after a fortnight they returned with new supplies for us. All during this time, Serith and Thurdun pleaded with their father, King Parthais, to abandon the place. But he was unmoved by their words and was determined to remain.

Then, on the evening of a new moon, a storm brewed far in the west. We watched it approach for all of the night until, when the first ray of the eastern sunrise met our promontory, the sky grew violent with wind, and the light of morning was dimmed to darkness as the storm came upon us. Firebolts split the sky, and hail pelted us, and the wind and rain blew away our tents and scattered us into the rocks and crevices for protection. We covered our ears against the terrible sound and kept our eyes shut fast against the blinding light, just as Elrasil told us he had done. After some while, just as Elrasil had told before, a lull came, and we looked up and beheld the black disk now shining as a brilliant blue-white star, and we perceived a steady ringing as if a giant rubbed his wet finger upon the rim of a mighty crystal goblet. And there appeared to us, far out over the abyss of sky, and floating in the swirling storm, a grand and mighty mansion, like a fortress. And a mysterious narrow bridge stretched out from the gateway to it, suspended, like the castle, by nothing that we could perceive. As soon as these things were revealed to us, a mighty blare of trumpets sounded forth, as mighty as the storm itself, and louder. At that moment, the far gates of the castle opened up, and from it emerged a small figure, alone, who walked slowly across the causeway. It was the same figure that Elrasil had described to us, a child, still in swaddling clothes. In one hand, he carried a wand of wheat and in the other was a sandglass, and it was many long moments for the child to walk the distance between the faraway castle to the gateway upon our summit. As he came upon the threshold of the gate before us, we stood in wonder at the sight of him. Our sovereign, Parthais, though restrained by his children, stepped forward to face the child.

"What manner of place is this?" he cried out.

But his words were lost in the maelstrom of noise and carried away on the powerful wind. Yet the child appeared not to see or hear Parthais and stood aside on the threshold and raised the wand of wheat and smote the threshold with it three times. And on the third time that he smote the threshold, a great mist bellowed forth from the open gates of the fortress and from it came galloping a terrible warrior. His robes and the livery of his horse were the color of crimson blood, edged in gold. His armor was black, and around his helmet curled the horns of a mighty ram, and upon his face-plate was the likeness of a skull. Upon his back was a great sword, and in his saddle cup and in his black-gloved hand was a tall lance of black, banded in red. Such was the dreadful aspect of the warrior, thundering forth on his cinder-hoovéd beast, that we were all filled with terror, and those of us with weapons drew them in readiness. But then we saw the rider pull forth his lance and draw it down upon the child who stood without motion and who showed no knowledge of the doom crashing down upon him. All of us that beheld this cried out in horror, yet our feet were unable to step forth to the child's defense in time to avert his murder. But as the lance tip came upon the child, he raised his stem of grain and smote aside the lance so that it shattered and split apart. Without care or concern, the tiny one then tapped the passing beast on its flank with his wand, and under this insignificant blow, the horse stumbled and fell along with its rider over the edge of the bridge, and the two terrible creatures plummeted down into the cloudy abyss. As if nothing had occurred of any significance, the child turned again toward us and raised his sandglass and turned it over so that its sand trickled from the top to the bottom of the glass.

All became silent, save the ringing of the archway. Even the flashes of lightning about the far castle held their bright and jagged place so that no sound came of them. No breath of air stirred, and there was no motion within the clouds or anywhere about the summit but the steady fall of grains in the glass.

But Parthais approached the child, stepping upon the threshold of the gate, and he knelt before the child, placing down before him his sword.

"Wondrous and terrible child," he said, "tell us what manner of place is this, that it appears so mysteriously. And what manner of child art thou to wield such power upon a grim warrior?"

The child turned his eyes upon Parthais, and with many voices, those of the young and of the old, of both male and female, he spoke.

"This is the entrance to the place of judgment, called Griferis."

"Is this wherein the dead come to be judged of their life?"

"No, it is the living we judge of their worthiness to rule others. And it is revealed only to those desiring fitness to rule."

"Who, then, would come, except those who wish to overthrow their sovereign?"

"Any may come hither, regardless of station or intent, both the wise and the foolish may be judged."

"Why shouldst any come who may take the throne otherwise?"

"The giving of thrones and kingdoms is not our concern or affair. Our task is merely to make ready the ruler-to-be."

"Tell us of the warrior which was smote before us and destroyed. How was it that we saw what we saw? How be it that a terrible warrior is so easily vanquished by a child?"

"The warrior was Ambition, and he rode upon Power. His lance was Cruelty, and his sword is called Wealth. He wore the red and gold trappings of Conspiracy, and the headgear of Force. Yet I wield the wand of Justice, made heavy with the fruit of True Prosperity, holding within its chaff the grains of Wisdom and Truth and Humility."

"Why, then, dost thou comest forth from yonder castle?"

"Only in my company, and as the grains of this glass still fall, may a person enter the place of Trial."

At these words, the child turned away and walked back to the mysterious castle. The doors of that place took him in and shut upon him with a great clap of thunder, and the storm once again beat upon those of us gathered, and the black clouds, split with lightning, engulfed the scene. After only a few moments, all noise dissipated, and the rain ceased to beat, and the clouds faded away unto the bright morning sun. Gone was the bridge, vanished was the fabulous castle, and dim black was the stone above the gate. And all who witnessed it were filled with wonder and amazement, and we stood for many hours pondering what we had seen and heard.

Part III:
Parthais

But Parthais the King grew agitated and was much concerned about the words of the child and entered into deep thought. Then he ordered all to make ready to depart immediately, and so we did, leaving in haste to his sudden mood. It took as long to come down from the mountain as it took to go up it, and a week more as well owing to an avalanche that blocked our way. But when we reached the village of Elrasil we did not tarry, even though it was evening and the night was cold, but at the insistence of Parthais we parted from Elrasil and his kinsmen and traveled onward and back to Vanara and unto his court. All during these travels, Parthais kept his own counsel and spoke little, seeming vexed and short of temper. When we returned once more to the court of Vanara, and to the White Palace, all worried over their King's mood, none more than his son Thurdun and his daughter Serith Ellyn who feared for their father's condition. Yet, he shut himself away from all company for many days and weeks, even unto winter, desiring to see no one, not even his own family. And often, so the servants told his children, mutterings could be heard from within his chambers, as if some other was within there with Parthais, and together they spoke and sometimes argued. Then, one day, he emerged with a fearsome aspect, pale and wild-eyed. He ordered his builders to come to him, and he summoned, too, his fell generals and his chief counselors.

"This I command," he told them. "Get ye to the far mountains and unto the place called Griferis and into the lands thereabout that peak. Make ye there an impossible way for anyone to ascend. Lay the paths with terrible pits, and at every turn place snares of great cunning. Destroy roadways ye may find, and cause the canyons that may be crossed to be filled with subtle traps. Destroy also the village of Elrasil and all those who dwell there. Bring the hunter's head unto me that I might see that he lives no more. Leave none of his kin or kith alive who may tell of Griferis or show the way unto the summit."

Thurdun and his sister Serith Ellyn who attended their father heard these orders and were filled with dismay and fear.

"Sire?" Thurdun asked. "Thy commands trouble my heart! What madness overtakes thee that thou wouldst slay the innocent? What fear hast thee of the mountain and the mysterious gate that thou should make of the land a deathtrap for the unwary and blameless?"

"Not for the blameless, nay!" cried out Parthais. "But it is come to my understanding that Griferis is an evil place, vying to usurp my throne and to cast down my house and make waste of our realm. Madness it would be for me not to act. What wouldst ye have me do, son and daughter? Not forever will the desert children rest, and in days that may come again we may needs to war with them. And I must then take up the sword in battle as is my place. Yet if some rebel passes Griferis, and comes to hold the power of that place, what would he not do to take the throne from me whilst we are away to defend the lands? Would ye have me be idle? Would ye have me do nothing that is within my sight to do? At least if I fall in battle, the throne would be preserved. Which between ye should then sit here?"

"It would be my sister," said Thurdun. "For I do not have the wisdom to rule, nor the place, being the younger."

"Oh, my brother, speak not of such! What state would our people be in should I rule them? Where should wisdom be then? But Father, why be not fair and content with destroying only the gate of Griferis? And why should not builders and soldiers be cunning with their deceptions and pits, so that none may dare intrude there, and be it at that alone, with warning to all not to trespass there? Why then, with that burden of cruelty, also take upon thy head the blood of Elrasil and his people? What have they done to deserve this of their King, except to show him safety and good fare and be as guides to their Sovereign, even to their suffering?"

"I do what I must do, for any else would be folly!"

"What is the greater folly?" cried Thurdun. "To poison thy children with thine obsession? To preserve a house with a dishonored name?"

"Speak not, nor any more!" Parthais bellowed back, laying his hand upon his sword and stepping toward Thurdun as if to draw it. "Get thee away, and be never again in my presence to gainsay me so! Go! Let not thy shadow fall again upon my doorstep!"

"Oh, Father!" cried Serith. "He is thine own son!"

"No more! And speak with a mind to care, daughter, if thou wish to remain so!"

Sobbing, Serith left Parthais and went to Thurdun her brother.

"Oh how I wish Mother were still among the living!" she said. "She would dissuade his madness and cool his temper!"

"I am thankful, sister, that she cannot see the fearsome aspect of his countenance, nor hear the terrible voice of his words. Nay, it is better that she has died upon the sword of our enemies to the south than to have this shame upon her. But do not fret. I will tell thee what we must do."

Then Thurdun told his sister that they should go together to Griferis, before the builders and soldiers of Parthais could arrive. "Elrasil and his people we shall warn," he told her, "and give them the means to flee to far parts, northward and east, to escape this threat. I shall defend their retreat. I, with any who may follow me. But thou, my sister, must climb Griferis and truly delve the secret of that place. Mayhap our father is not long to rule, for I am sure that such madness cannot be quelled by these acts, but must forever pace back and forth in his heart, seeing new threats in every shadow of thought. At last, it shall lead him and our land to ruin. Make thyself ready. Yes, listen, yes! This thou must do! Go and be tried by Griferis for worthiness to be Queen of our people."

After some weeks, Parthais stirred and asked where his daughter was. It was then that he was told that she had departed with Thurdun. Enraged, Parthais then sent out his warriors to find them, knowing that his children would defy his will.

By this time, the others Parthais had already sent had climbed the summit and found the gate thereupon. Taking their tools, they tried to destroy the gate. With their hammers and their chains they tried to crack the rock and pull it down, but it would not be moved or even scratched. So instead, as they descended, they made mischief with the paths and ways, and they worked and reworked the mountains and the passes. With chisel and pick, they made smooth ways rough and perilous, and they made easy ways to lead into dead-end walls looming high, or into sudden lance-bottomed pits. Delicate traps they laid all along the ways, even unto the precipice, sprung by the smallest movement to rain avalanche and to flood rocks upon any who might intrude, or to make the paths collapse into deep crevasses.

When at last they finished their work, they returned to Vanara and reported their work saying, "O, King! We have done as commanded and made a terrible place for any who may tread there. So dreadful and cunning are the obstacles we made, and so deadly are they, that even we who made them dare not disturb again those paths for fear of being crushed, or cut through by sharp spears, or dashed down into the deepest defiles."

"And what of Elrasil and his village?" Parthais asked of them. "Where is the sign I bid thee bring me?"

"King, we builders know not what became of them, for their place was abandoned and not even a mouse stirred there or anywhere in the hills and dales surrounding. The general that was sent and all his men even now seek them out, having vowed never to return to Vanara without completing thy command."

"And was there no sign of my children?"

"No, sire. None that we could read or discern."

Having news from messengers that Elrasil had escaped and all his village, too, Parthais grew in his rage, certain that it was the doings of his children, thwarting his will not only as their father, but doubly as their King. But he was also greatly disturbed by this news, and he went from his court and unto his high chambers and brooded there for many weeks while his kingdom fell into gloom and dread.

There was in those days a conjurer by the name of Tythos who practiced dark arts in the woods nearby to the southern mountains of Vanara. Tythos was one of the First Ones, as Parthais himself, and, it was said that he had even been a minion of Morgasir but had escaped Morgasir's doom when Beras destroyed his thralldoms. And, it was said, Tythos had since allied himself with Secundur, to be his servant. It was Tythos that King Parthais now called to his chambers.

"Summon thy master," Parthais ordered him. "For I wish to bestow a gift upon him."

Then Tythos went to the candle burning at the window of the chamber and with his hand he snuffed out the flame, saying, "As ye will it, my lord."

"I am here," said Secundur, wafting outward from the deep shadows of the chamber to stand, vague of shape, before Parthais. "I am here, as I have ever been. What have ye to say to me?"

"Take thee the lands of the north and west unto the place called Griferis," said Parthais. "Make therein thine own lands and spread there thine arts dark and foul, so that none living may pass through. Keep unto thyself any who venture there, and make it a place to be thine own."

Secundur laughed softly in Parthais's ear with grave-breath, cold and final, saying, "What would l have to do with that place? l, who may roam the earth wherever there be shadow or darkness? What more value to me would be the place ye speak of than any other?"

"None, save to defy Beras, whose gate is upon the high mountain there. And this gate was set forth to make his kings and his queens upon the earth and among the newcomers, Men, who now populate our eastern lands. ls spite's sake not enough for thee? l also give thee this: Go there and make a place of thine own desire, and l will send unto thee slaves from the desert, prisoners of my conquests. And l will provide to thee captives from amongst the Men to serve thee. Foul beast and lowly form thou canst fashion of them without reprisal, and, once upon every tenth winter of my rule, l shall send unto thee a prince and a princess of the high houses of my lands, fair and strong, to please and serve thee. Whilst ever l am upon the throne of Vanara, this pact l shall keep, so that none may be sent against thee, nor tread of my permission upon those lands."

To this Secundur agreed, and thus made a black pact with Parthais. And Secundur went immediately to those lands and set about his purpose. And there he yet abides, it is said, west and north of the lands of Vanara and west and south of the lands of Duinnor, in the unknown and forbidden places near the end of the earth.

But, unbeknownst to Parthais or any other in his court, Serith Ellyn did not go with Thurdun unto Elrasil's village, nor did she see or speak with any but her brother while they traveled. For when they left Vanara and fled to warn Elrasil, Serith Ellyn parted company before they came upon the village. With kiss and embrace, Thurdun bade farewell to his sister, and she to him, trusting in Beras to make their separate ways, Thurdun to rouse the people of Elrasil to flight, as Serith Ellyn climbed the heights to Griferis, to enter into the place of mystery.

Many, many years passed, and the rule of Parthais became ever more wicked and cruel. At the same time, his country was weakened by his severity and his mistrust of all around him. Oft it was that even those of high rank who met the displeasure of Parthais were never seen again. Thus high princes and princesses were taken away and given over to Secundur. Likewise, many prisoners, Men and Dragonkind and even Elifaen, were taken secretly away to that place.

And in the lands surrounding Griferis, a cruel and black kingdom arose, ruled by foul creatures, witches and goblins, and patrolled by vile warriors who lined the borders of those lands with the impaled bodies of their victims. That land came to be called Shatuum, and the little kingdom of Duinnor, which lost many of its settlements to the place, sent an army against it, but few returned to tell of the horrors they encountered. ln spite of Duinnor's entreaties, Parthais refused to join in the attack, heedless of the growing power that threatened from there. Pressed by the Dragonkind from the south and cut off from the northwest by Shatuum, Vanara suffered defeat after defeat, and many of the Firstborn who still lived were killed in useless battle. At last, when three hundred and thirty-one summers of the world had passed since Parthais ascended the throne of Cupeldain his father, and when Vanara teetered on the edge of collapse and complete ruin, a stranger appeared in his court. She was tall and beautiful and garbed in the dress of a powerful queen. When she was ushered before Parthais, and did not bow before him, his counselors were filled with fear and dismay, and the King was sorely offended.

"Why dost thou not bow before the sovereign?" one of the courtiers demanded.

"l bow before no sovereign but Aperion, true King of all Faere, whom Beras himself appointed, until the day that the King of Kings may come, whom also shall be appointed by Beras to rule over the earth as Aperion now does in the heavens."

Her words filled all who heard them with fear, all but Parthais, and he rose from his throne in a rage and took from his sword bearer his iron lance, and made to run it through the stranger. But she smote it away with a rod of wood which shattered the steel blade utterly and sent a bolt of bright lightning up his arm and into his heart. Parthais then fell to his knees, mortally wounded, but he did not yield. He took from his belt his dagger, but as he raised it against her, she struck him again about the wrist so that the wooden rod transformed, likened unto a serpent, and it twisted about his wrist and held it fast. Then were the eyes of Parthais opened, and he saw that it was his own daughter, Serith Ellyn, who had returned and who smote him.

"Daughter!" he groaned, struggling to free his hand from the wooden rod about his wrist that Serith Ellyn held.

"Call me not daughter," she cried. "Call me Retribution! My house thou hast made into a shameful place. My legacy thou hast poisoned by thy lust. My people thou hast misused, cheated, and murdered. Thou hast squandered their goodwill. Thou hast turned their goodly hearts dark with thy deeds of avarice, and thou hast weakened the realm by thine injustice and by foul deceits. It was their woe that called me forth, they who yearn for relief, who have cried out for deliverance from thy cruelty. And it was they who, in union with the Newcomers of the east and with the Kingdom of Duinnor, and that of Glareth, have banded together to oppose thee. This night, thy kingdom is overthrown, the throne of Vanara I claim for its people and in the name of Beras!"

Serith Ellyn then released Parthais from her grip, and with her sword she struck his head from his body. At that moment, the windows of the Palace blew outward, and every shadow fled the place, and all the candles and lamp-flames leapt upward and burned once again with clear bright light which filled the halls and every room and every tower. Those with her, fell warriors of Thurdun and many of the race of Men, and many, too, of the people of Elrasil, laid hands on the supporters of Parthais and slew them. Then Serith Ellyn ordered the body of Parthais her father and the bodies of his chief generals and counselors to be burned. Their bones and ashes she made to be cast with mortar into hard stone, and these stones were laid on the walks of the White Palace so that all who came and went would trod upon them. She met with all the people and begged their consent to continue the rule of Fairlinden over Vanara, and they rejoiced at her return and gladly confirmed her as Queen. Without delay, she set about to right the many wrongs of Parthais, to make compensation to those he made to suffer, and to punish those that Parthais had made lords of terror and earls of fraud. Yet so deep was the hurt and evil that Parthais fell into, that even Serith Ellyn, with all her power and grace, could not repair the deep wounds that he made in the world, nor could she confront Shatuum, the ultimate expression of her father's folly.

And that was how Griferis was found and then lost to the world, and how the place named Shatuum came to be a land of shadow. And all the powers of Serith Ellyn could not lift from that place the darkness and terror that had settled upon it. To this day, it is a forbidden land from which no wanderer has ever emerged. And from that place come loathsome beings, demons and witches, worms and warlocks, corrupted creatures that once were wolves or lions, and many others, some on four legs and some on two. Some were once living things, but they are now no longer living, yet neither are they dead. And it is said that Secundur abides patiently there, growing his dark thralldom, and sending his spies and provocateurs out from Shatuum into the bright world to test it, to measure it, or to prepare his sullen design.

This, then, concludes the last book of Nimwill, Scribe to King Parthais, a witness to these things, faithfully recording all that was, as it was.

The End

The House of Fairmyrtle
Pyros and Duiniece

Much of the following comes from the journals and diaries of Nianan who wrote down much of what her mother Byrniece told her. In the Second Age, long after her death, a collection of Nianan's personal papers were brought out of Tracia and taken to Vanara by Devan Seafar. The writings of Nianan, along with many other works relating to the House of Fairmyrtle, were later donated to Vanara's Royal Archives by Devan Seafar's descendant, Lord Brandis Seafar, who became Regent and Chancellor of Vanara under Queen Serith Ellyn. The following is based upon that collection of papers, which includes Devan Seafar's own notes pertaining to the House of Fairmyrtle.

Note: The Common Speech pronunciation and meaning of primary names is as follows:

Pyros -- PI rose (meaning fire-maker)
Duiniece -- do in ICY (icy river)
Byrniece -- burn ICY (fire and ice)
Nianan -- NI annan (meaning unknown)

Pyros was a Firstborn, conceived of the spirit of fire. His eyes were bright amber, his hair red and long, and his skin orange. During the Time Before Time, he loved to fly through the plains, and so enraptured with him were the tall blades of grass that they spontaneously burst into flame in the wake of his passage. At first the other Faerekind feared him and were angry at the quick destruction that he brought upon the grasslands and woodlands. Aperion laughed, saying that Pyros only released from those trees what was already there, giving the light and heat they borrowed from Sir Sun back into the air. But Pyros knew that he should not be too playful, for he loved his fellow Faerekind and would not willingly hurt them or the things they cared about.

When came the Fall, he was far away in the south deserts, cavorting with an old dragon that lived there, playing catch with balls of fire that they tossed back and forth to one another. He did not wish to give up the world, and so when Aperion took away his faithful host, the wings of Pyros turned to ash, and he fell to earth.

Like all Elifaen, he struggled to survive, and he seemed to suffer more from cold than others of his kind did. But, before the First Tongue faded from him, he listened carefully to dry sticks when they told him how to rub them together to make fire. And he heard the brittle leaves of autumn say how sparks from flint and steel would make them burn. And so Pyros became the Firemaker, and many Elifaen came to him, for he was so skilled that he could make fire from wet twigs and conjure it from flint and steel. Pyros did not guard his methods, and went widely about trading his knowledge for food and clothing for his friends, showing the Elifaen how to make fire-tools, and teaching everyone who wished to know all about fire-making.

One winter day, in the forests of the high Carthanes, Pyros walked along the banks of an ice-crusted stream, gathering flint as he went. Some he picked up and examined only to toss away, while others he put into his shoulder bag. He did this carefully, taking his time to find those best suited to his purpose.

"Why do you pick and choose your rocks so carefully when there are so many stones along the banks of my stream?" a gentle voice asked.

Startled, Pyros turned and looked around, but saw no one there.

"Because," he said, still looking for the source of the voice, "the ones I choose are much to my liking."

"Oh? But they are coarse and sharp, broken and jagged. Why do you pick those when there are so many beautiful and smooth ones for the taking?"

"Because, though rough in form, from them I may make fire and warmth."

"Oh? What is fire? And what is warmth?"

"Well," said Pyros. "If you show yourself to me, I will show you what fire is, and what warmth is, too."

Out of the middle of the stream nearby to Pyros rose a beautiful nymph. Her hair was long and blue-white, and her skin and eyes, too, and she was flecked with crystals of ice all over her naked form. Pyros was immediately taken by her beauty, and as she stepped up onto the bank beside him, he took off his cloak to put around her.

"Why do you do this?" she asked, touching the fur of the coat and letting it remain loose over her shoulders, as if she did not know what it was. "What is this that you put over me?"

"It is my coat. Do you not feel the cold?"

"If I knew what it was, perhaps I could tell you whether I felt it."

Pyros shook his head in wonder as her eyes searched his.

"I have watched people," she said, "who come to drink from the flowing water or who take fish from it. But I have never seen one like you with your red hair and your orange skin. And your eyes are like the sun's color upon the honey that bees make."

"I am Pyros, of the Fallen Ones. And I have never seen anyone like you," said Pyros. "Your hair is like bright moonlight upon snow, and your eyes like the high blue peak on yon distant mountain, and your skin is like the glittering sun on the morning frost."

"I am Duiniece, of the Fallen Ones," said the nymph. "What have you to show me about the rocks that you gather?"

"Come and see."

Pyros went to the nearby brush, pulled away many dead twigs, and broke them into a small pile on the ground. He took some thin bark from a myrtle, and he crumbled and tore it into a fine fluffy wad. Duiniece watched with interest as Pyros took from his bag a piece of steel that was part of an old broken sword. He picked up a rock, examined it, and crouched over the little pile that he had made, glancing up at Duiniece to see that she was watching.

It took Pyros only two strikes of the flint before a spark landed where he intended, and he blew upon it until smoke appeared and bright orange light glowed. Duiniece stepped back cautiously.

"Have no fear," said Pyros. "I will not let it harm you."

Then, blowing gently, he coaxed the flame into the twigs and soon had a little fire crackling.

Duiniece gazed with fascination at the fire, and Pyros stood, offering his hand.

"Come near," he said.

Her hand was cold and trembling when she took his, and he led her closer to the fire.

"Put out your hands, like this," he instructed, crouching and holding out his palms toward the fire. When she did as he did, her eyes grew wide with wonder, glancing at Pyros from time to time.

"It is a child of the sun," she said. "It has light and feels as the sun does in summer!"

"It is called fire," said Pyros. "And what you feel is called warmth. Truly you do not know these things?"

She shook her head, holding her hands closer and closer to the fire as the flecks of ice on her skin turned to water and dripped away. Pyros reached out and took her wrists, gently pulling her hands away.

"Do not reach too close," he said. "Or else you will feel great pain from its power, or even die from it."

"Is it a beast?" she asked. "Like the bear or the lion? It eats away the twigs and sticks."

"It is like a beast, yes," he answered. "But it lives only to eat, and when it has consumed its meal, it dies away. See?"

Indeed, the little fire had run its course and now flickered to nothing but smoke. Duiniece waved her hand in front of her wrinkled nose.

"It belches constantly," said Pyros, "and even afterwards, when it is gone, its meal still smells of its belch."

"Oh, how marvelous!" she laughed. "I have never seen or felt the like. And it is from the stones that you make the fire-beast come?"

"The stones are one way to make it come. There are other ways."

She took his arm and looked at him with excitement.

"Make it come again!"

And that was how Pyros and Duiniece met. So different from one another they were, but they soon fell in love. Years later, when the two were leaders of a great number of Elifaen, they took the name of the little tree from which Pyros stripped bark, calling themselves the House of Fairmyrtle. Together, Pyros and Duiniece joined their people together as Fairmyrtle, and with her knowledge of streams and rivers, she showed them how to catch fish and how to collect mussels to eat. With the fire that Pyros made, they learned to cook and to keep warm and to keep away the wild animals that hunted them. Life was still very difficult, and many of their people were killed by lions, bears, and other animals that they once lived with in peace. They gathered around their fires in their longhouses and talked about the time when they all had wings, and they shared stories and sang songs about those days and about their regret for not going with Aperion when he called to them. And they worked very hard to survive and to make their lives better. They learned to hunt and to plant crops. And Pyros traveled throughout the world, teaching fire-making and bringing back home with him tools and new knowledge. After many years, the House of Fairmyrtle was numbered in the thousands.

Then Aperion called again, and Pyros was willing to his call and was transported to high Mount Cassos. When he returned, he showed Duiniece his Seven gold-circled ruby objects.

"This is our way out from our toil and our strife," Pyros said to her.

"Perhaps, in Aperion's home, things are as they once were here," said Duiniece, "and our lost kin still have their wings."

"And, perhaps," said Pyros, "if we go there, our wings will be restored to us."

"Then we must make it so!"

But it was not so easy. When Pyros and Duiniece showed the Bloodcoins to their people, and explained about them, most were happy that some end to their plight might be near. A celebration took place, and all the old stories were retold, and all the old songs were sung, but now it was all with joy and thankfulness. The days and weeks following were filled with happiness and anticipation, so much so that they let their crops go ungathered and their fishnets go unused.

But there were others of their people who were wary. They loved their fields and forests, their streams and rivers, and had no wish to be parted from them, even though life was hard. It was to these that Secundur came, and in the shadows of the darkest reaches of the forest, he whispered doubt into their ears. He told them that Aperion's gift, the seven objects given to Pyros, was only another way to punish them. Secundur said that his teacher, Morgasir, had warned him about Aperion before Morgasir was destroyed. And, he said, the Dragonkind, who marauded and murdered, were Aperion's servants, sent to do harm to their people.

"Do not trust too much in Pyros and Duiniece," Secundur softly spoke to one of the Elifaen. To another he said, "Those things that Aperion gave will be the undoing of your kin."

To some of them, Secundur said, "Come with me, and I will show you how to speak to the things of the world once more. I will teach you, as I was taught, how to say words to make fire, how to be powerful like the animals, and how to take life's power from others."

This Secundur did amongst Fairmyrtle just as he did all over the earth, spreading lies and deceit, and luring away many. Those that followed him from the lands of Fairmyrtle and from other lands went into Secundur's secret places, dark and lightless, where he poisoned them with words so that they were no longer Elifaen. He filled them with lust for blood and violence, and took from them their offspring to feed upon gore and lies, until some became witches and others became lesser-demons.

While Secundur did these things, the people of Fairmyrtle slowly realized their mistake in thinking they might soon leave the earth and for putting off their chores; they would not be rejoining Aperion so very soon, and now they were weak and hungry. Pyros traveled to the west, seeking out others of the High Houses, to ask them how to use the Forty-Nine. But when he arrived in Vanara, he found turmoil. There the Elifaen were fighting amongst one another as much as against the Dragonkind who terrorized the western lands. He failed to find Cupeldain, and went to look for Katrina, but could not find her either. At last, hearing that Pyros went from place to place in Vanara, Lyrium sought him out. But what she had to say was a final blow to Pyros, for she told him how most of the others who led High Houses prized their Seven only as symbols of power, and had no desire to leave the earth.

"I see terrible things in store for us," she told him. "So go back to your people, and strive to live in peace as we in Vanara seem unable to do. I am sorry."

Disheartened, Pyros returned to his lands some months later, and found his people torn by feuds that had arisen in his absence. Some, it seemed, did not care that Duiniece had demanded that they resume their work. She and those friendly to her labored long to fish and to hunt for food. They did much to prepare the longhouses for winter, and to smoke meat and lay aside grain. But others continued to languish in renewed despair, thinking it all a waste. Entire groups leapt together, hand in hand, from cliffs to bring a swift end to their melancholy hearts, whilst others laid themselves down before lions.

Pyros was shocked and outraged at this conduct, yet the news he brought home with him did little to improve matters. Duiniece begged him to come away with her, to forsake everyone for faraway woods and streams, but he would not. He went about from family to family to encourage them not to give up, but to continue their labors, and to bear up to their condition, whether it may last a year or a thousand years. But it was to little avail. Winter was harsh, and many wasted away. Suicides were an epidemic until, at last, Pyros called all the people of Fairmyrtle together at a single great gathering. Knowing what he planned, Duiniece and others took aside the children so that only the adults of the people were gathered.

"Decide," Pyros said to them. "Those of you who wish to continue in life, stand with me. Those of you who wish for it to end, stand yonder. Decide now and forever! But be warned: should you stand with me as the House of Fairmyrtle, you shall not be a burden to others. You shall be loved and cherished. We will stand together to protect one another, and to help each other. As for the rest of you, stand yonder. But if you love your children and wish to remain with them, and are willing to work for them and to protect them, come hither and stand with me."

Even Pyros was surprised and dismayed at how many of his people stood apart and, by doing so, thus expressed their wish to end their lives. He looked at the great circle before him, then, when Duiniece came to his side and clutched his arm, he stared at her.

"Is it right? Can it be so many?" Pyros was heard to mutter. He looked around at the few who stood with him, many of them sobbing, and then he turned back to gaze at those who stood apart as tears now streamed down his own face. But he saw that they were decided, and he knew, for the sake of those who wished to carry on, what he must do. But he gave them one last chance.

"If not for your children, and for the friends and loved ones that stand with me here," he asked, "then what may entice you to change your minds?"

Only one spoke back to Pyros, saying, "If any could entice us, it would have been Secundur, who has lured away so many of our people. We would not go with him, but we no longer love this world. If it be in your means, then end us. For if we had courage enough we would have gone to the cliffs or to the lions as so many others have done."

Pyros nodded, and Duiniece clutched his arm all the harder. He used the last memory of the First Tongue left to him, lifted his face to the starry sky, and spoke.

"Be it as you wish!"

A column of blinding yellow light shot up from the ground beneath the crowd's feet and quickly ascended. Then it was gone, and where before the crowd had stood, now their figures glowed like embers, slowly going from yellow to red and then to black.

"It is done!" cried Pyros. "And we shall never again be happy."

Then he groaned and fell to his knees, covering his eyes with his hands as those left with him sobbed and wailed in grief.

Indeed, they were not a happy people. That very night, Secundur, who watched from the shadows and had ducked behind a rock when the bright light shot skyward, took advantage of their grief. By morning, new divisions were made, and some called Pyros a murderer. But Duiniece saw what had been done to her husband, for his heart was broken, and she berated those who criticized Pyros for doing what he thought was necessary for the survival of those who remained.

"Had you done more," she said, "things would not have come to such a pass. Blame not Pyros, who only granted them their wish. Blame yourselves for promoting that wish in them!"

At first, her cold words cowered them. But as the years passed, and Fairmyrtle began to recover, Pyros had little to say to those who questioned him. From time to time, someone who was outspoken against Pyros would disappear from their lands, with no trace to be found of them. Each time, just before the disappearance, they would have words with Duiniece, and she would conclude, in her icy manner, "If you do not love these lands, go from them. And good riddance!"

After a time, people began to whisper that Duiniece had something to do with the disappearances.

One day, a friend of Pyros came to bring him some blueberries he had picked. This friend rarely said anything at all, preferring to be silent. But this day he asked Pyros where Duiniece was.

"She bathes in the cold waterfall," said Pyros, "as she always does at this hour of the day. Why do you ask?"

"Because I wish to speak, but I do not wish for my words to fall upon any ears but your own."

"Speak, then."

"Does Duiniece speak truthfully to you in all things?"

"Yes. In all things, she does."

"And if she wishes not to speak to you, may she refuse to answer you?"

"She may refuse, if she wishes to. But she never has before."

"Then ask her what became of young Halaborn, whose parents went up in fire and whose forms still stand as hardened stone in that clearing along with the others who wished to depart."

"Halaborn? He dislikes me, I know. But I have not seen him for several days. How would Duiniece know what became of him?"

"It is for her to say, my lord. If she will do so. But if she will not, then ask where she was this morning before dawn, and why she left your bed."

"Are you impertinent?"

"No, my lord. I am a witness."

These last words sent chills down the spine of Pyros.

"I shall do as you say, if I must," he said.

"I do not say that you must, my lord. Only that you should."

And so, when Duiniece returned, Pyros privately questioned her on the whereabouts of Halaborn.

"Why should you ask?" responded Duiniece, her wet hair suddenly growing frosty, though it was summertime. "And how would I know where he is?"

"Then, if you will not say that, tell me where you went this morning before dawn?"

"I was restless, so I walked out through the woods and down to the stream," she told him as her skin glittered and cracked with frost.

While Duiniece turned cold, Pyros grew hot, and his eyes burned with impatience as his skin glowed. Then, just as he was about to lay his hands upon her, a rider came galloping into the village upon a buckmarl. Hearing the commotion of his arrival, Pyros left and went outside where he saw, dismounting, a fair Elifaen wearing bright armor.

"I come seeking Pyros," he cried out to the astonished people around.

"I am he," said Pyros, still so full of anger at his wife that he did not fear the warrior.

"I am Heneil, son of Silmain," said the warrior, bowing.

"Silmain? He who calls himself King of Vanara?"

"That is so, my lord. I come with tidings from my father. He wishes for each of the Seven High Houses to send their chief, and to gather together the Forty-Nine Keys from Aperion and to use them for the purpose of their making."

Duiniece, relieved at the interruption, was nonetheless as surprised and filled with disbelief as Pyros and everyone else who heard Heneil's words.

"Silmain, King, begs that you come away to Linlally, in Vanara, and to bring with you those Seven given to you in hopes of ending our strife on earth. Will you come?"

Without hesitating, Pyros said, "With gladness, I shall certainly come!"

Heneil was given a great welcome and a feast was prepared in his honor. At the feast, Heneil explained that some of the other High Houses must be convinced, but that Silmain hoped it could be done. This dampened everyone's spirits somewhat, but it was still with a sense of hope that, the next day, Pyros prepared for his departure. Turning to his wife, he kissed her.

"I do not wish for strife between us," he said to her. "But do nothing in my name that is not just, as I would see it to be just. Keep our people safe, and yourself, too. I love you above all others."

"I love you, too, my husband," said Duiniece. "And if I did wrong, it was with love for you in my heart. Keep safe, and be swift. I hope and pray for the best and every success. But if all goes against you, pray return with all haste. Here I shall be waiting for you. And, by the time you return, your child shall await also."

"A child? After all these years?"

"Yes, my husband. And it has been foretold to me that, by spring, you shall have a daughter."

"I am overjoyed!"

They kissed and hugged, and it was only the hope of fulfilling Aperion's charge that Pyros was able to tear himself away.

It was a long journey from the Carthanes in the east to Linlally in the west. And it would be years of fruitless debate. All during these years, messengers went back and forth between Pyros and Duiniece. He asked after his daughter, whom they called Byrniece, and after the welfare of Fairmyrtle. She inquired about the debates, and asked why it was taking so long. When he told her, she encouraged him to keep trying to convince Cupeldain and the others who resisted. Year after year passed, with progress and setbacks, over and again. Until, after twelve long years, Pyros sent word to Duiniece that he had failed, and that he was coming home at last, for he could no longer bear to be parted from his wife, and he yearned to greet the little girl who was his daughter.

Much had changed upon his return. Gone were many of the woods, replaced by fields and vineyards, and sheep grazed where deer once browsed the wildwood. Gone, too, were the wooden longhouses, and in their place stood stone homes. There were foundries smelting ore for iron and precious metals, and villages where jewels were mined. Horses now were tamed and hitched to wagons and ploughs, and many Elifaen rode them instead of buckmarls. Full of wonder, and somewhat dismayed at the changes he saw, Pyros was soon met by Duiniece herself, riding a snow-white horse at the head of a grand party of finely dressed Elifaen, a young girl riding at her side. It was a great homecoming, and Pyros lavished gifts that he had obtained in Vanara upon his daughter and upon his wife—jewels, and trinkets, and fine cloth for their gowns. And he brought many books and scrolls for his people, too, and, of course, his Seven that he had taken all the way to Vanara and back. When he came to the castle that was built for him by Duiniece, and was welcomed by a great crowd of onlookers, he held his Seven aloft for all to see.

"I and the others of the High Houses have failed," he cried out. "And thus all of our people throughout the world are failed."

The crowd went silent at his words, not knowing how to respond. But so happy was Pyros to be home amongst them, that he spoke again.

"But surely Fairmyrtle is the greatest of all of the High Houses. Out of such great struggles, look at what you have done. How well you look, how handsome and beautiful! How lovely are the vineyards and orchards that I have seen, and how fine your clothes. I am proud of you, and I now look forward to working with you at whatever labors need doing! Surely there is no fairer land than this, and no fairer people."

"Hail, King Pyros!" proclaimed the crowd enthusiastically. "Hail, Queen Duiniece!"

Pyros was taken aback at the declarations, having no notion of the extent of change in his absence. But over the course of the next few months, he learned. As he did so, he grew ever more unhappy. But he did not speak against the changes, for he did not understand them. Instead, while Duiniece and her ministers made their laws and enforced them, Pyros withdrew. He spent more and more time with his daughter, and less and less with his wife.

"You cannot appear uncaring before your people," Duiniece said to him one night. "You should make more appearances in court, and treat kindly the lords of our land who come to see us."

"I remember when there were no lords of our land," Pyros said. "I saw too many lords and ladies in the court of Silmain to have much liking for them, or much trust in them."

On another night, Pyros ventured to Duiniece, "Do you not wish that we could return to that mountain stream where we met? I could show you fire, all over again. And we could roast nuts for Byrniece to eat whilst we laugh and splash cold water at each other."

"I care not to go back there," Duiniece said. "I am much changed from then, and I like these warm blankets too much."

And so it went. The years passed. Nothing that one had to say seemed to satisfy the other, and neither could prompt the other to their own way of thinking. They did not argue or fight. But, as things may sometimes happen, Pyros grew cool toward his people, whilst Duiniece grew hot-tempered. And Byrniece, living under the same roof as such profound unhappiness, grew ever more unhappy herself with each passing day, even as she grew more beautiful.

Meanwhile, the lands of Fairmyrtle also suffered decline. Crops failed, game disappeared, and the ore and precious minerals ran out. More and more people left the lands to travel south and north and west. Others stole away to join those living along the coasts. Duiniece and Pyros worried a great deal about their dwindling population. But there was little they could do to prevent people from leaving, short of making slaves of them, and that was not something that they even contemplated. Byrniece grew ever restless, too, but her restlessness caused her to turn inward rather than seek happier lands. She found no satisfying suitor, and seemed to care little for her appearance, going about her home barefooted and in her sleeping gown. She went forth less often from the castle of her parents, choosing instead to spend her time at her window, staring out over the lands as the forests took back the vineyards, and the pastures grew over with briars.

From time to time, passing travelers brought news of the world outside their lands. And so they learned of the death of Silmain, and of the terrible wars with the Dragonkind that persisted. They learned how Cupeldain became the King of Vanara, and how he renewed the wars with the Dragonkind. Many, many years passed. News did not come often, but when it did, it was mostly about wars and earthquakes and other terrible things happening in the west.

Then came Heneil once again, this time with word that Cupeldain would seek to do what Silmain had failed to do. He gave to Pyros a scroll, written in Cupeldain's own hand. Cupeldain wrote that, like Silmain before him, he had grown weary of strife and longed to make his peace with Aperion by returning to him, by bringing together all of the Forty-Nine Bloodcoins and opening the Nimbus Illuminas for all Elifaen. Pyros read the scroll aloud to Duiniece and Byrniece, and to many courtiers who received Heneil. The court was silent and thoughtful, and considered the message.

"Tell us, then," said Pyros to Heneil, "how it is with the other High Houses. What prospects are there to bring about the Nimbus Illuminas?"

"Forsooth, Lord Pyros, I cannot say," Heneil bowed. "When my father failed, many were as disappointed as you. King Cupeldain's House of Fairlinden is resolved to try again, though. Fairfir and Fairmaple stand with him, as does, I think, Faircedar. Fairbirch and Fairwillow, though, are likely opposed. But Cupeldain hopes that Fairmyrtle may help convince them."

Pyros nodded.

"Then what say you, my wife?" Pyros asked Duiniece. "How does your heart feel on this matter? Should I go with Heneil once again to Vanara?"

"My husband, I cannot say," answered Duiniece. "I love my mountains and my streams, and I love the winter's cold. And I have fallen in love with warmth, too, as when you first showed it to me, and am fond of summertime. Before, when Silmain called, I thought things might be as they were before we lost our wings. But now I wonder whether it is a good thing to wish for. Is there winter snow in Aperion's abode? And icy streams for me to swim in? Are there grapes on summer hills such as we have in our lands, and good mead to enjoy? My heart is in the past, but also here. I do not know, for truth, in which place my heart more strongly rests or yearns for."

"If I may," Heneil bowed again, addressing Duiniece. "Perhaps you would consider coming to Linlally with your husband. Your words echo those of others, and the thoughts of many. Perhaps you could put those questions of your heart before the High Houses and thus have it openly discussed. Should the Nimbus Illuminas open a way from this earth, perhaps not all will be required to go away, but only those who strongly desire it. But if the way be not opened, then all must remain."

"I think it is a good thing that Lord Heneil suggests," said Pyros. "Would you then come with me?"

"Yes, my husband," Duiniece said. "But I have no wish to be away from our lands very long. If it is not decided very quickly, one way or the other, I will not tarry in Vanara."

"And, then, nor shall I," agreed Pyros. "You have your answer, Lord Heneil. We shall depart within the fortnight."

All who know the tale of Cupeldain also know what happened. The Seven High Houses gathered again in the beautiful palace of Linlally, but they could reach no decision. As autumn reached into winter, Secundur found willing ears to his rumors and his accusations. Duiniece and Pyros were unwilling to listen to him, for they suspected him of taking many of their people away from their lands. But they argued for using the Bloodcoins to open the Nimbus Illuminas, along with all but Ormace of Fairbirch and Therona of Fairwillow. Those two were convinced that if the Nimbus Illuminas was opened, all Elifaen would be forced to leave the world. And they were taken in by Secundur's lies, and accused the other High Houses of having the power to use only Seven of the Forty-Nine without the consent of the others. All knew this was untrue, but it came to pass that Ormace threatened to destroy his Seven unless all were redistributed so that all High Houses would have a share of those belonging to the others. When this was done, the gathering broke up, and Pyros and Duiniece departed for home. Duiniece sought to console her husband, but she, too, was depressed at the outcome. She was also wary, having seen Vanara's might and power, and she wondered how their little land would fare should the western Elifaen come east in force.

When they arrived back in the lands of Fairmyrtle, they found that Byrniece, in their absence, had managed things with ease, overseeing the people of Fairmyrtle with kindness and with an evenhanded approach to settling the few disputes that had arisen. But there was no ignoring that the lands were in decline, and to Duiniece, the House of Fairmyrtle seemed a weak and unaccomplished people compared to the Vanarans.

Many, many years passed, and each day seemed to Pyros to be longer than the day before. News came about Princess Islindia and how she was kidnapped by Secundur and how, when Secundur was thwarted, he blighted her splendid forest. Then came word that Ormace and his House of Fairbirch was destroyed, and his Seven Bloodcoins were lost. This news seemed to affect Duiniece not at all, but Pyros was distraught for months.

Then, once again, their people began to disappear. At first it was only a horse or a buckmarl that went missing. But then it was a farmer, or a child, or a blacksmith. Odd things were heard at night, in the woods and hills. And from the walls of their castle, Pyros and Duiniece saw strange lights within the encroaching forest. Bones were found. Human bones, with every appearance of having been cooked.

Witches were in the lands. They were Secundur's pupils, bred and nurtured by him for centuries in dark lairs all over the world. Then, to see what they might do, he released them all. It was thus the year 880 of the First Age when they crawled up out of the ground. With their vile lusts and insatiable appetites, they began their work.

No one really knew what these creatures were, or what to do about them, for nothing like them had ever been seen before. In some parts of the world, the witches served demons, capturing prisoners for the delight of their masters. But in the lands of Fairmyrtle, they answered only to their own dark will.

Pyros first saw one darting through a shady glade while he gathered blackberries at its edge, and he was filled with an instinctive horror as it bore down with its crooked gait on a hapless farmer who was passing from one field to another. Before Pyros could react or call out, the creature flew right through the poor man's chest. The farmer writhed in agony as the witch then devoured his face. Pyros turned and ran in terror as day sank into night. At first his only thought was to get to his wife and daughter, but as he fled home, he saw others of his people, and he began shouting, "Go inside! Close your windows and lock your doors! We are attacked!"

When he came to the base of the hill on which his castle stood, he slowed not at all, but he saw, climbing up the side of his stronghold, a wispy figure, moving like a gauzy spider. He flew inside, taking for the first time ever a sword into his hands, and he burst into his daughter's room just as the witch entered her window. The screams of Byrniece brought Duiniece running as Pyros struck at the creature. But, laughing hideously, the witch ran across the ceiling out of his reach, her stench filling the room. Pyros threw the sword at her, but it only lodged harmlessly into a beam. Duiniece pulled Byrniece away as Pyros picked up a poker from the fireplace and threw it, too, this time striking the witch so hard that she fell to the floor. Then she turned on him, her stance slanting. Her jaw, filled with jagged teeth like an animal, drooped down against her chest as she grinned.

"Ye, Pyros, must hae better 'an iron again me. For I knowest thee well, ye wha had once the pire o' flame!"

"And still do!" Pyros answered as the creature stepped closer and reached out for him, laughing as she came. Summoning all his mental might, he closed his eyes and spoke ancient words as he held up his hands, palms toward himself. He smiled and opened his eyes; the witch was now within reach of him. His hands burst into flames, and he grabbed hers. She recoiled, screaming as the flames raced across her. Byrniece buried her head on her mother's shoulder, but Duiniece immediately saw that something was terribly wrong. Pyros staggered backwards, releasing the witch, his hands smoking. The witch, meanwhile, giggled.

"Wae day ye say at that, great laird Pyros. Knowest ye not that I eat fiyer?"

Pushing Byrniece safely away, Duiniece leapt forward.

"Then eat this, bitch!"

She grabbed the creature's shoulders and immediately jets of sizzling steam shot out from every part of the witch. She writhed and squirmed, turning around to try to bite and scratch Duiniece, but Duiniece held her firmly. Suddenly, the witch stopped squirming, her coal-black eyes wide and glazed. There was a cracking sound, the fire went out from the witch's clothes, then the steam also halted. A moment later, the creature was completely frozen, from her matted hair to her clawed feet, her crooked, talon-tipped fingers still clawing the air. Duiniece pulled away, her own hands now smoking, and shoved the witch over to shatter into scores of icy chunks that scattered and slid across the floor. Duiniece hurried to Pyros, whose hands were terribly burned and blistered.

"Oh my dear Pyros!" she said, pulling him down to sit on the floor as she knelt and took his hands and placed them on her cold breasts. Byrniece, who was crying, came to kneel next to them, too upset for words.

"Oh, my love, my love!" Duiniece kept repeating, her tears rolling down like sleet from her eyes.

"You still love me?" he asked through his pain.

"Oh, yes! Oh, yes, I do! Oh!"

She kissed his lips, hot and cold together, and Byrniece put her arms around her parents as they all wept. After a long while, Pyros shook his head.

"I'm afraid you cannot save my hands," he said. "And I fear I have taken some fiery poison in."

"Hush, hush! Do not say that!"

"I am burning, do you not feel it? Even your loving touch cannot stop it. You must take the Bloodcoins and flee these lands. They are no longer safe if there are any other creatures such as that one. Take Byrniece and go, I beg you! Leave me and go! I cannot fight the flames that grow within me much longer. Oh, my love, my beautiful nymph! Byrniece, take your mother away. Can you not see?"

Indeed, Pyros was glowing, and he was now too hot for his daughter to touch, though Duiniece still held his hands against her. Her tears bounced down from her cheeks and tapped on the floor as her daughter pulled at her.

"Mother, Mother!" Byrniece cried out. "He is leaving us!"

"Go quickly!" cried out Pyros, his skin now shining, and his clothes beginning to smoke.

"No!" wailed Duiniece. But Byrniece was Elifaen, too, and pulled with strength that she did not know she had. She dragged her screaming mother away, going first to her parents' room to fetch the sack of Bloodcoins, holding onto her mother to prevent her from going back to Pyros. She took Duiniece up into her arms and fled down the stairs and out through the courtyard. Hearing a tremendous crack, she turned at the gate of the castle and looked back just as bright orange flames burst through her high bedroom windows and engulfed the castle.

Byrniece, carrying her mother, the both of them crying as they went, fled and fled, not knowing which way to go, until at last they arrived at a stone keep manned by some of their most loyal people. The doors had been buttressed and barricaded from within, and it took some doing to get them opened. Once inside, the men and women of the keep closed the heavy doors once again, and turned to the weeping wife and daughter of Pyros. Through their sobs, they told what had happened, and the Elifaen of the keep told them that they, too, had seen terrible and horrible creatures, and that they took refuge within the keep.

It was a terrible night of sadness and anxiety. Byrniece saw, though, that her mother slowly became stern of face, and took to pacing back and forth within the stronghold, sometimes going to the top to stand with the archers and others who stood watch. They heard awful screams and other noises coming out of the darkness from the nearby village, and they saw the red glow of the burning castle in the distance. They stood ready to let in any who came seeking refuge, but none came. At dawn, Duiniece ordered that they go forth together, well armed, to see what they could see, and to find others who had survived the night. This they did, and they found a few others of Fairmyrtle. But they also discovered smoking holes in the ground that emitted a putrid stench.

"It must be from these places that the creatures came," said Byrniece.

Late in the day, they topped a hill from where they could gaze across the valleys and mountains of their lands, and could see the long shadows of the peaks reaching out. They saw sooty trails of smoke, such as they had seen coming from the holes in the ground. The trails they saw counted in the dozens, rising thin into the summer sky. It was then that Duiniece turned to the others.

"You must leave these lands," she said to the hundred or so men and women with them. "My daughter is now leader of the House of Fairmyrtle, and she has the objects that were given to my husband by Aperion, and to her you must swear allegiance. No, daughter. Do not argue. Honor me by your obedience. These lands are blighted, and if they can poison your father, who was strong, unto death, surely they will do worse to those who stay here."

"But what do you intend? Why do you stay?" Byrniece asked. "And, besides, where should we go to?"

"Go east and perhaps south, into the flatter lands near the sea. Perhaps there you will find refuge amongst the Elifaen of the pine forests or the marshland Elifaen, or those who live upon the shore of the world. I shall stay and see to it that these creatures do not pursue you."

As Duiniece spoke, a cold mist formed around her, and flowed down along the ground like a gray cloak. Her daughter and all of the others of Fairmyrtle stepped away from her as the ground that Duiniece stood upon cracked and crackled, and hoarfrost formed on the grass at her feet.

"Do not hug me!" she said to Byrniece. "Though I long to embrace you, I cannot restrain my cold resolve. Go quickly!"

They did as Duiniece said, and ordered themselves to march quickly through the night. Byrniece took a sword and led the way south and east along well-worn paths. They tarried not at village or farmhouse except to take lamps and torches and to compel anyone they came upon to flee with them. Byrniece led them on quickly, and they spoke little, going as swiftly as they possibly could through the mountains. When dawn came, they were many leagues away, and they climbed up to a place on a high ridge above part of the narrow path they had followed, overlooking the place that would later be called the Narrows. They gathered, catching their breath at what they saw behind them. Leagues away, the forests of the Carthanes were white with ice and snow, though it was still summertime. Byrniece and those with her watched for a long while as the freezing mist spread slowly, far and near. They could even hear the distant crack and crumble of trees as the forest was torn apart by spreading ice. When they realized the noise and white blanket was coming closer and closer, they turned and hurried southward.

That summer, a great swath of the Carthanes was covered with killing frost and ice, from the plains nearby to Mount Halfis, northward for many leagues, eastward halfway to Lake Halgaeth, and southward into the northern range that would later be called the Thunder Mountains. Only the strongest trees survived, only the deepest burrowing creatures, or those that could outrun the ice or fly away. It remained uninhabitable, devoid of life, throughout the summer, autumn, and winter. And when spring came, the frost melted, the ice subsided, choking the streams and rivers with such water that the land was reformed. Slowly, the forest returned. Within only a few years, the land was wild once more, teeming with woodland life, and very little evidence remained of the people who had once called it their home. But Duiniece was never again to be seen or heard of.

Of Byrniece and her people who fled, little was heard until, in the early Second Age, they established themselves in the lands of Tracia, and aligned themselves with the Newcomers, the mortal race that had come into the world from the sea and who were industrious and short-lived. The House of Fairmyrtle remained small, though it became wealthy. But tragedy after tragedy was visited upon them. Byrniece wed a man, and had a son, who, in turn, had his own daughter, called Nianan. But a fever swept the lands, and Byrniece's husband died of it. That same year, her son and daughter-in-law were drowned when the ship bearing them to Glareth foundered and sank. The following year, while Byrniece was riding through her estate with several of her friends, a boar charged out from a copse and attacked her horse. The horse fell and Byrniece was crushed to death beneath it. Nianan, grief-stricken, withdrew from all society, allowing her trusted foreman, young Devan Seafar, to run her estate for her. She grew old, to the surprise of many, for they did not yet understand that only the child of a female Elifaen will be Elifaen. And, at last, in the 225th year of the Second Age, Nianan died. She had no husband and no child, and thus, upon her death, the House of Fairmyrtle was dissolved.

Before her body was even buried, the people of her estate, led by Devan Seafar, took her Bloodcoins and prepared to depart, aiming to take the Bloodcoins to Vanara. But as they were preparing their train, young King Kapol of the House of Alder arrived with many soldiers. He seized the Bloodcoins and had many of the Fairmyrtle people arrested on charges of thievery. When he announced that he would retain the Bloodcoins for safekeeping, word reached Vanara and immediately Queen Serith Ellyn sent emissaries to demand the Bloodcoins be delivered to Vanara. But Kapol steadfastly refused, saying that it was his right as King of Tracia to hold the Bloodcoins, and he promised to defend Tracia and the Bloodcoins against any outsiders, even if it meant going to war. In addition, Kapol openly persecuted any supporters of Fairmyrtle still found within Tracia.

In 278 S.A., during the Pinewood Uprising, the place where Kapol kept the Bloodcoins was discovered, attacked, looted, and burned by a large group of unknown robbers. Failure to protect the Bloodcoins brought further shame and outrage upon Kapol's House of Alder. When Kapol ignominiously threw his support to the House of Pinewood, his fate was sealed. He and Pinewood were soon defeated by a coalition of Men and Elifaen alike, Eastlanders, Glarethians, and volunteers from other Realms. King Kapol was dethroned by the victors, and his House and the House of Pinewood were abolished. Kapol would die in prison under suspicious circumstances, and his entire family was banished to Grisland Island and would live the rest of their days in exile. And none could say whatever became of the Bloodcoins of the House of Fairmyrtle. Devan Seafar, who had been imprisoned by King Kapol, was released. He and his people, many who were former servants of the House of Fairmyrtle, remained in Tracia for a time. During the Great Dragonkind Invasion, Devan Seafar's people fought valiantly against the raiders, and suffered terrible losses as a result. The survivors, including Devan Seafar himself, joined with Serith Ellyn at the Battle of Saerdulin which utterly defeated the Dragonkind in the east. Not long afterwards, Devan Seafar removed to Vanara, taking many artifacts and papers of the House of Fairmyrtle with him. The Bloodcoins of the House of Fairmyrtle, however, were never located.

The House of Fairmaple
Katrina and Her People

Legends surrounding Lady Katrina of the House of Fairmaple abound. There are many reasons for the persistent popular fascination concerning her, and for the many inventive tales that have arisen. She was the most aloof of any of the leaders of the Seven High Houses, mistrustful of power, of Vanara, and of the other High Houses. She also retained her use of the First Tongue long after most Elifaen had forgotten it, and was able to use the First Tongue to safeguard and protect her people for a long time. And, certainly, the mystery surrounding her fate and that of her people has served as a springboard for speculative tales.

Katrina was a Firstborn, said to have come into the world from the spirit of snow upon sunlit mountain forests. Her hair was golden yellow, and her eyes bright green, and her skin was as dark as coal. Legends say that the trees of her favorite mountains were enamored of her hair, so she gave locks of her hair to them to wear every autumn. When came the Fall, and she lost her wings, they gave to her sap from their own branches to drink in order to sustain her.

Katrina spoke the First Tongue long after most other Elifaen had forgotten it, and so she was able to speak to the natural objects of the world, to birds and animals and trees, and also hear their replies. She used this ability, it is said, to coax the forest to yield more nuts for the people that gathered to her, and to speak to the streams so that they made the fish within them leap into the air to be caught by her people. For this, she was considered a sorceress by many of those who could no longer speak the First Tongue.

She and her people settled into the mountains and forests north of Vanara in territories that would later become Duinnor. There they lived simply and as happily as they could, united under Katrina's House of Fairmaple.

When Aperion gave her the Seven Topaz Bloodcoins, she kept them in secret for many years without telling anyone why she was spirited away or what happened while she was apart from her people. Later, some would say that she spent much time trying to delve into the nature of her Bloodcoins, speaking to them with the First Tongue. But they would not reply to her. When word reached her how others of the High Houses were using their Bloodcoins as symbols of authority, she knew that she would have to tell her people about them. She did so fully, holding nothing back from them about what happened atop Mount Cassos when Aperion gave the objects. She told her people to be wary of any who used them for their own gain or power, and to trust no one who did so, for it was not for such things that the objects were made or given. But she listened as her people told her that they wished they could go to Aperion's abode and depart from the world, for it had become a hard and cruel place to live in, so unlike the Time Before Time when they could fly and all could speak the First Tongue.

During the years after the Forty-Nine were given by Aperion, the House of Fairmaple remained apart from other Elifaen, many of whom turned violently upon one another in their lust for power. When Silmain of Vanara declared himself King of the Faere, Katrina was angered by his claim. Silmain united the clans and Houses of Vanara and used his power to renew the wars with the Dragonkind. But Katrina was resolved to keep her people safe from Silmain and his wars. Katrina managed to do this, resisting Silmain's entreaties for her to render aid to him.

Meanwhile, having heard the desire of her people to have the Nimbus Illuminas opened so that they could depart the world, Katrina sent messengers to Lyrium, who had been a friend to her during the Time Before Time, asking if she or the other High Houses wished, as she did, to use their Bloodcoins. She was surprised when Lyrium answered that Silmain had tired of war and strife and was calling for the Seven High Houses to come to Linlally to do just what Katrina desired.

But, as all know, things did not go well. Ormace, Therona, Lucinda, and Cupeldain would not consent to the use of their Bloodcoins, and the effort failed. Disappointed, Katrina returned home with the bad news, telling her people the entire story of her time in Linlally and what happened there.

In the years that followed, the House of Fairbirch under Ormace made every effort to extend its reach from its lands in northern Vanara to Katrina's lands. At first, she withdrew her people farther north, but new settlements in the region of Duinnor prevented them from going far. Later, as Ormace kept up the pressure on Fairmaple, she armed her people and prepared them as well as she could for war, though they had no experience at it. But, not wishing to appear weak, she made it known to Ormace that, should he persist in sending his hunting parties northward into Fairmaple lands, it would be at their peril. When Ormace tested her resolve by sending a large party of three hundred Elifaen fighters into her lands, Katrina convinced bears and wolves and mountain lions to attack them. With Katrina leading the onslaught, riding upon the back of a great lion, they killed most of Ormace's intruders in a single night. Katrina permitted a handful to escape, but her army of animals chased the terrified Elifaen back into Fairbirch lands and to Ormace's castle. She surrounded his valley, and for seven days and nights her lions growled, her bears roared and bellowed, and her wolves howled so that, it was said, none dared leave their homes, and Ormace himself trembled in his castle. Satisfied that her message had been delivered and understood, she thanked her animal companions, promising that they would never need fear being hunted by her people, so long as they did not hunt hers. But when she returned to her people, they saw that she was troubled, and, being honest and forthcoming with them as always, she explained that the First Tongue was leaving her, and that it was a struggle for her to speak it to the animals or to understand what they said in return. Thus, she warned, she feared her power to protect them was waning.

Ormace remained fearful of Katrina for a long while, though he coveted her lands. Instead, he turned his attention to other matters, some of which included encouraging Silmain to seize lands across the River Iridelin, lands that Ormace hoped would be given over to him. When King Silmain marched across the river, the House of Fairbirch was with him. But in the bloody fighting that followed, Ormace proved too cruel for Silmain's liking, and he continually undermined Silmain's orders. Silmain appealed to Cupeldain for aid, and when Cupeldain brought his army to join Silmain's, Ormace was told to take his Fairbirch fighters away and leave the valley. This humiliated and infuriated Ormace. Yet, almost as soon as Ormace withdrew, Silmain and Cupeldain enjoyed victory after victory, and those lands became part of Vanara.

Hearing of these events, Katrina grew more uneasy, thinking that Ormace might now try to redouble his efforts against her, having lost his opportunity in the east. As it turned out, Ormace was more interested in using his army in the south against the Dragonkind, thinking that spoils taken there would bolster his wealth and power. Ormace carefully mended his relationship with King Silmain, and reached an accord so that Fairbirch would be on the forefront of new wars with the Dragonkind. Cupeldain, who commanded the largest army of all of the High Houses, mistrusted Ormace, but together Cupeldain and Ormace, along with many others, took their armies into the deserts. Wielding the great sword Ethliad, Silmain led them all, and they had many victories, but they were costly. The Dragonlands were vast, and the few cities and towns within reach of the Elifaen armies were well defended. Elsewhere, the Dragonkind systematically retreated, springing traps and counterattacks that took a great toll on the Elifaen. Yet the Vanarans were as stubborn in their hatred of the Dragonkind as ever they were, and they persistently raised new armies and waged new campaigns.

Then King Silmain was killed in battle. His death was blamed on the incompetence of Ormace, who failed to protect the flank of Silmain's army, allowing the Dragonkind to strike with devastating effect. Soon, Vanara was divided by new power struggles and feuds. Silmain's army collapsed, and his ministers scattered. Ormace vied for power, making it known that he coveted the throne of Silmain. Fighting broke out in Linlally, and Cupeldain withdrew his army from the Dragonlands and took it back to Vanara where he sought to enforce the peace. For the next few decades, amid growing chaos in Vanara, Cupeldain watched as his own people fractured, and many pressured him to take the throne. Cupeldain, however, wished to unite the Elifaen and hoped to install someone agreeable to all upon the vacant throne. Council after council was formed but they all failed to resolve the matter of leadership, while Ormace and a few others continued working to make the Palace at Linlally their own. Katrina watched from afar, continually sending messengers to Vanara to bring back news, fearing that Ormace, should he become King, would quickly march on her lands. However, the news that Katrina's spies and messengers brought back to her was only about new divisions and new strife as Vanara's people languished. Ormace, they said, could not muster the support needed to make himself king. All of the Vanaran Houses squabbled with one another, and, in spite of Cupeldain's efforts, sometimes there were bloody feuds amongst them.

Then, what Cupeldain failed to do, the Dragonkind did for him. Tajahnaman, King of the Dragonkind, led an invasion against Vanara, aiming to take the Blue Mountains and make strongholds there. Cupeldain was aware of the approaching army, and he spread word far and wide concerning it. Quickly, the Elifaen were reunited, and joined together under Cupeldain's banner to drive out the Dragonkind. Cupeldain, upon his return to Linlally, was hailed as a hero, and soon the people were calling for him to be crowned as their king. It took three years to convince him, but he eventually agreed and was made King of Vanara.

Katrina was relieved, for she knew that Cupeldain had no designs upon her lands or her people. The years that followed Cupeldain's coronation were peaceful ones for the House of Fairmaple, and Katrina was grateful that they lived so far from the wars that Vanara continually fought. She and her people remained wary and vigilant against Ormace, and she continued to send messengers and spies to gather news for her. No threat materialized, but she was saddened by the great losses that Vanara's people suffered with their wars and their feuds.

Then came an envoy from Cupeldain, begging Katrina to come to Linlally. Like Silmain, Cupeldain also wearied of the world and its strife, and he sought to have the Nimbus Illuminas opened. She gladly went, and found great support once more from Lyrium, Pyros, and now even Lucinda, besides Cupeldain himself. But Therona and Ormace were adamant in their opposition to the plan, and, as it turned out, they would have their way. Secundur also went about speaking privately with the leaders of the High Houses, spreading rumor and lies. Using these as a pretense, Ormace forced the Houses to redistribute their Bloodcoins, so that all would have one of every kind from every House, to ensure that none could use theirs without all of the others being used, too.

Katrina of the House of Fairmaple, like so many others, departed Vanara soon after the Forty-Nine were redistributed. She was sad and disappointed, and now she feared Ormace more than ever. Should he move against her people, she could hardly hope to use the First Tongue as she did before, for it had altogether faded from her. And Katrina thought that she could not rely upon Cupeldain or anyone else to come to her aid if Ormace tried to invade her lands or attempt to take her Bloodcoins from her. She expressed these concerns to her people, and they considered what they might do. It did not take them long to decide.

In late winter of the 811th year of the First Age, Katrina and all her people secretly went eastward, crossing the Middlemount until they came to Wayregyle on the northwestern slopes of the Carthanes. In those days, it was a dense forest, much like the lands they left behind, and that is where they settled. A few years later, Katrina received word that Ormace and his House was destroyed and his Bloodcoins were lost. Some of her people wondered if they should return to their old lands, but Katrina said she would not go back since she was still mistrustful of Cupeldain and did not wish to become embroiled in the intrigues of Vanara.

So Katrina and her people abided in Wayregyle for several centuries, keeping to themselves, shunning visitors who came from Vanara, and turning away strangers who came into their lands. She still sent out her spies and messengers to gather news and knowledge of the happenings within Vanara. Thus she learned that King Cupeldain, while traveling with his wife and a party of their friends, was ambushed by assassins. He and all his party were murdered. Though she was never friendly with Cupeldain, Katrina grieved nonetheless, for she knew that Cupeldain had changed since his early days. She knew that in the final years of his life, all Cupeldain desired was peace. And Katrina mourned also for those who were murdered with Cupeldain, and especially his gentle wife, Loura, who had always treated Katrina most graciously.

So it was that Cupeldain's son, Parthais, came to the throne, and King Parthais had little desire to conduct himself as his father had, but sought to interfere in the affairs of other Houses in order to bolster his own power. He sent several envoys to Wayregyle in an attempt to convince Katrina to return with her Bloodcoins to Vanara. But all such invitations were firmly rejected, and Parthais eventually turned his attentions elsewhere.

However, when Serith Ellyn and Thurdun were banished from Vanara, Thurdun went to Wayregyle, seeking to remind Katrina of her promise of allegiance to Cupeldain's House, and to enlist her aid against his own father, King Parthais. But, when Thurdun arrived, he found the region empty, the castles and villages abandoned, and only a few Men living there, who said it was just as they had found the place some dozen years before. The Men told Thurdun that some of the mountain Elifaen said that the former people of Wayregyle departed for the far northern lands, across the "duinnor," or northern river (that is, the Osterflo), aiming to make new settlements far away. Nothing else was ever learned concerning the people of the House of Fairmaple, Katrina, or her Bloodcoins.

The House of Faircedar

Lucinda

Lucinda was born to Chantay and Galanas in the Time Before Time. Chantay was born of the spirit of forest mists and Galanas was born of the spirit of mountain air. It is said that when the two fell in love, Lucinda was born to them under the rainbow of a waterfall. Lucinda, who had the silver hair of her mother and the blue eyes of her father, loved to fly through the forests, caressing the cedar boughs to yield their scent as she flew along.

When Galanas joined with Cupeldain to fight the Dragonkind, Lucinda went with him, although her mother stayed away. However, what Galanas and Lucinda saw sickened both of them, and they returned to Chantay just as Aperion summoned all the Faerekind. Galanas wanted to go with Aperion, but Chantay did not think it right to be made to give up her forests because of Cupeldain and the others. Even though Galanas pleaded with her, Chantay refused and Lucinda could not bear to abandon her mother. So all three remained and were Scathed of their wings.

Little is known of the years that followed, but during that time Chantay and Galanas united many others with them into a clan, and they formed the House of Faircedar, one of the first of the Seven High Houses. Their clan grew to be powerful and adept at hunting and fishing for food, and for making shelters in the mountains, and there was little discord amongst them. Life was difficult, as it was for all of the Elifaen, but Faircedar managed better than most. When Galanas was killed by a bear, Chantay and Lucinda became the leaders of their people.

Then Aperion came again to the earth, and when he called for the willing leaders of the Fallen Ones to come to him, Chantay heeded his call and was spirited away to Mount Cassos to hear what Aperion had to say. Chantay later told her daughter how Aperion knew beforehand that few Elifaen leaders would heed his call. He said that he was happy that the leaders of seven Houses came, even some of those who were responsible for the plight of the Elifaen. And so, Aperion said, the fate of all of the Fallen Ones, all Elifaen who had lost their wings, would now lay heavy upon those before him. The seven that came were Chantay, Ormace, Cupeldain, Lyrium, Katrina, Therona, and Pyros. Aperion praised them for coming, even those who had warred with the Dragonkind. He especially praised Cupeldain and Ormace for their bravery in coming to him, even though their hearts were still hardened against Aperion, and their hatred for the Dragonkind still burned.

Chantay later related how she and the other Elifaen were unable to speak. So brilliant was Aperion's light, and his voice spoke so powerfully in their hearts that they all fell to their knees in fear and wonder. Aperion then gave to each of them seven wondrous objects, fashioned of red gold with seven kinds of stones made into the center of them. To Chantay he gave seven of these objects, each with an amethyst jewel in its center. Then, through a vision, he showed them how the objects were to be used should the Elifaen ever wish to come away from the earth and rejoin the Faere in their new heavenly abode. The Nimbus Illuminas is what he showed them, a staff of light reaching to the sky, held up by the Forty-Nine Keys that he had given to them. But Aperion warned them to be united in their decision, for all Forty-Nine must be used together, and they could only be used one time. And he further warned them to bring all their peoples together quickly and to come away from the earth soon. If they abided without action for very long, he said, great strife would plague their Houses, and each passing year would become more difficult. He then returned each of the seven Elifaen to their people.

Aperion's warning came to pass for each of the seven High Houses. When Chantay showed her people the objects, and told how Aperion had given them to her, she said it was a sign of her authority over them. Many of Faircedar were jealous of Chantay's power, and her daughter Lucinda coveted the Seven Objects, and she tried to convince her mother to give her one or two to keep for her own so that the people of their House would know that Lucinda was second in power to Chantay. But Chantay refused, and she spent much of her time gazing at the seven amethyst-bejeweled objects, holding them up to the sun to see their luster and the color of their jewels. As the years passed, Chantay became more imperious, saying that it was Aperion's will that her people should obey her, since it was to her that he gave the Seven. But she often hid herself away, so that none could consult with her on matters of importance.

It fell to Lucinda, therefore, to lead Faircedar, but the people were reluctant to obey her, especially when she contradicted her mother's wishes. Seeing that the Seven would give her sway over them, Lucinda came to her mother in private and tried to wrest the objects from Chantay. In the angry struggle that ensued, Chantay repeatedly struck at Lucinda with a knife, stabbing her so that Lucinda's blood splattered the Seven. Hearing the struggle, several servants tried to intervene, but Chantay turned upon them, killing two of them before Lucinda picked up a sword and struck off her mother's head. Then, taking the Seven, Lucinda called together the chiefs of her people. Still bleeding from her wounds, she proclaimed that she had purchased the Seven with the blood of her mother and her own blood, too. She bade any who wished not to belong any more to Faircedar to depart, but all who remained were to obey her as their queen. That was how the Seven first came to be called Bloodcoins.

And so Lucinda was made Queen of Faircedar, although her House would ever be divided. When Silmain established his throne in Vanara, Lucinda sought to increase her power by wooing him from his wife. Silmain rebuffed her, though she was beautiful, so she turned her attentions to his sons. But Heneil and Pellen were not taken in by her guile. After many years, King Silmain tired of war and strife. He called together the Seven Houses, and he tried to convince them to use their Bloodcoins to open the Nimbus Illuminas and free all of the Elifaen. During these talks, which lasted for twelve years, Lucinda tried again to persuade Silmain to her bed, saying that if he took her as his lover and his wife, making her his queen over his own wife, then she would give him her support with the other High Houses. But this only made Silmain angry, for he saw that she was too greedy for power to give up the world and to permit her Seven to be used. Still, he tried to convince the other High Houses, but only three of the seven were for his plan (Lyrium of Fairfir, Katrina of Fairmaple, and Pyros of Fairmyrtle). Thus, Silmain failed.

Long years of war and struggle followed. During that time, Faircedar sought and formed new alliances, and was embroiled in many feuds. When King Silmain seized lands for Vanara across the Iridelin, there was an uprising against him that sparked feuds amongst the woodland Elifaen, between those who supported Silmain and others opposed to him. Lucinda's House did not participate directly, but she was sympathetic to those whose lands were taken. However, when her lands were raided and overrun by Dragonkind, Faircedar responded by joining with Silmain against them. Many of her people were killed in fighting over the next several centuries, and the lands of Faircedar were ruined, forcing Faircedar to establish a new estate near Linlally. At last, Silmain was killed in battle against the Dragonkind, and Cupeldain came to sit on the throne of Vanara.

Cupeldain continued the wars with the Dragonkind, and the House of Faircedar supported him. But when Cupeldain sought, like Silmain before him, to have the Forty-Nine Bloodcoins used to open the Nimbus Illuminas, Lucinda was undecided. Like Cupeldain, she had seen much suffering and bloodshed, but she hoped for peace. When they all met in Linlally, Secundur went amongst them, seeking to create discord. When Ormace accused Cupeldain and Lyrium of planning to use their own coins to force everyone out from the earth, Lucinda remembered how her mother had told her that all Forty-Nine must be used. She scolded Ormace for believing the lies of Secundur, and for spreading them, but Ormace was convinced of them. By threatening to destroy his seven emerald Bloodcoins, he forced the assembly of Houses to redistribute their coins so that none could use their own to open the Nimbus Illuminas. The great council then disbanded, and Lucinda departed, too, depressed and confused at how things came to be the way they were since the blissful days of the Time Before Time.

However, while at Linlally's court, Lucinda met an Elifaen named Heretios. The two fell in love, married, and would have three children, two sons and a daughter. Heretios was a scholar, and knew much concerning the lore of the Elifaen. He was sympathetic to Cupeldain, and served for a time as one of his counselors. When Lucinda and Heretios married, he gave up his position in court to oversee Faircedar lands.

When new feuds broke out in eastern Vanara, Lucinda threw her backing to the House of Hemlock which resisted the woodland Elifaen. Although her people did not fight, she supplied Hemlock and its allies with bows and swords to help them secure their lands.

Witches and demons then came into the world from unknown places, and Lucinda became a huntress, leading her people to help drive them out from Vanara. While she was occupied with this, the feuds in eastern Vanara grew more violent and threatened to spread into the rest of Vanara as more and more Houses took sides amid the terror spread by the witches and demons. Seeking to end the feuds, Cupeldain negotiated a truce between the warring clans and Houses. When it was tentatively agreed to, he went with his wife to visit the villages across the Iridelin, to seal the peace between them. While traveling through Hemlock lands, his party was set upon and captured by masked Elifaen. They murdered Cupeldain, his wife, and those with them by weighing them with chains and millstones and casting them into a forest lake. But one person escaped to Linlally with the news.

Parthais, Cupeldain's son, immediately went with an army into the region where he was met by members of the House of Hemlock saying they had captured the culprits. Those captured, though, professed their innocence, claiming that Hemlock was to blame for the murders. Parthais was skeptical, and he mistrusted them all. He ordered his army to camp on a hill overlooking the lake where his parents were murdered, and, to show his anger, he forced all villages and Houses within the region to send their chief men to him. When they came, Parthais questioned them, and he concluded that several villages, unhappy with the terms that Cupeldain forced upon them, were guilty of the murders. He ordered that the chief men and their wives be put to death, and he had them drowned in the same manner and in the same lake as had happened to Cupeldain. After the executions, Parthais had a wagon brought forth, and from it was taken a demon-serpent that had been captured in the Iridelin. Parthais ordered it released into the lake to gnaw away at the spirits of the dead and to make them restless and without peace. This horrified even his friends, for the spirits of Cupeldain and Loura, the parents of Parthais, also rested at the bottom of the lake. But it was Parthais's way of declaring that he, and none other, now ruled all of Vanara.

When Lucinda heard these things she was filled with misgivings. She feared that Faircedar's role in the feuds would not go unpunished. Upon his return to Linlally, Parthais ordered that all Elifaen Houses not favorable to him be taxed with heavy tributes in order to enjoy his protection. Lucinda suspected that it was a ploy to deplete Faircedar of its riches and to force them to give over the Bloodcoins of their House. So when war broke out between Altoria and Masurthia, and Parthais departed with an army to quash it, Lucinda fled Vanara with many of her people. They made their way to the distant eastern shores of the world, to Glareth by the Sea. They were welcomed by King Gardin of the House of Beech who had established a small coastal domain that would soon become the powerful Realm of Glareth. Although Gardin was a nephew to Parthais on his mother's side, he was no friend to Parthais since some of those executed by Parthais were his kin.

For several years after Lucinda's arrival, all was well with the House of Faircedar in Glareth. Gardin arranged for Lucinda to purchase lands for new estates, and her people enjoyed living in peace. However, when Parthais returned to Vanara from Altoria and was confirmed as King of Vanara, he secretly sent agents to Glareth to undermine the friendship between Faircedar and Beech. At the same time, other agents sent by Parthais made overtures to Lucinda in an effort to convince her of Parthais's goodwill, inviting her to return to Vanara with her Bloodcoins. Although Lucinda mistrusted Parthais, she did not know how he worked against her. By various intrigues, the relations between Faircedar and the House of Beech became increasingly strained. In 945 F.A., Faircedar was falsely implicated in a failed plot to overthrow King Gardin. Although Gardin did not believe the lies told by captured members of the conspiracy, who named Faircedar as organizers of the plot, the people of Glareth were convinced against Faircedar, including many of those who had not long before come with Lucinda out of Vanara.

Eventually things became untenable for the House of Faircedar within Glareth, and Lucinda accepted an offer by Masurthia's King Barindon to remove to his domain. Gardin, who remained friendly with Lucinda, warned her against the long voyage, and he did not trust the Masurthian ships that were sent to bring her to that land. However, Lucinda was decided. With all of her household and many of her people, she departed Glareth by the Sea bound for Masurthia in the year 947 of the First Age.

The voyage was beset with difficulties from the start. A fire on board one of the seven ships forced the fleet into Colleton, but the damage was too severe for the ship to be salvaged. Continuing on, the remaining ships were battered by storms, and during the foggy aftermath, they inadvertently sailed into the treacherous Grisland Strait where three of the ships ran aground and were pounded to bits by heavy seas. Heretios was killed, but Lucinda and her children were saved, and the remaining three ships limped into Forlandis where they waited out the winter.

In the late spring of the following year (948 F.A.), the three remaining Masurthian ships set out for the final leg of their voyage. Five days out, a typhoon struck and drove all three ships ashore. A month after Lucinda had departed Forlandis, a Masurthian fishing boat came upon the wreckage and found twelve survivors, all very weak from injuries and hunger. They reported that Lucinda had been drowned, and her daughter crushed by a falling spar, and that most of the other passengers and crew were drowned or died, too. They told how, after the storm had passed, and the dead were buried, the survivors salvaged what they could from the wrecked ships. But after waiting three weeks for rescue, Lucinda's two sons decided to trek cross-country in an attempt to reach the Masurthian Kingdom of Solsorna, and they took thirty strong men and women with them. As soon as could be done, the fishermen sailed to Solsorna and reported to King Barindon who immediately sent parties by sail and horseback to search for Lucinda's sons and to bring back the remaining survivors of the shipwrecks. But Lucinda's sons were never found, nor were any of those who went with them, and it was assumed that the Bloodcoins of Faircedar were lost with them.

Almost immediately, rumors and legends sprang up concerning the lost Bloodcoins of Faircedar. Some legends told that Lucinda's sons became terribly lost, being too young to find their way, and that they actually wandered north of their way to Lake Adin. There, so it was told, the two brothers quarreled and killed each other in fighting, and the Bloodcoins were buried somewhere within sight of Lake Adin's shore. Other legends tell how the two brothers were taken by the Cuwali tribes of the southern Bletharn Plains and were, with all their comrades, sacrificed to their gods while the Bloodcoins were taken as trinkets.

The House of Fairwillow
Queen Therona

Therona was born of the still waters, in lands that would later become the deserts of the Dragonkind. Her skin was pale-green, like the leaves of the drooping limbs of the trees that lined the banks of woodland ponds and lakes. Her hair was brown like the wild hares that played at the water's edge, and her eyes were silver, like the delicate flowers that bloomed nearby to these places. It is said that she rarely flew, preferring to swim or to languish beneath the willows.

When those lands were made into deserts, she was angry at Aperion who did nothing to put it right. She removed to other parts, across the Tulivana Mountains, to find other lakes and ponds to enjoy. But she nursed a powerful resentment against the Dragonkind who now lived in lands that once were hers. When she heard that they attacked the north, she feared they would spread their deserts, and she went with Cupeldain to fight them. When Aperion called the Faerekind away, she was unwilling to go with him and was Scathed.

During the Time of Strife, Therona gathered to her those who mistrusted Cupeldain and Silmain, and together they settled in lands that would be called Altoria. They prospered, learning to make boats and to navigate the rivers and coastal seas. Therona, by her charm and by her determination, rose to be leader of her people and named her House after her favorite tree, the willow. And so she was among those who, when Aperion called again, gathered upon Mount Cassos, and to Therona Aperion gave seven diamond Bloodcoins.

But Therona guarded her heart well, having no liking for Aperion or the other Elifaen, and when she was returned by Aperion to her people, she used her Bloodcoins to show her authority over them, saying that she was chosen by Aperion to be their queen.

By the time that Silmain called for the coming together of the High Houses, she had no desire to leave the world, as her life was comfortable and she suffered little. So she opposed Silmain's plan, and returned to her own people. Centuries later, when Cupeldain again called for the Nimbus Illuminas to be opened, she went again to Linlally. This time, only she and Ormace opposed the plan, and she feared that the others would force them to give up their Bloodcoins. She was pleased when Ormace threatened to destroy his Bloodcoins in order to force the redistribution of them, and she willingly backed Ormace. She gave up six of hers in exchange for one from each other High House, and then she returned to Altoria.

By tradition, Therona displayed her Bloodcoins to her ministers every twenty-four years to show her claim of authority under Aperion (a practice that would later be taken up by Queen Serith Ellyn of Vanara). However, during the war between Masurthia and Altoria, the Queen proclaimed that it was no longer safe to do so. They would remain unseen from thenceforth, even after Parthais enforced peace between the two realms. Growing suspicion and unrest led three of her ministers to force their way into the Royal Altorian Vaults in 967 F.A., where they discovered that the Bloodcoins were missing. This resulted in a broad uprising against Therona, who would not explain the missing Bloodcoins. In 968 F.A., facing dethronement and public humiliation, she abdicated to the popular Prince Felthain of the House of Mulberry, who placed her under guarded arrest and exiled her to a villa in northern Altoria. In 980 F.A., she was found dead. She had taken Sigh Mortabilis (foxdire), smuggled to her by her servants. She never revealed what became of her Seven Bloodcoins.

Nearly six hundred years later, it was widely rumored that the Third Unknown King of Duinnor had two sets of Bloodcoins in his possession, although the rumors were never confirmed nor denied by the King or his ministers. It has since been assumed that one of those sets of Bloodcoins had once been those of Therona of the House of Fairwillow.

See Also:

Biographical Sketches (Felthain)

The House of Fairbirch
Ormace and Eyrice

Ormace was born in the Time Before Time. It is not known what spirit of the earth formed him, but it was said that he had wings like those of a condor, long and broad, and he rarely enjoyed the company of the other Firstborn, preferring to fly high and alone over the broad world. But when Morgasir made the dragons come into the southern world, and vast lands were made waste by him, it was Ormace who saw it and took the news to the others of the Faerekind. And when Beras destroyed Morgasir, and freed the Dragonkind peoples from their thralldom, Ormace cared not for them. Nor did he care when his fellow Faerekind tried to destroy the Dragonkind by laying waste their lands, by drying up its rivers, and by making clouds yield their rain far in the west before reaching the southwestern lands. Ormace did not care, for he had all of the rest of the world to fly over.

But he fell in love with a beautiful Faere maiden called Eyrice who was born of the spirit of the rainbow. When he saw her flying back and forth over the desert lands, he was attracted by her beauty and by the many colors of her shimmering wings. From high above, he watched her and followed her as she went from place to place as if looking for something. At last, when she alit on a wide barren stretch of sandy dunes, he descended and landed beside her.

"I am Ormace," he said, "and I have watched you fly over these dry lands. Tell me, what is your name? And what is it that you seek?"

"I am Eyrice," she said. "I look for those friends of mine who once lived here, who once stretched from cloud to cloud after the rains, and were like an arc of many colors. Do you know the ones I mean?"

"I know of them," Ormace replied. "They live far north of here, in the skies that cover the green valleys and plains."

"They are kin of those I seek," said Eyrice. "But the ones I speak of lived in this region, and it was of their spirit that I was born into the world. I once danced and played with them, darting under their arcs of light. And though I never need rest, I often sat upon their high backs to survey the world with them. But now they are gone, along with the rain that often came with them, and these lands are dry and lonely."

"It is because of the Dragonkind that they are gone," said Ormace. "I speak of those who were once slaves of the fire-spitting worms that Beras destroyed. Those slaves survived, and walk with their feet upon the earth, for they have no wings to fly with. Some of our brethren and sisters were angered at them, and they made the mountains rub the clouds dry of their rain before reaching here."

"Why? Why would they do such a thing?"

"I do not know why, but I am sure that if they had known it would trouble one so beautiful as you, they would not have done it," said Ormace.

"Then I am to be lonely?"

"There is no need of that," said Ormace. "I will keep company with you for as long as you wish it. And, if you like, together we will fly to the far Northlands. I know a lake with waterfalls where five little rainbows live and play. Perhaps you would like to meet her, this lake, and see her little children?"

Eyrice nodded and took Ormace's hand, and together they flew to the far northern mountains where a great river poured down the slopes of Mount Cassos and emptied into a high lake atop a broad cliff. From there, the river poured out in five streams, falling far to a pool below where, around the base of the five falls, five little rainbows danced. Eyrice was delighted with them and joined in their play as Ormace circled high overhead, watching. Truly, he had never seen anything so beautiful as that, and most beautiful of all was Eyrice.

Indeed, it was Tiandari Lake that thus fell into five streaming waterfalls, and this was the lake where Silmain and Cupeldain worked to build a palace, along with Alonair and many other Faerekind. While they toiled, and many of the Faere came and went, Eyrice was content to play and dance with the little water-rainbows, and Ormace was happy to circle and circle, watching her.

"Won't you come join us?" asked Eyrice.

"No," said Ormace. "I am content to watch."

In fact, he grew shyer the more he watched because he grew more in love with Eyrice with each wave of her wings, with each sunlit sparkle that coursed over her skin, and with each laugh that passed from her lips.

Who can say how long she played? For in the Time Before Time, night and day were meaningless, and Lady Moon shown as brightly with her white light as her husband, Sir Sun, did with his yellow light, and so time was not known or marked. But at last, Eyrice flew to the banks of the pool into which the five Falls of Tiandari fell, and she sat on a glistening rock to gaze at her little rainbow friends. Gathering his courage, Ormace alit next to her.

"Why do you not play any longer? Do you tire of the little rainbows? Did they offend you in any way?"

"No, they are but children, and are content to play and play. But they are too small for me to sit upon, and too shallow for me to fly under," she said. "I miss my friends in the south. They were mighty in their breadth, spanning from the highest cloud to the ground. And while these five little ones are noisy and gay, their chatter is incessant. My friends spoke very little, and had little need to, but when they did, they had mighty thunder in their voices."

"I see," said Ormace. "And because you are sad, I am too. If I could restore your friends to you, I would do so. But such a feat is beyond me. However, I shall go and seek out Aperion. I shall ask him how the desert lands should have their rain back, and their clouds and rainbows, too."

And that is what Ormace did, flying high over the lands until he found Aperion, who was conversing with a gathering of the Faerekind that he had summoned. Aperion was questioning them on the same thing that Ormace came to ask, namely, how the lands that were stricken could be put back the way they had been before.

"I know not," said one of the Faere, "for when I pushed down into the earth to raise up stones and rocks into mountains, they came with me reluctantly, and were sorely angry at me for moving them."

"I, too," said another of the Faerekind, "helped in the making of the long cut in the world, and I was resisted by the rocks and stones that I delved out."

"And they told me," said another of those gathered before Aperion, "that they would never again willingly obey one of our kind for disturbing them so."

"Perhaps you, Aperion," suggested a voice that came from the shadows of a tree, "may speak with Beras, if he may hear you on the matter. For surely if you wish it, he shall grant it."

"I shall do so, Secundur," said Aperion. "But it would be better for these here who thus cursed those lands to put it right themselves."

"Yes, but the task is beyond them, it seems," answered Secundur.

And so Aperion departed, and flew upwards into the sky. Many of the Faerekind followed him, and Ormace did, too. But Secundur did not, preferring to remain in the deep shade that he was so fond of. Ormace, though, followed those that flew upward with Aperion, and he continued climbing higher and higher, beyond the path that Sir Sun walked, and even higher still. The other Faerekind gave up and returned to the earth, but Aperion kept on, climbing even higher, and Ormace continued to follow him. But at last, even with his long and mighty wings, Ormace could climb no more. So he circled and circled, so high over the world that even with his keen eyes he could barely see the ground.

It was during this time, no one knows how long it lasted, that Kalzar accepted the challenge of Alonair the Sculptor, and strove to cut and move the Great Stone. Still Ormace circled and circled, waiting for Aperion to return from Beras on high. And while Kalzar's efforts were foiled by the desert and by the impossibility of the challenge, Eyrice decided to return to the desert lands and search once again for her lost friends. She was still searching in the skies when she saw, far below, a shimmering swath of color moving across the sandy lands. Excitedly, she dove downward, but became perplexed the lower she came. Others of her kind, having seen the strange colors, too, swooped down with her to see what it was. It was, in fact, Kalzar's mighty army marching northward. Its banners were of every color of the rainbow, and the armor of his people was brightly burnished. Having never seen the likes of this, Eyrice glided lower to have a better look at the strange creatures that walked on their feet. But as she did so, a flock of strange narrow birds rose up from the army, whistling through the air. Several of these tore through her wings, and four of them lodged in her breast and her legs. She fell, dead from the arrows, and landed in the waters of a tiny oasis many miles away. Her many-colored wings spread out where she floated face down in the pool. Along the sun-drenched shore of the pond then sprouted new and strange flowers that grew over and choked the oasis. The blossoms, when they bloomed, were at first brown in color but gradually changed to red, then green, and at last they turned blue until finally becoming white before they withered. Thus were the first Cronosis, which would be called Semiluna, the Fortnight Flower.

As for Kalzar's army, all who know the story of how he attacked the north know also the outcome. Ormace, who still awaited Aperion, heard even from his great height the moan that went up from the Faerekind when Kalzar's army came upon them. He dove downward to find out what was amiss, and when he saw the bloodshed, his only thought was of Eyrice. But she was not where he had left her. Whilst the Dragonkind shot their arrows all around him and swung their swords at those of the Faere who did not know they should fly away, Ormace, in a panic, questioned first one, then another of the Faere as to Eyrice's whereabouts. But the first one did not know, and struggled to be let free of his grip so as to flee. The next pointed south before she was struck through the neck with an arrow and died in Ormace's arms. Ormace had never seen death before, and did not understand it. But he soon did, as he saw more and more fall around him. He dodged and banked as he flew southward, looking for Eyrice as, behind him, Cupeldain and the others of his kind armed themselves and beat back Kalzar's army.

Ormace found Eyrice. He sat in the oasis pond and turned her over and held her body against his, weeping most bitterly. He hardly noticed the army of Kalzar, retreating quickly around him, and they in their panic to escape Cupeldain had no thought to stop for drink or rest. It was only when one of Kalzar's soldiers fell dead beside him, clove in half by one of the Faerekind, that Ormace stirred. He took the sword from the dead soldier's hand and flew in pursuit of the others. Ormace, crying out scream after scream, chopped and slashed, he clawed and kicked and bit, and as many fell dead to him as to any other that day. Then, just when Ormace thought it possible to destroy them all, his head was blinded by a searing light, and his ears were filled with a trumpet's roar. He dropped the sword, covering his ears as his wings, which no longer obeyed him, took him far away from the place of battle.

Aperion delivered his ultimatum to the Faerekind. And Ormace was Scathed of his great wings, for he would not so soon give up his revenge. And after Aperion departed, it was a long struggle for Ormace, as it was for all of the Elifaen. He had to learn to walk, then to eat. To eat he learned to kill animals that had once been his friends, and he ate their meat and put their skins over his own to protect himself from cold and from rain. But he was strong and determined, and gathered strong and determined survivors with him. They did what they could, and more, to eat and to live. He enforced his will, sometimes cruelly, upon his tribe, and they made their home in the mountains of northern Vanara. He subjugated other nearby tribes, and brought many others into his service for their skills and knowledge. Eventually, he had a mighty clan, calling themselves Fairbirch.

In later years, the House of Fairbirch was one of those High Houses given a portion of the Forty-Nine Keys to the Nimbus Illuminas. But when it came to their use, Ormace would oppose the others. When Silmain sought to have them used, Ormace joined with Cupeldain and others to refuse. Later, when Cupeldain in turned wished to open the Nimbus Illuminas, it would be Ormace and Therona alone who stood opposed to the others. And Ormace, never forgetting that he wished for the destruction of the Dragonkind, threatened to destroy his Bloodcoins unless all were redistributed. When that was done, Ormace knew that he must increase his power in order to wreak his final vengeance upon those who had killed Eyrice. He agreed to assist in the wars, but his desire for vengeance was so great that it clouded his judgment. In battle, Silmain paid for Ormace's errors with his life. Afterwards, shamed by Cupeldain and dismissed from the field, he swore to increase his power by taking lands from Katrina's House of Fairmaple. That, too, ended in disaster, with many of his people killed by the beasts that she sent against him. In the last days of his House, he took to brooding, ever-seeking some way to make his will felt in Cupeldain's court, or to undermine any who might seek peace with the Dragonkind. It was said by some that he often received strange visitors into his castle, and one, especially, who shunned all manner of light. Some said it could be none other than Secundur who visited Ormace.

But the end of Ormace and the House of Fairbirch came about because of his love of Eyrice. There was a small valley, surrounded by high peaks, in northern Vanara. Whilst standing on an outcrop on a summer day, he saw how the slanting sun played on the streams that ran through the valley below him, shimmering with multicolored light just the same way that the wings of Eyrice had once done. It was there, in that deep valley, that Ormace made his castle and the center of the House of Fairbirch. It was from there that he launched his ill-fated ventures, and it was there that he retreated into brooding, staring at the surrounding snowy peaks. The place suited him, cut off by high and heavy snows and thick ice each winter. It was his decision to keep his people there, and to make it his home.

So, at last, in the year 835 of the First Age, there were many earthquakes and tremors felt throughout the world, and it was during one of these that a great avalanche fell into Ormace's valley, destroying his castle and burying it under tons of ice and rock and rubble. Hearing of this, Cupeldain sent an army of relief to the valley, but they found it covered over. Eventually, the castle would be excavated, and though many bones were uncovered, the Bloodcoins of the House of Fairbirch were never found.

The House of Fairfir
Lyrium and Heneil

Lyrium established the House of Fairfir. She worked very hard to convince Silmain and later Cupeldain to open the Nimbus Illuminas, but her efforts were doomed to fail. She eventually married Heneil, son of Silmain, and together they had twin daughters, Belmira and Elmira. Although she foresaw the catastrophe at Tulith Attis, she was unable to prevent it.

The following entries come to us from a set of documents discovered at the end of the Second Age among a trove of materials that had been hidden away in the private vaults of the former First Lord of High Chambers, Lord Banis of the House of Elmwood. The documents are incomplete, consisting of an unbound sheaf of handwritten materials. The author is unknown, but it seems apparent that it must have been someone very close to Lyrium, perhaps one or both of her daughters. The only other clue as to their origin comes from the fact that the rest of the materials included within the sheaf were unrelated documents and letters that had been stolen from the King's Post sometime around the year 860 of the Second Age (judging by the dates on some of the letters). Yet the diaries of Lord Banis clearly indicates that he himself did not come into possession of the documents until the year 870. How Banis came to possess them remains but one of the mysteries surrounding the documents.

Nevertheless, much was revealed by those documents. It seems apparent that Lord Banis must have read these materials and thus would have known the identity of the traitor of Tulith Attis. However, he could not reveal this knowledge (if he had any desire to do so) without also revealing that an associate of his, one Bailorg, would also be implicated in the fall of Tulith Attis. By the late Second Age, there was so much discontent with Lord Banis and the Sixth Unknown King that it seems evident that Banis could not risk further dissent by permitting the revelations within the documents to be made known. But why Banis chose to retain these rather than destroy them is a mystery.

We may never know the answers to the many questions those documents pose. The authorship of the documents remains in question. And if Banis had some reason for retaining the materials, he took it to the grave with him. As to the identity of the young boy at the end of the following passage, we can only assume that he was someone of great importance, perhaps even the seminal figure who rapidly rose to power some years later during the Year of the Red Door.

Lord Heneil

Heneil was a Firstborn twin, born to Silmain and Beryleve during the Time Before Time. His twin brother was Pellen. It is thought that during the time before the Fall, Heneil was a friend of Cupeldain and assisted in the building of the Palace of Linlally and many of the surrounding structures. When Aperion called away the Faerekind, Beryleve went with him, but Silmain and his sons remained to fight the Dragonkind and were Scathed.

Little is known about Silmain and his sons until the First Age, when Silmain emerged as one of the most powerful of the Elifaen. It is said that Silmain was jealous of the other Elifaen who had received from Aperion the Keys to the Nimbus Illuminas, the Bloodcoins, and he strove to attain power by uniting under him those other clans not pledged to the Seven High Houses. He gained a powerful ally in Cupeldain, and, in 143 F.A., he declared himself King of the Faere. He soon gained the support of many other Houses and launched an attack into the Dragonlands, during which Heneil played an important role as a warrior and leader. During these years, Heneil worked with Cupeldain to strengthen the fortifications of Linlally, and it was he who constructed the walls around Linlally's lake. However, he, along with his father and his brother, Pellen, grew disheartened by the continual wars and by the ongoing difficulties faced by the Elifaen.

When Silmain failed to gain support for opening the Nimbus Illuminas, Heneil's angry outbursts at those who opposed Silmain, including Cupeldain, sealed the divisions that would plague the Elifaen thereafter. In spite of this, Silmain and Heneil were forced to support continued war in the south against the Dragonkind.

During the years leading up to Silmain's death, Heneil served as his father's chief military advisor, leading armies across the Iridelin to seize lands that had been the domain of the woodland Elifaen who opposed Silmain. This act led to a general uprising in those "lands across the river," that turned into a two-year war. Pellen, Heneil's twin brother, joined the fight and led a fierce campaign against the woodland Elifaen, burning vast tracts of forest and destroying many towns.

When at last those lands were secured, Silmain and Heneil turned their attention once again to the south. It was largely due to Heneil's careful construction of keeps and defensive strongholds in the Blue Mountains that Vanara was able to push out the Dragonkind who had encroached there. Fighting continued for many years, and eventually Silmain was killed in battle.

Heneil was devastated by his father's death, and he blamed those who did not wish to bring together the Nimbus Illuminas to end their strife. However, both Heneil and Pellen made it known that they were not interested in accepting Silmain's throne. This announcement led to widespread disorder as several powerful Houses vied for supremacy in Vanara. The Elifaen quickly divided and formed alliances, which just as quickly fell apart. Murder and intrigue were rife in Vanara until, after over forty years of such strife, Heneil and Pellen supported Cupeldain of the House of Fairlinden, even though they had no wish to serve him.

During Cupeldain's reign, Heneil and his brother devoted themselves to less war-like pursuits. While Pellen traveled north to see those remote lands of Duinnor and Glareth, Heneil began to construct buildings and other structures in and around Linlally. He was as surprised as any when, in the year 810 of the First Age, Cupeldain called a great council to bring together the Nimbus Illuminas. Heneil threw his support behind Cupeldain, an act that rekindled friendship between the two Elifaen. Heneil worked feverishly behind the scenes to convince the other Elifaen to give over their Bloodcoins and to end the long suffering of their people. However, Secundur worked just as hard to thwart Heneil's efforts, going around and spreading rumors that led to greater discord and disagreement. Myrium and Lyrium, of the House of Fairfir, stood with Cupeldain, as did Pyros, Katrina, and Lucinda. But Therona and Ormace were adamant in their opposition. They were taken in by Secundur's whispers, and they maintained that Fairlinden and Fairfir were planning to use their Bloodcoins to open the Nimbus Illuminas without the consent of the others. Although Heneil, Cupeldain, and Lyrium tried to persuade them that such an act was impossible, Ormace was unmoved.

The crisis came when Ormace of the House of Fairbirch declared that he would destroy his Seven Bloodcoins rather than have them used. He produced a great hammer and made to strike one of his emerald Bloodcoins, but Lyrium threw herself over it. Angered by her act, Ormace lifted his hammer even higher over Lyrium as all cried out and implored Ormace to have mercy on her. Pellen, who was there, held back Myrium who tried to reach her sister, while Heneil drew his sword upon Ormace. Immediately, other weapons were produced and brandished amongst them. But Ormace had calculated this result, and it was then, with hammer still held aloft, that he made his proposal, as suggested by Secundur. In order to assure that none could use their Bloodcoins without the consent of the others, Ormace said, they were to redistribute them so that all would have a Bloodcoin from each House. And so, in order to prevent bloodshed amongst them, Cupeldain reluctantly conceded, along with Myrium and Lyrium. Pyros, Katrina, and Lucinda also had to agree, but Heneil was outraged. He went to Cupeldain and, whispering in his ear, begged permission to kill Ormace on the spot, saying that the others would not dare stand against them once Ormace was dead. But Cupeldain forbade it, telling Heneil that if Aperion allowed the Nimbus Illuminas to open, it surely would not be by an act of murder.

It was done. The Forty-Nine Bloodcoins of the Seven High Houses were divided so that each would have one of the others, but all would still have seven. Yet Heneil remained angry, and feared that Ormace might try to wrest the throne of Linlally from Cupeldain. With his sword still drawn in a threatening way, Heneil insisted that all of the High Houses present should swear their allegiance to Cupeldain's House of Fairlinden, in the presence of all others, and to support the House of Fairlinden forever. This they did, some reluctantly, others gladly. But Heneil had no trust for any of the leaders of the High Houses except Lyrium. Although he would serve the House of Fairlinden, he remained cautious and wary. And soon he would take up the sword once more.

Lady Lyrium

Lyrium and Myrium were Firstborn twins born of moonlight and starlight. They each had pale skin, long black hair, and eyes of glittering silver-gray. They enjoyed their company with one another, and cared not for the strife with the Dragonkind when it came. They were divided, though, when Aperion called the Faerekind away, with Myrium wishing to stay and Lyrium wishing to go. But neither could bear to be parted from one another, so they decided to stay and were Scathed.

In the years that followed, whilst all of the Elifaen suffered and learned to walk and to hunt and to do all of the things needed, Lyrium found that she had the gift of Sight, and Myrium the gift of song. But Lyrium, with her power, could foresee which streams would bear bountiful fish, and which trees would bear great numbers of nuts, and she saw many other things besides. This permitted Lyrium to ease the suffering of a great number of Elifaen, and she and her sister became the respected leaders of a clan of Elifaen that occupied the shores of the Iridelin River where it poured out from Linlally. Although they kept themselves aloof from the other Elifaen, for they did not trust them, their House of Fairfir became a respected and prosperous one. Lyrium, especially, was looked to for her leadership, and with her gift of Sight, she rarely failed to guide her people well.

However, as the years passed, it became apparent to Myrium that Lyrium struggled more and more to conjure her visions, and Lyrium confessed that the day might come when her skill may fail her altogether. This prompted Myrium to make new alliances with lesser Houses of the Elifaen, which strengthened their own.

When Aperion summoned the leaders of the Elifaen, and gave to the High Houses the Forty-Nine, he gave to Lyrium Seven that were made with amber. And Aperion also told Lyrium, without speaking aloud, that her gift would only slowly fade from her, since she, more than any of the others, still listened to the world and attended to its murmurings. Lyrium took heart by this, and determined to do what she could to obey Aperion and to encourage the others to use the Forty-Nine as he had instructed.

But it was not to be as Lyrium wished. The Seven High Houses seemed intent to remain apart from one another, and were little inclined to join together their Bloodcoins.

When Silmain became King and renewed the wars with the Dragonkind, Lyrium went to him and told him that she foresaw a time when he would regret doing so, and that he should instead seek to have the Forty-Nine brought together to open the Nimbus Illuminas. Although Silmain listened carefully to Lyrium, and had great respect for her, he did not agree. Silmain and Lyrium talked for a very long while, and one of Silmain's sons, Heneil, listened as they debated her suggestion. Ultimately, Silmain dismissed her by saying that until the Dragonkind were subjugated, he would not support her plan. Lyrium went away full of foreboding, but after she had departed, Heneil took to heart her words and pondered them carefully. Heneil knew his father's heart, but he slowly began urging Silmain to do as Lyrium wished. It would be many years before Silmain heeded her, but at last, weary of war and strife, he did. However, when Silmain called together the leaders of the Seven High Houses to use their Bloodcoins, only Lyrium, Pyros and Katrina were for it, and the effort failed.

Disappointed, Lyrium went away and told her sister what had happened. But Myrium was not too concerned, saying that if Aperion wished for any of them to depart, he would have made it so they could do so without the use of the Forty-Nine. Lyrium pondered this, but suspected that Myrium had become too attached to the world. And Lyrium knew that Myrium had become fond of Pellen, who was one of Silmain's sons, and she suspected, too, that Pellen did not wish to leave the world, either.

But Heneil came to Lyrium privately, saying that he would support his father the King in all that was asked of him, but that, if it could come about, he would rather go from the earth. He walked with Lyrium through the gardens of Vanara, and they talked all through the night. When morning came, and Heneil had to depart, Lyrium was in love.

Heneil and Lyrium would see each other again, many times. She tried to warn Heneil to protect his father and admonished him not to permit Ormace's army to go with him into the Dragonlands, but her message to Heneil arrived too late. As it turned out, the incompetence of Ormace resulted in Silmain's death in battle, and Lyrium was as sad as any that she had not prevented it. She feared that if either Pellen or Heneil took the throne, they would meet the same fate as their father. Whilst Myrium convinced Pellen not to accept the throne, there was no need for Lyrium to convince Heneil, for he had no lust for such power.

When Cupeldain was made king, Lyrium feared the worst. His zeal against the Dragonkind was well-known, though he ever watched for the well-being of Vanara. But Lyrium foresaw that he, too, would tire of war, and when at last Cupeldain called for the Forty-Nine to be brought together, Lyrium and Myrium went gladly to the Palace atop the high Falls of Tiandari.

Lyrium was made even happier when she found that five of the Seven High Houses were for the plan, and she worked very hard to convince Therona and Ormace to consent. But she did not know that Secundur also stalked the Palace halls, going from shadow to shadow and breathing lies and accusations to Ormace and Therona. As a result, Ormace accused the others of conspiring to use their Bloodcoins without his consent. He said that any one of them, with their Seven alone, could open the Nimbus Illuminas and force them all to leave. This was blatantly untrue, and Ormace knew it, for Aperion had told him otherwise just as he had told all of the others when first he gave the Forty-Nine to them.

"They must all be used together and at once," cried Cupeldain.

"None can use theirs alone," Pyros rejoined.

"It is not so!" Therona answered back.

"And we have it upon good authority that it is not," Ormace stated.

"Are you accusing Aperion of lying to us?" cried Katrina.

"You know better, Ormace," said Lucinda. "And I know that another breathes falsehoods and accusations to you, for he has also come to me, in the dark of night."

They argued, and Lyrium was aghast at the turn of events, hardly able to speak. She shook with fear and dread at what was taking place, and suddenly, as Myrium held her from fainting, Lyrium had a vision of what was about to happen.

"I shall not have it done!" cried out Ormace. He suddenly threw his Seven upon the marble floor and produced a great hammer. Lyrium tore herself away from Myrium and dove over Ormace's Bloodcoins to protect them from him.

"You witch!" Ormace shouted, raising his hammer to strike Lyrium. Heneil shouted and drew his sword and raised it to strike Ormace as Pellen restrained Myrium.

"Strike me and my hammer falls nonetheless!" Ormace said. Heneil froze, his sword still at the ready.

"Stop this at once!" cried out Cupeldain, coming to Ormace. "What would you have us do to convince you that we will not open the Nimbus Illuminas without your consent?"

"Take one of my Seven, each of you," said Ormace. "And give me one each of your own. And let it be likewise so that none may have Seven of the same color."

"Put away your sword, Heneil. And put away your hammer, Ormace. Come, Lyrium."

Cupeldain reached down and helped Lyrium up, who went sobbing into Myrium's arms. Cupeldain put onto the floor all his Seven beside those of Ormace.

"Let it be done," said Cupeldain.

And so it was, each putting all upon the floor, under Ormace's watchful eye and lifted hammer. Then, one by one, each took one of each type of Bloodcoin.

Then Heneil, still angry, forced all to swear allegiance to the House of Fairlinden, in hopes of preventing further strife amongst them. They all did so, but Heneil's anger was little quelled. Meanwhile, Lyrium sobbed, saying, almost incoherently, that it was their last chance to save their people. As all made ready to depart, she begged them not to go, pulling on their arms and going to her knees as she clung to them.

Unable to bear this, Heneil went to Cupeldain, who had slumped down onto his throne.

"Give me leave, my King, and I shall slay Ormace this instant. We shall have his Seven, and Therona's, too, and we shall make Aperion's way appear to us."

But Cupeldain looked at Heneil with pity in his eyes.

"Put away your sword, good prince," he said. "Do you think murder will open the way to Aperion's abode?"

"It would be just!" said Heneil. "You saw how little Ormace cared for Lyrium's life, and threatened her with his hammer. He has threatened Katrina and her people, too."

"Justice has nothing to do with it, Heneil," Cupeldain countered. "Ormace must come around as I have, and as Lucinda has done. With regret in his heart, and with weariness. Therona, likewise, must have it in her heart to give her Seven. Go to Lyrium. Her sister is too distraught herself to give comfort, but I know that Lyrium loves you and that you love her, and she will take comfort from your company."

Then, standing, Cupeldain cried out, "I desire to be alone. Leave me, I beg you all. Go in peace."

The Seven High Houses thus failed a second time to open the Nimbus Illuminas. Lyrium was distraught, and nearly inconsolable. But she was in love with Heneil, and he with her, and together they sought to comfort each other. Soon, Lyrium and Heneil married, and they had twin daughters, called Belmira and Elmira. Lyrium's sister and Heneil's brother, Myrium and Pellen, also married, and they had a son named Dalcadian.

Lyrium clung to hope, for Cupeldain was changed by his time in the world, and he longed for peace. She hoped that he would try again, someday, to bring together the Forty-Nine. But it was not to be. First, Lord Ormace was killed in an earthquake and his Bloodcoins were lost. An effort to excavate the ruins of Ormace's castle was made, financed and organized by Lyrium and Heneil. But unearthing Ormace's castle was a slow, tedious, and ultimately fruitless effort. His Bloodcoins could not be found. Then, while journeying across the Iridelin to conclude a peace agreement between feuding clans of Elifaen, Cupeldain and Loura were set upon and murdered. Nearly everyone traveling with Cupeldain was also murdered, including Lyrium's friend Shevalia and her husband Bychanter. Lyrium entered a state of dark melancholia. Myrium could not console her, and only Heneil seemed able to break through her sadness.

Parthais, Cupeldain's son, would become King of Vanara. And Heneil and Pellen were his strongest supporters, and went wherever Parthais wished them to go, warring with the Dragonkind or going with Parthais's army to put an end to conflicts in Altoria and Masurthia. The two brothers were with Parthais at the battle of Tamkal Plain, and they saw Parthais slay King Salkasin of the Dragonkind. But soon after that, Parthais began to grow unpredictable and morose, prone to anger and fits of jealousy while permitting corruption and violence amongst his ministers. All this made Heneil uneasy, so he took Lyrium and went into the north to live in Duinnor. There, he assisted others who fled the purges of Parthais, and advised the ruling lords of Duinnor to welcome such refugees. Heneil also worked to construct several castles, most of which would later become part of a great academy, and he helped design the defensive works around Duinnor, in case Parthais, who was angry at Duinnor, should attack. In all these things, Lyrium was uneasy, since she swore an oath to the House of Fairlinden. But Heneil said that the oath was to the House and not to Parthais. So, from afar, Heneil abided during the decline of Vanara while Parthais sunk further and further into madness and despotism. When Heneil heard that Parthais had banished his own son and daughter, Thurdun and Serith Ellyn, he made it known that he would never return to Vanara while Parthais sat upon its throne.

Then, some years later, Thurdun and Serith Ellyn, who were banished by their father, came secretly to Duinnor seeking Heneil and Lyrium, to tell them that they intended to wrest the throne from their father in order to save their people. They had raised a small army, with the help of disaffected Vanarans and the people of Elrasil the Hunter. Heneil gladly agreed to join them, as did Lyrium. Pellen and Myrium did likewise, and they soon added many followers to Thurdun and Serith Ellyn's army from among those exiles living in Duinnor.

They marched on Vanara, moving by night through the hills and hiding by day to avoid detection. On the night of their attack, their army came out of the north and east and swept swiftly through the lower city of Linlally, but there was little fighting as they were welcomed by the people who hoped for an end to their misery under Parthais. Serith Ellyn, with Thurdun, Lyrium, and Heneil with her, went ahead of the army as it spread out through lower Linlally, and they ascended up the Falls of Tiandari to the Palace. There Serith Ellyn slew her father and thus ended the First Age of the World.

The early years of the Second Age were happy ones for Heneil and his family. It was during this time that Belmira and Elmira were born, and Lyrium took great consolation from her children and from the love of Heneil. Indeed, by the 225th year of the Reign of Serith Ellyn, Vanara was beginning to thrive as never before. Accustomed as they were to a slow pace of change, many Elifaen were unsettled by the flurry of changes that took place after the fall of King Parthais. To others, Queen Serith Ellyn could not act fast enough to sweep away those whom her father had brought to power. But now the corrupt lords and ministers were gone, judges and magistrates, too, replaced by new leaders and new institutions to assure that the Queen's will, and the will of her people, would be carried out justly. Many who were banished by Parthais, or had fled his violent purges, were welcomed back and restored to their lands and their estates. The Queen especially assured returning scholars that, unlike her father, she would never allow any edict which would control what scholars of Vanara wrote or studied. She established new schools in which teachers were free to teach and scholars were free to study. She freed Vanara of the systems of corrupt patronage that Parthais had established, and she oversaw the passing of new laws to safeguard the people from unfair tribute. She freed all the roads from tolls, and all commerce from tariffs and duties in order to encourage renewed trade within and outside of Vanara. And she reinstated the old property tax methods that her grandfather, Cupeldain, had established, with every person given the right of appeal.

With all of these reforms, and many others, the population of Vanara was beginning to stabilize after many years of decline. And although there were fewer taxes overall, the coffers of the Crown grew steadily since tributes were no longer diverted to a few lords and traders that had previously enjoyed the protection of Parthais. Thus Vanara was able to finance an expansion of her armed forces, to build new roads and canals, to rebuild the towns and cities that Parthais had let fall into ruin, and fund several centers of learning. And so, for most, it was a time of great hope.

Heneil was busier than ever directing the reconstruction of Vanara's public buildings that Parthais had let fall into ruin. And he also assisted Prince Thurdun with the reorganization of Vanara's armed forces.

Heneil seemed happy enough in his new work, but Lyrium remained melancholy. She was glad that the reign of Parthais had ended, and that Vanara was prospering under Queen Serith Ellyn. But Lady Lyrium was gripped with terrible sadness and regret over the loss of so many of the Bloodcoins, those forty-nine objects given by Aperion to the Seven High Houses of the Elifaen as a way for the Elifaen to end their strife on earth and rejoin the Faerekind. Only twenty-one Bloodcoins remained, those given to Serith Ellyn's House of Fairlinden and to Lyrium's House of Fairfir, and to Pyros' House of Fairmyrtle. All of the others—those belonging to Ormace, Katrina, Lucinda, and Therona—were gone, along with their Houses. And those once held by Pyros had been seized by King Kapol of Tracia, since the House of Fairmyrtle had been recently dissolved upon the death of Nianan, the last remaining heir of Pyros. Even if King Kapol could be convinced to give up those Bloodcoins that he possessed, the loss of the others meant that the few remaining ones were useless.

Lyrium, who was blessed with the Gift of Sight, struggled very hard to discover where the lost Bloodcoins were. It was to no avail. Her visions were increasingly more difficult for her to conjure, and when they came, they were more difficult for her to interpret and understand. And not once did they ever contain any hint concerning the lost Bloodcoins.

She became increasingly resigned to the fact that the Elifaen had failed. They were now trapped upon the earth forever, and Lyrium mourned over all of the strife that could have been avoided.

She was much comforted, though, by her twin daughters, and she spent many happy hours with them each day. The children and the love that Lyrium and Heneil had for each other—the exuberance of their love well-known—was a powerful force that kept Lyrium from falling into hopeless despair. Perhaps now that Parthais was gone and Serith Ellyn showed no signs of falling into the despotism of her father, there might be a chance for her daughters to find happiness. If she herself could not find peace, perhaps she might find contentment. And if the persistent conflicts with the Dragonkind could ever be brought to a lasting end, perhaps all of Vanara's people might now have a chance for peace and contentment, too.

One morning in early autumn, not long after Heneil had departed their home to supervise the construction of bridges over the River Iridelin, a mysterious messenger arrived asking to speak with Lyrium. He was shown to her sitting room where she soon joined him. She saw at once that he was unusual. His skin was dark brown, his head completely shaven. By the slight stubble on his chin, she could see that he was one of the Newcomers, the race called Men, and although she was not practiced at such guesses, she imagined that he might be only thirty years of age. Even though it was a cold day out, he was dressed in a simple loose robe of sky-blue and wore only sandals on his feet. He bowed very low, and she curtseyed.

"Lady Lyrium," he said.

"Yes," she replied. "My servant tells me that you would not give your name."

"Members of my Order relinquish their names when vows are taken," he said.

"Oh? And what is the nature of your Order?"

"I am a servant of Beras, as are all of my Order." "Surely we all should be that."

"Indeed, my lady."

"And does your Order have a name?"

"No, my lady. It is as its members are, with no name other than that which seems suitable to use as the occasion merits."

Lyrium gazed carefully at the man.

"And to what do I owe the honor of this visit?"

"I have come, at the bidding of my master, the Oracle of Beras, to impart a message."

"Oh?"

"My master says to tell you that the days of the Elifaen are now on the wane. Men are on the rise. Their old world was destroyed, and the sea has cast them upon the shores of this world. Although they strive to build a new world for themselves, the world they will bring about is not of their design. Soon a new power amongst Men will rise up, a power that will reach over all of the earth. Six seasons shall come and go, says my master, some quickly, some very slowly. With each passing season, a new star will shine, one next to the previous. Until at last there will come the Seventh Season, the shortest of all, and the Seventh Star. Then the world will be remade, for better or for worse.

"My master says to you, Lady Lyrium of the House of Fairfir, that your Sight will wane as the last vestige of the Faerekind's power on earth wanes. But he says to you that since you, of all your people, have been most faithful to your charge, given unto you by Aperion, that your gift of Sight will diminish only but slowly. And he says that your Gift will serve you well if you are careful to coax it, and if you are careful to see rightly what is shown to you. He says to you, have a care to abide your Sight this very evening. It shall guide you to an object of great power. My master bids you take the object and keep it safe with those eight other objects of power that you now possess. Keep this object hidden, and keep all knowledge of it to yourself, telling no one about it until comes the time for you to use it. For with this new object, and with one other object that you already possess, you may test the Seventh Star before it shines. Know this: The Seventh Star shall come of the East, but shall arrive from the West. He shall be hidden from the world until it is come time for him to be known. When comes that time, go to him and offer the two objects of power to him. Thus, you shall see his worthiness. When you have seen his worthiness, lend to him your encouragement, for the Hidden One shall not know his own way for many years. And when he learns it, he shall yearn to refuse it. Yet his will be the duty, the way, and the might so that old promises may be kept, old grievances cast aside, and old strife turned to new hope."

"I don't understand," said Lyrium. "Seven seasons? Seven stars? East? West? What is the meaning of these words? And what object do you mean?"

"The meaning, Lady Lyrium, is for you to discern, as sign after sign is given unto you. My master says one last thing to you: Look first to your Sight. Then, in years to come, look to the north for news. For in that land the evidence of these words will show, upon Mount Onuma nearby to the City of Duinnor, and in the skies that ride above that city. Ponder things well, Lady Lyrium. And may peace be with you. That is all that my master says."

The monk looked upon Lyrium serenely with a kindly expression bearing the hint of a smile. Lyrium, for her part, was baffled.

"How comes your Oracle to know of me?" she asked. "And to send these words to me?"

"I know not the scope of his wisdom, nor can I conceive the matters that he knows. But he is the Oracle of Beras, so I know the font of my master's knowledge and insight."

"That is a most audacious thing to say," responded Lyrium.

"For if Beras has placed an Oracle upon the earth, surely we here in Vanara would know."

"Nay. With respect, dear lady, perhaps not. The entire breadth of the earth is under the Intent of Beras, as well as the wheel of the heavens with Sir Sun and Lady Moon attending. So it may be reasoned that this realm of Vanara is but a waypoint and not the path. Just as it might be said that Duinnor is but another place, but does not encompass all other places. And, therefore, a new temple comes to be built upon the earth, and a new Oracle to reside therein. These are the days when the course of events takes a turn. Just as your Queen has changed the course of Vanara, so, too, does Beras reshape history, moving to put aside the old in order to make way for the new, be it light or dark, be it for good or for ill by our judgment. Certainly it is not for those of us who tread the path to know at the beginning of our sojourn all that will be known at journey's end."

Lyrium shook her head, turning aside in thought. She absently looked out through a nearby window. For a long moment, she looked across the city at the distant high falls of Tiandari pouring forth in five long strands that fanned the morning light. When she turned back to the monk, he bowed.

"I bid you peace, Lady Lyrium. I must depart." "Wait. Wait just a moment."

Lyrium hurried from the room, leaving the monk somewhat surprised and perplexed. He went to the window, and he gazed at Tiandari just as Lyrium had done. He was still there when she returned bearing a purse.

"Allow me to show you out," she said.

When they reached the outside door, she held out her purse.

"Permit me to offer this to you and to your Order," she said, giving the purse to the monk. "I think that if you are truly an Order ordained by Beras, that you will exercise compassion upon those who are in need, those who have been harmed by others or who have, through no fault of their own, been abandoned, shunned, or left in want. In their name I give this to you, in regard for the message that was delivered unto me just now. Although it is not much compared to the need, it may be a start."

Now the monk smiled broadly, and accepted the purse.

"It is as the Oracle foresaw," he said, bowing once more. "He told me that the means by which our Order shall minister unto others will have its beginning with the House of Fairfir. Thank you, Lady Lyrium."

"Safe journey."

Lyrium watched the man walk away and pass through the gate and out of sight. When she closed the door and turned around, her little twin daughters, still in their nightgowns, were standing behind her in the hallway.

"Mother, where was he from?" asked one. "Mother, why did he come?" ask the other.

"I do not know where he came from, not exactly. He came to deliver a message."

"Of great importance, it must have been to you…" "…since the jewels you gave were none too few."

"Yes. An important message, indeed, I think. And the purse held only a few old jewels that have been gathering dust," she answered, gently pushing them ahead of her as she went through the vestibule. "Isn't it about time you two should get dressed?"

For the rest of the day, Lyrium pondered the message, the messenger, and the Oracle of Beras. By the time Heneil had returned late that evening, she had decided to say nothing to him about the visitor. After they had dined, and the children were in bed, she went to Heneil.

"My husband, tonight I feel the need to See," she said, "and

I have certain things that I wish to delve by doing so."

"Of course, my love," he said. "Would you like for me to abide nearby to you?"

"No. I do not think I shall need your assistance tonight. I shall go to our parlor and strive to see what I might See. But perhaps you would remain at your books and studies until I emerge?"

"Certainly. I will be happy to do so."

That evening, Lyrium's Sight came to her almost without any effort on her part. Indeed, as soon as she closed the door to the parlor, and before she could even kneel on the carpet to prepare herself, she Saw.

It was a snowy day that Lyrium saw, and a long stretch of road. In the distance, she could see the ruins of an ancient henge, many of its stones leaning precariously. Then she perceived a movement, and she spotted a small group of dogs, one that was full grown trailed by three little pups that jumped and pranced happily along through the snow. Just as they were crossing the road, a rider came galloping over the hill and bore down upon them. The pups, confused and bewildered by the oncoming horse, tried to scatter. The large dog, which Lyrium now saw was a great wolf, turned and snapped at her young just when the horse and rider were upon them. The horse, seeing or smelling the wolves, panicked and began rearing and bucking. Its rider shouted at the horse and flogged it with a crop, but in doing so he only made the horse more frantic, and it stumbled and fell, throwing the rider and falling onto one of the little pups, killing it instantly. The large wolf attacked the horse at once, and the man, uninjured, drew his sword and swung at the wolf. For a moment, the outcome was in doubt, for the wolf threw itself onto the man and both went tumbling, kicking up snow as they fought one another. Then the wolf got hold of the man's sword hand with its teeth and shook and pulled viciously. The man, screaming in agony, dropped his sword, and he kicked and punched at the wolf with his free hand. Whether the man pulled free, or the wolf let go, Lyrium could not tell, but as soon as the two were separated, the wolf began bounding away, going this way and that as if wounded and dizzy. The man leapt to his feet, clutching his mangled and bleeding hand, and he chased after the wolf. Meanwhile, his horse was long fled. The man stumbled and fell, got up, and continued to chase the wolf that was now running down the road in a drunken fashion. At last, the wolf veered off the road and into the nearby brush. The man fell again, and he did not get up, though he kept screaming and shouting for a long while. His voice eventually grew weak and barely audible until Lyrium could hear him no more.

Lyrium's vision darkened. She watched as Lady Moon rapidly rose up over the distant henge and pass quickly overhead as if racing the stars. Then Sir Sun appeared in the east just as quickly as his lady had passed. And when he was high overhead, he slowed his course through the daytime sky. Lyrium saw that the man was still prostrated in the roadway.

Another rider approached from the opposite direction. He stopped and dismounted to give the first man his attention. She watched as the second man returned quickly to his horse and pulled off a blanket, and he put it over the injured man. Tearing off strips from his own blouse, the traveler made a tourniquet around the injured man's hand, and then he tried to bandage the hand. When that was done, he hurried away into the nearby wood, soon returning with many sticks which he piled at the side of the road. Lyrium watched as the man went back and forth gathering a great supply of sticks and branches. He also brought armloads of pine straw and leaves, and, after arranging a thick mound upon the ground, he put another blanket down upon it. Then he set to work building a fire. As soon as the fire was crackling, he went back to the injured man and lifted him up. He carried the injured man in his arms to the fire and placed him beside it upon the bed of straw and leaves.

"Have no worry," the man said, "I will not abandon you. And as soon as you are able, I shall help you to a village just south of here where there is shelter and where I can give you better care."

"Do not waste your effort," said the injured man, "for I am ruined. Ruined!"

"I do not know what you can mean," was the reply. "The pain of your injury only makes things seem worse than they are. Once you are healed, you will think differently."

"No. It is not merely the injury itself, not merely the loss of my fingers," said the injured man. "And I do not mind that I am ruined and that my time has come at last to die. I have for many years done wicked things, and the wolf that bit me perhaps did me a great favor. By taking my finger, and the ring that was upon it, my mind is clear, free as it has not been for twenty years."

"Your words baffle me, sir."

"Pray, tell me, what is your name? Where are you from and bound for?"

"Pardon me, sir. My name is Harson Corvis. I am from Kalbrith, in Tracia Realm. I travel in search of trading opportunities, having sailed from Forlandis to Draymoor, thence overland to Linlally. I now travel to Duinnor City."

"Then you are a Man."

"Yes."

"So am I, and so my hand will not heal as it might if I were Elifaen," the injured man said. "My name is Tarsus Maklaran, of Duinnor. Perhaps you have heard of me?"

"No, sir. I do not recognize the name."

"No matter. It will soon be forgotten, anyway, for I have no children, and no legacy of valor or any great works to which my name will be attached."

"I beg you rest," said Harson. "I have food in my saddlebags, and a small pot for heating water. I shall soon have something warm for you to eat."

"Do not bother. Leave me and be on your way. I am not long for this world."

"I bother for both our sakes. I am hungry, too! And I shall not leave you."

"Then stay. Do not bring food. I grow weak, and am too faint to eat. Let me tell you my story, why I am ruined. Why I do not resent ending my days here, alone but for you."

Lyrium's vision was such that she watched from many yards away. Yet, when Tarsus spoke, she heard his words well, even though he spoke with difficulty.

"I am a lord of Duinnor," Tarsus said. "I am feared by all. But now that I will soon be out of the way, there will be turmoil for a time in Duinnor until others wrest for themselves the power that I wielded until late.

"Twenty-one years ago, my estate was one of the smallest in the realm, of no consequence. I paid tribute to the council of lords that has ruled Duinnor since the last king died, some hundred years ago. However, I learned of a sorcerer who was able to grant wishes for a sum of gold. His abode was in the mountains to the south of Forest Islindia, on the eastern side of the Iridelin. I went there, and I found the sorcerer. I bargained with him to grant my wish to know the thoughts of all and any who was in my presence. He was reluctant to do so, but I persisted. He said that granting such a wish could cause much misunderstanding, and that the power to hear the thoughts of others would have a corrupting influence. But I made little of his concerns, and I offered him a great amount of gold, the worth of my entire estate. At last I convinced him. He agreed to fashion a ring that would enable the wearer to do as I wished, to hear what others were thinking. But he made a condition, which was that any who was offered the ring and refused it would be granted one single wish, no matter what that wish was. So we made our bargain. He bade me give him one half of the gold immediately and then return to him in one year. That I did. And in a year's time I returned to him. He had fashioned a ring that he called the Ring of Hearing. Before he gave it to me, he said that it would only serve Mortal Men, and it would be utterly useless to an Elifaen. He reminded me of his concerns, saying that he doubted that I was wise enough to use the ring, that he feared I would eventually put it to evil use. And he also reminded me that if I refused the ring, I would be granted any wish whatsoever, anything at all that I desired. But I was adamant. I put all my gold before him, and demanded the ring. Indeed, I took the ring from him and immediately put it on."

"That's when it began. As soon as I put the ring on my finger, I saw what was in the sorcerer's mind. He planned to steal the ring back from me at the first opportunity, in order to destroy it. This knowledge infuriated me, and I flew into a rage. And I...I..."

Tarsus hesitated.

"It was the first time," he went on, "and the only time that I ever killed anyone with my own hands. But I murdered him. And I fled his abode and hurried back to Duinnor."

Harson tossed a few sticks onto the fire, but said nothing. "You do not believe me!" cried Tarsus. "But let me tell you more. I will not tell you the many ways that I used the ring, to increase my power, to usurp my fellow lords, to conspire against their conspiracies, and to blackmail and coerce any and all to do my bidding. I will not tell you the many ways in which my power, my wealth, and my position grew. But I was soon a mighty lord, respected. Feared. And after only a few short years, I was the chief ruling lord upon the council of Duinnor lords, and it was I who played one against the other for my own benefit.

"The sorcerer had, indeed, foretold the true consequence of wearing the Ring of Hearing. Not only did I do many vile things, and had many terrible things done by others in my sway, but I was constantly tortured. I never dared remove the ring, not even during sleep, for fear of what someone might be planning to do against me. My own family was not immune to my fears, and I banished them all until only I remained in my manor house. Even then, I was fearful of my servants. I slept as little as possible, and then only behind heavily barred doors, constantly waking to listen at the thoughts of my servants going about their work, fearing they might betray me and let my enemies into my abode.

"Year passed year, and steadily my madness grew. Until, at last, having no peace in Duinnor, I struck out alone to find some place away from people where I could find peace, where I could sleep a natural sleep. Where I might dare remove the ring from my finger."

"If you go to Duinnor," Tarsus went on, "carry the news of my death. See for yourself how that news is received, and let that be the confirmation of my tale. In all the years since I put the ring upon my finger, I have told no one about it at all, until this night. When the wolf bit my finger from my hand, and with it the Ring of Hearing, my madness came full upon me. Rather than tending to my wound, I let it bleed whilst I chased after the wolf to get back the ring. But I had not the strength. That is the state in which you found me. Now, in your presence, I know again the peace of my own thoughts alone. The easy and natural quiet of my own mind, unmingled with your thoughts. Ah! That is my sorry tale! For power I gave up the chance for a good and wholesome life. For power I made myself hated and feared, when I should have been a man of good works."

"You must not tax yourself," said Hanson, whom Lyrium saw was upset by the tale he had just heard. "You must allow me to make some hot food for us to partake of. When we have eaten, then we shall rest."

"Do as you wish," said Tarsus, turning over onto his back and putting his head down. Lyrium watched as Hanson went to his horse and took from the packs a little pot and a bag of victuals. But she could also see the tears that glittered down the face of Tarsus. He whispered, "And so it shall go to the Elifaen."

Hanson did not hear him say that, but Lyrium did. And Lyrium saw that, only a moment or two later, Tarsus was dead.

Suddenly, the moon and stars overhead shot across the sky, and the sun rose quickly in the east, just as before, then stopped. Lyrium saw Hanson making a grave. He had no pick or shovel, so instead he gathered rocks and piled them upon the dead man until he was covered over. Afterwards, he gathered up his things, and he rode away.

The vision had come in a flash, and it left just as suddenly. Lyrium found herself swaying with dizziness, back in her own parlor. She immediately sat on the nearest chair. After a moment's thought, she began to doubt what she had seen in her vision. And, for some reason, it was not the tale of Tarsus that lingered in her mind, but the memory of seeing the leaning stones of the ancient henge. She realized where the incident had taken place, or would take place if the vision had been one of the future. The words of the monk came back to her:

"...have a care to abide your Sight this very evening. It shall guide you to an object with which you may test the Seventh Star before it shines."

She sat for a long while, pondering what she should do. She suddenly stood and left the parlor, going to her husband. She found him within his study chamber, looking over some letters he had recently received. When he saw her, he looked up.

"Have you decided against trying to See this evening?" he asked.

"My Sight has already come to me," she answered. "And I must now go on a journey." "Where must you go?"

"North, along the old road toward Duinnor."

"To Duinnor?"

"No, I shan't go that far. I must go to Minion Gap, to the old henge that is nearby to the road."

"But why? Why must you go there?"

"I must heed what has come to me in my vision," Lyrium said. "I cannot say more, because there are many mysteries wrapped up in the vision. But this I can tell you: if my Sight is trustworthy, and if events unfold out accordingly, then a great change is taking shape."

"A great change? What kind of change?"

"The rise of a new power, I think."

"Oh!" said Heneil. "When do we depart?"

"I must go alone, Heneil," said Lyrium, squatting beside his chair and putting her hand in his. "I will be careful, and travel as quickly as my buckmarl can go. And I will return as soon as possible."

Heneil frowned. But he was well-acquainted with the mystery and marvels of Lyrium's gift of Sight. So he nodded.

"So be it," he said.

Lyrium rose, and turned to go.

"Tell me," she asked, "do you know the name Tarsus Maklaran?"

Heneil looked at her with concern.

"Yes, I do. He is a great lord of Duinnor, the chief lord of their ruling council," he said. "I hope you will have nothing to do with him!"

"I do not know. Why do you say that?"

"Because he is reputed to be vicious. They say he moves to make himself king."

"Oh," Lyrium said. "I do not think that will happen." "What makes you say that?"

"Because I think he is dead. Or if he is not dead, I think he soon shall be. But I can say no more for now. I depart in the morning."

Indeed, Lyrium departed on her buckmarl the next morning, after kissing her husband and her two daughters goodbye. She carried no weapons, and she took with her only a small bag of amulets that might help her See should the need arise. It would be a journey of over 300 miles, and she rode with some urgency, both day and night, stopping only to rest and feed her mount. She passed very few other travelers, and those that she came upon that were going north as she did, she passed by quickly and left them behind, not wishing to speak to anyone. By the time she reached Airemoor, it had been snowing for two days. She rode on through the town without stopping.

Early the following morning, some eight days after leaving home, she came to the place where an east-west path crossed the road, in the region called Minion Gap. She knew that she was near the old stone henge that she had seen in her vision, and she slowed her pace, riding carefully on until, around noontime, she could see the henge. It was atop a broad hill, a few furlongs eastward, and the gray stones, capped and coated with snow, were a stark contrast to the brightly lit sky. Halting, she gazed at the henge for a few moments.

All during her travel, she had tried to think of what it was that she should do once she had arrived. But now that she had reached her destination, she was no closer to knowing. For a moment, she wondered whether it had all been a mistake.

The light breeze shifted, and Lyrium smelled the distinct aroma of burnt wood. Nudging her mount on along the road, she looked carefully for the source and soon found, only a few yards off the road, the remnants of a recent fire. Dismounting, she hurried to it and saw that it had not been long since it had died out, for no snow was upon the ashes. Nearby was a pile of sticks, and there was also a small mound of straw and leaves, pressed down in the very way they would be had someone lain upon the pile. Turning this way and that, she finally saw the pile of rocks, some twenty yards farther away from the road, in a small clearing. Going to it, she saw that it had very recently been constructed, perhaps only a few hours earlier.

This was confirmation enough of the vision that her Sight had given her. She still did not know what to do. But she was certain that if the tale of Tarsus was true, then perhaps it was the Ring of Hearing that she was meant to find.

Lyrium walked back, looking carefully at the snow- covered road as she went. There was only one set of tracks, those of a horse that she was certain belonged to Harson Corvis. Farther along, she came to a place where the snow was scuffled and kicked about. A glint caught her eye and, reaching into the snow, she pulled out a short sword. Its hilt was covered with blood, and there was also blood on the blade. Continuing carefully, she saw tracks, those of a very small animal, like those of a wolf pup. And she saw another set of tracks, those of a larger wolf, coming back to the place where she had found the sword. There was something odd about the tracks, and she realized that the big wolf had been limping. Looking very carefully, she followed the tracks away from the road and into the sparse woods. And, every few feet, there was a smudge of red along the tracks.

Lyrium whistled to her buckmarl, and the creature came to her.

"Follow," she said, and the buckmarl obliged, trailing a few feet behind Lyrium. She continued following the wolf tracks eastward. After a few hundred yards, she realized where they were leading her. At the edge of the woods, at the base of the hill upon which stood the henge, she paused, gazing at the hilltop.

"Remain here," she said to her buckmarl. Then she cautiously proceeded out of the woods and up the hill, following the bloody tracks.

The henge loomed, made up of some thirty or so huge stones about twice Lyrium's height and arranged in a broad circle. She knew that such places were built before the Fall, when all of her kind spoke the First Tongue and could coax the stones of faraway mountains into the air. And she knew that some of the Faerekind had built many henges, but she did not know why. They were not as elegant or as finely made as some of the temples that were made during the Time Before Time, so she doubted that the henges were for that purpose. But thousands of years had passed since that age, and many of the henges that she knew of were like this one, with many of its stones sunken into the ground, or tilted, or completely fallen over. She came onto the broad flat top of the hill and approached the first stone. Shivers coursed up her spine.

She halted a few feet from the first stone, listening. She heard an odd sound coming from ahead, from within the circle of stones. Carefully approaching, she hid behind the stone and then leaned cautiously around it to look. Within the henge were many other stones, some that were rectangular in shape. At the base of one of these, she saw some movement, and she heard again the peculiar sound. When she realized what the sound was, she understood what she saw. It was whimpering. A mournful sound. A large she-wolf lay there, licking a motionless pup, whilst two other pups lay nearby, their heads on their front paws, watching. The she-wolf raised her head to the sky and let out a high-pitched howl that tapered off to a low whimper as she lowered her head once more to her dead pup. Another river of shivers flowed up and down Lyrium's back and arms, tingling her scars and setting the hair of her scalp on end.

For she heard words. Wolf-words. And she knew what they meant.

Summoning her courage, she stepped from behind the stone and let herself be seen. Immediately, the two pups yipped and snarled at her, standing protectively in front of their mother and their dead sibling.

"Silence!" barked the she-wolf. "And away with you! This is the one I have awaited."

The two pups cringed and hesitated.

"Be off!" she growled. The pups reluctantly skulked away. The she-wolf turned to Lyrium, and in a sudden mournful whimper, she said, "Approach Fallen Faerekind. You come to do me a great favor."

Lyrium hesitated. She wondered how she understood the wolf, for the First Tongue had left her eons ago.

"It is not the First Tongue you hear," said the she-wolf, "but my own language."

"How?" thought Lyrium, confused but slowly drawing near.

"It is because of this ring, lodged upon my tooth," said the she-wolf. "All night I have lain here with my dead son. All night I have heard the thoughts of two Men. One of them put this wound in me, here in my side. It was his horse that killed my pup. The other Man happened by later."

Lyrium immediately recalled the tale that Tarsus told, but before she could form a question, the wolf spoke again.

"I am called Moonwulf, because I was born on a night when Lady Moon was at her brightest and boldest," said the she- wolf. "And you wonder that I may speak in ways that you understand. I wonder, myself, and but for this accursed thing lodged in my mouth, I would be as ignorant as any other of my kind. For in a single night, I have been given the gift of hearing not only what Men say, and what they mean, but what they think, too. And not only Men. I now hear your thoughts, too. And all that those two men thought upon, memories that were recent and long ago, I heard and understood. And now all that you think upon I also understand."

"And since for the Elifaen, such as you," the wolf went on, "time moves slowly within the heart—such that many things may be thought of in the course of a short while—all that you have thus remembered and pondered, I know. I know your history. I know your dreams. I know your language, and the meaning of all of your words, even if you say none aloud. I know the names of your daughters, whom you call Elmira and Belmira. And I know that they are twins. Your husband's name is Heneil. And his brother, Pellen, is wed to your sister, called Myrium. And you and Myrium are twins, too."

"Why do I tell you this? I tell you so that you will have no fear of me. This is the way of it: I am made old beyond my years. My heart is made old overnight, burdened with the terrible memories of the two Men whom I came to know last night. And now, with yours mingled in, I do not think I can abide much longer, but will soon join my young one, here, in the place where wolves go when they die. And then my two daughters must fend for themselves. Come closer to me, I cannot speak loudly, for my breath leaves me quickly, and it is painful for me to draw. Come nigh unto me, and sit yourself there, upon that stone."

Lyrium did so, sitting only two or three feet from the she-wolf.

"You are not the first person to have Sight," said the she-wolf. "There have been others, many others. Some had other gifts, too. One was an Elifaen by the name of Xilos who once lived many leagues south of Vanara, in the mountains beyond Islindia's blighted forest. He had Sight, and he could foresee the outcome of certain things. He also had the gift of granting wishes. The manner of his gift was such that he had to give over the power of each wish into some work of his hands, being in metal, in wood, or in cloth or other material. Because he had Sight, he knew the outcome of his gift of granting wishes. And he knew from his Sight, too, that he would grant one wish that would be a foolish one. But his Sight did not tell him which one would be foolish. He was much in demand to those who knew how to find him. For one village far away by the Great Sea, he made a wondrous feather that would tell what weather was to come. For a lady of Glareth, he made a marvelous lantern that would glow brightly of its own accord, without flame, on nights when Lady Moon does not shine, or on nights when the sky is covered over with clouds. The lady's intention was to put the lantern into a high tower so that sailors far at sea might find their way home to their city, called Glareth by the Sea. Each time he granted such a wish, and made a thing to be the vessel of that wish, he feared it would be the one foolish time that he had foreseen. But he was doomed to grant wishes to any who found him out."

"Thus, at last, he made his mistake. To Tarsus Maklaran, Xilos granted the wish to know the thoughts of others, and he made the wish into a ring of iron. But, fearing great mischief, Xilos put his own wish into the iron ring as well as that of Tarsus Maklaran, so that any who could refuse the offer of the ring would be granted a wish, no matter how great the wish was. He also made the ring so that it would only reveal the thoughts of others if worn by a Man, for he feared his own kind, the Elifaen, more than he feared Men. However, Xilos did not foresee that the ring would also reveal the thoughts of Elifaen such as himself, thinking that only the thoughts of Men would be revealed to the wearer of the ring. Still, Xilos was racked with hesitation. He knew that he was bound by his bargain to give over the ring to Tarsus Maklaran, but he planned to find an opportunity to cut the ring from Tarsus Maklaran's hand and then to destroy the ring.

"All these things did Tarsus Maklaran learn when he slipped the Ring of Hearing onto his finger. He learned about Xilos and his gift of Sight. He learned also of all of the wonderful wishes, and things, that Xilos had made before. And, of course, he learned about the sorcerer's plan to take back the ring."

"The rest, you already know, for your own Sight has revealed that to you," said the she-wolf. "But I, Moonwulf, learned something that Xilos did not know, that Tarsus Maklaran could never have learned. I learned, to my woe, that the ring's magic would grant its power to any creature but Elifaen. Even to a wolf. So when I bit the hand of Tarsus Maklaran, and the ring lodged on my tooth, I immediately heard and understood his thoughts, his rage, and his desperation. I had never before felt such, nor did I ever before suspect that Men were capable of having feelings at all. I also learned his history, all about his deeds against his own kind, and all about his fears. Such was the power of those revelations that I went mad myself. And even though he had wounded me with his sword, I should have turned on him and killed him. I should have gone back for my young one immediately, perhaps to groom and caress life back into him. But I did not go back for my pup until this very morning, when my own fears and my own feelings overcame me, when I was almost too weak to bring him away."

"So I fetched him and carried him here by the nape of his neck, though he was already dead. That is not the way of my kind. I do not know why I did it."

Again, the she-wolf raised her head to howl, but it was a weak, plaintive moan. Then she licked her dead pup a time of two, and nudged it with her nose. She whimpered very softly, and then she looked back to Lyrium.

"You wonder how I knew you would come," the she-wolf said to Lyrium.

Lyrium nodded.

"Xilos foresaw it," said Moonwulf. "And Tarsus Maklaran saw what Xilos had foreseen. Xilos had a vision that the Ring of Hearing, if not destroyed, would be given unto an Elifaen lady, a Firstborn of the Faerekind, by a wolf. Xilos greatly feared this, thinking that should the Elifaen gain possession of the ring, it would be given unto Secundur and reforged to make a ring that would grant the Elifaen the power that Xilos had reserved within the ring for Men alone. But it was only after Xilos had forged the ring, and before he had given it over to Tarsus Maklaran, that his Sight told him the fate of the ring. That is the true reason why he determined to take the ring from Tarsus Maklaran as soon as he could do so. And that is what sealed his fate. And so, since Tarsus Maklaran knew all within the mind of Xilos, and because I, in turn, learned all that was within his mind, I have waited for you. Please take it."

Moonwulf opened her mouth fully, and Lyrium saw the ring. It had gotten caught on one of her canine teeth and wedged against an adjoining tooth. She hesitated.

"I am too weak," the she-wolf said. "I can barely lift my head, so I cannot attack you. But I wish to die a wolf, not as the creature this ring has made me. Take it from me, I beg you. And then remember what the monk told you."

Lyrium cautiously reached into the mouth of the wolf, grasped the ring, and tugged. It did not come out, so she quickly reached with her other hand and, using her fingers, pried it up and pulled harder. It came out, and she backed away, gripping it within her fist. The she-wolf panted for a moment, as if out of breath, then yowled loudly. Lyrium did not understand what it said. With her eyes on Lyrium, Moonwulf put her head down with her chin on her dead pup. After a moment, she exhaled heavily. Her eyes remained open, but the spark of life was gone.

Lyrium returned to Vanara, back to her home in Linlally a few hours before dawn, and she went immediately to her private chamber. She took up a small wooden box, no bigger than her hand, and opened it. Inside, resting on a small pillow, was a beautiful ring of silver, its band set with tiny bits of amber. It had been a gift from her sister. She removed the silver ring and put it on her finger. Then she took from her pouch the Ring of Hearing and put it into the box. Going to a long chest on the floor, she knelt and opened the lid. Inside, at the bottom of the chest, was Ethliad, the sword, wrapped in fine linen. On top of the sword was a box made of rosewood, no bigger than a large book. She opened it and gazed for a moment at the seven Bloodcoins within it. Then she closed it, and she put the box containing the Ring of Hearing on top of it. After a moment, she lowered the lid of the chest.

Lyrium stood and crossed the room to a chair and sat. She pondered all that she had learned and all that the monk had told her. She wondered, as she had done so many times during her journey back to Vanara, what great change the future held in store.

For a moment, she was filled with hope.

In 266 S.A., Heneil traveled east to meet the Newcomers, a mortal race that had come from the sea, who called themselves Men and were establishing towns and villages along the coasts. While there, Heneil constructed bridges and roadways to further trade and commerce. In 275 S.A., he and Lyrium settled in Attis, a pleasant crossroads of the trade routes near the headwaters of the River Saerdulin. A few years later, in 278 S.A., there was an uprising of forest Elifaen led by the House of Pinewood. Their targets were the settlements of the Newcomers, but Pinewood also interfered with all trade, robbing and killing Men and Elifaen alike as they terrorized the countryside of Tracia and the Eastlands. Heneil worked to rebuild and remodel the defenses on the heights overlooking Attis, called Tulith Attis. He also led several counterattacks on Pinewood strongholds. Within a couple of years, he had formed a loose-knit alliance with Men of the surrounding region.

Hearing that Heneil was uniting with Men, Tracia Realm under the rule of King Kapol of the House of Alder joined the fight on the side of Pinewood. Glareth soon afterwards allied itself to the Eastlands and sent forces to the Kingdom of Colleton to aid in its defense. Soon Duinnor, Vanara, Masurthia, and Altoria had also joined with Glareth, and their armies quickly defeated Pinewood and Tracia. The Houses of Pinewood and Alder were abolished, and the Tracian throne was given to Prince Dulmian of the House of Bayberry. Peace returned to the east, and armies withdrew to their own realms.

After the conflict was over, Attis thrived under Heneil's leadership. With a long view, he continued his work on the fortress, and also formed and trained a standing army for the defense of the region. All this, and the growing wealth and influence of Attis, sparked a rivalry between Attis and the Kingdom of Colleton, which was the seat of governance for the Eastlands Realm. The young King Inrick of Colleton tried to impose taxes and tolls on traders traveling through the region of Attis in order to force them through his own region, but with little success.

Lyrium, with her Gift of Sight, grew increasingly agitated by what her visions showed her, and she expressed to Heneil her concerns that there would be an attack on Attis. Even though there was peace in the lands, Heneil agreed to redouble his efforts on the fortress. Aiming to make a river approach more difficult for large boats, Heneil constructed a dam on the Saerdulin Falls, where Lake Halgaeth poured its waters into the river. As a result, the lake level rose, eventually spilling into the Bentwide, and the Saerdulin became difficult for any but the smallest of boats to navigate. This at first angered some Attis traders who relied on the river, but Heneil arranged for a new bridge across the Bentwide to be built. All these projects, prodigious though they were, took only twenty years to complete.

Meanwhile, Attis had become the wealthiest community in the Eastlands Realm, though not as populous or as large as Colleton. So grateful were the people that they gave Heneil a new name, calling him Amandoel, which in their old dialect meant The Builder.

Lyrium, throughout all these events, continued to have dark visions concerning Tulith Attis, which she shared with Heneil. She now feared that wolves and other attackers might enter Tulith Attis from the fortress's old river entrance, and she begged Heneil to seal all but the main gate of Tulith Attis. Instead, he devised a method of warning. Heneil thus had a Great Bell cast, and he placed it into the underground Bell Room. He constructed an Iron Door leading from the Bell Room into the fortress, one that could only be opened by speaking the First Tongue, which only a Firstborn Faerekind could speak, and he made it so that if it opened, it would ring the Great Bell. He brought a conjuror to the room who cast spells upon the bell, making it so that its warning would be heard far and wide, rising up through the ground and carrying to distant places through the air. Once that was done, however, the conjuror told Heneil that it would not be enough to save the fortress, for who would come when the bell rang if all were engaged in battle?

"I know that there are marble columns nearby, left by Alonair when he abandoned the world, before he could make them into statues," the conjuror said. "I know their secret, for I was with Alonair before the Fall when he brought them into the Thunder Mountains when we still had wings and all things were as light as a feather to us. And I know where they still are. Let us fetch them here, using your trade wagons and many men. Let us place them within your fortress, and then give unto me some of your soldiers, and I will place them into the protection of those columns. My spells will make it so that time will not pass for them until the moment when the Great Bell rings thrice, then they shall awaken to carry out your orders."

"Is such a thing possible?" Heneil asked.

"Yes," replied the conjuror. "For a sum of gold and silver in exchange, you shall see it done. But I warn you, no power but the Great Bell may awaken the soldiers, no matter the need of them that may arise. And, once they have done your bidding, they will be filled once more with the spirit of the stone, and with a strong desire to find Alonair, since it is of his stone that they shall be made."

Heneil was reluctant, and told the conjuror that he must consider the proposition. During the days that he thought about it, Pellen and Myrium arrived from Duinnor. Myrium was alarmed at the anxieties of her sister Lyrium, and went to Pellen and told him of Lyrium's terrible visions. And now Lyrium foresaw the Iron Door being opened and the fortress being filled with an army of attacking wolves. Pellen listened to Myrium and went to Heneil to learn more. But none knew that Pellen had been secretly asked by the King of Duinnor to obtain those Seven Bloodcoins held by Lyrium and Heneil. When Heneil told Pellen about the conjuror's proposition, Pellen saw his chance. He encouraged his brother to do as the conjuror said, and so Heneil did, telling those who volunteered to be placed within the stone to kill any intruders that they found within the fortress, and especially any wolves.

The conjuror was summoned, and the many marble columns were brought out of the mountains and into the fortress and placed all around the grounds within it. Each of Heneil's men stood next to one of the columns in battle gear. And the conjuror merged each man with each stone column so that, by all appearances, only the columns stood where before both a man and a column had been. Afterwards, Heneil paid the conjuror, but Pellen held him back from leaving Tulith Attis.

"One more thing you must do," Pellen said to the conjuror. "And I will pay you well."

It was then that Pellen told the conjuror his plan, and the conjuror agreed to it. Pellen went to Heneil, and told him, too, of his plan saying, "Let the conjuror make of me a statue, too, using the dust from the columns to fill me with the spirit of stone. And I shall stand within the Bell Room and guard it, too. And should any wolves enter there, I shall awaken to fight them."

"No, brother," Heneil told Pellen. "I would rather you be at my side should any enemy come."

But Pellen persisted for many days, and he even convinced Myrium his wife to also volunteer to stand as he would, in wait for when they would be needed. Others, too, high lords of Attis, did Pellen enlist into the plan.

But Heneil was opposed to it, and Lyrium had reservations, too.

When news arrived that a vast horde of Dragonkind approached the region, Heneil begged his brother Pellen to go to Duinnor and to Vanara for aid. Instead, Pellen redoubled his arguments, and at last convinced Heneil of his plan.

"Would I endanger my wife?" asked Pellen. "But by her enchantments and my sword, and those of the others who wish to guard the Bell Room, no intruder could hope to succeed even if they outnumbered those who were awakened from stone."

Lyrium was against it, for she mistrusted the conjuror who was to do the work. However, Pellen prevailed. Several other high lords of Attis were also selected, and they placed their own armed forces under the command of Heneil until they would be revived from the stone in which they would sleep until needed.

Pellen convinced Myrium to go first, to show the others that there was no danger in the process. She stood on the pedestal upon which she would remain, and the conjuror made his spells, casting dust he had gathered from Alonair's columns upon her. In an instant it was done. Everyone saw how beautiful Myrium remained, even though she was now made of stone, and they submitted themselves to the conjuror.

All these enchantments were made without any other witness than Pellen himself, and when all but Pellen were thus encased and asleep, Pellen sent for Heneil to see for himself their progress.

"Now, my brother," Pellen said to Heneil, "there is the place where I shall stand. And to do you honor, and to further baffle and frighten any enemy that may come, I have donned your spare armor and robes. Knowing your prowess at arms, and having fair skill of my own, the intruders will shrink away from me when I awake, thinking it is you who comes at them."

"You do me great honor, indeed, brother Pellen," replied Heneil. "Though I wish you would reconsider and remain unenchanted to stand with me at the hour of need."

"My mind is set on this," said Pellen. "And I would not have my wife Myrium await, but that I should wait with her."

"If you are certain," said Heneil. "But I see that the pedestal upon which you will stand is somewhat off from where it should be. Should it not be here, just across the doorway from Myrium?"

"I thought from there I could see best when I awoke where I should strike," replied Pellen.

"Yes, perhaps," nodded Heneil. "But I think here, across from Myrium, would be a better place from which to see."

"Then, stand you upon the pedestal and tell me," said Pellen.

Heneil stepped upon the pedestal and looked about the room.

"I cannot see from here the far door that leads down to the river landing," said Heneil. "I think the pedestal should be moved to where I suggest."

"Then let us do so," said Pellen.

The two strong brothers moved the pedestal to where Heneil suggested, and Heneil stood again upon it.

"Yes," said Heneil. "From here you may best see what comes."

"But you must stand as I will, leaning upon your sword," said Pellen, handing Heneil his sword, "so that your posture may be known and not hinder you."

Heneil took the sword, and put the tip of the blade at his feet and held it, nodding.

"Yes, I still see," he said. "Holding the sword will not hinder you."

But before he could leap down from the pedestal, the conjurer threw his dust upon Heneil and breathed his spells, and immediately Heneil was turned to stone.

That is how Pellen took the place of his brother Heneil. Going to Lyrium, in the dress and manner of his brother, he pretended to be Heneil and told her that all was done.

"It is as Pellen wished," Pellen said to Lyrium, "and he now stands nearby to Myrium. The Iron Door is closed, and the Bell awaits. All is ready. But where are our daughters?"

"I sent them away, Heneil," said Lyrium. "I had a terrible dream that they would be slain if I kept them here."

"Oh? And where did they go? For the Dragonkind press against us in greater strength every day."

"They went north and west, Heneil. To make their way through the high Carthanes and on to Vanara by safe and seldom used ways."

"That is just as well. And did you send the Seven Bloodcoins away with them?" Pellen asked.

"No, my love. They remain with us, for I did not wish to entrust those objects to anyone, fearing that our daughters would be endangered by any who chanced to learn of them."

"Wise lady! Then are they within the treasure vaults?"

"Yes, my husband. That is where they are. You should rest, now. The enemy will soon be nigh, and you will need your strength."

But Pellen refused, saying that he was needed by his army.

"Then take this gift that I have for you. Myrium helped me prepare it for you."

Lyrium took out a sword and offered it to Pellen, whom she still thought was her husband Heneil. When Pellen saw the sword, his eyes widened and he came to Lyrium as she held it out to him.

"Is this not my father's sword, sharp Ethliad? The very sword taken when he was slain, and lost to the world?"

"Yes, my love. It was revealed to me in a vision where I might find it, and so I traveled to the place where King Silmain died. There, upon the old and dusty battlefield in the desert lands, my Sight revealed where Ethliad was, and how it came to be hidden where it fell. So I found Ethliad, and I have held it in secret ever since, awaiting the man and the purpose worthy of it. I did not offer it before, fearing that its possession would corrupt those around you, who would be envious and might conspire to take it from you. I feared, too, my husband, that wielding such power might make you too much like your father. But now our need is great, and I know you to be a worthy man. Take it! And with it be truly invincible in battle! Worry not that it might be wrested from you and used against you. For my sister has laid a powerful enchantment upon Ethliad, so that if any but my own hand or the hand of Heneil wields it, that person shall be struck dead on the spot."

"But Lyrium," Pellen shrank from the sword she held out, "what if arrows strike me down and a hapless comrade reaches for it to defend himself?"

"My Heneil! That is unlikely, for you are a mighty warrior. But Myrium's spell is such that if you die in battle, Ethliad will lodge itself into the rocky ground so that only I may pull it free. And only then, after you are dead, may I bestow it upon another, thus breaking Myrium's spell. Thus be assured. Take it, my husband, and let it be as a scythe against our enemies, and you the reaper!"

Lyrium was puzzled by her husband's expression and his reluctance to take Ethliad.

"How be it that my own wife may doubt my prowess? I need no such thing for victory!" Pellen said, laughing nervously. "I shall show you and all others that I need not spells or enchantments to win over against the Dragonkind! Put Ethliad away! I will hear no more of it. Now I must go and see to our defenses, for I hear the horns of our horsemen who are returning from their forays against the enemy."

"Then let me fight beside you, my husband," Lyrium said. "I shall wield Ethliad, and none may stand before us."

"That is unwise, my lady," Pellen answered. "You are not trained in combat. And Ethliad is said to be as a flame to the moths of war, attracting combatants against it. No doubt, the enemy would ply against you with arrows and missiles. It is not needed, I tell you. And I enjoin you to stay with the other ladies of our people, safe within our stronghold."

Pellen departed. But Lyrium was immediately filled with dark suspicion, for Pellen did not answer her in tone or in gesture as Heneil would have. There was no tenderness in his voice, and his eyes would not meet hers in earnest gaze as he spoke. She put Ethliad away, pondering these things until she could bear her suspicions no longer. She went secretly out from the fortress, and along paths around the walls of Tulith Attis and down to the boat landing beside the River Saerdulin where the river entrance into the fortress was. She entered and climbed the long stairs upward and into the Bell Room and looked upon the eerie statues there, including her sister Myrium. Although Myrium appeared peaceful and beautiful, Lyrium's heart was filled with sadness upon seeing her. She could hardly restrain her tears when she reached out and touched Myrium's feet and felt them to be cold and hard, like the stone they were.

Then Lyrium turned to the statue made of Pellen, her sister's husband, and saw upon his finger a peculiar thing. It was the ring that she herself had given to Heneil on the day they were wed, and there was no other ring like it. Staring at the ring, she cried out and fell to her knees, weeping. For at that moment, she knew that she was betrayed. And when she remembered how Pellen asked her about the Seven Bloodcoins, she understood why he had come to Tulith Attis.

Being careful not to arouse Pellen's suspicion, Lyrium sought out the conjuror, and she asked him how the enchantment upon those within the Bell Room could be lifted.

"How may they be awakened," asked Lyrium, "without ringing the Great Bell or opening the Iron Door?"

"I answer only to gold," said the conjuror. "And unless you give me more than was given me to make my enchantments, I shall never answer you."

"Then I shall double the amount," said Lyrium, "but only if you first tell me."

"Swear it!"

"I do swear it!"

"Ha! The enchantments upon those of your household guard cannot be lifted by me, but only by the tolling of the Great Bell."

"I care not for them. I speak of the others, including my sister Myrium and my husband Heneil."

"Ah. You have guessed Pellen's intrigue against you! Then I will tell you, there is no awakening for them. They are dead, and were dead the moment they turned to stone. It was Pellen's order that it be so!"

The conjuror raised his handful of dust to throw at Lyrium, too, but Lyrium struck first, driving her hairpin of witchbane deep into the conjurer's eye, killing him instantly. As he fell, his dust scattered upon him, and his body was made into stone.

Knowing that Pellen had betrayed and murdered his brother and his own wife, Lyrium was filled with anger and went immediately to find Pellen, determined to kill him. But that was the very moment the Dragonkind made their first attack. Hurrying to the top of the western wall of Tulith Attis, she saw Pellen and the soldiers of Tulith Attis meet the Dragonkind, and she saw how fiercely they fought. Pellen drove the Dragonkind back, and returned victorious with his men to the cheers of Lyrium's people, who thought that he was Heneil. All of the people rejoiced, thinking themselves safe in the hands of their defenders.

Lyrium was deeply troubled, for Pellen now seemed to be their only hope. She went from the walls, acting the part of a loving wife by going to Pellen when he came back into the fortress. She gave him a kiss on the cheek and congratulated him on his victory. Lyrium saw that Pellen did not suspect that his ruse was known to her, and she departed to her chambers, leaving Pellen to be celebrated by her people, who cheered, "Heneil! Heneil! Heneil!"

But Lyrium, informed by her Sight, knew that Pellen could not long prevail against the Dragonkind hordes that were coming. She called aside her most trusted household guard and met secretly with them. Then she went quickly to the Treasure Room, and from there to her chambers where she summoned her maidservant, a fierce and cunning fighter named Faeanna. As soon as Faeanna came, Lyrium pressed a small bundle into her hands.

"Faeanna, these are the Seven Bloodcoins entrusted to the House of Fairfir. Take them! They are no longer safe and must be taken away, for this fortress will fall, and all within will die or be made captives. I will see to my own escape, when the time comes."

"But, my lady, have you not seen your husband's victories today? With his leadership, we have easily pushed back the Dragonkind, and—"

"Do not argue! You know me best of any, and know the power of my Sight. This fortress will fall, I say. So give heed to my words! You must take these Seven and go far away from here."

"But how are we to get away?"

"Put those under your cloak. Wear them under your blouse, under your cuirass, if you can. Let me help."

Lyrium quickly explained all while she helped Faeanna undress. As she spoke, she affixed the Bloodcoins in their wrapping around Faeanna's waist like a belt, and helped her put her garments back on. By the time that was done, Faeanna understood.

A little while later, Lyrium, Faeanna, and five members of her guard had all donned battle cloaks such as Heneil's men wore, and Lyrium took them to stand nearby to the gate of the fortress amid the crowds that gathered there. Pellen prepared to lead his men out on another foray against the Dragonkind, who had regrouped and were once again ransacking and destroying the town of Attis below the fortress. There, the enemy was busy leveling the town, using timber and stone from the destruction to build siege engines.

Lyrium and her party watched Pellen, whom all else thought was Heneil, and readied themselves. Amid cheers and cries of well-wishes, the fortress gate was opened, and Pellen marched out at the lead of two-thousand determined men. Lyrium waited until the last soldiers moved through the gate of the fortress, then, at Lyrium's nod, her party carefully mingled with the rearmost ranks. Once the gate was closed behind them, Lyrium's group stole away, going around the fortress and down to the river landing. There, Lyrium watched as the group boarded three small boats and took up their paddles.

"My lady," Faeanna said before boarding, "I shall do as you say. Have no fear for the things that I carry. They shall never fall into the hands of the enemy. When a year has passed, I shall await you at the agreed place, and you shall have your Seven back. This I promise: If it can be done at all, it shall be done."

"I give you my eternal thanks, dear Faeanna. These boats are light but strong, and soon you shall be far away, hidden by this moonless night. I shall make my own way when the time comes, taking as many with me as I can. Then I shall meet you at the appointed place. Now go! Quickly!"

"Farewell! May the gods protect you!"

"And you! Farewell!"

Lyrium kissed Faeanna. Faeanna boarded, and the boats eased out into the fast-moving currents. Lyrium watched the boats go, disappearing swiftly down river and into the darkness, then she turned back to the fortress and arrived when Pellen and his men were returning, victorious once more against the Dragonkind upon the field. She came in with them, and quickly went to her chambers to clean herself while the people within the fortress celebrated the day's victories.

Lyrium went to Pellen, saying to him, "Heneil, my husband. I witnessed your prowess upon the field. I hope you will continue to have easy victories in the days to come."

"And why should I not? The Dragonkind are weak and ill-led."

"I hope so, for as you know, we cannot allow our Seven to fall into their hands."

"They are safe within the vaults, my wife. So fear not for their safety!"

"But our scouts report a great army now approaches to join with the ones you have prevailed against."

"Yes, my wife. And let them come! They will scatter before our steel."

As history tells, they did not. Although Pellen fought bravely, the Dragonkind were too many, and they were well prepared. Within three days, the town of Attis was completely destroyed, the enemy's machines were hurling their missiles over the walls of Tulith Attis, and their ranks surrounded the fortress on every side. Again and again, Pellen led sorties out to push away the Dragonkind, until at last his tactics were understood and anticipated. Pellen grew weary, and the brave defenders of the fortress dwindled before the arrows and missiles that rained upon them.

At last, Pellen marched out for a desperate attempt to deal a crushing blow to the Dragonkind hordes. He and his men fought ferociously. They pushed the Dragonkind back across the craggy debris-strewn plain before Tulith Attis, and it seemed as if victory was at hand. But it was in vain. The Dragonkind generals anticipated Pellen's maneuvers, and feigned a retreat only to have greater forces move around and flank Pellen's army. Then the Dragonkind fully encircled Pellen's men and squeezed in, methodically cutting them down. While those on the walls watched in horror, the burgundy-cloaked patch of Men and Elifaen shrank before the engulfing tide until it was a mere dot within a sea of copper-colored armor, until even that dot disappeared.

Pellen, alone, remained. With his shield split asunder and thrown away, his breastplate dented and dripping with blood, he held aloft a dead Dragonkind against the blows that came at him, and with his notched and battle-jagged sword, he fought on. Suddenly the Dragonkind backed away, out of reach of his sword, and Pellen paused, panting and gasping for air, turning all about, preparing for their final push against him. Unfastening his helmet, he tossed it away.

"Come!" he cried at the wall of Dragonkind that surrounded him. "Come have me then!"

But they did not answer, nor did they strike at him. When he charged at them, they only moved away. He stumbled and fell to his knees, tears running down his face.

"Why do you wait?" he cried hoarsely, his eyes wild as he swung his sword weakly at the crowd of Dragonkind that tightly surrounded him. Then a Dragonkind general in resplendent armor and cloaks pushed through and paused, gazing upon Pellen.

"You then!" Pellen cried at him. "Shall I be your prize?"

The Dragonkind general did not reply. Instead, he turned and gestured to his soldiers. They then parted to let someone else come through to Pellen.

When Pellen saw who it was that entered the circle, he stared in disbelief and let his sword fall. It was Bailorg, agent of the Unknown King of Duinnor. For Pellen had promised the King that the Seven Bloodcoins of Fairfir would be delivered to Duinnor so that the King would have them as his own. And it was this Bailorg who had promised safe passage through the Dragonkind ranks, and had also promised glory and wealth should the Bloodcoins be delivered. And when Pellen saw Bailorg come to him, he knew that honor was lost to him, if it had not already fled when he murdered his wife, when he murdered his brother and all the others. When Bailorg smiled, Pellen knew that he was lost, that redemption in battle was gone.

At Bailorg's signal, Dragonkind came bearing new armor for Pellen to wear.

"Take this armor," Bailorg said. "It comes not from the King, but from another great lord of the west. Its giver anticipated that you would need it, and bids you put it on as a token of his goodwill. That lord, whose name we shall not say, sends you his word that, should you need refuge, his domain shall welcome you."

The armor brought to him was of finely wrought heavy black iron, embossed with a red hourglass upon the breastplate. The great helm was likewise of black, embossed in the form of a grim face with two horns protruding forward from the cheeks. It was fearsome armor, not of any Duinnor fashion that Pellen had ever known. In fact, it had been forged and fashioned not in Duinnor, but in Shatuum. And when Pellen touched it and felt how warm it was, a shiver coursed through his body.

"Put it on," said Bailorg. "And you shall not be known by any here who look upon you. Then go, order the gate of the fortress to be opened unto you, and let these Dragonkind in. And when all is done, we shall then have those things that the King of Duinnor demands!"

Lyrium watched the catastrophe from the walls of Tulith Attis with all of the others gathered there. As the field became silent, and the last of their defenders were gone from sight within the sea of besiegers, a dense fog settled over the land. So dense it was that those watching from Tulith Attis could no longer see the scene before them nor even any person standing but a few feet away. As those upon the wall mourned and wept, Lyrium hurried away. She went to her chambers and she put on her light armor that had never before been used, a gift from her husband, and she girded Ethliad upon herself, the first sword she had ever worn. Then she went about and gathered as many women and girls who could bear arms. Seeing her dressed so, as they had never seen her before, they were filled with fear and did as she instructed, arming themselves and following her lead.

While she did this, going from chamber to chamber, outside in the dense fog, a cheer went up at the gate and word soon spread: Heneil had miraculously survived and had somehow evaded the enemy. He had come back and called to the gatekeepers his name and gave the secret password that only he and the gatekeepers knew. People gathered to welcome Heneil as the gatekeepers drew up the portcullis, pulled away the buttresses, and swung open the heavy iron-shod gate. Just as it opened, Lyrium arrived, and when she saw what they did, she cried out in warning.

But it was too late. The thick gates were now being pushed in from without. There was a pause, and the people backed away in shock as a tall figure strode through, in black armor from head to toe, with a horned helmet covering his head, and a red hourglass upon his breastplate. Then, as the gates widened further, Dragonkind poured around the warrior. He carried a battleaxe, but swung it not at all, striding through the fray as the Dragonkind around him did their work.

No defense was possible within the bailey of the fortress, and all was violent confusion. Instead of withdrawing from the onslaught, Lyrium led her group along the base of the fortress walls, fighting their way to the gate. She was filled with a powerful desire to cut her way through to Pellen and slay him, but he was by now far from her.

Lyrium stayed with the group that she led. Though unpracticed, she swung Ethliad with terrible effect. It sliced through armor and sang through flesh, and with it Lyrium cleared a narrow path through the horde. As the river of Dragonkind poured in around them, she led her band against the current, through the inrush of their jubilant ranks, and out from the fortress. Of the two hundred with her, forty were already killed, and by the time she and Ethliad had fought through to the field of carnage before Tulith Attis, a dozen more were dead. As she and her followers sliced their way toward the far woods to the west, their numbers dwindled until only a few dozen were still with Lyrium. Up the far ridge, they fled, and the ranks of the enemy thinned, as the Dragonkind continued to throng toward the fortress.

On the other side of the ridge, they came upon a small stream, choked with the dead of their men. Seeing them, many of those still with Lyrium cried out and threw themselves upon their knees, wailing and weeping upon the banks. But Lyrium could not coax them away, and there was no time. She picked up a small child and carried him as she and a few others pushed on, tracking northward along the top of the low ridge. They made it to the shores of Lake Halgaeth, and came to Heneil's Wall, the dam that blocked all but a small trickle of the lake's water that flowed across it. Over its top they ran, but Dragonkind sentries saw them and set out after them. Across the dam and into the forest they fled, Lyrium holding the child close with one arm and swinging Ethliad with the other. But the woods were full of the enemy who joined in the pursuit of her party. They ran, stopping only to turn on their pursuers, then they ran again. It was a running fight for miles and miles through the darkness, through the deadly wood. At dawn, Lyrium suddenly found herself alone, and she stopped to look behind her. It was then that she noticed that the child was dead, pierced through by an arrow intended for her. She laid him down, tears streaming from her eyes. Of all those she led out from Tulith Attis, only she remained. But she heard her pursuers coming, and she shed her armor, stripping down to only her loincloth for speed, then resumed her flight as arrows flitted through the brush at her.

She wept as she ran. When she turned to face a swift-coming Dragonkind, she cried in anger and grief when she fought. Then she ran again, hardly able to see her way for the tears in her eyes. By noon, she was far away, and no one else pursued her. Still she ran and wept as she fled through the war-stricken lands. At last, near the end of day, she came to a bluff overlooking Lake Halgaeth to the west. There she fell upon her knees and sobbed.

Day passed into night, and the sound of Lyrium's weeping slowly diminished into the silence of the forest. Still she remained, her head down, her tears slowly drying.

At least Pellen would not have what he came for. At least, Lyrium hoped, Faeanna made it away with the Seven Bloodcoins. But Lyrium knew that reports of her own escape would reach Pellen. When he found the Bloodcoins gone, what would he do? Would he give chase? Would he, with his patience and cunning, track her down? He, like her, was Elifaen, and he would have all of eternity to find her.

Lyrium got to her feet, took Ethliad, and resumed her way. By stealth and by avoiding all she saw, whether Man or Elifaen, Lyrium made it away northward, first into Glareth Realm and around the northern shores of Lake Halgaeth. Then she climbed up into the high Carthanes. There, she hid Ethliad and approached a farmer's cottage to beg for clothes, covering herself with ferns for modesty's sake. An old woman took pity on her and shared food and some old ragged clothes. When Lyrium departed, and was well away from the cottage, she disguised herself as an old crone, befitting her clothes, and then found her way to a place called Darforin, which would later be called Chiselpeck. There, she traded fortune-telling and soothsaying for shelter, and she awaited Faeanna and the Bloodcoins. Months passed as she lived a miserly life, remaining in disguise the entire time. But Faeanna never came.

Word eventually reached the isolated people of Darforin of the battle at Tulith Attis. There were no survivors, it was told. And among the dead were the Elifaen sisters of Fairfir, Lady Lyrium and Lady Myrium, and both their husbands, the brothers Heneil and Pellen. The fortress had fallen to treachery and betrayal, it was told, and all of the defenders had been massacred. But no one knew who the traitor was.

Soon after, more news came. Great armies, it was told, had arrived from Vanara and Duinnor and Glareth. A great and terrible battle took place along the Saerdulin near the River Lerse. The Dragonkind were defeated, and the remnants of their massive army were being pursued back to their own desert lands. All the Realms had rallied, and few of the Dragonkind who came out of the deserts would ever see home again, as they were hunted down and killed like animals.

Soon after hearing the news, Lyrium, still in disguise, traveled back to the Eastlands and tried to locate Faeanna and any others that she had sent away with the Seven Bloodcoins. But she found only one, named Tyrillick, who was still alive and imprisoned by Men who thought him to be a deserter from Tulith Attis since he wore the livery of the House of Fairfir. Lyrium secured his release, and in private Tyrillick described how the boats had struck chains stretched across the Saerdulin by the Dragonkind. The boats were overturned, he said, and all aboard them were thrown into the swift waters and separated from one another. Tyrillick escaped capture, but could not find any of his comrades. Weeks later, he had been captured by Men, and, unable to explain himself, he was accused of desertion.

Fearing that Pellen may have survived, or that agents of the Dragonkind might pursue her, Lyrium took Tyrillick with her, and together they fled the Eastlands. They eventually made their way to Forest Islindia and were granted refuge by the King of the Wood and Islindia, his lonesome daughter. Later, Lyrium was joined by her two daughters and a few others of her household who were not at Tulith Attis when it fell. In an isolated part of the northernmost woods of Islindia's forest, Lyrium and the only remaining members of the ancient House of Fairfir remained. The years passed slowly, and the centuries likewise. The world changed, and many things were forgotten.

One night, while striving with her Sight to see the fate of her lost Seven, Lyrium's vision instead revealed to her a sick mortal child. The child's mother wept beside the sickbed as her helpless husband paced back and forth. It was a beautiful woman who wept, with long red hair, and as she wept she whispered a prayer. It was an ancient prayer, and Lyrium, Seeing and Hearing it, was surprised that the woman could know it. It was a plea that Beras might send his agents to fairly and justly decide the fate of her son, so that death would not arbitrarily take him, and so that the banshee that sang outside of their house would depart without her son.

When Lyrium emerged from her vision of Sight, she went immediately to her daughters, Elmira and Belmira.

"Daughters," she said to them, "you are summoned by prayer and by vision. As in the days of yore, agents of Beras are called upon to decide over life and death. You shall be those agents. Yet, it is not an Elifaen who is threatened by death, but a mortal child that you must go to. Go swiftly. See what you may see. Do what you may do. Take the wondrous carriage of King Ilex, and go swiftly!"

So this they did, flying out from Islindia in a marvelous coach. Its wheels did not turn as wheels of the earth do, each having a circumference greater than the measure of their rims. Out from the enchanted forest they sped, and in less than a day the sisters came to the far away Eastlands. By their own powers of listening, Belmira and Elmira heard the prayers of the child's mother, and they also heard the song of the banshee that sometimes comes to Men to take them from the living. Following these sounds, they found the child's humble home, which was in the upstairs rooms above a shop of sundries. A friend of the house opened the door to them, and led the sisters upstairs where they found the boy and his parents, just as Lyrium said they would.

"Stand with your husband, just there, if you will," said Belmira.

"Be very quiet. Please, be very still," said Elmira.

"You summoned us hither to look at your son…"

"…and that we shall do, and see what's to be done."

The boy's parents retreated from the bed, and when the two sisters approached it, they were mystified, for the child muttered softly in the First Tongue, which no Mortal can speak. They put their ears close to him to hear his words, and in his fevered delirium, the child spoke of going to the end of the world to visit a marvelous castle in the air. He spoke, too, of the Great Bell, saying that perhaps he should have left it alone.

These things stunned the two daughters of Lyrium, for though they were spoken with the voice of a small child, they pertained to things that such a little one should know nothing about.

Then the child briefly opened his eyes and looked at the two beautiful visitors, from one to the other, and said, with tears running down his little face, "If anyone is to be saved, I wish it would be my mother and not me."

Elmira glanced at the child's mother and father, and Belmira clutched her sister's hand, whispering to her, "Terrible power labors here, for I sense darkness in his speech."

"I sense the like, my sister dear," replied Elmira, "so an accord now let us reach."

"Ask ye now, his name to say, and we shall each call to him…"

"…and whom he hears shall have her way, to joyous life or banshee grim."

So, turning to the child's parents, Elmira and Belmira asked, "What true name may we call him by…"

"…to beckon him to live or die?"

The child's parents looked at each other, as if not knowing what to say. Then the child's father spoke.

"We can say only what we call the boy," he said, "for we don't rightly know his true name."

"He was named in the ancient way," said the boy's mother, her tears running all the more for this, "by a dying relative who took his true name to the grave so that none living can use it against him. Oh what have we done?"

Belmira and her sister looked at each other.

"Without his name, what may we do…"

"…to coax his spirit to me or to you?"

"Our debate is undone, it is not in our hands…"

"Is that why we came to these faraway lands?"

"Or may we together be joined into song…"

"…and put off the banshee before very long?"

"Yes, take it all night, or take it all day…"

"…we shall counter her voice, 'til she goes away."

Turning back to the feverish child, who was now tossing and turning in his delirium, the two ladies began to sing to him. It was a sweet lullaby, a simple tune, their voices in two-part harmony. Only he could hear their words, for they were sung to him as they bent over his bed, stroking his hot brow and his wet hair with their gentle hands. For a long while they sang, and the boy weakly opened his eyes to look at their smiling faces and kind eyes. As he looked at them, to their amazement he began to hum their tune, as though he had heard it before. Heartened by this, they sang all the more earnestly, and now tears streamed down their faces, too, so tenderly did they feel toward the child. He smiled and peacefully closed his eyes to sleep.

The two sisters brought their song to a close, and looked at one another, smiling. Belmira and Elmira came around from their sides of the bed and embraced at its foot, weeping softly upon each other's shoulders. They looked at one another, tilting their heads to listen. All was quiet. The banshee was gone.

When they turned to the parents, their smiles told all that they needed to know, and the mother rushed to the bed, kneeling and petting her son while the father bowed deeply to the ladies.

"What might I do to repay ye?" he said, trying to stifle the long-held tears, which nonetheless now streamed from his joyous eyes.

"Only love this child with all your heart," said Elmira.

"And go to him, now, while we depart," said Belmira.

And so the two sisters departed, talking incessantly to each other in their rhyming way until they came once again to Islindia's forest and to their mother. They told her all that had happened, all that was said, filling Lyrium with as much wonder as was in their own hearts. And for many years Lyrium pondered these things, and she sought to prepare for the day when she herself would see the boy.

Thus Ends the Tales of the High Houses

From these tales, many connections may be made between, or surmised about, the people and events described within *The Year of the Red Door*.   For Queen Serith Ellyn and Lady Lyrium in particular, whose Houses were the only remaining of the Seven, the wear of years and woes took their toll.   These tales show, too, why the Elifaen people, were melancholy and retrospective, being much disappointed in each other and themselves.   No wonder, then, that very few Elifaen elected to remain in this world when given the chance, and choice, to depart peacefully to be with their lost loved ones and heavenly kin.

Editor's Note:
In Ullin's notes, we found this observation:

>Something I have contemplated on.
>
>As is told within *The Year of the Red Door*, when we met Lyrium for the first time in Tallinvale, and she revealed her true appearance, Robby instantly "recognized her face from the likeness he had gazed upon in the bell room, carved in stone and painted in life-like illusion." But what was said next was interesting. Robby said to her "It was your statue that I saw in the fortress." "No," answered Lyrium. "That was my twin sister, Myrium."
>
>Lyrium did not say "that was *a statue of* my twin sister." She knew that it was Myrium herself, turned to stone by the cunning and vile Pellen. From what I now know, I can only surmise that Lyrium was still too terrified that, should she share her knowledge, doing so might betray her to Pellen, to his master in Shatuum, and to the Unknown King of Duinnor. Perhaps it was a slip on her part. Or perhaps, like much else that she wrought that evening, it was a test. She did not lie, and she might have been prepared to be questioned on the phrasing of her answer. I wonder if Collandoth caught it? If so, he said nothing to me about it. I think Lyrium was willing to allow people to think and believe what they might as long as doing so protected her secrets. And we now know that it was not through Lyrium that Robby learned the identity of the traitor of Tulith Attis.

Eighteen Objects of Power

Introduction

There have been many objects with magical or mysterious qualities throughout the history of the world. The actuality of some of these objects is common knowledge, and for others there are reliable historical accounts to verify that they existed or still exist. Others mentioned here are purely legendary, surrounded by tales from antiquity.

During the latter part of the Second Age, a treatise concerning these objects was written by Raynor the Melnari, a scholar of Duinnor, entitled "Legends and Tales of Magical Things." Raynor's work was academic in nature, and it remained relatively obscure for many years, with limited readership mostly among the scholars of the King's Academy.

In late 869 of the Second Age, the owner of a Duinnor printing concern came across the treatise. The following year an abridged version was printed and widely circulated. It reduced the number of objects from seventy-two to eighteen, and was written in a relaxed vernacular. It first appeared as an entertaining supplement to The Star, one of the popular broadsheets of Duinnor City. The text of the supplement, entitled, "Eighteen Objects of Power," appears below in its entirety, as a reproduction of the original.

Shortly after its publication, Raynor took issue with the Star's version of these things. In an open letter published by a competing printer, he said that the Supplement was misleading and grossly incomplete, and he advised everyone to read the original work that he had authored. Raynor also accused The Star of trivializing such things as described within the Supplement. Addressing the readers of The Star, he warned that many such objects were still in the world, and they continued to influence our lives and our fates.

The below is a reproduction of the original supplement, presented in a fashion as close to the original as possible, with changes in formatting in order to fit a smaller page than the original broadsheet version.

Special Supplement
To
The Star
Duinnor City's Leading Broadsheet

**Published on the
22nd Day of Fifthmonth, 870 S.A.**

As many of our faithful readers are interested in matters of the world and its history, the Proprietors of this broadsheet are happy to report that a substantial work concerning the magical objects of the world has been written by one of Duinnor's preeminent scholars, Raynor the Wise, who was at one time the minister of the King's Academy. We have taken the liberty of revising the work to be more suitable to the tastes of our readers who are not academics like the esteemed Raynor. Confident that our discriminating readers will enjoy such reviews, we are happy to share this Special Supplement, being a description of

Eighteen Objects of Power,
A concise but thorough Examination
of certain Uncanny Objects
that are known to Exist,
as well as others that are known only in
Tales and Legends full of Mystery and Wonder.

Who has not heard of the King's Golden Mantle?   And what long inhabitant of Our City has not on some occasion or other seen the King's Avatar?   Perhaps, too, you may have heard tales of flying carpets, or know about ink that tells only the truth.   And doubtless there are those still living among us who remember the fantastical Glowing Stone of Bazradur, which was once in the desert city of Calamandor, known to us as the Green Citadel.   Descriptions of these things and their powers abound, and in unsettled times such as these, it might be fanciful, or wise, to recollect such things.   So here we humbly list and describe eighteen of those objects for those of our readers who may wish to be reminded of such things, or for those who have perhaps never heard of them.

§

Nasakeeria's Ring of Fire

On the very doorstep of Duinnor is the mysterious and foreboding land of Nasakeeria, the border of which cannot be crossed by any living person lest he be consumed by the sudden appearance of the Ring of Fire. Indeed, it takes only one wayward step too close to the forbidden land to release searing hot flames which issue suddenly from the ground and burst upward into the sky all around the border of Nasakeeria, thus ringing that land in its entirety. Such is the power and intensity of the uprush of flame and heat that the hapless interloper has his flesh completely burned away in an instant. All that will remain will be the victim's brittle bones which are sent flying outward several yards from the border to land with those others that dared go before.

Our countrymen should know the Ring of Fire and the danger of Nasakeeria well enough, for it was into that place that a mighty army of Duinnor went in the year 322 of this Age, foolishly intent on speeding to the east to face the Dragonkind invaders of that year and taking no care to mind their path. As many as seven thousand soldiers who crossed over were killed, along with all the horses they rode, and their bones were cast out by the powerful blast to fall in piles just outside Nasakeeria's border. To this day, no one understands how the army was destroyed, since it would seem likely that as those in the lead of the army were consumed those behind would see and halt their advance into death. The lone messenger who returned to report the advance carried dispatches that indicated the army proceeded in five columns, each racing against the other, goaded by a substantial reward offered to those who first reached the beleaguered city of Fisenwold. But even this explanation fails to explain the catastrophe, and our people and our leaders were, according to story, shocked and baffled.

As is well known, the Fifth Unknown King took immediate action, dispatching another army to the east, a risky move that left Duinnor depleted of its defensive forces. Shortly after the crisis was over and the Dragonkind were defeated in the east, our former King began a massive project of erecting markers around Nasakeeria to warn away the hapless and the foolhardy.

The land of Nasakeeria, even its name, is a mystery. It is clearly occupied by some creatures, perhaps like those that make Shatuum their abode, for there are many reliable reports of activities, heard or sighted from a safe distance, that can only be the result of its sinister inhabitants. Here and there, some distance across the borders into that land, are towers that stand just over the treetops, or on lonely hills. Surely the creatures of Nasakeeria keep watch from those places and others. For many years, too, there have been heard the sound of drums coming from within that land. These sounds have been carefully studied by our Kingsmen, who regularly patrol the vicinity of Nasakeeria. It seems likely that the cadences heard are methods of communication, carrying news from one place to another. Certainly it seems reasonable that the Ring of Fire might be made to appear by the dark efforts of Nasakeeria's occupants, for that land has no natural barriers and, if it were not for the Ring of Fire, it could be easily entered and explored. Surely its inhabitants guard terrible secrets. Whatever those secrets are, let us hope that we are as protected from them, and from the inhabitants of Nasakeeria, as they are from us by the Ring of Fire.

§

The Avatar

We who live within the City of Duinnor can never be accustomed to that most uncanny and terrifying apparition, the Avatar of the King. Although it changes its form from one year to the next, the Avatar can hardly be mistaken for the object that it simulates, for it floats out of the King's Palace and glides purposely along our streets and avenues in a manner that no natural object may mimic. The Avatar has been with us since the very first Unknown King, but there is very little that we know about it. What seems apparent, however, is that the Avatar has something to do with the Rites of Renewal that the King must conduct each spring at the Temple of Beras that is nearby to our city.

As we know, but perhaps the foreign reader does not, the Avatar has taken hundreds of forms since it first appeared with the First Unknown King of Duinnor. And every form of the Avatar throughout the years has shared certain aspects with all other forms. It is always silent. It floats at least one or perhaps two feet from the ground, but no more than four feet. Except when accompanying the King to the Temple of Beras each spring, the Avatar has never been seen outside of our city. It is plain, too, that our King somehow communicates with the Avatar, giving the mysterious object instructions concerning who it is to summon to the King's High Chamber for an interview. And, finally, when confronted by the Avatar, no person can resist accompanying it to the King's Palace (which makes one wonder why the Avatar is almost always escorted by a small company of Kingsmen).

Rumors abound concerning why the Avatar takes one shape and not another for a given Regnal Year. For years, now, tales have been told that the shape and form of the Avatar represents some object (or animal, as the case may be) that will threaten the King's rule during that particular Regnal Year. Some even say that the King's efforts to preserve his power revolves each year around such things as the Avatar represents. Since the beginning of our current Year of the Red Door, such speculations have gained credibility due to the recent Royal Proclamation that no new door made within this city is to be red in color, and all old red doors are to be painted over in some other hue.

§

The Carriage of Ilex

Accounts of the Carriage of Ilex date from the year 810 of the First Age, a time before Men came to the World. It was then that Cupeldain, King of Vanara, summoned the High Houses and other parties to Linlally. They were to bring together and discuss the use of the legendary Forty-Nine Bloodcoins of the Elifaen. Since it was thought that the issues to be debated would affect all Elifaen, many powerful lords and kings were also invited to come even though they were not of High Houses. At the insistence of Ormace of the High House of Fairbirch, King Ilex of Halethiris was amongst those invited, to represent that powerful and ancient land.

To make the journey more comfortable for himself and his wife and daughter, King Ilex constructed a magical carriage for their transport. It was said to be larger on the inside than its outside proportions. Indeed, within the carriage was a large woodland garden, as one might find on a cool day of spring, lit with sunshine and moonlight. Pulled by powerful buckmarls, it traveled at an uncanny pace, covering many miles in but a few moments. As far as is known, the journey to Vanara and thence back to Halethiris was the only time King Ilex enjoyed the use of his carriage, for he has never since been seen outside of his forest domain.

Only a few years later, Halethiris was destroyed with all of its inhabitants. The place has since come to be called Forest Islindia, after the daughter of King Ilex. Some say that his spirit and hers still linger as forlorn apparitions filled with gloom and hatred within that forbidding region which is now ringed by razor-sharp thorns and filled with mists and shadow. Few enter Forest Islindia willingly, and none ever emerge. And no one can say for certain what became of King Ilex's magnificent carriage.

However, there has come to light three reports of its sighting, all of a questionable nature, and all of which occurred within a single year, 854 of this age, The Year of the Lion.

One report was from a group of travelers bound from Altoria to Duinnor. This group brought to Duinnor an account of an odd and eerie coach that they saw as they made their way along the Old South Road some few leagues north of the town of Edgewold. The coach came suddenly from the west, crossed the road before them, and continued eastward at an unbelievable pace, coming and going almost before they could comment to each other upon it. They also reported that the carriage left no track or sign of its passing, even though it had rained the same day and the ground was very soft.

A second report was an account given by a Post Rider returning from a long trek from Duinnor to Colleton on the Eastland's coast. He departed Duinnor in 854 on a long trek across the world to Colleton on the Eastlands' coast, but he did not return and deliver his official report until the following year. As he made his way eastward across the Bletharn Plain, and was nigh upon the ruins of Fisenwold, a strange carriage passed him by, coming silently behind him and upsetting his horse as it flew past toward the Thunder Mountains. He reported that his horse was so startled by the sudden appearance of the carriage, passing within a few yards of his own path, that it bucked violently and broke the straps that held the rider's saddlebags in place. It was so weird and silent and swift, he said, that he would have passed the whole incident off as a dream, thinking that he had fallen asleep in his saddle, but for the repairs that he had to make to his bags.

The third report did not arrive in Duinnor for at least seven more years, relayed by Devon Argales, a Tracian gentleman who came to our city seeking refuge from the unrest within his own lands. The story of his flight from Tracia and his eventual arrival in our city was recorded by his niece and eventually published as a booklet in the year 862 entitled, "North to Glareth, West to Duinnor."

As an interesting side note within that tale, Argales reported that as he traveled on horseback from Tracia to Glareth, he rode through the town of Passdale, which was along the road that he took. Traveling with haste, he arrived in that hamlet late into the night with no intention of stopping for rest or food. But, as it happened, Argales came upon a strange coach parked in the roadway outside a shop of that town. So strange and uncanny it was that he reined to a halt to stare upon it. With goosebumps coursing up and down his body, he even dared to dismount to inspect it more carefully. The coach was black, and its sides were in the shape of folded wings. Though it was a cloudy night, Argales reported that the stars painted upon it were so attractive and so hypnotic that he felt he was looking at a cloudless night-time sky through a forest clearing. He said that it was completely unattended, with no escort, no footmen, and no driver, and that the six buckmarls that were harnessed to it seemed to glow. They were harnessed and reined with delicate ribbons that could not have possibly pulled the weight of the coach. When he reached out to touch one of the docile beasts, a jarring sound came to his ears, like the scraping of iron against iron. Turning toward the source of the sound, he saw what he called a banshee standing but a few yards away, moaning and wailing with a dreadful voice. The witness's horse pulled at the reins, which were still in the man's hands, and, terrified, the Tracian mounted and galloped quickly away.

Argales was convinced that the coach was the banshee's method of transport. He, too, said that this incident happened during the Year of the Lion. But, as the Kingsman already mentioned, he traveled alone and there was no other witness than his horse.

If these reports are to be believed, they seem to imply that the Carriage of Ilex still goes forth from time to time. Whether it truly carries banshees or other uncanny creatures to and from Forest Islindia remains to be discovered.

§

The Cornucopia of Sudamoor

The Kingdom of Sudamoor, located on the northern shores of Lake Adin, has never been allied to any Realm since its mysterious founding nearly two thousand years ago. It is a small kingdom with a small population that, by all accounts, is happy and content to be isolated from the woes of the world. Travelers report that it is an unremarkable place, with farmers and fisher-folk going about their work in a land rather unsophisticated in craft and in culture. That land was not attacked by the Dragonkind during the Great Invasion of 322, as Sudamoor was probably too far out of the way of the invaders. The people of Sudamoor have never seen the need to ally themselves with any other Realm, and they have softly rebuffed all entreaties to do so.

It is there that exists a peculiar object, in the possession of the King of that land and passed down from king to king, all of whom are known as Sudamoor the First, Sudamoor the Second, and so forth, to the current King Sudamoor the Twelfth. This object is in the form of a very large, curled ram's horn. Such is its size that it would take several strong men to lift it, thus it housed within the throne room of King Sudamoor upon an ornate cradle.

Whenever there comes a time of want in those lands, whether due to harsh winters or the failure of crops, the King causes the horn to dispense food and sustenance to any who may need such, in abundance enough to prevent starvation and ill-health. Legend has it that Sudamoor shall always be in peace and will never be vexed by the woes of the world as long as the fruits of the Cornucopia are made freely available to its people. Indeed, this must be the case, for it seems that no one outside of that land cares to bring strife to it, and its people continue to live in the peace of their simple ways.

§

Ethliad, the Sword

Who has not heard of the fabulous sword of Silmain, first King of Vanara? Descriptions of it abound, and during King Silmain's time, he was proud to show it to any who cared to look upon it.

It was a fine sword, made by a smithy of Vanara sometime during the Age of Strife, and other than his name, Ethliad, nothing else is known about him. The sword was about four feet long from the pommel to the tip of the straight blade. A length of silver wire, intricately knotted and woven, wrapped about the tang, forming its grip, and ended in a large knotted ball that was its pommel. The silver winding was done in such a fashion that it was easily gripped by hands that were either large or small. It had no cross-guard or quillon, and the entire sword was said to weigh no more than a half-pound.

It was the blade of Ethliad, though, that was so marvelous. It was straight and flat, having no fuller or ridge, about three inches wide at the strong, tapering very gradually to the tip. The blade was unique in composition and quality, and its light weight was not the least of its mysteries. The blade was not polished, nor did it reflect any light, but was said to appear at first glance to be a mirror. Many accounts are given, however, that upon closer inspection, the blade appeared to be as a window, revealing live scenes of battle. Whether these were from the past or future, no one could say. And, as evidenced by the many battles that Silmain participated in, it never dulled, blood would not adhere to it, and it cut as easily through iron and steel as it did through water.

The sword came into the possession of Silmain near the end of the Age of Strife. With the sword, he not only faced down Elifaen opponents, but also led many armies to victory against the Dragonkind. Due in large measure to Ethliad, Silmain consolidated his power over the Elifaen of Vanara, and declared himself "King of the Faere." In his hand, the sword was instrumental in the defeat of both the Dragonkind who encroached into Vanara and those Elifaen who opposed Vanara's growing might. Knowing its value, Silmain was never without it, and, it is said, he even slept with it in his hand.

Ethliad was lost when Silmain was overwhelmed in battle against the Dragonkind in 454 F.A.. Immediately upon Silmain's death, disputes arose amongst the Elifaen. Many cast blame for Silmain's death upon the incompetence of Ormace, who was to protect Silmain's flank, while others blamed Cupeldain for not reaching Silmain in time. Meanwhile, Elifaen treasure hunters scoured the battleground in an effort to find Ethliad, and Cupeldain even dispatched a large, fast-moving force to cut off the retreating Dragonkind and to surround them, thinking they had made off with the sword. But when the Dragonkind they found were massacred, even after they surrendered, Ethliad was not found amongst them.

Although the whereabouts of Ethliad remains unknown, something of its fate was pieced together from eyewitness accounts and other information that has more recently come to light, and we are obliged to convey this news to our readers.

As it turned out, Ethliad was not taken by the Dragonkind. Silmain was killed when the battalion he led was surrounded by an overwhelming force. All of the men with Silmain were killed in a horrible battle, but, according to Dragonkind accounts that later became known, King Silmain continued to fight on, easily laying waste scores of his attackers with Ethliad. At last, an axe was thrown at Silmain which cut off his arm with such force that the sword he held flew from him. Silmain was quickly dispatched, according to the account, and the Dragonkind immediately set about searching for the powerful sword, looting the dead as they went. However, when they learned that Cupeldain's army was bearing down upon them, the Dragonkind gave up the field and fled the scene. Most would later be killed by Cupeldain's Fellfaere, but a few escaped, including the source of this account.

The whereabouts of Ethliad would remain a mystery for almost a thousand years, until the Second Age and the reign of the Second Unknown King of Duinnor. During that time, letters and dispatches were routinely intercepted by agents of the King, who was suspicious of conspiracies and plots against him. In one such item was an intriguing letter. This letter remained a secret until it was discovered many years later, which we will describe below.

The letter in question was written in an unusual script and in a careful and complex cipher. Much, but not all, of the letter was deciphered, and the writer and intended recipient remain unknown, though it was determined was that the letter was originally dispatched from somewhere within the Old Eastlands Realm and was to be delivered to a particular residence in Vanara. When the King's investigators traveled to that residence, they found it empty and could locate no one who knew anything concerning its occupants. It is no wonder that these efforts were made, for the letter described how Ethliad was found sometime after Silmain's death and prior to Cupeldain's reign. Here, then, is the main content of the letter, from a deciphered version:

"...and so, assured by visions that Ethliad would be needed, I was also shown in the same manner how I might find it. The visions were powerful, and revealed, too, that if I did not find and safeguard Ethliad, it might fall into unworthy hands. These visions came to me in the dark days after Silmain's death, before Cupeldain had ascended the throne.

"Traveling alone, and taking great care not to be discovered, I went into the desert lands and unto the battlefield where Silmain died. When I arrived, I found many skeletons and parts of skeletons of those who died there. Many of the remains were scattered by vultures and carrion, while others were lying in the same manner and repose as when they died. Almost all were of Dragonkind soldiers, piled and scattered widely across the hard-packed desert floor. Armor and weapons, corroded but very little, were likewise scattered all around. There, in the midst of this place of violent death, my Sight came upon me, and I saw each skeleton take flesh once again, pools of blood running backwards into wounds, and prostrated and piled bodies rise up to their feet. I watched in terror as all moved backwards in a dizzying blur. At last, I perceived Silmain himself,

Ethliad in hand, striving against the onslaught that came against him. Then my vision paused. Arrows were suspended in flight, sparks from swords hung like stars, and streams of blood were frozen in mid-air like small red clouds. Suddenly the battle resumed in the natural order of things, and just as Silmain swung Ethliad at an opponent, I saw his arm cut from his body by a flying axe. Silmain's sword arm was completely severed, and I saw Ethliad fly over the heads of his attackers and lodge deep into the horse of a Dragonkind captain. The horse threw its rider and then galloped swiftly away in pain. Silmain was immediately slain, but I looked no more upon him. Instead, I ran after the horse in an effort to catch it, though it outpaced me. But the horse's wound was a mortal one, with Ethliad lodged within the horse's shoulder up to the hilt, and the animal quickly grew weak and slowed. Some half-mile away, as I caught up with it, the creature stumbled and collapsed, falling upon Ethliad. And it thus died, covering the sword with its body. Then I saw time pass by rapidly, and the passing days were like flashes of lightning. By the unsteady light, I saw the flesh of the horse fall away until nothing but its skeleton remained. Then the light steadied, and there I stood, in the full heat of a desert sun. And there before me, resting amid the dusty remains of the horse's sun-bleached bones, was Ethliad.

"I took the sword, hiding it within the covers of my robes, and I fled that place, to keep Ethliad until that day when one worthy to wield it has come with a worthy cause which requires such a blade.

"Since it is my way to keep nothing from you, I tell you that I do not reveal this to your father, though I love him above all other men, and I long for him to have Ethliad. But I fear he would have the sword from me before the right time for its use. And, by having it, I fear he might be counseled and tempted by others to use it unwisely. So, for now, I keep Ethliad a secret from all but you. Other things, things of greater importance, have been entrusted to me, so I am accustomed to such burdens. However, should anything happen to me, I trust that with this knowledge, you will be guided as to what course of action to take."

The remaining page of the letter was only partially deciphered, but it apparently contained various statements concerning the writer's longing to see the recipient(s) once again, concluding with expressions of fondness and well-wishing.

Although the letter was stolen by the Second Unknown King sometime around the year 265 of the Second Age, the letter and accompanying documents describing it were uncovered only by accident in 496. when a cache of documents was found within the old archives of Duinnor and sent to the newly established King's Academy. Since the letter's rediscovery, additional efforts have been made to uncover the identities of those involved and the whereabouts of Ethliad, but to no avail.

§

The Flying Rug of Zan

Although Zan was a Dragonkind, it is said that he is practically unknown within the desert lands. Indeed, this legend comes to us from the Elifaen who once lived along the eastern shores of the earth. Men, who were Newcomers to the world and knew little about the Dragonkind, heard this tale from the woodland Elifaen they encountered. The tale has since gained popularity by the retelling and has likely been embellished over the long span of its existence.

During the time of Kalzar, there was a young weaver called Zan who lived in Tyrsharat, that most ancient of Dragonkind cities. Zan had come to the great city years earlier from his village far to the south. His father was a weaver, too, and Zan had learned all that he could before traveling to Tyrsharat intent on making his fortune.

Zan applied himself to his trade with diligence, enthusiasm, and skill. Although he was young, he was soon a master weaver in his own right, specializing in rugs and carpets of an ingenious design, fine and luxurious, and beautiful to behold. It was said that some of his rugs adorned the palace of Kalzar, and a few made their way into foreign parts, even to the faraway lands of the north.

Zan did not embroil himself in the many intrigues of the market, and he cared little for the pleasures of the bazaar. He asked only a fair price for his textiles, and he expected no more and no less. And while many of the other rug makers were jealous of Zan's skill, they did not begrudge him his place in the market, for he only sold one rug at a time, and there were plenty of customers for all.

So Zan paid little attention to the talk of conflict with the Faerekind of the North, and he cared little for the happenings of the world. He was content to work and sell his rugs in the bazaar, and as long as he made enough from each sale to pay for his rent, his food, and the yarn for his next rug, he was happy and satisfied, proud of his reputation and confident of his skill. So when many of the men of Tyrsharat were called away by Kalzar for a great expedition, Zan remained behind to continue his work.

Indeed, although many people were gone from Tyrsharat, business at the bazaar seemed to improve, for many wives now spent their faraway husbands' money more freely, and the concubines of the powerful were generous with the gold of their absent masters. But Zan noticed this, if at all, only in passing, so intent he was on his own occupation.

Thus Zan was completely unaware of Kalzar's war upon the Faerekind lands to the far north. Nor was he aware when Kalzar's army was beaten back by the Faerekind who flew deep into the Dragonlands taking revenge upon Zan's people for the attack instigated by the King of the Dragonlands. All during these events, Zan worked at his loom, weaving a new and marvelous rug, confident that the investment he had made in such fine yarn would be recovered many times over.

So there he was, weaving at his loom, oblivious of the war that came to Tyrsharat or the Faerekind who swooped down upon the city. But one of these Faerekind was killed by arrows and happened to fall upon the roof of Zan's shop, crashing through the roof and into his weaving room. The terrified Zan dove away as debris continued to fall upon him and upon the dead creature before him. As the dust settled, so did the Faerekind's wings, like those of a butterfly, and they became entangled in Zan's loom. Zan had never seen a dead person before, and, knowing nothing about the woes of the world or the conflict that surrounded his shop, he attempted to revive the Faerekind. But it was useless, so Zan turned his attention to his loom and tried to extricate the creature's wings from his rug, already well along when all this happened. But removing the wings from his work was impossible, for not only were they shredded and tangled into the warp, they were also knotted and kinked about the weft and twisted around the beams and shafts of his loom. Zan's efforts to disentangle the delicate material of the Faerekind's wings only seem to make matters worse. After much consideration, sitting and staring at the beautiful creature that lay dead in his shop, Zan was forced to cut away the wings.

After Zan completed the sad task of removing the wings from the Faerekind, he buried the body in his yard. It was only then that he noticed the noise of wailing all around, those of the dead and dying and their bereaved kin, and he ran from neighbor to neighbor, learning as he went about the war and the battle that had only just ended when all the attacking Faerekind suddenly flew away. Indeed, it had been a terrible day, and the entire city was filled with so many dead that Zan and his neighbors worked for a week to take corpses away to the funeral pyres of the city. Only after this time did he return to his home and shop to make repairs to his roof. So it was another few weeks before he sat once more on his stool and studied his loom and the disarray of his rug.

Zan's great problem was that he had spent every bit of gold and silver he had, and had borrowed even more, to purchase the fine yarn required for this rug. Unless he could finish the rug and find a buyer for it, he would certainly be ruined. Yet he could not remove the bits of Faerekind-wing from the weft and warp without cutting away his own precious yarn. Having little choice, he cut the fibers of the wings into fragments and twisted them into thin threads, carefully knotting them and weaving them into his rug.

A week later, Zan completed the rug, but he was unsatisfied with it. The bits of Faerekind wing gave the rug a mottled sheen that was not in keeping with his design. Yet there was nothing else he could do. He had no choice except to try to sell it for whatever he could get. But when he took it to the marketplace the following day, he could find no buyer for the rug. Indeed, many people gave him their sympathy, for it was apparent to them that his skills were much diminished, and the quality of his work not as it had once been. Many of the other weavers laughed outright at Zan and the odd and inappropriate pieces of thread woven into such luxurious yarn. Their derision drove many potential customers away. And besides, since the battle with the Faerekind had left so many of Zan's people dead, and had destroyed so many homes, there were few who had the means to buy rugs or anything else, much less one that was so undesirable.

Disheartened, and knowing that he faced ruin, Zan kept trying to sell the rug. When his rent came due, he sold his bed and all his furnishings to pay it. When his larder ran out, he traded nearly all of his clothes for food. But he could entice no one to buy the rug. Things continued as such until Zan was even forced to sell his loom and give up his shop just to pay what he owed for the expensive yarn he had used.

Now destitute, Zan took his rug and went to the city walls where he hoped to beg for food. When he arrived, however, the other beggars would not allow him a place, and so violent was their opposition to him that he had to flee from the city. Exhausted, hungry, and defeated, that night he spread his rug on a dune and sat upon it, gazing at the city. At last, weeping with hopelessness, he fell asleep upon the rug under the bright stars of the desert. He dreamed of better days, of when he was a boy and a weaver's apprentice far away in a small village in the southern lands of the desert. He awoke, remembering how he came to the great city, how he made a fine living and even hoped to take a wife. But now all Zan wanted was to go home.

"Oh, fie upon my fate!" he cried at the starry sky. "That the foul Faerekind have ruined me in such a way as this! They, who have wings and may go wherever they wish! Oh, rug! If I had the strength, I would leave this place and go home. But I am too old, now, and too weak to cross the great sands."

Suddenly, Zan felt the dune shift beneath him, and he thought he was sliding away. Sitting up, he was amazed to see that the dune was far below, and the rug was lifting him up and carrying him away to the south.

So it was that Zan discovered the strange and wonderful quality of his rug. By merely wishing his desire out loud, or saying where it was he wanted to go, the rug took him there, flying through the sky as swift as a bird and a smooth as silk. And it was not long before he took full advantage of the rug. Zan was able to swoop down, take food away from people, and to fly away before any could react. He also obtained new clothes that way, flying through the marketplace and snatching robes and hats and slippers as he flew by kiosks and merchants.

Within weeks, Zan had traveled all over the Dragonlands, taking what he wished and escaping with ease. He effortlessly took gold, jewels, fine clothes, and delicious food and wine. Zan soon had all the wealth that he could wish for, and he piled his stolen treasure within a hidden cave located in the Tulivana Mountains. It was not long, though, before he yearned for companionship, and so he determined to find himself a wife.

Dressing in the most splendid robes and riding his flying rug, Zan went looking. He flew over courtyards and among the palaces of the Dragonlands, hovering low to see the ladies and girls in the private gardens of great palaces, or floating outside the windows of elegant chambers to look upon the harems of the mighty. However, the women inevitably screamed or fainted when they saw him, and others fled, perhaps thinking he was one of the Faerekind who had come through the air to do them harm. Word of the flying marauder spread, and arrows were soon flying up at him wherever he went. So things did not go well for Zan.

After several weeks, and many narrow escapes from flying missiles, Zan decided to try other lands. In spite of his fear of the Faerekind, he turned his rug northward. When he passed over the Blue Mountains and on through what is now Vanara, he marveled at the land and its green forests, its streaming rivers, and its snowy mountains. It saddened him, too, for now he understood better how difficult it was for his own kind, scraping their existence from the harsh deserts while just a few leagues away was land for the taking, teeming with game and water. No wonder Kalzar wanted to conquer these lands.

When Zan flew low over a forest, he saw members of the Elifaen race for the first time. They were naked and dirty, with scars running down their backs where once they had wings. Many crawled on their hands and knees, digging for worms to eat, while others climbed trees to find fruit or nuts. He saw one group pulling tubers beside a stream when suddenly they were beset by others who came charging through woods. He watched them fight, some wielding rocks and others heavy sticks. When the waters of the stream turned red with blood, Zan flew away, going across the open plains and into the eastern mountains. There he saw more of the Elifaen struggling to survive just as the others he had seen. He kept going, eventually coming to a place where the land ended and where water stretched out as far as he could see. He was astonished to see so much water. He flew far out and high up, and when he got so far that he could barely make out the shore behind him, he still could not see the end of the waters.

Going back, he landed on a sandy beach and reached down to scoop some water in his hands to drink. It was salty, and he spat it out in surprise.

"You act as though you have never tasted the sea before," came a voice behind him. Turning, he saw a group of Elifaen sitting but a few yards away on a grassy dune. Though they could not have missed how he flew there and landed on his rug, they did not seem afraid of him, nor seem the least bit inclined to run away. There were about seven of them, all naked, men and women alike, and they all sat or reclined easily.

"Indeed, I have not," replied Zan. "This is the sea?"

"Yes. It is."

"I have heard of it, but I have never seen it before," said Zan. "I never heard that it was so big, though."

"Yes, it is very big."

"You are one of the desert people, are you not?" asked one of the ladies.

Zan was somewhat embarrassed to look upon her, though she seem not ashamed at all to be looked upon. And since she was so beautiful, with bronze skin and black hair streaked with green, he could hardly take his eyes from her.

"Yes. I am one of the Dragonkind."

"So you are what all the fuss was about?" asked one of the girls.

"What fuss?" asked Zan.

"Have you not heard? There was a war between some of your people and some of our people," said the Elifaen man who had spoken earlier. "Because of it, we lost our wings."

"Oh?" said Zan, glancing at his rug. "I did not know that. About your wings, I mean."

"It is true."

"And now we must walk as you do."

"When we are on the land, that is. But we prefer to swim in the sea."

"Although it is harder to do without our wings."

Zan looked from one to another as they spoke, but his eyes always went back to the one with the black and green hair.

"But we would not go with the others, the one who went away with Aperion and kept their wings. We love the sea, and we cannot not abide being far from it for very long."

"So we stayed, lost our wings, and returned here to live in and beside the sea."

Zan nodded. He was beginning to wonder how he understood them, for he had never heard words such as they spoke, and yet he understood everything they said.

"You speak strangely," he said. "But I understand you easily."

"We speak as we have always done," said one of them. "And we hear as we have always heard."

"So we understand you, and you understand us," said another.

"But it seems to be more difficult to say words as the days pass us by. Our words seem not to touch the things of the world as they once did."

"And it is harder for us to understand what the sea says, and what the fish say, and what the air and sand have to tell us."

Zan bent his head, listening.

"I do not hear them say anything at all," he commented, still listening.

"Hm. We have heard that the Dragonkind do not speak or hear as our people do."

"Why do you come here? Have you come to conquer us as others of your kind tried to do in the west?"

Zan nearly laughed as he said, "No. I am not a soldier, and I care not for such things. I am a weaver. Or else, I once was a weaver. Now I am wealthy and have no need of toil. I am on a quest to find a wife for myself, to live with me in luxury and comfort in my desert dwelling."

"Oh," said the beautiful lady that Zan continued to gaze at. "I do not know what a weaver is, and I have never seen the desert. Would you take me there on your magic leaf?"

"It is not a leaf. It is a rug, one that I made by weaving. If you would be my wife, I would gladly take you to the deserts and show you all there is to see."

The lady sprang to her feet and came running to Zan.

"Then let us go! It will be wonderful to see the desert."

"Do you know what a wife is?" asked Zan.

"No."

Zan looked at the others who only shrugged and shook their heads.

"I can learn to wife if you teach me," said the lady.

"Do you have a name?"

"I am called Wassani."

"Wassani. I am Zan."

"Zan."

"Yes. And I will take you, just have a seat upon my rug."

Wassani did so, and Zan sat beside her.

"Let us go west and south," said Zan to the rug.

"Let us go west and south," repeated Wassani.

The rug did not move at all.

"Let us go," he said again.

"Let us go," she repeated, too.

The rug did not move.

"Perhaps it is too heavy," he said, standing and stepping from the rug.

"Let us go," said Wassani.

Instantly, the rug rose up and shot away.

"Wait! Wait!" cried Zan.

But it was too late. The rug, with Wassani laughing, disappeared into the west, leaving Zan behind.

Needless to say, Zan was very unhappy at this turn. He cried and wept for days. But, eventually, he resigned himself to his fate. He learned to swim, although not as gracefully as the other Elifaen, who seemed not to miss Wassani at all. And he learned to find and eat fish and do other things. In turn, he taught the Elifaen about weaving, using vines and taking fibers from the nearby forest. And he taught them many other things, too, as the years passed. How to make shelter and clothing, how to eat nuts from the trees as he had seen other Elifaen do. And he taught them what he knew of the lore of his own people.

The years passed, but Wassani never returned. Zan continued to learn the ways of the forest and to teach what he knew to the Elifaen. When lightning struck a tree during a storm, he stole fire from it. Guarding the fire carefully, he showed the Elifaen how to use it to cook the animals they killed, and he showed them how they could light their way with it at night. From then on, his tribe guarded the fire very carefully, never allowing it to go out.

Other Elifaen came to live with them, and they formed a great forest tribe. And while Zan grew old, his Elifaen friends did not. They were amazed at how he became weak as the years passed by, how his hair became white and thin, and how his eyesight grew dim. At last, he went to sleep and did not wake up. The Elifaen were baffled, at first. But when they realized that he was dead, they had a great feast in his honor, cooking and sharing his flesh with one another, and talking all the while about Zan's life. They talked far into the night, retelling stories Zan had told to them, and telling each other about the marvelous rug that had brought Zan to live with them and had carried the beautiful Wassani away.

§

The Glowing Stone of Bazradur

Most of our readers have heard of the Green Citadel, the city of the Dragonlands that was besieged twice by our gallant soldiers. Both of those campaigns ended ignominiously, with much loss of life and sadness. However, the enemy's city was sacked on both occasions, and many relics and artifacts were brought back into the northern lands by those who returned. Several of these relics consist of pieces of the Glowing Stone of Bazradur for which the Green Citadel was named.

The Glowing Stone was a square block of marble that had the peculiar property to glow as brightly as a torch, giving off an intense green light with no heat. For centuries, it adorned a high tower within the city of Calamandor, which we call the Green Citadel, and it could be seen from several miles away by day, and many leagues by night. Legend says that the Glowing Stone was made by Bazradur, a Dragonkind alchemist who lived in Calamandor long ago, during the reign of Queen Nebalasa of the Dragonlands. Little is known of Bazradur, but legend has it that he assured Nebalasa that as long as the Glowing Stone remained within the city of Calamandor, it would never be attacked by the Elifaen. The light, which was as a beacon across the city, continued to sparkle by day and shine by night, until the tower which held it mysteriously crumbled in the year 790 of this the Second Age. As a result, the stone fell from the tower's apex and shattered. An attempt was made to reconstruct the tower and the stone, but from then on, the stone never glowed as it did before, giving off but a feeble light visible only on the darkest of nights.

To give credence to the legend, within fifty years of the stone's shattering, the city was indeed attacked and sacked by an invading army of our people in 837 S.A.. The tower that held the stone was captured after a fierce fight, the Glowing Stone was broken once more, and its pieces were taken away as prizes. It hardly seems necessary to acquaint our knowledgeable readers with the fate that befell our returning armies, only to say that very few who crossed the desert and laid waste to the city ever returned. And so, only a few shards of the Glowing Stone made it out of the Dragonlands. Four came to our own Realm, and can be seen to this day in the galleries of this city's Hanton Hall, a gift made to that place by our King. The fifth large piece made its way to Vanara where it is now part of Queen Serith Ellyn's treasure.

Some commentators have expressed a belief that the properties of the Glowing Stone of Bazradur must be similar to that of Luna's Lantern, an object to which we shall momentarily address our attention. However, the Glowing Stone of Bazradur glowed constantly, both day and night, whether the sky was clear or cloudy whereas Luna's Lantern did not.

§

Luna's Lantern

Luna's Lantern was a light or lamp, or some type of shining apparatus that belonged to the Sea Kings of Glareth. It glowed with captured moonlight, it is said, sending forth a very bright light of a silvery-blue hue. Luna's Lantern would only shine when Lady Moon was not in the night sky, or on those nights too overcast for her to be seen, in deference, it is said, to the beauty of the Night-time Mistress. It was mounted at the top of a special tower of Castle Glaria, once the residence of Glareth's Sea Kings of yore and now the abode of the Ruling Prince of that land. During the reign of the Sea Kings, Luna's Lantern beamed out over the sea as a steady beacon, guiding sailors safely to Glareth's port.

The origin of Luna's Lantern remains shrouded in mystery. However, according to legend, if it was ever lost or destroyed, then the rule of the Sea Kings would soon after come to an end. The legend proved true. An earthquake struck Glareth Realm in the year 354 S.A., the tower of Castle Glaria was overturned, and it fell into the churning sea along with Luna's Lantern. This was during King Thalamir's reign, and he would be the very last of the Sea Kings. The loss of Luna's Lantern may have also contributed to the death of Ishtorgus the Mariner, that famed Melnari who was so instrumental in bringing about Glareth's maritime power. Ishtorgus was lost at sea during a great storm, and his ship was unable to navigate safely to Glareth. Sailors on a nearby ship reported that the vessel carrying Ishtorgus was swallowed by a maelstrom that the storm roiled and churned upon the sea.

Many efforts to recover Luna's Lantern have been made, but with no success. However, witnesses say that they have seen peculiar lights in the deep waters at the base of the cliff beneath Castle Glaria, precisely where Luna's Lantern fell. These lights, they say, can only be seen on the darkest nights, when Lady Moon is nowhere to be seen when even her retinue of stars are blocked by dense clouds.

§

The Golden Mantle of Duinnor

Certainly our regular readers and all inhabitants of our city are quite familiar with the Golden Mantle of Duinnor, that exquisite robe which attires our King from head to toe. It shines with its own light of a painful intensity and uncanny quality. The King cannot therefore be looked upon for very long without the looker becoming muddled or even going mad, thus protecting our King from steady gaze. It is rumored that the Golden Mantle is also the source of the King's long life, His ability to hear the thoughts of others and to speak into their minds, and a constitution that does not require sleep, food, or drink.

This covering has been bestowed upon each Unknown King in turn by the Oracle of Beras, from the First Unknown King of our lands to the present Sixth King, and the power of the Golden Mantle is thought to be renewed each spring at the beginning of the King's new Ruling Year. The making of the Golden Mantle is a complete mystery, and it is rumored that even the monks of the Temple of Beras do not know its origin.

§

The Great Bell of Tulith Attis

Cast by craftsmen of the Eastlands under the direction of Heneil the Builder, the Great Bell was placed within an underground chamber of the fortress of Tulith Attis in the year 307 of the Second Age. It is said that a powerful incantation was placed upon the bell so that if it ever rang, its sound would pass through earth and air and be heard throughout the world. It was rumored that the sorcerer who laid the incantation summoned some portion of the essence out of all ringing things that ever were or ever would be, and that he put the essence within the iron of the bell. In this manner, all ringing things would sound out when the Great Bell tolled.

Heneil constructed the underground Bell Room in such a manner that there were only two ways to enter it. One way was up a long staircase leading from an outside landing at the base of the fortress where boats often moored bringing goods from down the River Saerdulin. The other way to and from the Bell Room was blocked by a massive Iron Door that could only be opened if commanded to do so by a person speaking the First Tongue. In this manner, should any intruder enter the fortress and attempt to pass through the Bell Room, their way would be blocked. Further, should the intruder be a Firstborn Elifaen with the power of the First Tongue, and thereby open the Iron Door, the Bell would ring, awakening the so-called Stony Guard to repel any such intruders.

The work on the Bell and the Iron Door was completed in the year 322 S.A., shortly before the Great Dragonkind Invasion of that year. As fate would have it, Tulith Attis would come under attack and would fall by treachery, but the Bell was not rung. Some have even speculated that the Great Bell had no enchantments upon it after all, and the tale of the Iron Door is also a fanciful yarn. We may never know, for all those present during the construction of the Great Bell and the Iron Door were lost in battle or in the notorious massacre which took place at Tulith Attis. Today, by all reports, the ill-fated fortress and the land immediately surrounding it have since remained abandoned and forsaken, while those lands only a few miles away are fertile and prosperous. It is likely that the Great Bell still rests within the ruins of that place, along with the Iron Door that was constructed to bring about its ringing. And if any enchantments still abide upon the summit of Tulith Attis, likely they are those rendered by the passage of time and the progress of rust, rendering the Iron Door purposeless and the Great Bell silent for all time.

§

Swyncraff

This object is sometimes called the Rod of Laeleth, after the mythical daughter of Aperion. It is thought to be made of the wood of Shadowbane, a rare tree once found only in forests of the Carthanes, but having since disappeared. It is a staff of four feet in length, capped by iron on either end.

Swyncraff has certain living qualities, like an animal, and obeys its master's commands, forming itself in the fashion desired whether supple as a rope, or stiff as steel, straight or bent. No known blade can cut it, nor can any knot tied by its master be released by any other person.

Legends say that it was first used by Laeleth as a walking stick, but that she gave it to Cupeldain as a consolation when he failed in his efforts to assemble the Forty-Nine Bloodcoins of the Nimbus Illuminas. Upon Cupeldain's death, Swyncraff passed to his son, Parthais. However, it is unclear whether or not Parthais knew of Swyncraff's nature, for he bestowed it to Serith Ellyn as a gift shortly after the beginning of his reign over Vanara. Sometime after she became Queen, Serith Ellyn gave it to Prince Thurdun, her brother.

To this day, esteemed visitors to Vanara who chance to meet Prince Thurdun no doubt have seen Swyncraff coiled over his shoulder. If they are lucky, the Prince may even entertain his guests with a demonstration of Swyncraff's nature.

§

The Ice Tree of Greenfar

Like the land or place of Greenfar itself, there are no accounts of this object of power that are deemed reliable. However, the persistent rumors of the Ice Tree of Greenfar seem remarkably uniform, even though from a variety of sources.

The few travelers who tell of Greenfar say that it is a quiet, peaceful town surrounded by a quiet, peaceful land, located somewhere nearby or even within Forest Islindia. There, the people enjoy all of the ordinary things of life whilst going about their day-to-day work. It is, by all accounts, an unremarkable place but for the Ice Tree that adorns the Great Hall of that town at the beginning of each winter's season. Within that hall is a well, and out of the well the tree emerges each year.

This tree is made of clear ice, and begins to form itself a fortnight before Midwinter's Day, when the water of the well within the Great Hall freezes and sends up a crystalline sprout. From that moment and for two weeks, the Ice Tree grows rapidly, day by day, just as a fir tree might do, but with a trunk, boughs, and branches all made of ice. On Midwinter's Day, the tree is thirty feet tall, almost reaching the ceiling of the Great Hall, reaching that height just as the inhabitants of Greenfar gather for their annual Midwinter's celebrations.

The icy tree has the peculiar property of reflecting and enhancing light into many colors and, once the celebrations are done, it does not melt, but sublimates directly into a mist, leaving no puddle, and wholly evaporating by a fortnight after Midwinter's Day. It is also said by some that as it disappears, slowly growing smaller and thinner, it rings with a soft and delicate sound akin to chimes.

§

The Red Feather of Callowain

Legend has it that Callowain was a village located somewhere along the coast of either Altoria or Masurthia. Although a small village of fishermen and farmers, its main feature was a huge red feather that hung from a very tall pole in the center of the village. By watching this feather, the villagers could know what weather, fair or foul, was coming. If it appeared wet and flew erratically about on its tether, a storm was coming. If it drooped while appearing wet, then only rain. If it curled, then very hot weather was in store, and if it grew thick and fluffy, then it would soon be cold. Thus the village farmers and fisher-folk could avoid bad weather and plan their work better than those in other villages. For this reason, a substantial portion of the village's resources were spent on guarding and protecting the Red Feather from members of other settlements.
It is said that during the Great Dragonkind Invasion of 322 S.A., Callowain was surprised and overrun by the invaders before the Red Feather could be removed and taken away. And, unfortunately, the marvelous Red Feather was consumed in flames when the village was burned by the ignorant and uncaring Dragonkind.

§

The Ring of Hearing

The Ring of Hearing is another one of those objects for which there is no substantive evidence. However, since rumors of its existence abound, we duly describe it for our reader's entertainment.

It is said to be a ring of plain iron that enables its wearer to know the thoughts of any person within his presence. One of the most popular tales concerning it relates that the Ring of Hearing was forged and crafted by a sorcerer in the late First Age and given to a lord of Duinnor. This lord paid the sorcerer handsomely to make the ring. And the lord ordered the sorcerer to fashion his enchantments upon the ring so that it would be of no use to any Elifaen who wore it, for the lord was fearful of the descendants of the Faerekind. But the sorcerer was loathe to create such an object as this, since it could easily be abused, and any wearer of the Ring of Hearing might be corrupted by its power. However, the lord who commissioned the sorcerer to make the ring was insistent, and he eventually permitted the sorcerer to make one condition upon the Ring of Hearing's power.

So the sorcerer took the lord's gold, and he forged the ring, making it so that it would be useless to any Elifaen that wore it. But the sorcerer added his own condition, too, which was that if any person who was offered the Ring of Hearing could refuse it, that person would be granted a wish, be it anything at all. The sorcerer hoped that the lord would thus be moved to refuse the ring, using his granted wish to acquire wealth or some other power.

However, the lord did not refuse the newly forged Ring of Hearing, but greedily took it from the sorcerer. When the lord put the ring on his finger, the very first thing he learned (from hearing the sorcerer's thoughts) was that the sorcerer planned to take the ring back from the lord at the first opportunity and destroy it. So the lord promptly slew the sorcerer and took back the gold he had given in payment for the ring.

This lord, who was a Newcomer (as Men were called in those days and sometimes still are) used the ring to gain power for himself and his people. As the years passed, he accumulated wealth, enforced his law, and was able to forestay those who conspired against him. Slowly, however, the lord became ever more afraid and mistrustful of his people and even his own family, going without sleep except behind strongly bolted doors. But he could never bring himself to remove the Ring of Hearing from his finger.

At last, being unable to find peace or comfort within his own lands, the ever-suspicious lord abruptly departed his estate within Duinnor and set out alone for Vanara where he hoped to find some peace from the vexing thoughts of others. Along the way, though, he was attacked by wolves, and his hand was bitten off, along with the finger upon which he wore the Ring of Hearing. The hand, the finger, and the ring were all swallowed by one of the wolves. The lord, badly wounded, fought away the other wolves and set off after the wolf that ate his hand. But the wolf escaped.

All this was related by the lord to a passing traveler who saw the lord's distress and rendered aid to the stricken man. While the stranger ministered to the lord's wounds, the lord told his tale. But the lord's wounds were mortal ones, and he died within only a few days.

The traveler buried the lord and continued on his way, coming eventually to Duinnor where he conveyed the tale to others. Those were the years before the Unknown Kings, when Duinnor was ruled by a group of lords who shared power. Upon hearing of the traveler's tale, they summoned him to repeat it to them, since the lord in question had been one of their most powerful opponents. When they heard the traveler speak, they were filled with relief at the demise of their enemy. But, as things turned out, with the Ring of Hearing gone, and the lord that had worn it, too, the ruling lords of Duinnor, no longer bound by fear of their now-dead enemy, quickly lost their unity and were soon feuding with one another. So they were not at all prepared when a new and mighty power suddenly arose and overthrew them all. As you may have guessed, that power was none other than the First Unknown King of Duinnor.

Having now heard this tale, some of our readers may naturally be inclined to wonder whether the Ring of Hearing was found by the First Unknown King, and subsequently taken by those Unknown Kings that followed. For surely the ability of the King to see into the hearts and minds of those in His presence is like the power of the Ring of Hearing. However, it is our duty to point out that our King not only sees the thoughts of those before Him, but He may speak His own thoughts into their minds, an ability not at all contained in the object we just described. No, it must be that the King's Golden Mantle, which we have already reviewed, is the source of His uncanny power of communication.

As for the Ring of Hearing, no one can say what became of the wolf that ate the ring, or whether the Ring of Hearing may have since been found by some other person. More likely, it was disgorged by the hungry wolf somewhere in the wild forests. And if it was made of plain iron, as the legend goes, surely the Ring of Hearing has by now gone completely deaf, having rusted away to nothing.

§

The Storm Bag

As our readers might observe, it seems that there was no shortage of sorcerers in days gone by. Whether there are still any about, we cannot say. But many of the Objects of Power seem to have had their origins at the hands of some wonder-worker or other. And so it is with the fabled Storm Bag, although here we find bits of a tale that have some substantive relation to actual facts.

As with some of the other Objects of Power, the Storm Bag seems to have been made by a sorcerer sometime prior to the beginning of the First Age of the world. From those days, called the Time of Strife by the Elifaen, come tales of a sorcerer who used the Storm Bag. These legends say that the sorcerer was able to conjure from the bag any kind of weather he desired. That is, until one day when he was struck and killed by a bolt of lightning that he himself had brought forth from the bag.

During the latter part of the First Age or the early years of this our Second Age, tales began circulating that an Elifaen of Vanara found the sorcerer's Storm Bag. The name of Bailorg has been associated with these tales, and that was the name of a person who was said to have used the contents of the Storm Bag to baffle and confuse his enemies. We do not know if the Bailorg of legend is the same person as Bailorg Delcorman, a somewhat shadowy figure who was once known in the courts of Duinnor and who, according to some accounts, sometimes served as a guide to those venturing into the southwestern mountains in the region of Shatuum. We shall say more about him momentarily.

As for the Storm Bag itself, the name is somewhat misleading for it was neither a bag nor did it contain storms. Rather, it was a small pouch from which the owner could draw forth any number of clay tokens. These tokens represented various weather conditions, some represented fog, others represented thunderstorms or snow, et cetera. To bring about the desired weather, the owner of the Storm Bag merely had to produce the appropriate token and throw it upon the ground. The desired weather conditions would then almost immediately occur. However, if legends are believed, once a token was used, it could not be retrieved to be used again, nor could the pouch be replenished with new tokens because the art of creating the tokens was lost with their creator.

It is thought that Bailorg Delcorman professed ownership of the Storm Bag by which he provided fair weather for traveling, thus making the arduous way easier for those whom he served as guide. Bailorg was the subject of some notoriety a few centuries ago when he agreed to lead a small party of adventurers into the frontier of Shatuum and to the border of that fearsome land. Only Bailorg returned, having accomplished his duty and was freed to return by those whom he had escorted. He reported that the party, which included the famous Navis of Elmwood, continued on into Shatuum without him. Further to that, Bailorg claimed that he used the last powers of his Storm Bag to assure the success of his mission, and to see his party to the border of Shatuum.

Certain court records have come to light that support this tale, indicating that our King granted Bailorg a reward of gold for his service and as compensation for the depletion of his Storm Bag. Those documents, which record Bailorg's testimony concerning the adventure, indicate that Bailorg used the Storm Bag once to bring a wind to push away fog and on another occasion to summon warm rain to melt snow that blocked a narrow pass.

All this occurred many, many years ago. Since Navis traveled to Shatuum on a mission to free his sister, Lady Esildre, from that place, and since she emerged on her own some years later, it is apparent that Navis and his party were lost within the shadowed land. As for Bailorg Delcorman, we have little to report.   He was seen within our city quite recently, and agents hired exclusively by this Establishment have made a diligent effort to locate him. It was this Establishment's hope to inquire of him any knowledge of these things, and to learn if he is, in fact, the same Bailorg mentioned in old legends. However, our search has turned up nothing whatsoever concerning his whereabouts.

§

The Torch of Solstice

Here is certainly a tale that will raise our readers' skeptical brow, for it is a fanciful one pertaining to the Torch of Solstice.

King Ilex of Halethiris had a brother who called himself Solstice. When Aperion Scathed the Elifaen of their wings, Solstice quite nearly succumbed to sadness and melancholia, for he so loved those of his brethren that Aperion left behind that he would not be parted from them. Yet, after the Fall of the Faere, Solstice found himself powerless to relieve their suffering, and it is said that he wept for a century. Seeing his grief, Aperion's heart was softened, and he took pity upon Solstice and those whom Solstice longed to comfort. He gave to Solstice a flame, conveyed upon a conical torch, so that wherever Solstice went, so, too, would go goodwill and good fellowship. When Newcomers came into the world, Solstice found their love for one another, in spite of their short lives, a great comfort. So moved by their acts of great kindness, he began to take on a form more akin to them than his own people, and he grew a beard and whiskers such as the Elifaen rarely have. And Solstice found that he was able to go in spirit to any place and to all gatherings where there was goodwill and love, no matter how small or large the gathering, and no matter when or where they may take place.

Some say that Solstice abides in the woods bordering Forest Islindia, that same place which was once called Halethiris before its destruction and before it became a forbidden place. From there, Solstice goes forth upon a wondrous sleigh drawn by mighty buckmarls to visit and to celebrate Midwinter's with the good folk of Greenfar. But there are many reports that he and his sleigh are also seen in many other parts of the world at the very same time of year and at other times, too. Often, such sightings are accompanied by the mysterious arrival of small gifts of a delightful nature, tiny ornate discs or marvelously illuminated scrolls, all bearing good wishes for the coming year that invariably come true. As well, there have been numerous reports, both here in Duinnor and elsewhere, of a jolly fellow who mysteriously appears at weddings and other celebrations, and sometimes in the camps of weary but happy travelers. Such is his kind and joyful demeanor that he is always offered a place at the table, or beside the campfire, situating his marvelous Torch nearby to shine upon the occasion.

§

True Ink

Any who have traveled to Vanara and have visited the Hall of Ministers in the city of Linlally must know of True Ink. For it is with that ink that the visitor must write his genuine and rightful name before he is permitted inside the Hall. In this way, the keepers of the Hall may know as a certainty who comes and goes from that place, for the ink used is True Ink, and what is written with True Ink will only remain visible if the truth has been written. It is suspected by some that True Ink is also used by Vanarans to obtain their uncanny knowledge of other matters, but it is so rare and expensive that it is unlikely that it could be so.

What we do know is that True Ink was discovered only a century or so ago. It is made of the oil from a rare plant only found within Vanara. The plant cannot be cultivated, and so it must be harvested in the wild. True Ink is so rare and valuable that harvesting the plant without the Queen's express permission carries the stiffest of penalties. The method of making True Ink from the gathered plants is a closely guarded secret, one that many agents and alchemists from other Realms undoubtedly seek to discover. Once prepared, True Ink is a delicate concoction. It spoils easily, and if it is mixed with dried ink it is rendered useless. The liquid cannot be transported unless it is kept within vials of raw amber, otherwise it cannot survive the bumps and jostles of travel. Because of this, Vanara has made every effort to secure all sources of amber, including those in other Realms and within the border mountains of the Dragonlands, presumably to prevent the transport of True Ink should any quantity be stolen.

For our part, the reader is assured that this Establishment uses a form of True Ink in all its publications. However, our source comes not from Vanara, nor is it refined from any rare plant, yet, as our readers can attest, every word remains visible to the eye. Rather, our ink flows naturally and freely from the steady honesty and trustworthiness of this establishment's Proprietors, who allow only the truth to pass through our presses and unto our readers.

§

The Unerring Arrow of Kalsabahyood

This is the tale of Kalsabahyood and his Unerring Arrow. It comes to us from the Dragonlands where, according to our sources, it is a popular legend.

According to legend, Kalsabahyood was a Dragonkind who somehow learned the First Tongue from the Faerekind during the Time Before Time. Speaking the First Tongue, he fashioned an arrow by coaxing the feathers from a blackbird onto a straight stick. Then by talking to a sharp piece of obsidian, he convinced it to join with the stick to be the arrowhead. With this arrow, Kalsabahyood became a famous hunter, never carrying a quiver like other hunters, only the one arrow. When hunting, he would pull it back on his bowstring, whispering to the arrow where it should go. When released, the arrow never failed to strike its target, no matter how far away it was or how fast the target was moving. But Kalsabahyood always hunted alone, and never allowed anyone to witness his skill with it, for he feared the arrow would be stolen from him. And so he hunted in the region that would later be called the Blue Mountains, going from the nearby desert and up into the mountains to hunt all by himself, and returning home with his game upon his shoulders. Thus he supported his family and village with the spoils of his hunts, and since they lived simply they had little want.

One day, when he had returned from a successful hunt and had delivered his quarry to his wife to cook, his neighbor plied him with wine and challenged Kalsabahyood to a shooting match. The wager would be that whosoever won the match would have his choice of the other's belongings. Kalsabahyood was reluctant and resisted the notion. However, at last drunken with wine, he consented to the contest, but only if it was held at night.

The night of the contest was agreed upon, and all of the people of the village were in attendance. Since Kalsabahyood was the one challenged, the choice of targets was his.

"Let it be that star yonder," he said, pointing up to a bright blue star in the west.

"That is a foolish target," his opponent said, "for no arrow can reach the heavens."

"Then you concede the match. And I'll have all your cattle."

"I will concede only if you go first," said his opponent.

"I will go first. And if I strike down that blue star, you must match the feat by striking down yon yellow star."

"I will do so," said his opponent. "And if we both miss, then the next target is to be of my own choosing."

"I agree," said Kalsabahyood.

So Kalsabahyood shot his arrow at the star, which promptly fell from the sky and was lost to sight beyond the far horizon. His opponent, of course, failed to duplicate the feat with the yellow star. And since the match was judged by all of the village people, Kalsabahyood's opponent had to give over all of his cattle.

Thus the Unerring Arrow was foolishly lost. Although Kalsabahyood's family was prosperous for a time, when drought came and feed withered, he and his family starved, along with all his village, for without his arrow, he was a poor hunter indeed. Soon after, his village was no more. Kalsabahyood and his Unerring Arrow are now remembered only in legends and in tales such as this one.

§

Thus Ends Our Review
of
Eighteen Objects of Power

It is the Proprietor's sincere hope that the reader has enjoyed the inclusion of this Supplement. As well, readers are also cordially invited to apply for a Special Illustrated Edition of these tales, which is soon to be printed using the highest quality vellum and bound in handsome leather, the aforesaid made available for the price of only Twenty Duinnor Silvers. Interested readers may remit payment in person or by agent within the offices of this Establishment, or in the Printing Shop just adjacent, where many other Fine Books may also be purchased.

§ § § § §

Reader's Companion Notes:

As is readily apparent, many objects of interest, if not power, were not mentioned at all in the above supplement. The Five Stars of Duinnor, ever-present to the readers of the broadsheet, were not even alluded to. And the Forty-Nine Bloodcoins of the Elifaen were mentioned only in passing. These exclusions were among the shortcomings of the supplement that drew Raynor's sharp criticism.

It might also be noted that on the night of the Eighth Day of Eighthmonth of the same year as the above supplement, all of the bells and chimes in and around Duinnor (as well as the rest of the world) began ringing all by themselves in a most strident manner without any apparent agitation or cause to make them do so. This ringing, which took place three times within only a few moments, was so loud and uncanny that it caused great alarm throughout Duinnor and, it is presumed, elsewhere. By the time the ringing ceased, all were in a panic, the gates of Duinnor City were shut, and the armed forces were summoned to defend the city against any attack. After several days, when no threat materialized, some were beginning to speculate whether the Great Bell of Tulith Attis had been rung. This speculation was fueled in part by the above supplement and by subsequent articles published in the various broadsheets of Duinnor.

As for other objects mentioned above, we know the fate of some of them. In this Companion, for example, are passages concerning Lyrium's acquisition of Ethliad and the Ring of Hearing. As well, we know from *The Year of the Red Door* that Swyncraff was given to Robby Ribbon by Queen Serith Ellyn and Thurdun, and that Robby rang the Great Bell of Tulith Attis. We also know, from Eldwin's tale (related to Robby in *The Year of the Red Door*) that Bailorg used the contents of the Storm Bag (although the bag itself is not named). So, too, does *The Year of the Red Door* describe the Ice Tree of Greenfar, Solstice's Torch, and Nasakeeria's Ring of Fire. Also, from information provided here in this Companion, we know more about True Ink, its use and nature.

However, we include this newspaper supplement, published in early 870, as an indication of the awareness and attitude of people of that day, and the limitations of their general knowledge pertaining to such objects.

We have had an opportunity to read Raynor's original work upon which The Star based its reporting. Raynor provided more information, listed a greater number of objects, and also included in his work some of his own opinions and observations about "magical" objects in general and these in particular. To Raynor, nuance was very important, and he proposed a few alternative explanations for things for his readers to ponder. Although we did consider Raynor's work when putting this Companion together, we deemed it altogether too lengthy and detailed, with much that would be of little interest to those primarily concerned with *The Year of the Red Door*. And, having already pushed the bounds somewhat on what we have included, we felt that the Supplement above would be better suited to our readers and audience. However, as we have stated elsewhere, those who are interested in Raynor's work can find copies of it in the Great Library of Darini, which is open to all visitors.

Reader's Companion Index

Afterword

We hope this Companion has been (and will continue to be) of service to you.

And we cordially invite you to ask questions, and to share your thoughts and comments!!   You can do so via any of the methods below:

Penflight Books
P.O. Box 857
125 Avery Street
Winterville, Georgia 30683-9998
USA

OR

infodesk@penflightbooks.com

We Respect Your Privacy!

We do not sell, trade, or share any addresses, emails, or other private information provided to us without express individual permission!   But you can rest assured that we make every attempt to read and respond to every single note, letter, and email that we receive!

For More, Including Maps, Videos, and Special Offers

Visit

TheYearOfTheRedDoor.com